# WILD JUSTICE & HUNGRY AS THE SEA

*Also by Wilbur Smith*

THE COURTNEYS
Birds of Prey
Monsoon
When the Lion Feeds
The Sound of Thunder
A Sparrow Falls

THE COURTNEYS OF AFRICA
The Burning Shore
Power of the Sword
Rage
A Time to Die
Golden Fox

THE BALLANTYNE NOVELS
A Falcon Flies
Men of Men
The Angels Weep
The Leopard Hunts in Darkness

*also*

The Dark of the Sun
Shout at the Devil
Gold Mine
The Diamond Hunters
The Sunbird
Eagle in the Sky
The Eye of the Tiger
Cry Wolf
Hungry as the Sea
Wild Justice
Elephant Song
River God
The Seventh Scroll
Warlock

# WILD JUSTICE

Wilbur Smith was born in Central Africa in 1933. He was educated at Michaelhouse and Rhodes University.

He became a full-time writer in 1964 after the successful publication of *When the Lion Feeds*, and has since written twenty-six novels, all meticulously researched on his numerous expeditions worldwide. His books are now translated into twenty-six languages.

He owns a farm and game reserve and has an abiding concern for the peoples and wildlife of his native continent, an interest strongly reflected in his novels.

# WILBUR SMITH

# WILD JUSTICE & HUNGRY AS THE SEA

PAN BOOKS

*Wild Justice* first published 1979
by William Heinemann Ltd and first published by Pan Books 1998
*Hungry As The Sea* first published 1978
by William Heinemann Ltd and first published by Pan Books 1998

This omnibus edition published 2002 by Pan Books
an imprint of Pan Macmillan Ltd
Pan Macmillan, 20 New Wharf Road, London N1 9RR
Basingstoke and Oxford
Associated companies throughout the world
www.panmacmillan.com

ISBN 0 330 41825 4



1 3 5 7 9 8 6 4 2

A CIP catalogue record for this book is available from
the British Library.

Typeset by SetSystems Ltd, Saffron Walden, Essex
Printed and bound in Great Britain by
Mackays of Chatham plc, Chatham, Kent

# WILD JUSTICE

Once again this book is for my wife
Danielle Antoinette

There were only fifteen joining passengers for the British Airways flight at Victoria Airport on the island of Mahé in the oceanic republic of the Seychelles.

Two couples formed a tight group as they waited their turn for departure formalities. They were all young, all deeply tanned and they seemed still carefree and relaxed by their holiday in that island paradise. However, one of them made her three companions seem insignificant by the sheer splendour of her physical presence.

She was a tall girl, with long limbs and her head set on a proud, shapely neck. Her thick, sun-gilded blonde hair was twisted into a braid and coiled high on top of her head, and the sun had touched her with gold and brought out the bloom of youth and health upon her skin.

As she moved with the undulating grace of one of the big predatory cats, bare feet thrust into open sandals, so the big pointed breasts joggled tautly under the thin cotton of her tee-shirt and the tight round buttocks strained the faded denim of her hacked-off shorts.

Across the front of her tee-shirt was blazoned the legend 'I AM A LOVE NUT' and below it was drawn the suggestive outline of a coco-de-mer.

She smiled brilliantly at the dark-skinned Seychellois immigration officer as she slid the green United States passport with its golden eagle across the desk to him, but when she turned to her male companion she spoke in quick fluent German. She retrieved her passport and led the others through into the security area.

Again she smiled at the two members of the Seychelles

Police Force who were in charge of the weapons search, and she swung the net carry bag off her shoulder.

'You want to check these?' she asked, and they all laughed. The bag contained two huge coco-de-mer; the grotesque fruit, each twice the size of a human head, were the most popular souvenirs of the Islands. Each of her three companions carried similar trophies in net bags, and the police officer ignored such familiar objects and instead ran his metal detector in a perfunctory manner over the canvas flight bags which made up the rest of their hand luggage. It buzzed harshly on one bag and the boy who carried it shamefacedly produced a small Nikkormat camera. More laughter and then the police officer waved the group through into the final Departure Lounge.

It was already crowded with transit passengers who had boarded at Mauritius, and beyond the lounge windows the huge Boeing 747 Jumbo squatted on the tarmac, lit harshly by floodlights as the refuelling tenders fussed about her.

There were no free seats in the lounge and the group of four formed a standing circle under one of the big revolving punkah fans, for the night was close and humid – and the mass of humanity in the closed room sullied the air with tobacco smoke and the smell of hot bodies.

The blonde girl led the gay chatter and sudden bursts of laughter, standing inches above her two male companions and a full head above the other girl, so that they were a focus of attention for the hundreds of other passengers. Their manner had changed subtly since they entered the lounge; there was a sense of relief as though a serious obstacle had been negotiated, and an almost feverish excitement in the timbre of their laughter. They were never still, shifting restlessly from foot to foot, hands fiddling with hair or clothing.

Although they were clearly a closed group, quarantined by an almost conspiratorial air of camaraderie, one of the transit passengers left his wife sitting and stood up from his seat across the lounge.

'Say, do you speak English?' he asked, as he approached the group.

He was a heavy man in his middle fifties with a thick thatch of steel-grey hair, dark horn-rimmed spectacles, and the easy confident manner of success and wealth.

Reluctantly the group opened for him, and it was the tall blonde girl who answered, as if by right.

'Sure, I'm American also.'

'No kidding?' The man chuckled. 'Well, what do you know.' And he was studying her with open admiration. 'I just wanted to know what those things are.' He pointed to the net bag of nuts that lay at her feet.

'They are coco-de-mer,' the blonde answered.

'Oh yeah, I've heard of them.'

'They call them "love nuts",' the girl went on, stooping to open the heavy bag at her feet. 'And you can see why.' She displayed one of the fruit for him.

The double globes were joined in an exact replica of a pair of human buttocks.

'Back end.' She smiled, and her teeth were so white they appeared as translucent as fine bone china.

'Front end.' She turned the nut, and offered for his inspection the perfect *mons veneris* complete with a feminine gash and a tuft of coarse curls, and now it was clear she was flirting and teasing; she altered her stance, thrusting her hips forward slightly, and the man glanced down involuntarily at her own plump *mons* beneath the tight blue denim, its deep triangle bisected by the fold of material which had rucked up into the cleft.

He flushed slightly and his lips parted with a small involuntary intake of breath.

'The male tree has a stamen as thick and as long as your arm.' She widened her eyes to the size and colour of blue pansies, and across the lounge the man's wife stood up and came towards them, warned by some feminine instinct. She was much younger than her husband and very heavy and awkward with child.

'The Seychellois will tell you that in the full moon the male pulls up its roots and walks around to mate with the females—'

'As long and as thick as your arm—' smiled the pretty little dark-haired girl beside her, ' – wow!' She was also teasing now, and both girls dropped their gaze deliberately down the front of the man's body. He squirmed slightly, and the two young men who flanked him grinned at his discomfort.

His wife reached him and tugged at his arm. There was a red angry rash of prickly heat on her throat and little beads of perspiration across her upper lip, like transparent blisters.

'Harry, I'm not feeling well,' she whined softly.

'I've got to go now,' he mumbled with relief, his poise and confidence shaken, and he took his wife's arm and led her away.

'Did you recognize him?' asked the dark-haired girl in German, still smiling, her voice pitched very low.

'Harold McKevitt,' the blonde replied softly in the same language. 'Neurosurgeon from Forth Worth. He read the closing paper to the convention on Saturday morning.' She explained. 'Big fish – very big fish,' and like a cat she ran the pink tip of her tongue across her lips.

Of the four hundred and one passengers in the final Departure Lounge that Monday evening three hundred and sixty were surgeons, or their wives. The surgeons, including some of the most eminent in the world of medicine, had come from Europe and England and the United States, from Japan and South America and Asia, for the convention that had ended twenty-four hours previously on the island of Mauritius, five hundred miles to the south of Mahé island. This was one of the first flights out since then and it had been fully booked ever since the convention had been convoked.

'British Airways announces the departure of Flight BA 070 for Nairobi and London; will transit passengers please board now through the main gate.' The announcement was in the soft singsong of the Creole accent, and there was a massed movement towards the exit.

'Victoria Control this is Speedbird Zero Seven Zero request push back and start clearance.'

'Zero Seven Zero you are cleared to start and taxi to holding point for runway Zero One.'

'Please copy amendment to our flight plan for Nairobi. Number of Pax aboard should be 401. We have a full house.'

'Roger, Speedbird, your flight plan is amended.'

The gigantic aircraft was still in its nose-high climb configuration and the seat belt and no-smoking lights burned brightly down the length of the first-class cabin. The blonde girl and her companion sat side by side in the roomy seats 1a and 1b directly behind the forward bulkhead that partitioned off the command area and the first-class galley. The seats that the young couple occupied had been reserved many months previously.

The blonde nodded to her companion and he leaned forward to screen her from the passengers across the aisle while she slipped one of the coco-de-mer from its net bag and held it in her lap.

Through its natural division the nut had been carefully sawn into two sections to allow removal of the milk and the white flesh, then the two sections had been glued together again just as neatly. The joint was only apparent after close inspection.

The girl inserted a small metal instrument into the joint and twisted it sharply, and with a soft click the two sections fell apart like an Easter egg.

In the nests formed by the double husk of the shells, padded with strips of plastic foam, were two smooth, grey, egg-like objects – each the size of a baseball.

They were grenades of East German manufacture, with the Warsaw Pact command designation MK IV(C). The outer layer of each grenade was of armoured plastic, of the type used in landmines to prevent discovery by electronic metal detectors. The yellow stripe around each grenade indicated that it was not a fragmentation type, but was designed for high impact concussion.

The blonde girl took a grenade in her left hand, unlatched her lap belt and slipped quietly from her seat. The other passengers paid her only passing interest as she ducked through the curtains into the galley area. However, the purser and the two stewardesses, still strapped into their fold-down seats, looked up sharply as she entered the service area.

'I'm sorry, madam, but I must ask you to return to your seat until the captain extinguishes the seat-belt lights.'

The blonde girl held up her left hand and showed him the shiny grey egg.

'This is a special grenade, designed for killing the occupants of a battle tank,' she said quietly. 'It could blow the fuselage of this aircraft open like a paper bag or kill by concussion any human being within fifty yards.'

She watched their faces, saw the fear bloom like an evil flower.

'It is fused to explode three seconds after it leaves my hand.' She paused again, and her eyes glittered with excitement and her breath was quick and shallow.

'You—' she selected the purser, ' – take me to the flight deck; you others stay where you are. Do nothing, say nothing.'

When she ducked into the tiny cockpit, hardly large enough to contain the members of the flight crew and its massed banks of instruments and electronic equipment, all three men turned to look back at her in mild surprise – and she lifted her hand and showed them what she carried.

They understood instantly.

'I am taking command of this aircraft,' she said, and then, to the flight engineer, 'Switch off all communications equipment.'

The engineer glanced quickly at his captain, and when he nodded curtly, began obediently to shut down his radios – the very high frequency sets, then the high frequency, the ultra high frequency—

'And the satellite relay,' the girl commanded. He glanced up at her, surprised by her knowledge.

'And don't touch the bug.' He blinked at that. Nobody, but nobody outside the company should have known about the special relay which, when activated by the button beside his right knee, would instantly alert Heathrow Control to an emergency and allow them to monitor any conversation on the flight deck. He lifted his hand away.

'Remove the fuse to the bug circuit.' She indicated the correct box above his head, and he glanced at the captain again, but her voice stung like the tail of a scorpion:

'Do what I tell you.'

Carefully he removed the fuse and she relaxed slightly.

'Read your departure clearance,' she instructed.

'We are cleared to radar departure on track for Nairobi and an unrestricted climb to cruise altitude of thirty-nine thousand feet.'

'When is your next "operations normal" due?'

Operations normal was the routine report to Nairobi

Control to assure them that the flight was proceeding as planned.

'In eleven minutes and thirty-five seconds.' The engineer was a young, dark-haired, rather handsome man with a deep forehead, pale skin and the quick, efficient manner instilled by his training.

The girl turned to the captain of the Boeing and their gazes locked as they measured each other. The captain's hair was more grey than black and cropped close to his big rounded skull. He was bull-necked, and had the beefy, ruddy face of a farmer or of a butcher – but his eyes were steady and his manner calm and unshakeable. He was a man to watch, the girl recognized instantly.

'I want you to believe that I am committed entirely to this operation,' she said, 'and that I would welcome the opportunity to sacrifice my life to my cause.' Her dark blue eyes held his without fear, and she read the first growth of respect in him. That was good, all part of her careful calculations.

'I believe that,' said the pilot, and nodded once.

'Your duty is to the four hundred and seventeen lives aboard this aircraft,' she went on. He did not have to reply. 'They will be safe, just as long as you follow my commands implicitly. That I promise you.'

'Very well.'

'Here is our new destination.' She handed him a small white typewritten card. 'I want a new course with forecast winds, and a time of arrival. Your turn onto the new heading to commence immediately after your next "operations normal" report in—' She glanced back at the engineer for the time.

'Nine minutes fifty-eight seconds,' he said promptly.

' – and I want your turn to the new heading to be very gentle, very balanced. We don't want any of the passengers to spill their champagne – do we?'

In the few minutes that she had been on the flight deck

she had already established a bizarre rapport with the captain; it was a blend of reluctant respect and overt hostility and of sexual awareness. She had dressed deliberately to reveal her body, and in her excitement her nipples had hardened and darkened, pushing out through the thin cotton shirt with its suggestive legend, and the musky woman's smell of her body again intensified by her excitement filled the confined cockpit.

Nobody spoke again for many minutes, then the flight engineer broke the silence.

'Thirty seconds to "operations normal".'

'All right, switch on the HF and make the report.'

'Nairobi Approach this is Speedbird Zero Seven Zero.'

'Go ahead Speedbird Zero Seven Zero.'

'Operations normal,' said the engineer into his headset.

'Roger, Zero Seven Zero. Report again in forty minutes.'

'Zero Seven Zero.'

The blonde girl sighed with relief. 'All right, shut down the set.' Then to the captain, 'Disengage the flight director and make the turn to the new heading by hand; let's see how gentle you can be.'

The turn was a beautiful exhibition of flying, two minutes to make a change of 76° of heading, the needles of the turn-and-balance indicator never deviating a hair's breadth, and when it was completed, the girl smiled for the first time.

It was a gorgeous sunny flash of very white teeth.

'Good,' she said, smiling directly into the captain's face. 'What is your name?'

'Cyril,' he replied after a moment's hesitation.

'You can call me Ingrid,' she invited.

There was no set routine to the days in this new command of Peter Stride's, except the obligatory hour on the range with pistol and automatic weapons. No member of Thor Command – not even the technicians – were spared daily range practice.

The rest of Peter's day had been filled with unrelenting activity, beginning with a briefing on the new electronic communications equipment that had just been installed in his command aircraft. This had taken half the morning, and he had been only just in time to join his striker force in the main cabin of the Hercules transport for the day's exercise.

Peter jumped with the first stick of ten men. They jumped from five hundred feet, the parachutes seeming to snap open only seconds before they hit the ground. However, the crosswind had been strong enough to spread them out a little even from that height. The first landing had not been tight enough for Peter. They had taken two minutes fifty-eight seconds from jump to penetration of the deserted administration block standing forlornly in one of the military zones of Salisbury Plain.

'If they had been holding hostages in here, we'd have arrived just in time to start mopping up the blood,' Peter told his men grimly. 'We'll do it again!'

This time they had cut one minute fifty seconds off their time, falling in a tightly steered pattern about the building – beating the time of Colin Noble's No 2 striker team by ten seconds.

To celebrate Peter had scorned the military transports and they had run the five miles to the airstrip, each man in full combat kit and carrying the enormous bundle of his used parachute silk.

The Hercules was waiting to fly them back to base, but it was after dark before they landed and taxied into Thor Command's security compound at the end of the main runway.

For Peter the temptation to leave the debriefing to Colin

Noble had been strong indeed. His driver would have picked up Melissa-Jane at East Croydon Station and she would already be waiting alone in the new cottage, only half a mile from the base gates.

He had not seen her for six weeks, not since he had taken command of Thor, for in all that time he had not allowed himself a single day's respite. He felt a tickle of guilt now, that he should be allowing himself this indulgence, and so he lingered a few minutes after the briefing to transfer command to Colin Noble.

'Where are you going for the weekend?' Colin demanded.

'She's taking me to a pop concert tomorrow night – The Living Dead, no less,' Peter chuckled. 'Seems I haven't lived until I hear the Dead.'

'Give M.J. my love, and a kiss,' Colin told him.

Peter placed high value on his new-found privacy. He had lived most of his adult life in officers' quarters and messes, constantly surrounded by other human beings. However, this command had given him the opportunity to escape.

The cottage was only four and a half minutes' drive from the compound but it might have been an island. It had come furnished and at a rental that surprised him pleasantly. Behind a high hedge of dog rose, off a quiet lane, and set in a sprawling rather unkempt garden, it had become home in a few weeks. He had even been able to unpack his books at last. Books accumulated over twenty years, and stored against such an opportunity. It was a comfort to have them piled around his desk in the small front room or stacked on the tables beside his bed, even though there had been little opportunity to read much of them yet. The new job was a tough one.

Melissa-Jane must have heard the crunch of gravel under the Rover's tyres, and she would certainly have been waiting for it. She came running out of the front door into the driveway, directly into the beam of the headlights, and

Peter had forgotten how lovely she was. He felt his heart squeezed.

When he stepped out of the car she launched herself at him and clung with both arms around his chest. He held her for a long moment, neither of them able to speak. She was so slim and warm, her body seeming to throb with life and vitality.

At last he lifted her chin and studied her face. The huge violet eyes swam with happy tears, and she sniffed loudly. Already she had that old-fashioned English porcelain beauty; there would never be the acne and the agony of puberty for Melissa-Jane.

Peter kissed her solemnly on the forehead. 'You'll catch your death,' he scolded fondly.

'Oh, Daddy, you are a real fusspot.' She smiled through the tears and on tip-toe she reached up to kiss him full on the mouth.

They ate lasagne and cassata at an Italian restaurant in Croydon, and Melissa-Jane did most of the talking. Peter watched and listened, revelling in her freshness and youth. It was hard to believe she was not yet fourteen, for physically she was almost fully developed, the breasts under the white turtle-neck sweater no longer merely buds; and she conducted herself like a woman ten years older, only the occasional gleeful giggle betraying her or the lapse as she used some ghastly piece of Roedean slang – 'grotty' was one of these.

Back at the cottage she made them Ovaltine and they drank it beside the fire, planning every minute of the weekend ahead of them and skirting carefully around the pitfalls, the unwritten taboos of their relationship which centred mostly on 'Mother'.

When it was time for bed she came and sat in his lap and traced the lines of his face with her fingertip.

'Do you know who you remind me of?'

'Tell me,' he invited.

'Gary Cooper – only much younger, of course,' she added hurriedly.

'Of course,' Peter chuckled. 'But where did you ever hear of Gary Cooper?'

'They had *High Noon* as the Sunday movie on telly last week.'

She kissed him again and her lips tasted of sugar and Ovaltine, and her hair smelled sweet and clean.

'How old are you, anyway, Daddy?'

'I'm thirty-nine.'

'That isn't really so terribly old.' She comforted him uncertainly.

'Sometimes it's as old as the dinosaurs—' and at that moment the bleeper beside his empty cup began its strident, irritating electronic tone, and Peter felt the slide of dread in his stomach.

Not now, he thought. Not on this day when I have been so long without her.

The bleeper was the size of a cigarette pack, the globe of its single eye glared redly, insistent as the audio-signal. Reluctantly Peter picked it up and, with his daughter still in his lap, he switched in the miniature two-way radio and depressed the send button.

'Thor One,' he said.

The reply was tinny and distorted, the set near the limit of its range.

'General Stride, Atlas has ordered condition Alpha.'

Another false alarm, Peter thought bitterly. There had been a dozen Alphas in the last month, but why on this night. Alpha was the first stage of alert with the teams embarked and ready for condition Bravo which was the GO.

'Inform Atlas we are seven minutes from Bravo.'

Four and a half of those would be needed for him to

reach the compound, and suddenly the decision to rent the cottage was shown up as dangerous self-indulgence. In four and a half minutes innocent lives can be lost.

'Darling,' he hugged Melissa-Jane swiftly, 'I'm sorry.'

'That's all right.' She was stiff and resentful.

'There will be another time soon, I promise.'

'You always promise,' she whispered, but she saw he was no longer listening. He dislodged her and stood up, the heavy jawline clenched and thick dark brows almost meeting above the narrow, straight, aristocratic nose.

'Lock the door when I'm gone, darling. I'll send the driver for you if it's Bravo. He will drive you back to Cambridge and I will let your mother know to expect you.'

He stepped out into the night, still shrugging into his duffle coat, and she listened to the whirl of the starter, the rush of tyres over gravel and the dwindling note of the engine.

The controller in Nairobi tower allowed the British Airways flight from Seychelles to run fifteen seconds past its reporting time. Then he called once, twice and a third time without reply. He switched frequencies to the channels reserved for information, approach, tower and, finally, emergency, on one at least of which 070 should have been maintaining listening watch. There was still no reply.

Speedbird 070 was forty-five seconds past 'operations normal' before he removed the yellow slip from his approach rack and placed it in the emergency 'lost contact' slot, and immediately search and rescue procedures were in force.

Speedbird 070 was two minutes and thirteen seconds past 'operations normal' when the telex pull sheet landed on the British Airways desk at Heathrow Control, and sixteen seconds later Atlas had been informed and had placed Thor Command on condition Alpha.

The moon was three days short of full, its upper rim only slightly indented by the earth's shadow. However, at this altitude it seemed almost as big as the sun itself and its golden light was certainly more beautiful.

In the tropical summer night great silver cloud ranges towered into the sky, and mushroomed into majestic thunder heads, and the moonlight dressed them in splendour.

The aircraft fled swiftly between the peaks of cloud, like a monstrous black bat on back-swept wings it bored into the west.

Under the port-side wing a sudden dark chasm opened in the clouds like the mouth of hell itself, and deep in its maw there was the faint twinkle of far light, like a dying star.

'That will be Madagascar,' said the captain, his voice over-loud in the quiet cockpit. 'We are on track.' And behind his shoulder the girl stirred and carefully transferred the grenade into her other hand before she spoke for the first time in half an hour.

'Some of our passengers might still be awake and notice that.' She glanced at her wristwatch. 'It's time to wake up the others and let them know the good news.' She turned back to the flight engineer. 'Please switch on all the cabin lights and the seat-belt lights and let me have the microphone.'

Cyril Watkins, the captain, was reminded once again that this was a carefully planned operation. The girl was timing her announcement to the passengers when their resistance would be at its lowest possible ebb; at two o'clock in the morning after having been awoken from the disturbed rest of intercontinental flight their immediate reaction was likely to be glum resignation.

'Cabin and seat-belt lights are on,' the engineer told her, and handed her the microphone.

'Good morning, ladies and gentlemen.' Her voice was warm, clear and bright. 'I regret having to waken you at such an inconvenient hour. However, I have a very important announcement to make and I want all of you to pay the most careful attention.' She paused, and in the cavernous and crowded cabins there was a general stir and heads began to lift, hair tousled and eyes unfocused and blinking away the cobwebs of sleep. 'You will notice that the seat-belt lights are on. Will you all check that the persons beside you are fully awake and that their seat belts are fastened. Cabin staff please make certain that this is done.'

She paused again; the belts would inhibit any sudden movement, any spontaneous action at the first shock. Ingrid noted the passage of sixty seconds on the sweep hand of her wristwatch before going on.

'First let me introduce myself. My name is Ingrid. I am a senior officer of the Action Commando for Human Rights—' Captain Watkins curled his lip cynically at the pompous self-righteous title, but kept silent, staring ahead into the starry, moonlit depths of space ' – and this aircraft is under my command. Under no circumstances whatsoever will any of you leave your seats without the express permission of one of my officers – if this order is disobeyed, it will lead directly to the destruction of this aircraft and all aboard by high explosive.'

She repeated the announcement immediately in fluent German, and then in less proficient but clearly intelligible French before reverting to English once again.

'Officers of the Action Commando will wear red shirts for immediate identification and they will be armed.'

As she spoke her three companions in the front of the first-class cabin were stripping out the false bottoms from their canvas flight bags. The space was only two inches deep by fourteen by eight, but it was sufficient for the broken-down twelve bore pistols, and ten rounds of buckshot cartridges. The barrels of the pistols were fourteen inches long, the bores were smooth and made of armoured plastic. This material would not have withstood the passage of a solid bullet through rifling or any of the newer explosive propellants but it had been designed for use with the lower velocity and pressures of multiple shot and cordite. The breech piece was of plastic as were the double pistol grips, and these clipped swiftly into position. The only metal in the entire weapon was the case-steel firing pin and spring, no bigger than one of the metal studs in the canvas flight bag, so they would not have activated the metal detectors of the security check at Mahé airport. The ten cartridges contained in each bag had plastic cases and bases; again only the percussion caps were of aluminium foil, which would not disturb an electrical field. The cartridges were packed in looped cartridge belts which buckled around the waist.

The weapons were short, black and ugly; they required reloading like a conventional shotgun, the spent shells were not self-ejecting and the recoil was so vicious that it would break the wrists of the user who did not bear down heavily on the pistol grips. However, at ranges up to thirty feet the destructive power was awesome, at twelve feet it would disembowel a man and at six feet it would blow his head off cleanly – yet it did not have the penetrating power to hole the pressure hull of an intercontinental airliner.

It was the perfect weapon for the job in hand, and within a few seconds three of them had been assembled and loaded and the two men had slipped on the bright scarlet shirts that identified them over their tee-shirts and moved to their positions – one in the back of the first-class cabin and one in the back of the tourist cabin, they stood with their grotesque weapons ostentatiously displayed.

The slim, pretty, dark-haired German girl stayed in her seat a little longer, working swiftly and neatly as she opened the remaining coco-de-mer and transferred their contents into two of the netting bags. These grenades differed only from the one carried by Ingrid in that they had double red lines painted around the middle. This signified that they were electronically fused.

Now Ingrid's clear young voice resumed over the cabin address system, and the long rows of passengers – all fully awake now – sat rigid and attentive, their faces reflecting an almost uniform expression of shock and trepidation.

' – The officer of the action commando who is moving down the cabin at this time is placing high explosive grenades—' The dark-haired girl started down the aisle, and every fifteen rows she opened one of the overhead lockers and placed a grenade in it, closed the locker and moved on. The passengers' heads revolved slowly in unison as they watched her with the fascination of total horror. 'A single one of those grenades has the explosive power to destroy this aircraft – they were designed to kill by concussion the crew of a battle tank protected by six inches of armour – the officer is placing fourteen of these devices along the length of this aircraft. They can be detonated simultaneously by an electronic transmitter under my control—' the voice contained a hint of mischief now, a little undercurrent of laughter ' – and if that happened they'd hear the bang at the North Pole!'

The passengers stirred like the leaves of a tree in a vagrant breeze; somewhere a woman began to weep. It was a strangled passionless sound and nobody even looked in her direction.

'But don't worry yourselves. That isn't going to happen. Because everybody is going to do exactly as they are told, and when it's all over you are going to be proud of your part in this operation. We are all partners in a noble and glorious mission, we are all warriors for freedom and for the dignity of man. Today we take a mighty step forward into the new world – a world purged and cleansed of injustice and tyranny and dedicated to the welfare of all its peoples.'

The woman was still weeping, and now a child joined her on a higher, more strident note.

The dark-haired girl returned to her seat and now she retrieved the camera that had activated the metal detector at Mahé airport. She slung it around her neck and crouched again to assemble the two remaining shot pistols; carrying them and the cartridge belts she hurried forward to the flight deck where the big blonde kissed her delightedly and unashamedly on the lips.

'Karen, *Liebling*, you were wonderful.' And then she took the camera from her and slung it around her own neck.

'This—' she explained to the captain ' – is not what it appears to be. It is the remote radio detonator for the grenades in the fuselage.'

He nodded without replying, and with obvious relief Ingrid disarmed the grenade that she had carried for so long by replacing the safety pin. She handed it to the other girl.

'How much longer to the coast?' she asked as she strapped and buckled the cartridge belt around her waist.

'Thirty-two minutes,' said the flight engineer promptly, and Ingrid opened the breech of the pistol, checked the load and then snapped it closed again.

'You and Henri can stand down now,' she told Karen. 'Try and sleep.'

The operation might last many days still, and exhaustion would be the most dangerous enemy they would have to contend with. It was for this reason alone that they had employed such a large force. From now on, except in an emergency, two of them would be on duty and two would be resting.

'You have done a very professional job,' said the pilot, Cyril Watkins, ' – so far.'

'Thank you.' Ingrid laughed, and over the back of his

seat placed a comradely hand on his shoulder. 'We have practised very hard for this day.'

Peter Stride dipped his lights three times as he raced down the long narrow alley that led to the gates of the compound without slowing the Rover, and the sentry swung the gate open just in time for him to roar through.

There were no floodlights, no bustling activity – just the two aircraft standing together in the echoing cavern of the hangar.

The Lockheed Hercules seemed to fill the entire building, that had been built to accommodate the smaller bombers of World War II. The tall vertical fin of its epinage reached to within a few feet of the roof girders.

Beside it the Hawker Siddeley HS 125 executive jet seemed dainty and ineffectual. The differing origins of the machines emphasized that this unit was a co-operative venture between two nations.

This was underscored once more when Colin Noble hurried forward to meet Peter as he cut the Rover's engine and lights.

'A grand night for it, Peter.' There was no mistaking the drawl of mid-Western America, although Colin looked more like a successful used-car salesman than a colonel in the U.S. Marines. In the beginning Peter had believed that this strict apportioning of material and manpower on equal national lines might weaken the effectiveness of Atlas. He no longer had those doubts.

Colin wore the nondescript blue overalls and cloth cap, both embroidered with the legend 'THOR COMMUNICATIONS' which deliberately made him look more of a technician than a soldier.

Colin was Peter's second in command. They had known each other only the six weeks since Peter had assumed command of Thor – but after a short period of mutual wariness the two men had formed one of those fast bonds of liking and mutual respect.

Colin was of medium height, but none the less a big man. First glance might have given the impression that he was fat, for his body had a certain toad-like spread to it. There was no fat upon his frame, however, it was all muscle and bone. He had boxed heavyweight for Princeton and the marines, and his nose above the wide laughing mouth had been broken just below the bridge, it was lumped and twisted slightly.

Colin cultivated the boisterous bluff manner of a career athlete, but his eyes were the colour of burned toffee and were brightly intelligent and all-seeing. He was tough and leery as an old alley cat. It was not easy to earn the respect of Peter Stride. Colin had done so in under six weeks.

He stood now between the two aircraft, while his men went about their Alpha preparation with quick understated efficiency.

Both aircraft were painted in commercial airline style, blue and white and gold, with a stylized portrait of the Thunder God on the tail fin and the 'THOR COMMUNICATIONS' title down the fuselage. They could land at any airport in the world without causing undue comment.

'What is the buzz, Colin?' Peter Stride demanded as he slammed the Rover's door and hurried to meet the American. It had taken him some time and conscious effort to adapt his language and mode of address to fit in with his new second-in-command. He had learned very early not to expect that, merely because he was the youngest major-general in the British army, Colonel Colin Noble was going to call him 'Sir' every time he spoke.

'Missing aircraft.' It could have been a train, an embassy,

even an ocean liner, Peter realized. 'British Airways. For Chrissake let's get out of the cold.' The wind was flapping the legs of Colin's overalls and tugging at his sleeves.

'Where?'

'Indian Ocean.'

'Are we set for Bravo?' Peter asked as they climbed into his command plane.

'All set.'

The interior of the Hawker had been restyled to make it a compact headquarters and communications centre.

There was comfortable seating for four officers directly behind the flight deck. Then the two electronic engineers and their equipment occupied a separate rear compartment, beyond which were the small toilet and galley in the extreme rear.

One of the technicians looked through the communicating door as Peter stooped into the cabin. 'Good evening, General Stride – we have a direct link with Atlas established.'

'Put him on the screen,' he ordered as he sank into the padded leather of his chair behind the small working desk.

There was a single fourteen-inch main television screen in the panel directly facing Peter, and above it four smaller six-inch screens for conference communication. The main screen came alive, and the image of the big noble leonine head firmed.

'Good afternoon, Peter.' The smile was warm, charismatic, compelling.

'Good evening, sir.'

And Dr Kingston Parker tilted his head slightly to acknowledge the reference to the time difference between Washington and England.

'Right at this moment we are in the dark completely. All we have is that BA 070 with four hundred and one passengers and sixteen crew on a flight from Mahé to Nairobi has not reported for thirty-two minutes.'

Parker was Chairman of the Intelligence Oversight Board, among other duties, and he reported directly to the President of the United States in that capacity. He was the President's personal and trusted friend. They had been in the same class at Annapolis, both of them had graduated in the top twenty but, unlike the President, Parker had gone directly into government.

Parker was an artist, a talented musician, the author of four scholarly works of philosophy and politics, and a grand master of chess. A man of overwhelming presence, of vast humanity and towering intelligence. Yet also he was a secret man, avoiding the glaring scrutiny of the media, hiding his ambitions, if ambitions he had – although the presidency of the United States would not be an impossible dream to such a man – only taking up with rare skill and strength any burden that was thrust upon him.

Peter Stride had met him personally on half a dozen occasions since being seconded to Thor. He had spent a weekend with Parker at his New York home, and his respect for the man had become boundless. Peter realized that he was the perfect head for such a complex concept as Atlas: it needed the philosopher's tempering influence over trained soldiers, it needed the tact and charisma of the diplomat to deal directly with the heads of two governments, and it needed that steely intellect to make the ultimate decision that could involve hundreds of innocent lives and incur fearsome political consequences.

Now swiftly and incisively he told Peter what little they knew of Flight 070 and what search and rescue routine was already in force, before going on, 'Without being alarmist, this does seem to be the perfect target. The flight carries most of the world's leading surgeons, and the convention was public knowledge eighteen months ago. Doctors have the necessary image to appeal to public sentiment and their nationalities are nicely mixed – American, British, French, Scandinavian, German, Italian – three of those countries have notoriously *soft* records with militant activity. It's a British aircraft, and the final destination would probably have been chosen to further complicate the issue and inhibit any counter-action.'

Parker paused, and a small crease of worry appeared for a moment in the broad smooth forehead.

'I have put Mercury on condition Alpha as well – if this is a strike the final destination could just as easily be eastwards of the aircraft's last reported position.'

Atlas's offensive arm comprised three identical units. Thor would be used only in Europe or Africa. Mercury was based on the American Naval base in Indonesia and covered Asia and Australasia, while Diana was in Washington itself and ready for counteraction in either of the American continents.

'I have Tanner of Mercury on the other relay now. I will be back to you in a few seconds, Peter.'

'Very well, sir.'

The screen went blank, and in the chair beside him Colin Noble lit one of his expensive Dutch cheroots and crossed his ankles on the desk in front of him.

'Seems the great god Thor came down to earth for a little poontang. When he'd finished pleasuring one of the vestal virgins he thought he'd let her know the honour she'd been given. "I'm Thor," he told her. "Tho am I," she agreed, "but it wath loth of fun."'

Peter shook his head sorrowfully. 'That's funny?' he asked.

'Helps to while away the time.' Colin glanced at his wristwatch. 'If this is another false alarm, it's going to make it thirteen straight.' He yawned. There was nothing to do. It had all been done before. Everything was in the ultimate state of readiness. In the huge Hercules transport, every item of a comprehensive arsenal of equipment was ready for instant use. The thirty highly trained soldiers were embarked. The flight crews of both aircraft were at their stations, the communications technicians had set up their links with satellites and through them to the available intelligence computers in Washington and London. It remained only to wait – the greater part of a soldier's life was spent waiting, but Peter had never become hardened to it. It helped now to have the companionship of Colin Noble.

In a life spent in the company of many men it was difficult to form close relationships. Here in the smaller closed ranks of Thor in shared endeavour they had achieved that and become friends, and their conversation was relaxed and desultory, moving casually from subject to subject, but without relaxing the undercurrent of alertness that gripped both men.

At one stage Kingston Parker came on the screen again to tell them that search and rescue aircraft had found no indications at the last reported position of 070, and that a photographic run by the 'Big Bird' reconnaissance satellite had been made over the same area, but that film would not be ready for appraisal for another fourteen hours. Speedbird 070 was now one hour six minutes past 'operations normal' and suddenly Peter remembered Melissa-Jane. He asked communications for a telephone line and dialled the cottage. There was no reply, so the driver would have collected her already. He hung up and rang Cynthia in Cambridge.

'Damn it, Peter. This really is most inconsiderate of you.' Freshly aroused from sleep, her voice was petulant, immediately awakening only antipathies. 'Melissa has been looking forward to this—'

'Yes, I know, and so have I.'

' – and George and I had arranged—' George, her new husband, was a Political History don; despite himself Peter quite liked the man. He had been very good to Melissa-Jane.

'The exigencies of the service.' Peter cut in lightly – and her voice took on a bitter edge.

'How often I had to listen to that – I hoped never to hear it again.' They were on the same futile old treadmill, and he had to stop it.

'Look, Cynthia. Melissa is on her way—'

In front of him the big television screen lit and Kingston Parker's eyes were dark with regret, as though he mourned for all mankind.

'I have to go,' Peter told the woman whom once he had loved, and broke the connection, leaning forward attentively towards the image on the screen.

'The South African radar defences have painted an unidentified target approaching their airspace,' Kingston Parker told him. 'Its speed and position correspond with those of 070. They have scrambled a Mirage flight to intercept – but in the meantime I'm assuming that it's a militant strike and we'll go immediately to condition Bravo, if you please, Peter.'

'We are on our way, sir.'

And beside him Colin Noble took his feet off the desk and thumped them together onto the floor. The cheroot was still clamped between his teeth.

The target was live and the pilot of the leading Mirage F.1 interceptor had his flight computer in 'attack' mode and all his weaponry – missiles and cannon – were armed. The computer gave him a time to intercept of thirty-three seconds, and the target's heading was constant at 210° magnetic and its ground speed at 483 knots.

Ahead of him the dawn was rising in wildly theatrical display. Avalanches of silver and pink cloud tumbled down the sky, and the sun, still below the horizon, flung long lances of golden light across the heavens. The pilot leaned forward against his shoulder straps and lifted the Polaroid visor of his helmet with one gloved hand, straining ahead for the first glimpse of the target.

His trained gunfighter's eye picked out the dark speck against the distracting background of cloud and sunlight and he made an almost imperceptible movement of the controls to avoid the direct head-on approach to the target.

The speck swelled in size with disturbing rapidity as they converged at combined speeds of nearly fifteen hundred miles per hour, and at the instant he was certain of his identification the leader took his flight, still in a tight 'finger five', up into a vertical climb from which they rolled out neatly five thousand feet above the target and on the same heading, immediately reducing power to conform in speed to the big aircraft far below.

'Cheetah, this is Diamond leader – we are visual, and target is a Boeing 747 bearing British Airways markings.'

'Diamond Leader, this is Cheetah, conform to target, maintain five thousand feet separation and avoid any threatening attitudes. Report again in sixty seconds.'

Major-General Peter Stride's executive jet was arrowing southwards and leaving its enormous protégé lumbering ponderously along in its wake. Every minute increased the distance between the two aircraft, and by the time they reached their ultimate destination – wherever that might be – there would probably be a thousand miles or more separating them.

However, the big Hercules's slow speed became a virtue when the need arose to take its heavy load of men and equipment into short unsurfaced strips in unlikely corners of the earth – perhaps in the 'hot and high' conditions that a pilot most dreads.

It was the Hawker's job to get Peter Stride to the scene of terrorist activity as swiftly as possible, and the general's job once there to stall and procrastinate and bargain until Colin Noble's assault team caught up with him.

The two men were still in contact, however, and the small central television screen in front of Peter was permanently lit with a view of the interior of the Hercules's main hold. When he lifted his head from his work, Peter Stride could see a picture of his troops, all in the casual Thor overalls, lounging or sprawled in abandoned attitudes of relaxation down the central aisle of the Hercules. They also were veterans at the hard game of waiting, while in the foreground Colin Noble sat at his small work desk, going through the voluminous check list for 'condition Charlie' which was the next state of alert when terrorist activity was confirmed.

Watching Colin Noble at work, Peter Stride found a moment to ponder once again the enormous cost of maintaining Atlas, most of it paid by the United States intelligence budget, and the obstacles and resistance that had been overcome to launch the project in the first place. Only the success of the Israelis at Entebbe and of the Germans at Mogadishu had made it possible, but there was still violent opposition in both countries to maintaining a dual national counteraction force.

With a preliminary click and hum the central screen of Peter's communications console came alive and Dr Parker spoke before his image had properly hardened.

'I'm afraid it's condition Charlie, Peter,' he said softly, and Peter was aware of the rush of his blood through his veins. It was natural for a soldier whose entire life had been spent in training for a special moment in time to welcome the arrival of that moment – yet he found contempt for himself in that emotion; no sane man should anticipate violence and death, and all the misery and suffering which attended them.

' – the South Africans have intercepted and identified 070. It entered their airspace forty-five seconds ago.'

'Radio contact?' Peter asked.

'No.' Parker shook his great head. 'It is declining contact, and we must assume that it is under the control of militants – so now I'm going to be at this desk until this thing is settled.' Kingston Parker never used the emotive word 'terrorist' and he did not like to hear it from his subordinates either.

'Never hate your adversary blindly,' he had told Peter once. 'Understand his motives, recognize and respect his strengths – and you will be better prepared to meet him.'

'What co-operation can we expect?' Peter asked.

'All African States that we have so far been able to contact have offered full co-operation, including overflight, landing and refuelling facilities – and the South Africans are being helpful. I have spoken to their defence minister and he has offered the fullest possible co-operation. They will refuse 070 landing clearance, of course, and I anticipate that it will have to go on to one of the black states farther north, which is probably the militants' intention anyway. I think you know my views about South Africa – but in this instance I must say they are being very good.'

Parker brought into the television shot a black briar pipe with a big round bowl, and began to stuff it with tobacco. His hands were large, like the rest of his body, but the fingers were long and supple as those of a pianist – which of course he was. And Peter remembered the scented smell of the tobacco he smoked. Even though he was a non-smoker, Peter had not found the odour offensive. Both men were silent, deep in thought, Parker frowning slightly as he seemed to concentrate on his pipe. Then he sighed and looked up again.

'All right, Peter. Let's hear what you have.'

Peter shuffled through the notes he had been making. 'I have prepared four tentative scenarios and our responses to each, sir. The most important consideration is whether this is a strike "à l'allemande" or "à l'italienne"—'

Parker nodded, listening; although this was well-travelled ground they must go over it again. A strike in the Italian fashion was the easier to resolve, a straight demand for cash. The German tradition involved release of prisoners, social and political demands that crossed national boundaries. They worked on for another hour before they were interrupted again.

'Good God.' It was a measure of Kingston Parker's astonishment that he used such strong language. 'We have a new development here—'

It was only when 070 joined the eastern airway and began to initiate a standard approach and let down, without however obtaining air traffic control clearance, that South African Airforce Command suddenly realized what was about to happen.

Immediately emergency silence was imposed on all the aviation frequencies while the approaching flight was bombarded by urgent commands to immediately vacate national airspace. There was no response whatsoever, and one hundred and fifty nautical miles out from Jan Smuts International Airport the Boeing reduced power and commenced a sedate descent to enter controlled airspace.

'British Airways 070 this is Jan Smuts Control, you are expressly refused clearance to join the circuit. Do you read me, 070?'

'British Airways 070 this is Airforce Command. You are warned that you are in violation of national airspace. You are ordered to climb immediately to thirty thousand feet and turn on course for Nairobi.'

The Boeing was a hundred nautical miles out and descending through fifteen thousand feet.

'Diamond Leader, this is Cheetah. Take the target under command and enforce departure clearance.'

The long sleek aircraft in its mottled green and brown battle camouflage dropped like a dart, rapidly overhauling the huge multi-engined giant, diving down just behind the tailplane and then pulling up steeply in front of the gaily painted red, white and blue nose.

Skilfully the Mirage pilot stationed his nimble little machine one hundred feet ahead of the Boeing and rocked his wings in the 'Follow me' command.

The Boeing sailed on serenely as though it had not seen or understood. The Mirage pilot nudged his throttles and the gap between the two aircraft narrowed down to fifty feet. Again he rocked his wings and began a steady rate-one turn onto the northerly heading ordered by Cheetah.

The Boeing held rock steady on its standard approach towards Johannesburg, forcing the Mirage leader to abandon his attempts to lead her away.

He edged back alongside, keeping just above the jet-blast of the Boeing's port engines until he was level with the cockpit and could stare across a gap of merely fifty feet.

'Cheetah, this is Diamond One. I have a good view into target's flight deck. There is a fourth person in the cockpit. It's a woman. She appears to be armed with a machine pistol.'

The faces of the two pilots were white as bone as they turned to watch the interceptor. The woman leaned over the back of the left-hand seat, and lifted the clumsy black weapon in an ironic salute. She smiled and the Mirage pilot was close enough to see how white her teeth were.

' – a young woman, blonde hair, *mooi, baie mooi*—' the Mirage pilot reported. 'Pretty – very pretty.'

'Diamond One, this is Cheetah. Position for head-on attack.'

The Mirage thundered instantly ahead and climbed away swiftly, the other four aircraft of the flight sweeping in to resume their tight 'finger five' formation as they went out in a wide turn ahead of the Boeing.

'Cheetah. We are in position for a head-on attack.'

'Diamond Flight. Simulate. Attack in line astern. Five-second intervals. Minimum separation. Do not, I say again, do not open fire. This is a simulated attack. I say again, this is a simulated attack.'

'Diamond One – understands simulated attack.'

And the Mirage F.1 winged over and dived, its speed rocketing around the mach scale, booming through the sonic barrier in a fearsomely aggressive display.

Cyril Watkins saw him coming from seven miles ahead.

'Jesus,' he shouted. 'This is real,' and he lunged forward to take manual control of the Boeing, to pull her off the automatic approach that the electronic flight director was performing.

'Hold her steady.' Ingrid raised her voice for the first time. 'Hold it.' She swung the gaping double muzzles of the shot pistol onto the flight engineer. 'We don't need a navigator now.'

The captain froze, and the Mirage howled down on them, seemed to grow until it filled the whole view through the windshield ahead. At the last possible instant of time the nose lifted slightly and it flashed only feet overhead, but the supersonic turbulence of its passage struck and tossed even that huge machine like a piece of thistledown.

'Here comes another,' Cyril Watkins shouted.

'I mean it.' Ingrid pressed the muzzles so fiercely into the back of the flight engineer's neck that his forehead struck the edge of his computer console, and there was the quick bright rose of blood on the pale skin.

The jet blasts struck the Boeing one after the other as the Mirages attacked. Ingrid clutched wildly for support with her free hand, but kept the pistol jammed into the navigator's neck. 'I mean it,' she kept shouting. 'I'll kill him,' and they could hear the screams of the passengers even through the bulkhead of the flight deck.

Then the last Mirage was passed and gone and the Boeing's flight director recovered from the battering of close separation and quickly realigned the aircraft on the radio navigational beacons of Jan Smuts Airport.

'They won't buzz us again.' Ingrid stepped back from the flight engineer, allowing him to lift his head and wipe away the trickle of blood on the sleeve of his shirt. 'They can't come again. We are into controlled airspace.' She pointed ahead. 'Look!'

The Boeing was down to five thousand feet, but the horizon was obscured by the haze of smog and summer heat. To the right rose the smooth silhouette of the Kempton Park Power Station cooling towers and, closer at hand, the poisonous yellow tablelands of the mine dumps squatted on the flat and featureless plain of the African highveld. Around them human habitation was so dense that hundreds of windowpanes caught the early morning sun and glittered like beacons.

Closer still was the long, straight, blue streak of the main runway of Jan Smuts Airport.

'Take her straight in on runway 21,' Ingrid ordered.

'We can't—'

'Do it,' snapped the girl. 'Air traffic control will have cleared the circuit. They can't stop us.'

'Yes, they can,' Cyril Watkins answered. 'Just take a look at the runway apron.'

They were close enough now to count five fuel tenders, to see the Shell company insignia on the tanks.

'They are going to block the runway.'

With the tankers were five brilliant red vehicles of the fire service and two big white ambulances. They bumped wildly over the grass verge of the runway and then, one after the other, tenders and fire control vehicles and ambulances parked at intervals of a few hundred yards down the white-painted centre line of the runway.

'We can't land,' said the captain.

'Take her off automatic and fly her in by hand.' The girl's voice was different, hard, cruel.

The Boeing was sinking through a thousand feet, lined up for runway 21 and directly ahead the revolving red beacons on top of the fire vehicles seemed to flash a direct challenge.

'I can't pile into them,' Cyril Watkins decided, and there was no longer hesitation nor doubt in his tone. 'I'm going to overshoot and get out of here.'

'Land on the grass,' the girl shrieked. 'There is open grass on the left of the runway – put her down there.'

But Cyril Watkins had leaned forward in his seat and rammed the bank of throttles forward. The engines howled and the Boeing surged into a nose-high climb.

The young flight engineer had swivelled his stool and was staring ahead through the windscreen. His whole body was rigid, his expression intense and the smear of blood across his forehead was in vivid contrast to the pallor of his skin.

With his right hand he gripped the edge of his desk, and the knuckles of his fist were white and shiny as eggshell.

Without seeming to move the blonde girl had pinned the wrist of that rigid right hand, pressing the muzzles of the pistol into it.

There was a crash of sound, so violent in the confines of the cabin that it seemed to beat in their eardrums. The weapon kicked up as high as the girl's golden head and there was the immediate acrid stench of burned cordite.

The flight engineer stared down incredulously at the desk top. There was a hole blown through the metal as big as a teacup, and the edges were jagged with bright bare metal.

The blast of shot had amputated his hand cleanly at the wrist. The severed member had been thrown forward into the space between the pilots' seats, with the shattered bone protruding from the mangled meat. It twitched like a crushed and maimed insect.

'Land,' said the girl. 'Land or the next shot is through his head.'

'You bloody monster,' shouted Cyril Watkins, staring at the severed hand.

'Land or you will be responsible for this man's life.'

The flight engineer clutched the stump of his arm against his belly and doubled over it silently, his face contorted by the shock.

Cyril Watkins tore his stricken gaze from the severed hand and looked ahead once more. There was wide open grass between the runway markers and the narrow taxiway. The grass had been mown knee-high, and he knew the ground beneath it would be fairly smooth.

Cyril's hand on the throttle bank pulled back smoothly, almost of its own volition, the engine thunder died away and the nose dropped again.

He held his approach aligned with the main runway until he was well in over the threshold lights. He did not want to alert the drivers of the blocking vehicles to his intention while they still had time to counter it.

'You murderous bitch,' he said under his breath. 'You filthy murderous bitch.'

He banked the Boeing steeply, realigned it with the long strip of open grass and cut the throttles completely, bringing her in nose-high and just a fraction above the stall, flaring out deliberately low and banging the Boeing down into the grass for positive touch down.

The huge machine settled to the rough strip, jolting and lurching wildly as Cyril Watkins fought the rudders to keep them lined up, holding his nose wheel off with the control yoke, while his co-pilot threw all her giant engines into reverse thrust and trod firmly down on the main landing gear brakes.

The fire engines and fuel tankers flashed past the starboard wing tip. The startled faces of their crews seemed very close and white – then 070 was past, her speed bleeding off sharply so her nose wheel dropped and she rocked and swayed gradually to a dead stop just short of the brick building which housed the approach and landing beacons, and the main radar installations.

It was 7.25 a.m. local time and Speedbird 070 was down.

'Well, they are down,' intoned Kingston Parker. 'And you can well understand the extreme efforts that were made to prevent them. Their choice of final destination settles one of your queries, Peter.'

'"À l'allemande"—' Peter nodded. 'It's got to be political. I agree, sir.'

'And you and I must now face in dreadful reality what we have discussed only in lofty theory—' Parker held a taper to his pipe and puffed twice before going on. ' – Morally justifiable militancy.'

'Again we have to differ, sir.' Peter cut in swiftly. 'There is no such thing.'

'Is there not?' Parker asked, shaking his head. 'What of the German officers killed in the streets of Paris by the French resistance?'

'That was war,' Peter exclaimed.

'Perhaps the group that seized 070 believes that they are at war—'

'With innocent victims?' Peter shot back.

'The *Haganah* took innocent victims – yet what they were fighting for was right and just.'

'I'm an Englishman, Dr Parker – you cannot expect me to condone the murder of British women and children.' Peter had stiffened in his chair.

'No,' Parker agreed. 'So let us not speak of the MauMau

in Kenya, nor of present-day Ireland then – but what of the French Revolution or the spreading of the Catholic faith by the most terrible persecution and tortures yet devised by man – were those not morally justifiable militancy?'

'I would prefer to call it understandable but reprehensible. Terrorism in any form can never be morally justifiable.' Provoked himself, Peter used the word deliberately to provoke and saw the small lift of Parker's thick bushy eyebrows.

'There is terrorism from above – as well as from below.' Parker picked up the word and used it deliberately. 'If you define terrorism as extreme physical or physiological coercion used to induce others to submit to the will of the terrorist – there is the legal terror threat of the gallows, the religious terror threat of hell fire, the paternal terror threat of the cane – are those more morally justifiable than the aspiration of the weak, the poor, the politically oppressed, the powerless victims of an unjust society? Is their scream of protest to be strangled—'

Peter shifted uncomfortably in his chair. 'Protest outside the law—'

'Laws are made by man, almost always by the rich and the powerful – laws are changed by men, usually only after militant action. The women's suffragette movement, the civil rights campaign in this country—' Parker broke off and chuckled. 'I'm sorry, Peter. Sometimes I confuse myself. It's often more difficult to be a liberal than it is to be a tyrant. At least the tyrant seldom has doubts.' Parker lay back in his chair, a dismissive gesture. 'I propose to leave you in peace for an hour or two now. You will want to develop your plans in line with the new developments. But I personally have no doubts now that we are dealing with politically motivated militants, and not merely a gang of old-fashioned kidnappers after a fast buck. Of one other thing I am certain: before we see this one through we will be forced to examine our own consciences very closely.'

'Take the second right,' said Ingrid quietly, and the Boeing swung off the grass onto the taxiway. There seemed to be no damage to her landing gear, but now that she had left her natural element, the aircraft had lost grace and beauty and became lumbering and ungainly.

The girl had never been on the flight deck of a grounded Jumbo before, and the height was impressive. It gave her a feeling of detachment, of being invulnerable.

'Now left again,' she instructed, and the Boeing turned away from the main airport building towards the southern end of the runway. The observation deck of the airport's flat roof was already lined with hundreds of curious spectators, but all activity on the apron was suspended. The waiting machines and tenders were deserted, not a single human figure on the tarmac.

'Park there.' She pointed ahead to an open area four hundred yards from the nearest building, midway between the terminal and the cluster of service hangars and the main fuel depot. 'Stop on the intersection.'

Grimly silent, Cyril Watkins did as he was ordered, and then turned in his seat.

'I must call an ambulance to get him off.'

The co-pilot and a stewardess had the flight engineer stretched out on the galley floor, just beyond the door to the flight deck. They were using linen table napkins to bind up the arm and try and staunch the bleeding. The stench of cordite still lingered and mingled with the taint of fresh blood.

'Nobody leaves this aircraft.' The girl shook her head. 'He knows too much about us already.'

'My God, woman. He needs medical attention.'

'There are three hundred doctors aboard—' she pointed out indifferently. 'The best in the world. Two of them may come forward and attend to him.'

She perched sideways on the flight engineer's blood-splattered desk, and thumbed the internal microphone.

Cyril Watkins noticed even in his outrage that it needed only a single demonstration and Ingrid was able to work the complicated communications equipment. She was bright and very well trained.

'Ladies and gentlemen, we have landed at Johannesburg Airport. We will be here for a long time – perhaps days, even weeks. All our patience will be tried, so I must warn you that any disobedience will be most severely dealt with. Already one attempt at resistance has been made – and in consequence a member of the crew has been shot and gravely wounded. He may die of this wound. We do not want a repetition of this incident. However, I must again warn you that my officers and I will not hesitate to shoot again, or even to detonate the explosives above your heads – if the need arises.'

She paused and watched a moment as two selected doctors came forward and knelt on each side of the flight engineer. He was shaking like a fever victim with shock, his white shirt splashed and daubed with blood. Her expression showed no remorse, no real concern, and her voice was calm and light as she went on.

'Two of my officers will now pass down the aisles and they will collect your passports from you. Please have these documents ready.'

Her eyes flicked sideways, as movement caught her eye. From beyond the service hangars a line of four armoured cars emerged in line ahead. They were the locally manufactured version of the French Panhard with heavily lugged tall tyres, a raked turret and the disproportionately long barrels of the cannons trained forward. The armoured vehicles circled cautiously and parked three hundred yards out, at the four points – wing tips, tail and nose – around the aircraft, with the long cannon trained upon her.

The girl watched them disdainfully until one of the doctors pushed himself in front of her. He was a short, chubby little man, balding – but brave.

'This man must be taken to a hospital immediately.'

'That is out of the question.'

'I insist. His life is in danger.'

'All our lives are in danger, doctor.' She paused and let that make its effect. 'Draw up a list of your requirements. I will see that you get them.'

'They have been down for sixteen hours now and the only contact has been a request for medical supplies and for a power link-up to the electrical mains.' Kingston Parker had removed his jacket and loosened the knot of his tie, but was showing no other ill effects of his vigil.

Peter Stride nodded at the image on the screen. 'What have your medics made of the supplies?' he asked.

'Looks like a gunshot casualty. Whole blood type AB Positive, that's rare but one of the crew is cross-matched AB Positive on his service record. Ten litres of plasmalyte B, a blood-giving set and syringes, morphine and intravenous penicillin, tetanus toxoid – all the equipment needed to treat massive physical trauma.'

'And they are on mains power?' Peter asked.

'Yes, four hundred people would have suffocated by now without the air-conditioning. The airport authority has laid a cable and plugged it into the external socket. All the aircraft's support system – even the galley heating – will be fully functional.'

'So we will be able to throw the switch on them at any time.' Peter made a note on the pad in front of him. 'But no demands yet? No negotiator called for?'

'No, nothing. They seem fully aware of the techniques of bargaining in this type of situation – unlike our friends, the host country. I am afraid we are having a great deal of trouble with the Wyatt Earp mentality—' Parker paused. 'I'm sorry, Wyatt Earp was one of our frontier marshals—'

'I saw the movie, and read the book,' Peter answered tartly.

'Well, the South Africans are itching to storm the aircraft, and both our ambassador and yours are hard pressed to restrain them. They are all set to kick the doors of the saloon open and rush in with six-guns blazing. They must also have seen the movie.'

Peter felt the crawl of horror down his spine. 'That would be a certain disaster,' he said quickly. 'These people are running a tight operation.'

'You don't have to convince me,' Parker agreed. 'What is your flying time to Jan Smuts now?'

'We crossed the Zambesi River seven minutes ago.' Peter glanced sideways through the perspex bubble window, but the ground was obscured by haze and cumulus cloud. 'We have another two hours ten minutes to fly – but my support section is three hours forty behind us.'

'All right, Peter. I will get back onto them. The South African Government has convened a full cabinet meeting, and both our ambassadors are sitting in as observers and advisers. I think I am going to be obliged to tell them about the existence of Atlas.'

He paused a moment. 'Here at last we are seeing Atlas justified, Peter. A single unit, cutting across all national considerations, able to act swiftly and independently. I think you should know that I have already obtained the agreement of the President and of your Prime Minister to condition Delta – at my discretion.'

Condition Delta was the kill decision.

' – but again I emphasize that I will implement Delta only as a last possible resort. I want to hear and consider the demands first, and in that respect we are open to negotiation – fully open—'

Parker went on speaking, and Peter Stride shifted slightly, dropping his chin into the cup of his hand to hide his irritation. They were into an area of dispute now – and once again Peter had to voice disagreement.

'Every time you let a militant walk away from a strike you immediately create the conditions for further strikes, to free the captive.'

'I have the clearance for condition Delta,' Parker reiterated with a trace of acid in his tone now, 'but I am making it clear that it will be used only with the greatest discretion. We are not an assassination unit, General Stride.' Parker nodded to an assistant off-screen. 'I am going through to the South Africans now to explain Atlas.' The image receded into darkness.

Peter Stride leapt up abruptly and tried to pace the narrow aisle between the seats, but there was insufficient headroom for his tall frame and he flung himself angrily into the seat again.

Kingston Parker stood up from his communications desk in the outer office of his suite in the west wing of the Pentagon. The two communications technicians scurried out of his way and his personal secretary opened the door to his inner office.

He moved with peculiar grace for such a large man, and there was no excess weight on his frame, his big heavy bones lean of flesh. His clothes were of fine cloth, well cut – the best that Fifth Avenue could offer – but they were worn almost to the point of shoddiness, the button-down collar slightly frayed, the Italian shoes scuffed at the toes as though material trappings counted not at all with him. Nevertheless he wore them with a certain unconscious panache, and he looked ten years younger than his fifty-three, only a few silver strands in the thick bushy mane of hair.

The inner office was Spartan in its furnishings, all of it U.S. Government issue, utilitarian and impersonal, only the books that filled every shelf and the grand piano were his own. The piano was a Bechstein grand and much too large for the room. Parker ran his right hand lightly across the keyboard as he passed it – but he went on to the desk.

He dropped into the swivel chair and shuffled through the dozen intelligence folders on his desk. Each of them contained the latest computer print-outs that he had requested. There were personal histories, appraisals, and character studies of all the personalities that had so far become involved in the taking of Speedbird 070.

Both the ambassadors – their pink files signified the highest security ratings, and were marked 'Heads of Departments only'. Four other files in lower echelon green were devoted to the South African Government personalities with decision-making capabilities in an emergency. The thickest file was that of the South African Prime Minister – and once again Parker noted wryly that the man had been imprisoned by the pro-British government of General Jan Smuts during World War II as a militant opponent of his country's involvement in that war. He wondered just how much sympathy he would have for other militants now.

There were files for the South African Ministers of Defence and of Justice, and still slimmer green files for the Commissioner of Police and for the Assistant Commissioner who had been given the on-site responsibility of handling the emergency. Of them all only the Prime Minister emerged as a distinct personality – a powerful bulldog figure, not a man easily influenced or dissuaded, and instinctively Kingston Parker recognized that ultimate authority rested here.

There was one other pink file at the bottom of the

considerable stack, so well handled that the cardboard cover was splitting at the hinge. The original print-out in this file had been requisitioned two years previously, with quarterly up-dates since that time.

'STRIDE PETER CHARLES' it was headed – and reclassified 'Head of Atlas only'.

Kingston Parker could probably have recited its contents by heart – but he untied the ribbons now, and opened it in his lap.

Puffing deliberately at his pipe he began to turn slowly through the loose pages.

There were the bare bones of the subject's life. Born 1939, one of twin war-time babies of a military family, his father killed in action three years later when the armoured brigade of guards he commanded was overrun by one of Erwin Rommel's devastating drives across the deserts of North Africa. The elder twin brother had inherited the baronetcy and Peter followed the well-travelled family course, Harrow and Sandhurst, where he must have disconcerted the family by his academic brilliance and his reluctance to participate in team sports – preferring the loner activities of golf and tennis and long-distance running.

Kingston Parker pondered that a moment. They were pointers to the man's character that had disconcerted him as well. Parker had the intellectual's generalized contempt for the military, and he would have preferred a man who conformed more closely to his ideal of the brass-headed soldier.

Yet when the young Stride had entered his father's regiment, it seemed that the exceptional intelligence had been diverted into conventional channels and the preference for independent thought and action held in check, if not put aside completely – until his regiment was sent to Cyprus at the height of the unrest in that country. Within a week of arrival the young Stride had been seconded, with his commanding officer's enthusiastic approval, to central army intelligence. Perhaps the commanding officer had already become aware of the problems involved in harbouring a wonder-boy in the tradition-bound portals of his officers' mess.

For once the military had made a logical, if not an outright brilliant, choice. Stride in the sixteen years since then had not made a single mistake, apart from the marriage which had ended in divorce within two years. Had he remained with his regiment that might have affected his career – but since Cyprus Stride's progress had been as unconventional and meteoric as his brain.

In a dozen different and difficult assignments since then, he had honed his gifts and developed new talents; rising against the trend of reduced British expenditure on defence, he had reached staff rank before thirty years of age.

At NATO Headquarters he had made powerful friends and admirers on both sides of the Atlantic, and at the end of his three-year term in Brussels he had been promoted to major-general and been transferred to head British Intelligence in Ireland, bringing his own particular dedication and flair to the job.

A great deal of the credit for containing the sweep of Irish terrorism through Britain was his, and his in-depth study of the urban guerrilla and the mind of the militant, although classified departmentally, was probably the definitive work on the subject.

The Atlas concept was first proposed in this study, and so it was that Stride had been on the short list to head the project. It seemed certain the appointment would be made – the Americans had been impressed with his study and his friends from NATO had not forgotten him. His appointment was approved in principle. Then at the last moment there had developed sudden and intense opposition to the appointment of a professional soldier to head such a sensitive agency. The opposition had come from both Whitehall and Washington simultaneously, and had prevailed.

Kingston Parker knocked out his pipe, and carried the file across the room and laid it open on the music rack of the piano. He seated himself at the keyboard and, still studying the printout sheets, began to play.

The stream of music, the lovely ethereal strains of Liszt, did not interrupt his thoughts but seemed to buoy them brightly upwards.

Parker had not wanted Stride, had considered from the very first that he was dangerous, sensing in him ambitions and motivations which would be difficult to control. Parker would have preferred his own nominees – Tanner, who now commanded the Mercury arm of Atlas, or Colin Noble – and had expected that Stride would have declined a command so far below his capability.

However, Stride had accepted the lesser appointment and headed Thor. Parker suspected that there was unusual motivation in this, and had made every effort to study the man at first hand. On five separate occasions he had ordered Stride to Washington, and focused upon him the full strength of his charisma and personality. He had even invited him to stay with him in his New York home, spending many hours with him in deep far-ranging discussions – from which he had developed a prudent respect for the man's mind, but had been able to reach no firm conclusions as to his future in Atlas.

Parker turned a page of the character appraisal. When he looked for the weakness in an opponent, Parker had long ago learned to start at the groin. With this man there was no evidence of any unnatural sexual leanings. Certainly he was not homosexual, if anything too much the opposite. There had been at least a dozen significant liaisons with the opposite sex since his divorce. However, all of these had been discreet and dignified. Although three of the ladies had been married, none of them were the wives of his subordinates in the armed services, nor of brother officers or of men who might be able to adversely affect his career.

The women he chose all had certain qualities in common – they all tended to be tall, intelligent and successful. One was a journalist who had her own syndicated column, another was a former fashion model who now designed and marketed her clothes through her own prestigious outlets in London and on the continent. Then there was an actress who was a leading female member of the Royal Shakespeare Company – Parker skimmed the list impatiently, for Parker himself had no sympathy nor patience with a man who succumbed to the dictates of his body.

Parker had trained himself to be totally celibate, channelling all his sexual energies into pursuits of the mind, while this man Stride, on the other hand, was not above conducting two or three of his liaisons concurrently.

Parker moved on to the second area of weakness. Stride's inheritance had been decimated by the punitive British death duties – yet his private income even after savage taxation was still a little over twenty thousand pounds sterling a year, and when this was added to his salary and privileges as a general officer, it enabled him to live in good style. He could even indulge in the mild extravagance of collecting rare books – and, Parker observed acidly, the greater extravagance of collecting rare ladies.

However, there was no trace of any illicit hoard – no Swiss bank accounts, no deposits of gold bullion, no foreign properties, no shares in off-share companies held by nominees – and Parker had searched diligently for them, for they would have indicated payments received, perhaps from foreign governments. A man like Stride had much to sell, at prices he could set himself – but it seemed he had not done so.

Stride did not smoke; Parker removed the old black briar from his own mouth, regarded it affectionately for a moment. It was his one indulgence, a harmless one despite what the surgeon-general of the United States had determined, and he took the stem firmly between his teeth again.

Stride took alcohol in moderation and was considered knowledgeable on the subject of wine. He raced occasionally, more as a social outing than as a serious punter, and the odd fifty pounds he could well afford. There was no evidence of other gambling. However, he did not hunt, nor did he shoot – traditional pursuits of the English gentleman. Perhaps he had moral objections to blood sports, Parker thought, though it seemed unlikely, for Stride was a superlative marksman with rifle, shotgun and pistol. He had represented Britain at the Munich Olympics as a pistol shot, winning a gold in the fifty metre class, and he spent at least an hour every day on the range.

Parker turned to the page of the print-out that gave the man's medical history. He must be superbly fit as well – his body weight at the age of thirty-nine was one pound less than it had been at twenty-one, and he still trained like a front-line soldier. Parker noticed that he had logged sixteen parachute jumps the previous month. Since joining Atlas he had no opportunity or time for golf, though when he was with NATO Stride had played off a handicap of three.

Parker closed the folder and played on softly, but neither the sensual polished feel of cool ivory beneath his fingertips nor the achingly lovely lilt of the music could dispel his sense of disquiet. Exhaustive as the report was, yet it left unanswered questions, like why Stride had downgraded himself to accept the command of Thor – he was not the kind of man who acted ill-advisedly. Yet the most haunting questions that nagged at Parker were just how strong were his qualities of resilience and independent thought, just how strongly was he driven by his ambitions and that penetrating intellect – and just how great a threat such a man would present to the evolution of Atlas into its ultimate role.

'Doctor Parker, sir—' his assistant knocked lightly and entered, ' – there are new developments.'

Parker sighed softly. 'I'm coming,' he said, and let the

last sad and beautiful notes fall from his long, powerful fingers before he stood up.

The Hawker slid almost silently down the sky. The pilot had closed down power at five thousand feet and made his final approach without touching the throttles again. He was ten knots above the stall as he passed over the boundary fence and he touched down twenty feet beyond the chevron markings of the threshold of runway One Fife, instantly applying maximum safe braking. One Fife was the secondary cross-wind runway and the Hawker's roll-out was so short that every part of the approach and landing had been screened by the buildings of the main airport terminal from where Speedbird 070 stood at the southern intersection of the main taxiway.

The pilot swung the Hawker through 360° and back-tracked sedately up runway 15, using just enough power to keep her rolling.

'Well done,' grunted Peter Stride, crouching behind the pilot's seat. He was almost certain that nobody aboard 070 had remarked their arrival.

'They've prepared a slot for us, with hook up to the electrical mains at the north—' Peter broke off as he saw the apron marshal waving them in with the bats, and beyond him a tight group of four men waiting. Three of them wore camouflage battle dress and the other the trim blue uniform, cap and gold insignia of a senior South African police officer.

The uniformed officer was the first to greet Peter as he came down the Hawker's fold-out air-stairs.

'Prinsloo.' He shook hands. 'Lieutenant-General.'

He ranked Peter, but it was a police, not a military appointment. He was a stocky man, with steel-rimmed spectacles, a little paunchy, and not less than fifty-five years of age. He had the rather heavy features, the fleshiness of jowl and lips, that Peter had noticed so often in Belgian and Dutch peasants during his NATO tour in the Netherlands. A man of the earth, dour and conservative.

'Let me introduce Commandant Boonzaier.' This was a military rank, equivalent to that of colonel, and he was a younger man, but with the same thick accent and his features cast in the same mould. A tall man, however, only an inch or so shorter than Peter – but both of the South Africans were suspicious and resentful, and the reason was immediately apparent.

'I have been instructed to take my orders from you, General,' and there was a subtle shift of position, the two officers ranging themselves beside Peter, but facing each other, and he was aware instantly that not all the hostility was directed at him. There had been friction between police and military already – and the basic value of Atlas was underlined yet again.

A single clean-cut line of command and of responsibility was absolutely essential – Peter's mind flicked back to the shoot-out at Larnaca Airport between Egyptian commandos and Cypriot national guardsmen, from which the hijackers of the grounded jet emerged unscathed while the airfield was littered with the burning wreckage of the Egyptian transport aircraft and dozens of dead and dying Cypriots and Egyptians.

The first principle of terrorist strategy was to strike at the point where national responsibilities were blurred. Atlas cut through that.

'Thank you.' Peter accepted command without flaunting it. 'My back-up team will land in just over three hours' time. We will, of course, use force only as a last resort – but if it comes to that, I will use exclusively Atlas personnel in any counter-strike. I would like to make that quite clear immediately.' And he saw the line of the soldier's mouth harden with disappointment.

'My men are the élite—'

'It's a British aircraft, most of the hostages are British or American nationals – it's a political decision, Colonel. But I would value your help in other areas.' Peter turned him aside tactfully.

'Firstly, I want you to suggest a position where I can place my surveillance equipment – and then we will go over the ground together.'

Peter had no difficulty selecting his forward observation post. The service manager's roomy, sparsely furnished office on the third floor of the terminal building overlooked the entire service area and the southern portion of the taxiway where the Boeing stood.

The windows had been left open when the offices were evacuated, so there was no need to change the external appearance of the room.

The overhang of the observation balcony on the floor above shaded the interior, and the office was deep enough to ensure that an observer out there in the bright glare of sunshine would not be able to see into the room, even with a powerful lens. The militants would expect surveillance from the glass control tower high above – any deception, however trivial, was worth while.

The surveillance equipment was lightweight and compact, the television cameras were neither of them bigger than a super 8-mm home movie camera and a man could carry in one hand both of the aluminium extension tripods. However, the cameras could zoom to 800-mm focal length, and they repeated on the screens of the command console in the cabin of the Hawker, while the image was simultaneously stored on videotape.

The audio intensifier was more bulky, but no heavier. It had a four-foot dish antenna, with the sound collector in the centre. The telescopic sight could aim the intensifier at a sound source with the accuracy of a sniper's rifle – could focus on the lips of a human being at eight hundred yards' distance and clearly record normal conversation at that range, passing sound directly to the command console and at the same time storing it on the big magnetic tape spools.

Two of Peter's communications team were posted here, with a plentiful supply of coffee and doughnuts, and Peter, accompanied by the South African colonel and his staff, went up in the elevator to the glass house of the control tower.

From the air traffic control tower there was an unobstructed view across the airfield and over the apron and service areas around the terminal. The observation platform below the tower had been cleared of all but military personnel.

' – I have road blocks at all the main entrances to the airfield. Only passengers with confirmed reservations and current tickets are being allowed through – no thrill seekers – and we are using only the northern section of the terminal for traffic.'

Peter nodded and turned to the senior controller. 'What is the state of your traffic pattern?'

'We have refused clearance to all private flights, incoming and departing. All domestic scheduled flights have been re-routed to Lanseria and Germiston airports, and we are landing and despatching only international scheduled flights – but the backlog has delayed departures by three hours.'

'What separation are you observing from 070?' Peter asked.

'Fortunately the international departures terminal is the farthest from the aircraft, and we are not using the taxiways or the apron of the southern section. As you see, we have cleared the entire area – except for those three S.A. Airways aircraft which are undergoing overhaul and servicing, there are no other aircraft within a thousand yards of 070.'

'I may have to freeze all traffic, if—' Peter paused, 'or should I say, when we have an escalation.'

'Very well, sir.'

'In the meantime, you may continue as you are at present.' Peter lifted his binoculars and once again very carefully examined the huge Boeing.

It stood in stately isolation, silent and seemingly abandoned. The bright, almost gaudy marking gave her a carnival air. Red and blue and crisp sparkling white in the brilliant sunlight of the highveld. She was parked fully broadside to the tower, and all her hatches and doors were still armed and locked.

Peter traversed slowly along the line of perspex windows down the length of the fuselage – but over each of them the sunshades had been firmly closed from the interior, turning them into the multiple eyes of a blinded insect.

Peter lifted his scrutiny slightly onto the windshield and side panels of the flight deck. These again had been screened with blankets, hung over them from inside, completely thwarting any glimpse of the crew or their captors – and certainly preventing a shot into the flight deck, although the range from the nearest corner of the terminal was not more than four hundred yards, and with the new laser sights one of Thor's trained snipers could pick through which eye of the human head he would put a bullet.

Snaking across the open tarmac of the taxiway was the thin black electrical cable that connected the aircraft to the mains supply, a long, vulnerable umbilical cord. Peter studied it thoughtfully, before turning his attention to the four Panhard armoured cars. A little frown of irritation crossed his forehead.

'Colonel, please recall those vehicles.' He tried not to let the irritation come through in his tone. 'With the turrets battened down, your crews will be roasting like Christmas geese.'

'General, I feel it my duty—' Boonzaier began, and Peter lowered the glasses and smiled. It was a charming, friendly grin that took the man by surprise, after the previous stern set of features – and yet the eyes were devoid of humour, cracking blue and hard in the craggy granite of the face.

'I want to defuse the atmosphere as much as possible.' The necessity to explain irked Peter, but he maintained the smile. 'Somebody with four great cannons aimed at him is more likely to make a bad decision, and pull the trigger himself. You may keep them in close support, but get them out of sight into the terminal car park, and let your men rest.'

With little grace the colonel passed the order over the walkie-talkie on his belt, and as the vehicles started up and slowly pulled away behind the line of hangars, Peter went on remorselessly.

'How many men have you got deployed?' He pointed to the line of soldiers along the parapet of the observation balcony, and then to the heads visible as specks between the soaring blue of the African sky and the silhouette of the service hangars.

'Two hundred and thirty.'

'Pull them out,' Peter instructed, 'and let the occupants of the aircraft see them go.'

'All of them?' incredulously.

'All of them,' Peter agreed, and now the smile was wolfish, 'and quickly, please, colonel.'

The man was learning swiftly, and he lifted the miniaturized walkie-talkie to his mouth again. There were a few moments of scurrying and confusion among the troops on the observation deck below before they could be formed up and marched away in file. Their steel helmets, like a bobbing line of button mushrooms, and the muzzles of their slung weapons would show above the parapet, and would be clearly visible to an observer in the Boeing.

'If you treat these people, these animals—' the colonel's voice was choked slightly with frustration, ' – if you treat them soft—'

Peter knew exactly what was coming, ' – and if you keep waving guns in their faces, you will keep them alert and on their toes, Colonel. Let them settle down a little and relax, let them get very confident.' He spoke without lowering the binoculars. With a soldier's eye for ground he was picking the site for his four snipers. There was little chance that he would be able to use them – they would have to take out every single one of the enemy at the same instant – but a remote chance might just offer itself, and he decided to place one gun on the service hangar roof, there was a large ventilator which could be pierced and would command the port side of the aircraft, two guns to cover the flight deck from both sides – he could use the drainage ditch down the edge of the main runway to get a man into the small hut that housed the approach radar and ILS beacons. The hut was in the enemy's rear. They might not expect fire from that quarter – point by point from his mental checklist Peter planned his dispositions, scribbling his decisions into the small leather-covered notebook, poring over the large-scale map of the airport, converting gradients and angles into fields of fire, measuring 'ground to cover' and 'time to target' for an assault force launched from the nearest vantage points, twisting each problem and evaluating it, striving for novel solutions to each, trying to think ahead of an enemy that was still faceless and infinitely menacing.

It took him an hour of hard work before he was satisfied. Now he could pass his decisions to Colin Noble on board the incoming Herc, and within four minutes of the big landing wheels hitting tarmac his highly trained team with their complex talents and skills would be in position.

Peter straightened up from the map and tucked the notebook under the flap of his button-down breast pocket. Once again he scrutinized every inch of the silent, battened-down aircraft through his glasses – but this time he allowed himself the luxury of gut emotion.

He felt the anger and the hatred rise from some hidden depth of his soul and flush his blood and tighten the muscles of his belly and thighs.

Once again he was confronted by the many-headed monster. It crouched out there in ambush, waiting for him as it had so often before.

He remembered suddenly the shards of splintered glass littering the cobbles of a Belfast street and glittering like diamond chips in the arc lamps, the smell of explosives and blood thick in the air.

He remembered the body of a young woman lying in the gutted interior of a fashionable London restaurant. Her lovely young body stripped by the blast of all but a flimsy pearl-coloured pair of French lace panties.

He remembered the smell of a family, father, mother and three small children, burning in the interior of their saloon car, the bodies blackening and twisting in a slow macabre ballet as the flames scorched them. Peter had not been able to eat pork since that day.

He remembered the frightened eyes of a child, through a mask of blood, a dismembered arm lying beside her, the pale fingers still clutching a grubby little rag doll.

The images flashed in disjointed sequences across his memory, feeding his hatred until it pricked and stung behind his eyes and he had to lower the binoculars and wipe his eyes with the back of his hand.

It was the same enemy that he had hunted before, but his instincts warned him that it had grown even stronger and more inhuman since last he had met and fought it. He tried to suppress the hatred now, lest it cloud his judgement, lest it handicap him during the difficult hours and days that he knew lay ahead – but it was too powerful, had been too long nurtured.

He recognized that hatred was the enemy's vice, that from it sprang their twisted philosophy and their monstrous actions, and that to descend to hatred was to descend to their sub-human levels – yet still the hatred persisted.

Peter Stride understood clearly that his hatred was not only for the ghastly death and mutilation that he had witnessed so often. More it was fostered by the threat that he recognized to an entire society and its civilized rule of law. If this evil should be allowed to triumph, then in the future laws would be made by the wild-eyed revolutionary, with a gun in his fist – the world would be run by the destroyers instead of the builders, and Peter Stride hated that possibility more even than the violence and the blood, and those he hated as a soldier hates. For only a soldier truly knows the horror of war.

His soldier's instinct now was to immediately engage the enemy and destroy him – but the scholar and philosopher in him warned that this was not the moment, and with an enormous effort of will he held that fighting man's instinct in check.

Yet still he was deeply aware that it was for this moment, for this confrontation of the forces of evil, that he had jeopardized his whole career.

When command of Atlas had been plucked away and a political appointee named in his place, Peter should have declined the offer of a lesser position in Atlas. There were other avenues open to him, but instead he had elected to stay with the project – and he hoped that nobody had guessed at the resentment he felt. God knows, Kingston Parker had no cause for complaint since then. There was no harder working officer on Atlas, and his loyalty had been tested more than once.

Now all that seemed worth while, and the moment for which he had worked had arrived. The enemy waited for him out there on the burning tarmac under an African sun, not on a soft green island in the rain nor in the grimy streets of a crowded city – but still it was the same old enemy, and Peter knew his time would come.

His communications technicians had Colin Noble on the main screen as Peter ducked into the Hawker's cabin that was now his command headquarters, and settled into his padded seat. On the top right screen was a panoramic view of the southern terminal area, with the Boeing squatting like a brooding eagle upon its nest in the centre of the shot. On the next screen beside it was a blow-up through the 800-mm zoom lens of the Boeing's flight deck. So crisp was the detail that Peter could read the maker's name on the tab of the blanket that screened the windshield. The third small screen held a full shot of the interior of the air traffic control tower. In the foreground the controllers in shirt sleeves sitting over the radar repeaters, and beyond them through the floor to ceiling windows still another view of the Boeing. All these were being shot through the cameras installed an hour earlier in the terminal building. The remaining small screen was blank, and Colin Noble's homely, humorous face filled the main screen.

'Now if only it had been the cavalry instead of the U.S. Marines,' Peter said, 'you'd have been here yesterday—'

'What's your hurry, pal. Doesn't look like the party has started yet.' Colin grinned at him from the screen and pushed his baseball cap to the back of his head.

'Damned right,' Peter agreed. 'We don't even know who is throwing the party. What's your latest estimate on arrival time?'

'We've picked up a good wind – one hour twenty-two minutes to fly now,' Colin told him.

'Right, let's get down to it,' Peter said, and he began his briefing, going carefully over the field notes he had taken. When he wanted to emphasize a point, Peter called for a change of shot from his cameramen, and they zoomed in or panned to his instruction, picking up the radar shed or the service hangar ventilator where Peter was siting his snipers. The image was repeated not only on the command console but in the cavernous body of the approaching Hercules so that the men who would be called to occupy those positions could study them now and prepare themselves thoroughly for the moment. The same images were hurled across the stratosphere to the circling satellite and from there bounced down to appear, only slightly distorted, on the screens of Atlas Command in the west wing of the Pentagon. Sagging like an old lion in his armchair, Kingston Parker followed every word of the briefing, rousing himself only when a long telex message was passed to him by his assistant, then he nodded a command to have his own televised image superimposed on Peter's command console.

'I'm sorry to interrupt you, Peter, but we've got a useful scrap here. Assuming that the militant group boarded 070 at Mahé, we asked the Seychelles Police to run a check on all joining passengers. There were fifteen of them, ten of whom were Seychelles residents. A local merchant and his wife, and eight unaccompanied children between nine and fourteen years of age. They are the children of expatriate civil servants employed on contract by the Seychelles Government, returning to schools in England for the new term.'

Peter felt the weight of dread bring down upon him like a physical burden. Children, the young lives seemed somehow more important, somehow more vulnerable. But Parker was reading from the telex flimsy in his left hand, the right scratching the back of his neck with the stem of his pipe.

'There is one British businessman, Shell Oil Company, and well-known on the island, and there are four tourists, an American, a Frenchman and two Germans. These last four appeared to be travelling in a group, the immigration and security officers remember them well. Two women and two men, all young. Names Sally-Anne Taylor, twenty-five years, American, Heidi Hottschauser, twenty-four and Gunther Retz, twenty-five, the two Germans and Henri Larousse, twenty-six, the Frenchman. The police have run a back check on the four. They stayed two weeks at the Reef Hotel outside Victoria, the women in one double room and the two men in another. They spent most of the time swimming and sunbathing – until five days ago when a small ocean-going yacht called at Victoria. Thirty-five foot, single-hander around the world, skippered by another American. The four spent time on board her every day of her stay, and the yacht sailed twenty-four hours before the departure of the 070.'

'If the yacht delivered their arms and munitions, then this operation has been planned for a long time,' Peter pondered, 'and damn well planned.'

Peter felt the tingling flush of his blood again, the form of the enemy was taking shape now, the outline of the beast becoming clearer, and always it was uglier and more menacing.

'You have run the names through the computer?' he asked.

'Nothing,' Parker nodded. 'Either there is no intelligence record of them, or the names and passports are false—'

He broke off as there was sudden activity on the screen that monitored the air traffic control tower, and another voice boomed out of the secondary speaker; the volume was set too high, and the technician at the control board adjusted it swiftly. It was a female voice, a fresh, clear young voice speaking English with the lilt and inflexion of the west coast of America in it.

'Jan Smuts tower, this is the officer commanding the task

force of the Action Commando for Human Rights that has control of Speedbird 070. Stand by to copy a message.'

'Contact!' Peter breathed. 'Contact at last.'

On the small screen Colin Noble grinned and rolled his cheroot expertly from one side of his mouth to the other. 'The party has begun,' he announced, but there was the razor edge in his voice not entirely concealed by his jocular tone.

The three-man crew had been moved back from the flight deck, and were held in the first class seats vacated by the group of four.

Ingrid had made the cockpit of the Boeing her headquarters, and she worked swiftly through the pile of passports, filling in the name and nationality of each passenger on the seating plan spread before her.

The door to the galley was open and except for the hum of the air-conditioning, the huge aircraft was peculiarly silent. Conversation in the cabins was prohibited, and the aisles were patrolled by the red-shirted commandos to enforce this edict.

They also ordered the use of the toilets: a passenger must return to his seat before another was allowed to rise. The toilet doors had to remain open during use, so that the commandos could check at a glance.

Despite the silence, there was a crackling atmosphere of tension down the full length of the cabin. Very few of the passengers, mostly the children, were asleep, but the others sat in rigid rows, their faces taut and strained – watching their captors with a mixture of hatred and of fear.

Henri, the Frenchman, slipped into the cockpit.

'They are pulling back the armoured cars,' he said. He was slim, with a very youthful face and dreaming poet's eyes. He had grown a drooping blond gunfighter's moustache, but the effect was incongruous.

Ingrid looked up at him. 'You are so nervous, *chéri.*' She shook her head. 'It will all be all right.'

'I am not nervous,' he answered her stiffly.

She chuckled fondly, and reached up to touch his face. 'I did not mean it as an insult.' She pulled his face down and kissed him, thrusting her tongue deeply into his mouth. 'You have proved your courage – often,' she murmured.

He dropped his pistol onto the desk with a clatter and reached for her. The top three buttons of her red cotton shirt were unfastened, and she let him grope and find her breasts.

They were heavy and pointed and his breathing went ragged as he teased out her nipples. They hardened erect like jelly beans – but when he reached down with his free hand for the zipper of her shorts, she pushed him away roughly.

'Later,' she told him brusquely, 'when this is over. Now get back into the cabin.' And she leaned forward and lifted a corner of the blanket that screened the side window of the cockpit. The sunlight was very bright but her eyes adjusted swiftly and she saw the row of helmeted heads above the parapet of the observation deck. So they were pulling back the troops as well. It was nearly time to begin talking – but she would let them stew in their own juice just a little longer.

She stood up, buttoned her shirt and adjusted the camera on its strap around her neck, paused in the galley to rearrange the shiny mass of golden hair – and then walked slowly back down the full length of the central aisle, pausing to adjust the blanket over a sleeping child, to listen attentively to the complaints of the pregnant wife of the Texan neurosurgeon.

'You and the children will be the first off this plane – I promise you.'

When she reached the prone body of the flight engineer, she knelt beside him.

'How is he?'

'He is sleeping now. I shot him full of morphine,' the fat little doctor muttered, not looking at her, so she could not read the hatred in his expression. The injured arm was elevated to control the bleeding, sticking up stiffly in its cocoon of pressure bandages, oddly foreshortened with the bright ooze of blood through the dressing.

'You are doing good—' She touched his arm. 'Thank you.' And now he glanced at her startled, and she smiled – such a radiant lovely smile, that he began to melt.

'Is that your wife?' Ingrid dropped her voice, so that he alone could hear – and he nodded, glancing at the plump little Jewish woman in the nearest seat. 'I will see she is amongst the first to leave,' she murmured, and his gratitude was pathetic. She stood and went on down the aircraft.

The red-shirted German stood at the head of the tourist cabin, beside the curtained entrance to the second galley. He had the intense drawn face of a religious zealot, dark burning eyes, long black hair falling almost to his shoulders – a white scar twisted the corner of his upper lip into a perpetual smirk.

'Kurt, everything is all right?' she asked in German.

'They are complaining of hunger.'

'We will feed them in another two hours – but not as much as they expect—' and she ran a contemptuous glance down the cabin. 'Fat,' she said quietly, ' – big fat bourgeoisie pigs,' and she stepped through the curtains into the galley and looked at him in invitation. He followed her immediately, drawing the curtains behind them.

'Where is Karen?' Ingrid asked, as he unbuckled his belt. She needed it very badly, the excitement and the blood had inflamed her.

'She is resting – at the back of the cabin.'

Ingrid slipped the button that held the front of her shorts

together and drew down the zipper. 'All right Kurt,' she whispered huskily, 'but quickly, very quickly.'

Ingrid sat in the flight engineer's seat; at her shoulder stood the dark-haired girl. She wore the cartridge belt across the shoulder of her bright red shirt, like a bandolier – and she carried the big ugly pistol on her hip.

Ingrid held the microphone to her lips, and combed the fingers of her other hand through the thick golden tangle of her tresses as she spoke.

' – One hundred and ninety-eight British subjects. One hundred and forty-six American nationals—' She was reading the list of her captives. 'There are one hundred and twenty-two women on board, and twenty-six children under the age of sixteen years.' She had been speaking for nearly five minutes and now she broke off and shifted in her seat, turning to smile at Karen over her shoulder. The dark-haired girl smiled in return and reached across to caress the fine mass of golden hair with a narrow bony hand, before letting it drop back to her side.

'We have copied your last transmission.'

'Call me Ingrid.' She spoke into the mike with the smile turning into a wicked grin. There was a moment's silence as the controller in the tower recovered from his shock.

'Roger, Ingrid. Do you have any further messages for us?'

'Affirmative, Tower. As this is a British aircraft and as three hundred and forty-four of my passengers are either British or American, I want a spokesman, representing the embassies of those countries. I want him here in two hours' time to hear my terms for the release of passengers.'

'Stand by, Ingrid. We will be back to you immediately we have been able to contact the ambassadors.'

'Don't horse around, Tower.' Ingrid's voice snapped. 'We both know damned well they are breathing down your neck.

Tell them I want a man here in two hours – otherwise I am going to be forced to put down the first hostage.'

Peter Stride was stripped down to a pair of bathing trunks, and he wore only canvas sneakers on his feet. Ingrid had insisted on a face-to-face meeting, and Peter had welcomed the opportunity to assess at close range.

'We'll be covering you every inch of the way there and back,' Colin Noble told Peter, fussing over him like a coach over his fighter before the gong. 'I'm handling the gunners, personally.'

The snipers were armed with specially hand-built .222 magnums with accurized barrels that threw small light bullets with tremendous velocity and striking power. The ammunition was match-grade, each round lovingly hand finished and polished. The infra-red telescopic sights were readily interchangeable with the laser sights, making the weapon deadly accurate either in daylight or at night. The bullet had a clean, flat trajectory up to seven hundred yards. They were perfectly designed mankillers, precision weapons that reduced the danger to bystanders or hostages. The light bullet would slam a man down with savage force, as though he had been hit by a charging rhinoceros, but it would break up in his body, and not over-penetrate to kill beyond the target.

'You're getting into a lather,' Peter grunted. 'They want to talk, not shoot – not yet, anyway.'

'The female of the species—' Colin warned, ' – that one is real poison.'

'More important than the guns are the cameras, and sound equipment.'

'I went up there and kicked a few arses. You'll get pictures that will win you an Oscar – my personal guarantee.' Colin checked his wristwatch. 'Time to go. Don't keep the lady waiting.' He punched Peter's shoulder lightly. 'Hang loose,' he said, and Peter walked out into the sunshine, lifting both hands above his shoulders, palms open, fingers extended.

The silence was as oppressive as the dry fierce heat, but it was intentional. Peter had frozen all air traffic, and had ordered the shut down of all machinery in the entire terminal area. He did not want any interference with his sound equipment.

There was only the sound of his own footfalls, and he stepped out briskly – but still it was the longest walk of his life, and the closer he got to the aircraft, the higher it towered above him. He knew that he had been required to strip almost naked, not only to ensure that he carried no weapons, but to place him at a disadvantage – to make him feel ill at ease, vulnerable. It was an old trick – the Gestapo always stripped the victim for an interrogation – so he held himself proud and tall, pleased that his body was so lean and hard and muscled like an athlete's. He would have hated to drag a big, pendulous gut and sagging old-man's tits across those four hundred yards.

He was half-way there when the forward door, just behind the cockpit, slid back and a group of figures appeared in the square opening. He narrowed his eyes: there were two uniformed figures, no three – British Airways uniforms, the two pilots and between them the shorter slimmer feminine figure of a stewardess.

They stood shoulder to shoulder, but beyond them he could make out another head, a blonde head – but the angle and the light were against him.

Closer, he saw that the older pilot was on the right, short-cropped grey curls, ruddy round face – that would be Watkins, the commander. He was a good man, Peter had studied his service record. He ignored the co-pilot and stewardess and strained for a glimpse of the figure beyond them, but it was only when he stopped directly below the open hatch that she moved to let him get a clear view of her face.

Peter was startled by the loveliness of that golden head, by the smooth gloss of young sun-polished skin and the thundering innocence of wide-set, steady, green eyes – for a moment he could not believe she was one of them, then she spoke.

'I am Ingrid,' she said. Some of the most poisonous flowers are the loveliest, he thought.

'I am the accredited negotiator for the British and American Governments,' he said, and switched his gaze to the beefy red face of Watkins. 'How many members of your commando are aboard?' he asked.

'No questions!' Ingrid snapped fiercely, and Cyril Watkins extended four fingers of his right hand down his thigh without a change of expression.

It was vital confirmation of what they already suspected, and Peter felt a rush of gratitude towards the pilot.

'Before we discuss your terms,' Peter said, 'and out of common humanity, I would like to arrange for the well-being and comfort of your hostages.'

'They are well cared for.'

'Do you need food or drinking water?'

The girl threw back her head and laughed delightedly. 'So you can dope it with laxative – and have us knee-deep in shit? Stink us out, hey?'

Peter did not pursue it. The doped trays had already been prepared by his doctor.

'You have a gunshot casualty on board?'

'There are no wounded aboard,' the girl denied flatly, cutting her laughter short – but Watkins made the circular affirmative sign of thumb and forefinger, effectively contradicting her, and Peter noticed the spots of dried blood on the sleeves of his white shirt. 'That's enough,' Ingrid warned Peter. 'Ask one more question and we'll break off—'

'All right,' Peter agreed quickly. 'No more questions.'

'The objective of this commando is the ultimate downfall of the brutally fascist, inhuman, neo-imperialistic regime that holds this land in abject slavery and misery – denying the great majority of the workers and the proletariat their basic rights as human beings.'

And that, thought Peter bitterly, even though it's couched in the garbled jargon of the lunatic left, is every bit as bad as it can be. Around the world hundreds of millions would have immediate sympathy, making Peter's task just that little bit more difficult. The hijackers had picked a soft target.

The girl was still speaking, with an intense, almost religious fervour, and as he listened Peter faced the growing certainty that the girl was a fanatic, treading the thin line which divided sanity from madness. Her voice became a harsh screech as she mouthed her hatred and condemnation, and when she had finished he knew that she was capable of anything – no cruelty, no baseness was beyond her. He knew that she would not stop even at suicide, the final act of destroying the Boeing, its passengers and herself – he suspected she might even welcome the opportunity of martyrdom, and he felt the chill of it tickle up along his spine.

They were silent now, staring at each other, while the hectic flush of fanaticism receded from the girl's face and she regained her breath, and Peter waited, controlling his own misgivings, waiting for her to calm herself and continue.

'Our first demand—' the girl had steadied and was watching Peter shrewdly now, ' – our first demand is that the statement I have just made be read on every television network in Britain and the United States, and also here upon the South African network.' Peter felt his loathing of that terrible little box rise to the surface of his emotions. That mind-bending electronic substitute for thought, that deadly device for freezing, packaging and distributing opinion. He hated it, almost as much as the violence and sensation it purveyed so effectively. 'It must be read at the next occurrence of 7 p.m. local time in Los Angeles, New York, London and Johannesburg—' Prime time, of course, and the media would gobble it up hungrily, for this was their meat and their drink – the pornographers of violence!

High above him in the open hatch the girl brandished a thick buff envelope. 'This contains a copy of that statement for transmission – it contains also a list of names. One hundred and twenty-nine names, all of them either imprisoned or placed under banning orders by this monstrous police regime. The names on this list are the true leaders of South Africa.' She flung the envelope, and it landed at Peter's feet.

'Our second demand is that every person on that list be placed aboard an aircraft provided by the South African Government. Aboard the same aircraft there will be one million gold Kruger Rand coins also provided by the same government. The aircraft will fly to a country chosen by the freed political leaders. The gold will be used by them to establish a government in exile, until such time as they return to this country as the true leaders of the people.'

Peter stooped and picked up the envelope. He was calculating swiftly. A single Kruger Rand coin was worth $170 at the very least. The ransom demand was, therefore, worth one hundred and seventy million dollars.

There was another calculation. 'One million Krugers will weigh well over forty tons,' he told the girl. 'How are they going to get all that on one aircraft?'

The girl faltered. It was a little comfort to Peter to realize that they hadn't thought out everything perfectly. If they made one small mistake, then they were capable of making others.

'The government will provide sufficient transport for all the gold and all the prisoners,' the girl said sharply. The hesitation had been momentary only.

'Is that all?' Peter asked; the sun was stinging his naked shoulders and a cold drop of sweat tickled down his flank. He had never guessed it could be this bad.

'The aircraft will depart before noon tomorrow, or the execution of hostages will begin then.' Peter felt the crawl of horror. 'Execution.' She was using the jargon of legality, and he realized at that moment that what she promised she would deliver.

'When those aircraft arrive at the destination chosen by the occupants, a pre-arranged code will be flashed to us, and all women and children aboard this aircraft will immediately be released.'

'And the men?' Peter asked.

'On Monday the sixth – three days from now, a resolution is to be tabled before the General Assembly of the United Nations in New York. It will call for immediate total mandatory economic sanctions on South Africa – including withdrawal of all foreign capital, total oil and trade embargoes, severance of all transport and communications links, blockade of all ports and air borders by a U.N. peace-keeping force – pending free elections under universal suffrage supervised by U.N. inspectors—'

Peter's mind was racing to keep ahead of the girl's demands. He knew of the U.N. motion, of course, it had been tabled by Sri Lanka and Tanzania. It would be vetoed in the Security Council. That was a certainty – but the girl's timing brought forward new and frightening considerations. The beast had changed shape again, and what he had heard sickened him. It surely could not be merely coincidence that the resolution was to be tabled within three days of this strike – the implications were too horrible to contemplate. The connivance, if not the direct involvement, of world leaders and governments in the strategy of terror.

The girl spoke again deliberately. 'If any member of the Security Council of the U.N. – America, Britain or France

– uses the veto to block the resolution of this General Assembly, this aircraft and all aboard her will be destroyed by high explosive.'

Peter had lost the power of speech. He stood gaping up at the lovely blonde child, for child she seemed, so young and fresh.

When he found voice again, it croaked hoarsely. 'I don't believe you could have got high explosive aboard this aircraft to carry out that threat,' he challenged her.

The blonde girl said something to somebody who was out of sight, and then a few moments later she tossed a dark round object down to Peter.

'Catch!' she shouted, and he was surprised by the weight of it in his hands. It took only a moment to recognize it.

'Electronically fused!' The girl laughed. 'And we have so many I can afford to give you a sample.'

The pilot, Cyril Watkins, was trying to tell him something, touching his own chest – but Peter was occupied with the explosive in his hands. He knew that a single one of these would be fully capable of destroying the Boeing and all aboard her.

What was Watkins trying to tell him? Touching his neck again. Peter transferred his attention to the girl's neck. She wore a small camera slung around her neck. Something connecting camera and grenade – perhaps? Is that what the pilot was trying to tell him?

But now the girl was speaking again. 'Take that to your masters, and let them tremble. The wrath of the masses is upon them. The revolution is here and now,' she said, and the door of the hatchway was swung closed. He heard the lock fall into place.

Peter turned and began the long walk back, carrying an envelope in one hand, a grenade in the other, and sick loathing in his guts.

Colin Noble's rugged frame almost filled the hatchway of the Hawker, and for once his expression was deadly serious, no trace of laughter in his eyes or at the corners of the wide friendly mouth.

'Doctor Parker is on the screen.' He greeted Peter who was still buttoning his overalls as he hurried to the command plane. 'We copied every word, and he was hooked into the system.'

'Christ, it's bad, Colin,' Peter grunted.

'That was the good news,' Colin told him. 'When you have finished with Parker, I've got the bad news for you.'

'Thanks, pal.' Peter shouldered his way past him into the cabin, and dropped into his leather command chair.

On the screen Kingston Parker was hunched over his desk, poring over the teleprinter sheet on which the entire conversation between Ingrid and Peter had been recorded, the cold empty pipe gripped between his teeth, the broad brow creased with the weight of his responsibility as he studied the demands of the terrorist commando.

The communications director's voice from off-screen alerted Parker.

'General Stride, sir.' And Parker looked up at the camera.

'Peter. This is you and me alone. I have closed the circuit and we will restrict to single tape recording. I want your first reaction, before we relay to Sir William and Constable—' Sir William Davies was the British Ambassador and Kelly Constable was the United States Ambassador to Pretoria.

'I want your first reaction.'

'We are in serious trouble, sir,' Peter said, and the big head nodded.

'What is the militant capability?'

'I am having my explosives team take down the grenade – but I have no doubt that they have the physical capability to destroy 070, and all aboard. I reckon they have an overkill potential of at least ten.'

'And the psychological capability.'

'In my view, she is the child of Bakunin and Jean Paul Sartre—' Again Parker nodded heavily and Peter went on. 'The anarchist conception that destruction is the only truly creative act, that violence is man recreating himself. You know Sartre said that when the revolutionary kills, a tyrant dies and a free man emerges.'

'Will she go all the way?' Parker insisted.

'Yes, sir.' Peter answered without hesitation. 'If she is pressed she'll go all the way – you know the reasoning. If destruction is beautiful, then self-destruction is immortality. In my view, she'll go all the way.'

Parker sighed and knocked the stem of his pipe against his big white teeth.

'Yes, it squares with what we have on her.'

'You have read her?' Peter asked eagerly.

'We got a first-class voice print, and the computer cross-matched with her facial structure print.'

'Who is she?' Peter cut in impatiently; he did not have to be told that the sound intensifier and the zoom video cameras had been feeding her voice and image into the intelligence computer even as she issued her demands.

'Her born name is Hilda Becker. She is a third-generation American of German extraction. Her father is a successful dentist widowed in 1959. The girl is thirty-one years old—' Peter had thought her younger, that fresh young skin had misled him. ' – I.Q. 138. University of Columbia 1965–68, Master's degree in Modern Political History. Member of SDS – that's Students for a Democratic Society—'

'Yes.' Peter was impatient. 'I know.'

' – Activist in Vietnam war protests. Worker for the draft evasion pipeline to Canada. One arrest for possession of marijuana 1967, not convicted. Implicated with Weathermen – and one of the leaders of on-campus rioting in the spring of 1968. Arrested for bombing of Butler University and released. Left America in 1970 for further study at

Dusseldorf. Doctorate in Political Economics 1972. Known association with Gudrun Ensslin and Horst Mahler of the Baader-Meinhof. Went underground in 1976 after suspicion of implication in the abduction and murder of Heinrich Kohler, the West German industrialist—' Her personal history was an almost classical development of the modern revolutionary, Peter reflected bitterly, a perfect picture of the beast. 'Believed to have received advanced training from the PFLP in Syria during 1976 and 1977. No recorded contact since then. She is a habitual user of cannabis-based drugs, reported voracious sexual activity with members of both sexes—' Parker looked up. 'That's all we have,' he said.

'Yes,' Peter repeated softly. 'She'll go all the way.'

'What is your further assessment?'

'I believe that this is an operation organized at high level – possibly governmental—'

'Substantiate!' Parker snapped.

'The co-ordination with U.N.O. proposals sponsored by the unaligned nations points that way.'

'All right, go on.'

'For the first time we have a highly organized and heavily supported strike that is not seeking some obscure, partisan object. We've got demands here about which a hundred million Americans and fifty million Englishmen are going to say in unison, "Hell, these aren't unreasonable."'

'Go on,' said Parker.

'The militants have picked a soft target which is the outcast pariah of Western civilization. That U.N. resolution is going to be passed a hundred to nil, and those millions of Americans and Englishmen are going to have to ask themselves if they are going to sacrifice the lives of four hundred of their most prominent citizens to support a government whose racial policies they abhor.'

'Yes?' Parker was leaning forward to stare into the screen. 'Do you think they'll do a deal?'

'The militants? They might.' Peter paused a moment and then went on. 'You know my views, sir. I oppose absolutely dealing with these people.'

'Even in these circumstances?' Parker demanded.

'Especially now. My views of the host country's policies are in accord with yours, Doctor Parker. This is the test. No matter how much we personally feel the demands are just, yet we must oppose to the death the manner in which they are presented. If these people win their objects, it is a victory for the gun – and we place all mankind in jeopardy.'

'What is your estimate for a successful counterstrike?' Parker demanded suddenly, and even though he had known the question must come, still Peter hesitated a long moment.

'Half an hour ago I would have put the odds at ten to one in our favour that I could pull off condition Delta with only militant casualties.'

'And now?'

'Now I know that these are not fuddle-headed fanatics. They are probably as well trained and equipped as we are, and they have had years to set this operation up.'

'And now?' Parker insisted.

'We have a four to one in our favour of getting them out with a Delta strike, with say less than ten casualties.'

'What is the next best chance?'

'I would say there is no middle ground. If we failed, we would be into a situation with one hundred per cent casualties – we would lose the aircraft and all aboard, including all Thor personnel involved.'

'All right then, Peter.' Parker leaned back in his chair, the gesture of dismissal. 'I am going to speak with the President and the Prime Minister, they are setting up the link now. Then I will brief the ambassadors – and be back to you within the hour.'

His image flickered into darkness, and Peter realized that

all his hatred was suppressed. He felt cold, and functional as the surgeon's blade. Ready to do the job for which he had trained so assiduously, and yet able to assess and evaluate the enemy and the odds against success.

He pressed the call button. Colin had been waiting beyond the soundproof doors of the command cabin, and he came through immediately.

'The explosives boys have taken down the grenade. It's a dandy. The explosive is the new Soviet CJ composition, and the fusing is factory manufacture. Professional stuff – and it will work. Oh, baby, will it ever work.'

Peter hardly needed this confirmation, and Colin went on as he flung himself untidily in the chair opposite Peter.

'We put the list of names and the text of the militant statement on the teleprinter for Washington—' He leaned forward and spoke into the cabin intercom. 'Run that loop – without sound first.' Then he told Peter grimly. 'Here's the bad news I promised.'

The loop of video tape began to run on the central screen. It had clearly been shot from the observation post in the office overlooking the service area.

It was a full shot of the Boeing, the background flattened by the magnification of the lens and swimming and wavering with heat mirage rising from the tarmac of the main runway beyond the aircraft.

In the foreground were Peter's own naked back and shoulders as he strode out towards the aircraft. The lens had again flattened the action so that Peter appeared to be marking time on the same spot without advancing at all.

Suddenly the forward hatch of the Boeing changed shape as the door was slid aside, and the cameraman instantly zoomed in for the closer shot.

The two pilots and the air hostess in the doorway, the camera checked for a few frames and then zoomed closer. The aperture of the lens adjusted swiftly, compensating for the gloom of the interior, and the shot was close and tight on the blonde girl's head for a heartbeat, then the head turned slightly and the lovely line of her lips moved as she spoke – it seemed like three words – before she turned back full face to the camera.

'Okay,' Colin said. 'Run it again – with neutral balance on the sound.'

The entire loop reran, the cabin door opened, there were the three hostages, the fine golden head turned, and then the words 'Let's slide,' from Ingrid, but there was background hiss and clutter.

'"Let's slide"?' Peter asked.

'Run it again with the bass density filter on the sound,' Colin ordered.

The same images on the screen, the golden head turning on the long neck.

'"It's slide."' Peter could not quite catch it.

'Okay,' Colin told the technician. 'Now with full filter and resonance modulation.'

The repetitive images, the girl's head, the full lips parting, speaking to somebody out of sight in the body of the aircraft.

Very clearly, unmistakably, she said, 'It's Stride.' And Peter felt it jolt in his belly like a fist.

'She recognized you,' said Colin. 'No, hell, she was expecting you!'

The two men stared at each other, Peter's handsome craggy features heavy with foreboding. Atlas had one of the highest security classifications. Only twenty men outside the close ranks of Atlas itself were privy to its secrets. One of those was the President of the United States – another was the Prime Minister of Great Britain.

Certainly only four or five men knew who commanded the Thor arm of Atlas – and yet there was no mistaking those words the girl had spoken.

'Run it again,' Peter ordered brusquely.

And they waited tensely for those two words, and when

they came they were in the clear lilt of that fresh young voice.

'It's Stride,' said Ingrid, and the screen went blank.

Peter massaged his closed eyelids with thumb and forefinger. He realized with mild surprise that he had not slept for nearly forty-eight hours, but it was not physical weariness that assailed him now but the suddenly overwhelming knowledge of treason and betrayal and of undreamed-of evil.

'Somebody has blown Atlas,' said Colin softly. 'This is going to be a living and breathing bastard. They'll be waiting for us at every turn of the track.'

Peter dropped his hand and opened his eyes. 'I must speak to Kingston Parker again,' he said. And when Parker's image reappeared on the main screen he was clearly agitated and angry.

'You have interrupted the President.'

'Doctor Parker—' Peter spoke quickly. ' – Circumstances have altered. In my opinion the chances of a successful Delta strike have dropped. We have no better than an even chance.'

'I see.' Parker checked the anger. 'That's important. I will inform the President.'

The lavatories were all blocked by this time, the bowls almost filled, and the stench permeated all the cabins despite the air-conditioning.

Under the strict rationing of food and water most of the passengers were suffering from the lethargy of hunger, and the children were petulant and weepy.

The terrible strain was beginning to show on the hijackers themselves. They were standing a virtual non-stop watch, four hours of broken rest followed by four of ceaseless vigil and activity. The red cotton shirts were rumpled and sweat-stained at the armpits, the sweat of nervous and physical strain, eyes bloodshot and tempers uncertain.

Just before nightfall, the dark-haired girl, Karen, had lost her temper with an elderly passenger who had been slow to respond to her command to return to his seat after using the toilet. She had worked herself up into an hysterical shrieking rage, and repeatedly struck the old man in the face with the short barrel of her shot pistol, laying his cheek open to the bone. Only Ingrid had been able to calm her, leading her away to the curtained tourist galley where she pampered and hugged her.

'It will be all right, *Liebchen*.' She stroked her hair. 'Only a little longer now. You have been so strong. In a few more hours we will all take the pills. Not long now.' And within minutes Karen had controlled the violent trembling of her hands, and although she was pale, she was able to take her position at the rear of the tourist cabin again.

Only Ingrid's strength seemed without limits. During the night she passed slowly down the aisles, pausing to talk quietly with a sleepless passenger, comforting them with the promise of imminent release.

'Tomorrow morning we will have an answer to our demands, and all the women and children will be free – it's going to be all right, you just wait and see.'

A little after midnight the little roly-poly doctor sought her out in the cockpit.

'The navigator is very ill,' he told her. 'Unless we get him to a hospital immediately we will lose him.'

Ingrid went back and knelt beside the flight engineer. His skin was dry and burning hot and his breathing rasped and sawed.

'It's renal failure,' said the doctor, hovering over them. 'Breakdown of the kidneys from delayed shock. We cannot treat him here. He must be taken to hospital.'

Ingrid took the semi-conscious flight engineer's uninjured hand. 'I'm sorry, but that's impossible.'

She went on holding his hand for another minute.

'Don't you feel anything?' the doctor demanded of her bitterly.

'I feel pity for him – as I do for all mankind,' she answered quietly. 'But he is only one. Out there are millions.'

The towering flat-topped mountain was lit by floodlights. It was high holiday season and the fairest cape in all the world was showing her beauty to the tens of thousands of tourists and holidaymakers.

On the penthouse deck of the tall building, named for a political mediocrity as are so many buildings and public works in South Africa, the cabinet and its special advisers had been in session for most of the night.

At the head of the long table brooded the heavily built figure of the Prime Minister, bulldog-headed, powerful and unmovable as one of the granite kopjes of the African veld. He dominated the large panelled room, although he had hardly spoken, except to encourage the others with a nod or a few gruff words.

At the far end of the long table sat the two ambassadors, shoulder to shoulder, to emphasize their solidarity. At short intervals the telephones in front of them would ring, and they would listen to the latest reports from their embassies or instructions from the heads of their governments.

On the Prime Minister's right hand sat the handsome moustached Minister of Foreign Affairs, a man with enormous charisma and a reputation for moderation and common sense – but now he was grim and hard faced.

'Your own governments have both pioneered the policy of non-negotiation, of total resistance to the demands of terrorists – why now do you insist that we take the soft line?'

'We do not insist, minister, we have merely pointed out the enormous public interest that this affair is generating in both the United Kingdom and in my own country.' Kelly Constable was a slim, handsome man, intelligent and persuasive, a democratic appointee of the new American administration. 'It is in your government's interest even more than ours to see this through to a satisfactory conclusion. We merely suggest that some accommodation to the demands might bring that about.'

'The Atlas Commander on the spot has assessed the chances of a successful counter-strike as low as fifty-fifty. My government considers that risk unacceptable.' Sir William Davies was a career diplomat approaching retirement age, a grey, severe man with gold-rimmed spectacles, his voice high pitched and querulous.

'My men think we can do better than that ourselves,' said the Minister of Defence, also bespectacled, but he spoke in the thick blunt accent of the Afrikaaner.

'Atlas is probably the best equipped and most highly trained anti-terrorist group in the world,' Kelly Constable said, and the Prime Minister interrupted harshly.

'At this stage, gentlemen, let us confine ourselves to finding a peaceful solution.'

'I agree, Prime Minister.' Sir William nodded briskly.

'However, I think I should point out that most of the demands made by the terrorists are directly in line with the representations made by the government of the United States—'

'Sir, are you expressing sympathy with these demands?' the Prime Minister asked heavily, but without visible emotion.

'I am merely pointing out that the demands will find sympathy in my country, and that my government will find it easier to exercise its veto on the extreme motion of the General Assembly on Monday if some concessions are made in other directions.'

'Is that a threat, sir?' the Prime Minister asked, a small humourless smile hardly softening the question.

'No, Prime Minister, it's common sense. If that U.N. motion was carried and implemented, it would mean the economic ruin of this country. It would be plunged into anarchy and political chaos, a ripe fruit for futher Soviet encroachment. My government does not desire that – however, nor does it wish to endanger the lives of four hundred of its citizens.' Kelly Constable smiled. 'We have to find a way out of our mutual predicament, I'm afraid.'

'My Minister of Defence has suggested a way out.'

'Prime Minister, if your military attack the aircraft without the prior agreement of both the British and American heads of state, then the veto will be withheld in the Security Council and regretfully we will allow the majority proposal to prevail.'

'Even if the attack is successful?'

'Even if the attack is successful. We insist that military decisions are made by Atlas only,' Constable told him solemnly; and then, more cheerfully, 'Let us examine the minimum concessions that your government would be prepared to make. The longer we can keep open the lines of communication with the terrorists, the better our chances of a peaceful solution. Can we offer to fulfil even one small item on the list of demands?'

Ingrid supervised the serving of breakfast personally. Each passenger was allowed one slice of bread and one biscuit with a cup of heavily sweetened coffee. Hunger had lowered the general resistance of the passengers, they were apathetic and listless once they had gobbled their meagre meal.

Ingrid went amongst them again, passing out cigarettes from the duty-free store. Talking gently to the children, stopping to sympathize with a mother – smiling and calm. Already the passengers were calling her 'the nice one'.

When Ingrid reached the first-class galley she called her companions to her one at a time, and they each ate a full breakfast of eggs and buttered toast and kippers. She wanted them as strong and alert as the arduous ordeal would allow. She could not begin to use the stimulants until midday. The use of drugs could only be continued for seventy-two hours with the desired effects. After that the subject would become unpredictable in his actions and decisions. Ratification of the sanctions vote by the Security Council of the United Nations would take place at noon New York time on the following Monday – that was seven p.m. local time on Monday night.

Ingrid had to keep all her officers alert and active until then, she dared not use the stimulants too early and risk physical disintegration before the decisive hour, and yet she realized that lack of sleep and tension were corroding even her physical reserves; she was jumpy and nervous, and when she examined her face in the mirror of the stinking first-class toilets, she saw how inflamed her eyes were, and for the first time noticed the tiny lines of ageing at the corners of her mouth and eyes. This angered her unreasonably. She hated the thought of growing old, and she could smell her own unwashed body even in the overpowering stench from the lavatory.

The German, Kurt, was slumped in the pilot's seat, his pistol in his lap, snoring softly, his red shirt unbuttoned to the waist and his muscular hairy chest rising and falling with each breath. He was unshaven and the lank, black hair fell over his eyes. She could smell his sweat, and somehow that excited her, and she studied him carefully. There was an air of cruelty and brutality about him, the machismo of the revolutionary, which always attracted her strongly – had perhaps been the original reason for her radical leanings so many years ago. Suddenly she wanted him very badly.

However, when she woke him with a hand down the front of his thin linen slacks, he was bleary-eyed and foul-breathed, not even her skilful kneading could arouse him, and in a minute she turned away with an exclamation of disgust.

As a displacement activity, she picked up the microphone, switched on the loudspeakers of the passenger cabins. She knew she was acting irrationally, but she began to speak.

'Now listen to me, everybody, I have something very important to tell you.' Suddenly she was angry with them. They were of the class that had devised and instituted the manifestly unjust and sick society against which she was in total rebellion. They were the fat, complacent bourgeoisie. They were like her father and she hated them as she hated her father. As she began to speak she realized that they would not even understand the language she was using, the language of the new political order, and her anger and frustration against them and their society mounted. She did not realize she was raving, until suddenly she heard as from afar the shriek of outrage in her own voice, like the death wail of a mortally wounded animal – and she stopped abruptly.

She felt giddy and light-headed, so she had to clutch at the desk top for support and her heart banged wildly against her ribs. She was panting as though she had run a long way, and it took nearly a full minute for her to bring herself under control.

When she spoke again, her tone was still ragged and breathless.

'It is now nine o'clock,' she said. 'If we do not hear from the tyrant within three hours I shall be forced to begin executing hostages. Three hours—' She repeated ominously, ' – only three hours.'

Now she prowled the aircraft like a big cat paces along the bars of its cage as feeding time approaches.

'Two hours,' she told them, and the passengers shrank away from her as she passed.

'One hour.' There was a bright sadistic splinter of anticipation in her voice. 'We will choose the first hostages now.'

'But you promised,' pleaded the fat little doctor as Ingrid pulled his wife out of her seat and the Frenchman hustled her forward towards the flight deck.

Ingrid ignored him, and turned to Karen. 'Get children, a boy and a girl—' she instructed, ' – oh yes, and the pregnant one. Let them see her big belly. They won't be able to resist that.'

Karen herded the hostages into the forward galley and forced them at pistol point to sit in a row upon the fold-down air-crew seats.

The door to the flight deck was open and Ingrid's voice carried clearly to the galley, as she explained to the Frenchman Henri, speaking in English.

'It is of the utmost importance that we do not allow a deadline to pass without retaliating strongly. If we miss one deadline, then our credibility is destroyed. It will only be necessary once, we must show the steel at least once. They must learn that every one of our deadlines are irrevocable, not negotiable—'

The girl began to cry. She was thirteen years old, able to understand the danger. The plump doctor's wife put her arm around her shoulders and hugged her gently.

'Speedbird 070—' the radio squawked suddenly, ' – we have a message for Ingrid.'

'Go ahead, Tower, this is Ingrid.' She had jumped up to take the microphone, pushing the door to the flight deck closed.

'The negotiator for the British and American governments has proposals for your consideration. Are you ready to copy?'

'Negative.' Ingrid's voice was flat and emphatic. 'I say

again negative. Tell the negotiator I will talk only face to face – and tell him we are only forty minutes to the noon deadline. He had better get out here fast,' she warned. She hooked the microphone and turned to Henri.

'All right. We will take the pills now – it has truly begun at last.'

It was another cloudless day, brilliant sunlight that was flung back in piercing darts of light from the bare metal parts of the aircraft. The heat came up through the soles of his shoes and burned down upon Peter's bare neck.

The forward hatch opened, as it had before, when Peter Stride was half-way across the tarmac.

This time there were no hostages on display, the hatchway was a dark empty square. Suppressing the urge to hurry, Peter carried himself with dignity, head up, jaw clenched firmly.

He was fifty yards from the aircraft when the girl stepped into the opening. She stood with indolent grace, her weight all on one leg, the other cocked slightly, long, bare, brown legs. She carried the big shot pistol on one hip, and the cartridge belt emphasized the narrow waist.

She watched Peter come on, with a half-smile on her lips. Suddenly a medallion of light appeared on her chest, a dazzling speck like a brilliant insect and she glanced down at it contemptuously.

'This is provocation,' she called. Clearly she knew that the bright speck was the beam thrown by the laser sight of one of the marksmen covering her from the airport building. A few ounces more of pressure on the trigger would send a .222 bullet crashing precisely into that spot, tearing her heart and lungs to bloody shreds.

Peter felt a flare of anger at the sniper who had activated his laser sight without the order, but his anger was tempered by reluctant admiration for the girl's courage. She could sneer at that mark of certain death upon her breast.

Peter made a cut out sign with his right hand, and almost immediately the speck of light disappeared as the gunner switched off his laser sight.

'That's better,' the girl said, and she smiled, running her gaze appraisingly down Peter's body.

'You've a good shape, baby,' she said, and Peter's anger flared again under her scrutiny.

'Nice flat belly—' she said, ' – good legs, and you didn't get those muscles sitting at a desk and pushing a pen.' She pursed her lips thoughtfully. 'You know I think you're a cop or a soldier. That's what I think, baby. I think you're a goddamned pig.' Her voice had a new harsh quality, and the skin seemed drier and drawn – older than it had been before.

He was close enough now to see the peculiar diamantine glitter in her eyes, and he recognized the tension that seemed to rack her body, the abrupt restless gestures. She was onto drugs now. He was certain of it. He was dealing with a political fanatic, with a long history of violence and death, whose remaining humane traits would be now entirely suppressed by the high of stimulant drugs. He knew she was more dangerous now than a wounded wild animal, a cornered leopard, a man-eating shark with the taste of blood exciting it to the killing frenzy.

He did not reply, but held her gaze steadily, keeping his hands in view, coming to a halt below the open hatchway.

He waited quietly for her to begin, and the itch of the drug in her blood would not allow her to stand still; she fidgeted with the weapon in her hands, touched the camera still hanging from around her neck. Cyril Watkins had tried to tell him something about that camera – and suddenly Peter realized what it was. The trigger for the fuses? he pondered, as he waited. Almost certainly, he decided, that was why it was with her every moment. She saw the direction of his eyes, and dropped her hand guiltily, confirming his conclusion.

'Are the prisoners ready to leave?' she demanded. 'Is the gold packed? Is the statement ready for transmission?'

'The South African Government has acceded to urgent representations by the governments of Great Britain and the United States of America.'

'Good.' She nodded.

'As an act of common humanity the South Africans have agreed to release all the persons on your list of detainees and banned persons—'

'Yes.'

'They will be flown to any country of their choice.'

'And the gold?'

'The South African Government refuses categorically to finance or to arm an unconstitutional foreign-based opposition. They refuse to provide funds for the persons freed under this agreement.'

'The television transmission?'

'The South African Government considers the statement to be untrue in substance and in fact and to be extremely prejudicial to the maintenance of law and order in this country. It refuses to allow transmission of the statement.'

'They have accepted only one of our demands—' The girl's voice took on an even more strident tone, and her shoulders jerked in an uncontrolled spasm.

'The release of political detainees and banned persons is subject to one further condition—' Peter cut in swiftly.

'And what is that—' The girl demanded, two livid burning spots of colour had appeared in her cheeks.

'In return for the release of political prisoners, they demand the release of all hostages, not only the women and children, all persons aboard the aircraft – and they will guarantee safe passage for you and all members of your party to leave the country with the released detainees.'

The girl flung back her head, the thick golden mane

flying wildly about her head as she screeched with laughter. The laughter was a wild, almost maniacal sound, and though it went on and on, there was no echo of mirth in her eyes. They were fierce as eagles' eyes, as she laughed. The laughter was cut off abruptly, and her voice was suddenly flat and level.

'So they think they can make demands, do they? They think they can draw the teeth from the U.N. proposals, do they? They think that without hostages to account for, the fascist governments of Britain and America can again cast their veto with impunity?'

Peter made no reply.

'Answer me!' she screamed suddenly. 'They do not believe we are serious, do they?'

'I am a messenger only,' he said.

'You're not,' she screamed in accusation. 'You're a trained killer. You're a pig!' She lifted the pistol and aimed with both hands at Peter's face.

'What answer must I take back?' Peter asked, without in any way acknowledging the aim of the weapon.

'An answer—' Her voice dropped again to an almost conversational level. 'Of course, an answer.' She lowered the pistol and consulted the stainless steel Japanese watch on her wrist. 'It's three minutes past noon – three minutes past the deadline, and they are entitled to an answer, of course.'

She looked around her with an almost bewildered expression. The drug was having side effects, Peter guessed. Perhaps she had overdosed herself, perhaps whoever had prescribed it had not taken into account the forty-eight sleepless hours of strain that preceded its use.

'The answer,' he prodded her gently, not wanting to provoke another outburst.

'Yes. Wait,' she said, and disappeared abruptly into the gloom of the interior.

Karen was standing over the four hostages on the fold-down seats. She looked around at Ingrid with smouldering dark eyes. Ingrid nodded once curtly, and Karen turned back to her prisoners.

'Come,' she said softly, 'we are going to let you go now.' Almost gently she lifted the pregnant woman to her feet with a hand on her shoulder.

Ingrid left her and passed swiftly into the rear cabins. She nodded again to Kurt, and with a toss of his head he flicked the lank locks of hair from his eyes and thrust the pistol into his belt.

From the locker above his head he brought down two of the plastic grenades. Holding one in each fist he pulled the pins with his teeth and held the rings hooked over his little fingers.

With his arms spread like a crucifix, he ran lightly down the aisle.

'These grenades are primed. Nobody must move, nobody must leave their seats – no matter whatever happens. Stay where you are.'

The fourth hijacker took up the cry from him, holding primed grenades in both hands above his head.

'Nobody move. No talking. Sit still. Everybody still.' He repeated in German and in French and his eyes had the same hard, glossy glitter of the drug high.

Ingrid turned back towards the flight deck.

'Come, sweetheart.' She placed an arm round the girl's shoulder, shepherding her towards the open hatchway – but the child shrank away from her with dread.

'Don't touch me,' she whispered, and her eyes were huge with terror. The boy was younger, more trusting. He took Ingrid's hand readily.

He had thick curly hair, and honey brown eyes as he looked up at her. 'Is my daddy here?' he asked.

'Yes, darling.' Ingrid squeezed his hand. 'You be a good boy now, and you'll see your daddy very soon.'

She led him to the open hatchway. 'Stand there,' she said.

Peter Stride was uncertain what to expect, as the boy stepped into the open hatchway high above him. Then next to him appeared a plump middle-aged woman in an expensive but rumpled, high-fashion silk dress, probably a Nina Ricci, Peter decided irrelevantly. The woman's elaborate lacquered hairstyle was coming down in wisps around her ears, but she had a kindly humorous face and she placed a protective arm about the boy-child's shoulders.

The next person was a taller and younger woman, with a pale sensitive skin; her nostrils and eyelids were inflamed pink from weeping or from some allergy and there were blotches of angry prickly heat on her throat and upper arms. Under the loose cotton maternity dress her huge belly bulged grotesquely, throwing her off balance; she stood with her thin white legs knock-kneed awkwardly – and blinked in the brilliant sparkling sunshine, her eyes still attuned to the shaded gloom of the cabin.

The fourth and last person was a young girl, and with a sudden blinding stab of agony below the ribs Peter thought it was Melissa-Jane. It took a dozen racing beats of his heart before he realized it was not her – but she had the same sweet Victorian face, the classical English skin of rose petals, the finely bred body of almost woman with delicate breast-buds and long coltish legs below narrow boyish hips.

There was naked terror in her huge eyes, and almost instantly she seemed to realize that Peter was her hope of salvation. The eyes turned on him pleading, hope starting to awaken.

'Please,' she whispered. 'Don't let them hurt us.' So softly that Peter could hardly catch the words. 'Please, sir. Please help us.'

But Ingrid was there, her voice rising stridently.

'You must believe that what we promise, we mean. You and your evil capitalist masters must understand completely that we will not let a single deadline pass without executions. We have to prove that for the revolution we are without mercy. You must be made to understand that our demands must be met in full, that they are not negotiable. We must demonstrate the price for missing a deadline.' She paused. 'The next deadline is midnight tonight. If our demands are not met in full by then – you must know the price you will be made to pay.' She halted again, and then her voice rose into that hysterical shriek. 'This is the price!' and she stepped back out of sight.

Helpless with dread, Peter Stride tried to think of some way to prevent the inevitable.

'Jump!' he shouted, lifting both hands towards the girl. 'Jump, quickly. I will catch you!'

But the child hesitated, the drop was almost thirty feet, and she teetered uncertainly.

Behind her, ten paces back, the dark-haired Karen and the blonde lion-maned girl stood side by side, and in unison they lifted the short, big bored pistols, holding them in the low double-handed grip, positioning themselves at the angle and range which would allow the mass of soft heavy lead beads with which the cartridges were packed to spread sufficiently to sweep the backs of the four hostages.

'Jump!' Peter's voice carried clearly into the cabin, and Ingrid's mouth convulsed in a nervous rictus, an awful parody of a smile.

'Now!' she said, and the two women fired together. The two shots blended in a thunderous burst of sound, a mind-stopping roar, and blue powder smoke burst from the gaping muzzles, flying specks of burning wadding hurled across the cabin, and the impact of lead shot into living flesh sounded like a handful of watermelon pips thrown against a wall.

Ingrid fired the second barrel a moment before Karen, so this time the two shots were distinct stunning blurts of sound, and in the dreadful silence that followed the two men in the passenger cabins were screaming wildly.

'Nobody move! Everybody freeze!'

For Peter Stride those fractional seconds seemed to last for long hours. They seemed to play on endlessly through his brain, like a series of frozen frames in a grotesque movie. Image after image seemed separated from the whole, so that forever afterwards he would be able to recreate each of them entire and undistorted and to experience again undiluted the paralysing nausea of those moments.

The pregnant woman took the full blast of one of the first shots. She burst open like an overripe fruit, her swollen body pulled out of shape by the passage of shot from spine to navel, and she was flung forward so she somersaulted out into space. She hit the tarmac in a loose tangle of pale thin limbs, and was completely still, no flicker of life remaining.

The plump woman clung to the boy beside her, and they teetered in the open doorway – around them swirled pale blue wisps of gunsmoke. Though she kept her balance, the tightly stretched beige silk of her dress was speckled with dozens of tiny wounds, as though she had been stabbed repeatedly with a sharpened knitting needle. The same wounds were torn through the boy's white school shirt, and little scarlet flowers bloomed swiftly around each wound, spreading to stain the cloth. Neither of them made any sound, and their expressions were startled and uncomprehending. The next blasts of sound and shot struck them solidly, and they seemed boneless and without substance as they tumbled forward, still locked together. Their fall seemed to continue for a very long time, and then they sprawled together over the pregnant woman's body.

Peter ran forward to catch the girl-child as she fell, and her weight bore him to his knees on the tarmac. He came to his feet running, carrying her like a sleepy baby, one arm under her knees and the other around her shoulders. Her lovely head bumped against his shoulder, and the fine silken hair blew into his face, half blinding him.

'Don't die,' he found himself grunting the words in time to his pounding feet. 'Please don't die.' But he could feel the warm wet leak of blood down his belly, soaking into his shorts, and dribbling down the front of his thighs.

At the entrance to the terminal buildings Colin Noble ran out a dozen paces and tried to take the child from his arms, but Peter resisted him fiercely.

Peter relinquished the frail, completely relaxed body to the Thor doctor, and he stood by without word or expression of regret as the doctor worked swiftly over her. Peter's face was stony and his wide mouth clamped in a hard line when the doctor looked up at last.

'I'm afraid she's dead, sir.'

Peter nodded curtly and turned away. His heels cracked on the echoing marble of the deserted terminal hall and Colin Noble fell in silently beside him. His face was as bleak and expressionless as Peter's, as they climbed into the cabin of the Hawker command aircraft.

'Sir William, you point at us for holding enemies of the State without trial.' The Foreign Minister leaned forward to point the accuser's finger. 'But you British discarded the citizen's right of Habeas Corpus when you passed the Prevention of Terrorism Act, and in Cyprus and Palestine you were holding prisoners without trial long before that. Now your H block in Ulster – is that any better than what we are forced to do here?'

Sir William, the British Ambassador, gobbled indignantly, while he collected his thoughts.

Kelly Constable intervened smoothly. 'Gentlemen, we are trying to find common ground here – not areas of dispute. There are hundreds of lives at stake—'

A telephone shrilled in the air-conditioned hush of the room and Sir William lifted the receiver to his ear with patent relief, but as he listened, all blood drained from his face, leaving it a jaundiced, putty colour.

'I see,' he said once, and then, 'very well, thank you,' and replaced the receiver. He looked down the length of the long polished imbuia wood table to the imposing figure at the end.

'Prime Minister—' his voice quavered a little ' – I regret to inform you that the terrorists have rejected the compromise proposals offered by your government, and that ten minutes ago they murdered four hostages—'

There was a gasp of disbelief from the attentive circle of listening men.

' – The hostages were two women and two children – a boy and a girl – they were shot in the back and their bodies thrown from the aircraft. The terrorists have set a new deadline – midnight tonight – for the acceptance of their terms. Failing which there will be further shootings.'

The silence lasted for almost a minute as head after head turned slowly, until they were all staring at the big hunched figure at the head of the table.

'I appeal to you in the name of humanity, sir.' It was

Kelly Constable who broke the silence. 'We must save the women and children at least. The world will not allow us to sit by as they are murdered.'

'We will have to attack the aircraft and free the prisoners,' said the Prime Minister heavily.

But the American Ambassador shook his head. 'My government is adamant, sir – as is that of my British colleague—' he glanced at Sir William, who nodded support ' – we cannot and will not risk a massacre. Attack the aircraft and our governments will make no attempt to moderate the terms of the U.N. proposals, nor will we intervene in the Security Council to exercise the veto.'

'Yet, if we agree to the demands of these – these animals—' the last words were said fiercely ' – we place our nation in terrible danger.'

'Prime Minister, we have only hours to find a solution – then the killing will begin again.'

'You yourself have placed the success chances of a Delta strike as low as even,' Kingston Parker pointed out, staring grimly at Peter Stride out of the little square screen. 'Neither the President nor I find those odds acceptable.'

'Doctor Parker, they are murdering women and children out there on the tarmac.' Peter tried to keep his tone neutral, his reasoning balanced.

'Very strong pressure is being brought to bear on the South African Government to accede to the terms for release of the women and children.'

'That will solve nothing.' Peter could not restrain himself. 'It will leave us with exactly the same situation tomorrow night.'

'If we can secure the release of the women and children, the number of lives at risk will be reduced, and in forty hours the situation might have changed – we are buying time, Peter, even if we have to pay for it with a heavy coin.'

'And if the South Africans do not agree? If we come to the midnight deadline without an agreement with the hijackers, what happens then, Doctor Parker?'

'This is a difficult thing to say, Peter, but if that happens—' Parker spread those long graceful hands in a gesture of resignation, ' – we may lose another four lives, but that is better than precipitating the massacre of four hundred. And after that the South Africans will not be able to hold out. They will have to agree to free the women and children – at any cost.'

Peter could not truly believe what he had heard. He knew he was on the very brink of losing his temper completely, and he had to give himself a few seconds to steady himself. He dropped his eyes to his own hands that were interlocked on the desk top in front of him. Under the fingernails of his right hand were black half moons, the dried blood of the child he had carried back from the aircraft. Abruptly he unlocked his fingers and thrust both hands deeply into the pockets of his blue Thor overalls. He took a long deep breath, held it a moment, then let it out slowly.

'If that was difficult to say, Doctor Parker – console yourself that it was a bloody sight harder to listen to.'

'I understand how you feel, Peter.'

'I don't think you do, sir.' Peter shook his head slowly.

'You are a soldier—'

' – and only a soldier knows how to really hate violence,' Peter finished for him.

'Our personal feelings must not be allowed to intrude in this.' Kingston Parker's voice had a sharp edge to it now. 'I must once again forcibly remind you that the decision for condition Delta has been delegated to me by the President and your Prime Minister. No strike will be made without my express orders. Do you understand that, General Stride?'

'I understand, Doctor Parker,' Peter said flatly. 'And we hope to get some really good videotapes of the next murders. I'll let you have copies for your personal collection.'

The other 747 had been grounded for servicing when the emergency began, and it was parked in the assembly area only a thousand yards from where Speedbird 070 stood, but the main service hangars and the corner of the terminal buildings effectively screened it from any observation by the hijackers.

Although it wore the orange and blue of South African Airways with the flying Springbok on the tail, it was an almost identical model to its sister ship. Even the cabin configurations were very close to the plans of Speedbird 070, which had been teleprinted from British Airways Headquarters at Heathrow. It was a fortunate coincidence, and an opportunity that Colin Noble had seized immediately. He had already run seven mock Deltas on the empty hull.

'All right, you guys, let's try and get our arses out of low gear on this run. I want to better fourteen seconds from the "go" to penetration—' His strike team glanced at one another as they squatted in a circle on the tarmac, and there were a few theatrical rollings of eyes. Colin ignored them. 'Let's go for nine seconds, gang,' he said and stood up.

There were sixteen men in the actual assault group – seventeen when Peter Stride joined them. The other members of Thor were technical experts – electronics and communications, four marksmen snipers, a weapons quartermaster, and a bomb disposal and explosives sergeant, doctor, cook, three engineering N.C.O.s under a lieutenant, the pilots and other flight personnel – a big team, but every man was indispensable.

The assault group wore single-piece uniforms of close fitting black nylon, for low night visibility. They wore their gas masks loosely around their necks, ready for instant use. Their boots were black canvas lace-ups, with soft rubber soles for silence. Each man wore his specialized weapons and equipment either in a back pack or on his black webbing belt. No bulky bulletproof flak jackets to impede mobility or to snag on obstacles, no hard helmets to tap against metal and tell tales to a wary adversary.

Nearly all the group were young men, in their early twenties, hand picked from the U.S. Marine corps or from the British 22.SAS regiment that Peter Stride had once commanded. They were superbly fit, and honed to a razor's edge.

Colin Noble watched them carefully as they assembled silently on the marks he had chalked on the tarmac, representing the entrances to the air terminal and the service hangars nearest to 070. He was searching for any sign of slackness, any deviation from the almost impossible standards he had set for Thor. He could find none. 'All right, ten seconds – to flares,' he called. A Delta strike began with the launching of phosphorus flares across the nose of the target aircraft. They would float down on their tiny parachutes, causing a diversion which would hopefully bunch the terrorists in the flight deck of the target aircraft as they tried to figure out the reason for the lights. The brilliance of the flares would also sear the retina of the terrorists' eyes and destroy night vision for many minutes afterwards.

'Flares!' shouted Colin, and the assault group went into action. The two 'stick' men led them, sprinting out directly under the gigantic tail of the deserted aircraft. Each of them carried a gas cylinder strapped across his shoulder, to which the long stainless steel probes were attached by flexible armoured couplings – these were the 'sticks' that gave them their name.

The leader carried compressed air in the tank upon his back at a pressure of 250 atmospheres, and on the tip of his twenty-foot probe was the diamond cutting bit of the air-drill. He dropped on one knee under the belly of the aircraft ten feet behind the landing gear and reached up to press the point of the air-drill against the exact spot, carefully plotted from the manufacturer's drawing, where the pressure hull was thinnest and where direct access to the passenger cabins lay just beyond the skin of alloy metal.

The whine of the cutting drill would be covered by the revving of the jet engines of aircraft parked in the southern terminal. Three seconds to pierce the hull, and the second 'stick' man was ready to insert the tip of his probe into the drill hole.

'Power off,' Colin grunted; at that moment electrical power from the mains to the aircraft would be cut to kill the air-conditioning.

The second man simulated the act of releasing the gas from the bottle on his back through the probe and saturating the air in the aircraft's cabins. The gas was known simply as FACTOR V. It smelled faintly of newly dug truffles, and when breathed as a five per cent concentration in air would partially paralyse a man in under ten seconds – loss of motor control of the muscles, unco-ordinated movement, slurred speech and distorted vision, were initial symptoms.

Breathed for twenty seconds the symptoms were total paralysis, for thirty seconds loss of consciousness; breathed for two minutes, pulmonary failure and death. The antidote was fresh air or, better still, pure oxygen, and recovery was rapid with no long-term after-effects.

The rest of the assault group had followed the 'stick' men and split into four teams. They waited poised, squatting under the wings, gas masks in place, equipment and weapons ready for instant use.

Colin was watching his stopwatch. He could not chance exposing the passengers to more than ten seconds of Factor V. There would be elderly people, infants, asthma sufferers aboard; as the needle reached the ten-second mark, he snapped.

'Power on.' Air-conditioning would immediately begin washing the gas out of the cabins again, and now it was 'Go!'

Two assault teams poured up the aluminium scaling ladders onto the wing roots, and knocked out the emergency window panels. The other two teams went for the main doors, but they could only simulate the use of slap-hammers to tear through the metal and reach the locking device on the interior – nor could they detonate the stun grenades.

'Penetration.' The assault leader standing in for Peter Stride on this exercise signalled entry of the cabins, and Colin clicked his stopwatch.

'Time?' asked a quiet voice at his shoulder, and he turned quickly. So intent on his task, Colin had not heard Peter Stride come up behind him.

'Eleven seconds, sir.' The courteous form of address was proof of Colonel Colin Noble's surprise. 'Not bad – but sure as hell not good either. We'll run it again.'

'Rest them,' Peter ordered. 'I want to talk it out a bit.'

They stood together at the full windows in the south wall of the air traffic control tower, and studied the big red, white and blue aircraft for the hundredth time that day.

The heat of the afternoon had raised thunderheads, great purple and silver mushroom bursts of cloud that reached to the heavens. Trailing grey skirts of torrential rain they marched across the horizon, forming a majestic backdrop that was almost too theatrical to be real, while the lowering sun found the gaps in the cloud and shot long groping fingers of golden light through them, heightening the illusion of theatre.

'Six hours to deadline,' Colin Noble grunted, and groped for one of his scented black cheroots. 'Any news of concessions by the locals?'

'Nothing. I don't think they will buy it.'

'Not until the next batch of executions.' Colin bit the end from the cheroot and spat it angrily into a corner. 'For two years I break my balls training for this, and now they tie our hands behind our backs.'

'If they gave you Delta, when would you make your run?' Peter asked.

'As soon as it was dark,' Colin answered promptly.

'No. They are still revved up high on drugs,' Peter demurred. 'We should give them time to go over the top, and start downing. My guess is they will dope again just before the next deadline. I would hit them just before that—' He paused to calculate. ' – I'd hit them at fifteen minutes before eleven – seventy-five minutes before the deadline.'

'If we had Delta,' Colin grunted.

'If we had Delta,' Peter agreed, and they were silent for a moment. 'Listen, Colin, this has been wearing me down. If they know my name, what else does that gang of freaks know about Thor? Do they know our contingency planning for taking an aircraft?'

'God, I hadn't worked it out that far.'

'I have been looking for a twist, a change from the model, something that will give us the jump even if they know what to expect.'

'We've taken two years to set it up tightly—' Colin looked dubious. 'There is nothing we can change.'

'The flares,' said Peter. 'If we went, we would not signal the Delta with the flares, we would go in cold.'

'The uglies would be scattered all through the cabins, mixed up with passengers and crew—'

'The red shirt Ingrid was wearing. My guess is, all four of them will be uniformed to impress their hostages. We would hose anything and everybody in red. If my guess is wrong, then we would have to do it Israeli style.'

Israeli style was the shouted command to lie down, and to kill anyone who disobeyed or who made an aggressive move.

'The truly important one is the girl. The girl with the camera. Have your boys studied the videotapes of her?'

'They know her face better than they do Fawcett Majors',' Colin grunted, and then, 'the bitch is so goddamned lovely – I had to run the video of the executions three times for them, twice in slow motion, to wipe out a little of the old chivalry bit.' It is difficult to get a man to kill a pretty girl, and a moment of hesitation would be critical with a trained fanatic like Ingrid. 'I also made them take a look at the little girl before they put her in a basket and took her down to the morgue. They're in the right mood.' Colin shrugged. 'But what the hell, Atlas isn't going to call Delta. We're wasting our time.'

'Do you want to play make-believe?' Peter asked, and then without waiting for an answer, 'Let's make believe we have a Delta approval from Atlas. I want you to set up a strike timed to "go" at exactly 10.45 local time tonight. Do it as though it was the real thing – get it right in every detail.'

Colin turned slowly and studied his commander's face, but the eyes were level and without guile and the strong lines of jaw and mouth were unwavering.

'Make-believe?' Colin Noble asked quietly.

'Of course,' Peter Stride's tone was curt and impatient, and Colin shrugged.

'Hell, I only work here,' and he turned away.

Peter lifted the binoculars and slowly traversed the length of the big machine from tail to nose, but there was no sign of life, every port and window still carefully covered

– and reluctantly he let his binoculars sink slightly until he was staring at the pitiful pile of bodies that still lay on the tarmac below the forward hatch.

Except for the electrical mains hook-up, the delivery of medicines and the two occasions when Peter himself had made the long trip out there, nobody else had been allowed to approach the machine. No refuelling, no refuse nor sanitary removals, no catering – not even the removal of the corpses of the murdered hostages. The hijackers had learned the lesson of previous hijacking attempts when vital information had been smuggled off the aircraft in refuse and sewerage at Mogadishu, and at Lod where the storming party had come disguised as caterers.

Peter was still gazing at the bodies, and though he was accustomed to death in its most obscene forms, these bodies offended him more deeply than any in his life before. This was a contemptuous flaunting of all the deepest rooted taboos of society. Peter was grimly content now with the decision of the South African police not to allow any television teams or press photographers through the main gates of the airport.

Peter knew that the world media were howling outrage and threats, protesting in the most extreme terms against the infringement of their God-given rights to bring into the homes of all civilized people images of dreadful death and mutilation, lovingly photographed in gorgeous colour with meticulous professional attention to all the macabre details.

Without this enthusiastic chronicling of their deeds, international terrorism would lose most of its impetus and his job would be a lot easier. For sneaking moments he envied the local police the powers they had to force irresponsibles to act in the best interests of society, then as he carried the thought a step further, he came up hard once again against the question of who was qualified to make such decisions on behalf of society. If the police made that decision and exerted it, was it not just another form of the terrorism it was seeking to suppress? 'Christ,' thought Peter angrily, 'I'm going to drive myself mad.'

He stepped up beside the senior air traffic controller.

'I want to try again,' Peter said, and the man handed him the microphone.

'Speedbird 070 this is the tower. Ingrid, do you read me? Come in, Ingrid.'

He had tried a dozen times to make contact in the last few hours, but the hijackers had maintained an ominous silence.

'Ingrid, come in please.' Peter kept trying, and suddenly there was the clear fresh voice.

'This is Ingrid. What do you want?'

'Ingrid, we request your clearance to have an ambulance remove the bodies,' Peter asked.

'Negative, Tower. I say again, negative. No one is to approach this aircraft.' There was a pause. 'We will wait until we have a round dozen bodies for you to remove—' The girl giggled, still on the drug high, ' – wait until midnight, and we'll make it really worth your while.' And the radio clicked into silence.

'We are going to give you dinner now,' Ingrid shouted cheerfully, and there was a stir of interest down the length of the cabin. 'And it's my birthday today. So you're going to have champagne – isn't that great!'

But the plump little Jewish doctor rose suddenly to his feet. His grey sparse hair stood up in comical wisps, and his face seemed to have collapsed, like melting candle wax, ravaged and destroyed by grief. He no longer seemed to be aware of what had been said or what was happening. 'You had no right to kill her.' His voice sounded like a very old man. 'She was a good person. She never hurt anyone—' He looked about him with a confused, unfocused look, and ran the fingers of one hand through his disordered hair. 'You should not have killed her,' he repeated.

'She was guilty,' Ingrid called back at him. 'Nobody is innocent – you are all the cringing tools of international capitalism—' Her face twisted, in an ugly spasm of hatred. ' – You are guilty, all of you, and you deserve to die—' She stopped short, controlled herself with an obvious effort of will, and then smiled again; going forward to the little doctor, she put an arm around his shoulders. 'Sit down,' she said, almost tenderly, 'I know just how you feel, please believe me, I wish there had been another way.'

He sank down slowly, his eyes vacant with sorrow and his fingers plucking numbly at themselves.

'You just sit there quietly,' Ingrid said gently. 'I'm going to bring you a glass of champagne now.'

'Prime Minister—' Kelly Constable's voice was husky with almost two days and nights of unceasing tension, ' – it's after ten o'clock already. We must have a decision soon, in less than two hours—'

The Prime Minister lifted one hand to silence the rest of it.

'Yes, we all know what will happen then.'

An airforce jet has delivered a copy of the videotape from Johannesburg, a thousand miles away, and the cabinet and the ambassadors had watched the atrocity in detail, recorded by an 800-mm lens. There was not a man at the table who did not have children of his own. The toughest right-wingers amongst them wavered uncertainly, even the puckish little Minister of Police could not meet the ambassador's eyes as he swept the table with a compelling gaze.

'And we all know that no compromise is possible, we must meet the demands in full or not at all.'

'Mr Ambassador—' the Prime Minister broke the silence at last, ' – if we agree to the terms, it will be only as an act of humanity. We will be paying a very high price indeed for the lives of your people – but if we agree to that price, can we be absolutely assured of your support – the support of both Britain and the United States – in the Security Council the day after tomorrow at noon?'

'The President of the United States has empowered me to pledge his support in return for your co-operation,' said Kelly Constable.

'Her Britannic Majesty's Government has asked me to assure you of the same support,' intoned Sir William. 'And our governments will make good the 170 million dollars demanded by the hijackers.'

'Still I cannot make the decision on my own. It is too onerous for one man,' the Prime Minister sighed. 'I am going to ask my ministers, the full cabinet—' he indicated the tense, grim faces around him, ' – to vote. I am going to ask you gentlemen to leave us alone now for a few minutes while we decide.'

And the two ambassadors rose together and bowed slightly to the brooding, troubled figure before leaving the room.

'Where is Colonel Noble?' Kingston Parker asked.

'He is waiting—' Peter indicated with a jerk of his head the sound-proof door of the Hawker's command cabin.

'I want him in on this, please,' Parker said from the screen, and Peter pressed the call button.

Colin Noble came in immediately, stooping slightly under the low roof, a chunky powerful figure with the blue Thor cap pulled low over his eyes.

'Good evening, sir.' He greeted the image on the screen and squeezed into the seat beside Peter.

'I'm glad Colonel Noble is here.' Peter's voice was crisp and businesslike. 'I think he will support my contention that the chances of a successful Delta counterstrike will be greatly enhanced if we can launch our attack not later than ten minutes before eleven o'clock.' He tugged back the cuff of his sleeve, and glanced at his watch. 'That is forty minutes from now. We reckon to catch the militants at the moment when the drug cycle is at its lowest, before they take more pills and begin to arouse themselves to meet their deadline. I believe that if we strike then, we will have an acceptable risk—'

'Thank you, General Stride—' Parker interrupted him smoothly, ' – but I wanted Colonel Noble present so there could be no misunderstanding of my orders. Colonel Noble—' Parker's eyes shifted slightly as he changed the object of his attention. 'Commander of Thor has requested an immediate Delta strike against Speedbird 070. I am now, in your presence, disapproving that request. Negotiations with the South African Government are at a critical state, and under no circumstances must there be either overt or covert hostile moves towards the militants. Do I make myself entirely clear?'

'Yes, sir.' Colin Noble's expression was stony.

'General Stride?'

'I understand, sir.'

'Very well. I want you to stand by, please. I am going to confer with the ambassadors. I will re-establish contact as soon as I have further concrete indications.'

The image receded rapidly, and the screen went dark. Colonel Colin Noble turned slowly and looked at Peter Stride, his expression changed slightly at what he saw, and quickly he pressed the censor button on the command console, stopping all recording tapes, killing the video cameras so there would be no record of his words now.

'Listen, Peter, you're in line for that NATO command, everybody knows that. From there the sky is the limit, pal. Right up there to the joint chiefs – just as far as you want to go.'

Peter said nothing, but glanced once more at the gold Rolex wristwatch. It was seventeen minutes past ten o'clock.

'Think, Peter. For God's sake, man. It's taken you twenty heart-breaking years of hard work to get where you are. They would never forgive you, buddy. You'd better believe it. They'll break you and your career. Don't do it, Peter. Don't do it. You're too good to waste yourself. Just stop and think for one minute.'

'I'm thinking,' said Peter quietly. 'I haven't stopped thinking since—' he checked, ' – always it comes back to this. If I let them die – then I am as guilty as that woman who pulls the trigger.'

'Peter, you don't have to beat your head in. The decision is made by someone else—'

'It would be easier to believe that, wouldn't it,' Peter snapped, 'but it won't save those people out there.'

Colin leaned across and placed a large hairy paw on Peter's upper arm. He squeezed slightly. 'I know, but it eats me to see you have to throw it all away. In my book, you're one of the tops, buddy.' It was the first time he had made any such declaration, and Peter was fleetingly moved by it.

'You can duck this one, Colin. It doesn't have to touch you or your career.'

'I never was very hot at ducking.' Colin dropped his hand away. 'I think I'll go along for the ride—'

'I want you to record a protest – no sense us all getting ourselves fired,' said Peter, as he switched on the recording equipment, both audio and video; now every word would be recorded.

'Colonel Noble,' he said distinctly, 'I am about to lead an immediate Delta assault on Flight 070. Please make the arrangements.'

Colin turned to face the camera. 'General Stride, I must formally protest at any order to initiate condition Delta without express approval from Atlas Command.'

'Colonel Noble, your protest is noted,' Peter told the camera gravely, and Colin Noble hit the censor button once again, cutting tapes and camera.

'Okay, that's enough crap for one day.' He came nimbly to his feet. 'Let's get out there and take the bastards.'

Ingrid sat at the flight engineer's desk, and held the microphone of the on-board loudspeaker system to her lips. There was a greyish tone beneath the sun-gilded skin; she frowned a little at the throbbing pulse of pain behind her eyes and the hand that held the microphone trembled slightly. She knew these were all symptoms of the drug hangover. She regretted now having increased the initial dosage beyond that recommended on the typed label of the tablet phial – but she had needed that extra lift to be able to carry out the first executions. Now she and her officers were paying the price, but in another twenty minutes she would be able to issue another round of tablets. This time she would stay exactly within the recommended dosage, and she anticipated the rush of it through her blood, the heightened vision and energy, the tingling exhilaration of the drug. She even anticipated the thought of what lay ahead; to be able to wield absolute power, the power of death itself, was one of life's most worthwhile experiences. Sartre and Bakunin and Most had discovered one of the great truths of life – that the act of destruction, of total destruction, was a catharsis, a creation, a reawakening of the soul. She looked forward, even through the staleness and ache of the drug let-down, she looked forward to the next executions.

'My friends—' she spoke into the microphone, ' – we have not heard from the tyrant. His lack of concern for your lives is typical of the fascist imperialist. He does not concern himself with the safety of the people, though he sucks and bloats himself on the blood and sweat—'

Outside the aircraft the night was black and close. Thunderheads blotted out half the sky, and every few minutes lightning lit the clouds internally. Twice since sundown abrupt fierce downpours of torrential rain had hammered briefly against the Boeing hull, and now the airport lights glinted on the puddled tarmac.

' – We have to show the face of unrelenting courage and iron purpose to the tyrant. We cannot afford to show even a moment's hesitation. We must now choose four more hostages. It will be done with the utmost impartiality – and I want you all to realize that we are now all part of the revolution together, you can be proud of that—'

Lightning exploded suddenly, much closer, a crackling greenish, iridescent flaming of the heavens that lit the field in merciless light, and then the flail of the thunder beat down upon the aircraft. The girl Karen exclaimed involuntarily and sprang nervously to her feet and crossed quickly to stand beside Ingrid. Her dark eyes were now heavily underscored by the dark kohl of fatigue and drug withdrawal; she trembled violently, and Ingrid caressed her absently the way she might calm a frightened kitten as she went on speaking into the microphone.

' – We must all of us learn to welcome death, to welcome the opportunity to take our place and add our contribution, no matter how humble it might be, to man's great reawakening.'

Lightning burst in fierce splendour once again, but Ingrid went on talking into the microphone, the senseless words somehow hypnotic and lulling so that her captives sat in quietly lethargic rows, not speaking, unmoving, seeming no longer capable of independent thought.

'I have drawn lots to choose the next martyrs of the revolution. I will call out the seat numbers and my officers will come to fetch you. Please co-operate by moving quickly forward to the first-class galley.' There was a pause, and then Ingrid's voice again. 'Seat number 63B. Please stand up.'

The scarred German in the red shirt and with the lank black hair hanging over his eyes had to force the thin, middle-aged man to his feet, twisting his wrist up between his shoulder blades. The man's white shirt was crumpled and he wore elastic braces over his shoulders and old-fashioned narrow trousers.

'You can't let them,' the man pleaded with his fellow passengers, as Henri pushed him up the aisle. 'You can't let them kill me, please.' And they looked down at their laps. Nobody moved, nobody spoke.

'Seat number 43F.' It was a handsome dark-haired woman in her middle thirties, and her face seemed to dissolve slowly as she read the number above her seat, and she covered her mouth with one hand to prevent herself crying out – but from the seat exactly across the aisle from her a sprightly old gentleman with a magnificent mane of silver-grey hair rose swiftly to his feet and adjusted his tie.

'Would you care to change seats with me, madam?' he said softly in a clipped English accent, and strode down the aisle, on long, thin, stork-like legs, contemptuously brushing past the blond moustached Frenchman who came hurrying forward to escort him. Without a glance to either side, and with thin shoulders thrown back, he disappeared through the curtains into the forward galley.

The Boeing had a blind spot that extended back from the side windows of the flight deck at an angle of 20° to the tail, but the hijackers were so well equipped and seemed to have considered every eventuality in such detail that there was no reason to fear that they had worked out some arrangement to keep the blind spot under surveillance.

Peter and Colin discussed the possibility quietly as they stood in the angle of the main service hangar, and both of them carefully studied the soaring shape of the Boeing tailplane and the sagging underbelly of the fuselage for the glint of a mirror or some other device. They were directly behind the aircraft and there was a little over four hundred yards to cover, half of that through knee-high grass and the rest over tarmac.

The field was lit only by the blue periphery lights of the taxiway, and the glow of the airport buildings.

Peter had considered dousing all the airport lights, but discarded the idea as self-defeating. It would certainly alert the hijackers, and would slow the crossing of the assault team.

'I can't see anything,' Colin murmured.

'No,' agreed Peter and they both handed their night glasses to a hovering NCO – they wouldn't need them again. The assault team had stripped all equipment down to absolute essentials.

All that Peter carried was a lightweight eleven-ounce VHF transceiver for communicating with his men in the terminal building – and in a quick-release holster on his right hip a Walther PK 38 automatic pistol.

Each member of the assault team carried the weapon of his own choice. Colin Noble favoured the Browning Hi-power .45 for its massive killing power and large fourteen-round magazine, while Peter liked the pinpoint accuracy and light recoil of the 9-mm parabellum Walther with which he could be certain of a snap head-shot at fifty metres.

One item was standard equipment for all members of the assault team. Every one of their weapons was loaded with Super Velex explosive bullets which trebled the knock-down power at impact, breaking up in the human body and thereby reducing the risk of over-penetration and with it the danger to innocents. Peter never let them forget they would nearly always be working with terrorist and victim closely involved.

Beside Peter, Colin Noble unclipped the thin gold chain from around his neck which held the tiny Star of David, twinkling gold on the black bush of his chest hair. He slipped the ornament into his pocket and buttoned down the flap.

'I say, old chap—' Colin Noble gave an atrocious imitation of a Sandhurst accent ' – shall we toddle along then?'

Peter glanced at the luminous dial of his Rolex. It was sixteen minutes to eleven o'clock. The exact moment at which my career ends, he thought grimly, and raised his right arm with clenched fist, then pumped it up and down twice, the old cavalry signal to advance.

Swiftly the two men raced out ahead, absolutely silent on soft rubber soles, carrying their probes at high port to prevent them clattering against tarmac or against the metal parts of the aircraft, dark hunchbacked figures under the burden of the gas cylinders they carried.

Peter gave them a slow count of five, and while he waited he felt the adrenalin charge his blood, every nerve and muscle of his body coming under tension, and he heard his own words to Kingston Parker echo in his ears like the prophecy of doom.

'There is no middle ground. The alternative is one hundred per cent casualties. We lose the aircraft, the passengers and all the Thor personnel aboard her.'

He thrust the thought aside, and repeated the signal to

advance. In two neat files, bunched up close and well in hand, the assault teams went out, at the run. Three men carrying each of the aluminium alloy scaling ladders, four with the sling-bags of stun grenades, others with the slap hammers to tear out the door locks, and each with his chosen weapon – always a big calibre handgun – for Peter Stride would trust nobody with an automatic weapon in the crowded interior of a hijacked aircraft, and the minimum requirement for every member of the assault teams was marksmanship with a pistol that would enable him to pick a small moving target and hit it repeatedly and quickly without endangering innocents.

They ran in almost total silence; the loudest sound was Peter's breathing in his own ears, and he had time now for a moment's regret. It was a gamble which he could never win, the best that could happen was the utter ruin of his life's work, but he steeled himself brutally and thrust aside the thought. He ran on into the night.

Just ahead of him now, silhouetted by the lights of the terminal building, the dark figures of the 'stick' men were in position under the bulging silver belly; and lightning flared suddenly, so that the tall silver thunderheads rippled with intense white fire, and the field was starkly lit, the double column of black-clad figures standing out clearly against the paler grass. If they were observed, it would come now, and the crash of thunder made Peter's nerves jump, expecting detonation and flame of a dozen percussion grenades.

Then it was dark again, and the sponginess of wet grass beneath his feet gave way to flat hard tarmac. Then suddenly they were under the Boeing fuselage, like chickens under the protective belly of the hen, and the two columns split neatly into four separate groups and still in tight order every man dropped onto his left knee, and at the same moment, with the precision of repeated rehearsals, every member of the team lifted his gas mask to cover his nose and mouth.

Peter swept one quick glance back at them, and then depressed the transmit button on his transceiver. He would not speak a word from now until it was over; there was always a remote possibility that the hijackers were monitoring this frequency.

The click of the button was the signal to the members of his team in the terminal – and almost immediately, there was a rising whistling howl of jet engines running up.

Even though the aircraft were parked up in the northern international departures area, they had been turned so the jet exhausts were pointed at the service area, and there were five intercontinental jet liners co-operating. The combined sound output of twenty big jet engines was deafening even at that range – and Peter gave the open hand signal.

The 'stick' man was waiting poised, and at the signal he reached up and placed the drill bit against the belly of the fuselage. Any sound of the compressed air spinning the drill was effectively drowned, and there was only the slight jerk of the long probe as it went through the pressure hull. Instantly the second 'stick' man placed the tip of his probe into the tiny hole, and glanced at Peter. Again the open hand signal, and the gas was spurting into the hull. Peter was watching the sweep hand of his watch.

Two clicks on the transmit button, and the lights behind the row of shaded portholes blinked out simultaneously as the mains power was cut – and the air-conditioning in the Boeing's cabins with it.

The howl of combined jet engines continued a few seconds longer and Peter signalled the ladder men forward.

Gently the rubber-padded tops of the ladders were hooked onto the leading edges of the wings and into the door sills high above them by black-costumed, grotesquely masked figures working with deceptively casual speed.

Ten seconds from discharge of the Factor V gas into the hull, and Peter clicked thrice. Instantly mains power to the Boeing was resumed and the lights flicked on. Now the air-conditioning was running again, washing the gas swiftly from the cabins and flight deck.

Peter drew one long, slow deep breath and tapped Colin's shoulder. They went up the ladders in a concerted silent rush, Peter and Colin leading the teams to each wing surface.

'Nine minutes to eleven,' said Ingrid to Karen. She lifted her voice slightly above the din of jet engines howling somewhere out there in the night. Her throat was dry and sore from the drug withdrawal and a nerve jumped involuntarily in the corner of her eye. Her headache felt as though a knotted rope was being twisted slowly tighter around her forehead. 'It looks as though Caliph miscalculated. The South Africans aren't going to give in—' She glanced with a small anticipatory twist of her lips back through the open door of the flight deck at the four hostages sitting in a row on the fold-down seats. The silver-haired Englishman was smoking a Virginia cigarette in a long amber and ivory holder, and he returned her gaze with disdain, so that Ingrid felt a prickle of annoyance and raised her voice so he could hear her next words. 'It's going to be necessary to shoot this batch also.'

'Caliph has never been wrong before.' Karen shook her head vehemently. 'There is still an hour to deadline—' and at that instant the lights flickered once and then went out. With all the portholes shaded the darkness was complete, and the hiss of the air-conditioning faded into silence before there was a murmur of surprised comment.

Ingrid groped across the control panel for the switch

which transferred the flight deck onto the power from the aircraft's own batteries, and as the soft ruddy glow of the panel lights came on her expression was tense and worried.

'They've switched off the mains,' she exclaimed. 'The air-conditioning – this could be Delta.'

'No.' Karen's voice was shrill. 'There are no flares.'

'We could be—' Ingrid started but she could hear the drunken slur in her own voice. Her tongue felt too large for her mouth, and Karen's face started to distort before her eyes, the edges blurring out of focus.

'Karen—' she said, and now in her nostrils the unmistakable aroma of truffles and on her tongue the taste of raw mushrooms.

'Christ!' she screamed wildly and lunged for the manual oxygen release. Above each seat the panels dropped open and the emergency oxygen masks dangled down into the cabins on their corrugated hoses.

'Kurt! Henri!' Ingrid shrieked into the cabin intercom. 'Oxygen! Take oxygen! It's Delta. They are going to Delta.'

She grabbed one of the dangling oxygen masks and sucked in deep pumping breaths, cleansing the numbing paralysing gas from her system. In the first-class galley one of the hostages collapsed slowly forward and tumbled onto the deck, another slumped sideways.

Still breathing oxygen, Ingrid unslung the camera from around her neck, and Karen watched her with huge terrified dark eyes. She lifted the oxygen mask from her face to ask:

'You're not going to blow, Ingrid?'

Ingrid ignored her and used the oxygen in her lungs to shout into the microphone.

'Kurt! Henri! They will come as soon as the mains are switched on again. Cover your eyes and ears for the stun grenades and watch the doors and wing windows.' Ingrid slapped the oxygen mask back over her mouth and panted wildly.

'Don't blow us up, Ingrid,' Karen pleaded around her mask. 'Please, if we surrender Caliph will have us free in a month. We don't have to die.'

At that moment the lights of the cabin came on brightly, and there was the hiss of the air-conditioning. Ingrid took one last breath of oxygen and ran back into the first-class cabin, jumping over the unconscious figures of the hostages and of two air hostesses. She grabbed another of the dangling oxygen masks above a passenger seat and looked down the long fuselage.

Kurt and Henri had obeyed her orders. They were breathing oxygen from the roof panels. The German was ready at the port wing panel, and Henri waited at the rear doorway hatch – both of them had the short big-mouthed shot pistols ready, but their faces were covered with the yellow oxygen masks, so Ingrid could not see nor judge their expressions.

Only a small number of the passengers had been quick enough and sensible enough to grab the dangling oxygen masks and remain conscious – but hundreds of others slumped in their seats or had fallen sideways into the aisles.

A thicket of dangling, twisting, swinging oxygen hoses filled the cabin like a forest of lianas, obscuring and confusing the scene, and after the darkness the cabin lights were painfully bright.

Ingrid held the camera in her free hand, for she knew that they must continue breathing oxygen. It would take the air-conditioning many minutes longer to cleanse the air of all trace of Factor V, and she held a mask over her mouth and waited.

Karen was beside her, with her shot pistol dangling from one hand and the other pressing a mask to her mouth.

'Go back and cover the front hatch,' Ingrid snapped at her. 'There will be—'

'Ingrid, we don't have to die,' Karen pleaded, and with a

crash the emergency exit panel over the port wing burst inward, and at the same instant two small dark objects flew threw the dark opening into the cabin.

'Stun grenades!' Ingrid howled. 'Get down!'

Peter Stride was light and jubilant as an eagle in flight. His feet and hands hardly seemed to touch the rungs of the ladder, now in the swift all-engulfing rush of action there were no longer doubts, no more hesitations – he was committed, and it was a tremendous soaring relief.

He went up over the smooth curved leading edge of the wing with a roll of his shoulders and hips, and in the same movement was on his feet, padding silently down the broad glistening metal pathway. The raindrops glittered like diamonds under his feet, and a fresh wind tugged at his hair as he ran.

He reached the main hull, and dropped into position at the side of the panel, his fingertips finding the razor-tight joint while his number-two man knelt swiftly opposite him. The grenade men were ready facing the panel, balanced like acrobats on the curved slippery upper surface of the great wing.

'Under six seconds.' Peter guessed at the time it had taken them to reach this stage from the 'go'. It was as swift and neat as it had never been in training, all of them armed by the knowledge of waiting death and horror.

In unison Peter and his number two hurled their combined strength and weight onto the releases of the emergency escape hatch, and it flew inwards readily, for there was no pressurization to resist, and at exactly the same instant the stun grenades went in cleanly, thrown by the waiting grenade men, and all four members of Peter's team bowed like Mohammedans in prayer to Mecca, covering eyes and ears.

Even outside the cabin, and even with ears and eyes

covered, the thunder of the explosions was appalling, seeming to beat in upon the brain with oppressive physical force, and the glare of burning phosphorus powder painted an X-ray picture of Peter's own fingers on the fleshy red of his closed eyelids. Then the grenade men were shouting into the interior, 'Lie down! Everybody down!' They would keep repeating that order Israeli style as long as it lasted.

Peter was a hundredth of a second slow, numbed by the blast, fumbling slightly at the butt of the Walther, thumbing the hammer as it snapped out of the quick-release holster, and then he went in – feet first through the hatch, like a runner sliding for home base. He was still in the air when he saw the girl in the red shirt running forward brandishing the camera, and screaming something that made no sense, though his brain registered it even in that unholy moment. He fired as his feet touched the deck and his first shot hit the girl in the mouth, punching a dark red hole through the rows of white teeth and snapping her head back so viciously that he heard the small delicate bones of her neck crackle as they broke.

Ingrid used both arms to cover eyes and ears, crouching forward into the appalling blast of sound and light that swept through the crowded cabins like a hurricane wind, and even when it had passed she was reeling wildly clutching for support at a seat back, trying to steady herself and judge the moment when the attackers were into the hull.

Those outside the hull would escape the direct force of the explosives she was about to detonate; there was a high survival chance for them. She wanted to judge the moment when the entire assault team penetrated the hull, she wanted maximum casualties, she wanted to take as many with her as possible, and she lifted the camera above her head with both hands.

'Come on!' she shrieked, but the cabin was thick with swirling clouds of white acrid smoke, and the dangling hoses twisted and writhed like the head of the Medusa. She heard the thunder of a shot pistol and somebody screamed, voices were chanting, 'Lie down! Everybody down!'

It was all smoke and sound and confusion, but she watched the dark opening of the emergency hatchway, waiting for it, finger on the detonator button of the camera. A supple black-clad figure in a grotesque mask torpedoed feet first into the cabin, and at that same instant Karen shrieked beside her.

'No, don't kill us,' and snatched the camera from Ingrid's raised hands, jerking it away by the strap, leaving Ingrid weaponless. Karen ran down the aisle through the smoke, still screaming, 'Don't kill us!' holding the camera like a peace offering. 'Caliph said we would not die.' She ran forward screaming frantically. 'Caliph—' and the black-clad and masked figure twisted lithely in the air, arching his back to land feet first in the centre of the aisle; as his feet touched the deck so the pistol in his right hand jerked up sharply but the shot seemed muted and unwarlike after the concussion of the stun grenades.

Karen was running down the aisle towards him, screaming and brandishing the camera, when the bullet took her in the mouth and wrenched her head backwards at an impossible angle. The next two shots blended into a single blurt of sound, fired so swiftly as to cheat the hearing, and from such close range that even the Velex explosive bullets ripped the back out of Karen's shirt and flooded it with a brighter wetter scarlet as they erupted from between her shoulder blades. The camera went spinning high across the cabin, landing in the lap of an unconscious passenger slumped in one of the central seats between the aisles.

Ingrid reacted with the instinctive speed of a jungle cat, diving forward, flat on the carpet aisle below the line of fire;

shrouded by the sinking white smoke of the grenades she wriggled forward on her belly to reach the camera.

It was twenty feet to where the camera had landed, but Ingrid moved with the speed of a serpent; she knew that the smoke was hiding her, but she knew also that to reach the camera she would have to come to her feet again and reach across two seats and two unconscious bodies.

Peter landed in balance on the carpeted aisle, and he killed the girl swiftly, and danced aside, clearing space for his number two to land.

The next man landed lightly in the space Peter had made for him, and the German in the red shirt jumped out from the angle of the rear galley and hit him in the small of the back with a full charge of buckshot. It almost blew his body into two separate parts, and he seemed to break in the middle like a folding penknife as he collapsed against Peter's legs.

Peter whirled at the shot, turning his back on Ingrid as she crawled forward through the phosphorous smoke.

Kurt was desperately trying to pull down the short, thick barrel of the pistol, for the recoil had thrown it high above his head. His scarlet shirt was open to the navel, shiny hard brown muscle and thick whorls of black body hair, mad glaring eyes through a greasy fringe of black hair, the scarred lip curled in a fixed snarl.

Peter hit him in the chest, taking no chance, and as he reeled backwards still fighting to aim the pistol, Peter hit again, in the head through the temple just in front of the left ear; the eyelids closed tightly over those wild eyes, his features twisted out of shape like a rubber mask and he went down face first into the aisle.

'Two.' Peter found that, as always in these desperate moments, he was functioning very coldly, very efficiently.

His shooting had been as reflexively perfect as if he were walking a combat shoot with jump-up cardboard targets.

He had even counted his shots, there were four left in the Walther.

'And two more of them,' he thought, but the smoke was still so thick that his visibility was down to under fifteen feet, and the swirling forest of dangling oxygen hose still agitated by the grenade blasts cut down his visibility further.

He jumped over the broken body of his number two, the blood squelching under his rubber soles, and suddenly the chunky black figure of Colin Noble loomed across the cabin. He was in the far aisle, having come in over the starboard wing. In the writhing smoke he looked like some demon from the pit, hideous and menacing in his gas mask. He dropped into the marksman's crouch, holding the big Browning in a double-handed grip, and the clangour of the gun beat upon the air like one of the great bronze bells of Notre Dame.

He was shooting at another scarlet-shirted figure, half seen through the smoke and the dangling hoses, a man with a round boyish face and drooping sandy moustache. The big Velex bullets tore the hijacker to pieces with the savagery of a predator's claws. They seemed to pin him like an insect to the central bulkhead, and they smashed chunks of living flesh from his chest and splinters of white bone from his skull.

'Three,' thought Peter. 'One left now – and I must get the camera.'

He had seen the black camera in the hands of the girl he had killed, had seen it fall, and he knew how deadly important it was to secure the detonator before it fell into the hands of the other girl, the blonde one, the dangerous one.

It had been only four seconds since he had penetrated the hull, yet it seemed like a dragging eternity. He could hear the crash of the slap-hammers tearing out the door locks, both fore and aft. Within seconds there would be Thor assault teams pouring into the Boeing through every opening, and he had not yet located the fourth hijacker, the truly dangerous one.

'Get down! Everybody down!' chanted the grenade men, and Peter spun lightly, and ran for the flight deck. He was certain the blonde girl would be there at the control centre.

Then, in front of him lay the girl he had shot down, the long, dark hair spread out around her pale, still terrified face. Her hair was already sodden with dark blood, and the black gap in her white teeth made her look like an old woman. She blocked the aisle with a tangle of slim boneless limbs.

The forward hatch crashed open as the lock gave way, but there were still solid curtains of white smoke ahead of him. Peter gathered himself to jump over the girl's body, and at that instant the other girl, the blonde girl, bounded up from the deck, seeming to appear miraculously from the smoke, like some beautiful but evil apparition.

She dived half across the block of central seating, groping for the camera, and Peter was slightly off balance, blocking himself in the turn to bring his gun hand on to her. He changed hands smoothly, for he was equally accurate with either, but it cost him the tenth part of a second, and the girl had the strap of the camera now and was tugging desperately at it. The camera seemed to be snagged, and Peter swung on her, taking the head shot for she was less than ten paces away, and even in the smoke and confusion he could not miss.

One of the few passengers who had been breathing oxygen from his hanging mask, and was still conscious, ignored the chanted orders 'Get down! Stay down!' and suddenly stumbled to his feet, screaming, 'Don't shoot! Get me out of here! Don't shoot!' in a rising hysterical scream. He was directly between Peter and the red-shirted girl, blocking Peter's field of fire, and Peter wrenched the gun off him at the moment that he fired. The bullet slammed into the roof, and the passenger barged into Peter, still screaming.

'Get me out! I want to get out!'

Peter tried desperately to clear his gun hand, for the girl had broken the strap of the camera and was fumbling with the black box. The passenger had an arm around Peter's gun arm, was shaking him wildly, weeping and screaming.

From across the central block of seats, Colin Noble fired once. He was still in the starboard aisle and the angle was almost impossible, for he had to shoot nine inches past Peter's shoulder, and through the forest of dangling hose.

His first shot missed, but it was close enough to flinch the girl's head violently, the golden hair flickered with the passage of shot, and she stumbled backwards, groping with clumsy fingers for the detonator.

Peter chopped the hysterical passenger in the throat with the stiffened fingers of his right hand and hurled him back into his seat, trying desperately to line up for a shot at the girl – knowing he must get the brain and still her fingers instantly.

Colin fired his second shot, one hundredth of a second before Peter, and the big bullet flung the girl aside, jerking her head out of the track of Peter's shot.

Peter saw the strike of Colin's bullet, it hit her high in the right shoulder, almost in the joint of the scapula and the humerus, shattering the bone with such force that her arm was flung upwards in a parody of a communist salute, twisting unnaturally and whipping above her head; once again the camera was flung aside and the girl's body was thrown violently backwards down the aisle as though she had been hit by a speeding automobile.

Peter picked his shot, waiting for a clean killing hit in the head as the girl tried to drag herself upright – but before he could fire, a mass of black-costumed figures swarmed out of the smoke, and covered the girl, pinning her kicking and screaming on the carpet of the aisle. The Thor team had come in through the forward hatch, just in time to save her life, and Peter clipped the Walther into his holster and stooped to pick up the camera gingerly. Then he pulled off his mask with his other hand.

'That's it. That's all of them,' he shouted. 'We got them all. Cease fire. It's all over.' Then into the microphone of the transceiver, 'Touch down! Touch down!' The code for total success. Three of his men were holding the girl down, and despite the massive spurting wound in her shoulder, she fought like a leopard in a trap.

'Get the emergency chutes down,' Peter ordered, and from each exit the long plastic slides inflated and drooped to the tarmac – already his men were leading the conscious passengers to the exits and helping them into the slide.

From the terminal building a dozen ambulances with sirens howling, gunned out across the tarmac. The back-up members of Thor were running out under the glare of floodlights, cheering thinly. 'Touch down! Touch down!'

Like prehistoric monsters the mechanical stairways lumbered down from the northern apron, to give access to the body of the Boeing.

Peter stepped up to the girl, still holding the camera in his hands, and he stood looking down at her. The icy coldness of battle still gripped him, his mind felt needle sharp and his vision clear, every sense enhanced.

The girl stopped struggling, and looked back at him. The image of a trapped leopard was perfect. Peter had never seen eyes so fierce and merciless, as she glared at him. Then she drew her head back like a cobra about to strike, and spat at him. White frothy spittle splattered down the front of Peter's legs.

Colin Noble was beside Peter now, pulling off his gas mask.

'I'm sorry, Peter. I was going for the heart.'

'You'll never hold me,' shrieked the girl suddenly. 'I'll be free before Thanksgiving!'

And Peter knew she was right. The punishment that a befuddled world society meted out to these people was usually only a few months' imprisonment, and that often suspended. He remembered the feel of the dying child in his arms, the warm trickle of her blood running over his belly and legs.

'My people will come for me,' the girl spat again, this time into the face of one of the men who held her down. 'You will never hold me. My people will force you to free me.'

Again she was right, her capture was a direct invitation for further atrocity, the wheel of vengeance and retribution was set in motion. For the life of this trapped and vicious predator, hundreds more would suffer, and dozens more would die.

The reaction was setting in now, the battle rage abating, and Peter felt the nausea cloying his bowels. It had been in vain, he thought; he had thrown away a lifetime's strivings and endeavour to win only a temporary victory. He had checked the forces of evil, not beaten them – and they would regroup and attack again, stronger and more cunning than ever, and this woman would lead them again.

'We are the revolution.' The girl lifted her uninjured arm in the clenched fist salute. 'We are the power. Nothing, nobody can stop us.'

When this woman had fired a load of buckshot through the swollen body of the pregnant woman it had distorted her shape completely. The image was recaptured entire and whole in Peter's memory, the way she had burst open like the pod of a ripe fruit.

The blonde woman shook the clenched fist into Peter's face.

'This is only the beginning – the new era has begun.'

There was a taunt and a sneering threat in her voice, uttered in complete confidence – and Peter knew it was not misplaced. There was a new force unleashed in the world, something more deadly than he had believed possible, and Peter had no illusions as to the role that blind fortune had played in his small triumph. He had no illusion either that the beast was more than barely wounded; next time it would be more powerful, more cunning, having learned from this inconsequential failure – and with the reaction from battle came a powerful wave of dread and despair that seemed to overwhelm his soul. It had all been in vain.

'You can never win,' taunted the woman, splattered with her own blood, but undaunted and unrepentant, seeming to read his very thoughts.

'And we can never lose,' she shrieked.

'Gentlemen.' The South African Prime Minister spoke with painful deliberation. 'My cabinet and I are firmly of the opinion that to accede to the terrorists' demands is to take a seat on the back of the tiger, from which we will never be able to dismount.' He stopped, hung his great granite-hewn head for a moment and then looked up at the two ambassadors. 'However, such is the duty we owe to humanity and the dignity of human life, and such is the pressure which two great nations can bring to bear upon one much smaller, that we have decided unanimously to agree in full to all the conditions necessary for the release of the women and children—'

A telephone on the table top in front of the American Ambassador began to shrill irritatingly, and the Prime Minister paused, frowned slightly.

'However, we place complete faith in the undertaking

given by your governments—' He stopped again for the telephone insisted. ' – You had better answer that, sir—' he told Kelly Constable.

'Excuse me, Prime Minister.' The American lifted the receiver, and as he listened an expression of utter disbelief slowly changed his features. 'Hold the line,' he said into the receiver, and then, covering the mouthpiece with his hand, he looked up. 'Prime Minister – it is a very great pleasure to inform you that three minutes ago the Thor assault team broke into Flight 070 and killed three of the terrorists – they wounded and captured a fourth terrorist, but there were no casualties among the passengers. They got them all out, every last one of them. Safe and sound.'

The big man at the head of the table sagged with relief in his seat, and as the storm of jubilation and self-congratulation broke about him, he started to smile. It was a smile that transformed his forbidding features, the smile of an essentially fatherly and kindly man. 'Thank you, sir,' he said, still smiling. 'Thank you very much.'

'You are guilty of blatant dereliction of your duty, General Stride,' Kingston Parker accused grimly.

'My concern was entirely with the lives of hostages and the force of moral law.' Peter answered him quietly; it was less than fifteen minutes since he had penetrated the hull of the Boeing in a blaze of fire and fury. His hands were still shaking slightly and the nausea still lay heavily on his guts.

'You deliberately disobeyed my specific orders.' Parker was an enraged lion, the mane of thick shot-silver hair seemed to bristle, and he glowered from the screen; the vast power of his personality seemed to fill the command cabin of the Hawker. 'I have always had grave reservations as to your suitability for the high command with which you have been entrusted. I have already expressed those reservations in writing to your superiors, and they have been fully justified.'

'I understand by all this that I have been removed from command of Thor,' Peter cut in brusquely, his anger seething to the surface, and Parker checked slightly.

Peter knew that even Kingston Parker could not immediately fire the hero of such a successful counter-strike. It would take time, a matter of days, perhaps, but Peter's fate was sealed. There could be no doubt of that, and Parker went on to confirm this.

'You will continue to exercise command under my direct surveillance. You will make no decision without referring directly back to me, no decision whatsoever. Do you understand that, General Stride?'

Peter did not bother to reply; he felt a wildly reckless mood starting to buoy his sagging spirits, a sense of freedom and choice of action such as he had never known before. For the first time in his career he had deliberately disobeyed a superior officer, and luck or not, the outcome had been a brilliant success.

'Your first duty now will be to withdraw all Thor units, and swiftly and in as good an order as possible. The militant you have taken will be returned to London for questioning and trial—'

'Her crimes were committed here. She should be tried here for murder – I have already had demands from the local—'

'Arrangements are being made with the South African authorities.' Parker's anger had not abated but he had it better under control. 'She will return to Britain aboard your command aircraft, with the Thor doctor in attendance.'

Peter remembered what had happened to the terrorist Leila Khaled, dragged from the El Al airliner where she was being held by Israeli security agents. As a guest of the British police, she had spent six short days in captivity, and then been released in a blaze of publicity and glory, heroine of the communications media, Joan of Arc of terror – released to plan and execute the death and destruction of hundreds more innocents, to lead the attack on the foundations of civilization, to shake the columns that held aloft the rule of law and society.

'I want this woman in London within twenty-four hours. She is to be strictly guarded at all times against retaliation. We cannot afford another bloodbath – like the one you led on 070.'

Peter Stride walked very erect, very tall into the echoing, marble-columned domestic departures hall of the airport, and his men called to him as he came.

'Well done, sir.'

'Great stuff, General.'

'Way to go—'

They were tending the released passengers, re-assembling their scattered gear, dismantling the security and communications equipment and packing it away – within the hour they would be ready to pull out – but now they left their tasks to crowd about him, competing to shake his hand.

The passengers realized that this must be the architect of their salvation and they cheered him as he passed slowly through the hall, and now he was smiling, acknowledging their pitiful gratitude, stopping to talk with an old lady, and submitting to her tearful embrace.

'God bless you, my boy. God bless you.' And her body trembled against him. Gently Peter set her aside and went on, and though he smiled it was with his lips only, for there was steel in his heart.

There were Thor guards on the main administrative offices on the mezzanine floor armed with submachine guns, but they stood aside for him and Peter went through.

Colin Noble was still in his black skin-tight assault suit with the big .45 on his hip, and a cheroot clamped between his teeth.

'Take a look at this lot,' he called to Peter. The desk was covered with explosives and weapons. 'Most of it's iron-curtain stuff – but God alone knows where they got these.' He indicated the double-barrelled shot pistols. 'If they had these custom built, it would have cost them plenty.'

'They have got plenty,' Peter answered drily. 'The ransom for the OPEC ministers was one hundred and fifty million dollars, for the Braun brothers twenty-five million, for Baron Altmann another twenty million – that's the defence budget for a nation.' He picked up one of the shot pistols and opened the breech. It had been unloaded.

'Is this the one she used to gun down the hostages?'

Colin shrugged. 'Probably, it's been fired through both barrels.' Colin was right, there were black specks of burned powder down the short smooth bores.

Peter loaded it with buckshot cartridges from the pile on the desk, and walked on down the long office with the covered typewriters on the deserted desks and the airline travel posters decorating the wall.

Along one wall the three bodies of the hijackers were laid out in a neat row, each encapsulated in its separate translucent plastic envelope.

Two Thor men were assembling the contents of their pockets – personal jewellery, meagre personal effects – and they were packing them into labelled plastic bags.

The body of Peter's Number Two was against the far wall, also in his plastic body-bag, and Peter stooped over him. Through the plastic he could make out the features of the dead man's face. The eyes were wide and the jaw hung open slackly. Death is always so undignified, Peter thought, and straightened up.

Still carrying the shot pistol, Peter went on into the inner office, and Colin Noble followed him.

They had the girl on another stretcher, a plasma drip suspended above her, and the Thor doctor and his two orderlies were working over her quietly, but the young doctor looked up irritably as Peter pushed open the door, then his expression changed as he recognized Peter.

'General, if we are going to save this arm, I have to get her into theatre pretty damned quickly. The joint of the shoulder is shattered—'

The girl rolled the lovely head towards Peter. The thick springing golden hair was matted with drying blood, and there was a smear of it across one cheek.

Now her face was completely drained of all colour, like the head of an angel carved out of white marble. The skin had a waxen, almost translucent, lustre and only the eyes were still fierce, not dulled by the painkilling drugs that they had injected into her.

' – I have asked the South Africans for co-operation—' the doctor went on, ' – they have two top orthopaedic surgeons standing by, and they have offered a helicopter to fly her into the Central Hospital at Edenvale.'

Already she was being treated, even by Thor, as the major celebrity she was. She had taken her first step along the rose-strewn pathway to glory, and Peter could imagine how the media would extol her beauty – they had gone berserk with extravagant praise for the swarthy ferrety-eyed Leila Khaled with her fine dark moustache – they would go over the top for this one.

Peter had never known any emotion so powerful as the emotion that gripped him now.

'Get out,' he said to the doctor.

'Sir?' The man looked startled.

'Get out,' Peter repeated, 'all of you.' And he waited until the opaque glass door closed behind them, before he spoke to the girl in conversational tones.

'You have made me abandon my own principles, and descend to your level.'

The girl watched him uncertainly, her eyes flickered to the shot pistol that Peter held dangling from his right hand.

'You have forced me, a career soldier, to disobey the orders of a superior officer in the face of the enemy.' He paused. 'I used to be a proud man, but when I have done what I must do now I will no longer have much of which to be proud.'

'I demand to see the American Ambassador,' said the girl huskily, still watching the pistol. 'I am an American citizen. I demand the protection—'

Peter interrupted her, again speaking quickly. 'This is not revenge. I am old and wise enough to know that revenge has the most bitter taste of all human excesses.'

'You cannot do it—' The girl's voice rose, the same strident tones, but now shriller still with fear. 'They will destroy you.'

But Peter went on as though she had not spoken. 'It is not revenge,' he repeated. 'You, yourself, gave the reason clearly. If you continue to exist, they will come to get you back. As long as you live, others must die – and they will die stripped of all human dignity. They will die in terror, the same way you murdered—'

'I am a woman. I am wounded. I am a prisoner of war,' screamed the girl, trying to struggle upright.

'Those are the old rules,' Peter told her. 'You tore up the book, and wrote a new one – I am playing to your rules now. I have been reduced to your level.'

'You cannot kill me,' the girl's voice range wildly. 'I still have work—'

'Colin,' Peter said quietly, without looking at the American. 'You'd better get out now.'

Colin Noble hesitated, his right hand on the butt of the Browning, and the girl rolled her head towards him imploringly.

'You can't let him do it.'

'Peter—' Colin said.

'You were right, Colin,' Peter spoke quietly. 'That kid did look a lot like Melissa-Jane.'

Colin Noble dropped his hand from the pistol and turned to the door. Now the girl was shrieking obscenity and threat, her voice incoherent with terror and hatred.

Colin closed the door softly and stood with his back to it. The single crash of shot was shockingly loud, and the stream of filthy abuse was cut off abruptly. The silence was even more appalling than the harrowing sounds which had preceded it. Colin did not move. He waited four, five seconds before the door clicked open and General Peter Stride came out into the main office. He handed the shot pistol to Colin and one barrel was hot in his hand.

Peter's handsome aristocratic features seemed ravaged, as though by a long wasting disease. The face of a man who had leapt into the abyss.

Peter Stride left the glass door open, and walked away without looking back. Despite the terrible expression of despair, he still carried himself like a soldier and his tread was firm.

Colin Noble did not even look through the open door.

'All right,' he called to the doctor. 'She's all yours now.' And he followed Peter Stride down the broad staircase.

There was a long hard gallop over good going and open pasture to the crest of the ridge, with only one gate. Melissa-Jane led on her bay filly, her Christmas gift from Uncle Steven. She was in the midst of the passionate love affair that most pubescent girls have with horses, and she looked truly good astride the glistening thoroughbred. The cold struck high colour into her cheeks and the braid of honey-coloured hair thumped gaily down her back at each stride. She had blossomed even in the few weeks since last Peter had seen her – and he realized with some awe and considerable pride that she was fast becoming a great beauty.

Peter was up on one of Steven's hunters, a big rangy animal with the strength to carry his weight, but the gelding was slogging hard to hold the flying pair that danced ahead of him.

At the hedge, Melissa-Jane scorned the gate, gathered the filly with fine strong hands and took her up and over. Her little round bottom lifted out of the saddle as she leaned into the jump, and clods of black earth flew from the filly's hooves.

As soon as she was over she swivelled in the saddle to watch him, and Peter realized that he was under challenge. The hedge immediately appeared to be head-high and he noticed for the first time how the ground fell away at a steep angle beyond. He had not ridden for almost two years, and it was the first time he had been up on this gelding – but the horse went for the jump gamely, and they brushed the top of the hedge, landed awkwardly, stumbled with Peter up on his neck for an appalling instant of time in which he was convinced he was to take a toss in front of his daughter's critical eye; caught his balance, held the gelding's head up and they came away still together.

'Super-Star!' Melissa-Jane shouted laughing, and by the time he caught her she had dismounted under the yew tree at the crest, and was waiting for him with her breath steaming in the crisp calm air.

'Our land once went right as far as the church—' Peter pointed to the distant grey needle of stone that pricked the belly of the sky, ' – and there almost to the top of the downs.' He turned to point in the opposite direction.

'Yes.' Melissa-Jane slipped her arm through his as they stood close together under the yew. 'The family had to sell it when Grandfather died. You told me. And that's right too. One family shouldn't own so much.'

Peter glanced down at her, startled. 'My God, a communist in the family. An asp in the bosom.'

She squeezed his arm. 'Don't worry, Daddy darling. It's Uncle Steven who is the bloated plutocrat. You're not a capitalist – you aren't even employed any more—' And the instant she had said it, her laughter collapsed around her and she looked stricken. ' – Oh, I didn't mean that. I truly didn't.'

It was almost a month now since Peter's resignation had been accepted by the War Office, but the scandal had not yet run out of steam.

The first heady paeans of praise for the success of Thor's Delta strike had lasted only a few days. The glowing editorials, the full front pages, the lead news item on every television channel, the effusive messages of congratulations from the leaders of the Western governments, the impromptu triumph for Peter Stride and his little band of heroes, had quickly struck an odd note, a sudden souring of the ecstasies.

The racist Government of South Africa had actually agreed to the release of political prisoners *before* the assault, one of the hijackers had been taken alive, and died of gunshot wounds received in the terminal buildings. Then one of the released hostages, a freelance journalist who had been covering the medical convention in Mauritius and was returning aboard the hijacked aircraft, published a sensational eye-witness account of the entire episode, and a dozen other passengers supported his claims that there had been screams from the fourth hijacker, screams for mercy, before she was shot to death after her capture.

A storm of condemnation and vilification from the extreme left of the British Labour Government had swept through the Westminster parliament, and had been echoed by the Democrats in the American Congress. The very existence of the Thor Command had come under scrutiny and been condemned in extravagant terms. The Communist parties of France and Italy had marched, and the detonation of an M.26 hand grenade – one of those stolen by the Baader-Meinhof gang from the American base in Metz – amongst the crowd leaving the Parc des Princes football stadium in Paris had killed one and injured twenty-three. A telephone call to the offices of *France Soir* by a man speaking accented French claimed that this fresh atrocity was revenge for the murder of four hijackers by the Imperialist execution squad.

Pressure for Peter's discharge had come initially from the Pentagon, and there was very little doubt that Dr Kingston Parker was the accuser, though, as head of Atlas, he was never identified, total secrecy still surrounding the project. The media had begun to demand an investigation of all the circumstances surrounding Thor. ' – And if it is ascertained that criminal irregularities did indeed exist in the conduct of the operation, that the person or persons responsible be brought to trial either by a military tribunal or the civil courts.' Fortunately the media had not yet unravelled the full scope of Atlas Command. Only Thor was under scrutiny; they did not yet suspect the existence of either Mercury or Diana.

Within the War Office and the governments of both America and Britain, there had been much sympathy and support for Peter Stride – but he had made it easier for his friends and for himself by tendering his resignation. The resignation had been accepted, but still the left was clamouring for more. They wanted blood, Peter Stride's blood.

Now Melissa-Jane's huge pansy violet eyes flooded with the tears of mortification. 'I didn't mean that. I truly didn't.'

'One thing about being out of a job – I have more time to be with my favourite girl.' He smiled down at her, but she would not be mollified.

'I don't believe the horrible things they are saying. I know you are a man of honour, Daddy.'

'Thank you.' And he felt the ache of it, the guilt and the

sorrow. They were silent a little longer, still standing close together, and Peter spoke first.

'You are going to be a palaeontologist—' he said.

'No. That was last month. I've changed my mind. I'm not interested in old bones any more. Now I'm going to be a doctor, a child specialist.'

'That's good.' Peter nodded gravely. 'But let's go back to old bones for a moment. The age of the great reptiles. The dinosaurs – why did they fade into extinction?'

'They could not adapt to a changing environment.' Melissa-Jane had the answer promptly.

Peter murmured, ' – A concept like honour. Is it outdated in today's world, I wonder?' Then he saw the puzzlement, the hurt in her eyes, and he knew they had wandered onto dangerous ground. His daughter had a burning love for all living things, particularly human beings. Despite her age, she had a developed political and social conscience, distinguished by total belief in shining ideals and the essential beauty and goodness of mankind. There would be time in the years ahead for the agony of disillusion. The term 'man or woman of honour' was Melissa-Jane's ultimate accolade. No matter that it could be applied to any of her current heroes or heroines – the Prince of Wales, or the singer of popular songs with an outrageous name that Peter could never remember, to Virginia Wade, the former Wimbledon champion, or to the Fifth Form science teacher at Roedean who had aroused Melissa-Jane's interest in medicine – Peter knew that he should feel proper gratitude for being included in this exalted company.

'I will try to live up to your opinion of me.' He stooped and kissed her, surprised at the strength of his love for this child-woman. 'And now it's too cold to stand here any longer, and Pat will never forgive us if we are late for lunch.'

They clattered over the stone cobbles of the stable yard, riding knee to knee, and before he dismounted, Peter indulged himself in the pleasure of his favourite view of the house that had always been home, even though it belonged now, together with the title, to Steven, the older brother, older by three hours only, but older none the less.

The house was red brick with a roof that ran at fifty different unlikely angles. It missed being hideous by a subtle margin and achieved a fairytale enchantment. Peter could never grudge it to Steven, who loved the sprawling edifice with something close to passion.

Perhaps the desire to own the house and to restore it to its former magnificence was the goad which had pricked Steven to the superhuman effort that a British resident must make against taxation and socialist restrictions in order to amass anything like a fortune.

Steven had made that effort and now Abbots Yew stood immaculate and well-beloved in glorious gardens, and Sir Steven kept baronial style.

His affairs were so complicated, spread over so many continents that even the British taxman must have been daunted. Peter had once skirted this subject with his twin brother, and Steven had replied quietly.

'When a law is patently unjust, such as our tax law is, it's the duty of an honest man to subvert it.'

Peter's old-fashioned sense of rightness had baulked at such logic, but he let it pass.

It was strange that it had worked this way for the two brothers, for Peter had always been the brilliant one, and the family had always referred to 'Poor Steven'. Nobody was very surprised when Steven left Sandhurst amid dark whispers halfway through his final year – but two years later Steven was already a millionaire while Peter was a lowly second lieutenant in the British Army. Peter grinned without rancour at the memory. He had always been particularly fond of his elder brother – but at that moment his train of thought was interrupted as his eye caught the mirror-like finish of the silver limousine parked at the end of the stable yard. It was one of those long Mercedes-Benz favoured by pop stars, Arab oil men, or heads of state. The chauffeur was uniformed in sober navy blue and was busy burnishing the paintwork to an even higher gloss. Even Steven did not run to that sort of transportation, and Peter felt mildly intrigued. House guests at Abbots Yew were always interesting. Steven Stride did not concern himself with those who did not wield either power, wealth or extraordinary talent. Beyond the Mercedes 600 was parked another smaller model; this one was black and the two men in it had the hard closed faces that marked them as bodyguards.

Melissa-Jane rolled her eyes at the automobile. 'Another bloated plutocrat, I expect,' she muttered. It was the currently favoured term of extreme disapproval, a great advance on 'grotty' which had preceded it, Peter could not help thinking as he helped his daughter unsaddle and then rub down the horses. They went up through the rose garden, arm in arm, and then laughing together into the main drawing-room.

'Peter old boy!' Steven came to meet him, as tall as his brother, and once he had been as lean, but good living had thickened his body while at the same time the strains of being a professional deal maker had greyed his hair at the temples and laced his moustache with silver bristles. His face was not quite a mirror image of Peter's, slightly more fleshy and florid – but the twin resemblance was still strongly marked, and now his face was alive with pleasure.

'Thought you'd broken your bloody neck, what!' Steven carefully cultivated the bluff manner of the country squire to shield his quick and shrewd intelligence.

Now he turned to Melissa-Jane and hugged her with barely a touch of incestuous pleasure. 'How did Florence Nightingale go?'

'She's a darling, Uncle Steven. I will never be able to thank you.'

'Peter, I would like you to meet a very charming lady—'

She had been talking to Patricia Stride, Steven's wife, and now as she turned, the winter sunshine through the bay windows behind lit her with a soft romantic aura.

Peter felt as though the earth had tilted under his feet, and a fist closed around his ribs constricting his breathing and inhibiting the action of his heart.

He recognized her immediately from the photographs in the official file during the long-drawn-out kidnapping and subsequent murder of her husband. At one stage it had seemed that the kidnappers had crossed the Channel with their victim, and Thor had gone to condition Alpha for almost a week. Peter had studied the photographs that had been assembled from a dozen sources, but even the glossy coloured portraits from *Vogue* and *Jours de France* had not been able to capture the magnificence of the woman.

Surprisingly, he saw his own immediate recognition reflected. There was no change in her expression, but it flared briefly like dark-green emerald fire in her eyes. There was no question in Peter's mind but that she had recognized him, and as he stepped towards her he realized she was tall, but the fine proportion of her body had not made that immediately apparent. Her skirt was of a fine wool crêpe which moulded the long, stately legs of a dancer.

'Baroness, may I present my brother. General Stride.'

'How do you do, General.' Her English was almost perfect, a low husky voice, the slight accent very attractive, but she pronounced his rank as three distinct syllables.

'Peter, this is Baroness Altmann.'

Her thick glossy black hair was scraped back severely from the forehead with a perfect arrowhead of widow's peak at the centre, emphasizing the high Slavic cheekbones and the unblemished perfection of her skin – but her jawline was too square and strong for beauty, and the mouth had an arrogant determined line to it. Magnificent, but not beautiful – and Peter found himself violently attracted. The breathless wholesale feeling he had not experienced for twenty years.

She seemed to epitomize everything he admired in a woman.

Her body was in the condition of a trained athlete. Beneath the oyster silk of her blouse her arms were delicately sculpted from toned muscle, the waist narrow, the breasts very small and unfettered, their lovely shape pressing clearly through fine material, her clean lightly tanned skin glowed with health and careful grooming. All this contributed to his attraction.

However, the greater part was in Peter's own mind. He knew she was a woman of extraordinary strength and achievement, that was pure aphrodisiac for him, and she exuded also the challenging air of being unattainable. The regal eyes mocked his evident masculinity with the untouchable aloofness of a queen or a goddess. She seemed to be smiling inwardly, a cool patronizing smile at his admiration, which she realized was no more than her due. Quickly Peter reviewed what he knew of her.

She had begun her association with the Baron as his private secretary, and in five years had become indispensable to him. The Baron had recognized her ability by rapidly elevating her to the boards of directors, first of some of the group's lesser subsidiaries, and finally to that of the central holding company. When the Baron's physical strength had begun to decline in his losing battle with an inexorable cancer, he came to rely more upon her, trust well placed as it soon turned out. For she ran the complex empire of heavy industrial companies, of electronics and armaments corporations, of banking and shipping and property developments, like the son he never had. When he married her he was fifty-eight years of age, almost thirty years her senior, and she had been a perfect wife as she had been a perfect business partner.

She had assembled and personally delivered the massive ransom demanded by his abductors, against the advice of the French police, going alone and unguarded to a meeting with merciless killers, and when they had returned the Baron's fearfully mutilated corpse to her, she had mourned him and buried him and continued to run the empire she had inherited, with vision and strength so far beyond her years.

She was twenty-nine years old. No, that had been two years ago, Peter realized, as he bowed over her hand, not quite touching the smooth cool fingers with his lips. She would be thirty-one years old now. She wore a single ring on her wedding finger, a solitaire diamond, not a particularly large diamond, not more than six carats but of such a perfect whiteness and fire that it seemed to be endowed with its own life. It was the choice of a woman of immense wealth and even greater style.

As Peter straightened, he realized that she was appraising him as carefully as he was her. It seemed that he would be unable to conceal anything from those slanted emerald eyes, but he returned her gaze steadily, knowing without conceit that he could withstand any such scrutiny; still intrigued, however, with the certainty that she had known him.

'Your name has been much in the news recently,' she said, as if in explanation.

There were sixteen for lunch, including Steven and Pat's three children and Melissa-Jane. It was a happy, relaxed meal, but the Baroness was seated at a distance that made it impossible for Peter to speak directly to her, and though he strained to follow her conversation, her voice was low and addressed mostly to Steven and the editor of one of the national daily newspapers who flanked her. Peter found himself fully occupied in fending off the breathless attention of the pretty but feather-brained blonde on his left. She was a starlet who had married well and divorced even better. She had been handpicked by Pat Stride. Peter's sister-in-law was indefatigable in her efforts to find him a suitable replacement for Cynthia. Twelve years of straight failures had not daunted her in the least.

There was still time for Peter to notice that though the Baroness sipped once or twice at her wine, the level in the glass never fell, and she picked only lightly at her plate.

Though Peter watched her covertly, the Baroness never glanced once in his direction. It was only as they went through for coffee that she came directly and unaffectedly to his side.

'Steven tells me there are Roman ruins on the estate,' she said.

'I could show them to you. It is a lovely walk up through the woods.'

'Thank you. I do have some business to discuss with Steven before that; shall we meet at three o'clock?'

She had changed into a loose tweed skirt and jacket that would have looked bulky on a shorter or plumper woman, and high boots in the same lavender tinted brown. Under it she wore a cashmere roll-neck jersey, and a scarf of the same fine wool hung down her back. A wide-brimmed hat with a bright feather in the band was pulled down over her eyes.

She walked in silence, hands thrust deeply into the big pockets of her jacket, making no effort to protect the expensive boots from mud, thorns of damp bracken. She moved with a flowing, long-legged grace, swinging from the hips so that her shoulder and head seemed to float beside Peter, at a not much lower level than his own. Had she not been a world leader in finance and industry, she might have made a great model, he decided. She had a talent for making clothes look important and elegant, while treating them with indifference.

Peter respected her silence, pleased to be able to step out to match her pace, as they went up through the dark dripping woods that smelt of leaf mould and cold rain, the oaks bare and moss-pelted, seeming to beseech a purple-grey sky with arthritic limbs held high.

They came out on the higher open ground without having stopped once, although the path had been steep and the ground soft underfoot.

She was breathing deeply but evenly, and she had coloured just sufficiently to flatter the high Slavic cheeks. She must be in peak physical condition, he thought.

'Here they are.' Peter indicated the barely discernible grass-covered ditch that circled the hilltop. 'They are not very impressive, but I didn't want to warn you in advance.'

She smiled now. 'I have been here before,' she said in that intriguing husky accent.

'Well, we are off to a flying start. We have both deceived each other at our first meeting—' Peter chuckled.

'I came all the way from Paris,' she explained. 'It was most inconvenient really – the business I had to discuss with Sir Steven could have been completed by telephone in five minutes. What I had to discuss with you could only be done face by face—' She corrected herself immediately. 'I am sorry, face to face.' It was a rare slip. Steven had been strangely insistent that Peter spend this particular weekend at Abbots Yew, and was certainly party to this encounter.

'I am flattered by the interest of such a beautiful lady—'

Instantly she frowned, and with a gesture of irritation cut short the compliment as frivolous.

'Very recently you were approached by the Narmco section of Seddler Steel with an offer to head their Sales Division,' she said, and Peter nodded. Since his resignation had been accepted by the War Office, there had been many offers. 'The terms of employment offered were extraordinarily generous.'

'That is true.'

'You prefer the cloistered academic life, perhaps?' she asked, and though Peter's expression did not change, he was taken off balance. It seemed impossible that she could know of the offer of the Chair of Modern Military History that he had been offered by a leading American university, an offer with which he was still toying idly.

'There are some books I want to read and write,' Peter said.

'Books. You have an important collection, and I have read those you have written. You are an interesting contradiction, General Stride. The man of direct action, and at the same time of deep political and social thought.'

'I confuse myself at times,' Peter smiled. 'So what chance do you have to understand me?'

She did not rise to the smile. 'A great deal of your writing coincides with my own conviction. As for your action, if I had been a man and in your position, I might have acted as you did.'

Peter stiffened, resenting any allusion to the taking of Flight 070, and again she seemed to understand instinctively.

'I refer to your entire career, General. From Cyprus to Johannesburg – and including Ireland.' And he relaxed slightly.

'Why did you refuse the Narmco offer?' she asked.

'Because it was presented with the unstated conviction that I could not refuse. Because the terms were so generous that they left a strange unsatisfying odour in my nostrils. Because I believe that I would have been required to perform duties in line with the reputation I seem to have acquired since the taking of Flight 070.'

'What reputation is that?' She leaned slightly towards him, and he smelled her particular aroma. The way perfume reacted upon that petally-smooth skin, heated by the exertion of the climb up the hill. She smelled faintly of crushed lemon blossom and clean healthy mature woman. He felt himself physically aroused by it, and had an almost undesirable impulse to reach out and touch her, to feel the warmth and glossiness of her skin.

'A man who makes accommodations, perhaps,' he answered her.

'What did you think you might have been asked to do?'

This time he shrugged. 'Perhaps carry bribes to my one-time colleagues in NATO Command, to induce them to consider favourably the products of Narmco.'

'Why would you believe that?'

'I was once a decision-making officer in that Command.'

She turned away from him and looked out across the special greens of an English winter landscape, the orderly fields and pastures, the dark wedges and geometrical shapes of the woods and copses.

'Do you know that through Altmann Industries and other companies I control a majority shareholding in Seddler Steel, and naturally in Narmco?'

'No,' Peter admitted. 'But I cannot say I am surprised.'

'Did you know that the offer from Narmco was in reality from me personally?'

This time he said nothing.

'You are quite right, of course, your contacts with the upper echelon of NATO and with the British and American high commands would have been worth every centime of the extravagant salary you were offered. As for bribes—' She smiled then suddenly, and it altered her face entirely, making her seem many years younger, and there was a warmth and a sense of fun that he would not have suspected, ' – this is a capitalist society, General. We prefer to talk about commissions and introducer's fees.'

He found himself smiling back at her, not because of what she had said, but simply because her smile was irresistible.

'However, I give you my solemn word that you would never have been expected to offer or carry – no, since Lockheed were indiscreet, it has changed. Nothing disreputable could ever be traced back to Narmco, and certainly not to the top men there. Certainly not to you.'

'It's all academic now,' Peter pointed out. 'I've refused the offer.'

'I disagree, General Stride.' The brim of the hat covered her eyes as she looked down. 'I hope that when you hear what I had hoped to achieve you may reconsider. I made the error of trying to keep us at arms' length to begin with. I relied on the generosity of the offer to sway you. I do not usually misjudge people so dismally—' and she looked up and smiled again, and this time reached out and touched his arm. Her fingers were like her limbs, long and slim, but they were delicately tapered and the nails were shaped and lacquered to a glossy fleshy pink. She left them on his arm as she went on speaking.

'My husband was an extraordinary man. A man of vast vision and strength and compassion. Because of that they tortured and killed him—' her voice had sunk to a hoarse catchy whisper ' – they killed him in the most vile manner—' She stopped, but made no attempt to turn her head away, she was unashamed of the tears that filled both eyes but did not break over the lower lids. She did not even blink, and it was Peter who looked away first. Only then she moved her hand, slipping it lightly into the crook of Peter's elbow and coming beside him so her hip almost touched his.

'It will rain soon,' she said, her voice level and controlled. 'We should go down.' And as they started, she went on talking.

'The butchers who did that to Aaron went free, while an impotent society looked on. A society which has systematically stripped itself of defence against the next attack. America has virtually disbanded its intelligence system, and so shackled and exposed what is left that it is powerless. Your own country is concerned only with its particular problems, as are we in the rest of Europe – there is no international approach to a problem that is international in scope. Atlas was a fine concept, limited as it was by the fact that it was a force that could only be used in retaliation and then only in special circumstances. However, if they ever suspect that it exists, the denizens of the left will mass to tear it down like a hunting pack of hyena.' She squeezed his arm lightly, and looked sideways at him with a solemn slant of the emerald eyes. 'Yes, General, I do know about Atlas – but do not ask me how.'

Peter said nothing, and they entered the forest, stepping carefully, for the path was slick and steep.

'After the death of my husband, I began to think a great deal about how we could protect the world that we know, while still remaining within the laws which were first designed to do that. With Altmann Industries I had inherited a comprehensive system of international information-gathering; naturally it was attuned almost entirely to commercial and industrial considerations—' She went on talking in that low intense voice that Peter found mesmeric, describing how she had gradually used her massive fortune and influence to reach across borders closed to most to gain the overall view of the new world of violence and intimidation. ' – I was not tied by considerations such as that of Interpol, forbidden by suicidal laws to involve itself in any crime that has political motivation. It was only when I was able to pass on what I had learned that I found myself coming up against the same self-destructive state of mind that masquerades as democracy and individual freedom. Twice I was able to anticipate a terrorist strike and to warn the authorities, but intention is not a crime, I was told, and both the culprits were quietly escorted to the border and turned free to prepare themselves almost openly for the next outrage. The world must wait and cringe for the next stroke, prohibited from making any pre-emptive strike to prevent it, and when it comes they are hampered by confused national responsibilities and by the complicated concept of minimum force—' The Baroness broke off. 'But you know all this! You have written in depth of the same subject.'

'It's interesting to hear it repeated.'

'I will come soon enough to the interesting part – but we are almost back at the house.'

'Come,' Peter told her, and led her past the stables to the swimming pool pavilion. The surface of the heated pool steamed softly, and lush tropical plants were in odd contrast to the wintry scene beyond the glass walls.

They sat side by side on a swing seat, close enough to be able to talk in subdued tones, but the intense mood was broken for the moment. She took off her hat, scarf and jacket, and tossed them onto the cane chair opposite, and she sighed as she settled back against the cushions.

'I understand from Sir Steven that he wants you to go into the bank.' She slanted her eyes at him. 'It must be difficult to be so sought after.'

'I don't think I have Steven's reverence for money.'

'It's a readily acquired taste, General Stride,' she assured him. 'One that can become an addiction.'

At that moment the children of both Stride brothers arrived in a storm of shouted repartee and laughter, which moderated only marginally when they realized that Peter and the Baroness were in the swing seat.

Steven's youngest son, bulging over the top of his costume with puppy-fat and with silver braces on his front teeth, rolled his eyes in their direction and in a stage whisper told Melissa-Jane, '*Je t'aime, ma chérie*, swoon! swoon!' His accent was frighteningly bad and he received a hissed rebuke and a shove in the small of the back that hurled him into the deep end of the pool.

The Baroness smiled. 'Your daughter is very protective—' she turned slightly to examine Peter's face again ' – or is it merely jealousy?' Without waiting for an answer she went straight on to ask another question. Against the background of shouts and splashes, Peter thought he had misheard.

'What did you say?' he asked carefully, certain that his expression had revealed nothing, and she repeated.

'Does the name Caliph mean anything to you?'

He frowned slightly, pretending to consider, while his memory darted back to the terrible micro-seconds of mortal combat, of smoke and flame and gunfire and a dark-haired girl in a scarlet shirt screaming:

'Don't kill us! Caliph said we would not die. Caliph—' And his own bullets stopping the rest of it, smashing into the open mouth. The word had haunted him since then, and he had tried a thousand variations, looking for sense and meaning, considering the possibility that he had misheard. Now he knew he had not.

'Caliph?' he asked, not knowing why he was going to deny it, merely because it seemed vital that he keep something in reserve, that he were not carried headlong on the torrent of this woman's presence and personality. 'It's a Mohammedan title – I think it literally means the heir of Mohammed, the successor to the prophet.'

'Yes.' She nodded impatiently. 'It's the title of a civil and religious leader – but have you heard it used as a code name?'

'No. I am sorry, I have not. What is the significance?'

'I am not sure, even my own sources are obscure and confused.' She sighed, and they watched Melissa-Jane in silence. The child had been waiting for Peter's attention, and when she had it she ran lightly out along the springboard and launched herself, light as a swallow in flight, into a clean one-and-a-half somersault, entering the water with hardly a ripple and surfacing immediately with fine pale hair slick down across her face, immediately looking again for Peter's approval.

'She's a lovely child,' said the Baroness. 'I have no

children. Aaron wanted a son – but there was not one.' And there was real sorrow in the green eyes that she masked quickly. Across the pool Melissa-Jane climbed from the pool and quickly draped a towel around her shoulders, covering her bosom which was now large enough and yet so novel as to provide her with a constant source of embarrassment and shy pride.

'Caliph,' Peter reminded the Baroness quietly, and she turned back to him.

'I first heard the name two years ago, in circumstances I shall never forget—' She hesitated. 'May I take it that you are fully aware of the circumstances surrounding my husband's kidnapping and murder? I do not wish to repeat the whole harrowing story – unless it is necessary.'

'I know it,' Peter assured her.

'You know that I delivered the ransom, personally.'

'Yes.'

'The rendezvous was a deserted airfield near the East German border. They were waiting with a light twin-engined aircraft, a Russian-built reconnaissance machine with its markings sprayed over—' Peter remembered the meticulous planning and the special equipment used in the hijacking of 070. It all tallied. ' – There were four men, masked. They spoke Russian, or rather two of them spoke Russian. The other two never spoke at all. It was bad Russian—' Peter remembered now that the Baroness spoke Russian and five other languages. She had a Middle European background. Peter wished he had studied her intelligence file more thoroughly. Her father has escaped with her from her native Poland when she was a small child. ' – Almost certainly, the aircraft and the Russian were intended to cover their real identity,' she mused. 'I was with them for some little time. I had forty-five million Swiss francs to deliver and even in notes of large denomination it was a bulky and heavy cargo to load aboard the aircraft. After the first few minutes, when they realized that I had no police escort, they relaxed and joked amongst themselves as they worked at loading the money. The word "Caliph" was used in the English version, in a Russian exchange that roughly translates as "He was right again" and the reply "Caliph is always right". Perhaps the use of the English word made me remember it so clearly—' She stopped again, grief naked and bleak in the green eyes.

'You told the police?' Peter asked gently, and she shook her head.

'No. I don't know why not. They had been so ineffectual up to that time. I was very angry and sad and confused. Perhaps even then I had already decided that I would hunt them myself – and this was all I had.'

'That was the only time you heard the name?' he asked, and she did not reply immediately. They watched the children at play – and it seemed fantasy to be discussing the source of evil in such surroundings, against a background of laughter and innocent high spirits.

When the Baroness answered, she seemed to have changed direction completely.

'There had been that hiatus in international terrorism. The Americans seemed to have beaten the hijacking problem with their Cuban agreement and the rigorous airport searches. Your own successful campaign against the Provisional wing of the IRA in this country, the Entebbe raid and the German action at Mogadishu were all hailed as breakthrough victories. Everybody was beginning to congratulate themselves that it was beaten. The Arabs were too busy with the war in the Lebanon and with inter-group rivalries. It had been a passing thing.' She shook her head again. 'But terrorism is a growth industry – the risks are less than those of financing a major movie. There is a proven sixty-seven per cent chance of success, the capital outlay is minimal, with outrageous profits in cash and publicity, with instant results – and potential power not even calculable. Even in the event of total failure, there is still a better than fifty per cent survival rate for the participants.' She smiled again, but now there was no joy and no warmth in it. 'Any businessman will tell you it's better than the commodity markets.'

'The only thing against it is that the business is run by amateurs,' Peter said, 'or by professionals blinded by hatred or crippled by parochial interests and limited goals.'

And now she turned to him, wriggling around in the canvas swing seat, curling those long legs up under her in that double-jointed woman's manner, impossible for a man.

'You are ahead of me, Peter.' She caught herself. 'I am sorry, but General Stride is too much to say, and I have the feeling I have known you so long.' The smile now was fleeting but warm. 'My name is Magda,' she went on simply. 'Will you use it?'

'Thank you, Magda.'

'Yes.' She picked up the thread of conversation again. 'The business is in the hands of amateurs – but it is too good to stay that way.'

'Enter Caliph,' Peter guessed.

'That is the whisper that I have heard; usually there is no name. Just that there was a meeting in Athens, or Amsterdam or East Berlin or Aden – only once have I heard the name Caliph again. But if he exists already he must be one of the richest men in the world, and soon he will be the most powerful.'

'One man?' Peter asked.

'I do not know. Perhaps a group of men – perhaps even a government. Russia, Cuba, an Arab country? Who knows yet?'

'And the goals?'

'Money, firstly. Wealth to tackle the political objectives – and finally power, raw power.' Magda Altmann stopped herself, and made a self-deprecating gesture. 'This is guesswork again, my own guessing – based only on past performance. They have the wealth now, provided by OPEC and – myself amongst others. Now he or they have started on the political objectives, a soft target first. An African racist minority government unprotected by powerful allies. It should have succeeded. They should have won an entire nation – a mineral-rich nation – for the price of a dozen lives. Even had they failed to gain the main prize, the consolation prize was forty tons of pure gold. That's good business, Peter. It should have succeeded. It *had* succeeded. The Western nations actually put pressure on the victims, and forced them to accede to the demands – it was a trial run, and it worked perfectly, except for one man.'

'I am afraid,' said Peter softly, 'as afraid as I have ever been in my life.'

'Yes, I am also, Peter. I have been afraid ever since that terrible phone call on the night they took Aaron, and the more I learn the more afraid I become.'

'What happens next?'

'I do not know – but the name he has chosen has the hint of megalomania, perhaps a man with visions of godlike domination—' She spread her fine narrow hands and the diamond flashed white fire. ' – We cannot hope to fathom the mind of a man who could embark on such a course. Probably he believes that what he is doing is for the eventual good of mankind. Perhaps he wants to attack the rich by amassing vast wealth, to destroy the tyrant with universal tyranny, to free mankind by making it a slave to terror. Perhaps he seeks to right the wrongs of the world with evil and injustice.'

She touched his arm again, and this time the strength of those long fingers startled Peter. 'You have to help me find him, Peter. I am going to put everything into the hunt, there will be no reservations, all the wealth and influence that I control will be at your disposal.'

'You choose me because you believe that I murdered a wounded woman prisoner?' Peter asked. 'Are those my credentials?' And she recoiled from him slightly, and stared at him with the slightly Mongolian slant of eyes, then her shoulders slumped slightly.

'All right, that is part of it, but only a small part of it. You know I have read what you have written, you must know that I have studied you very carefully. You are the best man available to me, and finally you have proved that your involvement is complete. I know that you have the strength and skill and ruthlessness to find Caliph and destroy him – before he destroys us and the world we know.'

Peter was looking inwards. He had believed that the beast had a thousand heads, and for each that was struck off a thousand more would grow – but now for the first time he imagined the full shape of the beast, it was still in ambush, not clear yet, but there was only a single head. Perhaps, after all, it was mortal.

'Will you help me, Peter?' she asked.

'You know I will,' he answered quietly. 'I do not have any choice.'

She flew in the brilliance of high sunlight reflected from snowfields of blazing white, jetting through her turns with flowing elegance, carving each turn with a crisp rush of flying snow, swaying across the fall line of the mountain in an intricate ballet of interlinked movement.

She wore a slim-fitting skin suit of pearly grey, trimmed in black at the shoulders and cuffs, she was shod with gleaming black Heierling snowbirds, and her skis were long, narrow, black Rossignol professionals.

Peter followed her, pressing hard not to lose too much ground, but his turns were solid Christies without the stylish fallback unweighting of the jet turn which gave her each time a fractional gain.

The dun he ran like a stag of ten
But the mare like a new roused fawn

Kipling might have been describing them, and she was a hundred yards ahead of him as they entered the forest.

The pathway was barred with the shadows of the pines, and sugary ice roared under his skis as he pushed the narrow corners dangerously fast. Always she was farther ahead, flickering like a silver-grey wraith on those long lean legs, her tight round buttocks balancing the narrow waist and swinging rhythmically into the turns, marvellous controlled broadsides where the icy roadway denied purchase, coming out fast and straight, leaning into the rush of the wind, and her faint sweet laughter came back to Peter as he chased. There is an expertise that must be learned in childhood, and he remembered then that she was Polish, would probably have skied before she was weaned, and suppressed the flare of resentment he always felt at being outclassed by another human being, particularly by the woman who was fast becoming his driving obsession.

He came round another steeply banked turn, with the sheer snow wall rising fifteen feet on his right hand and on his left the tops of the nearest pines at his own level, so steep the mountain fell away into the valley.

The ice warning signs flashed past, and there was a wooden bridge, its boards waxen, opalescent with greenish ice. He felt control go as he hit the polished iron-hard surface. The bridge crossed a deep sombre gorge, with a frozen waterfall skewered to the black mountain rock by its own cruel icicles, like crucifixion nails.

To attempt to edge in, or to stem the thundering rush across the treacherous going, would have invited disaster, to lean back defensively would have brought him down instantly and piled him into the sturdy wooden guide rails. At the moment he was lined up for the narrow bridge Peter flung himself forward so that his shins socked into the pads of his boots, and in a swoop of terror and exhilaration he went through, and found that he was laughing aloud though his heart leaped against his ribs and his breathing matched the sound of the wind in his own ears.

She was waiting for him where the path debouched onto the lower slopes. She had pushed her goggles to the top of her head, and stripped off her gloves, both sticks planted in the snow beside her.

'You'll never know how much I needed that.' She had flown into Zurich that morning in her personal Lear jet. Peter had come in on the Swissair flight from Brussels, and they had motored up together. 'You know what I wish, Peter?'

'Tell me,' he invited.

'I wish that I could take a whole month, thirty glorious days, to do what I wish. To be ordinary, to be like other people and not feel a moment's guilt.'

He had seen her on only three occasions in the six weeks since their first meeting at Abbots Yew. Three too brief and, for Peter, unsatisfying meetings.

Once in his new office suite at the Narmco headquarters in Brussels, again at La Pierre Bénite, her country home outside Paris, but then there had been twenty other guests for dinner. The third time had been in the panelled and tastefully decorated cabin of her Lear jet on a flight between Brussels and London.

Though they had made little progress as yet in the hunt for Caliph, Peter was still exploring the avenues that had occurred to him and had cast a dozen lines, baited and hooked.

During their third meeting Peter had discussed with her the need to restructure her personal safety arrangements. He had changed her former bodyguards, replacing them with operatives from a discreet agency in Switzerland which trained its own men. The director of the agency was an old and trusted friend.

They had come to this meeting now so that Peter might report back on his progress to Magda. But for a few hours the snow had seduced them both.

'There is still another two hours before the light goes.' Peter glanced across the valley at the village church. The gold hands of the clock showed a little after two o'clock. 'Do you want to run the Rheinhorn?'

She hesitated only a moment. 'The world will keep turning, I'm sure.' Her teeth were very white, but one of them was slightly crooked, a blemish that was oddly appealing as she smiled up at him. 'Certainly it will wait two hours.'

He had learned that she kept unbelievable hours, beginning her day's work when the rest of the world still slept, and still hard at it when the offices of Altmann Industries in Boulevard Capucine were deserted, except her own office suite on the top floor. Even during the drive up from Zurich she had gone through correspondence and dictated quietly to one of her secretaries. He knew that at the chalet across the valley her two secretaries would be waiting already, with a pile of telex flimsies for her consideration and the line held open for her replies.

'There are better ways to die than working yourself to death.' He was suddenly out of patience with her single-mindedness, and she laughed easily with high colour in her cheeks and the sparkle of the last run in the green eyes.

'Yes, you are right, Peter. I should have you near to keep reminding me of that.'

'That's the first bit of sense I've had from you in six weeks.' He was referring to her opposition to his plans for her security. He had tried to persuade her to change established behaviour patterns, and though the smile was still on her lips, her eyes were deadly serious as she studied his face.

'My husband left me a trust—' she seemed suddenly sad beneath the laughter ' – a duty that I must fulfil. One day I should like to explain that to you – but now we only have two hours.'

It was snowing lightly, and the sun had disappeared behind the mountains of rock and snow and cloud as they walked back through the village. The lights were burning in the richly laden shop windows and they were part of the gaily clad stream returning from the slopes, clumping along the frozen sidewalks in their clumsy ski boots, carrying skis and sticks over one shoulder and chattering with the lingering thrill of the high piste that even the lowering snow-filled dusk could not suppress.

'It feels good to be free of my wolves for a while.' Magda caught his arm as her snowbirds skidded on dirty ridged ice, and after she had regained her balance she left her gloved hand there.

Her wolves were the bodyguards that Peter had provided, the silent vigilant men who followed her either on foot or in a second car. They waited outside her offices while she worked, and others guarded the house while she slept.

That morning, however, she had told Peter, 'Today I have as a companion a gold medal Olympic pistol champion, I don't need my wolves.'

Narmco marketed its own version of the 9-mm parabellum pistol. It was called 'Cobra', and after a single morning in the underground range Peter had taken a liking to the weapon. It was lighter and flatter than the Walther he was accustomed to, easier to carry and conceal, and the single action mechanism saved a flicker of time with the first shot, for there was no need to cock the action. He had had no trouble obtaining a permit to carry one as a trade sample, although it was necessary to check it before every commercial flight, but it carried neatly in a quick-release shoulder holster.

He had felt theatrical and melodramatic at first, but with a little sober thought had convinced himself that to follow on Caliph's tracks unarmed was shortening the odds against himself.

Now it was becoming habit, and he was barely aware of the comforting shape and weight in his armpit, until Magda spoke.

'I am close to dying from thirst,' she went on, and they racked their skis and went into the jovial warmth and clouds of steam that billowed from one of the coffee shops that lined the main street.

They found a seat at a table already crowded with young people, and they ordered glasses of steaming hot *Glühwein*.

Then the four-piece band thumped out a popular dance tune and their table companions swarmed onto the tiny dance floor.

Peter raised a challenging eyebrow at her and she asked with amusement, 'Have you ever danced in ski boots?'

'There has to be a first time for everything.'

She danced like she did everything else, with complete absorption, and her body was strong and hard and slim against his.

It was completely dark as they climbed the narrow track above the village and went in through the electronically controlled gate in the protective wall around the chalet.

It was somehow typical of her that she had avoided the fashionable resorts, and that externally the chalet seemed not much different from fifty others that huddled in the edge of the pine forest.

There was patent relief amongst her entourage at her return, and she seemed almost defiant at their concern as though she had just proved something to herself – but still she did not change from her sports clothes before disappearing into the office suite on the first floor with her two male secretaries. 'I work better with men,' she had explained to Peter once. As Peter dressed in slacks, blazer and silk roll-neck after a scalding shower, he could still hear the clatter of the telex machine from the floor below, and it was an hour later when she called him on the house telephone.

The entire top floor was her private domain and she was standing at the windows looking out over the snow-fuzzed lights of the valley as he entered.

She wore green slacks tucked in après-ski boots, and a blouse of the same colour, a perfect match for her eyes. The moment Peter entered, she pressed a concealed switch and the curtains slid silently closed, then she turned to him.

'A drink, Peter?' she asked.

'Not if we are going to talk.'

'We are going to talk,' she said positively, and indicated the soft squashy leather armchair across from the fireplace. She had resisted the traditional Swiss cuckoo-clock and knotty pine decor, and the carpeting was thick Wilton to match the curtains, the furniture low and comfortable but modern, sporty and good fun, the very best made to appear natural and unaffected, blending easily with the modern art on the walls and abstract sculpture in marble and grained wood.

She smiled suddenly at him. 'I had no idea that I had found myself a gifted Sales Director for Narmco – I really am impressed with what you have done in so short a time.'

'I had to establish a plausible cover—' Peter deprecated the compliment. 'And I used to be a soldier – the job interests me.'

'You English!' she told him with mock exasperation. 'Always so modest.' She did not seat herself but moved about the room; although never at rest, neither did she give the feeling of restlessness. 'I am informed that there is to be a definite NATO testing of Kestrel – after almost two years of procrastination.'

Kestrel was Narmco's medium-range ground-to-ground infantry portable missile.

'I am further informed that the decision was made to test after you had met with some of your former colleagues.'

'The whole world runs on the old boy system—' Peter chuckled, ' – you should know that.'

'And you are on old boy terms with the Iranians?' She cocked her head at him.

'That was a small stroke of luck. Five years ago I was on a staff college course with their new military adviser.'

'Luck again.' She smiled. 'Isn't it strange that luck so often favours those who are clever and dedicated and who move faster than the pack?'

'I have had less luck in other directions,' Peter pointed out, and immediately there was no trace of laughter left upon her lips nor in the emerald eyes, but Peter went on. 'So far I have been unsuccessful with the contact we spoke about on our last meeting—'

They had discussed the possibility of access to the Atlas computer link, of requisitioning a printout on 'Caliph' from the Central Intelligence bank, if there was one programmed.

'As I explained, there was the one remote possibility of access, somebody who owed me a favour. He was of no help. He believes that if there is a "Caliph" listing, it's blocked and buzzed.' Which meant that any unauthorized requisition would sound an alarm in intelligence control. 'We'd trigger a Delta condition in Atlas if we put in a printout requisition.'

'You did not give him the name?' Magda asked sharply.

'No. No names, just a general discussion over dinner at Brooks's – but all the implications were there.'

'Do you have any further avenues – ?'

'I think so. One more, but it's a last resort,' Peter said. 'Before we come to that, though, perhaps you can tell me if you have anything further from your sources.'

'My sources—' Magda had never made more explicit descriptions, and Peter had instinctively known not to pry. There was a certain finality to the way she said it. 'My sources have been mostly negative. The seizure of the Netherlands Embassy in Bonn was unconnected with

Caliph. It was exactly what it purported to be – South Moluccan extremists. The hijackers of Cathay Airlines and Transit Airlines were both enthusiastic amateurs, as evidence the methods and the outcome—' She smiled drily and drifted back across the room to touch the Hundedwasser collage that hung on the side wall, rearranging the hang of the frame in an essentially feminine gesture. ' – There is only one recent act that has the style of Caliph.'

'Prince Hassied Abdel Hayek?' Peter asked, and she turned to face him, thrusting out one hip with her hand upon it, the nails very red against the light-green cloth and the marquise cut diamond sparkling.

'What did you make of it?' she asked. The Prince had been shot dead, three bullets of .22 calibre in the back of the head while asleep in his rooms on the Cambridge campus. A nineteen-year-old grandson of King Khalid of Saudi Arabia, not one of the particular favourites of the king, a bespectacled scholarly youth who seemed content to remain outside the mainstream of palace power and politics. There had been no attempt at abduction, no sign of a struggle, no evidence of robbery – the young Prince had no close friends nor apparent enemies.

'It does not seem to have reason or motive,' Peter admitted. 'That's why I thought of Caliph.'

'The deviousness of Caliph—' Magda turned away and her haunches rippled under the elastic of her green slacks. There was no ruck line of panties, and her buttocks were perfect spheres, with the shadow of the deep cleft between them showing through the thin material. Peter watched her legs as she paced, realizing for the first time that her feet were long and narrow as her hands, fine and graceful bones in perfect proportion.

'If I told you that Saudi Arabia last week made clear to the other members of OPEC that, far from supporting a rise in the price of crude, she will press for a *five per cent* reduction in the world price at the organization's next meeting—'

Peter straightened up in his chair slowly and Magda went on softly ' – and that she will be supported by Iran in her proposal. If I told you that, what would you think?'

'The King has other, more favoured grandchildren – grandsons and sons as well, brothers, nephews—'

'Seven hundred of them,' Magda agreed, and then went on musing. 'The Shah of Iran has children that he divorced one wife to obtain—'

'The Shah paid his hundred-million-dollar ransom promptly to save his oil minister during the Carlos abduction – what would he do for his own children?' Peter stood up now, unable to stay still with the itch of new ideas.

'And the King of Saudi-Arabia is an Arab. You know how Mohammedans are about sons and grandsons.' Magda came to stand so close to him that he could feel the warmth of her flesh through the narrow space between them, and her perfume subtly underlined the ripe sweet woman's smell of her body, disturbing him, but strangely heightening his awareness. 'Perhaps King Khalid has also been reminded of his own mortality.'

'All right.' Peter hunched his shoulders and frowned in concentration. 'What are we suggesting? That Caliph has struck another easy formula? Two men who control the economic destiny of the Western world? Two men who make decisions at the personal level, who are not answerable to cabinets or causes or governments?'

'Men who are therefore vulnerable to personal terrorism, who have records of appeasement to terrorist pressure.' Magda paused. 'The old truths are still good. "Uneasy lies the head that wears a crown." Both the Shah and the King will be no strangers to the fear of the assassin's blade. They will understand the law of the knife, because they have always lived by it.'

'Hell, you have to admire it.' Peter shook his head. 'There is no need to take and hold hostages. No need for exposure. You kill one obscure member of a large royal family, and you promise that there will be others, each one more important, closer to the head.'

'Both families have a high profile. The Shah loves the bright lights. He's up at Gstaad right this moment. It would need only a sniper up in the treeline to pick one of his children. His sister Shams is in Mauritius now. As for the King's family – any time you want to drop into the Dorchester you'll find one of his sons or grandsons sipping coffee in the public lounge. They are soft targets, and there are plenty of them. You might even have to kill two princelings or three – but secretly the world will feel that they had it coming to them anyway. There will not be oceans wept for men who have themselves held the world to ransom.'

Peter's frown smoothed away, and he grinned wryly. 'Not only do you have to admire it – you've got to have a sneaking sympathy for the object. A dead brake to the crippling inflation of the world, a slowing of disruptive imbalance in trade.'

And Magda's expression was fierce as he had never seen it before. 'That is the trap, Peter. To see the end only, and to harden yourself to the means. That was the trap that Caliph set with the taking of 070. His demands coincided with those of the Western powers, and they placed additional pressure on the victim. Now, if we are correct and Caliph is pressuring the oil dictators for a moderation of their demands, how much more support can he expect from the Western capitalist powers?'

'You are a capitalist,' Peter pointed out. 'If Caliph succeeds you will be one of the first to benefit.'

'I'm a capitalist, yes. But before that I am a human being, and a thinking human being. Do you really believe that if

Caliph succeeds now that this will be the last we hear of him?'

'Of course not.' Peter spread his hands in resignation. 'Always his demands will be harsher – with each success he must become bolder.'

'I think we can have that drink now,' Magda said softly, and turned away from him. The black onyx top of the coffee table slid aside at her touch to reveal the array of bottles and glasses beneath.

'Whisky, isn't it?' she asked, and poured a single malt Glenlivet into one of the cut glass tumblers. As she handed it to him their fingers touched and he was surprised at how cool and dry her skin felt.

She poured half a flute glass of white wine and filled it with Perrier water. As she replaced the wine bottle in the ice bucket, Peter saw the label. It was Le Montrachet 1969. Probably the greatest white wine in the world, and Peter had to protest at the way in which she had desecrated it.

'Alexander Dumas said it should be drunk only on bended knee and with head reverently bared—'

' – He forgot the mineral water,' Magda purred with throaty laughter. 'Anyway you can't trust a man who employed other people to write his books for him.' She lifted the adulterated wine to him. 'Long ago I decided to live my life on my own terms. To hell with Messrs Dumas and Caliph.'

'Shall we drink to that?' Peter asked, and they watched each other over the rims. The level of Magda's glass had not lowered and she set the glass aside, moving across to adjust the bowl of hothouse tulips in the chunky free-form crystal bowl.

'If we are right. If this is Caliph at work – then it disturbs the instinctive picture I had formed of him.' Peter broke the silence.

'How?' she asked without looking up from the flowers.

'Caliph – it's an Arabic name. He is attacking the leader of the Arab world.'

'The deviousness of Caliph. Was the name deliberately chosen to confuse the hunters – or perhaps there are other demands apart from the oil price – perhaps pressure is also being put on Khalid for closer support of the Palestinians, or one of the other extremist Arab movements. We do not know what else Caliph wants from Saudi Arabia.'

'But then, the oil price. It is Western orientated. Somehow it has always been accepted that terrorism is a tool of the far left,' Peter pointed out, shaking his head. 'The hijacking of 070 – even the kidnapping of your husband – were both aimed against the capitalist society.'

'He kidnapped Aaron for the money, and killed him to protect his identity. The attack on the South African Government, the attack on the oil cartel, the choice of name, all point to a person with god-like pretensions.' Magda broke the head off one of the tulips with an abrupt, angry gesture, and crushed it in her fist. She let the petals fall into the deep onyx ashtray. 'I feel so helpless, Peter. We seem to be going round in futile circles.' She came back to him as he stood by the curtained windows. 'You said earlier that there was one sure way to flush out Caliph?'

'Yes,' Peter nodded.

'Can you tell me?'

'There was an old trick of the Indian shikari. When he got tired of following the tiger in thick jungle without a sight of the beast, he used to stake out a goat and wait for the tiger to come to it.'

'A goat?'

'My Zodiacal sign is Capricorn – the goat.' Peter smiled slightly.

'I don't understand.'

'If I were to put the word out that I was hunting Caliph—' He smiled again. 'Caliph knows me. The hijacker spoke my name, clearly, unmistakenly. She had been warned. So I believe that Caliph would take me seriously enough to consider it necessary to come after me.'

He saw the lingering colour drain dramatically from her high cheeks, and the sudden shadow in the depths of her eyes.

'Peter—'

'That's the only way I'm going to get close to him.'

'Peter—' She placed her hand on his forearm, but then she could not go on. Instead she stared at him silently and her eyes were green and dark and unfathomable. He saw there was a pulse that throbbed softly in her long graceful neck, just below the ear. Her lips parted, as though she were about to speak. They were delicately sculptured lips, and she touched them with the pink tip of her tongue, leaving them moist and soft and somehow defenceless. She closed them, without speaking, but the pressure of her fingers on his arm increased, and the carriage of her whole body altered. Her back arched slightly so her lower body swayed towards him and her chin lifted slightly.

'I have been so lonely,' she whispered. 'So lonely, for so very long. I only realized how lonely today – while I was with you.'

Peter felt a choking sensation in his throat, and the prickle of blood behind his eyes.

'I don't want to be lonely again, ever.'

She had let her hair come down. It was very thick and long. It fell in a straight rippling curtain shot through with glowing lights, to her waist.

She had parted it in the centre; a thin straight line of white scalp divided the great black wings and they framed her face, making it appear pale and childlike with eyes too large and vulnerable, and as she came towards where Peter lay the glossy sheets of hair slid silently across the brocade of her gown.

The hem of the gown swept the carpet, and her bare toes peeped out from under it with each step. Narrow finely boned feet, and the nails were trimmed and painted with a colourless lacquer. The sleeves of the gown were wide as batwings and lined internally with satin, the collar buttoned up in a high Chinese style.

Beside the bed she stopped and her courage and poise seemed to desert her, her shoulders slumped a little and she clasped the long narrow fingers before her in a defensive gesture.

'Peter, I don't think I am going to be very good at this.' The throaty whisper was barely audible, and her lips trembled with the strength of her appeal. 'And I want so badly to be good.'

Silently he reached out one hand towards her, palm upwards. The bedclothes covered him to the waist, but his chest and arms were bare, lightly tanned and patterned with dark wiry body hair. As he reached for her the muscle bunched and expanded beneath the skin, and she saw that there was no surplus flesh on his waist, nor on his shoulders and upper arms. He looked lean and hard and tempered, yet supple as the lash of a bullwhip, and she did not respond immediately to the invitation, for his masculinity was overpowering.

He folded back the thick down-filled duvet between them, and the sheet was crisp and smoothly ironed in the low rosy light.

'Come,' he ordered gently, but she turned away and with her back to him she undid the buttons of the embroidered gown, beginning at the throat and working downwards.

She slipped the gown from her shoulders, and held it for a moment in the crook of her elbows. The smooth pale flesh gleamed through the fall of dark hair, and she seemed to steel herself like a diver bracing for the plunge into unknown depths.

She let the gown drop with a rustling slide down the full length of her body, and it lay around her ankles in a shallow puddle of peacock colours.

She heard him gasp aloud, and she threw the hair back from her shoulders with a toss of the long, swan-white neck. The hair hung impenetrably to the small of her back; just above the deep cleft of her lower body it ended in a clean line and her buttocks were round and neat and without blemish, but even as he stared the marble smoothness puckered into a fine rash of gooseflesh as though his eyes had physically caressed her, and she had responded with an appealingly natural awareness that proved how her every sense must be aroused and tingling. At the knowledge Peter felt his heart squeezed. He wanted to rush to her and sweep her into his arms, but instinct warned him that she must close the last gap herself, and he lay quietly propped on one elbow, feeling the deep ache of wanting spread through his entire body.

She stooped to pick up the gown, and for a moment the long legs were at an awkward coltish angle to each other and the spheres of her buttocks altered shape. No longer perfectly symmetrical, but parted slightly, and in the creamy niche they formed with her thighs there was an instant's heart-stopping glimpse of a single dense tight curl of hair and the light from beyond tipped the curl with glowing reddish highlights, then she had straightened again, once more lithe and tall, and she dropped the robe across the low couch and in the same movement turned back to face Peter.

He gasped again and his sense of continuity began to break up into a mosaic of distinct, seemingly unconnected images and sensations.

Her breasts were tiny as those of a pubescent child, but

the nipples were startlingly prominent, the colour and texture of ripening young berries, dark wine-red, already fully erect and hard as pebbles.

The pale plain of her belly, with the deep pit of the navel at its centre, that ended at last on the plump darkly furred mound pressed into the deep wedge between her thighs, like a small frightened living creature crouching from the stoop of the falcon.

The feel of her face pressed to his chest, and the tickle of her quick breath stirring his body hair, the almost painful grip of slim powerful arms locked with desperate strength around his waist.

The taste of her mouth as her lips parted slowly, softly, to his and the uncertain flutter of her tongue becoming bolder, velvety on top and slick and slippery on the underside.

The sound of her breathing changing to a deep sonorous pulse in his ears, seeming to keep perfect time with his own.

The smell of her breath, heavy with the aromatic musk of her arousal, and blending with the orangy fragrance of her perfume and the ripe woman smell of her body.

And always the feel of her – the warmth and the softness, the hardness of toned muscle and the running ripple of long dark hair about his face and down his body, the crisp electric rasp of tight, tense curls parting to unbearable heat and going on for ever to depths that seemed to reach beyond the frontier of reality and reason.

And then later the stillness of complete peace that reached out from the centre where she lay against his heart and seemed to spread to the farthest corners of his soul.

'I knew that I was lonely,' she whispered. 'But I did not realize just how terribly deeply.' And she held him as though she would never relinquish her grip.

Magda woke him in the cold utter darkness three hours before dawn, and it was still dark when they left the chalet. The headlights of the following Mercedes that carried her wolves swept the interior of their saloon through each bend in the steep twisting road down from the mountains.

On take-off from Zurich Magda was in the Lear jet's left-hand seat, flying as pilot-in-command, and she handled the powerful machine with the sedate lack of ostentation which marks the truly competent aviator. Her personal pilot, a grizzled and taciturn Frenchman, who was flying now as her co-pilot, evidently held her skill in high regard and watched over her with an almost fatherly pride and approval as she cleared Zurich controlled airspace and levelled out at cruise altitude for Paris Orly before she left him to monitor the auto-pilot and came back to the main cabin. Though she sat beside Peter in the black calfskin armchairs, her manner was unchanged from the way it had been during their last flight together in this machine – reserved and polite – so that he found it difficult to believe the wonders they had explored together the previous night.

She worked with the two dark-suited secretaries opposite her, speaking her fluent rippling French with the same enchanting trace of accent that marked her English. In the short time since he had joined Narmco, Peter had been forced to make a crash revision of his own French. Now once again he could manage, if not with éclat, at least with competence, in technical and financial discussion. Once or twice Magda turned to him for comment or opinion, and her gaze was serious and remote, seeming as impersonal and efficient as an electronic computer – and Peter understood that they were to make no show of their new relationship before employees.

Immediately she proved him wrong, for her co-pilot called her over the cabin speaker.

'We will join the Orly circuit in four minutes, Baroness.'

And she turned easily and naturally and kissed Peter's cheek, still speaking French.

'Pardon me, *chéri*. I will make the landing. I need the flying time in my logbook.'

She greased the sleek swift aircraft onto the runway as though she was spreading butter on hot toast. The co-pilot had radioed ahead so that when she parked in the private hangar there were a uniformed immigration *policier* and a *douanier* already waiting.

As they came aboard, they saluted her respectfully and then barely glanced at her red diplomatic passport. They took a little longer with Peter's blue and gold British passport, and Magda murmured to Peter with a trace of a smile.

'I must get you a little red book. It's so much easier.' Then to the officials. 'It is a cold morning, gentlemen, I hope you will take a glass.' And her white-jacketed steward was hovering already. They left the two Frenchmen removing their kepis and pistol belts, settling down comfortably in the leather armchairs to make a leisurely selection of the cigars and cognac that the steward had produced for their approval.

There were three cars waiting for them, parked in the back of the hangar with drivers and guards. Peter's lip curled as he saw the Maserati.

'I told you not to drive that thing,' he said gruffly. 'It's like having your name in neon lights.'

They had argued about this vehicle while Peter was reorganizing her personal security, for the Maserati was an electric silver-grey, one of her favourite colours, a shimmering dart of metal. She swayed against him with that husky little chuckle of hers.

'Oh, that is so very nice to have a man being masterful again. It makes me feel like a woman.'

'I have other ways of making you feel like that.'

'I know,' she agreed, with a wicked flash of green eyes.

'And I like those even better, but not now – please! What in the world would my staff think!' Then seriously, 'You take the Maserati, I ordered it for you, anyway. Somebody may as well enjoy it. And please do not be late this evening. I have especially made it free for us. Try and be at La Pierre Bénite by eight o'clock – will you please?'

By the time Peter had to slow for the traffic along the Pont Neuilly entrance to Paris, he had accustomed himself to the surging power and acceleration of the Maserati, and, as she had suggested, he was enjoying himself. Even in the mad Parisian traffic he used the slick gear box to knife through the merest suspicion of an opening, bulling out of trouble or overtaking with the omnipotent sense of power that control of the magnificent machine bestowed upon its driver.

He knew then why Magda loved it so dearly, and when he parked it at last in the underground garage on the Champs-Elysées side of Concorde he grinned at himself in the mirror.

'Bloody cowboy!' he said, and glanced at his Rolex. He had an hour before his first appointment, and as a sudden thought unclipped the holster of the Cobra and, with the pistol still in it, locked it in the glove compartment of the Maserati. He grinned again as he pondered the inadvisability of marching into French Naval Headquarters armed to the teeth.

The drizzle had cleared, and the chestnut trees in the Elysèe gardens were popping their first green buds as he came out into Concorde. He used one of the call boxes in the Concorde Metro station to make a call to the British Embassy. He spoke to the Military Attaché for two minutes, and when he hung up he knew the ball was probably already in play. If Caliph had penetrated the Atlas Command deeply enough to know him personally as the commander of Thor – then it would not be too long before he knew that the former commander had picked up the spoor. The

Military Attaché at the Paris Embassy had other more clandestine duties than kissing the ladies' hands at diplomatic cocktail parties.

Peter reached the main gates of the Marine Headquarters on the corner of the rue Royale with a few minutes to spare, but already there was a secretary waiting for him below the billowing Tricolour. He smoothed Peter's way past the sentries, and led him to the armaments committee room on the third floor overlooking a misty grey view of the Seine and the gilded arches of the Pont Neuf. Two of Peter's assistants from Narmco were there ahead of him with their briefcases unpacked and the contents spread upon the polished walnut table.

The French Flag captain had been in Brussels, and on one unforgettable evening he had conducted Peter on a magic carpet tour of the brothels of that city. He greeted him now with cries of Gallic pleasure and addressed him as 'tu' and 'toi' – which all boded very well for the meeting ahead.

At noon precisely, the French captain moved that the meeting adjourn across the street to a private room on the first floor of Maxim's, blissful in the certainty that Narmco would pick up the tab, if they were really serious about selling the Kestrel rocket motors to the French Navy.

It required all Peter's tact not to make it obvious that he was taking less than his share of the Clos de Vougeot or of the Rémy Martin, and more than once he found that he had missed part of the discussion which was being conducted at a steadily increasing volume. He found that he was thinking of emerald eyes and small pert bosoms.

From Maxim's back to the Ministry of Marine, and later it required another major act of diplomacy on Peter's part when the captain smoothed his moustache and cocked a knowing eye at Peter. 'There is a charming little club, very close and wonderfully friendly—'

By six o'clock Peter had disentangled himself from the

Frenchman's company, with protestations of friendship and promises to meet again in ten days' time. An hour later Peter left his two sales assistants at the Hôtel Meurice after a quick but thorough summation of the day's achievements. They were, all three, agreed that it was a beginning but a long, long road lay ahead to the ending.

He walked back along Rivoli; despite the frowsiness of a long day of endless talk and the necessity for quick thinking in a language which was still strange on the tongue, despite a slight ache behind the eyes from the wine and cognac and despite the taste of cigar and cigarette smoke he had breathed, he was buoyed by a tingling sense of anticipation, for Magda was waiting, and he stepped out briskly.

As he paused for traffic lights, he caught a glimpse of his own reflection in a shop window. He was smiling without realizing it.

While he waited on the ramp of the parking garage for his turn to pay and enter the traffic stream, with the Maserati engine whispering impatiently, he glanced in the rear view mirror. He had acquired the habit long ago when one of the captured Provo death lists had begun with his name; since then he had learned to look over his shoulder.

He noticed the Citroën two back in the line of vehicles because the windshield was cracked and there was a scrape which had dented the mudguard and exposed a bright strip of bare metal.

He noticed the same black Citroën still two back as he waited for pedestrian lights in the Champs-Elysées, and when he ducked his head slightly to try and get a look at the driver, the headlights switched on as though to frustrate him and at that moment the lights changed and he had to drive on.

Going around the Étoile, the Citroën had fallen back four places in the grey drizzling dusk of early autumn, but he spotted it once again when he was halfway down the Avenue de la Grande Armée, for by now he was actively searching for it. This time it changed lanes and slipped off the main thoroughfare to the left. It was immediately lost in the maze of side streets and Peter should have been able to forget it and concentrate on the pleasure of controlling the Maserati, but there lingered a sense of foreboding and even after he had shot the complicated junction of roads that got him onto the periphery route and eventually out on the road to Versailles and Chartres, he found himself changing lanes and speed while he scanned the road behind in the mirror.

Only when he left Versailles and was on the Rambouillet road did he have a clear view back a mile down the straight avenue of plane trees, and he was certain there was no other vehicle on the road. He relaxed completely and began to prepare himself for the final turn off that would bring him at last to La Pierre Bénite.

The shiny wet black python of road uncoiled ahead of him and then humped abruptly. Peter came over the rise at 150 kilometres an hour and instantly started to dance lightly on brake and clutch, avoiding the temptation of tramping down hard and losing adhesion on the slippery uneven tarmac. Ahead of him there was a gendarme in a shiny white plastic cape, wet with rain, brandishing a torch with a red lens; there were reflective warning triangles bright as rubies, a Peugeot in the ditch beside the road with headlights glaring at the sky, a dark blue police Kombi van half blocking the road, and in the stage lit by the Kombi's headlights two bodies were laid out neatly, and all of it hazed by the soft insistent mantle of falling rain – a typical roadside accident scene.

Peter had the Maserati well in hand, bringing her neatly down through the gears to a crawl, and as he was lowering the side window, the electric motor whining softly and the icy gust of night air into the heated interior, the gendarme gestured with the flashlight for him to pull over into the narrow gap between hedge and the parked Kombi, and at that moment the unexpected movement caught Peter's eye. It was one of the bodies lying in the roadway under the headlights. The movement was the slight arch of the back that a man makes before rising from the prone position.

Peter watched him lift his arm, not more than a few inches, but it was just enough for Peter to realize he had been holding an object concealed down the outside of his thigh, and even in the rain and the night Peter's trained eye recognized the perforated air-cooled sleeve enclosing the short barrel of a fold-down machine pistol.

Instantly his brain was racing so that everything about him seemed to be taking place in dreamy slow motion.

The Maserati! he thought. They're after Magda.

The gendarme was coming round to the driver's side of the Maserati, and he had his right hand under the white plastic cape, at the level of his pistol belt.

Peter went flat on the gas pedal, and the Maserati bellowed like a bull buffalo shot through the heart. The rear wheels broke from the wet surface, and with a light touch Peter encouraged the huge silver machine to swing like a scythe at the gendarme. It should have cut him down, but he was too quick. As he dived for the hedge, Peter saw that he had brought the pistol out from under his cape but was too busy at that moment to use it.

The side of the Maserati touched the hedge with a fluttering rustle of foliage, and Peter lifted his right foot, caught the enraged charge of the machine and swung her the other way. The moment she was lined up he hit the gas again, and the Maserati howled. This time she burned blue rubber smoke off her rear wheels.

There was a driver at the wheel of the blue police Kombi, and he tried to pull across to block the road completely, but he was not fast enough.

The two vehicles touched, with a crackle and scream of metal that jarred Peter's teeth, but what concerned him was that the two bodies in the headlights were no longer flat.

The nearest was on one knee and he was swinging the short stubby machine pistol – it looked like a Stirling or the new Sidewinder, but he was using the fold-down wire butt, wasting vital fractions of a second to get the weapon to his shoulder. He was also blocking the field of fire of the man who crouched behind him with another machine pistol pinned to his hip, pointing with index finger and forearm, ready to trigger with his second finger – 'That's the way it should be done.' Peter recognized professional skill, and his brain was running so swiftly that he had time to applaud it.

The Maserati cannoned off the police Kombi, and Peter lifted his right foot to take traction off the rear wheels, and spun the wheel the hard lock to the right. The Maserati swung her tail with a screech of rubber and went into a left side slide towards the two figures in the road, and Peter ducked down below the level of the door. He had deliberately induced the left-hand slide, so that he had some little protection from the engine compartment and bodywork.

As he ducked he heard the familiar sound, like a giant ripping heavyweight canvas, an automatic weapon throwing bullets at a cyclic rate of almost two thousand rounds a minute, and the bullets tore into the side of the Maserati, beating in the metal with an ear-numbing clangor, while glass exploded in upon Peter like the glittering spray as a storm-driven wave strikes a rock. Glass chips pelted across his back, and stung his cheek and the back of his neck. They sparkled like a diamond tiara in his hair.

Whoever was doing the shooting had certainly emptied the magazine in those few seconds, and now Peter bobbed up in his seat, slitting his eyes against the cloud of glass splinters. He saw a looming nightmare of dark hedges and spun the wheel back to hold the Maserati. She swayed to the limits of her equilibrium and Peter had a glimpse of the two gunmen in the road rolling frantically into the half-filled ditch, but at that moment his offrear wheel hit the lip and he was slammed up short against his safety belt with a force that drove the air from his lungs, and the Maserati reared like a stallion smelling the mare and tail-walked, swinging in short vicious surges back and forth across the road, as he desperately fought for control with gear and brake and wheel. He must have spun full circle, Peter realized, for there was a giddy dazzle of light beams and of running and rolling figures, everything hazy and indistinct in the rain, then the open road ahead again, and he sent the car at it with a great howling lunge, at the same moment glancing up at his mirror.

In the headlights he saw the burned blue clouds of smoke and steam thrown up by his own tyres, and through it the figure of the second gunman obscured from the waist by the ditch. He had the machine pistol at his waist, and the muzzle flash bloomed about him.

Peter heard the first burst hit the Maserati and he could not duck again, for there was a bend ahead in the rain, coming up at dazzling speed and he clenched his jaws waiting for it.

The next burst hit the car, like the sound of hail on a tin roof, and he felt the rude tugging, numbing jerk in his upper body.

'Tagged!' he realized. There was no mistaking it, he had been hit before. The first time when he led a patrol into an EOKA ambush a very long time ago, and at the same moment he was evaluating the hit calmly finding he still had use of both hands and all his senses. Either it was a ricochet, or the bullet had spent most of its force in penetrating the rear windshield and seat back.

The Maserati tracked neatly into the bend, and only then he felt the engine surge and falter. Almost immediately the sharp stink of gasoline filled the cab of the Maserati.

'Fuel line,' he told himself, and there was the warm, uncomfortable spread of his own blood down his back and side, and he placed his wound low in the left shoulder. If it had penetrated it would be a lung hit, and he waited for the coppery salt taste of blood in his throat or the bubbling froth of escaping air in his chest cavity.

The engine beat checked again, surged and checked, as it starved for fuel. That first traversing burst of automatic fire must have ripped through the engine compartment, and Peter thought wryly that in the movies the Maserati would have immediately erupted in spectacular pyrotechnics like a miniature Vesuvius – though in reality it didn't happen like that, still gasoline from the severed lead would be spraying over plugs and points.

One last glance backwards, before the bend hid it and he saw three men running for the police van – three men and the driver, that was lousy odds. They would be after him immediately, and the crippled machine made a final brave leap forward that carried them five hundred yards more, and then it died.

Ahead of him, at the limits of the headlight beam, Peter saw the white gates of La Pierre Bénite. They had set the ambush at the point where they could screen out most extraneous traffic, and gather only the silver Maserati in their net.

He cast his mind back swiftly, recalling the lie of the land beyond the main gates of the estate. He had been here only once before, and it had been dark then also – but he had the soldier's eye for ground, and he remembered thick forest on both sides of the road, down to a low bridge over a narrow fast flowing stream with steep banks, a hard left hander and a climb up to the house. The house was half a mile beyond the gates, a long way to go with a body hit and at least four armed men following, and no guarantee that he would be safe there either.

The Maserati was coasting down the slight incline towards the gates, slowing as it ran out of momentum, and now there was the hot smell of oil and burning rubber. The paintwork of the engine hood began to blister and discolour. Peter switched off the ignition to stop the electric pump spraying more fuel onto the burning engine and he slipped his hand into his jacket. He found the wound where he had expected it – low and left. It was beginning to sting and his hand came away sticky and slick with blood. He wiped it on his thigh.

Behind him was the reflected glow of headlights in the rain, a halo of light growing stronger. At any moment they would come through the bend, and he opened the glove compartment.

The 9-mm Cobra gave some little comfort as he slipped it from its holster and thrust it into the front of his belt. There was no spare magazine and the breech was empty, a safety consideration which he now regretted, for it left him with only nine rounds in the magazine – one more might make a lot of difference.

Pretty little fingers of bright flame were waving at him from under the bonnet of the engine compartment, finding the hinge and joint, probing the ventilation slot on the top surface. Peter released his seat belt, held open the door and steered with his other hand for the verge. Here the road was banked and dropped away steeply.

He flicked the wheel back the opposite way and let the change of direction eject him neatly, throwing him clear, while the Maserati swerved back into the centre of the road and rolled away, slowing gradually.

He landed as though from a parachute drop, feet and knees together cushioning the impact and then rolled into it. Pain flared in his shoulder and he felt something tear. He came up in a crouch and ran doubled over for the edge of the woods, and the burning auto lit the dark trees with flickering orange light.

The fingers of his left hand felt swollen and numb as he pumped a round into the chamber of the Cobra, and at that moment the headlights beyond the bend flared with shocking brilliance and Peter had the illusion of being caught in front stage centre of the Palladium. He went down hard on his belly in the soft rain-sodden earth, but still his wound jarred and he felt the warm trickle of running blood under his shirt as he crawled desperately for the tree line.

The police van roared down the stretch of road. Peter flattened and pressed his face to the earth, and it smelled of leaf mould and fungus. The van roared past where he lay.

Three hundred yards down the road the Maserati had coasted to a halt, two wheels still on the road, the offside wheels over the verge so she stood at an abandoned angle, burning merrily.

The van pulled up at a respectful distance from it, aware of the danger of explosion, and a single figure, the gendarme in his plastic cape, ran forward, took one look into the cab and shouted something. The language sounded like French, but the flames were beginning to drum fiercely and the range too long to hear clearly.

The van locked into a U-turn, bumped over the verge, and then started back slowly. The two erstwhile accident victims, still carrying their machine pistols, running ahead like hounds on leash, one on each side of the road, heads down as they searched for signs in the soft shoulders of the road. The white-caped gendarme rode on the running-board of the van, calling encouragement to the hunters.

Peter was up again, doubled over, heading for the edge of the forest, and he ran into the barbed wire fence at full stretch. It brought him down heavily. He felt the slash of steel through the cloth of his trousers, and as he gathered himself again, he thought bitterly. One hundred and seventy guineas. The suit had been tailored in Savile Row. He crawled between the strands of armed wire, and there was a shout behind him. They had picked up his spoor, and as he dodged across the last few yards of open ground, another sharper, more jubilant shout.

They had spotted him in the towering firelight of the blazing Maserati, and again there was the tearing rip of automatic fire; but it was extreme range for the short barrel and low velocity ammunition. Peter heard passing shot like a whisper of bats' wings in the darkness above him and then he reached the first trees and ducked behind one of them.

He found he was breathing deeply, but with a good easy rhythm. The wound wasn't handicapping him yet, and he was into the cold reasoning rage that combat always instilled in him.

The range to the barbed wire fence was fifty metres, he judged, it was one of his best distances – International pistol standard out-of-hand with a 50-mm X circle – but there were no judges out here and he took a double-handed grip, and let them run into the fence just as he had done.

It brought two of them down, and the cries of angry distress were definitely in French; as they struggled to their feet again they were precisely back-lit by the flames, and the Cobra had a luminous foresight. Peter went for the mid-section of one of the machine gunners.

The 9-mm had a vicious whipcrack report, and punched into flesh and bone with 385 foot-pounds of energy. The strike of the bullet sounded like a watermelon hit with the full swing of a baseball bat. It lifted the man off his feet, and threw him backwards, and Peter swung onto the next target, but they were pros. Even though the fire from the edge of the woods had come as a complete surprise, they reacted instantly, and disappeared flat against the dark earth. They gave him no target, and Peter was too low on ammunition to throw down holding fire.

One of them fired a burst of automatic and it tore bark and wood and leaves along the edge of the trees. Peter fired at the muzzle flash only once as a warning and then ducked away and, keeping his head down to avoid lucky random fire, sprinted back into the woods.

They would be held up for two or three minutes by the fence and by the threat of coming under fire again, and Peter wanted to open some ground between them during that time.

The glow of the burning Maserati kept him well orientated and he moved quickly towards the river; however, before he had covered two yards he was starting to shiver uncontrollably. His two-piece city suit was soaked by the persistent drizzle and by the shower from each bush he brushed against. His shoes were light calf leather with leather soles and he had stepped in puddles of mud, and the knee-high grass was sodden. The cold struck through his clothing; he could feel his wound stiffening agonizingly and the first nauseating grip of shock tightened his belly, but he paused every fifty yards or so and listened for sounds of pursuit. Once he heard the sound of a car engine from the direction of the road, passing traffic probably, and he wondered what they would make of the abandoned police vehicle and the blazing Maserati. Even if it was reported to the real police, it would be all over before a patrol arrived and Peter discounted the chance of assistance from that quarter.

He was beginning now to be puzzled by the total lack of any sign of further pursuit, and he looked for and found a good stance in which to wait for it. There was a fallen oak tree and he wriggled in under the trunk, with a clear avenue of retreat, good cover and a low position from which any pursuer would be silhouetted against the sky glow of the burning Maserati. There were only three pursuers now, and seven cartridges in the Cobra. If it were not for the cold and the demoralizing ache through his upper body, he might have felt more confident, but the nagging terror of the hunted animal was still on him.

He waited five minutes, lying completely still, every sense tuned to its finest, the Cobra held out in extended double grip, ready to roll left or right and take the shot as it came. There was no sound but the drip and plop of the rain-soaked woods.

Another ten minutes passed before it occurred to him suddenly that the pursuers must now realize that the wrong quarry had sprung their trap. They were setting for Magda Altmann, and it must be clear to them that they had a man, and an armed one at that. He pondered their reaction. Almost certainly they would pull out now, or had already done so.

Instead of a lady worth twenty or thirty million dollars in ransom money, they must realize they had one of her employees, probably an armed bodyguard, who was driving the Maserati either as a decoy or merely as delivery driver. Yes, he decided, they would pull out – take their casualty and melt away, and Peter was sure they would leave no clues to their identity. He would have enjoyed the opportunity to question one of them, he thought, and grimaced at a new lance of pain in the shoulder.

He waited another ten minutes, utterly still and alert, controlling the spasms of cold and reaction that shook him, then he rose quietly and moved back towards the river. The Maserati must have burned out completely now for the sky was black again and he had to rely on his own sense of direction to keep orientated. Even though he knew he was alone, he paused every fifty yards to listen and look.

He heard the river at last. It was directly ahead and very close. He moved a little faster and almost walked off the bank in the dark. He squatted to rest for a moment, for the shoulder was very painful now, and the cold was draining his energy.

The prospect of wading the river was particularly uninviting. The rain had fallen without a break for days now, and the water sounded powerful and swift – it would certainly be icy cold, and probably shoulder deep rather than waist deep. The bridge must be only a few hundred yards downstream, and he stood up and moved along the bank.

Cold and pain can sap concentration very swiftly, and Peter had to make a conscious effort to keep himself alert, and he felt for every foothold before transferring his weight forward. He held the Cobra hanging at full stretch of his right arm, but ready for instant use, and he blinked his eyes clear of the fine drizzle of rain and the cold sweat of pain and fear.

Yet it was his sense of smell that alerted him. The rank smell of stale Turkish tobacco smoke on a human body, it was a smell that had always offended him, and now he picked it up instantly, even though it was just one faint whiff.

Peter froze in mid stride while his brain raced to adjust to the unexpected. He had almost convinced himself that he was alone.

Now he remembered the sound of a car engine on the main road, and he realized that men who had set up such an elaborate decoy – the faked motor accident, the police van and uniform – would certainly have taken the trouble to plot and study the ground between the ambush point and the victim's intended destination.

They would know better than Peter himself the layout of woods and river and bridge, and would have realized immediately they had taken their first casualty that futility of blundering pursuit through the dark. It was the smart thing to circle back and wait again, and they would choose the river bank or the bridge itself.

The only thing that troubled Peter was their persistence. They *must* know it was not Magda Altmann, and then even in this tense moment of discovery he remembered the Citroën that had followed him down the Champs-Elysées – nothing was what it appeared to be, and slowly he completed the step in which he had frozen.

He stood utterly still, poised every muscle and every nerve screwed to its finest pitch, but the night was black and the rush of the river covered all sound. Peter waited. The other man will always move if you wait long enough, and he waited with the patience of the stalking leopard, although the cold struck through to his bones and the rain slid down his cheeks and neck.

The man moved at last. The squelch of mud and the unmistakeable brush of undergrowth against cloth, then silence. He was very close, within ten feet, but there was no glimmer of light, and Peter shifted his weight carefully to face the direction of the sound. The old trick was to fire one shot at the sound and use the muzzle flash to light the target for a second shot which followed it in almost the same instant of time – but there were three of them and at ten feet that machine pistol could cut a man in half. Peter waited.

Then from upstream there was the sound of a car engine again, still faint but fast approaching. Immediately somebody whistled faintly, a rising double note in the night up towards the bridge, clearly some prearranged signal. A car door banged shut, much closer than the sound of the approaching engine and a starter whirred, another harsher engine roared into life, headlights flared through the rain, and Peter blinked as the whole scene ahead of him lit up.

A hundred yards ahead the bridge crossed the stream, the surface of the water was shiny and black as new-mined coal as it flowed about the supporting piles.

The blue van had parked on the threshold of the bridge, obviously to wait for Peter, but now it was pulling out, probably alarmed by the approach of the other more powerful engine from the direction of La Pierre Bénite. The driver was heading back towards the main road, the phoney gendarme scrambling alongside with his cape flapping as he tried to scramble through the open offside door – and out of the darkness, close to Peter, a voice cried out with alarm.

'*Attendez*!' The third man had no desire to be left by his companions, and he ran forward, abandoning all attempt at concealment. He had his back to Peter now, waving the machine pistol frantically, clearly outlined by the headlights of the van, and the range was under ten feet. It was a dead shot, and Peter went for it instinctively – and only at the very instant of trigger pressure that would have sent a 95 gram bullet between his shoulder blades was Peter able to check himself.

The man's back was turned and the range would make it murder; Peter's training should have cured him of such nice gentlemanly distinctions. However, what really held his trigger finger was the need to know. Peter had to know who these people were and who had sent them, and what they had been sent to do, who they were after.

Now that the man was being deserted, he had abandoned all stealth and was running as though he were chasing a bus, and Peter saw the chance to take him. Roles had been exchanged completely, and Peter darted forward, transferring the Cobra to his injured left hand.

He caught the man in four paces, keeping low to avoid his peripheral vision, and he whipped his good right arm around the throat, going for the half nelson and the spin that would disorientate the man before he slammed the barrel of the Cobra against the temple.

The man was quick as a cat, something warned him – perhaps the squelch of Peter's sodden shoes, and he ducked his chin onto his chest rolling his shoulders and beginning to turn back into the line of Peter's attack.

Peter missed the throat and caught him high, the crook of his elbow locking about the man's mouth, and the unexpected turn had thrown him slightly off balance. If he had had full use of his left arm, he could still have spun his victim, but in an intuitive flash he realized that he had lost the advantage, already the man was twisting his head out of the armlock, bulking his shoulders, and by the feel of him, Peter knew instantly that he was steel-hard with muscle.

The barrel of the machine pistol was short enough to enable him to press the muzzle into Peter's body just as soon as he completed his turn; it would tear Peter to pieces like a chain saw.

Peter changed his grip slightly, no longer opposing the man's turn, but throwing all his weight and the strength of his right arm into the same direction; they spun together like a pair of waltzing dancers, but Peter knew that the moment they broke apart the man would have the killing advantage again.

The river was his one chance, he realized that instinctively, and before the advantage passed back from him to his adversary, he hurled himself backwards, keeping his grip on the man's head.

They went out into black space, falling together in a short gut-swooping drop with Peter underneath. If there was rock below the steep bank of the river, he realized he would be crushed by the other's weight.

They struck the surface of the fast black water, and freezing cold struck like a club so that Peter almost released the air from his lungs as a reflex.

The shock of cold water seemed to have stunned the man in his grip momentarily, and Peter felt the whoosh of air from his lungs as he let go. Peter changed his grip, wedging his elbow under the chin, but not quite able to get at the throat – immediately the man began the wild panic-stricken struggles of somebody held under icy water with empty lungs.

He had lost the machine pistol, for he was tearing at Peter's arms and face with both hands as the water swirled them both end over end down towards the bridge.

Peter had to keep him from getting air, and as he held his own precious single breath, he tried to get on top and stay there.

Fingers hooked at his closed eyes, and then into his mouth as the man reached back desperately over his own shoulders. Peter opened his mouth slightly and the other man thrust his fingers deeply in, trying to tear at his tongue. Immediately Peter locked his teeth into the fingers with a force that made his jaw ache at the hinges, and his mouth filled with the sickening warm spurt of the other man's blood.

Fighting his own revulsion, he hung on desperately with teeth and arms. He had lost his own weapon, dropping it into the black flood from numbed and crippled fingers, and the man was fighting now with the animal strength of his starved lungs and mutilated fingers; every time he tried to yank his hand out of Peter's mouth the flesh tore audibly in Peter's ears and fresh blood made him gag and choke.

They came out on the surface and through streaming eyes Peter had one glimpse of the bridge looming above him. The blue van had disappeared, but Magda Altmann's Mercedes limousine was parked in the centre of the bridge, and in the wash of its headlights he recognized her two bodyguards. They were leaning far out over the guardrail, and Peter had a moment's dread that one of them might try a shot – then they were flung into the concrete piles of the bridge with such force that they lost the deathlock they had upon each other.

The back eddy beyond the bridge swung them in towards the bank. Gasping and swallowing with cold and exhaustion and pain, Peter fought for footing on gravel and rock. The machine-gunner had found bottom also and was stumbling desperately towards the bank. In the headlights of the limousine Peter saw Magda's two bodyguards racing back across the bridge to head him off.

Peter realized that he would not be able to catch the man before he reached the bank.

'Carl!' he screamed at the bodyguard who was leading. 'Stop him. Don't let him get away.'

The bodyguard vaulted over the guardrail, landing cat-like in complete balance, with the pistol double-handed at the level of his navel.

Below him the machine-gunner dragged himself waist deep towards the bank. It was only then that Peter realized what was going to happen.

'No!' He choked on blood and water. 'Take him alive. Don't kill him, Carl!'

The bodyguard had not heard, or had not understood. The muzzle blast seemed to join him and the wallowing figure in the river below him, a blood-orange rope of flame and thunderous explosion. The bullets smacked into the machine-gunner's chest and belly like an axeman cutting down a tree.

'No!' Peter yelled helplessly. 'Oh Jesus, no! No!'

Peter lunged forward and caught the corpse before it slid below the black water, and he dragged it by one arm to the bank. The bodyguards took it from him and hauled it up, the head lolling like an idiot's, and the blood diluted to pale pink in the reflected headlights.

Peter made three attempts to climb the bank, each time slithering back tiredly into the water, then Carl reached down and gripped his wrist.

Peter knelt on the muddy bank, still choking with the water and blood he had swallowed, and he retched weakly.

'Peter!' Magda's voice rang with concern, and he looked up and wiped his mouth on the back of his forearm. She had slipped out of the back door of the limousine and was running back along the bridge, long-legged in black boots and ski-pants, her face dead white with concern and her eyes frantic with worry.

Peter pushed himself onto his feet and swayed drunkenly. She reached him and caught him, steadying him as he teetered.

'Peter, oh God, darling. What happened—'

'This beauty and some of his friends wanted to take you for a ride – and they got the wrong address.'

They stared down at the corpse. Carl had used a .357 magnum and the damage was massive. Magda turned her head away.

'Nice work,' Peter told the bodyguard bitterly. 'He's not going to answer any questions now, is he?'

'You said to stop him.' Carl growled as he reloaded the pistol.

'I wonder what you would have done if I'd said to really clobber him.' Peter began to turn away with disgust, and pain checked him. He gasped.

'You're hurt.' Magda's concern returned in full strength. 'Take his other arm,' she ordered Carl, and they helped him over the parapet to the limousine.

Peter stripped off the torn and sodden remains of his clothing and Magda wrapped him in the Angora wool travel rug before examining his wound under the interior light of the cab.

The bullet hole was a perfect little blue puncture in the smooth skin, already surrounded by a halo of inflammation, and the bullet was trapped between his ribs and the sheet of flat, hard trapezium muscles. She could see the outline of it quite clearly, the size of a ripe acorn in his flesh, swollen out angry purple.

'Thank God—' she whispered, and unwound the Jean Patou scarf from her long pale throat. She bound the wound carefully. 'We'll take you directly to the hospital at Versailles. Drive fast, Carl.'

She opened the walnut-fronted cocktail cabinet in the bodywork beside her and poured half a tumbler of whisky from the crystal decanter.

It washed the taste of blood from Peter's mouth and then went warmly all the way down his throat to soothe the cramps of cold and shock in his belly.

'What made you come?' he asked, his voice still rough with the fierce spirit, the timely arrival nagged at his sense of rightness.

'The police at Rambouillet had a report of a car smash – they knew the Maserati, and the inspector rang La Pierre Bénite immediately. I guessed something bad—'

At that moment they reached the gates at the main road. The remains of the Maserati lay smouldering on the side of the road; around it like boy scouts around a camp fire were half a dozen gendarmes in their white plastic capes and pillbox kepis. They seemed uncertain of what they should do next.

Carl slowed the limousine and Magda spoke tersely through the window to a sergeant, who treated her with immense respect. '*Oui*, madame la Baronne, *d'accord. Tout à fait vrai*—' She dismissed him with a final nod, and he and his men saluted the departing limousine.

'They will find the body at the bridge—'

'There may be another one on the edge of the forest there—'

'You are very good, aren't you?' She slanted her eyes at him.

'The really good ones don't get hit,' he said, and smiled at her. The whisky had taken some of the sting and stiffness out of the wound and unknotted his guts. It was good to still be alive, he started to appreciate that again.

'You were right about the Maserati then – they were waiting for it.'

'That's why I burned it,' he told her, but she did not answer his smile.

'Oh, Peter. You'll never know how I felt. The police told me that the driver of the Maserati was still in it and had been burned. I thought – I felt as though part of me had been destroyed. It was the most terrifying feeling—' She shivered. 'I nearly did not come, I didn't want to see it. I nearly sent my wolves, but then I had to know – Carl saw you in the river as we turned onto the bridge. He said it was you, I just couldn't believe it—' She stopped herself and shuddered at the memory. 'Tell me what happened, tell me all of it,' she demanded and poured more whisky into his tumbler.

For some reason that he was not sure of himself, Peter did not mention the Citroën that had followed him out of Paris. He told himself that it could not have been relevant. It must have been a coincidence, for if the driver of the Citroën had been one of them he would have been able to telephone ahead and warn the others that Baroness Magda Altmann was not in the Maserati, so that would have meant that they were not after her – but after him, Peter Stride, and that didn't make sense because he had only set himself up as bait that very morning, and they would not have had time yet. He stopped the giddy carousel of thoughts – shock and whisky, he told himself. There would be time later to think it all out more carefully. Now he would simply believe that they were waiting for Magda, and he had run into their net. He told it that way, beginning from the moment that he had seen the police van parked in the road. Magda listened with complete attention, the huge eyes clinging to his face, and she touched him every few moments as if to reassure herself.

When Carl parked under the portico of the emergency entrance of the hospital, the police had radioed ahead and there were an intern and two nurses waiting for Peter with a theatre trolley.

Before she opened the door to let them take Peter, Magda leaned to him and kissed him full on the lips.

'I'm so very glad to have you still,' she whispered, and then with her lips still very close to his ear she went on. 'It was Caliph again, wasn't it?'

He shrugged slightly, grimaced at the stab of pain, and answered, 'I can't think of anyone else offhand that would do such a professional job.'

Magda walked beside the trolley as far as the theatre doors, and she was beside his bed in the curtained cubicle as he struggled up through the deadening, suffocating false death of the anaesthetic.

The French doctor was with her, and he produced the gruesome blood-clotted souvenir with a magician's flourish.

'I did not have to cut,' he told Peter proudly. 'Probe only.' The bullet had mushroomed impressively, had certainly lost much of its velocity in penetrating the bodywork of the Maserati. 'You are a very lucky man,' the doctor went on. 'You are in fine condition, muscles like a racehorse that stopped the bullet going deep. You will be well again very soon.'

'I have promised to look after you, so he is letting you come home now.' Magda hovered over him also. 'Aren't you, doctor?'

'You will have one of the world's most beautiful nurses.' The doctor bowed gallantly towards Magda with a certain wistfulness in his expression.

The doctor was right, the bullet wound gave him less discomfort than the tears in his thighs from the barbed wire, but Magda Altmann behaved as though he were suffering from an irreversible and terminal disease.

When she did have to go up to her office suite in the Boulevard des Capucines the next day, she telephoned three times for no other reason than to make sure he was still alive and to ask for his size in shoes and clothing. The cavalcade of automobiles carrying her and her entourage were back at La Pierre Bénite while it was still daylight.

'You are keeping civil service hours,' he accused when she came directly to the main guest suite overlooking the terraced lawns and the artificial lake.

'I knew you were missing me,' she explained, and kissed

him before beginning to scold him. 'Roberto tells me you have been wandering around in the rain. The doctor said you were to stay in bed. Tomorrow I will have to stay here to take care of you myself.'

'Is that a threat?' he grinned at her. 'For that sort of punishment I would let Caliph shoot another hole—'

Swiftly she laid her fingers on his lips. 'Peter, *chéri*, don't joke like that.' And the shadow that passed across her eyes was touched with fear, then immediately she was smiling again. 'Look what I have bought you.'

Peter's valise had been in the trunk of the Maserati, and she had replaced it with one in black crocodile from Hermes. To fill it she must have started at the top end of the Faubourg St Honoré and worked her way down to the Place Vendôme.

'I had forgotten how much fun it is to buy presents for one who you—' She did not finish the sentence, but held up a brocade silk dressing-gown. ' – Everybody in St Laurent knew what I was thinking when I chose this.'

She had forgotten nothing. Shaving gear, silk handkerchiefs and underwear, a blue blazer, slacks and shoes from Gucci, even cufflinks in plain gold, each set with a small sapphire.

'You have such blue eyes,' she explained. 'Now I will go and make myself respectable for dinner. I told Roberto we would eat here, for there are no other guests tonight.'

She had changed from the gunmetal business suit and turban into floating cloud-light layers of gossamer silk, and her hair was down to her waist, more lustrous than the cloth.

'I will open the champagne,' she said. 'It needs two hands.'

He wore the brocade gown, with his left arm still in a sling, and they stood and admired each other over the top of the champagne glasses.

'I was right.' She nodded comfortably. 'Blue is your

colour. You must wear it more often.' And he had to smile at the quaint compliment, and touched her glass with his. The crystal pinged musically and they saluted each other before they drank. Immediately she set the glass aside, and her expression became serious.

'I spoke with my friends in the Sûreté. They agree that it was a kidnap attempt against me, and because I asked it, they will not trouble you to make a statement until you feel better. I told them to send a man tomorrow to speak to you. There was no sign of the second man you shot at on the edge of the woods, he must have been able to walk or been carried by his friends.'

'And the other man?' Peter asked. 'The dead one.'

'They know him well. He had a very ugly past. Algeria with the paras. The mutiny.' She spread her hands eloquently. 'My friends were very surprised that he had not killed you when he tried to do so. I did not say too much about your own past. It is better, I think?'

'It's better,' Peter agreed.

'When I am with you like this, I forget that you also are a very dangerous man.' She stopped and examined his face carefully. 'Or is it part of the reason I find you so—' she searched for the word ' – so compelling? You have such a gentle manner, Peter. Your voice is so soft and—' She shrugged. 'But there is something in the way you smile sometimes, and in certain light your eyes are so blue and hard and cruel. Then I remember that you have killed many men. Do you think that is what attracts me?'

'I hope it is not.'

'Some women are excited by blood and violence – the bullfight, the prize ring, there are always as many women as men at these, and I have watched their faces. I have thought about myself, and still I do not know it all. I know only that I am attracted by strong men, powerful men. Aaron was such a man. I have not found many others since then.'

'Cruelty is not strength,' Peter told her.

'No, a truly strong man has that streak of gentleness and compassion. You are so strong, and yet when you make love to me it is with extreme gentleness, though I can always feel the strength and cruelty there, held in bate, like the falcon under the hood.'

She moved away across the room furnished in cream and chocolate and gold, and she tugged the embroidered bell-pull that dangled from the corniced ceiling with its hand-painted panels, pastoral scenes of the type that Marie Antoinette had so admired. Peter knew that much of the furnishing of La Pierre Bénite had been purchased at the auction sales with which the revolutionary committee dispersed the accumulated treasures of the House of Bourbon. With the other treasures there were flowers, wherever Magda Altmann went there were flowers.

She came back to him as Roberto, the Italian butler, supervised the entry of the dinner trolley, and then Roberto filled the wine glasses himself, handling the bottles with white gloves as though they were part of the sacrament, and stationed himself ready to serve the meal, but Magda dismissed him with a curt gesture and he bowed himself out silently.

There was a presentation-wrapped parcel at Peter's place setting, tissue paper and an elaborately tied red ribbon. He looked up at her inquiringly as she served the soup into fragile Limoges bowls.

'Once I began buying presents, I could not stop myself,' she explained. 'Besides, I kept thinking that bullet might have been in my back.' Then she was impatient. 'Are you not going to open it?'

He did so carefully, and then was silent.

'Africa, it is your speciality, is it not?' she asked anxiously. 'Nineteenth-century Africa?'

He nodded, and reverently opened the cover of the volume in its bed of tissue paper. It was fully bound in maroon leather, and the state of preservation was quite extraordinary, only the dedication on the flyleaf in the author's handwriting was faded yellow.

'Where on earth did you find this?' he demanded. 'It was at Sotheby's in 1971. I bid on it then.' He had dropped out of the bidding at five thousand pounds.

'You do not have a first edition of Cornwallis Harris?' she asked again anxiously, and he shook his head, examining one of the perfectly preserved colour plates of African big game.

'No, I do not. But how did you know that?'

'Oh, I know as much about you as you do yourself,' she laughed. 'Do you like it?'

'It is magnificent. I am speechless.' The gift was too extravagant, even for someone of her fortune. It troubled him, and he was reminded of the comedy situation of the husband who brings home flowers unexpectedly and is immediately accused by his wife. 'Why do you have a guilty conscience?'

'Do you truly like it? I know so little about books.'

'It is the one edition I need to complete my major works,' he said. 'And it is probably the finest specimen left outside the British Museum.'

'I'm so glad.' She was genuinely relieved. 'I was truly worried.' And she put down the silver soup ladle and lifted both arms to welcome his embrace.

During the meal she was gay and talkative, and only when Roberto had wheeled away the trolley and they settled side by side on the down-filled couch before the fire did her mood change again.

'Peter, today I have been unable to think of anything but this business – you and me and Caliph. I have been afraid, and I am still afraid. I keep thinking of Aaron, what they did to him – and then I think of you and what nearly happened.'

They were silent, staring into the flames and sipping

coffee from the demi-tasses, then suddenly she had changed direction again. He was growing accustomed to these mercurial switches in thought.

'I have an island – not one island, but nine little islands – and in the centre of them is a lagoon nine kilometres wide. The water is so clear you can see the fish fifty feet down. There is an airstrip on the main atoll. Just under two hours' flying time to Tahiti. Nobody would ever know we were there. We could swim all day, walk in the sand, make love under the stars. You would be king of the islands, and I would be your queen. No more Altmann Industries – I would find somebody as good or better than myself to run it. No more danger. No more fear. No more Caliph – no more—' She stopped abruptly, as though she had been about to commit herself too far, but she went on quickly. 'Let's go there, Peter. Let's forget all this. Let's just run away and be happy together, for ever.'

'It's a pretty thought.' He turned to her, feeling deep and genuine regret.

'It would work for us. We would make it work.'

And he said nothing, just watching her eyes, until she looked away and sighed.

'No.' She mirrored his regret. 'You are right. Neither of us could ever give up living like that. We have to go on – but, Peter, I am so afraid. I am afraid of what I know about you and of what I do not know. I am afraid of what you do not know about me, and what I never can tell you – but we must go on. You are right. We have to find Caliph, and then destroy him. But, oh God, I pray we do not destroy ourselves, what we have found together – I pray we will be able to keep that intact.'

'The best way to conjure up emotional disaster is to talk about it.'

'All right, let's play riddles instead. My turn first. What is the most miserable experience known to the human female?'

'I give up.'

'Sleeping alone on a winter's night.'

'Salvation is at hand,' he promised her.

'But what about your poor shoulder?'

'If we combine our vast talents and wisdom, I am sure we will manage something.'

'I think you are right,' she purred and nestled against him like a sleek and silken cat. 'As always.'

There is always a delightfully decadent feeling about buying underwear for a beautiful woman, and Peter was amused by the knowing air of the middle-aged sales lady. She clearly had her own ideas about the relationship, and slyly produced a tray filled with filmy lace and iniquitously expensive wisps of silk.

'Yes,' Melissa-Jane approved rapturously. 'Those are exactly—' She held one of them to her cheek, and the sales lady preened at her own foresight. Peter hated to disillusion her, and he played the role of sugar-daddy a few moments longer as he glanced up at the mirror behind her head.

The tail was still there, a nondescript figure in a grey overcoat, browsing through a display of brassieres across the hall with the avid interest and knowledgeable air of a closet queen.

'I don't really think your mother will approve, darling,' Peter said, and the sales woman looked startled.

'Oh, please, Daddy. I will be fourteen next month.'

They had had a tail on him since he had arrived at Heathrow the previous afternoon, and Peter could not decide who they were. He began to regret he had not yet replaced the Cobra he had lost in the river.

'I think we'd better play it safe—' Peter told his daughter, and both Melissa-Jane and the sales lady looked crestfallen.

'Not bloomers!' Melissa-Jane wailed. 'Not elastic legs.'

'Compromise,' Peter suggested. 'No elastic legs – but no lace, not until you're sixteen. I think painted fingernails is enough for right now.'

'Daddy, you can be so medieval, honestly!'

He glanced at the mirror again, and they were changing the guard across the sales hall. The man in the shabby grey overcoat and checked woollen scarf drifted away and disappeared into one of the lifts. It would take some little time for Peter to spot his replacement – and then he grinned to himself; no it would not. Here he came now. He wore a tweed sports jacket in a frantic hounds tooth pattern, above Royal Stewart tartan trews and a grin like an amiable toad.

'Son of a gun. This is a surprise.' He came up behind Peter and hit him an open-handed blow between the shoulder blades that made Peter wince. At least he knew who they were at last.

'Colin.' He turned and took the massive paw with its covering of wiry black hair across the back. 'Yes, it is a surprise. I've been falling over your gorillas since yesterday.'

'Oafs,' Colin Noble agreed amiably. 'All of them, oafs!' And turned to seize Melissa-Jane. 'You're beautiful,' he told her and kissed her with more than avuncular enthusiasm.

'Uncle Colin. You come straight from heaven.' Melissa-Jane broke from the embrace and displayed the transparent panties. 'What do you think of these?'

'It's you, honey. You've just got to have them.'

'Tell my father, won't you?'

Colin looked around the Dorchester suite and grunted. 'This is really living. You don't get it this good in this man's army.'

'Daddy is truly becoming a bloated plutocrat – just like Uncle Steven,' Melissa-Jane agreed.

'I notice that you and Vanessa and the other comrades all wear lace panties,' Peter counter-attacked his daughter.

'That's different.' Melissa-Jane back-tracked swiftly, and hugged the green Harrod's package defensively. 'You can have a social conscience without dressing like a peasant, you know.'

'Sounds like a good life.' Peter threw his overcoat across the couch and crossed to the liquor cabinet. 'Bourbon?'

'On the rocks,' said Colin.

'Is there a sweet sherry?' Melissa-Jane asked.

'There is Coke,' Peter answered. 'And you can take it through to your own room, young lady.'

'Oh Daddy, I haven't seen Uncle Colin for ages.'

'Scat,' said Peter, and when she had gone, 'sweet sherry, forsooth.'

'It's a crying bastard when they start growing up – and they look like that.' Colin took the glass from Peter and rattled the ice cubes together as he lay back in the armchair. 'Aren't you going to congratulate me?'

'With pleasure.' Peter took his own glass and stood at the windows, against the backdrop of bare branches and grey misty skies over Hyde Park. 'What did you do?'

'Come on, Pete! Thor – they gave me your job, after you walked out.'

'Before they fired me.'

'After you walked out,' Colin repeated firmly. He took a sip of the Bourbon and gargled it loudly. 'There are a lot of things we don't understand – "Ours not to reason why, ours but to do and die." Shakespeare.'

He was still playing the buffoon, but the small eyes were as honey bright and calculating as those of a brand new teddy bear on Christmas morning. Now he waved his glass around the suite.

'This is great. Really it's great. You were wasted in Thor – everybody knew that. You must be pulling down more than all the joint-chiefs put together now.'

'Seven gets you five that you've already seen a Xeroxed copy of my contract of employment with Narmco.'

'Narmco!' Colin whistled. 'Is that who you're working for? No kidding, Pete baby, that's terrific!'

And Peter had to laugh, it was a form of capitulation. He came across and took the seat opposite Colin.

'Who sent you, Colin?'

'That's a lousy question—'

'That's just an opener.'

'Why should somebody have sent me? Couldn't I just want to chew the fat with an old buddy?'

'He sent you because he worked it out that I might bust the jaw of anybody else.'

'Sure now and everybody knows we love each other like brothers.'

'What's the message, Colin?'

'Congratulations, Peter baby, I am here to tell you that you have just won yourself a return ticket to the Big Apple.' He placed one hand across his heart and sang with a surprisingly mellow baritone. 'New York, New York, it's a wonderful town.'

Peter sat staring impassively at Colin, but he was thinking swiftly. He knew he had to go. Somehow he was certain that something was surfacing through muddied waters, the parts were beginning to click together. This was the sort of thing he had hoped for when he put the word on the wind.

'When?'

'There is an airforce jet at Croydon right now.'

'Melissa-Jane?'

'I've got a driver downstairs to take her home.'

'She's going to hate you.'

'Story of my life,' Colin sighed. 'Only the dogs love me.'

They played gin-rummy and drank teeth-blackening airforce coffee, all the way across the Atlantic. Colin Noble did most of the talking, around the stub of his cheroot. It was shop, Thor shop, training and personnel details, small anecdotes about men and things they both knew well – and he made no effort to question Peter about his job and Narmco, other than to remark that he would have Peter back in London for the series of Narmco meetings he had arranged starting on the following Monday. It was a deliberate and not very subtle intimation of just how much Atlas knew about Peter and his new activities.

They landed at Kennedy a little after midnight, and there was an army driver to take them to a local Howard Johnson for six hours' sleep, that kind of deep black coma induced by jet-lag.

Peter still felt prickly-eyed and woollen-headed as he watched with a feeling of disbelief as Colin devoured one of those amazing American breakfasts of waffles and maple syrup, wieners and bacon and eggs, sugar cakes and sticky buns, washed down with countless draughts of fruit juice and coffee. Then Colin lit his first cheroot and announced, 'Hell, now I know I'm home. Only now I realize I've been slowly fading away with malnutrition for two years.'

The same army driver was waiting for them at the front entrance of the motel. The Cadillac was an indication of their status in the military hierarchy. Peter looked out with detachment from the air-conditioned and padded interior onto the brooding ghettoes of Harlem. From the elevated highway along the East River, it reminded Peter of a deserted battle ground – where a few survivors lurked in dark doorways or scuttled along the littered and pitted sidewalks in the cold misty morning. Only the graffiti that adorned the bare brick walls had passion and vitality.

Their drive caught the junction of Fifth and One Hundred and Eleventh Street, and ran south down the park past the Metropolitan Art Museum in the thickening rush-hour traffic, then slipped off and into the cavernous mouth of a parking garage beneath one of the monolithic structures that seemed to reach to the grey cold heavens.

The garage entrance was posted 'Residents Only', but the doorman raised the electronically controlled grid and waved them through. Colin led Peter to the bank of elevators and they rode up with the stomach-dropping swoop while the lights above the elevator door recorded their ascent to the very top of the building.

There they stepped out into a reception area protected by ornamental, but none the less functional screens.

A guard in military police uniform and wearing a side-arm surveyed them through the grille and checked Colin's Atlas pass against his register before allowing them through.

The apartment occupied the entire top level of the building, for there were hanging gardens beyond the sliding glass panels and a view across the sickening canyons of space to the other tall structures farther down Island – the Pan Am building and the twin towers of the World Trade Center.

The decor was Oriental, stark interiors in which were displayed works of art that Peter knew from his previous visit were of incalculable value – antique Japanese brush paintings on silk panels, carvings in jade and ivory, a display of tiny netsuke – and in an atrium through which they passed was a miniature forest of Bonsai trees in their shallow ceramic bowls, the frozen contortions of their trunks and branches a sign of their great age.

Incongruously, the exquisite rooms were filled with the thunder of von Karajan leading the Berlin Philharmonic Orchestra through the glories of the Eroica.

Beyond the atrium was a plain door of white oak, and Colin Noble pressed the buzzer beside the lintel and almost immediately the door slid open.

Colin led into a long carpeted room, the ceiling of which was covered with acoustic tiles. The room contained besides the crowded bookshelves and work table an enormous concert piano, and down the facing wall an array of hi-fi turntables and loudspeakers that would have been more in place in a commercial recording studio.

Kingston Parker stood beside the piano, a heroic figure, tall and heavy in the shoulder, his great shaggy head hanging forward onto his chest, his eyes closed and an expression of almost religious ecstasy glowing upon his face.

The music moved his powerful frame the way the storm wind sways a giant of the forest. Peter and Colin stopped in the doorway, for it seemed an intrusion on such a private, such an intimate moment, but it was only a few seconds before he became aware of them and lifted his head. He seemed to shake off the spell of the music with the shudder that a spaniel uses to shake itself free of water when it reaches dry land, and he lifted the arm of the turntable from the spinning black disc.

The silence seemed to tingle after the great crashing chords of sound.

'General Stride,' Kingston Parker greeted him. 'Or may I still call you Peter?'

'Mr Stride will do very nicely,' said Peter, and Parker made an eloquent little gesture of regret, and without offering to shake hands indicated the comfortable leather couch across the room.

'At least you came,' he said, and as Peter settled into the couch, he nodded.

'I have always had an insatiable curiosity.'

'I was relying on that,' Kingston Parker smiled. 'Have you breakfasted?'

'We've had a snack,' Colin cut in but Peter nodded.

'Coffee then,' said Parker, and spoke quietly into the intercom set, before turning back to them.

'Where to begin?' Parker combed the thick greying hair back with both hands, leaving it even more tousled than it had been.

'Begin at the beginning,' Peter suggested. 'As the King of Hearts said to Alice.'

'At the beginning—' Parker smiled softly. ' – All right, at the beginning I opposed your involvement with Atlas.'

'I know.'

'I did not expect that you would accept the Thor command, it was a step backwards in your career. You surprised me there, and not for the first time.'

A Chinese manservant in a white jacket with brass buttons carried in a tray. They were silent as he offered coffee and cream and coloured crystal sugar and then, when he had gone, Parker went on.

'At that time, my estimate of you, General Stride, was that although you had a record of brilliance and solid achievement, you were an officer of rigidly old-fashioned thought. The Colonel Blimp mentality more suited to trench warfare than to the exigencies of war from the shadows – the kind of wars that we are fighting now, and will be forced to fight in the future.'

He shook the great shaggy head and unconsciously his fingers caressed the smooth cool ivory keyboard, and he settled down on the stool before the piano.

'You see, General Stride, I saw the role of Atlas to be too limited by the original terms of reference placed upon it. I did not believe that Atlas could do what it was designed for if it was only an arm of retaliation. If it had to wait for a hostile act before it could react, if it had to rely entirely on other organizations – with all their internecine rivalries and bickerings – for its vital intelligence. I needed officers who were not only brilliant, but who were capable of unconventional thought and independent action. I did not believe you had those qualities, although I studied you very carefully. I was unable to take you fully into my confidence.'

Parker's slim fingers evoked a fluent passage from the keyboard as though to punctuate his words, and for a moment he seemed completely enraptured by his own music, then he lifted his head again.

'If I had done so, then the conduct of your rescue operation of Flight 070 might have been completely different. I have been forced radically to revise my estimate of you, General Stride – and it was a difficult thing to do. For by demonstrating those qualities which I thought you lacked, you upset my judgement. I admit that personal chagrin swayed my reasoned judgement – and by the time I was thinking straight again you had been provoked into offering your resignation—'

'I know that the resignation was referred to you personally, Doctor Parker – and that you recommended that it be accepted.' Peter's voice was very cold, the tone clipped with controlled anger – and Parker nodded.

'Yes, you are correct. I endorsed your resignation.'

'Then it looks as though we are wasting our time here and now.' Peter's lips were compressed into a thin, unforgiving line, and the skin across his cheeks and over the finely chiselled flare of his nostrils seemed tightly drawn and pale as porcelain.

'Please, General Stride – let me explain first.' Parker reached out one hand to him as though to physically restrain him from rising, and his expression was earnest, compelling. Peter sank back into the couch, his eyes wary and his lips still tight.

'I have to go back a little first, in order to make any sense at all.' Parker stood up from the piano and crossed to the rack of pipes on the work table between the hi-fi equipment. He selected one carefully, a meerschaum mellowed to the colour of precious amber. He blew through the empty pipe and then tramped back across the thick carpet to stand in front of Peter.

'Some months before the hijacking of 070 – six months to be precise, I had begun to receive hints that we were entering a new phase in the application of international terrorism. Only hints at first, but these were confirmed and followed by stronger evidence.' Parker was stuffing the meerschaum from a leather wallet as he spoke, now he zipped this closed and tossed it onto the piano top. 'What we were looking at was a consolidation of the forces of violence under some sort of centralized control – we were not sure what form this control was taking.' He broke off and studied Peter's expression, seemed to misinterpret it for utter disbelief, for he shook his head. 'Yes, I know it sounds far-fetched, but I will show you the files. There was evidence of meetings between known militant leaders and some other shadowy figures, perhaps the representatives of an Eastern government. We were not sure then, nor are we now. And immediately after this a complete change in the conduct and apparent motivation of militant activity. I do not really have to detail this for you. Firstly the systematic accumulation of immense financial reserves by the highly organized and carefully planned abduction of prominent figures, starting with the ministers of OPEC, then leading industrialists and financial figures—' Parker struck a match and puffed on his pipe and perfumed smoke billowed around his head. ' – So that it appeared that the motivation had not really changed and was still entirely self gain or parochial political gain. Then there was the taking of 070. I had not confided in you before and once you were on your way to Johannesburg it was too late. I could do nothing more than try to control your actions by rather heavy-handed commands. I could not explain to you that we suspected that this was the leading wave of the new militancy, and that we must allow it to reveal as much as possible. It was a terrible decision, but I had to gamble a few human lives for vital information – and then you acted as I had believed you were incapable of acting.' Parker removed his pipe from his mouth and he smiled; when he smiled you could believe anything he said and forgive him for it, no matter how outrageous. 'I admit, General Stride, that my first reaction was frustrated rage. I wanted your head, and your guts also. Then suddenly I began using my own head instead. You had just proved you were the man I wanted, my soldier capable of unconventional thought and action. If you were discredited and cast adrift, there was just a chance that this new direction of militancy would recognize the same qualities in you that I had been forced to recognize. If I allowed you to ruin your career, and become an outcast – an embittered man, but one with vital skills and invaluable knowledge, a man who had proved he could be ruthless when it was necessary—' Parker broke off and made that gesture of appeal. ' – I am sorry, General Stride, but I had to recognize the fact that you would be very attractive to—' he made an impatient gesture ' – I do not have a name for them, shall we just call them "the enemy". I had to recognize the fact that you would be of very great interest to the enemy. I endorsed your resignation.' He nodded sombrely. 'Yes, I endorsed your resignation, and without your own knowledge you became an Atlas agent at large. It seemed perfect to me. You did not have to act a role – you believed it yourself. You were the outcast, the wronged and discredited man ripe for subversion.'

'I don't believe it,' Peter said flatly, and Parker went back to the work table, selected an envelope from a Japanese ceramic tray and brought it back to Peter.

It took Peter a few moments to realize that it was a Bank Statement – Crédit Suisse in Geneva – the account was in his name, and there were a string of deposits. No withdrawals or debits. Each deposit was for exactly the same amount, the net salary of a major-general in the British Army.

'You see,' – Parker smiled – 'you are still drawing your Atlas salary. You are still one of us, Peter. And all I can say is that I am very sorry indeed that we had to subject you to the pretence – but it seems it was all worth while.'

Peter looked up at him again, not entirely convinced, but with the hostility less naked in his expression.

'What do you mean by that, Doctor Parker?'

'It seems that you are very much back in play again.'

'I am Sales Director for Northern Armaments Company,' he said flatly.

'Yes, of course, and Narmco is part of the Altmann Industrial Empire – and Baron Altmann and his lovely wife are, or rather were, an extraordinarily interesting couple. For instance, did you know that the Baron was one of the top agents of Mossad in Europe?'

'Impossible,' Peter shook his head irritably. 'He was a Roman Catholic. Israeli intelligence does not make a habit of recruiting Catholics.'

'Yes,' Parker agreed. 'His grandfather converted to Catholicism – and changed the name of the family home to La Pierre Bénite. It was a business decision, that we are certain of, there was not much profit in being Jewish in nineteenth-century France. However, the young Altmann was much influenced by his grandmother and his own mother. He was a Zionist from a very early age, and he unswervingly used his enormous wealth and influence in that cause – right up until the time of his murder. Yet he did it so cunningly, with such subtlety that very few people were aware of his connections with Judaism and Zionism. He never made the mistake of converting back to his ancestral religion, realizing that he could be more effective as a practising Christian.'

Peter was thinking swiftly. If this was true, then it all had changed shape again. It must affect the reasons for the

Baron's death – and it would change the role of Magda Altmann in his life.

'The Baroness?' he asked. 'Was she aware of this?'

'Ah, the Baroness!' Kingston Parker removed his pipe from between his teeth, and smiled with reluctant admiration. 'What a remarkable lady. We are not certain of very much about her – except her beauty and her exceptional talents. We know she was born in Warsaw. Her father was a professor of medicine at the university there, and he escaped to the West when the Baroness was still a child. He was killed a few years later, a traffic accident in Paris. Hit and run driver, while the professor was leaving his faculty in the Sorbonne. A small mystery still hangs around his death. The child seems to have drifted from family to family, friends of her father, distant relatives. She already was showing academic leanings, musical talent, at thirteen a chess player of promise – then for a period there is no record of her. She seems to have disappeared entirely. The only hint is from one of her foster mothers, a very old lady now, with a fading memory. "I think she went home for a while – she told me she was going home."' Parker spread his hands. 'We do not know what that means. Home? Warsaw? Israel? Somewhere in the East?'

'You have researched her very carefully,' Peter said. What he had heard had left him uneasy.

'Of course, we have done so to every contact you have made since leaving Atlas Command. We would have been negligent not to do so – but especially we have been interested in the Baroness. She has been the most fascinating, you understand that, I am sure.'

Peter nodded, and waited. He did not want to ask for more. Somehow it seemed disloyal to Magda, distrustful and petty – but still he waited and Parker went on quietly.

'Then she was back in Paris. Nineteen years of age now – a highly competent private secretary, speaking five languages fluently, beautiful, always dressed in the height of fashion, soon with a string of wealthy, influential and powerful admirers – the last of these was her employer, Baron Aaron Altmann.' Parker was silent then, waiting for the question, forcing Peter to come to meet him.

'Is she Mossad also?'

'We do not know. It is possible – but she has covered herself very carefully. We are rather hoping you will be able to find that out for us.'

'I see.'

'She must have known that her husband was a Zionist. She must have suspected that it had something to do with his abduction and murder. Then there are the missing six years of her life – from thirteen to nineteen, where was she?'

'Is she Jewish?' Peter asked. 'Was her father Jewish?'

'We believe so, although the professor showed no interest in religion and did not fill in the question on his employment application to the Sorbonne. His daughter showed the same lack of religious commitment – we know only that her marriage to the Baron was a Catholic ceremony followed by a civil marriage in Rambouillet.'

'We have drifted a long way from international terrorism,' Peter pointed out.

'I do not think so.' Kingston Parker shook his big shaggy head. 'The Baron was a victim of it, and almost as soon as you – one of the world's leading experts on militancy and urban warfare – as soon as you are associated with her there is an assassination attempt, or an abduction attempt made on the Baroness.'

Peter was not at all surprised that Parker knew of that night on the road to La Pierre Bénite – it was only a few days since Peter's arm had been out of the sling.

'Tell me, Peter. What was your estimate of that affair? I have seen an excerpt of the statement that you made to the French police – but what can you add to that?'

Peter had a vivid cameo memory of the Citroën that had

followed him out of Paris, and then almost simultaneously the tearing sound of automatic fire in the night.

'They were after the Baroness,' Peter said firmly.

'And you were driving her car?'

'That's right.'

'You were at the place at the time that the Baroness usually passed?'

'Right.'

'Who suggested that? You?'

'I told her that the car was too conspicuous.'

'So you suggested taking it down to La Pierre Bénite that night.'

'Yes.' Peter lied without knowing why he did so.

'Did anybody else know that the Baroness would not be driving?'

'Nobody.' Except her bodyguards, the two chauffeurs who had met them on their return from Switzerland, Peter thought.

'You are certain?' Parker persisted.

'Yes,' Peter snapped. 'Nobody else.' Except Magda, only Magda. He pushed the thought aside angrily.

'All right, so we must accept that the Baroness was the target – but was it an assassination or an abduction attempt? That could be significant. If it was assassination, it would indicate that it was the elimination of a rival agent, that the Baroness was probably also a Mossad agent, recruited by her husband. On the other hand, an abduction would suggest that the object was monetary gain. Which was it, Peter?'

'They had blocked the road—' he said, but not completely he remembered. 'And the police impersonator signalled me to stop—' or at least to slow down, he thought, slow down sufficiently to make an easy target before they started shooting ' – and they did not open fire until I made it clear that I was not going to stop.' – But they had been ready to begin shooting at the instant Peter made the decision to send the Maserati through the roadblock. The intention of the two machine-gunners had seemed evident. ' – I would say the object was to seize the Baroness alive.'

'All right,' Parker nodded. 'We will have to accept that for the time being.' He glanced at Colin. 'Colonel Noble? You had a question?'

'Thank you, Doctor. We haven't heard from Peter in what terms he was approached by Narmco or the Baroness. Who made the first contact?'

'I was approached by a London firm who specializes in making top executive placements. They came directly from the Narmco Board—' And I turned them down flat, he thought. It was only later at Abbots Yew—

'I see.' Colin frowned with disappointment. 'There was no question of a meeting with the Baroness?'

'Not at that stage.'

'You were offered the sales appointment – no mention of any other duties, security, industrial intelligence—'

'No, not then.'

'Later?'

'Yes. When I met the Baroness, I realized her personal security arrangements were inadequate. I made changes.'

'You never discussed her husband's murder?'

'Yes, we did.'

'And?'

'And nothing.' Peter was finding it difficult to improvise answers, but he used the old rule of telling as much of the truth as possible.

'There was no mention by the Baroness of a hunt for her husband's murderers? You were not asked to use your special talents to lead a vendetta?'

Peter had to make a swift decision. Parker would know of his leak to the British military attaché in Paris – the bait he had so carefully placed to attract Caliph. Of course Parker would know: he was head of Atlas with access to the

Central Intelligence computer. Peter could not afford to deny it.

'Yes, she asked me to relay any information which might point to her husband's murderers. I asked G.2 in Paris for any information he might have. He couldn't help me.'

Parker grunted. 'Yes. I have a note that G.2 filed a routine report – but I suppose her request was natural enough.' He wandered back to his work table to glance at a pad on which was scribbled some sort of personal shorthand.

'We know of eight sexual liaisons that the Baroness formed prior to her marriage, all with politically powerful or wealthy men. Six of them married men—'

Peter found himself trembling with anger so intense that it surprised him. He hated Parker for talking like this of Magda. With a huge effort he kept his expression neutral, the hand in his lap was relaxed and the fingers spread naturally, though he felt a driving desire to bunch it and drive it into Parker's face.

' – all these affairs were conducted with utmost discretion. Then during her marriage there is no evidence of any extra-marital activity. Since the Baron's murder there have been three others, a minister in the French Government, an American businessman – head of the world's second largest oil company—' He dropped the pad back on the desk and swung back to face Peter. 'And recently there has been one other.' He stared at Peter with a bright penetrating gaze. 'The lady certainly believes in mixing business with pleasure. All her partners have been men who are able to deliver very concrete proof of their affections. I think this rule probably applies to her latest choice of sexual partner.'

Colin Noble coughed awkwardly, and shifted in his chair, but Peter did not even glance at him, he went on staring impassively at Kingston Parker. He and Magda had made very little secret of their relationship – still it was bitterly distasteful to have to discuss it with anybody else.

'I think that you are in a position now to gather vital intelligence. I think that you are very near the centre of this nameless and formless influence – I think that you will be able to make some sort of contact with the enemy, even if it is only another military brush with them. The only question is whether or not you find any reason, emotional or otherwise, that might prevent you fulfilling this duty?' Kingston Parker cocked his head on one side, making the statement into a question.

'I have never let my private life interfere with my duty, Doctor,' Peter said quietly.

'No,' Kingston Parker agreed. 'That is true. And I am sure that now you know a little more about Baroness Altmann you will appreciate just how vital is our interest in that lady.'

'Yes, I do.' Peter had his anger under control completely. 'You want me to use a privileged relationship to spy on her. Is that correct?'

'Just as we can be sure she is using the same relationship to her own ends—' Parker broke off as an odd thought seemed to occur. 'I do hope I have not been too blunt, Peter. I haven't destroyed some cherished illusion.' Now Parker's attitude was dismissive. The interview was over.

'At my age, Doctor – a man has no more illusions.' Peter rose to his feet. 'Do I report to you direct?'

'Colonel Noble will make the arrangements for all communications.' Kingston Parker held out his hand. 'I would not have asked this of you if I had a choice.'

Peter did not hesitate, but took the hand. Parker's hand was cool and dry. Although he made no show of it, Peter could sense the physical power in those hard pianist's fingers.

'I understand, sir,' said Peter – and he thought grimly, and even if that is also a lie, I'm going to understand pretty damned soon.

Peter made the excuse of tiredness to avoid the gin-rummy game, and pretended to sleep during most of the long trans-Atlantic flight. With his eyes closed he tried to marshal his thoughts into some sort of pattern, but always they seemed to come around full circle and leave him chasing his tail. He could not even achieve any certainty about his feelings and loyalties to Magda Altmann. They seemed to keep changing shape every time he examined them, and he found himself brooding on irrelevancies. 'Sexual liaisons' – what a ridiculously stilted expression Parker had used, and why had it angered Peter so much? Eight liaisons before marriage, six with married men, two others since marriage – all wealthy or powerful. He found himself trying to flesh out these bare statistics, and with a shock of bitter resentment imagined those faceless, formless figures with the slim smooth body, the tiny, perfectly shaped breasts, and the long smoky fall of shimmering hair. He felt somehow betrayed, and immediately scorned himself for this adolescent reaction.

There were other more dire questions and chances that Kingston Parker had raised, the Mossad connection, the six missing years in Magda's life – and yet he came back again to what had happened between them. Was she capable of such skilful deception, or was it not deception? Was he merely suffering from hurt pride now, or somehow unbeknown to him had she been able to force him into a more vulnerable position? Had she succeeded in making him fall in love with her?

How did he feel about her? At last he had to face that question directly and try to answer it, but when they landed again he still had no answer, except that the prospect of seeing her again pleased him inordinately and the thought that she had deliberately used him to her own ends and was capable of discarding him as she had done those others left him with an aching sense of dismay. He dreaded the answer for which he had to search, and suddenly he remembered her suggestion of an island to which they could escape together. He realized then that she was a victim of the same dread, and with a clairvoyant shudder he wondered if they were somehow preordained to destroy each other.

There were three separate messages from her at the Dorchester. She had left the Rambouillet number, each time. He telephoned immediately he reached the suite.

'Oh, Peter. I was so worried. Where were you?' And it was hard to believe her concern was faked, and it was even harder to discount the pleasure when, the following noon, she met him at Charles de Gaulle Airport herself instead of sending a chauffeur.

'I needed to get out of the office for an hour,' she explained, and then she tucked her hand into the crook of his elbow and pressed herself against him. 'That's a lie, of course. I came because I couldn't wait the extra hour to see you.' Then she chuckled huskily. 'I am behaving shamelessly, I can't imagine what you must think of me!'

They were with a party of eight that evening, dinner at Le Doyen and then the theatre at the Palais de Chaillot. Peter's French was still not up to Molière, so he took his pleasure in surreptitiously watching Magda, and for a few hours he succeeded in suppressing all those ugly questions; only on the midnight drive back to La Pierre Bénite did he begin the next move in the complicated game.

'I couldn't tell you on the telephone—' he said in the intimate darkness and warmth of her limousine. 'I had an approach from Atlas. The head of Atlas summoned me to New York. That's where I was when you called. They are also onto Caliph.'

She sighed then, and her hand stole into his. 'I was waiting for you to tell me, Peter,' she said simply, and she sighed again. 'I knew you'd gone to America, and I had a terrible premonition that you were going to lie to me. I don't know what I would have done then.' And Peter felt a lance of conscience driven up under his ribs, and with it the throb of concern – she had known of his journey to New York, but how? Then he remembered her 'sources'.

'Tell me,' she said, and he told her – everything, except the nagging question marks which Kingston Parker had placed after her name. The missing years, the Mossad connection with the Baron, and those ten nameless men.

'They don't seem to know that Caliph uses that name,' Peter told her. 'But they seem to be pretty certain that you are hunting him, and you've hired me for that purpose.'

They discussed it quietly as the small cavalcade of cars rushed through the night, and later when she came to his suite, they went on talking, holding each other as they whispered in the night, and Peter was surprised that he could act so naturally, that the doubts seemed to evaporate so easily when he was with her.

'Kingston Parker still has me as a member of Atlas,' Peter explained. 'And I did not deny it, nor protest. We want to find Caliph, and if I still have status with Atlas it will be useful, of that I am certain,'

'I agree. Atlas can help us – especially now that they are also aware that Caliph exists.'

They made love in the dawn, very deeply satisfying love that left bodies and minds replete, and then keeping her discretion she slipped away before it was light, but they met again an hour later for breakfast together in the Garden Room.

She poured coffee for him, and indicated the small parcel beside his plate.

'We aren't quite as discreet as we think we are, *chéri*.' She chuckled. 'Somebody seems to know where you are spending your evenings.'

He weighed the parcel in his right palm; it was the size of a roll of 35-mm film, wrapped in brown paper, sealed with red wax.

'Apparently it came special delivery yesterday evening.' She broke one of the crisp croissants into her plate, and smiled at him with that special slant of her green eyes.

The address was typed on a stick-on label, and the stamps were British, franked in south London the previous morning.

Suddenly Peter was assailed with a terrifying sense of foreboding; the presence of some immense overpowering evil seemed to pervade the gaily furnished room.

'What is it, Peter?' Her voice cracked with alarm.

'Nothing,' he said. 'It's nothing.'

'You suddenly went deadly pale, Peter. Are you sure you are all right?'

'Yes. I'm all right.'

He used his table knife to lift the wax seal and then unrolled the brown paper.

It was a small screw-topped bottle of clear glass, and the liquid it contained was clear also. Some sort of preservative, he realized immediately, spirits or formaldehyde.

Hanging suspended in the liquid was a soft white object.

'What is it?' Magda asked.

Peter felt cold tentacles of nausea closing around his stomach.

The object turned slowly, floating free in its bottle, and there was a flash of vivid scarlet.

'Does your mother allow you to wear nail varnish now, Melissa-Jane?' He heard the question echoed in his memory, and saw his daughter flirt her hands, and the scarlet flash of her nails. The same vivid scarlet.

'Oh yes – though not to school, of course. You keep forgetting I'm almost fourteen, Daddy.'

The floating white object was a human finger. It had been severed at the first joint, and the preservative had bleached the exposed flesh a sickly white. The skin had puckered and wrinkled like that of a drowned man. Only the painted fingernail was unaltered, pretty and festively gay.

The nausea caught Peter's throat, choking him and he heaved and retched drily as he stared at the tiny bottle.

The telephone rang three times before it was answered.

'Cynthia Barrow.' Peter recognized his ex-wife's voice, even though it was ragged with strain and grief.

'Cynthia, it's Peter.'

'Oh, thank God, Peter. I have been trying to find you for two days.'

'What is it?'

'Is Melissa-Jane with you, Peter?'

'No.' He felt as though the earth had lurched under his feet.

'She's gone, Peter. She's been gone for two nights now. I'm going out of my mind.'

'Have you informed the police?'

'Yes, of course.' The edge of hysteria was in her voice.

'Stay where you are,' Peter said. 'I'm coming to England right now, but leave any message for me at the Dorchester.' He hung up quickly, sensing that her grief would overflow at any moment and knowing that he could not handle it now.

Across the ormolu Louis Quatorze desk Magda was pale, tense, and she did not have to ask the question, it was in the eyes that seemed too large for her face.

He did not have to reply to that question. He nodded once, an abrupt jerky motion, and then he dialled again and while he waited he could not take his eyes from the macabre trophy that stood in its bottle in the centre of the desk.

'Colonel Noble.' Peter snapped into the mouthpiece. 'Tell him it's General Stride and it's urgent.'

Colin came on within the minute. 'Peter, is that you?'

'They've taken Melissa-Jane.'

'Who? I don't understand.'

'The enemy. They've taken her.'

'Jesus God! Are you sure?'

'Yes, I'm sure. They sent me her finger in a bottle.'

Colin was silent for a few seconds, and then his voice was subdued. 'That's sick. Christ, that's really sick.'

'Get onto the police. Use all your clout. They must be keeping quiet on it. There has been no publicity. I want to be in on the hunt for these animals. Get Thor involved, find out what you can. I'm on my way now. I'll let you know what flight I am on.'

'I'll keep a listening watch at this number round the clock,' Colin promised. 'And I'll have a driver meet you.' Colin hesitated. 'Peter, I'm sorry. You know that.'

'Yes. I know.'

'We will all be with you, all the way.'

Peter dropped the receiver onto its arm, and across the desk Magda stood up resolutely.

'I'll come with you to London,' she said, and Peter reached out and took her hand.

'No,' he said gently. 'Thank you, but no. There will be nothing for you to do.'

'Peter, I want to be with you through this terrible thing. I feel as though it's all my fault.'

'That's not true.'

'She's such a lovely child.'

'You will be more help to me here,' said Peter firmly. 'Try through all your sources, any little scrap of information.'

'Yes, very well.' She accepted the decision, without further argument. 'Where can I find you if I have anything?'

He gave her Colin Noble's private number at Thor, scribbling it on the pad beside the telephone. 'Either there or at the Dorchester,' he said.

'At least I will come with you as far as Paris,' she said.

The news had broken by the time Peter landed at Heathrow Airport. It was on the front page of the *Evening Standard* and Peter snatched a copy off the news stand and read it avidly during the drive up to London.

> The victim was abducted at the front gate of her home in Leaden Street, Cambridge at eleven o'clock on Thursday. A neighbour saw her speak to the occupants of a maroon Triumph saloon car, and then enter the back door of the vehicle, which drove off immediately.
>
> 'I thought there were two people in the car,' Mrs Shirley Callon, 32, the neighbour, told our correspondent, 'and Melissa-Jane did not seem alarmed. She appeared to enter the Triumph quite willingly. I know that her father, who is a senior officer in the army, often sends different cars to fetch her or bring her home. So I thought nothing about it.'
>
> The alarm was not raised for nearly twenty-four hours, as the missing girl's mother also believed that she might be with her ex-husband.
>
> Only when she was unable to contact Major-General Stride, the girl's father, did she inform the police. The Cambridge police found a maroon Triumph abandoned in the car park at Cambridge railway station. The vehicle had been stolen in London the previous day, and immediately a nation-wide alert was put in force for the missing girl.
>
> Chief-Inspector Alan Richards is the police officer in charge of the investigation and any person who may be able to provide information should telephone—

There followed a London number and a detailed description of Melissa-Jane and the clothes she was wearing at the time she disappeared.

Peter crumpled the newspaper and dropped it on the front seat. He sat staring ahead, cupping his anger to him like a flame, husbanding it carefully – because the heat was infinitely more bearable than the icy despair which waited to engulf him.

Inspector Alan Richards was a wiry little man, more like a jockey than a policeman. He had a prematurely wizened face, and he had combed long wisps of hair across his balding pate to disguise it. Yet his eyes were quick and intelligent, and his manner direct and decisive.

He shook hands when Colin Noble introduced them. 'I must make it very clear that this is a police matter, General. However, in these very special circumstances I am prepared to work very closely with the military.'

Swiftly Richards went over the ground he had already covered. He had mounted the investigation from the two offices set aside for him on the third floor of Scotland Yard, with a view over chimney pots of the spires of Westminster Abbey and the Houses of Parliament.

Richards had two young policewomen answering the telephone calls coming in through the number they had advertised in the Press and on television. So far they had accepted over four hundred of these. 'They range from long shots to the completely crazy, but we have to investigate all of them.' For the first time his expression softened. 'It's going to be a long, slow process, General Stride, but we have a few more leads to follow come through.'

The inner office was furnished in the same nondescript Public Works Department furniture, solid and characterless, but there was a kettle boiling on the gas ring, and Richards poured the tea as he went on.

'Three of my men are taking the kidnap car to pieces. We are sure it is the right car. Your ex-wife has identified a purse found on the floor of the vehicle. It is your daughter's. We have lifted over six hundred fingerprints, and these are being processed. It will take some time until we can isolate each and hope for an identification of any alien prints. However, two of these correspond to prints lifted from your daughter's room – Sugar? Milk?'

Richards brought the cup to Peter as he went on.

' – The neighbour, Mrs Callon, who saw the pick-up, is working on an identikit portrait of the driver, but she did not get a very good view of him. That is a very long shot.'

Richards sipped his tea. 'However, we will show the final picture on television and hope for another lead from it. I am afraid that in cases like this, this is all we can do. Wait for a tip, and wait for the contact from the kidnappers. We do not expect the contact will be made through your ex-wife but of course we have a tap on her telephone and men watching over her.' Richards spread his hands. 'That's it, General Stride. Now it's your turn. What can you tell us? Why should anybody want to snatch your daughter?'

Peter exchanged a glance with Colin Noble, and was silent as he collected his thoughts, but Inspector Richards insisted quietly:

'I understand you are not a very wealthy man, General – but your family? Your brother?'

Peter dismissed the idea with a shake of his head. 'My brother has children of his own. They would be the more logical targets.'

'Vengeance? You were very active against the Provos in Ireland. You commanded the recapture of Flight 070.'

'It's possible.'

'You are no longer connected with the army, I understand.'

Peter was not going to be drawn further in that direction. 'I do not think this type of guesswork will profit us much. We will know the motive as soon as the kidnappers make their demands known.'

'That is true.' Richards rattled his teacup, a little nervous gesture. 'They could not have sent you her—' He broke off as he saw Peter's expression change. ' – I'm sorry, General. It is horrible and terribly distressing, but we have to accept the finger as proof that your daughter is still alive and that the contact, when it comes, will be made to you. It was an expression of their earnest intention, and a threat – but—'

The telephone on his desk rang shrilly and Richards snatched it up.

'Richards!' he snapped, and then listened at length, occasionally grunting encouragement to the caller. When he hung up the receiver he did not speak immediately, but offered Peter a rumpled pack of cigarettes. When Peter refused, the policeman lit one himself and his voice was diffident.

'That was the laboratory. You know your daughter was a white cell donor, don't you?'

Peter nodded. It was part of Melissa-Jane's social commitment. If she had not been tactfully dissuaded, she would have donated her blood and marrow by the bucketful.

'We were able to get a tissue typing from the Cambridge hospital. The amputated finger matches your daughter's tissue type. I'm afraid we must accept that it is hers – I cannot imagine that the kidnappers would have gone to the lengths of finding a substitute of the same type.'

Peter had been secretly cherishing the belief that it was a bluff. That he had been sent the fingertip from a corpse, from a medical sample, from the casualty ward of a city hospital – and now as that hope died he was assailed by the cold spirit-sapping waves of despair. They sat in silence for fully a minute, and now it was Colin Noble who broke it.

'Inspector, you are aware of the nature of the Thor Command?'

'Yes, of course. There was a great deal of publicity at the time of the Johannesburg hijacking. It is an anti-terrorist unit.'

'We are probably the most highly trained specialists in

the world at removing hostages safely from the hands of militants—'

'I understand what you are trying to tell me, Colonel,' Richards murmured drily. 'But let us track down our militants first, and then any rescue attempts will be entirely under the control of the Commissioner of Police.'

It was after three o'clock in the morning when Peter Stride checked in with the night receptionist at the Dorchester Hotel in Park Lane.

'We have been holding your suite since midday, General.'

'I'm sorry.' Peter found himself slurring his words, exhaustion and nervous strain, he realized. He had only left Police Headquarters when he could convince himself that everything possible was being done, and that he could place complete trust in Chief-Inspector Richards and his team. He had Richards's solemn undertaking that he would be informed, no matter at what time of day or night, as soon as there was any new development.

Now he signed the register, blinking at the gritty swollen feeling of his eyelids.

'There are these messages for you, General.'

'Thank you again, and goodnight.'

In the elevator he glanced at the mail the clerk had given him.

The first was a telephone slip.

'Baroness Altmann asks you to return her call to either the Paris or Rambouillet number.'

The second was another telephone slip.

'Mrs Cynthia Barrow called. Please call her at Cambridge 699 – 313.'

The third was a sealed envelope, good-quality white paper, undistinguished by crest or monogram.

His name had been printed in capitals, very regular lettering, an old-fashioned copper-plate script. No stamp, so it would have been delivered by hand.

Peter split the flap with his thumb, and withdrew a single sheet of lined writing paper, again good but undistinguished. There would be a stack of these sheets in any stationery department throughout the United Kingdom.

The writing was the same regular, unnatural script, so that Peter realized that the writer had used a stencil to form each letter, one of those clear plastic cut-out stencils obtainable from any toy store or stationery department. A completely effective method of disguising handwriting.

> A finger you have already, next you will have the hand, then another hand, then a foot, then another foot – and at last the head.
>
> The next package will arrive on April 20th, and there will be another delivery every seven days.
>
> To prevent this you must deliver a life for a life. The day Dr Kingston Parker dies, your daughter will return to you immediately, alive and suffering no further harm.
>
> Destroy this letter and tell nobody, or the head will be delivered immediately.

The letter was signed with the name which had come to loom so largely in Peter's life:

'CALIPH'

The shock of it seemed to reach to the extremities of his soul. To see the name written. To have complete confirmation of all the evil that they had suspected, to see the mark of the beast deeply printed and unmistakable.

The shock was made greater, almost unbearable, by the contents of the letter. Peter found that such cruelty, such utter ruthlessness, tested his credibility to its limits.

The letter was fluttering in his hands, and he realized with a start of surprise that he was shaking like a man in high fever. The porter carrying his black crocodile valise was staring at him curiously, and it required a huge physical effort to control his hands and fold the sheet of white paper.

He stood rigidly, as though on the parade ground, until the elevator door opened and then he marched stiffly down the passage to his suite. He gave the porter a banknote, without glancing at it, and the moment the latch clicked closed, he unfolded the sheet again, and standing in the centre of the living-room floor scanned the stilted script again, and then again until the words seemed to melt together and lose coherence and meaning.

He realized that for the first time in his life he was in complete panic, that he had lost all resolution and direction.

He took a deep breath and closed his eyes, counting slowly to one hundred, emptying his mind completely, and then giving himself the command:

'Think!'

All right, Caliph knew his movements intimately. Even to when he was expected at the Dorchester. Who knew that? Cynthia, Colin Noble, Magda Altmann and the secretary at Rambouillet who had made the reservation, Colin's secretary at Thor, the Dorchester staff, and anybody else who had made even an idle study of Peter's movements would know he always stayed at the Dorchester. That was a cul-de-sac.

'Think!'

Today was April fourth. There were sixteen days before Caliph sent him Melissa-Jane's severed hand. He felt the panic mounting again, and he forced it back.

'Think!'

Caliph had been watching him, studying him in detail, assessing his value. Peter's value was that he could move unsuspected in high places. He could reach the head of Atlas by simply requesting an audience. More than that, he could probably get access to any head of state if he wanted it badly enough.

For the first time in his life Peter felt the need for liquor. He crossed quickly to the cabinet and fumbled with the key. A stranger's face stared at him out of the gilt-framed mirror above it. The face was pale, haggard, with deep parentheses framing the mouth. There were plum-coloured bruises of fatigue below the eyes, and the gaunt, bony jaw was gun-metal blue with a new beard – and the sapphire blue of the eyes had a wild deranged glitter. He looked away from his own image. It only increased his sense of unreality.

He poured half a tumbler of Scotch whisky, and drank half of it straight off. He coughed at the sting of the liquor and a drop of it broke from the corner of his mouth and trickled down his chin. He wiped it away with his thumb, and turned back to study the sheet of white paper again. It was crumpled already, where he had gripped it too hard. He smoothed it carefully.

'Think!' he told himself. This was how Caliph worked, then. Never exposing himself. Picking his agents with incredible attention to detail. Fanatics, like the girl, Ingrid who had led the taking of Flight 070. Trained assassins, like the man he had killed in the river at La Pierre Bénite. Experts in high places, like General Peter Stride. Studying them, assessing them and their capabilities, and finally finding their price.

Peter had never believed the old law that every man had his price. He had believed himself above that general rule. Now he knew he was not – and the knowledge sickened him.

Caliph had found his price, found it unerringly. Melissa-Jane. Suddenly Peter had a vivid memory of his daughter on horseback, swivelling in the saddle to laugh and call back to him.

'Super-Star!' And the sound of her laughter on the wind.

Peter shivered, and without realizing it he crumpled the sheet of paper to a ball in his fist.

Ahead of him he saw the road that he was destined to follow. With a new flash of insight, he realized that he had already taken his first steps along the road. He had done so when he had put the gun to the blonde killer in the terminal of Johannesburg Airport, when he had made himself judge and executioner.

Caliph had been responsible for that first step on the road to corruption, and now it was Caliph who was driving him farther along it.

With a sudden prophetic glimpse ahead, Peter knew it would not end with the life of Kingston Parker. Once he was committed to Caliph, it would be for ever – or until one of them, Peter Stride, or Caliph, was completely destroyed.

Peter drank the rest of the whisky in the tumbler.

Yes, Melissa-Jane was his price. Caliph had made the correct bid. Nothing else would have driven him to it.

Peter picked the booklet of matches off the liquor cabinet and like a sleepwalker moved through to the bathroom. He twisted the sheet of paper into a taper and lit the end of it, holding it over the toilet bowl. He held it until the flame scorched his fingers painfully, then dropped it into the bowl and flushed the ash away.

He went back into the lounge, and refilled the glass with whisky. He picked the comfortable armchair below the window and sank into it. Only then did he realize how very weary he was. The nerves in his thighs quivered and twitched uncontrollably.

He thought about Kingston Parker. A man like that had an incalculable amount to offer mankind. It will have to look like an assassination attempt aimed at me, Peter thought. One that finds the wrong victim.

'A bomb,' Peter thought. He hated the bomb. Somehow

it seemed to be the symbol of the senseless violence which he hated. He had seen it used in Ireland and in London town, and he hated it. The undirected destruction, mindless, merciless.

'It will have to be a bomb,' he decided, and with surprise he found that his hatred had found a new target. Again for the first time ever, he hated himself for what he was going to do.

Caliph had won. He knew that against an adversary of that calibre there was no chance they would find where Melissa-Jane was hidden. Caliph had won, and Peter Stride sat the rest of the night planning an act which he had dedicated his life, until then, to prevent.

'I cannot understand why we haven't had the demand contact yet.' Inspector Richards ran his hand distractedly across his pate, disturbing the feathery wisps that covered it and leaving them standing out at a startled angle. 'It's five days now. Still no demands.'

'They know where to contact Peter,' Colin Noble agreed. 'The interview he gave covered that.'

Peter Stride had appeared on BBC TV to broadcast an appeal to the kidnappers not to maim his daughter further, and to the general public to offer any information that might lead to her rescue.

On the same programme they had displayed the police identikit portrait of the driver of the maroon Triumph prepared by the one witness.

The response had been overwhelming, jamming the switchboard at Inspector Richards's special headquarters, and a mixed bag had fallen into the net.

A fourteen-year-old runaway had the police barge into the Bournemouth apartment where she was in bed with her thirty-two-year-old lover. She was returned weeping bitterly to the bosom of her family, and had again disappeared within twenty-four hours.

In North Scotland the police sadly bungled a raid on a remote cottage hired by a man with the same lank dark hair and gunfighter's moustache as the identikit portrait. He turned out to be a cottage-industry manufacturer of LSD tablets, and he and his four assistants, one of them a young girl who vaguely fitted the description of Melissa-Jane in that she was female and blonde, had scattered across the Highlands before being overtaken and borne to earth by sweating pounding members of the Scottish Constabulary.

Peter Stride was furious. 'If it had been Melissa-Jane, they would have had fifteen minutes in which to put her down—' He raged at Richards. 'You've got to let Thor go in to the next raid.'

Through the Thor communications net he spoke directly to Kingston Parker on the video screens.

' – We'll put all our influence into it,' Parker agreed, and then with deep compassion in his eyes, 'Peter, I'm living every minute of this with you. I cannot escape the knowledge that I have placed you into this terrible situation. I did not expect the attack would come through your daughter. I think you know that you can call on me for any support you need.'

'Thank you, sir,' said Peter and for a moment felt his resolve weaken. In ten days he would have to execute this man. He steeled himself by thinking of a puckered dead-white finger floating in its tiny bottle.

Kingston Parker's influence worked immediately. Six hours later the order came down from Downing Street via the Commissioner of Police, that the next raid on a suspect hideout would be conducted by Thor Command.

The Royal Air Force placed two helicopters at Thor's disposal for the duration of the operation, and Thor's assault unit went into intensive training for penetration and removal under urban conditions. Peter trained with them, he and Colin swiftly re-establishing the old rapport of concerted action.

When they were not practising and refining the exit and assembly from the hovering helicopters, Peter spent much of his time in the enclosed pistol range, trying to drown his awareness in the crash of gunfire, but the days passed swiftly in a series of false alarms and misleading clues.

Each night when Peter examined his face in the mirror above the liquor cabinet, it was more haggard, the blue eyes muddied by fatigue and terrible gut-eroding terror of what the next day might bring forth.

There were six days left when Peter left the hotel room before breakfast, caught the tube at Green Park and left it again at Finsbury Park. In a garden supplies shop near the station he purchased a twenty-pound plastic bag of ammonium nitrate garden fertilizer. He carried it back to the Dorchester in a locked Samsonite suitcase and stored it in the closet behind his hanging trenchcoat.

That night, when he spoke to Magda Altmann, she pleaded once again to be allowed to come to London.

'Peter, I know I can be of help to you. Even if it's just to stand beside you and hold your hand.'

'No. We've been over that.' He could hear the brutal tone in his own voice, but could not control it. He knew that he was getting very close to the edge. 'Have you heard anything?'

'I'm sorry, Peter. Nothing, absolutely nothing. My sources are doing all that is possible.'

Peter bought the dieseline from a pump at the Lex Garage in Brewer Street. He took five litres in a plastic screw-topped container that had contained a household detergent. The pump attendant was a pimply teenager in dirty overalls. He was completely uninterested in the transaction.

In his bathroom Peter worked on the dieseline and the nitrate from the garden shop. He produced twenty-one pounds of savagely weight-efficient high explosive that was, none the less, docile until activated by a blasting cap – such as he had devised with a flashlight bulb.

It would completely devastate the entire suite, utterly destroying everybody and everything in it. However, the damage should be confined to those three rooms.

It would be a simple matter to lure Kingston Parker to the suite under the pretence of having urgent information about Caliph to deliver, information so critical that it could only be delivered in person and in private.

That night the face in the mirror above the liquor cabinet was that of a man suffering from a devouring terminal disease, and the whisky bottle was empty. Peter broke the seal on a fresh bottle; it would make it easier to sleep, he told himself.

The wind came off the Irish Sea like the blade of a harvester's scythe, and the low lead-coloured cloud fled up the slopes of the Wicklow hills ahead of it.

There were weak patches in the cloud layer through which a cold and sickly sun beamed swiftly across the green forested slopes. As it passed so the rain followed – icy grey rain slanting in on the wind.

A man came up the deserted street of the village. The tourists had not yet begun the annual invasion, but the 'Bed and Breakfast' signs were already out to welcome them on the fronts of the cottages.

The man passed the pub, in its coat of shocking salmon pink paint – and lifted his head to read the billboard above the empty car park. 'Black is Beautiful – drink Guinness' it proclaimed, and the man did not smile but lowered his head and trudged on over the bridge that divided the village in two.

On the stone balustrades of the bridge a midnight artist

had used an aerosol paint can to spray political slogans in day-glo colours.

'BRITS OUT' on the left-hand balustrade and 'STOP H BLOCK TORTURE' on the other. This time the man grimaced sourly.

Below him the steely grey water boiled about the stone piers before hissing down towards the sea.

The man wore a cyclist's plastic cape and a narrow-brimmed tweed cap pulled down over his eyes. The wind dashed at him, flogging the skirts of the cape against his Wellington boots.

He seemed to cringe to the wind, hunching down against its cold fury, as he trudged on past the few buildings of the village. The street was deserted, though the man knew that he was being watched from curtained windows.

This village on the lower slopes of the Wicklow hills, a mere thirty miles from Dublin, would not have been his choice. Here isolation worked against them, making them conspicuous. He would have preferred the anonymity of the city. However, his preferences had never been asked for.

This was only the third time he had left the house since they had arrived. Each time it had been for some emergency provision, something that a little more forethought might have prevented, which should have been included when the old house was stocked for their stay. That came from having to rely on a drinking man, but here again he had not been consulted.

He was discontented and in a truculent, smouldering mood. It had rained most of the time, and the oil-fired central heating was not working, the only heating was the smoking peat fires in the small fireplaces in each of the two big rooms they were using. The high ceilings and sparse furnishings had made the rooms more difficult to warm – and he had been cold ever since they had arrived. They were using only the two rooms, and had left the rest of the house locked and shuttered. It was a gloomy building, with the smell of damp pervading it. He had only the company of a whining alcoholic, day after cold rainy day. The man was ripe and over-ripe for trouble, for any diversion to break the grinding monotony – but now he was reduced to errand boy and house servant, roles for which he was unsuited by temperament and training, and he scowled darkly as he trudged over the bridge towards the village store, with its row of petrol pumps standing before it like sentries.

The storekeeper saw him coming, and called through into the back of the shop.

'It's himself from down at the Old Manse.'

His wife came through, wiping her hands on her apron, a short plump woman with bright eyes and ready tongue.

'City people have no more sense than they need, out in this weather.'

'Sure and it's not baked beans nor Jameson whiskey he's after buying.'

Speculation about the new occupant of the Old Manse had swiftly become one of the village's main diversions, with regular bulletins broadcast by the girl on the local telephone exchange – two overseas telephone calls, by the postman – no mail deliveries, by the dustman – the disposals into the dustbins were made up mainly of empty Heinz baked beans cans and Jameson whiskey bottles.

'I still think he's from the trouble up north,' said the shopkeeper's wife. 'He's got the look and the sound of an Ulster man.'

'Hush, woman.' Her husband cautioned her. 'You'll bring bad luck upon us. Get yourself back into the kitchen now.'

The man came in out of the rain and swept the tweed cap off his head, beating the water from it against the jamb of the door. He had black straight hair, cut into a ragged fringe above the dark Irish visage and fierce eyes, like those of a falcon when first the leather hood is slipped.

'The top of the morning to you, Mr Barry,' the shopkeeper greeted him heartily. 'Like as not it will stop raining, before it clears.'

The man they knew as Barry grunted, and as he slipped the waterproof cape from his shoulders, swept the cluttered interior of the little general dealer's store with a quick, all-embracing glance.

He wore a rough tweed jacket over a cable-stitched jersey and brown corduroys tucked into the top of the Wellington boots.

'You finished writing on your book, have you?' Barry had told the milkman that he was writing a book about Ireland. The Wicklow hills were a stronghold of the literary profession, there were a dozen prominent or eccentric writers living within twenty miles, taking advantage of Ireland's tax concessions to writers and artists.

'Not yet,' Barry grunted, and went across to the shelves nearest the till. He made a selection of half a dozen items and laid them on the worn counter top.

'When it's good and wrote I'm going to ask the library to keep a copy for me,' the shopkeeper promised, as though that was exactly what a writer would want to hear, and began to ring up the purchases on his register.

Barry's upper lip was still unnaturally smoother and paler than the rest of his face. He had shaved away the dark droopy moustache the day before arriving in the village, and at the same time had cut the fringe of his hair that hung almost to his eyes.

The shopkeeper picked up one of the purchases and looked inquiringly at Barry, but when the dark Irish face remained impassive and he volunteered no explanation, the shopkeeper dropped his eyes self-consciously and rang up the package with the other purchases and dropped it into a paper carrier.

'That will be three pounds twenty pence,' he said, and closed the cash drawer with a clang, waiting while Barry slung the cape over his shoulders and adjusted the tweed cap.

'God be with you then, Mr Barry.'

There was no reply and the shopkeeper watched him set off back across the bridge before he called his wife again.

'He's a surly one, all right, he is.'

'He's got him a girlfriend down there.' The shopkeeper was bursting with the importance of his discovery. 'He's up to a nice little bit of hanky-panky.'

'How do you know that?'

'He was after buying women's things – you know.' He hooded a knowing eye.

'No, I don't know,' his wife insisted.

'For the curse – you know. Women's things,' and his wife glowed with the news, and began to untie her apron.

'You're sure now?' she demanded.

'Would I ever be lying to you?'

'I think I'll go across to Mollie for a cuppa tea,' said his wife eagerly; the news would make her the woman of the hour throughout the village.

The man they knew as Barry trudged into the narrow, high-walled lane that led up to the Old Manse. It was only the heavy boots and voluminous cape that gave him a clumsy gait, for he was a lithe, lean man in prime physical condition, and under the brim of his cap the eyes were never still, hunter's eyes probing and darting from side to side.

The wall was twelve feet high, the stonework blotched with silver-grey lichen, and although it was cracked and sagging at places, yet it was still substantial and afforded complete privacy and security to the property beyond.

At the end of the lane there was a pair of rotten and warping double doors, but the lock was a bright new brass Yale and the cracks in the wood and the gaping seams had been covered with fresh white strips of pine so that it was impossible to see into the interior of the garage.

Barry unlocked the brass Yale lock and slipped through, pulling the latch closed behind him.

There was a dark blue Austin saloon car parked facing the doors for immediate departure. It had been stolen in Ulster two weeks before, resprayed and fitted with a roof rack to alter its appearance, and with new licence plates. The engine had been tuned and checked and Barry had paid nearly twice its market value.

Now he slipped behind the wheel and turned the key in the ignition. The engine fired and caught immediately. He grunted with satisfaction; seconds could mean the difference between success and failure, and in his life failure and death were synonymous. He listened to the engine beat for half a minute, checking the oil pressure and fuel gauges before switching off the engine again and going out through the rear door of the garage into the overgrown kitchen yard.

The old house had the sad unloved air of approaching dereliction. The fruit trees in the tiny orchard were sick with fungus diseases and surrounded by weed banks.

The thatch roof was rotten-green with moss, and the windows were blindman's eyes, unseeing and uncaring.

Barry let himself in through the kitchen door and dropped his cape and cap on the scullery floor and set the carrier on the draining board of the sink. Then he reached into the cutlery drawer and brought out a pistol. It was a British officer's service pistol, had in fact been taken during a raid on a British Army arsenal in Ulster three years previously.

Barry checked the handgun with the expertise of a long familiarity and then thrust it into his belt. He had felt naked and vulnerable for the short time that he was without the weapon – but he had reluctantly decided not to risk carrying it in the village.

Now he tapped water into the kettle, and at the sound a voice called through from the dim interior.

'Is that you?'

'None other,' Barry answered drily, and the other man came through and stood in the doorway to the kitchen.

He was a thin, stooped man in his fifties with the swollen inflamed face of the very heavy drinker.

'Did you get it?' His voice was husky and rough with whiskey, and he had a seedy run-down air, a day's stubble of grey hairs that grew at angles on the blotchy skin.

Barry indicated the package on the sink.

'It's all there, doctor.'

'Don't call me that, I'm not a doctor any more,' the man snapped irritably.

'Oh, but you are a damned fine one. Ask the girls who dropped their bundles—'

'Leave me alone, damn you.'

Yes, he had been a damn fine doctor. Long ago, before the whiskey, now however it was the abortions and the gunshot wounds of fugitives, and jobs like this one. He did not like to think about this one. He crossed to the sink and sorted through the packages.

'I asked you for adhesive tape,' he said.

'They had none. I brought the bandage.'

'I cannot—' the man began, but Barry whirled on him savagely, his face darkening with angry blood.

'I've had a gutsful of your whining. You should have brought what you needed, not sent me to get it for you.'

'I did not expect the wound—'

'You didn't expect anything but another dram of Jamesons, man. There is no adhesive tape. Now get on with it and tie the bitch's hand up with the bandage.'

The older man backed away swiftly, picked up the packages and shuffled through into the other room.

Barry made the tea and poured it into the thick china mug, spooned in four spoons of sugar and stirred noisily, staring out of the smeared panes. It was raining again. He thought that the rain and the waiting would drive him mad.

The doctor came back into the kitchen, carrying a

bundle of linen soiled with blood and the yellow ooze of sepsis.

'She is sick,' he said. 'She needs drugs, antibiotics. The finger—'

'Forget it,' said Barry.

From the other room there was a long-drawn-out whimper, followed by the incoherent gabble of a young girl deep in the delirium induced by fever and hypnotic drugs.

'If she is not taken to proper care, I won't be responsible.'

'You'll be responsible,' Barry told him heavily. 'I'll see to that.'

The doctor dropped the bundle of linen into the sink and let the water run over it.

'Can I have a drink now?' he asked.

Barry made a sadistic display of consulting his watch.

'No. Not yet,' he decided.

The doctor poured soapflakes into the sink.

'I don't think I can do the hand,' he whispered, shaking his head. 'The finger was bad enough – but I can't do the hand.'

'You'll do the hand,' said Barry. 'Do you hear me, you whiskey-guzzling old wreck? You'll do the hand, and anything else I tell you to do.'

Sir Steven Stride offered a reward of fifty thousand pounds to anyone giving information that led to the recovery of his niece, and the offer was widely reported on television and in the press with reprints of the identikit portrait. It led to a revival of the flagging public interest in the case.

Inspector Richards had been able to reduce his telephone answering staff to one the last few days, but with the renewed spate of informers and speculators, he had to ask for the other policewoman to return to the third floor, and he had two sergeants processing the material that flowed in.

'I feel like Littlewoods,' he growled to Peter. 'Everybody taking a ticket on the pools, or getting his three-pence worth of advertising.' He picked up another message slip. 'Here is another claim for responsibility – the Democratic People's Party for the Liberation of Hong Kong – Have we ever heard of them before?'

'No, sir.' The senior sergeant looked up from his lists. 'But that makes one hundred and forty-eight confessions or claims for responsibility so far.'

'And 'Enry the Eighth was on again half an hour ago.' One of the girls at the switchboard turned and smiled around her mouthpiece. 'Hasn't missed a day.'

'Enry the Eighth was a sixty-eight-year-old pensioner who lived in a council estate in South London. His hobby was confessing to the latest spectacular crime from rape to bank robbery, and he had called regularly every morning.

'Come and get me,' he challenged each time. 'But I warn you I won't come peaceful like—' When the local constable had made a courtesy call, while on his regular beat, 'Enry the Eighth had his suitcase packed and ready to go. His disappointment was heart-rending when the bobby tactfully explained that they weren't going to arrest him, but when the bobby assured him that they would be keeping him under close surveillance as the Commissioner considered him a very dangerous man, he brightened up considerably and offered the constable a cup of tea.

'The trouble is we dare not dismiss any of it, even the real loonies, it all has to be checked out,' Richards sighed, and motioned Peter to go through to the inner office.

'Still nothing?' Richards asked. It was an unnecessary question. They had a tap on his telephone, at the hotel and at Thor Headquarters, to record any contact from the kidnappers.

'No, nothing,' Peter lied, but the lie had become easy now – just as he had learned to accept whatever else was necessary for Melissa-Jane's release.

'I don't like it, General. I really don't like the fact that there has been no attempt to contact you. I don't want to be despondent, but every day of silence makes it look more like an act of vengeance—' Richards broke off and covered his embarrassment by lighting a cigarette. 'Yesterday the Deputy-Commissioner telephoned me. He wanted my opinion as to how much longer I thought it necessary to maintain this special unit.'

'What did you tell him?' Peter asked.

'I told him that if we did not have some firm evidence within ten days, at least some sort of demand from the kidnappers – then I would have to believe that your daughter was no longer alive.'

'I see.' Peter felt a fatalistic calm. He knew. He was the only one who knew. There were four days to Caliph's deadline, he had worked out his timetable. Tomorrow morning he would request his urgent meeting with Kingston Parker. He expected it would take less than twelve hours to arrange it, he would make it too attractive for Parker to refuse.

Parker would have to come, but against the remote possibility that he did not, Peter had left himself three clear days before the deadline in which to put into action his alternative plan. This would mean going to Kingston Parker. The first plan was the better, the more certain – but if it failed, Peter would accept any risk.

Now he realized that he had been standing in the centre of Richards's office, staring vacantly at the wall above the little inspector's head. He started as he realized that Richards was staring at him with a mingling of pity and concern.

'I am sorry, General. I understand how you feel – but I cannot keep this unit functioning indefinitely. We just do not have enough people—'

'I understand.' Peter nodded jerkily, and wiped his face with an open hand. It was a weary, defeated gesture.

'General, I think you should see your doctor. I really do.' Richards's voice was surprisingly gentle.

'That won't be necessary – I'm just a little tired.'

'A man can take just so much.'

'I think that's what these bastards are relying on,' Peter agreed. 'But I'll be all right.'

From the next door office there was the almost constant tinkle of telephone bells, and the murmur of female voices as the two policewomen answered the incoming stream of calls. It had become a steady background effect, so that when the call for which they had prayed and pleaded and waited finally came, neither of the two men was aware of it, and there was no excitement on the switchboard.

The two girls sat side by side on swivel stools in front of the temporary switchboard. The blonde girl was in her middle twenties, she was pretty and pert, with big round breasts buttoned primly under her blue uniform jacket. The blonde hair was twisted into a bun at the back of her neck to free her ears, but the headset made her appear older and businesslike.

The bell pinged and a panel lit in front of her; she plugged in the switch and spoke into the headset.

'Good morning. This is the Police Special Information Unit—' She had a pleasant middle-class accent, but was unable to keep the trace of boredom out of it. She had been on this job for twelve days now. There was the warning tone of a public telephone and then the click of small change fed into the slot.

'Can you hear me?' The accent was foreign.

'Yes, sir.'

'Listen carefully. Gilly O'Shaughnessy has her—' No, it was an imitation, the foreign accept slipped a little with the pronunciation of the name.

'Gilly O'Shaughnessy,' the police girl repeated.

'That's right. He's holding her at Laragh.'

'Spell that, please.' Again the accent slipped as the man spelled the name.

'And where is that, sir?'

'County Wicklow, Ireland.'

'Thank you, sir. What is your name, please?'

There was the clack of a broken connection and the hum of the dialling tone. The girl shrugged, and scribbled the message on the pad before her, glancing at her wrist-watch simultaneously.

'Seven minutes to tea time,' she said. 'Roll on death, battle with the angels.' She tore the sheet off the pad and passed it over her shoulder to the burly, curly-headed sergeant who sat behind her.

'I'll buy you a sticky bun,' he promised.

'I'm on a diet,' she sighed.

'That's daft, you look a treat—' The sergeant broke off. ' – Gilly O'Shaughnessy. Why do I know that name?'

The older sergeant looked up sharply.

'Gilly O'Shaughnessy?' he demanded. 'Let me see that.' And he snatched the sheet, scanning it swiftly, his lips moving as he read the message. Then he looked up again.

'You know the name because you've seen it on the wanted posters, and heard it on the telly. Gilly O'Shaughnessy, strewth man, he's the one who bombed the Red Lion at Leicester, and shot the Chief Constable in Belfast.'

The curly-headed policeman whistled softly. 'This looks like a hot one. A real hot one—' But his colleague was already barging into the inner office without the formality of knocking.

Richards had the connection to the Dublin police within seven minutes.

'Impress upon them that there must be no attempt—' Peter fretted, while they waited, and Richards cut him short.

'All right, General. Leave this to me. I understand what has to be done—' At that moment the Dublin connection was made, and Richards was transferred quickly to a Deputy-Commissioner. He spoke quietly and earnestly for nearly ten minutes before he replaced the receiver.

'They will use the local constabulary, not to waste time in sending a man down from Dublin. I have their promise that no approach will be made if a suspect is located.'

Peter nodded his thanks. 'Laragh,' he said. 'I have never heard of it. It cannot have a population of more than a few hundred.'

'I've sent for a map,' Richards told him, and when it came they studied it together.

'It's on the slopes of the Wicklow hills – ten miles from the coast—' And that was about all there was to learn from the large-scale map.

'We'll just have to wait for the Dublin police to call back—'

'No,' Peter shook his head. 'I want you to call them again, and ask them to contact the surveyor-general. He must have trig maps of the village, aerial photographs, street layouts. Ask them to get them down with a driver to Enniskerry Airfield—'

'Should we do that now? What if this turns out to be another false alarm.'

'We'll have wasted a gallon of petrol and the driver's time—' Peter was no longer able to sit still, he jumped out of the chair and began to pace restlessly about the office; it was too small for him suddenly, he felt as though he were on the point of suffocation. 'I don't think it is, however. I have the smell of it. The smell of the beast.'

Richards looked startled and Peter deprecated the exaggerated phrase with a dismissive gesture. 'A manner of speech,' he explained, and then stopped as a thought struck him. 'The helicopters will have to refuel, they haven't got the range to make it in one hop, and they are so bloody slow!' He paused and reached a decision, then leaned across Richards's desk to pick up the telephone and dialled Colin Noble's private number at Thor.

'Colin.' He spoke curtly with the tension that gripped him like a mailed fist. 'We've just had a contact. It's still unconfirmed, but it looks the best yet.'

'Where?' Colin broke in eagerly.

'Ireland.'

'That's to hell and gone.'

'Right, what's the flight time for the whirly birds to reach Enniskerry?'

'Stand by.' Peter heard him talking to somebody else – probably one of the R.A.F. pilots. He came back within the minute.

'They will have to refuel en route—'

'Yes?' Peter demanded impatiently.

'Four and a half hours,' Colin told him.

'It's twenty past ten now – almost three o'clock before they reach Enniskerry. With this weather it will be dark before five.' Peter thought furiously; if they sent the Thor team all the way to Ireland on a false trail – and while they were there the correct contact was made in Scotland, or Holland, or—

'It's got the smell. It's got to be right,' he told himself, and took a deep breath. He could not order Colin Noble to go to Bravo. Peter was no longer commander of Thor.

'Colin,' he said. 'I think this is it. I have the deep-down gut feel for it. Will you trust me and go to Bravo now? If we wait even another half hour we'll not get Melissa-Jane out before nightfall – if she is there.'

There was a long silence, broken only by Colin Noble's light quick breath.

'Hell, it can only cost me my job,' he said easily at last. 'Okay, Pete baby, it's Bravo, we'll be airborne in five minutes. We'll pick you up from the helipad in fifteen minutes; be ready.'

The cloud was breaking up, but the wind was still bitter and spiteful, and up on the exposed helipad it cut cruelly through Peter's trench coat, blazer and roll-neck jersey. They looked out across the churned surface of the River Thames, eyes watering in the wind, for the first glimpse of the helicopters.

'What if we have a confirmation before you reach Enniskerry?'

'You can reach us on the R.A.F. frequencies, through Biggin Hill,' Peter told him.

'I hope I don't have bad news for you.' Richards was holding his bowler hat in place with one hand, the skirts of his jacket slapping around his skinny rump and his face blotchy with the cold.

The two ungainly craft came clattering in, low over the rooftops, hanging on the whirling silver coins of their rotors.

At a hundred feet Peter could plainly recognize the broad shape of Colin Noble in the open doorway of the fuselage, just forward of the brilliant R.A.F. roundels, and the down-draught of the rotors boiled the air about them.

'Good hunting.' Richards raised his voice to a shout. 'I wish I was coming with you.'

Peter ran forward lightly, and jumped before the helicopter gear touched the concrete pad. Colin caught him by the upper arm and helped to swing him aboard without removing the cheroot from his wide mouth.

'Welcome aboard, buddy. Now let's get this circus on the road.' And he hitched the big .45 pistol on his hip.

'She's not eating.' The doctor came through from the inner room and scraped the plate into the rubbish bin below the sink. 'I'm worried about her. Very worried.'

Gilly O'Shaughnessy grunted but did not look up from his own plate. He broke a crust off the slice of bread and very carefully wiped up the last of the tomato ketchup. He popped the bread into his mouth and followed it with a gulp of steaming tea, and while he chewed it all together, he leaned back on the kitchen chair and watched the other man.

The doctor was on the verge of cracking up. He would probably not last out the week before his nerve went completely; Gilly O'Shaughnessy had seen better men go to pieces under less strain.

He realized then that his own nerves were wearing away.

It was more than just the rain and the waiting that was working on him. He had been the fox for all of his life, and he had developed the instincts of the hunted animal. He could sense danger, the presence of the pursuers, even when there was no real evidence. It made him restless to stay longer in one place than was necessary, especially when he was on a job. He had been here twelve days, and it was far too long. The more he thought about it the more uneasy he became. Why had they insisted he bring the brat to this isolated, and therefore conspicuous, little dead-end? There was only one road in and out of the village, a single avenue of escape. Why had they insisted that he sit and wait it out in this one place? He would have liked to keep moving. If he had had the running of it, he would have bought a second-hand caravan, and kept rolling from one park to another – his attention wandered for a few moments as he thought how he would have done it – if he had been given the planning of it.

He lit a cigarette and gazed out of the rain-blurred window panes, hardly aware of the muttered complaints and misgivings of his companion. What they should have done was crop the brat's fingers and bottle all of them to send to her father at intervals, and then they should have held a pillow over her face and buried her in the vegetable garden or weighted her and dumped her out beyond the hundred-fathom line of the Irish Sea – that way they would not have had to bother with a doctor, and the nursing—

Everything else had been done with professional skill, starting with the contact they had made with him in the *favela* of Rio de Janeiro, where he was hiding out in a sleazy one-room shack with the half-caste Indian woman, and down to his last fifty quid.

That had given him a real start, he thought he had covered his tracks completely, but they had him made. They had the passport and travel papers in the name of Barry, and they did not look like forgeries. They were good papers, he was sure of it, and he knew a lot about papers.

Everything else had been as well planned, and swiftly delivered. The money – a thousand pounds in Rio, another five thousand the day after they grabbed the brat, and he was confident that the final ten would be there as it was promised. It was better than an English gaol, the 'Silver City' as the Brits called their concentration camp at the Maze. That was what Caliph had promised, if he didn't take the job.

Caliph, now that was a daft name, Gilly O'Shaughnessy decided for the fiftieth time as he dropped the stub of his cigarette into the dregs of his teacup and it was extinguished with a sharp hiss. A real daft name, but somehow it had the ability to put a chill on the blood, and he shivered not only from the cold.

He stood up and crossed to the kitchen window. It had all been done with such speed and purpose and planning – everything so clearly thought out, that when there was a lapse it was more troubling.

Gilly O'Shaughnessy had the feeling that Caliph did nothing without good reason – then why had they been ordered to back themselves into this dangerously exposed bottleneck, without the security of multiple escape routes, and to sit here and wait?

He picked up the cyclist cape and tweed cap. 'Where are you going?' the doctor demanded anxiously. 'I'm going to take a shufti,' Gilly O'Shaughnessy grunted as he pulled the cap down over his eyes.

'You're always prowling around,' the doctor protested. 'You make me nervous.'

The dark Irishman pulled the pistol from under his jacket and checked the load before thrusting it back into his belt. 'You just go on playing nursemaid,' he said brusquely. 'And leave the man's work to me.'

The small black Austin crawled slowly up the village street, and the rain hammered on the cab and bonnet in tiny white explosions that blurred the outline, giving the machine a softly focused appearance, and the streaming windscreen effectively hid the occupants. It was only when the Austin parked directly in front of Laragh's only grocery store and both front doors opened that the curiosity of watchers from behind the curtained windows all down the street was satisfied.

The two members of the Irish constabulary wore the service blue winter uniform with darker epaulettes. The soft rain speckled the patent leather peaks of their caps as they hurried into the shop.

'Good morning, Maeve, me old love,' the sergeant greeted the plump red-faced lady behind the counter.

'Owen O'Neill, I do declare—' She chuckled as she recognized the sergeant – there had been a time, thirty years before, when the two of them had given the priest some fine pickings at the confessional. 'And what brings you all the way up from the big city?'

That was a generous description of the quaint seaside resort town of Wicklow, fifteen miles down the road.

'The sight of your blooming smile—'

They chatted like old friends for ten minutes, and her husband came through from the little storeroom when he heard the rattle of teacups.

'So what is new in Laragh, then?' the sergeant asked at last. 'Any new faces in the village?'

'No, all the same faces. Nothing changes in Laragh, bless the Lord for that.' The shopkeeper wagged his head. 'No, indeed – only new face is the one down at the Old Manse, he and his lady friend—' he winked knowingly ' – but seeing as how he's a stranger, we aren't after counting him.'

The sergeant ponderously delved for his notebook, opened it and extracted a photograph from it; it was the usual side view and full face of police records. He held the name covered with his thumb as he showed it to them.

'No.' The woman shook her head positively. 'Himself down at the manse is ten years older than that, and he does not have a moustache.'

'This was taken ten years ago,' said the sergeant.

'Oh, well, why didn't you say so.' She nodded. 'Then that's him. That's Mr Barry for certain sure.'

'The Old Manse, you say.' The sergeant seemed to inflate visibly with importance, as he put the photograph back into his notebook. 'I'm going to have to use your telephone now, dear.'

'Where will you be after telephoning?' The shopkeeper asked suspiciously.

'Dublin,' the sergeant told him. 'It's police business.'

'I'll have to charge you for the call,' the shopkeeper warned him quickly.

'There,' said the wife as they watched the sergeant making his request to the girl on the village switchboard. 'I told you he had the look of trouble, didn't I. The first time I laid eyes on him I knew he was from up in the North, and carrying trouble like the black angel.'

Gilly O'Shaughnessy kept close in under the stone wall, keeping out of the slanting rain and out of the line of sight of a casual watcher on the slope beyond the river. He moved carefully and quietly as a tomcat on his midnight business, stopping to examine the earth below the weakened or tumbled places in the wall where a man could have come over, studying the wet drooping weeds for the brush marks where a man might have passed.

At the farthest corner of the garden, he stepped up onto the leaning main stem of an apple tree to see over the wall, wedging himself against the lichen-encrusted stone, so that the silhouette of his head did not show above the wall.

He waited and watched for twenty minutes, with the absolute animal patience of the predator, then he jumped down and went on around the perimeter of the wall, never for a moment relaxing his vigilance, seemingly oblivious to the discomfort of the cold and the insistent rain.

There was nothing, not the least sign of danger, no reason for the nagging disquiet – but still it was there. He reached another vantage point, the iron gate that led into the narrow walled alley, and he leaned against the stone jamb, cupping his hands to protect match and cigarette from the wind, and then shifting slightly so he could see through the crack between wall and gate and cover the walled lane, and the road beyond as far as the bridge.

Once again he assumed the patient watching role, closing his mind against the physical discomfort and letting his eyes and his brain work at their full capacity.

Not for the first time he pondered the unusual system of signals and exchanges of material that Caliph had insisted upon.

The payments had been made by bearer deposit certificates, in Swiss francs, sent through the post to his Rio address and then to his collection address in London.

He had made one delivery to Caliph, the bottle and its contents – and two telephone calls. The delivery had been made within two hours of grabbing the girl, while she was still under the effects of the initial shot of the drug. The doctor – Dr Jameson, as Gilly O'Shaughnessy liked to think of him – had done the job in the back of the second car. It had been waiting in the car park at Cambridge railway station, a little green Ford delivery van with a completely enclosed rear compartment. They had moved the girl from the maroon Triumph to the Ford in the covering dusk of the autumn evening, and they had parked again in the lot of a roadside café on the A10 while Dr Jameson did the job. All the instruments had been ready for him in the van, but he had botched it badly, his hands shaking with nerves and the need for liquor. The brat had bled copiously, and now the hand was infected.

Gilly O'Shaughnessy felt his irritation rising sharply when he thought of the doctor. Everything he touched seemed to turn to disaster.

He had delivered the bottle to a pick-up car that had been exactly where he was told it would be, and it had dipped its headlights in the prearranged signal. Gilly had hardly stopped, but merely drawn up alongside and handed the bottle across, then driven straight into the West, and caught the early morning ferry long before any general alarm was out for the girl.

Then there were the telephone calls. They worried Gilly O'Shaughnessy as much as anything else in this whole bloody business. He had made the first call immediately they reached Laragh. It was an international call, and he had to say one sentence: 'We arrived safely.' And then hang up. A week later a call to the same number, and again only one sentence: 'We are enjoying ourselves.' And then immediately break the connection.

Gilly remembered how each time the girl on the local exchange had called him back to ask if the contact had been satisfactory – and each time she had sounded puzzled and intrigued.

It was not the way Caliph had worked up until then, it was leaving a trail for the hunters to follow and he would have protested – if there had been somebody to protest to, but there was only the international telephone number, no other way of contacting Caliph. He decided as he stood by the gate that he would not make the next telephone call to that number which was due in four days' time.

Then he remembered that was the day the hand was due – and he would probably receive his orders for delivery of the hand when he made the call – but he didn't like it. Not even for the money – and suddenly his mind went back to an incident long ago.

They had wanted to pass false information to the English, details of an intended operation – which would in fact take place at a different place and a different time. They had fed the detailed but duff information to a young unreliable Provo, one who they knew would not hold out under interrogation, and they had put him in a safe house in the Shankhill Road – and that was where the English took him.

Gilly O'Shaughnessy felt a little electric prickle run down his spine like ghost-fire, and that feeling had never let him down before – never. He looked at his cheap Japanese wristwatch; it was almost four o'clock, and evening was lowering on the hills of grey and cold green. When he looked up again, there was movement on the road.

From the top of the hill a vehicle was following the curve of the road, down towards the bridge. It was a small black saloon car, and it went out of sight behind the hedge.

Gilly O'Shaughnessy watched for it to reappear without particular interest, still worrying about those two telephone calls. Trying to find the need for them, why Caliph should want to take that chance.

The small black car turned onto the bridge, and came directly down towards the Manse, but the light was wrong and Gilly could make out only the shape of two heads beyond the rhythmically flogging windscreen wipers.

The car began to slow up, coming down almost to walking speed, and Gilly straightened up instinctively, suddenly completely alert as he peered through the slit. There was the pale blur of faces turned towards him, and the car slowed almost to a halt. The nearest side window was lowered slowly and for the first time he could see clearly into the interior. He saw the peak of the uniform cap, and the silver flash of a cap badge above the straining white face. The ghost-fire flared up Gilly O'Shaughnessy's spine and he felt his breath suddenly scalding his throat.

The small black car disappeared beyond the corner of the stone wall, and he heard it accelerate away swiftly.

Gilly O'Shaughnessy whirled with the cape ballooning around him and he ran back to the house. He felt very cold and sure and calm now that the moment of action had come.

The kitchen was empty and he crossed it in half a dozen strides, and threw open the door to the second room.

The doctor was working over the bed and he looked up angrily.

'I've told you to knock.'

They had argued this out before. The doctor still retained some bizarre vestige of professional ethics in his treatment of his patient. He might surgically mutilate the child for the money he so desperately needed, but he had protested fiercely when Gilly O'Shaughnessy had lingered at the doorway to ogle the maturing body whenever the doctor stripped it for cleansing, treatment or for the performance of its natural functions.

The dark Irishman had half-heartedly attempted to force him to back down, but when he had encountered surprisingly courageous opposition he had abandoned his voyeuristic pleasures and had returned to the inner room only when called to assist.

Now the child lay face down on the soiled sheets. Her blonde hair was matted and snarled into greasy tresses; the doctor's attempts at cleanliness were as bumbling and ineffectual as his surgery.

The infection and the use of drugs had wasted the flesh off the tender young body, each knuckle of her spine stood out clearly and her naked buttocks seemed pathetically vulnerable, shrunken and pale.

Now the doctor pulled the grubby sheet up to her shoulders, and turned to stand protectively over her. It was an absurd gesture, when you looked at the untidy, stained dressing that bound up her left hand – and Gilly O'Shaughnessy snarled at him fiercely.

'We are getting out.'

'You can't move her now,' protested the doctor. 'She's really sick.'

'Suit yourself,' Gilly agreed grimly. 'Then we'll leave her.' He reached under the dripping cape, and brought out the pistol. He thumbed back the hammer and stepped up to the bed. The doctor grabbed at his arm, but Gilly pushed him away easily, sending him reeling back against the wall.

'You are right, she'll be a nuisance,' he said, and placed the muzzle of the pistol against the base of the child's skull.

'No,' shrieked the doctor. 'No, don't do that. We'll take her.'

'We are leaving as soon as it's dark.' Gilly stepped back and uncocked the pistol. 'Be ready by then,' he warned.

The two helicopters flew almost side by side, with the number two only slightly behind and higher than the leader; below them the Irish Sea was a sheet of beaten lead flecked with feathers of white water.

They had refuelled at Caernarvon and had made good time since leaving the Welsh coast, for the wind drove them on, but still the night was overtaking them and Peter Stride fretted, glancing at his wristwatch every few seconds.

It was only ninety miles of open water to cross, but to Peter it seemed like the entire Atlantic. Colin slumped beside him on the bench that ran the length of the hold, with the cold stump of a cheroot in the corner of his mouth in deference to the 'No smoking' light that burned on the bulkhead behind the flight deck. The rest of the Thor team had adopted their usual attitudes of complete relaxation, some of them sprawled on the deck using their equipment as pillows, the others stretched out full length on the benches.

Peter Stride was the only one tensed up, as though his blood fizzed with nervous energy. He stood up once again to peer through the perspex window, checking the amount of daylight and trying to judge the height and position of the sun through the thick cloud cover.

'Take it easy,' Colin counselled him as he dropped back into his seat. 'You will give yourself an ulcer.'

'Colin, we've got to decide. What are our priorities on this strike?' He had to shout above the racket of wind and motor.

'There are no priorities. We have only one object – to get Melissa-Jane out, and out safely.'

'We aren't going to try for prisoners to interrogate?'

'Peter baby, we are going to hit anything and everything that moves in the target area, and we are going to hit them hard.'

Peter nodded with satisfaction. 'They will only be goons anyway, you can be certain that their paymaster will not let them connect to him – but what about Kingston Parker, he would want prisoners?'

'Kingston Parker?' Colin removed the stub of cheroot from his mouth. 'Never heard of him – around here it's Uncle Colin makes the decisions.' And he grinned at Peter, that friendly lopsided grin, and at that moment the flight engineer crossed the cabin and yelled at Colin.

'Irish coast ahead – we'll be landing at Enniskerry in seven minutes, sir.'

Air traffic control at Enniskerry had been apprised of the emergency. They stacked the other traffic in holding pattern above circuit altitude and cleared the two R.A.F. helicopters for immediate landing.

They came clattering out of the low grey cloud and rain, and settled on the hangar apron. Immediately a police car with headlights burning in the gloom, sped out from between the hangars and parked beside the leading machine. Before the rotors had stopped turning, two members of the Irish Constabulary and a representative of the surveyor general's office were scrambling up into the camouflaged fuselage.

'Stride.' Peter introduced himself quickly. He was dressed now in Thor assault gear, the one piece fitted black suit and soft boots, the pistol on its webbing belt strapped down to his right thigh.

'General, we've had a confirmation,' the police inspector

told him while they were still shaking hands. 'Local people have identified O'Shaughnessy from a police photograph. He is staying in the area all right.'

'Have they found where?' Peter demanded.

'They have, sir. It's an old rambling building on the edge of the village—' He motioned the bespectacled surveyor to come forward with the file he was clutching to his chest. There was no chart table in the stripped-out hull of the helicopter, and they spread the survey map and photographs on the deck.

Colin Noble ordered across the team from the second helicopter, and twenty men crowded into a huddle about the maps. 'There, that's the building.' The surveyor placed a circle on the map with a blue pencil.

'Right,' grunted Colin. 'We've got good fixes – we pick up either the river or the road and follow it to the bridge and the church. The target is between them.'

'Haven't we got a blow-up of the building, a plan of the interior?' one of the Thor team asked.

'Sorry, there wasn't time to do a proper search,' the surveyor apologized.

'The local police reported again a few minutes ago, and we got a relay on the radio. They say the house is enclosed by a high stone wall and that there are no signs of activity.'

'They haven't been near it?' Peter demanded. 'They were strictly ordered not to approach the suspects.'

'They drove past once on the public road.' The inspector looked slightly abashed. 'They wanted to make certain that—'

'If it's O'Shaughnessy, he needs only one sniff and he'll be gone—' Peter's expression was stony, but his eyes sparkled blue with anger. ' – Why can't these people do what they are told?' He turned quickly to the helicopter pilot in his yellow life jacket and helmet with its built-in microphone and earphones.

'Can you get us in?'

The pilot did not answer immediately but glanced up at the nearest window; a fresh gout of rain splashed against the pane.

'It will be dark in ten minutes, or even earlier, and the ceiling is down to the deck now, we only got down here using the airport V.O.R. beacons—' He looked dubious. ' – There is nobody aboard who will recognize the target, hell – I don't know – I could get you in at first light tomorrow.'

'It has to be tonight, now. Right now.'

'If you could get the local police to mark the target—' the pilot suggested, ' – with torches or a flare.'

'There is no chance of that – we have to go in cold, and the longer we sit here talking the less our chances. Will you give it your best shot?' Peter was almost pleading, the go decision is one that cannot be forced on a pilot, even air traffic control cannot force a pilot-in-command to operate beyond his personal judgement.

'We will have to try and keep ground contact all the way; it's classic conditions for trouble, rising terrain and deteriorating weather—'

'Try it—' Peter said, ' – please.'

The pilot hesitated five seconds longer.

'Let's go!' he said abruptly, and there was a concerted rush for the hatchway as the second Thor team made for the other machine, and the police and surveyor made certain they were not included on the passenger list.

Turbulence slogged the helicopter like the punches of a heavyweight prize fighter, and she dipped and staggered to them with a nauseatingly giddy action. The ground flickered past under them, very close, and yet darkly insubstantial in the wild night. The headlights of a solitary vehicle on a lonely country road, the cluttered lights of a village, each a distinct yellow rectangle they were so close, these were the only landmarks with any meaning – the rest was dark patches of woods, the threads of hedges and stone walls drawn lightly across sombre fields, and every few minutes even that was gone as a fresh squall of grey clouds and rain washed away all vision, and the pilot concentrated all his attention on the dull glow of the flight instruments arranged in their distinctive T layout in front of him.

Each time they emerged from cloud, the light seemed to have diminished and the dark menace of earth loomed more threateningly as they were forced lower and lower to keep contact.

Peter was squeezed into the jump seat of the helicopter's flight deck, between the two pilots, and Colin crowded in behind him, all of them peering ahead, all silent and tense as the ungainly machines lumbered low and heavy over the earth, groping for the shoreline.

They hit the coast, the ghostly white line of surf flared with phosphorescence only fifty feet below them, and the pilot swung them to run south with it – and seconds later another brighter field of lights appeared below them.

'Wicklow,' said the pilot, and his co-pilot called the new heading; now they had made a fix they could head for Laragh directly.

They swung onto the new heading, following the road inland.

'Four minutes to target,' the co-pilot shouted at Peter, stabbing ahead with his finger, and Peter did not try to answer in the clatter and roar of the rotors, but he reached down and checked the Walther in its quick-release holster; it came out cleanly in his fist.

Gilly O'Shaughnessy threw his few personal possessions into the blue canvas airways grip, a change of underclothing and his shaving gear. Then he pulled the iron bedstead away from the wall, ripped back the skirting board and cleared out the hiding-place he had made there by removing a single brick.

There were the new papers and passports. Caliph had even provided papers for the brat – Helen Barry – his daughter. Caliph had thought of everything. With the papers was six hundred pounds sterling in travellers' cheques, and a package of spare ammunition for the pistol. He thrust these into the pocket of his jacket, and took one last look around the bare bleak room. He knew that he had left nothing to lead the hunters, because he never carried anything that could be used to identify him. Yet he was obsessed by the need to destroy all sign of his passing. He had long ago ceased to think of himself by the name of Gilly O'Shaughnessy. He had no name, and only one purpose – that purpose was destruction. The magnificent passion to reduce all life to decay and mortification.

He could recite by heart most of Bakunin's *The Revolutionary Catechism*, especially the definition of the true revolutionary:

> The lost man, who has no belongings, no outside interest, no personal ties of any sort – not even a name. Possessed of but one thought, interest and passion – the revolution. A man who has broken with Society, broken with its laws and conventions. He must despise the opinions of others, and be prepared for death and torture at any time. Hard towards himself, he must be hard to others, and in his heart there must be no place for love, friendship, gratitude or even honour.

As he stood now in the empty room, he saw himself in a

rare moment of revelation, as the man he had set out to become – the true revolutionary, and his head turned for a moment to indulge in the vanity of regarding his own image in the mirror screwed to the peeling wallpaper above the iron bedstead.

It was the dark cold face of the lost man, and he felt proud to belong to that élite class, the cutting edge of the sword, that was what he was.

He picked up the canvas grip, and strode through into the kitchen.

'Are you ready?' he called.

'Help me.'

He dropped the grip and stepped to the window. The last of the light was fading swiftly, glowing pink and mother-of-pearl within the drooping, pregnant belly of the sky. It seemed so close he could reach out and touch it. Already the trees of the unkempt orchard were melding into the darkness as the night encroached.

'I cannot carry her on my own,' the doctor whined, and he swung away from the window. It was time to go again. In his life there was always the moving onwards, and always the hunters baying hard upon his scent. It was time to run again, run like the fox.

He went through into the second room. The doctor had the child wrapped in a grey woollen blanket, and he had tried to lift her from the bed, but had failed. She was sprawled awkwardly, half onto the floor.

'Help me,' repeated the doctor.

'Get out of the way.' Gilly O'Shaughnessy pushed him roughly aside, and stooped over the girl. For a second their faces were within inches of each other.

Her eyes were opened, half conscious, although the pupils were widely dilated by the drug. The lids were pink-rimmed and there were little butter-yellow lumps of mucus in the corners. Her lips were dried to white scales, and cracked through to the raw flesh at three places.

'Please tell my daddy,' she whispered. 'Please tell him I'm here.'

His nostrils flared at the sick sour smell of her body, but he picked her up easily with an arm under her knees and the other under her shoulders, and carried her out across the kitchen, kicking open the door so the lock burst and it slammed back against its hinges.

Quickly he carried her across the yard to the garage, with the doctor staggering along after them carrying a carton of medical supplies and equipment against his chest, cursing miserably at the cold, and sliding and slipping in the treacherous footing.

Gilly O'Shaughnessy waited while the doctor opened the rear door of the car, and then he bundled her in so roughly that the child cried out weakly. He ignored her and went to the double garage doors and dragged them open. It was so dark now that he could not see as far as the bridge.

'Where are we going?' bleated the doctor.

'I haven't decided yet,' Gilly told him brusquely. 'There is a safe house up North, or we might go back across the sea to England—' He thought of the caravan again, that was a good one—

'But why are we leaving now, so suddenly?'

He did not bother to reply but left the garage and ran back into the kitchen. Always he was obsessed by the need to cover his tracks, to leave no sign for the hunters.

Though he had brought little with him, and was taking that now, yet he knew the old house contained signs, even if it was only his fingerprints. There was also the single remaining appetite for destruction to assuage.

He ripped the wooden doors off the kitchen cupboards and smashed them to splinters under his heel, piled them in the centre of the wood floor. He crumpled the newspapers piled on the table and added them to the pile, threw the table and chairs upon it.

He lit a match and held it to the crumpled newsprint. It flared readily, and he straightened and opened the windows and doors. The flames fed on the cold fresh air and climbed greedily, catching on the splintered doors.

Gilly O'Shaughnessy picked up the canvas grip and stepped out into the night, crouching to the wind and the rain – but halfway to the garage he straightened again abruptly and paused to listen.

There was a sound on the wind, from the direction of the coast. It might have been the engine note of a heavy truck coming up the hills, but there was a peculiar thin whistling sound mingled with the engine beat, and the volume of sound escalated too sharply to be that of a lumbering truck. It was coming on too swiftly, the sound seemed to fill the air, to emanate from the very clouds themselves.

Gilly O'Shaughnessy stood with his face lifted to the fine silver drizzle, searching the belly of the clouds, until a throbbing regular glow began to beat like a pulse in the sky, and it was a moment until he recognized it as the beacon light of a low-flying aircraft, and at the same moment he knew that the shrill whistle was the whirling of rotors bringing the hunters.

He cried aloud in the certainty of betrayal and onrushing death. 'Why? God, why?' He called to the god he had so long ago denied, and he began to run.

'It's no good.' The pilot twisted his neck to shout at Peter without taking his eyes from the flight instruments which kept the great ungainly machine level and on course. They had lost contact with the other machine.

'We are socked in, blind.' The cloud frothed over the

canopy like boiling milk over the lip of the pot. 'I'm going to have to climb out, and head back for Enniskerry before we run into my number two.'

The risk of collision with the other helicopter was now real and imminent.

The beacon light throbbed above them, reflected off the impenetrable press of soft cloud – but the other pilot would not see it until too late.

'Hold on. Just another minute,' Peter shouted back at him, his expression tortured in the glow of the instrument panel. The entire operation was disintegrating about him, would soon end in tragedy or in fiasco, but he must go on.

'It's no good—' the pilot began, and then shouted with fright and hurled the helicopter over onto its side, at the same instant altering pitch and altitude so the machine shuddered and lurched as though she had run into a solid obstruction, and then bounded upwards, gaining a hundred feet in a swoop.

The spire of a church had leapt at them out of the cloud, like a predator from ambush, and now it flickered by only feet from where they crouched in the flight deck, but it had disappeared again instantly as they roared past.

'The church!' Peter yelled. 'That's it! Turn back.'

The pilot checked the machine, hovering blindly in the chaos of rain and cloud churned to a fury by the down-draught of their own rotor.

'I can't see a damned thing,' shouted the pilot.

'We've got one hundred and seventy feet on the radio altimeter,' his co-pilot called; that was actual height from the ground and still they could see nothing below them.

'Get us down. For God's sake, get us down,' Peter pleaded.

'I can't take the chance. We don't have any idea of what is under us.' The pilot's face was sickly orange in the instrument glow, his eyes the dark pits of a skull. 'I'm climbing out and heading back—'

Peter reached down and the butt of the Walther jumped into his hand, like a living thing. He realized coldly that he was capable of killing the pilot, to force the co-pilot to land – but at the moment there was a hole in the cloud, just enough to make out the dark loom of the earth below them.

'Visual,' Peter shouted. 'We've visual, get us down!' And the helicopter sank swiftly, breaking out suddenly into the clear.

'The river.' Peter saw the glint of water. 'And the bridge—'

'There's the churchyard—' Colin roared eagerly, ' – and that's the target.'

The thatched roof was a black oblong, and light spilled from the windows of one side of the building, so they could see the high enclosing wall. The pilot spun the helicopter on its axis like a compass needle, and dived towards the building.

Colin Noble scrambled down into the cabin, shouting to his team. 'Delta! We are going to Delta—' And the flight engineer slid the hatch cover open. Immediately a fine swirling mist filled the cabin as the down-draught of the rotors churned the rain filled air.

The Thor team were on their feet, forming up on each side of the open hatch, while Colin towered over the flight engineer as he took lead position – 'point' as he always called it.

The dark earth rushed up to meet them, and Colin spat out the cheroot stub and braced himself in the doorway.

'Hit anything that moves,' he yelled. 'But for Chrissake watch out for the kid. Let's go, gang. Let's go!'

Peter was jammed into the jump seat by the swooping drop of the machine, unable to follow, wasting precious seconds – but he had a clear view ahead through the canopy.

The light in the windows of the building wavered unnaturally, and Peter realized that it was burning. Those were flames, and his concern was heightened by the knowledge, but he did not have a chance to ponder this new development. In the shadows of the walled yard he saw movement, just the dark blur of it in the glow of the flames, and what was left of the daylight – but it was the shape of a man, running, crouched low, disappearing almost immediately into one of the outbuildings that flanked the narrow stone walled lane.

Peter dragged himself out of the seat against the G force, scrambling awkwardly down into the cabin as the helicopter dropped the last few feet, and then hung, swaying slightly, suspended ten feet above the open yard at the rear of the house – and black-clad figures spilled out of her, dropping lightly onto their feet and racing forward as they touched ground, seeming to disappear again miraculously through the doors and windows of the building. Even in the grinding tension of the moment Peter felt the flare of pride in the way it was done, instant and seemingly effortless penetration, the lead man using the sandbags to break in glass and wooden shutters and the man behind him going in with a clean controlled dive.

Peter was the last man left aboard, and something made him check in the open hatchway before jumping. Perhaps it was that glimpse of movement outside the main building that he had been given; he looked back that way, and suddenly lights leapt in solid white lances down the walled lane – the headlights of a motor vehicle, and at the same moment the vehicle launched itself from the dark derelict outbuilding and rocketed away down the lane.

Peter teetered in the open hatch, for he had been in the very act of jumping, but he caught his balance now, grabbing wildly at the nylon line above the door. The vehicle slowed for the turn into the main road at the bridge – and Peter caught the flight engineer and shook his shoulder violently, pointing after the escaping vehicle. His lips were inches from the man's face.

'Don't let it get away!' he screamed, and the flight engineer was quick and alert; he spoke urgently into his microphone, directly to the pilot in the flight deck above them, and obediently the helicopter swung around and the beat of the engines changed as the rotors altered pitch and roared in forward thrust – the machine lunged forward, skimming the garage roof by mere feet and then hammered out into the night in pursuit of the dwindling glow of headlights.

Peter had to hang out of the hatchway to see ahead, and the wind clamoured around his head and tore at his body, but they were swiftly overhauling the vehicle as it raced down the twisting narrow road towards the coast.

It was two hundred yards ahead, and the dark tree tops seemed to rush by at the same level as the hatch in which Peter stood. A hundred yards ahead now, the headlights blazing through the drivel of rain, etching fleeting cameos of hedges and starkly lit stone walls from the night.

They were close enough now for Peter to make out that it was a smallish vehicle with an estate car body, not quite large enough to be a station wagon – the driver was throwing it through the curves and twists of the road with reckless skill, but the helicopter crept up behind him.

'Tell him to switch off the beacon light.' Peter swung inboard to shout in the flight engineer's ear. He did not want to warn the driver that he was being followed, but as the engineer lifted the microphone to his mouth the headlights snapped out into darkness. The driver had become aware, and after the brilliance of the headlights the night seemed totally dark, and the car disappeared into it.

Peter felt the helicopter lurch, as the pilot was taken by surprise, and his own dismay was a lance.

We have lost them, he thought, and he knew that it was suicide to fly on in darkness only a few feet above t treetops, but the pilot of the helicopter steadied the and then suddenly the earth below them was lit by a b of stark white light that startled Peter until he realized that the pilot had switched on his landing lights. There were two of them, one on each side of the fuselage; they were aimed down and slightly forward.

The escaping car was caught fairly in their brilliance.

The helicopter dropped lower, edging in between the telegraph poles and trees that lined the narrow road.

Now Peter could see that the car was a dark blue Austin, with a carrying rack bolted to the long roof. It was that carrying rack which decided him. Without it no human being could have hoped for purchase on the smooth rounded roof of the lurching, swaying car.

The doctor in the back seat of the Austin had been the one who spotted the helicopter. The engine noise and the drumming of the wind had covered the whistling whine of the rotors, and Gilly O'Shaughnessy had chuckled with grim triumph and self-congratulation. He had deliberately waited for the helicopter to discharge its load of fighting men before he had switched on his headlights and roared out of the garage into the lane.

He knew it would be many minutes before the assault team realized that the burning house was empty and that it would take as long again to regroup and board the helicopter to continue the hunt – and by that time he would be clear; there was a safe house in Dublin – or there had been, four year previously. Perhaps it was blown now; in that case he would have to get rid of the brat and Dr Jameson, a bullet each in the back of the head, and drive the Austin into the Irish Sea.

The wild exhilaration of danger and death was upon him ...in, the waiting was over at last and he was living again ...way he had chosen – the fox running ahead of the ...ds, he was alive again, with his right foot thrust flat to the floor boards and the Austin rocketing through the night.

The girl was screaming weakly from the back seat, in pain and panic; the doctor was trying to quieten her, and Gilly laughed aloud. The tyres screeched wildly as he skidded out in the turn, brushing the hedge with the side before he was through.

'They are following,' screamed the doctor, as he straightened the car into the next stretch, then Gilly glanced back over his shoulder. He could see nothing through the rear windows.

'What?'

'The helicopter—'

Gilly lowered his window and, driving with one hand, thrust his head out. The flashing aircraft beacon was close behind and above, and he ducked back in and looked ahead to make sure that the road ran straight, then he switched off the headlights.

In total darkness he did not diminish speed, and now when he laughed it was a wild and reckless sound.

'You're mad,' the doctor shrieked. 'You'll kill us all!'

'Right you are, doctor!' But his night vision was clearing and he caught the Austin before she wandered into the stone wall on the left-hand side, and at the same moment he jerked the pistol from under his cape and laid it on the seat beside him.

'There is not going to be—' he began and then broke off as the blinding light burst over them. The helicopter had switched on its landing lights – the road ahead was brightly lit, and he skidded into the next turn with rubber squealing.

'Stop!' the doctor pleaded, trying to hold the semiconscious child from being hurled about in the swaying cab. 'Let's give up now, before they kill us.'

'They've got no fighting men on board,' Gilly yelled back at him. 'There's nothing they can do.'

'Give up,' the doctor whined. 'Let's get out of this alive.'

And Gilly O'Shaughnessy threw back his head and roared with laughter.

'I'm keeping three bullets, doctor, one for each of us—'

'They're right on top of us.'

Gilly snatched up the pistol and once again thrust his head and right shoulder out, twisting to look upwards.

The eye-searing lights beamed down upon him, very close above. It was all he could see and he fired at them, the crash of the shots lost in the clattering whistling roar of the rotors and the tearing rush of the wind.

Poised in the hatchway, Peter counted the bright orange spurts of gunfire. There were five of them, but there was no sound of passing shot, no thump of the strike.

'Get lower!' he shouted at the engineer, reinforcing the order with urgent hand signals, and obediently the big machine sank down upon the racing Austin.

Peter gathered himself, judging his moment carefully, and when it came he launched himself clear of the hatchway, and his guts seemed to cram into his throat as he dropped.

He dropped with all four limbs spread and braced to land together, but for a moment he thought he had misjudged it and would fall behind the Austin, into the metalled roadway, to be crushed and shredded by the forward impetus of the low-flying helicopter.

Then the Austin swerved and checked slightly and Peter crashed into its roof with stunning force; he felt the metal buckle and sag under him, and then he was rolling and slipping sideways. His whole left side was numbed by the force of impact, and he clutched wildly with his right hand, his fingernails tearing at the paintwork, but still he slid towards the edge, his legs kicking wildly in dark rushing space.

At the last instant before he was hurled into the roadway, his clawed fingers hooked in the framework of the roof rack, and he hung bat-like from his one arm. It had taken only a small part of a second, and immediately the driver of the Austin realized that there was a man on the roof. He slewed the little car from one side of the road to the other, short wrenching turns that brought her over on two outside wheels before slamming back and twisting the other way. The tyres squealed harsh protest, and Peter was flung brutally back and forth, the muscle and tendons of his right arm popping and creaking with the strain of holding on – but feeling was flooding swiftly back into his numbed left side.

He had to move quickly, he could not survive another of those wrenching swerves, and he gathered himself, judged the Austin's momentum, and used it to roll and grab with his free hand; at the same moment the toes of his soft boots found purchase on one of the struts of the roof carrier, and he pressed himself belly down, clinging with both arms and legs to the wildly swinging machine.

The Austin checked and steadied as a steep turn appeared ahead in the arc lights of the helicopter which still hung over them. The driver shot the car into the corner, and ahead of them was a long extended drop as the road twisted down the hills towards the coast.

Peter half lifted himself and was about to slide forward when the metal six inches in front of his nose exploded outwards, leaving a neatly punched hole through the roof, and tiny fragments of flying metal stung his cheek; at the same moment the concussion of the pistol shot beat in upon his eardrums. The driver of the Austin was firing blindly up through the coachwork, and he had misjudged Peter's position above him by inches. Peter threw himself desperately to one side, for an instant almost losing his grip on the struts of the carrier – and another pistol bullet clanged out through the metal roof, that one would have taken him through the belly, and Peter had a fleeting image of the kind of wound that it would have inflicted, the bullet would have been mushroomed and deformed by the roof and would have broken up inside his body.

Desperately Peter threw himself back the opposite way, trying to outguess the gunman below him, and once again the crash of the shot and the metal roof erupted in a little jagged pockmark, flecking the paintwork away so the rim of the bullet hole shone like polished silver shilling. Again it would have hit him, if he had not moved.

Peter rolled again, tensing his belly muscles in the anticipation of the tearing, paralysing impact, expecting the gun shot – which did not come. Only then he remembered the wasted pistol fire the driver had thrown up at the hovering helicopter. He had emptied his pistol and as the realization dawned on Peter there was another completely compelling sound, very faint in the drumming rush of the wind and the engine roar – but unmistakable. It was the sound of a young girl screaming and it galvanized Peter as nothing else, even the threat of death, could have done.

He came up on toes and fingers, like a cat, and he went forward and to the right, until he was directly above the driver's seat.

The girl screamed again, and he recognized Melissa-Jane's voice. There was no question of it, and he slipped the Walther from its quick-release holster and cocked the hammer with the same movement, one glance ahead and they were rushing down on another turn in the narrow road. The driver would be using both hands to control the swaying and bucking little machine.

'Now!' he told himself, and dropped forward, so that he was peering backwards and upside-down through the windscreen directly into the driver's pale face and at a distance of only eighteen inches.

In the thousandth part of a second Peter recognized the dark, wolfish features and the cold, merciless eyes of the killer. He had hunted this man for many years and studied his photograph endlessly when the hunting of the Provo terrorists had been his life's work.

Gilly O'Shaughnessy was driving with both hands, the pistol still gripped in one of them and the chamber open for reloading. He snarled at Peter like an animal through the bars of its cage, and Peter fired with the muzzle of the Walther touching the glass of the windscreen.

The glass starred into a glittering sheet, white and opaque, and then it collapsed inwards with the force of the wind, filling the interior of the Austin with flying diamond chips of sparkling glass.

Gilly O'Shaughnessy had thrown up both hands to his face, but bright blood burst from between them, spattering his chest and soaking swiftly into the lank black hair.

Still hanging upside down across the Austin's cab, Peter thrust the Walther in through the shattered windscreen until it almost touched the man's body and he fired twice more into his chest, where the explosive Velex bullets would break up against bone, and would not overpenetrate to harm anybody else in the interior. Melissa-Jane's screams still rang clearly in his ears, as he killed Gilly O'Shaughnessy. He did it as coldly as a veterinary surgeon would put down a rabid dog, and with as little pleasure, and the bullets punched Gilly O'Shaughnessy back on the bucket seat, head lolling from side to side, and Peter expected the howl of the engine to cut out now as the dead man's foot slipped from the accelerator.

It did not happen. There was no change in the engine beat, the body had slid forward and jammed, the knee under the dashboard bearing down fully on the pedal, and the little car flew down the slope of the hill, the stone walls on each side blurring past as though down a tunnel in the depths of the earth.

Peter wriggled forward and thrust both arms through the shattered windscreen and caught the untended wheel as it began to spin aimlessly. He checked the Austin and swung her back into the road but she had been driven to her limits, rocking and swaying crazily before she righted herself and flew down the hill.

It was almost impossible to judge the control needed to keep her on the road.

Peter was hanging head down, gripping only with knees and toes, and he had to manipulate the wheel from this inverted position with his upper arms sawing across the teeth of jagged glass still remaining in the frame of the windscreen.

The wind whipped and clawed him, and Gilly O'Shaughnessy's body flopped forward bonelessly onto the wheel, jamming it at a critical moment, so that while Peter used one hand to shove him backwards, the side of the Austin touched the stone wall with a screech of rending metal and a shower of orange sparks. Peter wrenched her back into the road, and she began a series of uncontrolled broadsides, swinging wildly from side to side, touching the wall with another jarring shock, then swinging back sideways to bounce over the verge, then back again.

She was going over, Peter knew it, and he would be crushed under the metal roof and smeared along the abrasive surface of the macadam road. He should jump now, and take his chances – but grimly he stayed with the crazed machine, for Melissa-Jane was in her and he could not leave.

She survived one more skid, and ahead Peter had the glimpse of a barred wooden gate in the wall. Deliberately he turned the front wheels into the direction of the next skid, no longer trying to counteract it, but aggravating it –

steering directly for the gate, and the Austin smashed into it.

A wooden beam cartwheeled over Peter's head, and a scalding cloud of steam from the shattered radiator stung his face and hands, and then the Austin was into the open field, bouncing and thudding over the rocks that studded it, the drag of soft muddy earth slowing her, and the steep slope of the hillside against her – within fifty feet the front end dropped heavily into a drainage ditch, and the little car shuddered to a halt, canted at an abandoned angle.

Peter slipped over the side and landed on his feet. He jerked open the rear door and a man half fell from the cab. He dropped onto his knees in the mud, blubbering incoherently and Peter drove his right knee into his face. Bone and cartilage crunched sharply and there was the crackle of breaking teeth. His voice was cut off abruptly and, as he dropped, Peter chopped him with the stiffened blade of his right hand, a controlled blow – judged finely to immobilize but not to kill, and before the unconscious body dropped, Peter had gone in over it.

He lifted his daughter out of the Austin, and the frail wasted body felt unsubstantial in his arms, and the heat of fever and infection burned against his chest.

He was possessed by an almost uncontrollable desire to crush her body to him with all the strength of his arms, but instead he carried her as though she was made of some precious and fragile substance, stepping carefully over the uneven rocky surface of the field to where the helicopter was settling cumbersomely out of the darkness.

The Thor doctor was still aboard her; he jumped clear before the helicopter touched and ran towards Peter in the brilliant glare of the landing lights.

Peter found he was crooning softly.

'It's all right now, darling. It's all over now. It's all finished, my baby – I'm here, little one—'

Then Peter made another discovery. It was not sweat running down his cheeks and dripping from his chin, and he wondered unashamedly when last it was he had wept. He could not remember, and it did not seem important, not now, not with his daughter in his arms.

Cynthia came down to London, and Peter relived some of those horrors from their marriage.

'Everybody around you always has to suffer, Peter. Now it's Melissa-Jane's turn.'

He could not avoid her, nor her martyred expression, for she was always at Melissa-Jane's bedside. While he bore her recriminations and barbed accusations, he wondered that she had ever been gay and young and attractive. She was two years younger than he was but she already had the shapeless body and greying mind that made her seem twenty years older.

Melissa-Jane responded almost miraculously to the antibiotics, and although she was still weak and skinny and pale, the doctor discharged her on the third day, and Peter and Cynthia had their final degrading haggling and bargaining session which Melissa-Jane settled for them.

'Mummy, I'm still so afraid. Can't I go with Daddy – just for a few days?'

Finally Cynthia agreed with sighs and pained airs that left them both feeling a little guilty. On the drive down to Abbots Yew, where Steven had invited them for as long as was necessary for Melissa-Jane's convalescence, she sat very quietly beside Peter, her left hand still in the sling and the finger wearing a small neat white turban. She spoke only after they had passed the Heathrow turn off on the M4.

'All the time I knew you were going to come. I can't remember much else. It was always dark and giddymaking –

things kept changing. I'd look at a face and it would fade away, and then we'd be somewhere else—'

'It was the drug they were giving you,' Peter explained.

'Yes, I know that. I remember the prick of the needle—' Reflexively she rubbed her upper arm, and shivered briefly. 'But even with the drug I always knew you were going to come. I remember lying in the darkness listening for your voice—'

There was the temptation to try to pretend it had never happened, and Melissa-Jane had not spoken about it until now – but Peter knew she must be allowed to talk it out.

'Would you like to tell me about it?' he invited gently, knowing that it was essential to the healing process. He listened quietly as she spilled out drug-haunted memories, disjointed scraps of conversation and impressions. The terror was back in her voice when she spoke of the dark one.

'He looked at me sometimes. I remember him looking at me—' And Peter remembered the cold killer's eyes.

'He is dead now, darling.'

'Yes, I know. They told me.' She was silent for a moment, and then went on. 'He was so different from the one with grey hair. I liked him, the old one. His name was Doctor Jameson.'

'How did you know that?' Peter asked.

'That's what the dark one called him.' She smiled. 'Doctor Jameson, I remember he always smelled like cough mixture and I liked him—'

The one who had done the amputation, and would have taken her hand as well, Peter thought grimly.

'I never saw the other one. I knew he was there, but I never saw him.'

'The other one?' Peter turned to her sharply. 'Which other one, darling?'

'There was another one – and even the dark one was afraid of him. I knew that, they were all afraid of him.'

'You never saw him?'

'No, but they were always talking about him, and arguing about what he would do—'

'Do you remember his name?' Peter asked, and Melissa-Jane frowned in concentration.

'Did he have a name?' Peter prompted.

'Usually they just talked about *him*, but, yes, I remember now. The dark one called him "Casper".'

'Casper?'

'No, not that, not Casper. Oh, I can't remember.' Her voice had risen, a shrill note in terror that ripped at Peter's nerves.

'Don't worry about it.' He tried to soothe her, but she shook her head with frustration.

'Not Casper, a name like that. I knew he was the one who really wanted to hurt me – they were just doing what he told them. He was the one I was truly afraid of.' Her voice ended with a sob, and she was sitting bolt upright in the seat.

'It's over now, darling.' Peter swung into the verge of the road and braked to a halt. He reached for her but she was rigid in his arms and at his touch she began to shake uncontrollably. Peter's alarm flared, and he held her to his chest.

'Caliph!' she whispered. 'That's his name. Caliph.' And she relaxed against him softly, and sighed. The shaking stopped slowly. Peter went on holding her, trying to control the terrible consuming waves of anger that engulfed him, and it was some little time before he realized suddenly that Melissa-Jane had fallen asleep.

It was as though uttering the name had been a catharsis for her terror, and now she was ready to begin the healing inside.

Peter laid her gently back in the seat and covered her with the angora rug before he drove on, but every few seconds he glanced across to make sure she was at peace.

Twice Peter called Magda Altmann from Abbots Yew, both times to her private number, but she was unobtainable and there was no message for him. That was five days he had not been able to reach her, not since the Delta Strike which had freed Melissa-Jane. She seemed to have disappeared completely, and Peter pondered the implications during the quiet days when he was almost always alone with his daughter.

Then Dr Kingston Parker arrived at Abbots Yew, and Sir Steven Stride was delighted to have as his guest such a distinguished statesman.

Kingston Parker's giant personality seemed to fill the beautiful old home. When he put himself out, his graciousness was irresistible. Steven was delighted with him, particularly when he discovered that despite Parker's image as a liberal and his well-known concern with human rights, he was also a champion of the capitalist system, and determined that his country should take more seriously its responsibilitics as leader of the Western world. They both deplored the loss of the B1 bomber and the delaying of the neutron bomb programme, and the restructuring of America's intelligence agencies. They spent much of the first afternoon in Steven's redwood-panelled study exploring each other's views, and came out of it fast friends.

When they emerged, Parker completed his conquest of the Stride household by showing he shared with Patricia Stride a scholarly knowledge and love of antique porcelain. His concern and warmth for Melissa-Jane and his relief at her safety were too spontaneous not to be entirely genuine. His conquest of that young lady's affections was complete when he went down with her to the stables to meet Florence Nightingale and prove that he was also a fair judge of horseflesh.

'He's a lovely man. I think he is truly an honourable man,' Melissa-Jane told Peter, when he went up to her bedroom to bid her goodnight – 'And he's so kind and funny—' Then, lest there be any question of disloyalty, 'But you are still my most favourite man in all the world.'

Her cure and convalescence seemed almost complete, and as Peter went down to rejoin the company he marvelled again at the resilience of young flesh and young minds.

As usual at Abbots Yew there was glittering and stimulating company at dinner, with Kingston Parker at its centre, but afterwards he and Peter exchanged a single glance down the length of Pat Stride's silver- and candle-decorated table and they left them to the port and cognac and cigars and slipped out unobtrusively into the walled rose garden.

While they paced side by side on the crunching gravel pathway, Kingston Parker stoked his meerschaum and then began to talk quietly. Once his bodyguard coughed in the shadows where he waited just out of range of their subdued voices, but that was the only intrusion and the spring night was still and balmy. Their conversation seemed utterly incongruous in these surroundings, talk of death and violence, the use and abuse of power, and the manipulations of vast fortunes by a single mysterious figure.

'It's been five days since I arrived in England—' Kingston Parker shrugged. 'One does not rush through the echoing passages of Whitehall. There was much to discuss—' Peter knew that he had met with the Prime Minister on two separate occasions ' – and it wasn't just Atlas business, I'm afraid—' Parker was one of the President's confidants. They would have taken full advantage of his visit to exchange views with the British Government. 'However, we did discuss Atlas in depth and detail. You know very well that Atlas has opponents and critics on both sides of the Atlantic. They tried very hard to squash it, and when they could not they saw to it that its power and duties were severely curtailed—' Parker paused and his pipe gurgled. He flicked out the juices from the mouthpiece onto the gravel path. 'The opponents of Atlas are all highly intelligent concerned and informed men. Their motives and their reasoning in opposing Atlas are laudable. I find myself a little in sympathy despite myself. If you create a strike force such as Atlas, where enormous powers are placed in the hands of a single man or a small élite leadership, you could very well be creating a Frankenstein – a monster more frightening than you are setting out to destroy.'

'That depends on the man who controls it, Dr Parker. I believe that they have the right man.'

'Thank you, Peter.' Parker turned his big shaggy head and smiled. 'Won't you please call me Kingston.'

Peter nodded agreement, while Parker went on. 'Atlas has had some spectacular successes – at Johannesburg and now in Ireland – but that makes it more dangerous. There will be a readier acceptance of the whole concept by the public; if Atlas asks for wider powers, it is more likely they would be granted. And, believe me, if it is to do the job it needs wider powers, Peter. I find myself torn down the centre—'

'And yet,' Peter pointed out, 'we cannot take on the most dangerous animal in the world, man the killer, we cannot do it without arming ourselves in every possible way.'

Kingston Parker sighed. 'And if Atlas achieves those powers, who can say when they will be abused, when will the rule of force supersede the rule of law?'

'The rules have changed. The rule of law is so often powerless in the face of those who have no respect for the law.'

'There is another aspect, Peter. One that I have thought about half my life. What about the rule of unjust law? The laws of oppression and greed. A law that enslaves or deprives a man because of the colour of his face or the god he worships? If a duly constituted parliament makes racial laws – or if the General Assembly of the United Nations declares that Zionism is a form of Imperialism and must be outlawed. – What if a handful of men gain control of the world's resources and legally manipulate them in a manner dictated by personal greed to the detriment of all mankind, such as the Committee of the OPEC, the Shah and the King of Saudi Arabia—' Kingston Parker made a helpless gesture, spreading those long sensitive fingers. 'Must we respect those laws? The rule of law, even unjust law, is it sacrosanct?'

'Balance,' said Peter. 'There has to be a balance between law and force.'

'Yes, but what is the balance, Peter?' He abruptly closed his hands into fists. 'I have asked for greater powers for Atlas, wider scope for its use, and I think these will be granted. When they are, we will have need of good men, Peter.' Kingston Parker reached out and took Peter's shoulder in a surprisingly powerful grip. 'Just men, who can recognize when the rule of law has either failed or is unjust, and who have the courage and the vision to act to restore the balance that you spoke of a moment ago.'

His hand was still on Peter's shoulder and he left it there. It was a natural gesture, without affectation.

'I believe you are one of those men.' He let the hand drop, and his manner changed. 'Tomorrow I have arranged that we meet with Colonel Noble. He has been busy breaking down and examining the entire Irish operation, and I hope he will have come up with something for us to get our teeth into. Then there is much else to discuss. Two o'clock at Thor Command, will it suit you, Peter?'

'Of course.'

'Now let's go in and join the company.'

'Wait.' Peter stopped him. 'I have something I must tell you, Kingston. It's been tearing at my guts, and after you have heard it you may alter your opinion of me – my suitability for my role at Atlas.'

'Yes?' Parker turned back and waited quietly.

'You know that the people who kidnapped my daughter

made no demands for her return, made no attempt to contact me or the police to negotiate.'

'Yes,' Parker answered. 'Of course. It was one of the puzzling things about the whole business.'

'It was untrue. There was a contact and a demand.'

'I don't understand.' Parker frowned and thrust his face closer to Peter's, as though trying to study his expression in the poor light from the windows.

'The kidnappers contacted me. A letter which I destroyed—'

'Why?' Parker shot at him.

'Wait. I'll explain,' Peter replied. 'There was a single condition for my daughter's release, and a deadline of two weeks. If I did not meet the condition by that time, they would have sent me parts of my daughter's body – her hands, her feet, and finally her head.'

'Diabolical,' Parker whispered. 'Inhuman. What was the condition?'

'A life for a life,' said Peter. 'I was to kill you in exchange for Melissa-Jane.'

'Me!' Parker started, throwing back his head with shock. 'They wanted me?'

Peter did not reply, and they stood staring at each other, until Parker raised his hand and combed at his hair, a distracted gesture.

'That changes it all. I will have to think it out carefully – but it makes a whole new scenario.' He shook his head. 'Me. They were going for the head of Atlas. Why? Because I was the champion of Atlas, and they opposed its formation? No! That's not it. There seems only one logical explanation. I told you last time I saw you that I suspected the existence of a central figure – the puppetmaster who was taking control of all known militant organizations and welding them into a single cohesive and formidable entity. Well, Peter, I have been hunting this figure. I have learned much to confirm my suspicions since last we met. I believe this person, or assembly of persons, does in fact exist – part of the new powers I have asked for Atlas were to be used to hunt and destroy this organization before it does grave damage – before it succeeds in so terrifying the nations of the world that it becomes itself a world power—' Parker stopped as though to gather his thoughts, and then went on in quiet, more measured tones. 'I think now that this is absolute proof that it does exist, and that it is aware of my suspicions and intentions to destroy it. When I set you up as Atlas agent at large, I believed you would make contact with the enemy – but, God knows, I did not expect it to come like this.'

He paused again, considering it. 'Incredible!' he marvelled. 'The one person whom I would never have suspected, you Peter. You could have reached me at any time, one of the few people who could. And the leverage! Your daughter – the protracted mutilations – I may have just misjudged the cunning and ruthlessness of the enemy.'

'Have you ever heard the name Caliph?' Peter asked.

'Where did you hear that?' Parker demanded harshly.

'The demand letter was signed Caliph, and Melissa-Jane heard her captors discussing it.'

'Caliph.' Parker nodded. 'Yes, I have heard the name, Peter. Since I last spoke to you. I have heard the name. Indeed I have.' He was silent again, sucking distractedly on his pipe, then he looked up. 'I will tell you how and when tomorrow when we meet at Thor, but now you have given me much to keep me awake tonight.'

He took Peter's arm and led him back towards the house. Warm yellow light and laughter spilled out from the downstairs windows, welcoming and gay, but both of them were withdrawn and silent as they trudged up the smoothly raked path.

At the garden door Kingston Parker paused, holding Peter back from entering.

'Peter, would you have done it?' he asked gruffly.

Peter answered him levelly without attempting to avoid his eyes. 'Yes, Kingston, I would have done it.'

'How?'

'Explosives.'

'Better than poison,' Parker grunted. 'Not as good as the gun.' And then angrily, 'We have to stop him, Peter. It is a duty that supersedes every other consideration.'

'What I have just told you does not alter our relationship?' Peter asked. 'The fact that I would have been your assassin – does not change it?'

'Strangely enough, it merely confirms what I have come to believe of you, Peter. You are a man with the hard ruthless streak we need, if we are to survive.' He smiled bleakly. 'I might wake up sweating in the night – but it doesn't alter what we have to do – you and I.'

Colin Noble with his cheroot, and opposite him Kingston Parker with the amber meerschaum, seemed to be in competition as to who could soonest render the air in the room incapable of supporting human life. It was already thick and blue, and the temporary headquarters of Thor Command lacked air-conditioning – but within minutes Peter had become so immersed in what he was hearing that the discomfort was forgotten.

Colin Noble was going over the details of the Irish operation, and all that had been gleaned from it.

'The house, the Old Manse, was burned to the ground, of course. The Irish constabulary had twenty men sifting through the ashes—' He spread his hands. 'A big nix. Nothing at all.'

'Next the contents of the Austin and its – provenance – how do you like that word, Peter baby? Provenance, that's a classy word.'

Parker smiled indulgently. 'Please go on, Colin.'

'The Austin was stolen in Dublin, and resprayed and fitted with the roof carrier. It contained nothing, no papers, nothing in the glove compartment or boot, it had been stripped and cleaned out by an expert—'

'The men,' Parker prompted him.

'Yes, sir. The men. The dead one first. Name of Gerald O'Shaughnessy, also known as "Gilly", born Belfast 1946—' As he spoke Colin picked up the file that lay on the table in front of him. It was five inches thick. ' – Do we want to read all of it? It's a hell of a story. The guy had a track record—'

'Only as far as it concerns Atlas,' Parker told him.

'There is no evidence as to when or how he became involved with this business—' Colin sketched the facts swiftly and succinctly. ' – So we end with the contents of his pockets. Six hundred pounds sterling, thirty-eight rounds of .38 ammunition, and papers in the name of Edward and Helen Barry – forged, but beautifully forged.' Colin closed the file with a slap. 'Nothing,' he repeated. 'Nothing we can use. Now the other man. Morrison – Claude Bertram Morrison – celebrated abortionist and dedicated alcoholic. Struck off the medical rolls in 1969—' Again he recounted the sordid history swiftly and accurately. ' – His price for the digital surgery was three thousand pounds – half in advance. Hell, that's cheaper than the Blue Cross.' Colin grinned but his eyes were black and bright with anger. 'I am pleased to report that he can expect a sentence of approximately fifteen years. They are going to throw the book at him. There is only one item of any possible interest which he could give us. Gilly O'Shaughnessy was the leader from whom he took his orders, O'Shaughnessy in turn took his orders from somebody called—' He paused dramatically. 'Yes, that's right. The name we have all heard before. Caliph.'

'Just one point here,' Kingston Parker interrupted.

'Caliph likes to use his name. He signs it on his correspondence. Even his lowliest thugs are given the name to use. Why?'

'I think I can answer that.' Peter stirred and raised his head. 'He wants us to know that he exists. We must have a focal point for our fear and hatred. When he was merely a nameless, faceless entity he was not nearly as menacing as he is now.'

'I think you are right.' Parker nodded his head gravely. 'By using the name he is building up a store of credibility which he will draw upon later. In future when Caliph says he will kill or mutilate we know he is in deadly earnest, there will be no compromise. He will do exactly as he promises. The man, or men, are clever psychologists.'

'There is just one aspect of the Irish operation we have not yet considered,' Peter broke in, frowning with concentration. 'That is – who was it that tipped us off, and what was the reason for that telephone call?'

They were all silent, until Parker turned to Colin.

'What do you think of that one?'

'I have discussed it with the police, of course. It was one of the first things that puzzled us. The police believe that Gilly O'Shaughnessy picked his hideout in Ireland because he was familiar with the terrain, and had friends there. It was his old stamping ground when he was with the Provos. He could move and disappear, get things fixed.' Colin paused and saw the sceptical expression on Peter's face. 'Well, look at it this way, Peter baby. He had a woman negotiate the lease on the Old Manse – Kate Barry, she called herself and signed it on the lease – so that was one ally. There must have been others, because he was able to buy a stolen and reworked automobile – he would have had difficulty doing that in Edinburgh or London without the word getting about.'

Peter nodded reluctantly. 'All right, having the Irish connection helped him—'

' – But there was the other side of the coin. O'Shaughnessy had enemies, even in the Provos. He was a ruthless bastard with a bloody record. We can only believe that one of those enemies saw the chance to make a score – the one who sold him the stolen auto, perhaps. We have had the recording of the tip-off call examined by language experts and had a run against the voice prints on the computer. Nothing definite. The voice was disguised, probably through a handkerchief and nose plugs, but the general feeling is that it was an Irishman who made the call. The boffins from the telephone department were able to test the loading of the line and guess it was a call from a foreign country – very likely Ireland, although they cannot be certain of that.'

Peter Stride raised one eyebrow slightly, and Colin chuckled weakly and waved the cheroot at him in a wide gesture of invitation.

'Okay. That's my best shot,' he said. 'Let's hear you do better. If you don't like my theories, you must have one of your own.'

'You are asking me to believe it was all a coincidence; that O'Shaughnessy just happened to run into an old enemy who just happened to tip us off twenty-four hours before the deadline for Melissa-Jane's hand to be amputated. Then it just so happened that we reached Laragh at exactly the same moment as O'Shaughnessy was pulling out and making a run for it. Is that what you want me to believe?'

'Something like that,' Colin admitted.

'Sorry, Colin. I just don't like coincidence.'

'Shoot!' Colin invited. 'Let's hear how it really happened.'

'I don't know,' Peter grinned placatingly. 'It is just that I have this feeling that Caliph doesn't deal in coincidence either. I have this other feeling that somehow Gilly O'Shaughnessy had the death mark on his forehead from the beginning. I have this feeling it was all part of the plan.'

'It must be great fun to have these feelings.' Colin was prickling a little. 'But they sure as hell aren't much help to me.'

'Take it easy.' Peter held up one hand in surrender. 'Let's accept tentatively that it happened your way, then—'

'But?' Colin asked.

'No buts – not until we get some more hard evidence—'

'Okay, buster.' There was no smile on Colin's face now, the wide mouth clamped in a grim line. 'You want hard evidence, try this one for size—'

'Hold it, Colin,' Parker shot in quickly, authoritatively. 'Wait for a moment before we come to that.' And Colin Noble deflated with a visible effort, the cords in his throat smoothing out and the line of mouth relaxed into the old familiar grin as he deferred to Kingston Parker.

'Let's backtrack here a moment,' Parker suggested. 'Peter came up with the name Caliph. In the meantime we had picked up the same name – but from an entirely different source. I promised Peter I would tell him about our source – because I think it gives us a new insight into this entire business.' He paused and tinkered with his pipe, using one of those small tools with folding blades and hooks and spikes with which pipe smokers arm themselves. He scraped the bowl and knocked a nub of half-burned tobacco into the ashtray, before peering into the pipe the way a rifleman checks the bore of his weapon. Peter realized that Parker used his pipe as a prop for his performances, the way a magician distracts his audience with flourishes and mumbo-jumbo. He was not a man to underestimate, Peter thought again for the hundredth time. Kingston Parker looked up at him and smiled, a conspiratorial smile as if to acknowledge that Peter had seen through his little act.

'Our news of Caliph comes from an unlikely direction – or rather, considering the name, a more likely direction. East. Riyadh to be precise. Capital city of Saudi Arabia, seat of King Khalid's oil empire. Our battered and beleaguered

Central Intelligence Agency has received an appeal from the King following the murder of one of his grandsons. You recall the case, I'm sure—' Peter had a strange feeling of *déjà-vu* as he listened to Kingston Parker confirming exactly the circumstances that he and Magda Altmann had discussed and postulated together, was it only three weeks before? ' – You see the King and his family are in a very vulnerable position really. Did you know that there are at least seven hundred Saudi princes who are multi-millionaires, and who are close to the King's affections and power structure? It would be impossible to guard that many potential victims adequately. It's really damned good thinking – you don't have to seize a hostage with all the attendant risks. There is virtually an unlimited supply of them walking around, ripe for plucking, and an inexhaustible supply of assassins to be either pressured or paid to do the job, just as long as you have the information and leverage, or just enough money. Caliph seems to have all that.'

'What demand has been made upon Khalid?' Peter asked.

'We know for certain that he has received a demand, and that he has appealed to the CIA for assistance to protect and guard his family. The demand came from an agency or person calling himself Caliph. We do not know what the demand is – but it may be significant that Khalid and the Shah of Persia have both agreed that they will not support a crude oil price increase at the next pricing session of OPEC, but on the contrary they will push for a five per cent decrease in the price of crude.'

'Caliph's thinking has paid off again,' Peter murmured.

'It looks like it, doesn't it.' Parker nodded, and then chuckled bitterly. 'And once again you get the feeling, as with his demands to the South African Government, that his final objective is desirable – even if the way he goes about procuring it is slightly unconventional, to say the least.'

'To say the very least,' Peter agreed quietly, remembering

the feel of Melissa-Jane's fever-racked body against his chest.

'So there is no doubt now that what we feared, is fact. Caliph exists—' said Parker.

'Not only exists, but flourishes,' Peter agreed.

'Alive and well with a nice house in the suburbs.' Colin lit the stub of his cheroot before going on. 'Hell! He succeeded at Johannesburg. He is succeeding at Riyadh – where does he go from there – why not the Federation of Employers in West Germany? The Trade Union leaders in Great Britain? – Any group powerful enough to affect the fate of nations, and small enough to be terrorized as individuals.'

'It's a way to sway and direct the destiny of the entire world – you just cannot guard all the world's decision-makers from personal attack,' Peter agreed. 'And it's no argument to point out that because his first two targets have been South Africa and the oil monopoly, then the long term results will be to the benefit of mankind. His ultimate target will almost certainly be the democratic process itself. I don't think there can be any doubt that Caliph sees himself as a god. He sees himself as the paternal tyrant. His aim is to cure the ills of the world by radical surgery, and to maintain its health by unrestrained force and fear.'

Peter could remain seated no longer. He pushed back his chair and crossed to the windows, standing there in the soldier's stance, balanced on the balls of his feet with both hands clasped lightly behind his back. There was an uninspiring view of the high barbed-wire fence, part of the airfield and the corrugated sheet wall of the nearest hangar. A Thor sentry paced before the gates with a white M.P. helmet on his head and side arm strapped to his waist. Peter watched him without really seeing him, and behind him the two men at the table exchanged a significant glance. Colin Noble asked a silent question and Parker answered with a curt nod of affirmative.

'All right, Peter,' Colin said. 'A little while back you asked for hard facts. I promised to give you a few.'

Peter turned back from the window and waited.

'Item One. During the time that Gilly O'Shaughnessy held Melissa-Jane in Laragh, two telephone calls were made from the Old Manse. They were both international calls. They both went through the local telephone exchange. The first call was made at seven p.m. local time on the first of this month. That would have been the first day that they could have reached the hideout. We have to guess it was an "All Well" report to the top management. The second call was exactly seven days later again at seven o'clock local time precisely. To the same number. We have to guess that it was another report, "All is still well". Both calls were less than one minute in duration. Just time enough to pass a pre-arranged code message—' Colin broke off and looked again at Kingston Parker.

'Go on,' Parker instructed.

'The calls were to a French number. Rambouillet 47–87–47.'

Peter felt it hit him in the stomach, a physical blow, and he flinched his head, for a moment closing both his eyes tightly. He had called that number so often, the numerals were graven on his memory.

'No.' He shook his head, and opened his eyes. 'I'm not going to believe it.'

'It's true, Peter,' Parker said gently.

Peter walked back to his seat. His legs felt rubbery and shaky under him. He sat down heavily.

The room was completely silent. Neither of the other two looked directly at Peter Stride.

Kingston Parker made a gesture to Colin and obediently he slid the red box file, tied with red tapes, across the cheap vinyl-topped table.

Parker untied the tapes and opened the file. He shuffled the papers, scanning them swiftly. Clearly he was adept at speed reading and was able to assimilate each typed double-spaced page at a glance – but now he was merely waiting for Peter to recover from the shock. He knew the contents of the red file almost by heart.

Peter Stride slumped in the steel-framed chair with its uncushioned wooden seat, staring sightlessly at the bulletin board on the opposite wall on which were posted the Thor rosters.

He found it hard to ride the waves of dismay that flooded over him. He felt chilled and numbed, the depth of this betrayal devastated him, and when he closed his eyes again he had a vivid image of the slim, tender body with the childlike breasts peeping through a silken curtain of dark hair.

He straightened in his seat, and Kingston Parker recognized the moment and looked up at him, half closing the file and turning it towards him.

The cover bore the highest security gradings available to Atlas Command – and below them was typed:

ALTMANN MAGDA IRENE. Born KUTCHINSKY

Peter realized that he had never known her second name was Irene. Magda Irene. Hell, they were really ugly names – made special only by the woman who bore them.

Parker turned the file back to himself and began to speak quietly.

'When last you and I met, I told you of the special interest we had in this lady. That interest has continued, unabated, since then, or rather it has gathered strength with every fresh item of information that has come to us.' He opened the file again and glanced at it as if to refresh his memory. 'Colin has been very successful in enlisting the full co-operation of the intelligence agencies of both our countries, who in turn have been able to secure that of the French and – believe it or not – the Russians. Between the four countries we have been able to at last piece together the woman's history—' He broke off. 'Remarkable woman,' and shook his head in admiration. 'Quite incredible really. I can understand how she is able to weave spells around any man she chooses. I can understand, Peter, your evident distress. I am going to be utterly blunt now – we have no time nor space in which to manoeuvre tactfully around your personal feelings. We know that she has taken you as a lover. You notice that I phrase that carefully. Baroness Altmann takes lovers, not the other way around. She takes lovers deliberately and with careful forethought. I have no doubt that once she has made the decision, she accomplishes the rest of it with superb finesse.'

Peter remembered her coming to him and the exact words she had used. 'I am not very good at this, Peter, and I want so badly to be good for you.'

The words had been chosen with the finesse that Kingston Parker had just spoken of. They were exactly turned to make herself irresistible to Peter – and afterwards she had given the gentle lie to them with the skill and devilish cunning of her hands and mouth and body.

'You see, Peter. She had special and expert training in all the arts of love. There are probably few women in the Western world who know as much about reading a man, and then pleasing him. What she knows she did not learn in Paris or London or New York—' Kingston Parker paused and frowned at Peter. 'This is all theory and hearsay, Peter. You are in a better position to say just how much of it is false?'

The ultimate skill in pleasing a man is to fuel his own belief in himself, Peter thought, as he returned Parker's inquiring gaze with expressionless eyes. He remembered how with Magda Altmann he had felt like a giant, capable of anything. She had made him feel like that with a word, a smile, a gift, a touch – that was the ultimate skill.

He did not answer Parker's question. 'Go on please,

Kingston,' he invited. Externally, he had himself completely under control now. His right hand lay on the table top, with the fingers half open, relaxed.

'I told you that even as a child she showed special talents. In languages, mathematics – her father was an amateur mathematician of some importance – chess and other games of skill. She attracted attention. Especially she attracted attention because her father was a member of the Communist Party—' Parker broke off as Peter lifted his head in sharp inquiry. ' – I'm sorry, Peter. We did not know that when last we met. We have learned it since from the French, they have access to the party records in Paris it seems, and it was confirmed by the Russians themselves. Apparently the child used to accompany her father to meetings of the Party, and soon showed a precocious political awareness and understanding. Her father's friends were mostly party members, and after his death – there still remains a mystery around his death. Neither the French nor the Russians are forthcoming on the subject. – Anyway, after his death, Magda Kutchinsky was cared for by these friends. It seemed she was passed on from family to family—' Kingston Parker slid a postcard-sized photograph from a marbline envelope and passed it across the table to Peter, ' – from this period.'

It showed a rather skinny girl in short skirts and dark stockings, wearing the yoked collar and straw bonnet of the French schoolgirl. Her hair was in two short braids, tied with ribbons, and she held a small fluffy white dog in her arms. The background was a Parisian summer park scene, with a group of men playing *boule* and chestnut trees in full leaf.

The child's face was delicately featured with huge beautiful eyes, somehow wise and compassionate beyond her age, and yet still imbued with the fresh innocence of childhood.

'You can see she already had all the markings of spectacular beauty.' Kingston Parker grunted, and reached across to take back the photograph. For a moment Peter's fingers tightened instinctively; he would have like to have kept it, but he relaxed and let it go. Parker glanced at it again and then slipped it back into the envelope.

'Yes. She attracted much interest, and very soon an uncle from the old country wrote to her. There were photographs of her father and the mother she had never known, anecdotes of her infancy and her father's youth. The child was enchanted. She had never known she had an uncle. Her father had never spoken of his relatives, but now at last the little orphan found she had family. It took only a few more letters, exchanges of delight and affection, and then it was all arranged. The uncle came to fetch her in person – and Magda Kutchinsky went back to Poland.' Parker spread his hands. 'It was easy as that.'

'The missing years,' Peter said, and his voice sounded strange in his own ears. He cleared his throat and shifted uncomfortably under Parker's piercing but understanding gaze.

'No longer missing, Peter. We have been fed a little glimmering of what happened during those years – and we have been able to fill in the rest of it from what we knew already.'

'The Russians?' Peter asked, and when Parker nodded, Peter went on with a bitter tang to his voice. 'They seem to be very forthcoming, don't they? I have never heard of them passing information – at least not valuable information – so readily.'

'They have their reasons in this case,' Parker demurred. 'Very good reasons as it turns out – but one will come to those in due course.'

'Very well.'

'The child returned with her uncle to Poland, Warsaw. And there was an extravagant family reunion. We are not certain if this was her real family, or whether the child was provided with a foster family for the occasion. In any event, the uncle soon announced that if Magda would submit to examination there was an excellent chance that she would be provided with a scholarship to one of the élite colleges of the USSR. We can imagine that she passed her examination with great distinction and her new masters must have congratulated themselves on their discovery.

'The college is on the shores of the Black Sea near Odessa. It does not have a name, nor an old school tie. The students are very specially selected, the screening is rigorous and only the brightest and most talented are enrolled. They are soon taught that they are an élite group, and are streamed in the special direction that their various talents dictate. In Magda's case it was languages and politics, finance and mathematics. She excelled and at the age of seventeen graduated to a higher, more specialized branch of the Odessa college. There she was trained in special memory techniques, the already bright mind was honed down to a razor edge. I understand that one of the less difficult exercises was to be given access to a list of a hundred diverse items for sixty seconds. The list had to be repeated from memory, in the correct order, twenty-four hours later.' Parker shook his head again, expressing his admiration.

'At the same time she was also trained to fit naturally into upper-class international Western society. Dress, food, drink, cosmetics, manners, popular music and literature, cinema, theatre, democratic politics, business procedures, the operation of stocks and commodities markets, the more mundane secretarial skills, modern dancing, the art of love-making and pleasuring men – that and much else, all of it taught by experts – flying, skiing, weapons, the rudiments of electronics and mechanical engineering and every other skill that a top-class agent might have to call upon.

'She was the star of her course and emerged from it much as the woman you know. Poised, skilled, beautiful, motivated – and deadly.

'At the age of nineteen she knew more, was capable of

more, than most other human beings, male or female, twice her age. The perfect agent, except for a small flaw in her make-up that only showed up later. She was too intelligent and too personally ambitious.' Kingston Parker smiled for the first time in twenty minutes. ' – Which of course is a pseudonym for greed. Her masters did not recognize it in her, and perhaps at that age it was only latent greed. She had not yet been fully exposed to the attractions of wealth – nor of unlimited power.'

Kingston Parker broke off, leaned across the table towards Peter. He seemed to change direction then, smiling an inward knowledgeable smile, as though pondering a hidden truth.

'Greed for wealth alone belongs essentially to the lower levels of human intelligence. It is only the developed and advanced mind that can truly appreciate the need for power—' He saw the protest in Peter's expression. ' – No, no, I don't mean merely the power to control one's own limited environment, merely the power of life and death over a few thousand lives – not that, but true power. Power to change the destiny of nations, power such as Caesar or Napoleon wielded, such as the President of the United States wields – that is the ultimate greed, Peter. A magnificent and noble greed.'

He was silent a moment, as though glimpsing some vision of splendour. Then he went on:

'I digress. Forgive me,' and turned to Colin Noble. 'Do we have some coffee, Colin? I think we could all do with a cup now.'

Colin went to the machine that blooped and gurgled and winked its red eye in the corner, and while he filled the cups, the charged atmosphere in the room eased a little, and Peter tried to arrange his thoughts in some logical sequence. He looked for the flaws and weak places in the story but could find none – instead he remembered only the feel of her mouth, the touch of her hands on his body. Oh

God, it was a stab of physical pain, a deep ache in the chest and groin, as he remembered how she had coursed him like a running stag, driving and goading him on to unvisited depths of his being. Could such skills be taught, he wondered, and if so, by whom? He had a horrifying thought of a special room set on the heights above the Black Sea, with that slim, vulnerable tender body practising its skills, learning love as though it were cookery or small arms practice – and then he shut his mind firmly against it, and Kingston Parker was speaking again, balancing his coffee cup primly with his pinky finger raised, like an old maid at a tea party.

'So she arrived back in Paris and it fell at her feet. It was a triumphant progress.' Kingston Parker prodded in the file with his free hand, spilling out photographs of Magda – Magda dancing in the ballroom of the Elysée Palace, Magda leaving a Rolls-Royce limousine outside Maxim's in the rue Royale, Magda skiing, riding, beautiful, smiling, poised – and always there were men. Rich, well-fed, sleek men.

'I told you once there were eight sexual liaisons.' Kingston Parker used that irritating expression again. 'We have had reason to revise that figure. The French take a very close interest in that sort of thing, they have added to the list.' He flicked over the photographs. 'Pierre Hammond, Deputy Minister of Defence—' And another. 'Mark Vincent, head of mission at the American Consulate—'

'Yes,' Peter cut in short, but still there was a sickly fascination in seeing the faces of these men. He had imagined them accurately, he realized, without particular relish.

'Her masters were delighted – as you can imagine. With a male agent it is sometimes necessary to wait a decade or more for results while he moles his way into the system. With a young and beautiful woman she has her greatest value when those assets are freshest. Magda Kutchinsky gave them magnificent value. We do not know the exact extent of her contributions – our Russian friends have not bared everything to us, I'm afraid, but I estimate that it was about this time they began to realize her true potential. She had the magical touch, but her beauty and youth could not last for ever—' Kingston Parker made a deprecating gesture with the slim pianist's hands. ' – We do not know if Aaron Altmann was a deliberate choice by her masters. But it seems likely. Think of it – one of the richest and most powerful men in Western Europe, one who controlled most of the steel and heavy engineering producers, the single biggest armaments complex, electronics – all associated and sensitive secondary industries. He was a widower, childless, so under French law his wife could inherit his entire estate. He was known to be fighting a slowly losing battle with cancer, so his life term was limited – and he was also a Zionist and one of the most trusted and influential members of Mossad. It was beautiful. Truly beautiful,' said Kingston Parker. 'Imagine being able to undermine a man of that stature, perhaps being able to double him! Though that seemed an extravagant dream – not even the most beautiful siren of history could expect to turn a man like Aaron Altmann. He is a separate study on his own, another incredible human being with the strength and courage of a lion – until the cancer wore him out. Again I digress, forgive me. Somebody, either the Director of the NKVD in Moscow, or Magda Kutchinsky's control at the Russian Embassy in Paris, who was, incidentally, the Chief NKVD Commissar for Western Europe, such was her value, or Magda Kutchinsky herself, picked Aaron Altmann. Within two years she was indispensable to him. She was cunning enough not to use her sexual talents upon him immediately. Altmann could have any woman who took his fancy, and he usually did. His sexual appetites were legendary, and they probably were the cause of his remaining childless. A youthful indiscretion resulted in a venereal disease with complications. It was later completely cured, but the damage was irreversible, he never produced an heir.'

He was a man who would have toyed with her and cast her aside as soon as he tired of her, if she had been callow enough to make herself immediately available to him.

First, she won his respect and admiration. Perhaps she was the first woman he had ever met whose brain and strength and determination matched his own—

Kingston Parker selected another photograph and passed it across the table. Fascinated, Peter stared at the black and white image of a heavily built man with a bull neck, and a solid thrusting jaw. Like so many men of vast sexual appetite, he was bald except for a Friar Tuck frill around the cannon ball dome of his skull. But there were humorous lines chiselled about his mouth, and his eyes, though fierce, looked as though they too could readily crinkle with laughter lines. Portrait of Power, Peter thought.

'When at last she gave him access to her body, it must have been like some great electrical storm.' Kingston Parker seemed to be deliberately dwelling on her past love affairs, and Peter would have protested had not the information he was receiving been so vital. 'This man and woman must have been able to match each other once again. Two very superior persons, two in a hundred million probably – it is interesting to speculate what might have happened if they had been able to produce a child.' Kingston Parker chuckled. 'It would probably have been a mongolian idiot – life is like that.'

Peter moved irritably, hating this turn in the conversation, and Parker went on smoothly.

'So they married, and NKVD had a mole in the centre of Western industry. Narmco, Altmann's armaments complex, was manufacturing top secret American, British and French missile hardware for NATO. The new Baroness was on the Board, was in fact Deputy Chairman of Narmco. We can be sure that armaments blueprints were passed, not by the sheet but by the truckload. Every night, the leaders and decision-makers of the Western world sat at the new

Baroness's board and swilled her champagne. Every conversation, every nuance and indiscretion was recorded by that specially trained memory, and slowly, inevitably, the Baron's strength was whittled away. He began to rely more and more upon her. We do not know exactly when she began to assist him with his Mossad activities – but when it happened the Russians had succeeded in their design. In effect they had succeeded in turning Baron Aaron Altmann, they had his right hand and his heart – for by this time the dying Baron was completely besotted by the enchantress. They could expect to inherit the greater part of Western European heavy industry. It was all very easy – until the latent defect in the Baroness's character began to surface. We can only imagine the alarm of her Russian masters when they detected the first signs that the Baroness was working for herself alone. She was brighter by far than any of the men who had up until that time controlled her, and she had been given a taste of real power. The taste seemed very much to her liking. We can only imagine the gargantuan battle of wills between the puppetmasters and the beautiful puppet that had suddenly developed a mind and ambitions of her very own – quite simply her ambition now was to be the most wealthy and powerful woman since Catherine of Russia, and the makings were almost within her pretty hands – except—'

Kingston Parker stopped; like a born storyteller, he knew instinctively how to build up the tension in his audience. He rattled his coffee cup.

'This talking is thirsty business.' Colin and Peter had to rouse themselves with a physical effort. They had been mesmerized by the story and the personality of the storyteller. When Parker had his cup refilled, he sipped at it, then went on speaking.

'There was one last lever her Russian masters had over her. They threatened to expose her. It was quite a neat stroke, really. A man like Aaron Altmann would have acted like an enraged bull if he had known how he had been deceived. His reaction was predictable. He would have divorced Magda immediately. Divorce is difficult in France – but not for a man like the Baron. Without his protection Magda was nothing, less than nothing, for her value to the Russians would have come to an end. Without the Altmann Empire her dreams of power would disappear like a puff of smoke. It was a good try – it would have worked against an ordinary person, but of course they were not dealing with an ordinary person—'

Parker paused again; it was clear he was as wrapped up by the story as they were, and he was drawing out the pleasure of the telling of it.

'I have been doing a lot of talking,' he smiled at Peter. 'I'm going to let you have a chance now, Peter. You know her a little, you have learned a lot more about her in the last hour. Can you guess what she did?'

Peter began to shake his head – and then it crashed in upon him with sickening force, and he stared at Parker, the pupils of his eyes dilating with the strength of his revulsion.

'I think you have guessed.' Parker nodded. 'Yes, we can imagine that by this stage she was becoming a little impatient herself. The Baron was taking a rather long time to die.'

'Christ, it's horrible.' Peter grunted, as though in pain.

' – From one point of view, I agree.' Parker nodded. 'But if you look at it like a chess player, and remember she is a player of Grand Master standard, it was a brilliant stroke. She arranged that the Baron be kidnapped. There are witnesses to the fact that she insisted on the Baron accompanying her that day. He was feeling very bad, and he did not want to go sailing, but she insisted that the sun and fresh air would be good for him. He never took his bodyguard when he went sailing. There were just the two of them. A very fast cruiser was waiting offshore—' He spread his hands. ' – You know the details?'

'No,' Peter denied it.

'The cruiser rammed the yacht. Picked the Baron out of the water, but left the Baroness. An hour later there was a radio message to the coastguard; they went out and found her still clinging to the wreckage. The kidnappers were very concerned that she survived.'

'They may have wanted a loving wife to bargain with,' Peter suggested swiftly.

'That is possible, of course, and she certainly played the role of the bereaved wife to perfection. When the ransom demand came it was she who forced the Board of Altmann Industries to ante up the twenty-five million dollars. She personally took the cash to the rendezvous – alone.' Parker paused significantly.

'She didn't need the money.'

'Oh, but she did,' Parker contradicted. 'The Baron was not in his dotage, you know. His hands were still very firmly on the reins – and the purse strings. Magda had as much as any ordinary wife could wish for, furs, jewellery, servants, clothes, cars, boats – pocket money, around two hundred thousand dollars a year, paid to her as a salary from Altmann Industries. Any ordinary wife would have been well content – but she was not an ordinary wife. We must believe she had already planned how to carry forward her dreams of unlimited power – and it needed money, not thousands but millions. Twenty-five million would be a reasonable stop-gap, until she could get her pretty little fingers on the big apple. – She drove with the cash, in thousand-Swiss-franc bills, I understand; she drove alone to some abandoned airfield and had a plane come pick it up and fly it out to Switzerland. Damned neat.'

'But—' Peter searched for some means of denial. ' – But the Baron was mutilated. She couldn't—'

'Death is death, mutilation may have served some obscure purpose. God knows, we're dealing with an Eastern mind, devious, sanguinary – perhaps the mutilation was merely to make any suspicion of the wife completely far-fetched – just as you immediately used it to protect her.'

He was right, of course. The mind that could plan and execute the rest of such a heinous scheme would not baulk at the smaller niceties of execution. He had no more protest to make.

'So let us review what she had achieved by this stage. She was rid of the Baron, and the restrictions he placed upon her. An example of these restrictions, for we will find it significant later: she was very strongly in favour of Narmco banning the sale of all weapons and armaments to the South African Government. The Baron, ever the businessman, looked upon that country as a lucrative market. There was also the South African sympathy for Zionism. He overruled her, and Narmco continued to supply aircraft, missiles and light armaments to that country right up until the official UN resolution to enforce a total arms embargo, with Francc ratifying it. Remember, the Baroness's anti-South African attitude. We come to it again later.

'She was rid of the Baron. She was rid of her Russian control, well able to maintain a small army to protect herself. Even her former Russian masters would hesitate to take revenge on her. She was a French Grande Dame now. She had gained significant working capital – twenty-five million for which she was not accountable to another living human being. She had gained an invincible power base at Altmann Industries. Although she was still under certain checks and safeguards from the Board of Directors, yet she had access to all its information-gathering services, to its vast resources. As the head of such a colossus she had the respect of and sympathy of the French Government, and as a fringe benefit – limited but significant access to their intelligence systems. Then there was the Mossad connection: was she not the heir to Aaron Altmann's position—'

Peter suddenly remembered Magda speaking of her 'sources' – and never identifying them. Was she really able to use the French and Israeli intelligence as her own private agencies? It seemed impossible. But he was learning swiftly that when dealing with Magda Altmann, anything was possible – as Kingston Parker had pointed out, she was not an ordinary person – but Parker was speaking again.

'There was a period then of consolidation, a time when she gathered up the reins that Aaron had dropped. There were changes amongst the top management throughout Altmann Industries as she replaced those who might oppose her with her own minions. A time of planning and organizing, and then the first attempt to govern and prescribe the destiny of nations. She chose the nation which most offended her personal view of the new world she was going to build. We will never know what made her choose the name of Caliph—'

'You have to be wrong.' Peter squeezed his eyelids closed with thumb and forefinger. 'You just don't know her.'

'I don't think anybody knows her, Peter,' Kingston Parker murmured, and fiddled with his pipe. 'I'm sorry, we are going pretty fast here. Do you want to back up and ask any questions?'

'No, it's all right.' Peter opened his eyes again. 'Go on, will you, Kingston?'

'One of the most important lessons that Baroness Altmann had learned was the ease with which force and violence can be used, and their tremendous effect and profitability. Bearing this lesson in mind, the Baroness chose her first act as the new ruler of mankind, and the choice was dictated by her early political convictions, those convictions formed at her father's knee and at the Communist Party meetings that she had attended as a precocious child in Paris. There is a further suggestion that the choice was reinforced by the Altmann banking corporation's interests in South African gold sales, for by this time the Baroness had tempered her socialist and communist leanings with a good healthy dollop of capitalistic self-interest. We can only guess, but if the scheme to bring out forty tons of gold – and a black-based government-in-exile – had succeeded, it would not have taken very long for Caliph to gain control of both government and gold—' Parker shrugged. ' – We just cannot say how ambitious, even grandiose, those plans were. But we can say that Caliph, or the Baroness, recruited her team for the execution of the plan with the skill she brought to anything she handled.' He broke off, and smiled. 'I think all three of us remember the taking of Flight 070 vividly enough not to have to go once more over the details. Let me just remind you that it would have succeeded, in fact it had actually succeeded, when Peter here made his unscheduled move that brought it all down. But it succeeded. That was the important thing. Caliph could afford to congratulate herself. Her information was impeccable. She had chosen the right people for the job. She even knew the name of the officer who would command the anti-terrorist force which would be sent to intervene, and her psychology had been excellent. The execution of the four hostages had so shocked and numbed the opposition that they were powerless – the cup had been dashed from her lips by one man alone. Inevitably her interest in that man was aroused. Possibly with feminine intuition she was able to recognize in him the qualities which could be turned to her own purpose. She had that indomitable streak in her make-up that is able to recognize even in the dust of disaster that material for future victory—' Parker shifted his bulk, and made a small deprecatory gesture. ' – I hope this will not seem immodest if I bring myself into the story as this stage. I had been given the hint that something like Caliph existed. In fact this may not have been her first act after the killing of Aaron Altmann. Two other successful kidnappings have her style – one of them the OPEC ministers in Vienna – but we cannot be sure. I had been warned and I was waiting for Caliph to surface. Dearly I would have loved a chance to interrogate one of the hijackers—'

'They would have had nothing to tell you,' Peter interjected brusquely. 'They were merely pawns, like the doctor we captured in Ireland.'

Parker sighed. 'Perhaps you are right, Peter. But at the time I believed that our only lead to Caliph had been severed. Later when the thing had been done and I had recovered from the shock of it, it suddenly occurred to me that the lead was still there – stronger than ever. You were that lead, Peter. That was why I recommended that your resignation be accepted. If you had not resigned, I would have forced you out anyway, but you played along superbly by resigning—' He smiled again. ' – I have never thanked you for that.'

'Don't mention it,' said Peter grimly. 'I like to be of service.'

'And you were. Almost immediately you were on the loose, the Baroness began making her approach. First she collected every known fact about you. Somehow she even got a computer run on you. That's a fact. An unauthorized run was made on the Central Intelligence computer four days after your resignation. She must have liked what she got, for there was the Narmco offer – through conventional channels. Your refusal must have truly excited her interest, for she used her connections to have herself invited down to Sir Steven's country house.' Parker chuckled. 'My poor Peter, you found yourself without warning in the clutches of one of history's most accomplished enchantresses. I know enough about the lady to guess that her approach to you was very carefully calculated from the complete information that she had on you. She knew exactly what type of woman attracted you. Fortunately, she fitted the general physical description—'

'What is that?' Peter demanded. He was unaware that he had a specific type of physical preference.

'Tall, slim and brunette,' Parker told him promptly.

'Think about it,' he invited. 'All your women have been that.'

He was right, of course, Peter realized. Hell, even at thirty-nine years of age it was still possible to learn something about yourself.

'You're a cold-blooded bastard, Kingston. Did anybody ever tell you that?'

'Frequently.' Kingston smiled. 'But it's not true, and compared to Baroness Altmann I am Father Christmas.' And he became serious again. 'She wanted to find out what we at Atlas know about her activities. She knew by this stage that we had our suspicions, and through you she had an inside ear. Of course, your value would deteriorate swiftly the longer you were out of Thor – but you could still be useful in a dozen other ways. As a bonus you could be expected to do a good job at Narmco. All her expectations were fulfilled, and exceeded. You even thwarted an assassination attempt on her life—'

Peter lifted an eyebrow in inquiry.

' – On the road to Rambouillet that night. Here we are only guessing, but it's a pretty well-informed guess. The Russians had by this time despaired of returning her to the fold. They had also suspicions as to her role as Caliph. They decided on a radical cure for their one-time star agent. They either financed and organized the assassination attempt themselves, or they tipped off Mossad that she had murdered Aaron Altmann. I would be inclined to believe that they hired the killers themselves – because the Mossad usually do their own dirty work. Anyway, with NKVD or Mossad as paymasters, an ambush was set up on the Rambouillet road and you drove into it. I know you don't like coincidence, Peter, but I believe it was merely coincidence that you were driving the Baroness's Maserati that night.'

'All right,' Peter murmured. 'If I swallow the rest of the hog, that little crumb goes down easily enough.'

'That attempt severely alarmed the Baroness. She was not certain who had been the author. I think she believed it was Atlas Command, or at the very least that we had something to do with it. Almost immediately after that you were able to confirm our interest in her, and our knowledge that Caliph existed. I invited you to America, Colin brought you to meet me, and when you returned you either told her about it, or in some way confirmed her suspicions of Atlas Command and Kingston Parker. I am guessing again – but how close am I, Peter? Be honest.'

Peter stared at him, trying to keep his face expressionless while his mind raced. That was exactly how it had happened.

'We were all hunting Caliph. You saw no disloyalty in discussing it with her.' Parker prompted him gently, and Peter nodded once curtly.

'You believed that we had common goals,' Parker went on with deep understanding and compassion. 'You thought we were all hunting Caliph. That is right.'

'She knew I had been to America to see you before I told her. I don't know how – but she knew,' Peter said stiffly. He felt like a traitor.

'I understand,' Parker said simply. He reached across the table and once again placed his hand on Peter's shoulder. He squeezed it while he looked into Peter's eyes, a gesture of affirmation and trust. Then he laid both hands on top of the table.

'She knew who was the hunter then, and she knew enough about me to know I was dangerous. You were probably the only man in the world who could reach me and do the job – but you had to be motivated. She picked the one and only lever that would move you. She picked it unerringly – just as she had done everything else. It would have worked – in one stroke she would have gotten rid of the hunter, and she would have acquired a top-class assassin. When you had done the job, you would have belonged to

Caliph for all time. She would have used you to kill again and again, and each time you killed you would be more deeply enmeshed in her net. You really were a very valuable prize, Peter. Valuable enough for her to find it worthwhile to use her sexual wiles upon you.'

He saw the lumps of clenched muscle at the corner of Peter's jaw, and the fire in his eyes.

'You are also a very attractive man, and who knows but she felt the need to combine business and pleasure? She is a lady with strongly developed sexual appetites.'

Peter felt a violent urge to punch him in the face. He needed some outlet for his rage. He felt belittled, soiled and used.

'She was clever enough to realize that the sex was not enough of a hold to force you to commit murder. So she took your daughter, and immediately had her mutilated – just as at Johannesburg she had executed hostages without hesitation. The world must learn to fear Caliph.'

There was no smile on Parker's face now.

'I truly believe that if you had not been able to deliver my head by the deadline, she would not have hesitated to carry out the next mutilation, and the one after that.'

Again Peter was assailed by a wave of nausea as he remembered that shrivelled white lump of flesh with the scarlet fingernail floating horribly in its tiny bottle.

'We were saved from that by the most incredible piece of luck. The Provo informer,' said Parker. 'And again the understandable eagerness of the Russians to co-operate with us. It is a wonderful opportunity for them to hand us their problem. They have let us have an almost full account of the lady and her history.'

'But what are we going to do about it?' Colin Noble asked. 'Our hands are tied. Do we just have to wait for the next atrocity – do we have to hope we will get another lucky break when Caliph kills the next Arab prince, or machine-guns the Shah's sister?'

'That will happen – unless they push through the OPEC decision,' Parker predicted levelly. 'The lady has converted very easily to the capitalist system now that she owns half of Europe's industry. A reduction in the oil price would benefit her probably more than any other individual on earth – and at the same time it will also benefit the great bulk of humanity. How nicely that squares all her political and personal interests.'

'But if she gets away with it—' Colin insisted, ' – what will be her next act of God?'

'Nobody can predict that,' Parker murmured, and they both turned their heads to look at Peter Stride.

He seemed to have aged twenty years. The lines at the corners of his mouth were cut in deeply like the erosion of weathered granite. Only his eyes were blue and alive and fierce as those of a bird of prey.

'I want you to believe what I am going to say now, Peter. I have not told you all this to put pressure on you,' Parker assured him quietly. 'I have told you only what I believe is necessary for you to know – to protect yourself if you should elect to return to the lion's den. I am not ordering you to do so. The risks involved cannot be overestimated. With a lesser man I would term it suicidal. However, now that you are forewarned, I believe you are the one man who could take Caliph on her own ground. Please do not misunderstand what I mean by that. I am not for a moment suggesting assassination. In fact I expressly forbid you to even think in that direction. I would not allow it, and if you acted independently, I would do my utmost to see that you were brought to justice. No, all I ask is that you keep close to Caliph and try to outguess her. Try to expose her so we can lawfully act to take her out of action. I want you to put out of your mind the emotional issues – those hostages at Johannesburg, your own daughter – try to forget them, Peter. Remember we are neither judge nor executioner—' Parker went on speaking quietly and insistently, and Peter watched his lips with narrowed eyes, hardly listening to the words, trying to think clearly and see his course ahead – but his thoughts were a children's carousel, going around and around with fuss and fury but returning with every revolution to the one central conclusion.

There was only one way to stop Caliph. The thought of attempting to bring someone like Baroness Magda Altmann to justice – in a French court – was laughable. Peter tried to force himself to believe that vengeance had no part in his decisions, but he had lived too long with himself to be able to pull off such a deceit. Yes, vengeance was part of it – and he trembled with the rage of remembrance, but it was not all of it. He had executed the German girl Ingrid, and Gilly O'Shaughnessy – and had not regretted the decision to do so. If it was necessary for them to die – then surely Caliph deserved to die a thousand times more.

And there is only one person who can do it, he realized.

Her voice was quick and light and warm, with just that fascinating trace of accent; he remembered it so well, but had forgotten the effect it could have upon him. His heart pounded as though he had run a long way.

'Oh, Peter. It's so good to hear your voice. I have been so worried. Did you get my cable?'

'No, which cable?'

'When I heard that you had freed Melissa-Jane. I sent you a cable from Rome.'

'I didn't get it – but it doesn't matter.'

'I sent it to you via Narmco – in Brussels.'

'It's probably waiting for me there. I haven't been in touch.'

'How is she, Peter?'

'She is fine now—' He found it strangely difficult to use

her name, or any form of endearment. He hoped that the strain would not sound in his voice. 'But we went through a hell of a time.'

'I know. I understand. I felt so helpless. I tried so hard, that's why I was out of contact, Peter *chéri*, but day after day there was no news.'

'It's all over now,' Peter said gruffly.

'I don't think so,' she said swiftly. 'Where are you calling from?'

'London.'

'When will you come back?'

'I telephoned Brussels an hour ago. Narmco wants me back urgently. I am taking a flight this afternoon.'

'Peter, I have to see you. I've been too long without you – but, oh *mon Dieu*, I have to be in Vienna tonight. – Wait, let me see, if I sent the Lear to fetch you now we could meet, even for an hour. You could take the late flight from Orly to Brussels and I could go on to Vienna with the Lear – please, Peter. I missed you so. We could have an hour together.'

One of the airport sub-managers met Peter as he disembarked from the Lear and led him to one of the VIP lounges above the main concourse.

Magda Altmann came swiftly to meet him as he stepped into the lounge – and he had forgotten how her presence could fill a room with light.

She wore a tailored jacket over a matching skirt, severe gun-metal grey and tremendously effective. She moved like a dancer on long graceful legs which seemed to articulate from the narrow waist – and Peter felt awkward and heavy-footed, for the awareness that he was in the presence of evil sat heavily upon him, weighting him down.

'Oh, Peter. What have they done to you?' she asked with quick concern flaring in those huge compassionate eyes. She reached up to touch his cheek.

The strain and horror of the last days had drawn him out to the edge of physical endurance. His skin had a greyish, sickly tone against which the dark new beard darkening his jaws contrasted strongly. There were more fine silver threads at his temples, gull's wings against the thicker darker waves of his hair, and his eyes were haunted. They had sunk deeply into their sockets.

'Oh, darling, darling,' she whispered, low enough so that the others in the room could not hear her, and she reached up with her mouth for his.

Peter had carefully schooled himself for this meeting. He knew how important it was that he should not in any way betray the knowledge he had. Magda must never guess that he had found her out. That would be deadly dangerous. He must act completely naturally. It was absolutely vital, but there was just that instant's remembrance of his daughter's pale wasted fever-racked features, and then he stooped and took Magda's mouth.

He forced his mouth to soften, as hers was soft and warm and moist, tasting of ripe woman and crushed petals. He made his body welcoming as hers was melting and trusting against his – and he thought he had succeeded completely until she broke from his embrace and leaned back, keeping those slim strong hips still pressed against his. She studied his face again, a swift probing, questioning gaze, and he saw it change deep in her eyes. The flame going out of them leaving only a cold merciless green light, like the beautiful spark in the depths of a great emerald.

She had seen something; no there had been nothing to see. She had sensed something in him, the new awareness. Of course, she would have been searching for it. She needed only the barest confirmation – the quirk of expression on his mouth, the new wariness in his eyes, the slight stiffness and reserve in his body – all of which he thought he had been able to control perfectly.

'Oh, I am glad you are wearing blue now.' She touched the lapel of his casual cashmere jacket. 'It does suit you so well, my dear.'

He had ordered the jacket with her in mind, that was true – but now there was something brittle in her manner. It was as though she had withdrawn her true self, bringing down an invisible barrier between them.

'Come.' She turned away, leading him to the deep leather couch below the picture windows. Some airport official had been able to find flowers, yellow tulips, the first blooms of spring, and there was a bar and coffee machine.

She sat beside him on the couch, but not touching him, and with a nod dismissed her secretary. He moved across the room to join the two bodyguards, her grey wolves, and the three of them remained out of earshot, murmuring quietly amongst themselves.

'Tell me, please, Peter.' She was still watching him, but the cold green light in her eyes had been extinguished – she was friendly and concerned, listening with complete attention as he went step by step over every detail of Melissa-Jane's kidnapping.

It was an old rule of his to tell the complete truth when it would serve – and it served now, for Magda would know every detail. He told her of Caliph's demand for Kingston Parker's life, and his own response.

'I would have done it,' he told her frankly, and she hugged her own arms and shuddered once briefly.

'God, such evil can corrupt even the strongest and the best—' and now there was understanding softening her lips.

Peter went on to tell her of the lucky tip-off and the recovery of Melissa-Jane. He went into details of the manner in which she had been abused, of her terror and the psychological damage she had suffered – and he watched

Magda's eyes carefully. He saw something there, emphasized by the tiny frown that framed them. He knew that he could not expect feelings of guilt. Caliph would be far beyond such mundane emotion – but there was something there, not just stagey compassion.

'I had to stay with her. I think she needed those few days with me,' he explained.

'Yes. I am glad you did that, Peter.' She nodded, and glanced at her wristwatch. 'Oh, we have so little time left,' she lamented. 'Let's have a glass of champagne. We have a little to celebrate. At least Melissa-Jane is alive, and she is young and resilient enough to recover completely.'

Peter eased the cork and when it popped he poured creaming pale yellow Dom Perignon into the flutes, and smiled at her over the glass as they saluted each other.

'It's so good to see you, Peter.' She was truly a superb actress; she said it with such innocent spontaneity that he felt a surge of admiration for her despite himself. He crushed it down and thought that he could kill her now and here. He did not really need a weapon. He could use his hands if he had to, but the Cobra parabellum was in the soft chamois leather holster under his left armpit. He could kill her, and the two bodyguards across the room would gun him down instantly. He might take one of them, but the other one would get him. They were top men. He had picked them himself. They would get him.

'I'm sorry we will not be together for very long,' he countered, still smiling at her.

'Oh, *chéri*. I know, so am I.' She touched his forearm, the first touch since the greeting embrace. 'I wish it were different. There are so many things that we have to do, you and I, and we must forgive each other for them.'

Perhaps the words were meant to have a special significance; there was a momentary flash of the warm green fire in her eyes, and something else – perhaps a deep and unfathomable regret. Then she sipped the wine, and lowered the long curled lashes across her eyes, shielding them from his scrutiny.

'I hope we will never have anything terrible to forgive—'

For the first time he faced the act of killing her. Before it had been something clinical and academic, and he had avoided considering the deed itself. But now he imagined the impact of an explosive Velex bullet into that smooth sweet flesh. His guts lurched, and for the first time he doubted if he were capable of it.

'Oh, Peter, I hope so. More than anything in life, I hope that.' She lifted her lashes for a moment, and her eyes seemed to cling to his for an instant, pleading for something – forgiveness, perhaps. If he did not use the gun, then how would he do it, he wondered. Could he stand the feeling of cartilage and bone snapping and crackling under his fingers, could he hold the blade of knife into her flat hard belly and feel her fight it like a marlin fights the gleaming curved hook of the gaff?

The telephone on the bar buzzed, and the secretary picked it up on the second ring. He murmured into it.

'*Oui, oui. D'accord.*' And hung up. 'Ma Baronne, the aircraft is refuelled and ready to depart.'

'We will leave immediately,' she told him, and then to Peter, 'I am sorry.'

'When will I see you?' he asked.

She shrugged, and a little shadow passed over her eyes. 'It is difficult. I am not sure – I will telephone you. But now I must go, Peter. Adieu, my darling.'

When she had gone, Peter stood at the windows overlooking the airfield. It was a glorious spring afternoon, the early marguerites were blooming wild along the grassy verges of the main runways, like scattered gold sovereigns, and a flock of black birds hopped amongst them, probing and picking for insects, completely undisturbed by the jet shriek of a departing Swissair flight.

Peter ran his mind swiftly over the meeting. Carefully

identifying and isolating the exact moment when she had changed. When she had ceased to be Magda Altmann and become Caliph.

There was no doubt left now. Had there ever been, he wondered, or had it merely been his wish to find doubt?

Now he must harden himself to the act. It would be difficult, much more difficult than he had believed possible. Not once had they been alone, he realized then – always the two grey wolves had hovered around them. It was just another sign of her new wariness. He wondered if they would ever be alone together again – now that she was alerted.

Then abruptly he realized that she had not said 'Au revoir, my darling' but instead she had said 'Adieu, my darling'.

Was there a warning in that? A subtle hint of death – for if Caliph suspected him, he knew what her immediate reaction must be. Was she threatening, or had she merely discarded him, as Kingston Parker had warned that she would?

He could not understand the desolate feeling that swamped him at the thought that he might never see her again – except through the gunsight.

He stood staring out of the window, wondering how his career and his life had begun to disintegrate about him since first he had heard the name Caliph.

A polite voice at his shoulder startled him and he turned to the airport sub-manager. 'They are calling the KLM flight to Brussels now, General Stride.'

Peter roused himself with a sigh and picked up his overcoat and the crocodile skin Hermes briefcase that had been a gift from the woman he must kill.

There was such a volume of correspondence and urgent business piling the long desk in his new office that Peter had an excuse to put aside the detailed planning of the pre-emptive strike against Caliph.

To his mild surprise he found himself enjoying the jostle and haggle, the driving pace and the challenge of the market place. He enjoyed pitting wits and judgement against other sharp and pointed minds, he enjoyed the human interaction – and for the first time understood the fascination which this type of life had exerted over his brother Steven.

Three days after arriving back at his desk, the Iranian Air Force made their first order of the Narmco Kestrel missiles. One hundred and twenty units, over a hundred and fifty million dollars' worth. It was a good feeling, and could grow stronger, could finally become addictive, he realized.

He had always looked upon money as rather a nuisance, those degrading and boring sessions with bank managers and clerks of the income tax department, but now he realized that this was a different kind of money. He had glimpsed the world in which Caliph existed, and realized how once a human being became accustomed to manipulating this kind of money, then dreams of godlike power became believable, capable of being transmuted into reality.

He could understand, but could never forgive, and so at last, seven days after his return to Brussels, he forced himself to face up to what he must do.

Magda Altmann had withdrawn. She had made no further contact since that brief and unsatisfactory hour at Orly Airport.

He must go to her, he realized. He had lost his special inside position which would have made the task easier.

He could still get close enough to kill her, of that he was certain. Just as he had the opportunity to do so at Orly. However, if he did it that way it would be suicidal. If he survived the swift retribution of her guards, there would be the slower but inexorable processes of the law. He knew without bothering to consider it too deeply that he would be unable to use the defence of the Caliph story. No court would believe it. It would sound like the rantings of a maniac without the support of Atlas or the Intelligence systems of America and Britain. That support would not be forthcoming – of that he was certain. If he killed Caliph they would be delighted, but they would let him go to the guillotine without raising a voice in his defence. He could imagine the moral indignation of the civilized world if they believed that an unorthodox organization such as Atlas was employing assassins to murder the prominent citizens of a foreign and friendly nation.

No. He was on his own, completely. Parker had made that quite clear. And Peter realized that he did not want to die. He was not prepared to sacrifice his life to stop Caliph – not unless there was no other way. There had to be another way, of course.

As he planned it he thought of the victim only as Caliph – never as Magda Altmann. That way he was able to bring a cold detachment to the problem. The where, the when, and the how of it.

He had complicated the task by replanning her personal security, and his major concern when he did so had been to make her movements as unpredictable as possible. Her social calendar was as closely guarded as a secret of state, there were never any forward press reports of attendance at public or state events.

If she were invited to dine at the Élysée Palace, the fact was reported the day after, not the day before – but there were some annual events that she would never miss. Together they had discussed these weaknesses in her personal security.

'Oh, Peter – you cannot make a convict of me.' She had laughed in protest when he mentioned them. 'I have so few real pleasures – you would not take them from me, would you?'

The first seasonal showing of Yves St Laurent's collections, that she would never miss – or the Grande Semaine of the spring racing season which culminates with the running of the Grand Prix de Paris at Longchamp. This year she had high hopes of victory with her lovely and courageous bay mare, Ice Leopard. She would be there. It was absolutely certain.

Peter began to draw up the list of possible killing grounds, and then crossed off all but the most likely. The estate at La Pierre Bénite, for instance. It had the advantage of being familiar ground for Peter. With a soldier's eye he had noticed fields of fire across the wide terraced lawns that dropped down to the lake; there were stances for a sniper in the forests along the far edge of the lake, and in the little wooded knoll to the north of the house which commanded the yard and stables. However, the estate was well guarded and even there the victim's movements were unpredictable. It would be possible to lie in ambush for the week when she was in Rome or New York. Then again the escape route was highly risky, through a sparsely populated area with only two access roads – both easily blocked by swift police action. No, La Pierre Bénite was crossed from the list.

In the end Peter was left with the two venues that had first sprung to mind – the members' enclosure at Longchamp or Yves St Laurent's premises, at 46 Avenue Victor Hugo.

Both had the advantages of being public and crowded, circumstances favouring pickpockets and assassins, Peter thought wryly. Both had multiple escape routes, and crowds into which the fugitive could blend. There were good stances for a sniper in the grandstands and buildings overlooking the members' enclosure and the saddling paddock at Longchamp or in the multi-storied buildings opposite No 46 in Avenue Victor Hugo.

It would probably be necessary to rent an office suite in one of the buildings – with the attendant risks, even if he used a false name, which put the probability slightly in favour of the racecourse. However, Peter delayed the final decision until he had a chance to inspect each site critically.

There was one last advantage in doing it this way. It would be a stand-off kill. He would be spared the harrowing moments of a kill at close range, with handgun or knife or garrotte.

There would be the detached view of Caliph through the lens of a telescopic sight. The flattened perspectives and the altered colour balances always made for a feeling of unreality. The intervening distance obviated the need for confrontation. He would never have to watch the green light go out in those magnificent eyes, nor hear the last exhalation of breath through the soft and perfectly sculptured lips that had given him so much joy – quickly he thrust those thoughts aside. They weakened his resolve, even though the rage and the lust for vengeance had not abated.

If he could get one of the Thor .222 sniper rifles it would be the perfect tool for this task. With the extra long, accurized barrels designed for use with match grade ammunition and the new laser sights, the weapon could throw a three-inch group at seven hundred yards.

The sniper had only to depress the button on the top of the stock with the forefinger of his left hand. This activated the laser and the beam swept precisely down the projected flight of the bullet. It would show as a bright white coin the size of a silver dime. The sniper looked for the spot of light through the telescopic lens of the sight, and the moment it was exactly on the target he pressed the trigger. Even an unskilled marksman could hardly miss with this sight, in Peter's hands it would be infallible – and Colin Noble would give him one. Not only would Colin give him one, hell, he would probably have it delivered with the compliments of the American Marine Corps by the senior military attaché of the U.S. Embassy in Paris.

Yet Peter found himself drawing out the moment of action, going over his plans so often and with such a critical eye that he knew he was procrastinating.

The sixteenth day after his return to Brussels was a Friday. Peter spent the morning on the NATO range north of the city at a demonstration of the new electronic shield that Narmco had developed to foil the radar guidance on short-range anti-tank missiles. Then he helicoptered back with the three Iranian officers who had attended the demonstration and they lunched at Épaule de Mouton, a magnificent and leisurely meal. Peter still felt guilty spending three hours at the lunch table, so he worked until eight o'clock that evening, on the missile contracts.

It was long after dark when he left through the rear entrance, taking all his usual precautions against the chance that Caliph had an assassin waiting for him in the dark streets. He never left at the same time nor followed the same route, and this evening he bought the evening papers from a *marchand du tabac* in the Grand'Place and stopped to read them at one of the outdoor cafés overlooking the square.

He began with the English papers, and the headlines filled the page from one side to the other; black and bold, they declared:

DROP IN PRICE OF CRUDE OIL

Peter sipped the whisky thoughtfully as he read the article through, turning to Page Six for the continuation.

Then he crumpled the newsprint in his lap, and stared at the passing jostle of spring tourists and early evening revellers.

Caliph had achieved her first international triumph.

From now on there would be no bounds to her ruthless rampage of power and violence.

Peter knew he could delay no longer. He made the go decision then, and it was irrevocable. He would arrange to visit London on Monday morning, there was excuse enough for that. He would ask Colin to meet him at the airport, and it would be necessary to tell him of his plan. He knew he could expect full support. Then he could move on to Paris for the final reconnaissance and choice of killing ground. There was still two weeks until the showing of the spring collections – two weeks to plan it so carefully that there would be no chance of failure.

He felt suddenly exhausted, as though the effort of decision had required the last of his reserves. So exhausted that the short walk back to the hotel seemed daunting. He ordered another whisky and drank it slowly before he could make the effort.

Narmco maintained two permanent suites at the Hilton for their senior executives and other important visitors. Peter had not yet made the effort of finding private accommodation in the city, and he was living out of the smaller of the two suites. It was merely a place to wash and sleep and leave his clothes, for he could not shake off the feeling of impermanence, of swiftly changing circumstances by which he found himself surrounded.

My books are in storage again, he thought with a little chill of loneliness. His collection of rare and beautiful books had been in storage for the greater part of his life, as he roamed wherever his duty took him, living out of barracks and hotel rooms. His books were his only possessions, and as he thought about them now he was filled with an unaccustomed longing to have a base, a place that was his own – and immediately he thrust it aside, smiling cynically at himself as he strode through the streets of another foreign city, alone again.

It must be old age catching up with me, he decided.

There had never been time for loneliness before – but now, but now? Unaccountably he remembered Magda Altmann coming into his arms and saying quietly:

'Oh, Peter, I have been alone for so long.'

The memory stopped him dead, and he stood in the light of one of the street lamps, a tall figure in a belted trench coat with a gaunt and haunted face.

A blonde girl with lewdly painted lips sauntered towards him down the sidewalk, pausing to murmur a proposition, and it brought Peter back to the present.

'*Merci*.' He shook his head in curt refusal and walked on.

As he passed the bookstall in the lobby of the Hilton, a rack of magazines caught his attention and he stopped at the shelf of women's magazines. There would be announcements of the Paris haute couture showings soon, and he thumbed the pages of *Vogue* looking for mention of Yves St Laurent's show – instead he was shocked by the image of a woman's face that leapt out of the page at him.

The elegant cheekbone structure framing the huge slanted Slavic eyes. The shimmering fall of dark hair, the feline grace of movement frozen by the camera flash.

In the photograph she was in a group of four people. The other woman was the estranged wife of a pop singer, the sulky expression, slightly skew eyes and bee-stung lips a landmark on the Parisian social scene. Her partner was a freckled, boyish-faced American actor in a laid-back velvet suit with gold chains around his throat, more famous for his sexual exploits than his film roles. They were not the type of persons with whom Magda Altmann habitually associated, but the man beside her, on whose arm she leaned lightly, was much more her style. He was fortyish, dark and handsome in a fleshy heavily built way, with dense wavy hair, and he exuded the special aura of power and confidence that befitted the head of the biggest German automobile manufacturing complex.

The caption below the photograph had them attending

the opening of an exclusive new Parisian discotheque – again this was not Magda Altmann's habitual territory, but she was smiling brilliantly at the tall handsome German, so obviously enjoying herself that Peter felt a stinging shaft of emotion thrust up under his ribs. Hatred or jealousy – he was not certain – and he slapped the magazine closed and returned it to its rack.

In the impersonal antiseptically furnished suite he stripped and showered, and then standing naked in the small lounge of the suite he poured himself a whisky. It was his third that evening.

Since the kidnapping he had been drinking more than ever before in his life, he realized. It could exert an insidious hold when a man was lonely and in grave doubt. He would have to begin watching it. He took a sip of the smoky amber liquid and turned to look at himself in the mirror across the room.

Since he had been back in Brussels, he had worked out each day in the gymnasium at the NATO officers' club where he still had membership, and his body was lean and hard with a belly like a greyhound's – only the face was ravaged by strain and worry – and, it seemed, by some deep unutterable regret.

He turned back towards the bedroom of the suite, and the telephone rang.

'Stride,' he said into the mouthpiece, standing still naked with the glass in his right hand.

'Please hold on, General Stride. We have an international call for you.'

The delay seemed interminable with heavy buzzing and clicking on the line, and the distant voices of other operators speaking bad French or even worse English.

Then suddenly her voice, but faint and so far away that it sounded like a whisper in a vast and empty hall.

'Peter, are you there?'

'Magda?' He felt the shock of it, and his voice echoed

back at him from the receiver; there was the click before she spoke again, that switch of carrier wave that told him they were on a radio telephone link.

'I have to see you, Peter. I cannot go on like this. Will you come to me, please, Peter?'

'Where are you?'

'Les Neuf Poissons.' Her voice was so faint, so distorted, that he asked her to repeat it.

'Les Neuf Poissons – The Nine Fishes,' she repeated. 'Will you come, Peter?'

'Are you crying?' he demanded, and the silence echoed and clicked and hummed so he thought they had lost contact, and he felt a flare of alarm so his voice was harsh as he asked again. 'Are you crying?'

'Yes.' It was only a breath, he might have imagined it.

'Why?'

'Because I am sad and frightened, Peter. Because I am alone, Peter. Will you come, please will you come?'

'Yes,' he said. 'How do I get there?'

'Ring Gaston at La Pierre Bénite. He will arrange it. But come quickly, Peter. As quickly as you can.'

'Yes. As soon as I can – but where is it?'

He waited for her reply, but now the distances of the ether echoed with the sound of utter finality.

'Magda? Magda?' He found himself shouting desperately, but the silence taunted him and reluctantly he pressed a finger down on the cradle of the telephone.

'Les Neuf Poissons,' he repeated softly, and lifted the finger. 'Operator,' he said, 'please get me a call to France Rambouillet 47–87–47.' And while he waited he was thinking swiftly.

This was what he had been subconsciously waiting for, he realized. There was a feeling of inevitability to it, the wheel could only turn – it could not roll sideways. This was what had to happen.

Caliph had no alternative. This was the summons to

execution. He was only surprised that it had not come sooner. He would see why Caliph would have avoided the attempt in the cities of Europe or England. One such attempt well planned and executed with great force had failed that night on the road to Rambouillet. It would have been a warning to Caliph not to underestimate the victim's ability to retaliate – for the rest, the problems would have been almost the same as those that Peter had faced when planning the strike against Caliph herself.

The when and the where and the how – and Caliph had the edge here. She could summon him to the selected place – but how incredibly skilfully it had been done. As he waited for the call to Rambouillet, Peter marvelled at the woman afresh. There seemed no bottom to her well of talent and accomplishments – despite himself, knowing full well that he was listening to a carefully rehearsed act, despite the fact that he knew her to be a ruthless and merciless killer, yet his heart had twisted at the tones of despair in her voice, the muffled weeping perfectly done, so he had only just been able to identify it.

'This is the residence of Baroness Altmann.'

'Gaston?'

'Speaking, sir.'

'General Stride.'

'Good evening, General. I was expecting your call. I spoke to the Baroness earlier. She asked me to arrange your passage to Les Neuf Poissons. I have done so.'

'Where is it, Gaston?'

'Les Neuf Poissons – it's the Baroness's holiday island in the Îles sous le Vent – it is necessary to take the UTA flight to Papeete-Faaa on Tahiti where the Baroness's pilot will meet you. It's another hundred miles to Les Neuf Poissons and unfortunately the airstrip is too short to accommodate the Lear jet – one has to use a smaller aircraft.'

'When did the Baroness go to Les Neuf Poissons?'

'She left seven days ago, General,' Gaston answered, and

immediately went on in the smooth, efficient secretarial voice to give Peter the details of the UTA flight. ' – The ticket will be held at the UTA check-in counter for you, General, and I have reserved a non-smoking seat at the window.'

'You think of everything. Thank you, Gaston.'

Peter replaced the receiver, and found that his earlier exhaustion had left him – he felt vital and charged with new energy. The elation of a trained soldier facing the prospect of violent action, he wondered, or was it merely the prospect of an end to the indecision and the fear of unknown things? Soon, for good or for evil, it would be settled and he welcomed that.

He went through into the bathroom and pitched the whisky that remained in his glass into the handbasin.

The UTA DC 10 made its final approach to Tahiti-Faaa from the east, slanting down the sky with the jagged peaks of Moorea under the port wing. Peter remembered the spectacularly riven mountains of Tahiti's tiny satellite island as the backdrop of the musical movie *South Pacific* that had been filmed on location here. The volcanic rock was black and unweathered so that its crests were as sharp as sharks' fangs.

They arrowed down across the narrow channel between the two islands, and the runway seemed to reach out an arm into the sea to welcome the big silver machine.

The air was heavy and warm and redolent with the perfume of frangipani blossoms, and there were luscious brown girls swinging and swaying gracefully in a dance of welcome. The islands reached out with almost overpowering sweetness and friendliness – but as Peter picked his single light bag out of the hold luggage and started for the exit doors, something unusual happened. One of the Polynesian customs officers at the gate exchanged a quick word with his companion and then politely stepped into Peter's path.

'Good afternoon, sir.' The smile was big and friendly, but it did not stretch as far as the eyes. 'Would you be kind enough to step this way.' The two customs men escorted Peter into the tiny screened office.

'Please open your bags, sir.' Swiftly but thoroughly they went through his valise and crocodile-skin briefcase; one of them even used a measuring stick to check both cases for a hidden compartment.

'I must congratulate you on your efficiency,' said Peter, smiling also, but his voice tight and low.

'A random check, sir.' The senior officer answered his smile. 'You were just unlucky to be the ten thousandth visitor. Now, sir, I hope you won't object to a body search?'

'A body search?' Peter snapped, and would have protested further, but instead he shrugged and raised both arms. 'Go ahead.'

He could imagine that Magda Altmann was as much the Grande Dame here as she was in mother France. She owned the entire island group, and it would need only a nod to have an incoming visitor thoroughly searched for weapons of any sort.

He could imagine also that Caliph would be very concerned that the intended victim should be suitably prepared for execution, lest he should inadvertently become the executioner.

The one customs officer checked his arms and flanks from armpit to waist, while the other knelt behind him and checked inside the outside of his legs from crotch to ankle.

Peter had left the Cobra in the safe deposit box in the Hilton in Brussels. He had anticipated something like this, it was the way Caliph would work.

'Satisfied?' he asked.

'Thank you for your co-operation, sir. Have a lovely stay on our island.'

Magda's personal pilot was waiting for Peter in the main concourse, and hurried forward to shake his hand.

'I was worried that you were not on the flight.'

'A small delay in customs,' Peter explained.

'We should leave immediately, if we are to avoid a night landing on Les Neuf Poissons – the strip is a little difficult.'

Magda's Gates Lear was parked on the hardstand near the service area, and beside it the Norman Britten Tri-Islander looked small and ungainly, a stork-like ugly aircraft capable of the most amazing performance in short take-off and landing situations.

The body of the machine was already loaded with crates and cartons of supplies, everything from toilet rolls to Veuve Cliquot champagne, all tied down under a wide-meshed nylon net.

Peter took the right-hand seat, and the pilot started up and cleared with control, then to Peter:

'One hour's flying. We will just make it.'

The setting sun was behind them as they came in from the west and Les Neuf Poissons lay like a precious necklace of emeralds upon the blue velvet cushion of the ocean.

There were nine islands in the characteristic circular pattern of volcanic formation, and they enclosed a lagoon of water so limpid that every whorl and twist of the coral outcrops showed through as clearly as if they were in air.

'The islands had a Polynesian name when the Baron purchased them back in 1945,' the pilot explained in the clearly articulated rather pedantic French of the Midi. 'They were given by one of the old kings as a gift to a missionary he favoured and the Baron purchased them from his widow. The Baron could not pronounce the Polynesian name so he changed it—' The pilot chuckled. ' – The Baron was a man who faced the world on his own terms.'

Seven of the islands were merely strips of sand and fringes of palms, but the two to the east were larger with hills of volcanic basalt glittering like the skin of a great reptile in the rays of the lowering sun.

As they turned onto their downwind leg, Peter had a view through the window at his elbow of a central building with its roof of palm thatch elegantly curved like the prow of a ship in the tradition of the islands, and around it half-hidden in luscious green gardens were other smaller bungalows. Then they were over the lagoon and there were a clutter of small vessels around the long jetty which reached out into the protected waters – Hobie-cats with bare masts, a big powered schooner which was probably used to ship the heavy stores such as dieseline down from Papeete, power boats for skiing and diving and fishing. One of them was out in the middle of the lagoon, tearing a snowy ostrich feather of wake from the surface as it ran at speed; a tiny figure towed on skis behind it lifted an arm and waved a greeting. Peter thought it might be her, but at that moment the Tri-Islander banked steeply onto its base leg and he was left with only a view of cumulus cloud bloodied by the setting sun.

The runway was short and narrow, hacked from the palm plantation on the strip of level land between beach and hills. It was surfaced with crushed coral. They made their final approach over a tall palisade of palm trees. Peter saw that the pilot had not exaggerated by calling it a little difficult. There was a spiteful crosswind rolling in and breaking over the hills and it rocked the Tri-Islander's wings sickeningly. The pilot crabbed her in, heading half into the wind, and as he skimmed in over the palm tops, closed the throttles, kicked her straight with the rudders, lowered a wing into the wind to hold her from drifting and dropped her neatly fifty feet over the threshold, perfectly aligned with the short runway so she kissed and sat down solidly; instantly the pilot whipped the wheel to full lock into the crosswind to prevent a ground loop and brought her up short.

'*Parfait!*' Peter grunted with involuntary admiration, and the man looked slightly startled as though the feat deserved no special mention. Baroness Altmann employed only the very best.

There was an electric golf cart driven by a young Polynesian girl waiting at the end of the strip amongst the palm trees. She wore only a pareo wrapped around her body below the armpits, a single length of crimson and gold patterned cloth that fell to mid thigh. Her feet were bare, but around her pretty head she wore a crown of fresh flowers – the maeva of the islands.

She drove the golf cart at a furious pace along narrow winding tracks through the gardens that were a rare collection of exotic plants, skilfully laid out, so that there was an exquisite surprise around each turn of the path.

His bungalow was above the beach with white sand below the verandah and the ocean stretching to the horizon, secluded as though it were the only building on the island. Like a child the island girl took his hand, a gesture of perfect innocence, and led him through the bungalow, showing him the controls for the air-conditioning, lighting and the video screen, explaining it all in lisping French patois, and giggling at his expression of pleasure.

There was a fully stocked bar and kitchenette, the small library contained all the current best-sellers, and the newspapers and magazines were only a few days old. The offerings on the video screen included half a dozen recent successful features and Oscar winners.

'Hell, Robinson Crusoe should have landed here,' Peter chuckled, and the girl giggled and wriggled like a friendly little puppy in sympathy.

She came to fetch him again two hours later, after he had showered and shaved and rested and changed into a light cotton tropical suit with open shirt and sandals.

Again she held his hand and Peter sensed that if a man had taken the gesture as licence the girl would have been hurt and confused. By the hand she led him along a path that was demarcated by cunningly concealed glow lights, and the night was filled with the murmur of the ocean and the gentle rustle and clatter of palm fronds moving in the wind.

Then they came to the long ship-roofed building he had seen from the air. There was soft music and laughter, but when he stepped into the light the laughter stopped and half a dozen figures turned to him expectantly.

Peter was not sure what he had expected, but it was not this gay, social gathering, tanned men and women in expensive and elegant casual wear, holding tall frosted glasses filled with ice and fruit.

'Peter!' Magda Altmann broke from the group, and came to him with that gliding hip-swinging walk.

She wore a soft, shimmering, wheaten-gold dress, held high at the throat with a thin gold chain, but completely nude across the shoulders and down her back to within an inch of the cleft of her buttocks. It was breathtaking for her body was smooth as a rose petal and tanned to the colour of new honey. The dark hair was twisted into a rope as thick as her wrist and piled up onto the top of her head, and she had touched her eyes with shadows so they were slanting and green and mysterious.

'Peter,' she repeated, and kissed him lightly upon the lips, a brush like a moth's wing, and her perfume touched him as softly, the fragrance of Quadrille flowering with the warmth and magic of her body.

He felt his senses tilt. With all he knew of her, yet he was still not hardened to her physical presence.

She was cool and groomed and poised as she had ever been, there was no trace at all of the confusion and fearsome loneliness that he had heard in those muffled choked-down sobs from halfway across the world – not until she stepped back to tilt her head on one side, surveying him swiftly, smiling lightly.

'Oh, *chéri*, you are looking so much better. I was so worried about you when last I saw you.'

Only then he thought he was able to detect the shadows deep in her eyes, and the tightness at the corners of her mouth.

'And you are more beautiful than I remembered.'

It was true, so he could say it without reserve, and she laughed, a single soft purr of pleasure.

'You never said that before,' she reminded him, but still her manner was brittle. Her show of affection and friendliness might have convinced him at another time, but not now. 'And I am grateful.'

Now she took his arm, her fingers in the crook of his elbow, and she led him to the waiting group of guests as though she did not trust herself to be alone with him another moment lest she reveal some forbidden part of herself.

There were three men and their wives: an American Democrat senator of considerable political influence, a man with a magnificent head of silver hair, eyes like dead oysters, and a beautiful wife at least thirty years his junior who looked at Peter the way a lion looks at a gazelle and held his hand seconds longer than was necessary.

There was an Australian, heavy in the shoulder and big in the gut. His skin was tanned leathery and his eyes were framed in a network of wrinkles. They seemed to be staring through dust and sun glare at distant horizons. He owned a quarter of the world's known uranium reserves, and cattle stations whose area was twice the size of the British Isles. His wife was as tanned and her handshake was as firm as his.

The third man was a Spaniard whose family name was synonymous with sherry, an urbane and courtly Don, but with that fierce Moorish rake to his thin features. Peter had read somewhere that the sherry and cognac ageing in this man's cellars was valued at over five hundred million dollars, and that formed only a small part of his family's investments. His wife was a darkly brooding Spanish beauty with an extraordinary streak of chalk white through the peak of her otherwise black hair.

As soon as the group had assimilated Peter, the talk turned back easily to the day's sport. The Australian had boated a huge black marlin that morning, a fish over one thousand pounds in weight and fifteen feet from the point of its bill to the tip of its deep sickle tail, and the company was elated.

Peter took little part in the conversation, but watched Magda Altmann covertly. Yet she was fully aware of his scrutiny; he could see it in the way she held her hand, and the tension in her whole long slim body, but she laughed easily with the others and glanced at Peter only once or twice, each time with a smile, but the shadows were in the green depths of her eyes.

Finally she clapped her hands. 'Come, everybody, we are going to open the feast.' She linked arms with the senator and the Australian and led them down onto the beach. Peter was left to cope with the senator's wife, and pushed her bosom against his upper arm and ran her tongue lightly over her lips as she clung to him.

Two of the Polynesian servants were waiting beside a long mound of white beach sand, and at Magda's signal they attacked it with shovels, swiftly exposing a thick layer of seaweed and banana leaves from which poured columns of thick and fragrant steam. Below that was a rack of banyan wood and palm fronds which suspended the feast over another layer of seaweed and live coals.

There were exclamations of delight as the aroma of chicken and fish and pork mingled with those of breadfruit and plantains and spices.

'Ah, a success,' Magda declared gaily. 'If any air is allowed to enter the bake we lose it all. It burns, poof! And we are left with only charcoal.'

While they feasted and drank the talk and laughter became louder and less restrained, but Peter made the single drink last the evening and waited quietly – not joining the conversation and ignoring the blandishments of the senator's wife.

He was waiting for some indication of when and from what direction it would come. Not here, he knew, not in this company. When it came it would be swift and efficient as everything else that Caliph did. And suddenly he wondered at his own conceit, that had allowed him to walk, entirely unarmed and unsupported, into the arena selected and prepared by his enemy. He knew his best defencc was to strike first, perhaps this very night if the opportunity offered. The sooner the safer, he realized, and Magda smiled at him across the table set under the palm trees and laden with enough food to feed fifty. When he smiled back at her, she beckoned with a slight inclination of her head, and then while the men argued and bantered loudly, she murmured an apology to the women and slipped unobtrusively into the shadows.

Peter gave her a count of fifty before he followed her. She was waiting along the beach. He saw the flash of her bare smooth back in the moonlight and he went forward to where she stood staring out across the wind-ruffled waters of the lagoon.

He came up behind her, and she did not turn her head but her voice was a whisper.

'I am so glad you came, Peter.'

'I am so glad you asked me to.'

He touched the back of her neck, just behind her ear. The ear had an almost elfin point to it that he had not noticed before and the unswept hair at her nape was silken under his fingertips. He could just locate the axis, that delicate bone at the base of the skull which the hangman aims to crush with the drop. He could do it with the pressure of thumb and it would be as quick as the knot.

'I am so sorry about the others,' she said. 'But I am getting rid of them – with almost indecent haste, I'm afraid.' She reached up over her shoulder and took his hand from her neck, and he did not resist. Gently she spread the hand, and then pressed the open palm to her cheek. 'They will leave early tomorrow. Pierre is flying them back to Papeete, and then we will have Les Neuf Poissons to ourselves – just you and I—' And then that husky little chuckle.' – And thirty-odd servants.'

He could understand exactly why it would be that way. The only witnesses would be the faithful retainers of the Grande Dame of the islands.

'Now we must go back. Unfortunately my guests are very important, and I cannot ignore them longer – but tomorrow will come. Too slowly for me, Peter – but it will come.'

She turned in the circle of his arms and kissed him with a sudden startling ferocity, so his lips were crushed against his teeth, and then she broke from him and whispered close to his ear.

'Whatever way it goes, Peter, we have had something of value, you and I. Perhaps the most precious thing I have had in my life. They can never take that away from me.'

And then she was out of his arms with that uncanny speed and grace of movement and gliding back along the path towards the lights. He followed her slowly, confused and uncertain as to what she had meant by those last words, concluding finally that the purpose had been exactly that – to confuse and unbalance him, and at that moment he sensed rather than heard movement behind him, and instantly whirled and ducked.

The man was ten paces behind him, had come like a leopard, silently from the cover of a fall of lianas and flowering creepers beside the path; only some animal instinct had warned Peter – and his body flowed into the fighting stance, balanced, strung like a nocked arrow, at once ready both to attack and meet attack.

'Good evening, General Stride.' Peter only just managed to arrest himself, and he straightened slowly but with each hand still extended stiffly at his side like the blade of a meat cleaver, and as lethal.

'Carl!' he said. So the grey wolves had been close, within feet of them, guarding their mistress even in that intimate moment.

'I hope I did not alarm you,' said the bodyguard – and though Peter could not see the man's expression, there was a faint mockery in his voice. If there was confirmation needed, complete and final, this was it. Only Caliph would have need of a guard on a romantic assignment. Peter knew then beyond any doubt that either he or Magda Altmann would be dead by sunset the following evening.

Before going into the bungalow he made a stealthy prowling circuit of the bushes and shrubs that surrounded it. He found nothing suspicious but in the interior the bed had been prepared and his shaving gear cleaned and neatly rearranged. His soiled clothing had been taken for cleaning and the other clothing had been pressed and rearranged more neatly than his own unpacking. He could not therefore be certain that his other possessions had not been searched, but it was safe to presume they had. Caliph would not neglect such an elementary precaution.

The locks on doors and windows were inadequate, had probably not been used in years, for there had been no serpents in this paradise, not until recently. So he placed chairs and other obstacles in such a way that an intruder should stumble over them in the dark, and then he rumpled the bed and arranged the pillows to look like a sleeping figure, but took a single blanket to the long couch in the private lounge. He did not really expect an attempt before the other guests left the island, but if it came he would confuse Caliph's scenario as much as possible.

He slept fitfully, jerking awake when a falling palm frond rattled across the roof, or the moon threw picture shadows on the wall across the room. Just before dawn he fell into a deeper sleep and his dreams were distorted and nonsensical, only the sharp clear image of Melissa-Jane's terror-stricken face and her silent screams of horror remained with him when he woke. The memory roused in him the cold lust for vengeance which had abated a little in the weeks since her rescue, and he felt reaffirmed, possessed of a steely purpose once more, determined to resist the softening, fatal allure of Caliph.

He rose in the slippery pearl light of not yet dawn, and went down to the beach. He swam out a mile beyond the reef, and had a long pull back against a rogue current, but he came ashore feeling good and hard and alert as he had not been in weeks.

All right, he thought grimly. Let it come. I'm as ready as I'll ever be.

There was a farewell breakfast for the departing guests, on the sugary sands of the beach that had been swept smooth by the night tide – pink Laurent Perrier champagne and hothouse strawberries flown in from Auckland, New Zealand.

Magda Altmann wore brief green pants that showed off her long shapely legs to perfection, and a matching 'boob tube' across her small neat breasts – but her belly and shoulders and back were bare. It was the body of a finely trained athlete, but drawn by a great artist.

She seemed unnaturally elated to Peter, her gaiety was slightly forced and the low purring laughter just a little too ready – and with a saw-edge to it. It was almost as though she had made some hard decision, and was steeling herself to carry it through. Peter thought of them as true opponents who had trained carefully for the coming configuration – like prize fighters at the weigh-in.

After the breakfast they rode up in a cavalcade of electric carts to the airfield. The senator, revved-up with pink champagne and sweating lightly in the rising heat, gave Magda an over-affectionate farewell, but she skilfully avoided his hands and shunted him expertly into the Tri-Islander after the other passengers.

Pierre, Magda's pilot, stood on the brakes at the end of the runway while he ran all three engines up to full power. Then he let her go, and the moment she had speed he rotated her into a nose-high obstacle-clearance attitude. The ungainly machine jumped into the sky and went over the palms at the end of the short strip with five hundred feet to spare – and Magda turned to Peter ecstatically.

'I hardly slept last night,' she admitted, as she kissed him.

'Neither did I,' Peter told her – and then he added silently ' – for the same reasons, I'm sure.'

'I've planned a special day for us,' she went on. 'And I don't want to waste another minute of it.'

The head boatman had Magda's big forty-five-foot Chris-craft Fisherman singled up at the end of the jetty. It was a beautiful boat, with long low attacking lines that made it seem to be flying even when on its mooring lines, and loving care had very obviously been lavished upon it. The paintwork was unmarked and the stainless steel fittings were polished to a mirror finish. The boatman beamed happily when Magda commended him with a smile and a word.

'Tanks are full, Baronne. The scuba bottles are charged and the light rods are rigged. The water-skis are in the main racks, and the chef came down himself to check the ice-box.'

However, his wide white smile faded when he learned that Magda was taking the boat out alone.

'Don't you trust me?' she laughed.

'Oh, of course, Baronne—' But he could not hide his

chagrin at having to give over his charge – even to such a distinguished captain.

He handled the lines himself, casting her off, and calling anxious last-minute advice to Magda as the gap between jetty and vessel opened.

'*Ne t'inquiet pas*!' she laughed at him, but he made a dejected figure standing on the end of the jetty as Magda slowly opened up both diesels and the Chris-craft came up on the plane and seemed almost to break free of the surface. Her wake was scored deep and clean and straight through the gin-clear water of the lagoon, a tribute to the design of her hull, and then it curved out gracefully behind them as Magda made the turn between the channel markers and lined her up for the passage through the reef, and out into the open Pacific.

'Where are we going?'

'There is an old Japanese aircraft carrier lying in a hundred feet of water beyond the reef. Yankee aircraft sank her back in 'forty-four – It is a beautiful site for scuba diving. We will go there first—'

How? Peter wondered. Perhaps one of the scuba bottles had been partially filled with carbon monoxide gas. It was simply done, with a hose from the exhaust of the diesel generator: simply pass the exhaust gases through a charcoal filter to remove the taste and smell of unconsumed hydrocarbons and the remaining carbon monoxide gas would be undetectable. Fill the bottle to 30 atmospheres of pressure then top it up with clean air to its operating pressure of 110 atmospheres. It would be swift, but not too swift to alarm the victim, a gentle long sleep. When the victim lost his mouthpiece, the bottles would purge themselves of any trace of the gas. That would be a good way to do it.

'After that we can go ashore on Île des Oiseaux. Since Aaron stopped the islanders stealing the eggs to eat, we've got one of the biggest nesting colonies of terns and noddies and frigate birds in the Southern Pacific—'

Perhaps a speargun. That would be direct and effective. At short range, say two feet, even below the surface, the spear arrow would go right through a human torso – in between the shoulder blades and out through the breast bone.

'– And afterwards we can water-ski—'

With an unsuspecting skier in the water, awaiting the pick-up, what could be more effective than opening up both those tremendously powerful diesels to the gates and running the victim down? If the hull did not crush him, the twin screws turning at 500 revolutions per minute would cut him up as neatly as a loaf of pre-sliced bread.

Peter found himself intrigued with the guessing-game. He found himself regretting the fact that he would never know what she intended, and he looked back from where they stood side by side on the tall flying bridge of the Chris-craft. The main island was lowering itself into the water; already they were out of sight of anybody who did not have a pair of powerful binoculars.

Beside him Magda pulled the retaining ribbon out of her hair, and shook loose a black rippling banner that streamed in the wind behind her.

'Let's do this for ever,' she shouted above the wind and the boom of the engines.

'Sold to the lady with the sexy backside,' Peter shouted back, and he had to remind himself that she was one of the most carefully trained killers he would ever meet. He must not allow himself to be lulled by the laughter and the beauty – and he must not allow her to make the first stroke. His chances of surviving that were remote.

He glanced back again at the land. Any minute now, he thought, and moved as though to glance over the side, getting slightly into her rear, but still in the periphery of her vision; she shifted slightly towards him still smiling.

'At this state of the tide there are always amberjack in the channel. I promised the chef I would bring him a couple of them kicking fresh,' she explained. 'Won't you go down and get two of the light rods ready, *chéri*? The feather lures are in the forward starboard seat locker.'

'Okay,' he nodded.

'I'll throttle back to trolling speed when I make the turn into the channel – put the lines in then.'

'*D'accord.*' And then on an impulse. 'But kiss me first.'

She held up her face to him, and he wondered why he had said that. It was not to take farewell of her. He was sure of that. It was to lull her just that fraction, and yet as their lips met he felt the deep ache of regret that he had controlled for so long and as her mouth spread slowly and moistly open under his, he felt as though his heart might break then. For a moment he felt that he might die himself before he could do it; dark waves of despair poured over him.

He slid his hand over her shoulder to the nape of her neck and her body flattened against his; he caressed her lightly, feeling for the place, and then settling thumb and forefinger – a second, another second passed, and then she pulled him back softly.

'Hey, now!' she whispered huskily. 'You stop that before I pile up on the reef.'

He had not been able to do it with his bare hands. He just could not do it like that – but he had to do it quickly, very quickly. Every minute delayed now led him deeper and deeper into deadly danger.

'Go!' she ordered, and struck him a playful blow on the chest. 'We've got time for that later – all the time in the world. Let's savour it, every moment of it.'

He had not been able to do it, and he turned away. It was only as he went down the steel ladder into the cockpit of the Chris-craft that it suddenly occurred to him that during the lingering seconds of that kiss the fingers of her right hand had cupped lovingly under his chin. She could have crushed his larynx, paralysing him with a thumb driven up into the soft vulnerable arch of his throat at the first offensive pressure of his thumb and forefinger.

As his feet hit the deck of the cockpit another thought came to him. Her other hand had lain against his body, stroking him softly under the ribs. That hand could have struck upwards and inwards to tear through his diaphragm – his instincts must have warned him. She had been poised for the stroke, more so than he was; she had been inside the circle of his arms, inside his defences, waiting for him – and he shivered briefly in the hot morning sun at the realization of how close he had been to death.

The realization turned instantly to something else, that slid down his spine cold as water down a melting icicle. It was fear, not the crippling fear of the craven, but fear that edged him and hardened him. Next time he would not hesitate – he could not hesitate.

He was instinctively carrying out her instructions as his mind raced to catch up with the problem. He lifted the lid of the seat locker. In the custom-fitted interior were arranged trays of fishing gear, swivels of brass and stainless steel in fifty different sizes; sinkers shaped for every type of water and bottom; lures of plastic and feathers, of enamel and bright metal; hooks for gigantic bill fish or for fry – and in a separate compartment in the side tray a bait knife.

The knife was a fifty-dollar Ninja with a lexan composition handle, chequered and moulded for grip. The blade was seven inches of hollow ground steel, three inches broad at the hilt and tapering to a stiletto point. It was a brutal weapon, you could probably chop through an oak log with it, as the makers advertised. Certainly it would enter human flesh and go through bone as though it were Cheddar cheese.

It balanced beautifully in Peter's fist as he made one testing slash and return cut with it. The blade hissed in the air, and when he tested the edge too hurriedly it stung like a razor and left a thin line of bright blood across the ball of his thumb.

He kicked off his canvas sneakers, so the rubber soles did not squeak on the deck. He was dressed now in only a thin cotton singlet and boxer-type swimming trunks, stripped down for action.

He went up the first three rungs of the ladder on bare silent feet, and lifted his eyes above the level of the flying bridge.

Magda Altmann stood at the controls of the Chris-craft, conning the big vessel into the mouth of the channel, staring ahead in complete concentration.

Her hair still flew in the wind, snaking and tangling into thick shimmering tresses. Her naked back was turned to him, the deeply defined depression running down her spine and the crest of smooth hard muscle rising on each side of it.

One leg of her pants had rucked up slightly exposing a half-moon of round white buttock, and her legs were long and supple as a dancer's as she balanced on the balls of her narrow feet, raising herself to see ahead over the bows.

Peter had been gone from the bridge for less than ten seconds, and she was completely unaware, completely unsuspecting.

Peter did not make the same mistake again; he went up the ladder in a single swift bound, and the bellow of the diesels covered any sound he might have made.

With the knife you never take the chance of the point turning against bone, if you have a choice of target.

Peter picked the small of the back, at the level of the kidneys where there was no bone to protect the body cavity.

It is essential to put the blade in with all possible power; this decreases the chance of bone-deflection and it peaks the paralysing effect of impact-shock.

Peter put the full weight of his rush behind the thrust.

The paralysis is total if the blade is twisted a half-turn at the same instant that the blade socks in hilt-deep.

The muscles in Peter's right forearm were bunched in anticipation of the moment in which he would twist the blade viciously in her flesh, quadrupling the size and the trauma of the wound.

The polished stainless steel fascia of the Chris-craft's control panel reflected a distorted image, like those funny mirrors of the fairground. Only at the moment that Peter had committed himself completely, at the moment when he had thrown all his weight into the killing stroke, did he realize with a sickening flash that she was watching him in the polished steel control panel; she had been watching him from the moment he reappeared at the head of the ladder.

The curved surface of the steel distorted her face, so that it appeared to consist only of two enormous eyes; it distracted him in that thousandth part of a second before the point of the blade entered flesh. He did not see her move.

Blinding, numbing agony shot down his right flank and arm, from a point in the hollow where his collar bone joined the upper arm, while at the same instant something hit him on the inside of his forearm just below the elbow. The knife stroke was flung outwards, passing an inch from her hip, and the point of the blade crashed into the control panel in front of her, scoring the metal with a deep bright scratch, but Peter's numbed fingers could not keep hold on the hilt. The weapon spun from his grip, ringing like a crystal wine glass as it struck the steel handrail and rebounded over the side of the bridge into the cockpit behind him. He realized that she had struck backwards at him, not turning to face him but using only the reflection in the control panel to judge her blow with precision into the pressure point of his shoulder.

Now pain had crippled him and the natural reaction was

to clutch at the source of it. Instead with some reflexive instinct of survival he flung up his left hand to protect the side of his neck and the next blow, also thrown backwards, felt as though it had come from a full-blooded swing of a baseball bat. He hardly saw it, it came so fast and hard there was just the flicker of movement across his vision, like the blur of a hummingbird's wing, and then the appalling force of it crushing into the muscle of his forearm.

Had it taken him in the neck where it was aimed, it would have killed him instantly; instead it paralysed his other arm, and she was turning into him now effortlessly, matching his bull strength with a combination of speed and control.

He knew he must try and keep her close, smother her with his weight and size and strength and he hooked at her with the clawed crippled fingers of his knife hand; they caught for a moment and then she jerked free. He had ripped away the flimsy strip of elasticized cloth that covered her breasts, and she spun lightly under and out of the sweep of his other arm as he tried desperately to club her down with his forearm.

He saw that her face was bone-white with the adrenalin overdose coursing her blood. Her lips were drawn back into a fixed snarl of concentration and fury and her teeth seemed as sharp as those of a female leopard in a trap.

It was like fighting a leopard; she attacked him with an unrelenting savagery and total lack of fear, no longer human, dedicated only to his total destruction.

The long hair swirled about him, at one moment flicking like a whiplash into his eyes to blind and unbalance him, and she weaved and dodged and struck like a mongoose at the cobra, every movement flowing into the next, her taunting red-tipped breasts dancing and jerking with each blow she hurled at him.

With a jar of disbelief, Peter realized that she was beating him down. So far he had managed barely to survive each blow that he caught on arm and shoulder; each time her bare feet crashed into his thigh or lower belly, each time her knees drove for his groin and jarred against the bone of his pelvis, he felt a little more of his strength dissipate, felt his reactions becoming more rubbery, just that instant slower. He had countered her attack with luck and instinct, but any instant she must land solidly and drop him, for she was never still, cutting him with hands and feet, keeping him off balance – and he had not hurt her yet, had not touched her with any of his counter-strokes. Still there was no feeling in his hands and fingers. He needed respite, he needed a weapon, and he thought desperately of the knife that had fallen into the cockpit behind him.

He gave ground to her next attack, and the bridge rail caught him in the small of the back; at the same moment another of her strokes – aimed at the soft of his throat – deflected off his arm and crunched into his nose. Instantly his eyes flooded with tears, and he felt the warm salt flood of blood over his upper lip and down the back of his throat; he doubled over swiftly, then in the same movement he threw himself backwards, like a diver making a one-and-a-half from the three-metre board. The rail behind him helped his turn in the air, and he had judged it finely. He landed like a cat on both feet on the deck of the cockpit ten feet below the bridge, flexing at the knees to absorb the shock, and flicking the tears from his eyes, wringing his arms to return blood and feeling.

As he spun into a crouch he saw the knife. It had slid down the cockpit into the stern scuppers. He went for it.

The dive had taken her by surprise, just as she was poised for the final killing stroke to the back of his exposed neck, but she swirled to the head of the ladder and gathered herself while below her Peter launched himself across the cockpit for the big ugly Ninja knife.

She went for him feet first, dropping from ten feet, and the bare soles of her feet hit him together, the impetus of her falling body enhanced by the stabbing kick that she released at the moment that she hit him.

She caught him high in the back, hurling him forward so that the top of his head cracked into the bulkhead and darkness rustled through his head. He felt his senses going, and it required all of his resolve to roll over and pull his knees swiftly to his chest, to guard himself against the next killing stroke. He caught it on his shins, and once again launched himself after the knife. His fingers felt swollen and clumsy on the rough chequered surface of the hilt, and at the moment they touched he unwound his doubled-up body like a steel coil spring, lashing out with both feet together. It was a blind stroke, delivered in complete desperation.

It was the first solid blow he had landed; it caught her at the moment when she had already launched herself into her next onslaught; both his feet slammed into her belly just below the ribs, and had the flesh there been soft or yielding it would have ended it; but she was just able to absorb the force of it with flat hard muscle – though it hurled her backwards across the cockpit with the breath hissing from her lungs and the long slim body doubling over in an agonized convulsion.

Peter realized that this was the only chance that he had had, and the only one he would ever have – yet his body was racked with such pain that he could hardly drag himself up onto his elbow, and his vision swam and blurred with tears and blood and sweat.

He did not know how he had managed it, some supreme exertion of will, but he was on his feet with the knife in his hand, instinctively extending the blade down the back of his right thigh to keep it protected until the moment it had to be used, crouching as he went in, left arm raised as a shield – and knowing that now he had to end it swiftly, he could not go on longer. This was his last effort.

Then she had a weapon also. Moving so swiftly that it had happened before she was halfway across the cockpit, she had knocked the retaining clip off the boat hook that stood in the rack beside the cabin entrance.

It was eight feet of heavy varnished ash, with an ornate but vicious brass head, and she cut at him with it, a low swinging warning blow to hold him off while she forced air back into her empty lungs.

She was recovering swiftly, much more swiftly than Peter himself. He could see the cold killing light rekindle in her eyes. He knew he could not go on much longer, he must risk it all in one last total effort.

He threw the knife, aiming at her head. The Ninja, not designed as a throwing weapon, rolled out of line of flight, hilt foremost – but still it forced her to lift the staff of the boat hook and deflect it. It was the distraction he had wanted.

Peter used the momentum of his throw to go in under the swinging staff, and he hit her with his shoulder while her arms were raised.

Both of them reeled backwards into the cabin bulkhead, and Peter groped desperately for a grip. He found it in the thick lustrous tresses of her hair, and he wove his fingers into it.

She fought like a dying animal with strength and fury and courage that he could never have believed possible, but now at last he could pit his superior weight and strength directly against hers.

He smothered her against his chest, trapping one arm between their bodies, while he was able to pull her head backwards at an impossible angle, exposing the long smooth curve of her throat.

And then he scissored his thighs across her, so that those lethal feet and legs were unable to reach him, and they crashed over onto the deck.

She managed with an incredible effort to swing her weight so that she landed on top of him, her breasts sliding against his chest, lubricated by sweat and blood that dribbled down from his nose, but Peter heaved all his remaining strength into his shoulders and rolled back on top of her.

They were locked breast to chest and groin to groin in some bizarre parody of the act of love, only the stock of the boat hook between them.

Peter twisted down hard on the rope of hair in his left hand, pinning her head to the deck so that her eyes were only six inches from his and blood from his nose and mouth dripped onto her upturned face.

Neither of them had spoken a word, the only sound the hiss and suck of laboured breathing, the explosive grunt of a blow delivered or the involuntary gasp of pain as it landed.

They glared into each other's eyes, and at that moment neither of them was a human being, they were two animals fighting to the death, and Peter shifted quickly so the stock of the boat hook fell across her unprotected throat. She had not been ready for that and she ducked her chin too late.

Peter knew he could not dare to release his grip on her hair, nor the arm around her body, nor the scissors that enfolded her legs. He could feel the steely tension of her whole body, that required all his own strength to hold. If he relaxed his grip in the slightest, she would twist away, and he would not have the strength to go on after that.

With the elbow of the hand that held her hair, he began to bear down on the ash staff of the boat hook, slowly crushing down into her throat.

She knew it was over then, but still she fought on. As she weakened Peter was able to transfer more and more of his weight onto the stock of the boat hook. Slowly blood suffused her face, turning it dark mottled plum, her lips quivered with each painful rasping breath and a little frothy saliva broke from the corners of her mouth and ran back down her cheek.

Watching her die was the most horrible thing Peter had ever had to do. He shifted cautiously, going for the few extra ounces of weight which would force the heavy wooden stock down that last eighth of an inch and crush in her throat, and she recognized the moment in her eyes.

She spoke for the first time. It was a croak slurred through swollen and gaping lips.

'They warned me.' He thought he had misheard her, and he checked the final thrust downwards which would pinch out the last spark of life. 'I couldn't believe it.' The faintest whisper, only just intelligible. 'Not you.'

Then the last resistance went out of her, her body relaxed, the complete acceptance of death at last. The fierce green light went out in her eyes, replaced at the very end with a sadness so heavy that it seemed to acknowledge the ultimate betrayal of all goodness and trust.

Peter could not force himself to make the final thrust downwards that would end it. He rolled off her and flung the heavy wooden stock across the cockpit. It crashed into the bulkhead and he sobbed as he crawled painfully across the deck, turning his back to her completely, knowing that she was still alive and therefore still as dangerous as she had ever been – yet no longer caring. He had gone as far as he could go. It didn't matter any more if she killed him; something in him even welcomed the prospect of release.

He reached the rail and tried to drag himself onto his feet, expecting at any moment the killing blow into the nape of his neck as she attacked him again.

It did not come, and he managed to get onto his knees, but his whole body was trembling violently so that his teeth chattered in his jaws and every strained and bruised tendon and muscle screamed for surcease. Let her kill me, he thought, it doesn't matter. Nothing matters now.

Half supporting himself on the rail, he turned slowly and his vision swam and flickered with patches of darkness and little shooting stars of crimson and white flame.

Through the swirl of senses at the end of their usefulness,

he saw that she was kneeling in the centre of the cockpit, facing him.

Her naked torso was splattered and smeared with his blood and the smooth tanned skin oiled with slippery sweat of near death. Her face was still and swollen and inflamed, wreathed in a great tangle of matted and disordered hair. There was a flaming livid weal across her throat where the stock had crushed her, and as she fought for breath her small pert breasts lifted and dropped to the painful pumping of her chest.

They stared at each other, far beyond speech, driven to the very frontiers of their existence.

She shook her head, as though trying desperately to deny the horror of it all, and at last she tried to speak; no sound came and she licked her lips and lifted one slim hand to her throat as though to ease the pain of it.

She tried again, and this time she managed one word. 'Why?'

He could not reply for fully half a minute, his own throat seemed to have closed, grown together like an old wound. He knew that he had failed in his duty and yet he could not yet hate himself for it. He formed the words in his own mind, as though he were trying to speak a foreign language, and when he spoke his voice was a stranger's broken and coarsened by the knowledge of failure.

'I couldn't do it,' he said.

She shook her head again, and tried to frame the next question. But she could not articulate it, only one word came out, the same word again.

'Why – ?'

And he had no answer for her.

She stared at him, then slowly her eyes filled with tears; they ran down her cheeks and hung from her chin like early morning dew on the leaf of the vine.

Slowly she pitched forward onto the deck, and for many

seconds he did not have the strength to go to her, and then he lurched across the deck and dropped to his knees beside her; he lifted her upper body in his arms suddenly terrified that he had succeeded after all, that she was dead.

His relief soared above the pain of his battered body as he felt her breathing still sawing through her damaged throat, and as her head lolled against his shoulder he realized that fat oily tears still welled out from between her closed eyelids.

He began to rock her like a child in his arms, a completely useless gesture, and only then did her words begin to make any sense to him.

'They warned me,' she had whispered.

'I couldn't believe it,' she had said.

'Not you.'

He knew then that had she not spoken he would have gone through with it. He would have killed her and weighted her body and dropped it beyond the 1,000-fathom line – but the words, although they did not yet make sense, had reached deep into some recess of his mind.

She stirred against his chest. She said something, it sounded like his name. It roused him to reality. The big Chris-craft was still roaring blindly through the channels and reefs of the outer passage.

He laid her back gently on the deck, and scrambled up the ladder to the flying bridge. The whole of that horrific conflict had taken less than a minute, from his knife-stroke to her collapse under him.

The steering of the Chris-craft was locked into the automatic pilot and the vessel had run straight out through the channel into the open sea. It reinforced his knowledge that she had been ready for his attack. She had been acting that total concentration in steering the vessel, luring him into the attack while the Chris-craft was on automatic pilot and she was ready to throw that backward blow at him.

It did not make sense, not yet. All that he knew was that

he had made some terrible miscalculation. He threw out the switch of the automatic steering, and shut down both throttles to the idle position before disengaging the main drive. The diesels burbled softly, and she rounded up gently into the wind and wallowed beam-on to the short steep blue seas of the open ocean.

Peter took one glance back over the stern. The islands were just a low dark smudge on the horizon, and then he was stumbling back to the ladder.

Magda had dragged herself into a half sitting position, but she recoiled swiftly as he came to her and for the first time he saw fear pass like cloud shadow across her eyes.

'It's all right,' he told her, his own voice still ragged. Her fear offended him deeply. He did not want her ever to be afraid of him again.

He took her up in his arms, and her body was stiff with uncertainty, like that of a cat picked up against its will, but too sick to resist.

'It's all right,' he repeated awkwardly, and carried her down into the saloon of the Chris-craft. His own body felt battered as though his very bones were bruised and cracked, but he handled her so tenderly that slowly the resistance went out of her and she melted against him.

He lowered her onto the leather padded bench, but when he tried to straighten up she slid one arm around his neck and restrained him, clinging to him.

'I left the knife there,' she whispered huskily. 'It was a test.'

'Let me get the medicine chest.' He tried to pull away.

'No.' She shook her head and winced at the pain in her throat. 'Don't go away, Peter. Stay with me. I am so afraid. I was going to kill you if you took the knife. I nearly did. Oh, Peter, what is happening to us, are we both going mad?'

She held him desperately and he sank to his knees on the deck and bowed over her.

'Yes,' he answered her, holding her to his chest. 'Yes, we

must be going mad. I don't understand myself or any of it any more.'

'Why did you have to take the knife, Peter? Please – you must tell me. Don't lie, tell me the truth, I have to know why.'

'Because of Melissa-Jane – because of what you had done to her—'

He felt her jerk in his arms as though he had struck her again. She tried to speak but now her voice was only a croak of despair, and Peter went on to explain it to her.

'When I discovered that you were Caliph, I had to kill you.'

She seemed to be gathering herself for some major effort, but then when she spoke it was still in that scratchy broken whisper.

'Why did you stop yourself, Peter?'

'Because—' He knew the reason then. ' – Because suddenly I knew that I loved you. Nothing else counted.'

She gasped and was silent again for nearly a minute.

'Do you still think that I am Caliph?' she asked at last.

'I don't know. I don't know anything any more – except that I love you. That's all that matters.'

'What happened to us, Peter?' She lamented softly. 'Oh God, what has happened to us?'

'Are you Caliph, Magda?'

'But Peter, you tried to kill me. That was the test with the knife. You are Caliph.'

Under Magda's direction Peter took the Chris-craft in through a narrow passage in the coral reef that surrounded Île des Oiseaux, while the seabirds wheeled about them in a raucous cloud, filling the air with their wingbeats.

He anchored in five fathoms in the protected lee, and

then called the main island on the VHF radio, speaking to the head boatman.

'The Baronne has decided to sleep on board overnight,' he explained. 'Don't worry about us.'

When he went down to the saloon again Magda had recovered sufficiently to be sitting up. She had pulled on one of the terry towelling track suits from the clothes locker, and she had wound a clean towel around her throat to protect it and to hide the fierce fresh bruise that was already staining her skin like the squeezed juice of an over-ripe plum.

Peter found the medicine box in a locker above the toilet bowl of the heads, and she protested when he brought two Temprapain capsules for the pain, and four tablets of Brufin for the swelling and bruising of her throat and body.

'Take them,' he commanded and held the glass while she did so.

Then he carefully unwrapped the towel from her throat and lightly rubbed a creamy salve into the bruise with his fingertips.

'That feels better already,' she whispered, but now she had lost her voice almost entirely.

'Let's have a look at your stomach.' He pushed her down gently on her back on the long padded bench and unzipped the top of the towelling suit to the waist. The bruise where he had kicked her had spread from just below her small pale breasts to the tiny sculpted navel in the flat hard plane of her belly; again he massaged the soothing cream into her skin and she sighed and murmured with the comfort of it. When he finished she was able to hobble, still painfully doubled over, to the heads. She locked herself in for fifteen minutes while Peter tended his own injuries, and when she emerged again she had bathed her face and combed out her hair.

He poured two crystal old-fashioned glasses half full of Jack Daniel's Bourbon and he handed one to her as she sank onto the padded bench beside him. 'Drink it. For your throat,' he ordered, and she drank and gasped at the sting of the liquor and set the glass aside.

'And you, Peter?' she husked with sudden concern. 'Are you all right?'

'Just one thing,' he said. 'I'd hate you to get really mad at me.' Then he smiled, and she started to chuckle but choked on the pain and ended up clinging to him.

'When can we talk?' he asked her gently. 'We have to talk this out.'

'Yes, I know, but not yet, Peter. Just hold me for a while.' And he was surprised at the comfort that it afforded him. The warm woman shape pressed to him seemed to ease the pain of body and of mind, and he stroked her hair as she nuzzled softly against his throat.

'You said you loved me,' she murmured at last, making it a question. Seeking reassurance, as lovers always must.

'Yes. I love you. I think I knew it all along, but when I learned that you were Caliph, I had to bury it deep. It was only there at the end I had to admit to myself.'

'I'm glad,' she said simply. 'Because you see I love you also. I thought I would never be able to love. I had despaired of it, Peter. Until you. And then they told me you would kill me. That you were Caliph. I thought then I would die – having found you and then lost you. It was too cruel, Peter. I had to give you the chance to prove it wasn't true!'

'Don't talk,' he commanded. 'Just lie there and listen. There is nothing wrong with my voice, so I will tell it first. The way it was with me, and how I knew you were Caliph.'

And he told it to her, holding her to him and speaking softly, steadily. The only other sounds in the cabin were the slap of the wavelets against the hull and the subdued hum of the air-conditioning unit.

'You know everything up to the day Melissa-Jane was taken, all of it. I told you all of it, without reservation and without lying, not once—' He started, and then he went on to tell her in detail of the hunt for Melissa-Jane.

' – I think something must have snapped in my mind during those days. I was ready to believe anything, to try anything to get her back. I would wake up in the night and go to the toilet and vomit with the thought of her hand in a glass jar.'

He told her how he had planned to kill Kingston Parker to meet Caliph's demands, exactly how he intended doing it, the detailed how and where, and she shuddered against him.

'The power to corrupt even the best,' she whispered.

'Don't talk—' he admonished her, and went on to tell her of the tip-off that had led them at last to the Old Manse in Laragh.

'When I saw my daughter like that, I lost what little was left of my reason. When I held her and felt the fever and heard her scream with lingering terror, I would have killed—' He broke off and they were silent until she protested with a small gasp and he realized that his hand had closed on her upper arm and his fingers were biting into her flesh with the force of his memories.

'I'm sorry.' He relaxed his grip, and lifted the hand to touch her cheek. 'Then they told me about you.'

'Who?' she whispered.

'The Atlas Command.'

'Parker?'

'Yes, and Colin Noble.'

'What did they tell you?'

'They told me how your father brought you to Paris when you were a child. They told me that even then you were bright and pretty and special—' He began to recite it for her. ' – When your father was killed—' and she moved restlessly against his chest as he said it ' – you went to live with foster parents, all of them members of the party, and in the end you were so special that they sent somebody to take you back to Poland. Somebody who posed as your uncle—'

'I believed he was—' She nodded. ' – For ten years I believed it. He used to write to me—' She stopped herself with an effort, was silent a moment and then, ' – he was all I ever had after Papa.'

'You were selected to go to Odessa,' Peter went on, and felt her go very still in his arms, so he repeated it with the harshness unconcealed in his tone, ' – to the special school in Odessa.'

'You know about Odessa?' she whispered. 'Or you think you know – but nobody who has never been there could ever really know.'

'I know they taught you to—' He paused, imagining again a beautiful young girl in a special room overlooking the Black Sea, learning to use her body to trap and beguile a man, any man. ' – They taught you many things.' He could not make the accusation.

'Yes,' she murmured. 'Many, many things.'

'Like how to kill a man with your hands.'

'I think that subconsciously I could not bring myself to kill you, Peter. God knows you should not have survived. I loved you, even though I hated you for betraying me, I could not really do it—'

She sighed again, a broken gusty sound.

' – And when I thought that you were going to kill me – it was almost a relief. I was ready to accept that, against living on without the love that I thought I had found.'

'You talk too much.' He stopped her. 'You'll damage your throat further.' He touched her lips with his fingers, to silence her, and then went on. 'And at Odessa you became one of the chosen, one of the élite.'

'It was like entering the church, a beautiful mystic thing—' she whispered. 'I cannot explain it. I would have done everything or anything for the State, for what I knew was right for "Mother Russia".'

'All of this is true?' He marvelled that she made no effort to deny it.

'All of it,' she nodded painfully. 'I will never lie to you again, Peter. I swear it.'

'Then they sent you back to France – to Paris?' he asked, and she nodded.

'You did your job, even better than they had expected you to do it. You were the best, the very best. No man could resist you.'

She did not answer, but she did not lower her eyes from his. It was not a defiance but merely a total acceptance of what he was saying.

'There were men. Rich and powerful men—' His voice was bitter now. He could not help himself. 'Many, many men. Nobody knows how many, and from each of them you gathered harvest.'

'Poor Peter,' she whispered. 'Have you tortured yourself with that?'

'It helped me to hate you,' he said simply.

'Yes, I understand that. There is nothing that I can give you for your comfort – except this. I never loved a man until I met you.'

She was keeping her word. There were no more lies nor deceptions now. He was certain of it.

'Then they decided that you could be used to take over control of Aaron Altmann and his Empire—'

'No,' she whispered, shaking her head. 'I decided on Aaron. He had been the only one man who I had not been able to—' Her voice pinched out and she took a sip of the bourbon and let it trickle slowly down her throat before she went on. 'He fascinated me. I had never met a man like that before. So strong, such raw power.'

'All right,' Peter agreed. 'You might even have grown tired of the other role by then—'

'It's hard work being a courtesan—' She smiled for the first time since he had begun speaking, but it was a sad self-mocking smile.

'You went about it exactly the right way. First you made yourself indispensable to him. Already he was a sick man, beginning to need a crutch, somebody he could trust entirely. You gave him that—'

She said nothing, but memories passed across her eyes, changing the green shadows like sunlight through a deep still pool.

' – And when he trusted you there was nothing you could not supply to your masters. Your value had increased a hundredfold.'

He went on talking quietly while outside the day died in a fury of crimsons and royal purples, slowly altering the light in the cabin and dimming it down so that her face was all that existed in the soft gloom. A pale intense expression, listening quietly to the accusations, to the recitation of betrayals and deceits. Only occasionally she made a little gesture of denial, a shake of her head or the pressure of fingers on his arms. Sometimes she closed her eyes briefly as though she could not accept some particularly cruel memory, and once or twice an exclamation was wrung from her in that strained and tortured whisper.

'Oh God, Peter! It's true!'

He told her how she had gradually developed the taste for the power she was able to wield as Aaron Altmann's wife, and how that flourished as Aaron's strength declined. How she at last even opposed the Baron on some issues.

'Like that of supplying arms to the South African Government,' Peter said, and she nodded and made one of her rare comments.

'Yes. We argued. That was one of the few times we argued.' And she smiled softly, as though at a private memory that she could not share even with him.

He told her how the taste of power and the trappings of

power gradually eroded her commitment to her earlier political ideals, how her masters slowly realized they were losing their hold over her and of the pressures they attempted to apply to force her back into the fold. 'But you were too powerful now to respond to the usual pressures. You had even succeeded in penetrating Aaron's Mossad connections, and had that protection.'

'This is incredible!' she whispered. 'It's so close, so very close that it is the truth.' He waited for her to elaborate, but instead she motioned him to continue.

'When they threatened to expose you to the Baron as a communist agent, you had no choice but to get rid of him – and you did it in such a way that you not only got rid of the threat to your existence but you also achieved control of Altmann Industries, and to put the cherry on the top of the pie you got yourself twenty-five million in operating capital. You arranged the abduction and killing of Aaron Altmann, you paid yourself the twenty-five million and personally supervised its transfer, probably to a numbered account in Switzerland—'

'Oh God, Peter!' she whispered, and in the dark of the cabin her eyes were fathomless and huge as the empty cavities of a skull.

'Is it true?' Peter asked for confirmation for the first time.

'It's too horrible. Go on please.'

'It worked so well that it opened up a new world of possibilities for you. Just about this time you truly became Caliph. The taking of Flight 070 was possibly not the first stroke after the kidnapping of Aaron Altmann – there may have been others. Vienna and the OPEC ministers, the Red Brigade activities in Rome – but 070 was the first time you used the name Caliph. It worked, except for the dereliction of duty by a subordinate officer.' He indicated himself. 'That was all that stopped it – and that was how I attracted your attention originally.'

Now it was almost totally dark in the cabin and Magda

reached across and switched on the reading light beside them, adjusting the rheostat down to a soft golden glow. In its light she studied his face seriously as he went on.

' – By this time you were aware through your special sources, probably the Mossad connection and almost certainly through the French SID, that somebody was onto Caliph. That somebody turned out to be Kingston Parker and his Atlas organization, and I was the ideal person to firstly confirm that Parker was the hunter – and secondly, to assassinate him. I had the special training and talents for the job, I could get close to him without arousing his suspicions, and I needed only to be sufficiently motivated—'

'No,' she whispered, unable to take her eyes from his face.

'It holds together,' he said. 'All of it.' And she had no reply.

'When I received Melissa-Jane's finger, I was ready for anything—'

'I think I am going to be sick.'

'I'm sorry.' He gave her the glass and she drank the shot of dark liquor it contained, gagging a little on it. Then she sat for a few moments with her eyes closed and her hand on her bruised throat.

'All right?' he asked at last.

'Yes. All right now. Go on.'

'It worked perfectly – except for the tip-off to the hide-out in Ireland. But nobody could have foreseen that, not even Caliph.'

'But there was no proof!' she protested. 'It was all conjecture. No proof that I was Caliph.'

'There was,' he told her quietly. 'O'Shaughnessy, the head of the gang that kidnapped Melissa-Jane, made two telephone calls. They were traced to Rambouillet 47–87–47.'

She stared at him wordlessly.

'He was reporting to his master – to Caliph, you see.' And he waited for her reply. There was none, so after a minute of silence he went on to tell her the arrangements he had made for her execution – the sites he had chosen at Longchamp race course and in the Avenue Victor Hugo, and she shuddered as though she had felt the brush of the black angels' wings across her skin.

'I would have been there,' she admitted. 'You chose the two best sites. Yves has arranged a private showing for me on the sixth of next month. I would have gone to it.'

' – Then you saved me the trouble. You invited me here. I knew that it was an invitation to die, that you knew I had become aware, that I had learned you were Caliph. I saw it in your eyes during that meeting at Orly Airport, I saw it proven by the way you were suddenly avoiding me, the way you were giving me no opportunity to do the job I had to do.'

'Go on.'

'You had me searched when I landed at Tahiti-Faaa.'

She nodded.

'You had the grey wolves search my room again last night, and you set it up for today. I knew I had to strike first, and I did.'

'Yes,' she murmured. 'You did.' And rubbed her throat again.

He went to recharge the glasses from the concealed liquor cabinet behind the bulkhead, and came back to sit beside her.

She shifted slightly, moving inside the circle of his arm, and he held her in silence. The telling of it had exhausted him, and his body ached relentlessly, but he was glad it was said, somehow it was like lancing a malignant abscess – the release of poisons was a relief, and now the healing process could begin.

He could feel his own exhaustion echoed in the slim body that drooped against him, but he sensed that hers was deeper, she had taken too much already – and when he lifted her in his arms again she made no protest, and he carried her like a sleeping child through to the master cabin and laid her on the bunk.

He found pillows and a blanket in the locker below. He slid into the bunk with her, under the single blanket, and she fitted neatly into the curve of his body, pressing gently against him, her back against his chest, her hard round buttocks against the front of his thighs, and her head pillowed into the crook of his arm, while with his other arm he cuddled her close and his hand naturally cupped one of her breasts. They fell asleep like that, pressing closely, and when he rolled over she moved without waking, reversing their positions, moulding herself to his back and pressing her face into the nape of his neck, clasping him with one arm and with a leg thrown over his lower body as though to enfold him completely.

Once he woke and she was gone, and the strength of his alarm surprised him, a hundred new doubts and fears assailed him from the darkness, then he heard the liquid purr in the bowl of the heads and he relaxed. When she returned to the bunk, she had stripped off the terry towelling track suit and her naked body felt somehow very vulnerable and precious in his arms.

They woke together with sunlight pouring into the cabin through one porthole like stage lighting.

'My God – it must be noon.' She sat up, and tossed back the long mane of dark hair over her tanned bare shoulders – but when Peter tried to rise, he froze and groaned aloud.

'*Qu'a tu, chéri?*'

'I must have got caught in a concrete mixer,' he moaned. His bruises had stiffened during the night, torn muscle and strained sinews protested his slightest movement.

'There is only one cure for both of us,' she told him. 'It's in three parts.'

And she helped him off the bunk as though he was an

old man. He exaggerated the extent of his injuries a little to make her chuckle. The chuckle was a little hoarse, but her voice was stronger and clearer and she favoured her own bruises only a little as she led him up onto the deck. Her powers of recuperation were those of a young and superbly fit thoroughbred animal.

They swam from the diving platform over the Chris-craft's stern.

'It's working,' Peter admitted as the support of warm salt-water soothed his battered body. They swam side by side, both naked, slowly at first and then faster, changing the sedate breast-stroke for a hard overarm crawl, back as far as the reef, treading water there and gasping at the exertion.

'Better?' she panted with her hair floating around her like the tendrils of some beautiful water plant.

'Much better.'

'Race you back.'

They reached the Chris-craft together and clambered up into the cockpit, cascading water and laughing and panting, but when he reached for her, she allowed only a fleeting caress before pulling away.

'First Phase Two of the cure.'

She worked in the galley with only a floral apron around her waist which covered the dark bruises of her belly.

'I never thought an apron could be provocative before.'

'You are supposed to be doing the coffee,' she admonished him and gave him a lewd little bump and grind with her bare backside.

Her omelettes were thick and golden and fluffy, and they ate them in the early sunlight on the upper deck. The trade wind was sheep-dogging a flock of fluffy silver cloud across the heavens, and in the gaps the sky was a peculiar brilliant blue.

They ate with huge appetites, for the bright new morning seemed to have changed the mood of doom that had overpowered them the previous night. Neither of them wanted to break this mood, and they chattered inconsequential nonsense, and exclaimed at the beauty of the day and threw bread crusts to the seagulls, like two children on a picnic.

At last she came to sit in his lap, and made a show of taking his pulse.

'The patient is much improved,' she announced; 'is now probably strong enough for Phase Three of the cure.'

'Which is?' he asked.

'Peter *chéri*, even if you *are* English, you are not that dense.' And she wriggled her bottom in his lap.

They made love in the warm sunlight, on one of the foam mattresses, with the trade wind teasing their bodies like unseen fingers.

It began in banter and with low gurgles of laughter, little gasps of rediscovery, and murmurs of welcome and encouragement – then suddenly it changed, it became charged with almost unbearable intensity, a storm of emotion that sought to sweep all the ugliness and doubt. They were caught up in the raging torrent that carried them helplessly beyond mere physical response into an unknown dimension from which there seemed no way back, a total affirmation of their bodies and their minds that made all else seem inconsequential.

'I love you,' she cried at the very end, as though to deny all else that she had been forced to do. 'I have loved only you.' It was a cry torn from the very depths of her soul.

It took a long time for them to return from the far place to which they had been driven, to become two separate people again, but when they did somehow they both sensed that they would never again be completely separated; there had been a deeper more significant union than just that of their two bodies, and the knowledge sobered them and yet, at the same time, gave them both new strength and a deep elation that neither had to voice – it was there, and they both simply knew it.

They slid the big inflatable Avon S 650 dinghy over the stern, and went ashore, pulling the rubber craft above the high-water level and mooring it to one of the slanting palm boles.

Then they wandered inland, picking their way hand in hand between the seabird nests that had been crudely scraped in the earth. Half a dozen different species of birds were breeding together in one sprawling colony that covered most of the twenty-acre island. Their eggs varied from cool pale blue as big as that of a goose's, to others the size of a pullet's and speckled and spotted in lovely free-form designs. The chicks were either grotesquely ugly with bare parboiled bodies or were cute as Walt Disney animations. The entire island was pervaded by an endless susurration of thousands of wings and the uproar of squawking, screeching, feuding and mating birds.

Magda knew the zoological names of each species, its range and its habits, and its chances of survival or extinction in the changing eco-systems of the oceans.

Peter listened to her tolerantly, sensing that behind this chatter and studied gaiety she was steeling herself to answer the accusations that he had levelled at her.

At the far end of the island was a single massive takamaka tree, with dense green foliage spreading widely over the fluffy white sand. By now the sun was fiercely bright and the heat and humidity smothered them like a woollen blanket dipped in hot water.

They sought the shade of the takamaka gratefully, and sat close together on the sand staring out across the unruffled waters of the lagoon to the silhouette of the main island, five miles away. At this range and angle there was no sign of the buildings nor of the jetty, and Peter had an illusion of the primeval paradise with the two of them the first man and woman on a fresh and innocent earth.

Magda's next words dispelled that illusion entirely.

'Who ordered you to kill me, Peter? How was the

command given? I must know that before I tell you about myself.'

'Nobody,' he answered.

'Nobody? There was no message like the one you received ordering you to kill Parker?'

'No.'

'Parker himself or Colin Noble? They did not order you to do it – or suggest it?'

'Parker expressly ordered me not to do it. You were not to be touched – until you could be taken in jeopardy.'

'It was your own decision?' she insisted.

'It was my duty.'

'To avenge your daughter?'

He hesitated, would have qualified it, then nodded with total self-honesty. 'Yes, that was the most part of it, Melissa-Jane, but I saw it also as my duty to destroy anything evil enough to envisage the taking of 070, the abduction of Aaron Altmann and the mutilation of my daughter.'

'Caliph knows about us. Understands us better than we understand ourselves. I am not a coward, Peter, but now I am truly afraid.'

'Fear is the tool of his trade,' Peter agreed, and she moved slightly, inviting physical contact. He placed one arm about her bare brown shoulders and she leaned lightly against him.

'All that you told me last night was the truth, only the inferences and conclusions were false. Papa's death, the lonely years with strangers as foster-parents – of that period my clearest memories are of lying awake at night and trying to muffle the sound of my weeping with a false blanket. The return to Poland, yes, that was right, and the Odessa school – all of that. I will tell you about Odessa one day, if you truly want to hear it – ?'

'I don't think I do,' he said.

'Perhaps you are wise; do you want to hear about the return to Paris?'

'Only what is necessary.'

'All right, Peter. There were men. That was what I had been selected and trained for. Yes, there were men—' She broke off, and reached up to take his face between her hands, turning it so she could look into his eyes. 'Does that make a difference between us, Peter?'

'I love you,' he replied firmly.

She stared into his eyes for a long time looking for evidence of deceit, and then when she found none, 'Yes. It is so. You really mean that.'

She sighed with relief and laid her head against his shoulder, speaking quietly with just that intriguing touch of accent and the occasional unusual turn of phrase.

'I did not like the men, either, Peter. I think that was why I chose Aaron Altmann. One man, yes I could still respect myself—' She shrugged lightly. 'I chose Aaron, and Moscow agreed. It was, as you said, delicate work. First I had to win his respect. He had never respected a woman before. I proved to him I was as good as any man, at any task he wished to set me. After I had his respect, all else followed—' She paused and chuckled softly. ' – Life plays naughty tricks. I found firstly that I liked him, then I grew to respect him also. He was a great ugly bull of a man, but the power . . . A huge raw power, like some cosmic force, became the centre of my existence.' She lifted her head to touch Peter's cheek with her lips in reassurance. 'No. Peter, I never came to love him. I never loved before you. But I stood in vast awe of him, like a member of a primitive tribe worships the lightning and the thunder. It was like that. He dominated my existence – more than a father, more than a teacher, as much as a god – but less, very much less than a lover. He was crude and strong. He did not make love, he could only rut and tup like the bull he was.'

She broke off and looked seriously at him. 'Do you understand that, Peter? Perhaps I explained it badly?'

'No,' he assured her. 'You explained it very well.'

'Physically he did not move me, his smell and the hairiness. He had hair on his shoulders and like a pelt down his back. His belly was bulging and hard as iron—' She shivered briefly. ' – But I had been trained to be able to ignore that. To switch off something in the front of my brain. Yet in all other ways he fascinated me. He goaded me to think forbidden thoughts, to open vaults of my mind that my training had securely locked. All right, he taught me about power and its trappings. You accused me of that, Peter, and I admit it. The flavour of power and money was to my taste. I like it. I like it very much indeed. Aaron introduced me to that. He showed me how to appreciate fine and beautiful things, for he was only physically a bull and he had a wonderful appreciation of the refinements of life – he made me come completely alive. Then he laughed at me. God, I can still hear the bellow of his laughter, and see that great hairy belly shaking with it.'

She paused to remember it, almost reverently, and then she chuckled her own husky little laugh.

'"My fine little communist lady,"' he mocked me. 'Yes, Peter, it was I who was deceived, he had known from the beginning who I was. He also knew about the school at Odessa. He had accepted me as a challenge, certainly he loved me – or his version of love, but he took me knowingly and corrupted my pure ideological convictions. Only then did I learn that all the information which I had been able to pass to Moscow had been carefully screened by Aaron. He doubled me, as I had been sent to double him. He was Mossad, but of course you know that. He was a Zionist, you know that also. And he made me realize that I was a Jewess, and what it meant to be that. He showed me every fatal flaw in the doctrine of Universal Communism, he convinced me of democracy and the Western Capitalist system and then he recruited me to Mossad—'

She stopped again, and shook her head vehemently.

' – To believe that I could have wished to destroy such a

one. That I could have ordered his abduction and mutilation – Towards the end, when he was getting weak, when the pain was very bad, that was the closest I ever came to loving him, the way a mother loves a child. He became pathetically dependent upon me; he used to say the only thing that could lull the pain was my touch. I used to sit for hours rubbing that hairy belly – feeling that awful thing growing bigger inside him each day, like a cauliflower or a grotesque foetus. He would not let them cut it. He hated them, "butchers" he called them. "Butchers with their knives and rubber tubes – "'

She broke off and Peter realized that her eyes were filled with tears. He hugged her a little more firmly and waited for her to recover.

'It must have been about this time that Caliph made contact with Aaron. Thinking back I can remember the time when he became suddenly terribly agitated. It made little sense to me then, but he held long diatribes about right-wing tyranny being indistinguishable from tyranny of the left. He never mentioned the name Caliph, I do not think Caliph had yet used that name – and I do believe that Aaron would eventually have told me of the contact in detail, if he had lived. It was the way he was, even with me, he could be as wary and subtle as he could be overpowering. He would have told me of Caliph – but Caliph saw to it that he did not.'

She pulled away from Peter's arms so she could again see his face.

'You must understand, *chéri*, that much of this I have learned only recently – in the last few weeks. Much of it I can only piece together like a jig puzzle – pardon, a jig-saw puzzle.' She corrected herself swiftly. 'But this is what must have happened. Caliph contacted Aaron with a proposition. It was a very simple proposition. He was invited to become a partner of Caliph. Aaron was to make a substantial financial contribution to Caliph's war-chest, and to place his privileged knowledge and lines of influence at Caliph's disposal. In return he would have a hand in engineering Caliph's brave new world. It was a miscalculation on Caliph's part, perhaps the only mistake he has made up to now. He had misjudged Aaron Altmann. Aaron turned him down flat – but much more dangerously Caliph had made the mistake of revealing his identity to Aaron. I expect that he had to do that in an effort to convince Aaron. You see, Aaron was not a man who would indulge in a game of code-names and hidden identities. That much Caliph had divined correctly. So he had to confront Aaron face to face, and when he discovered that Aaron would not join in a campaign of murder and extortion – no matter how laudable the ultimate ends – Caliph had no choice. He took Aaron, killed him after torturing him hideously for information that could have been useful, mainly information about his Mossad connection I imagine. Then he persuaded me to pay the ransom. He won two major tricks with a single card. He silenced Aaron, and he gained the twenty-five million for his war-chest.'

'How did you learn this? If only you had explained to me before—' Peter heard the bitterness in his own voice.

'I did not know it when we first met, *chéri*, please believe me. I will tell you how I learned it, but please be patient with me. Let me tell it as it happened.'

'I am sorry,' he said simply.

'The first time I heard the name "Caliph" was the day I delivered the ransom. I told you about that, didn't I?'

'Yes.'

'So we come now to your part. I heard of you for the first time with the Johannesburg hijacking of Flight 070. I thought that you might be the one to help me hunt down Caliph. I found out about you, Peter. I was even able to have a computer printout on you—' She paused, and there was that mischievous flash in her eye again. ' – I will admit to being very impressed with the formidable list of your ladies.'

Peter held up both hands in a gesture of surrender.

'Never again,' he pleaded. 'Not another word – agreed?'

'Agreed.' She laughed, and then, 'I'm hungry, and my throat is sore again with all this talking.'

They crossed the island again, with their bare feet baking on the sun-heated sand, and went back on board the Chris-craft.

The chef had stocked the refrigerator with a cornucopia of food, and Peter opened a bottle of Veuve Cliquot champagne.

'You've got expensive tastes,' he observed. 'I don't know if I can afford to keep you – on my salary.'

'I'm sure we could arrange a raise from your boss,' she assured him with the twinkle in her eyes. In tacit agreement they did not mention Caliph again until they had eaten.

' – There is one other thing you must understand, Peter. I am of Mossad, but I do not control them. They control me. It was the same with Aaron. Both of us were and are very valuable agents, possibly amongst the most valuable of all their networks, but I do not make decisions, nor am I able to have access to all their secrets.

'Mossad's single-minded goal is the safety and security of the state of Israel. It has no other reason for existence. I was certain that Aaron had made a full report to Mossad of Caliph's identity, that he had detailed the proposition that Caliph had proposed – and I suspect that Mossad had ordered Aaron to co-operate with Caliph—'

'Why?' Peter demanded sharply.

'I do not know for certain – but I can think of two reasons. Caliph must have been such a powerful and influential man that his support would have been valuable. Then again I suspect that Caliph had pro-Israeli leanings, or professed to have those leanings. Mossad finds allies where it can, and does not question their morals. I think they ordered Aaron to co-operate with Caliph – but—'

'But?' Peter prompted her.

'But you do not order a man like Aaron to go against his deepest convictions, and under that forbidding exterior Aaron Altmann was a man of great humanity. I think that the reason for his agitation was the conflict of duty and belief that he was forced to endure. His instinct warned him to destroy Caliph, and his duty—'

She shrugged, and picked up her fluted champagne glass, twisting it between those long slim fingers and studying the pinpricks of bubbles as they rose slowly through the pale golden wine. When she spoke again she had changed direction disconcertingly.

'A thousand times I had tried to discover what was so different between you and me than with the other men I have known. Why none of them could move me – and yet with you it was almost instantaneous—' She looked up at him again as though she was still seeking the reason. ' – Of course, I knew so much about you. You had the qualities I admire in another human being, so I was disposed favourably – but there are other qualities you cannot detail on a computer printout nor capture in a photograph. There was something about you that made me—' She made a helpless gesture as she searched for the word. ' – You made me tingle.'

'That's a good word,' Peter smiled.

'And I had never tingled before. So I had to be very sure. It was a new experience to want a man merely because he is gentle and strong and—' she chuckled, ' – just plain sexy. You are sexy, you know that, Peter, but also you are something else—' She broke off. 'No, I am not going to flatter you any more. I do not want you to get swollen ankles—' mixing the French idiom quaintly with the English, and this time not correcting herself. She went straight on. 'Caliph must have realized that I had recruited a dangerous ally. He made the attempt to kill you that night on the Rambouillet road—'

'They were after you,' Peter cut in.

'Who, Peter? Who was after me?'

'The Russians – by that time they knew you were a double agent.'

'Yes, they knew—' She cocked her head and narrowed her eyes. 'I had thought about it, of course, and there had been two previous attempts on me, but I do not think the attempt on the Rambouillet road was Russian.'

'All right, Caliph then, but after you – not me,' Peter suggested.

'Perhaps, but again I do not think so. My instinct tells me they had the right target. They were after you.'

'I would have to agree,' Peter said. 'I think I was followed when I left Paris that evening—' and he told her about the Citroën. ' – I think they knew that I was alone in the Maserati.'

'Then we accept it was Caliph,' she stated flatly.

' – or Mossad,' Peter murmured, and her eyes slowly widened, turning a darker thoughtful green as Peter went on.

'What if Mossad did not want an Atlas man getting close to their star agent, they didn't want you to have an ally in your hunt for Caliph? What if they just didn't want me cluttering up the carefully rehearsed scenario?'

'Peter, it's very deep water—'

' – and there are packs of sharks.'

'Let's leave that night on the Rambouillet road for the moment,' she suggested. 'It merely complicates the story I am trying to tell you.'

'All right,' Peter agreed. 'We can come back to it, if we have to.'

'The next significant move was the abduction of Melissa-Jane,' she said, and Peter's expression changed, becoming flat and stony.

'The choice of the victim was genius-inspired,' she said. 'But it required no special knowledge of you or your domestic arrangements. There was no secret that you had an only child, and it needed but a casual appraisal of your character to understand how powerful a lever she could be—' Magda dipped the tip of her finger into the champagne and then sucked it thoughtfully, pursing her lips and frowning slightly.

'You must understand that by this time I had faced the fact that I was in love with you. The gift was supposed to affirm that—' She flushed slightly under her honey tan, and it was appealing and child-like. He had never seen her blush before and it twisted something in his chest.

'The book,' he remembered. 'The Cornwallis Harris first edition.'

'My first love gift ever. I bought it when I finally admitted it to myself – but I was determined that I would not admit it to you. I am old-fashioned enough to believe the man must speak first.'

'I did.'

'God, I'll never forget it,' she said fervently, and they both thought of the savage confrontation the previous day which had ended incongruously in a declaration of love.

'I try to be unconventional,' he said, and she shook her head smiling.

'You succeed, *mon amour*, oh how you succeed.' Then she sobered again. 'I was in love with you. Your distress was mine. The child was a lovely girl, she had captivated me when we met – and on top of all that I felt deadly responsible for her plight. I had inveigled you into joining my hunt for Caliph, and because of that you had lost your daughter.'

He bowed his head slightly, remembering how he had believed that she had engineered it. She recognized the gesture.

'Yes, Peter. For me it was the cruellest stroke. That you

should believe it of me. There was nothing that I would not have done to give her back to you – and yet there seemed nothing that I could do. My contacts with French intelligence had nothing for me. They had no inkling of how or where the child was being held – and my control at Mossad was unaccountably evasive. Somehow I had the feeling that Mossad had the key to the kidnapping. If they were not directly involved they knew more than anybody else. I have already explained that I believed Aaron had given them the identity of Caliph. If that was so, then they must know something that could have helped you to recover your child – but from Paris I was powerless to gather that information. I had to go in person to Israel and confront my control there. It was the one chance that I could get them to co-operate. They might believe my value as an agent was worth enough to give me a lead to Melissa-Jane—'

'You threatened Mossad with resignation?' Peter asked wonderingly. 'You would have done that for me?'

'Oh, Peter, don't you understand? I loved you – and I had never been in love before. I would have done anything for you.'

'You make me feel humble,' he said.

She did not reply, but let the statement stand as though she were savouring it, then she sighed contentedly and went on. 'I left everything in Paris. I have an established routine for disappearing when it is necessary. Pierre took me to Rome in the Lear; from there I telephoned you but I could not tell you what I was going to do. Then I switched identity and took a commercial flight to Tel Aviv. My task in Israel was difficult, much more difficult than I had bargained for. It was five days before my control would see me. He is an old friend. No! perhaps not a friend, but we have known each other a long time. He is the deputy-director of Mossad. That is how highly they value my services, to give me such an important controller, but still it took five days before he would see me, and he was cold.

There was no help they could give me, he said. They knew nothing.' She chuckled. 'You have never seen me when I want something really badly, Peter. Ha! – What a battle. There is much I knew that would embarrass Mossad with her powerful allies of the West – with France and Great Britain and the U.S.A. – I threatened to hold a Press conference in New York. He became less cold, he told me that the security of the State took precedence over all personal feelings, and I said something very rude about the security of the State, and reminded him of some outstanding business which I would happily leave outstanding. He became warmer – but all this was taking time, days, many days, too many days. I was going crazy. I remembered how they had found Aaron's body, and I could not sleep at night for worrying about that lovely child. And you, oh Peter, you will never know how I prayed to a god that I was not too sure of. You will never know how I wanted to be with you to comfort you. I wanted so desperately just to hear your voice – but I could not break my cover from Tel Aviv. I could not even telephone you, nor send you a letter—' She broke off. ' – I hoped you would not believe bad things of me. You would not believe that I did not care. That I was not prepared to help you. I could only hope that I would be able to bring you some information of value to prove it was not true – but I never dreamed that one day you would believe that it was I who had taken your daughter and tortured her.'

'I am sorry,' he said quietly.

'No, do not say you are sorry. We were both Caliph's playthings. There is no blame on you.' She laid her hand upon his arm and smiled at him. 'It was not you alone who believed bad things. For at last I had prevailed on my Mossad control to give me some little scraps of information. At first he denied completely that they had ever heard of Caliph, but I risked lying to him. I told him that Aaron had told me he had reported the Caliph contact. He gave ground. Yes, he admitted. They knew of Caliph, but they did not know who he was. I hammered on, demanding to see my controller each day, driving him as mad as I was – until he threatened to have me deported even. But each time we met I wheedled and bullied a little more from him.

'At last he admitted, "All right, we know Caliph but he is very dangerous, very powerful – and he will become more powerful – God willing, he will become one of the most powerful men in the world, and he is a friend of Israel. Or rather we believe he is a friend of Israel."

'I bullied some more and he told me, "We have put an agent close to Caliph, very close to him, and we cannot jeopardize this agent. He is a valuable agent, very valuable but very vulnerable to Caliph. We cannot take the chance that Caliph could trace information back to him. We have to protect our man."

'Now I threatened, and he told me the agent's code-name to protect both of us should we ever have to make contact. The code-name is "CACTUS FLOWER".'

'That was all?' Peter asked, with evident disappointment.

'No, my control gave me another name. As a sop – and as a warning. The name they gave me was so close to Caliph as to be virtually the same. Again he warned me that he was giving me the name for my own protection.'

'What was it?' Peter demanded eagerly.

'Your name,' she said softly. 'Stride.'

Peter made an irritable gesture of dismissal. 'My name is nonsensical. Why would I kidnap and mutilate my own daughter – and Cactus Flower. He might as well have said, "Kentucky Fried Chicken". '

'Now it's my turn to say I'm sorry.'

Peter caught himself, realizing suddenly that he had been too quick to dismiss these scraps of information. He stood up and paced the deck of the Chris-craft with choppy, agitated steps, frowning heavily. 'Cactus Flower,' he repeated. 'Have you ever heard it before?'

'No,' she shook her head.

'Since then?'

'No,' again.

He searched his memory, trying for a sympathetic echo. There was none.

'All right.' He accepted that as having no immediate value. 'We'll just remember it for now. Let's come to my name – Peter Stride. What did you make of that?'

'It didn't mean anything then, except as a shock. Strangely enough I did not immediately think of you, but I thought of confusion between the kidnapper and the victim.'

'Stride?' he asked. 'Peter Stride? I don't understand.'

'No, well – Melissa-Jane is a Stride also.'

'Yes, of course. They didn't give you the name Peter Stride then?'

'No. Just Stride.'

'I see.' Peter stopped in mid-pace as an idea struck him – and stared out thoughtfully to where the ocean met a blue horizon.

'But they gave me your full name later,' she interrupted his thoughts.

'When?'

'After we received the news that Melissa-Jane had been rescued. Of course, I wanted to return to Paris immediately – to be with you. I was able to get onto a flight from Ben-Gurion Airport six hours after we heard the news. My heart was singing, Peter. Melissa-Jane was safe, and I was in love. I was going to be with you very soon. At the airport, while I was going through the security check before departure, the policewoman took me aside – to the security office. My control was waiting for me there. He had rushed out from Tel Aviv to catch me before I left for home, and he was very worried. They had just received an urgent message from Cactus Flower. General Peter Stride was now definitely Caliph-motivated, and would assassinate me at the first opportunity, he told me. And I laughed at him – but he was deadly serious. "My dear Baroness, Cactus Flower is a first-class man. You must take this warning seriously," he kept repeating.'

Magda shrugged. 'I still did not believe it, Peter. It was impossible. I loved you, and I knew you loved me – although perhaps you had not yet realized that yourself. It was crazy. But on the aircraft I had time to think. My control at Mossad has never been wrong before. Can you imagine my dilemma now – how dearly I wanted to be with you, and yet I was now terrified – not that you would kill me. That did not seem important – but that you would truly turn out to be Caliph. That was what really frightened me. You see, I had never loved a man before. I don't think I could have stood it.'

She was quiet for a while, remembering the pain and confusion, and then she shook her head so that the thick fall of dark shimmering hair rustled around her shoulders.

'Once I reached Paris, my first concern was to learn that you and Melissa-Jane were safe at Abbots Yew, and then I could begin to try and find out how much substance there was in Cactus Flower's warning – but until I could decide on how safe it was I could not take the chance of being alone with you. Every time you attempted to contact me, I had to deny you, and it felt as though some little part of me was dying.'

She reached across and took his hand now, opened the fingers and bowed her head to kiss the palm and then held it to her cheek as she went on.

'A hundred times I convinced myself that it could not be true, and I was on the point of going to you. Oh, Peter – finally I could take it no longer. I decided to meet you at Orly that day and find out one way or the other, end the terrible uncertainty. I had the grey wolves with me, as you remember, and they had been warned to expect trouble – I didn't tell them to watch you,' she explained quickly, as if trying to dispel any memory of disloyalty, 'but if you had tried to get at me they would have—' She broke off, and let his hand fall away from her cheek. 'The moment you walked into the private lounge at Orly, I saw it was true. I could sense it, there was an aura of death around you. It was the most frightening and devastating moment of my life, you looked like a different man – not the Peter Stride I knew – your whole face seemed to be altered and restructured by hatred and anger. I kissed you goodbye, because I knew we could never meet again.' Remembering it her face darkened with sadness, as though a cloud shadow had passed over them. 'I even thought that I had to protect myself by—' She gagged the words. ' – You were part of Caliph, you see, and it would have been the wise thing to do. I admit that I thought of it, Peter. Have you killed, before you could kill me – but it was only a thought and it did not go farther than that. Instead I went on with the business of living, work has always been an opiate for me. If I work hard enough I can forget anything – but this time it didn't turn out that way. I've said it before, but it explains so much that I will say it again. I had never been in love before, Peter, and I could not turn it off. It tormented me, and I cherished doubts – about Cactus Flower's warning and what I had seen so clearly in the lounge at Orly Airport. It couldn't be, it just couldn't be true – I loved you and you loved me, and you just couldn't be plotting to kill me. I almost convinced myself of that.'

She laughed curtly, but it had no humour in the sound, only the bitterness of disillusion.

'I came out here—' she made a gesture that embraced sea and sky and islands ' – to be away from the temptation of going to you. A sanctuary where I could recover from my wounds and begin to get over you. But it didn't work, Peter. It was worse here. I had more time to think, to torture myself with wild speculation and grotesque theories. There was only one way. Finally I recognized that. I would bring you out here and give you the chance to kill me.' She laughed again, and now there was the old husky warmth in it. 'It was the most crazy thing I have ever done in my life – but thank God, I did it.'

'We went right to the very brink,' Peter agreed.

'Peter, why didn't you ask me outright if I was Caliph?' she wanted to know.

'The same reason you didn't ask me outright if I was plotting to kill you.'

'Yes,' she agreed. 'We were just caught up in the web that Caliph had spun for us. I have only one more question, Peter *chéri*. If I was Caliph, do you truly believe that I would have been so stupid as to give my telephone number at Rambouillet to the man who kidnapped Melissa-Jane, and instruct him to ring me for a friendly chat whenever he felt like it?'

Peter looked startled, 'I thought—' he began, then stopped. ' – No, I didn't think. I wasn't thinking clearly at all. Of course, you wouldn't have done that – and yet, even the cleverest criminals make the most elementary mistakes.'

'Not those who have been trained at the Odessa school,' she reminded him, and seemed immediately to regret the words, for she went on quickly. 'So there is my side of the story, Peter. I may have left something out – if you can think of anything, then ask me, darling, and I'll try to fill in any missing pieces.'

And so they started once again at the very beginning, and went over the ground minutely, searching for anything they might have overlooked at the first telling of it, this time exhaustively re-examining each fact from every angle, both of them applying their trained minds to the full without being able to come up with more than they already had.

'One thing we must never let out of sight for a moment is the quality of the opposition.' Peter summed it up as the sun began lowering itself towards the western horizon, its majestic progress flanked by cohorts of cumulo-nimbus cloud rising into towering anvil heads over the scattered islands, like silent nuclear explosions.

'There are layers upon layers, reasons behind reasons, the kidnapping of Melissa-Jane was not merely to force me to assassinate Kingston Parker, but you as well – the proverbial two birds – with a third bird to follow. If I had succeeded I would have been hooked into Caliph for ever.'

'Where do you and I go from here, Peter?' she asked, tacitly transferring ultimate decision-making to him.

'How about home, right now,' he suggested. 'Unless you fancy another night out here.'

Peter found that his possessions had been discreetly moved from the guest bungalow to the owner's magnificent private quarters on the north tip of the island.

His toilet articles had been laid out in the mirrored master bathroom, which flanked that of the mistress. His clothing, all freshly cleaned and pressed, was in the master's dressing-room where there was one hundred and fifty-five feet of louvred hanging space – Peter paced it out and calculated it would take three hundred suits of clothing. There were specially designed swinging shelves for another three hundred shirts and racks for a hundred pairs of shoes although all were empty.

His light cotton suit looked as lonely as a single camel in the midst of the Sahara desert. His shoes had been burnished to a gloss that even his batman had never been able to achieve. Despite himself he searched the dressing-room swiftly for the signs of previous occupancy – and was ridiculously relieved to find none.

'I could learn to rough it like this,' he told his reflection in the mirror as he combed the damp, darkly curling locks off his forehead.

The sitting-room off the suite was on three levels, and had been decorated with cane furniture and luxuriant tropical plants growing in ancient Greek wine amphoras or in rockeries that were incorporated into the flowing design of the room. The creepers and huge glossy leaves of the plants toned in artistically with jungle-patterned curtaining and the dense growth of exotic plants beyond the tall picture windows – yet the room was cool and inviting, although the sound of air-conditioning was covered by the twinkle of a waterfall down the cunningly contrived rock face that comprised one curved wall of the room. Tropical fish floated gracefully in the clear pools into which the waterfall spilled, and the perfume of growing flowers pervaded the room, and their blooms glowed in the subdued lighting.

One of the little golden Polynesian girls brought a tray of four tall frosted glasses for Peter to choose from. They were all filled with fruit and he could smell the sweet warm odour of rum mingled with the fruit. He guessed they would be almost lethal and asked for a whisky, then relented with the girl's eyes flooded with disappointment.

'I make them myself,' she wailed.

'In that case—' He sipped while she waited anxiously.

'*Parfait*!' He exclaimed, and she giggled with gratification, and went off wriggling her bottom under the brief pareo like a happy puppy.

Magda came then in a chiffon dress so gossamer-light that it floated about her like a fine green sea mist, through which her limbs gleamed as the light caught them.

He felt the catch in his breathing as she came towards him, and he wondered if he would ever accustom himself to the impact of her beauty.

She took the glass from his hand and tasted it.

'Good,' she said, and handed it back. But when the girl brought the tray she refused with a smile.

They moved about the room, Magda on his arm as she pointed out the rarer plants and fishes.

'I built this wing after Aaron's death,' she told him, and he realized that she wanted him to know that it contained no memories of another man. It amused him that she should find that important – and then he remembered his own furtive search of the dressing-room for signs of a lover before him, and the amusement turned inward.

One wall of the private dining-room was a single sheet of armoured glass, beyond which the living jewels of coral fish drifted in subtly-lit sea caverns and the fronds of magnificent sea plants waved in gentle unseen currents.

Magda ordered the seating changed so they could be side by side in the low lovers' seat facing the aquarium.

'I do not like you to be far away any more,' she explained, and she picked special titbits from the serving dishes for his plate.

'This is a speciality of Les Neuf Poissons. You will eat it nowhere else in the world.' She selected small deep-sea crustaceans from a steaming creole sauce of spices and coconut cream and at the end of the meal she peeled chilled grapes from Australia with those delicate fingers, using the long shell-pink nails with the precision of a skilled surgeon to remove the pips and then placing them between his lips with thumb and forefinger.

'You spoil me,' he smiled.

'I never had a doll when I was a little girl,' she explained, smiling.

A circular stone staircase led to the beach fifty feet below the dining-room and they left their shoes on the bottom step and walked bare-footed on the smooth, damp sand, compacted as hard as cement by the receding tide. The moon was a few days past full, and its reflection drew a pathway of yellow light to the horizon.

'Caliph must be made to believe that he has succeeded,' Peter said abruptly, and she shivered against him.

'I wish we could forget Caliph for one night.'

'We cannot afford to forget him for a moment.'

'No, you are right. How do we make him believe that?'

'You have to die—' He felt her stiffen.

' – or at least appear to do so. It has to look as though I killed you.'

'Tell me,' she invited quietly.

'You told me that you have special arrangements for when you want to disappear.'

'Yes, I do.'

'How would you disappear from here if you had to do so?'

She thought for only a moment. 'Pierre would fly me to Bora-Bora. I have friends there. Good friends. I would take the island airline to Tahiti-Faaa on another passport – and then a scheduled airline in the same name to California or New Zealand.'

'You have other papers?' he demanded.

'Yes, of course.' She sounded so surprised by the question, that he expected her to ask ' – doesn't everybody?'

'Fine,' he said. 'And we'll arrange a suspicious accident here. A scuba diving accident, shark attack in deep water, no corpse.'

'What is the point of all this, Peter?'

'If you are dead – Caliph is not going to make another attempt to have you killed.'

'Good!' she agreed.

'So you stay officially dead until we flush Caliph out,' Peter told her, and it sounded like an order but she did not demur as he went on. 'And if I carry out Caliph's evident wishes by killing you, it's going to make me a very valuable asset. I will have proved myself, and so he will cherish me. It will give me another chance to get close to him. At least it will give me a chance to check out a few wild hunches.'

'Don't let's make my death too convincing, my love. I

am a great favourite of the police on Tahiti,' she murmured. 'I'd hate to have you end up under the guillotine at Tuarruru.'

Peter woke before her and raised himself on one elbow over her to study her face, delighting to find new planes and angles to her high broad cheekbones, gloating in the velvety texture of her skin, so fine that the pores were indefinable from farther than a few inches. Then he transferred his attention to the curve of her eyelashes that interlocked into a thick dark palisade seeming to seal her eyelids perpetually in sleep – yet they sprang open suddenly, the huge black pools of her pupils shrinking rapidly as she focused, and for the first time he realized that the irises were not pure green but were flecked and shot through with gold and violet.

The surprise of finding him over her changed slowly to pleasure, and she stretched her arms out over her head and arched her back, the way a lazy panther does when it rouses itself. The satin sheet slid down to her waist and she prolonged the stretch a little longer than was necessary, a deliberate display of her body.

'Every other morning of my life that I woke without you there was wasted,' she murmured huskily, and raised her arms still at full stretch to him, folding them gracefully around his neck, still holding her back arched so that the prominent dark-red nipples brushed lightly against the crisp dark mat of curls that covered his own chest.

'Let's pretend this will last for ever,' she whispered, with her lips an inch from his, and her breath was rich as an overblown rose, heavy with the smell of vital woman and rising passion; then her lips spread softly, warmly against his and she sucked his tongue deeply into her mouth, with a low moan of wanting – and the hard slim body began to work against his, the hands breaking from his neck and hunting down his spine, long curved nails pricking and goading him just short of pain. His own arousal was so swift and so brutally hard that she moaned again, and the tension went out of her body, it seemed to soften and spread like a wax figure held too close to the flame, her eyelids trembling closed and her thighs falling apart.

'So strong—' she whispered, deep in her throat and he reared up over her, feeling supreme, invincible.

'Peter, Peter,' she cried. 'Oh yes like that. Please like that.' Both of them striving triumphantly for the moment of glory when each was able to lose self and become for a fleeting instant part of the godhead.

Long afterwards they lay side by side in the enormous bed, both of them stretched out flat upon their backs, not touching except for the fingers of one hand intertwined as their bodies had been.

'I will go away—' she whispered, ' – because I have to, but not now. Not yet.'

He did not reply, the effort was beyond him, and her own voice was languorous with a surfeit of pleasure.

'I will make a bargain with you. Give me three days more. Only three days, to be happy like this. For me it is the first time. I have never known this before, and it may be the last time—'

He tried to rouse himself to deny it, but she squeezed his fingers for silence and went on.

' – It may be the last,' she repeated. 'And I want to have it all. Three days, in which we do not mention Caliph, in which we do not think of the blood and striving and suffering out there. If you give me that I will do everything that you want me to do. Is it a bargain, Peter? Tell me we can have that.'

'Yes. We can have that.'

'Then tell me you love me again, I do not think I can hear you say it too often.'

He said it often during those magic days, and she had spoken the truth, each time he told her she accepted with as much joy as the last time, and always each seemed to be within touching distance of the other.

Even when tearing side by side across the warm flat waters of the lagoon, leaning back with straight arms on the tow lines, skis hissing angrily and carving fiercely sparkling wings of water from the surface as they wove back and forth in a *pas de deux* across the streaming, creaming water, laughing together in the wind and the engine roar of the Chris-craft, Hapiti the Polynesian boatman on the flying bridge looking back with a great white grin of sympathy for their joy.

Finning gently through mysterious blue and dappled depths, the only sound the wheezing suck and blow of their scuba valves and the soft clicking and the eternal echoing susurration that is the pulse beat of the ocean, holding hands as they sank down to the long abandoned hull of the Japanese aircraft carrier, now overgrown with a waving forest of sea growth and populated by a teeming fascinating multitude of beautiful and bizarre creatures.

Flying silently down the sheer steel cliff of the canted flight deck, which seemed to reach down into the very oceanic depths, so that there was the eerie fear of suddenly being deprived of support and falling down to where the surface light blued out in nothingness.

Pausing to peer through their glass face-plates into the still gaping wounds rent into the steel by aerial bombs and high explosive, and then entering through those cruel caverns cautiously as children into a haunted house and emerging victoriously with carrier nets of trophies, coins and cutlery, brass and porcelain.

Strolling on the secluded beaches of the outer islands, still hand in hand, naked in the sunlight.

Fishing the seething tide-race through the main channel at full spring tide, and shouting with excitement as the big golden amberjack came boiling up in the wake, bellies flashing like mirrors, to hit the dancing feather lures, and send the Penn reels screeching a wild protest, and the fibreglass rods nodding and kicking.

Out in the humbling silences of the unrestricted ocean, when even the smudge of the islands disappeared beyond the wave crests for minutes at a time, with only the creak and whisper of the rigging, the trembling pregnancy of the main sail, and the rustle as the twin hulls of the big Hobie cat knifed the tops off the swells.

Strolling the long curving beaches in the moonlight, searching for the heavenly bodies that so seldom show through the turbid skies of Europe – Orion the hunter and the Seven Sisters – exclaiming at the stranger constellations of this hemisphere governed by the great fixed cross in the southern heavens.

Each day beginning and ending in the special wonder and mystery of the circular bed, in loving that welded their bodies and their souls together each time more securely.

Then on the fourth day day Peter woke to find her gone, and for a moment experienced an appalling sensation of total loss.

When she came back to him he did not recognize her for a breath of time.

Then he realized that she had cut away the long dark tresses of her hair, cropped it down short so that it curled close against her skull, like the petals of a dark flower. It had the effect of making her seem even taller. Her neck like the stem of the flower, longer, and the curve of the throat accentuated so that it became delicate and swan-like.

She saw his expression, and explained in a matter-of-fact tone.

'I thought some change was necessary, if I am to leave under a new identity. It will grow again, if you want it that way.'

She seemed to have changed completely herself, the

languid amorous mood given way to the brisk business-like efficiency of before. While they ate a last breakfast of sweet yellow papaya and the juice of freshly squeezed limes she explained her intentions, as she went swiftly through the buff envelope that her secretary had silently laid beside her plate.

There was a red Israeli diplomatic passport in the envelope.

'I will be using the name Ruth Levy—' and she picked up the thick booklet of airline tickets, ' – and I have decided to go back to Jerusalem. I have a house there. It's not in my name, and I do not think anybody else outside of Mossad is aware of it. It will be an ideal base, close to my control at Mossad. I will try to give you what support I can, try to get further information to assist you in the hunt—'

She passed him a typed sheet of notepaper.

' – That is a telephone number at Mossad where you can get a message to me. Use the name Ruth Levy.'

He memorized the number while she went on talking, and then shredded the sheet of paper.

'I have modified the arrangements for my departure,' she told him. 'We will take the Chris-craft across to Bora-Bora. It's only a hundred miles. I will radio ahead. My friends will meet me off the beach after dark.'

They crept in through a narrow passage in the coral with all the lights on the Chris-craft doused, Magda's boatman using only what was left of the waning moon and his own intimate knowledge of the islands to take her in.

'I wanted Hapiti to see me go ashore alive,' she whispered quietly, leaning against Peter's chest to draw comfort from their last minutes together. 'I did not exaggerate the danger you might be in if the local people thought what we want Caliph to think. Hapiti will keep his mouth shut—' she assured him,' – and will back up your story of a shark attack, unless you order him to tell the truth.'

'You think of everything.'

'I have only just found you, monsieur,' she chuckled. 'I do not want to lose you yet. I have even decided to speak a word to the Chief of Police on Tahiti, when I pass through. He is an old friend. When you get back to Les Neuf Poissons, have my secretary radio Tahiti—'

She went on quietly, covering every detail of her arrangements, and he could find no omissions. She was interrupted by a soft hail from out of the darkness and Hapiti throttled the diesels back to idle. They drifted down closer to the loom of the island. A canoe bumped against the side, and Magda turned quickly in his arms, reaching up for his mouth with hers.

'Please be careful, Peter,' was all that she said, and then she broke away and stepped down into the canoe as Hapiti handed down her single valise. The canoe pushed away immediately, and was lost in the dark. There was nothing to wave at, and Peter liked it better that way, but still he stared back over the stern into the night as the Chris-craft groped blindly for the channel again.

There was a hollow feeling under his ribs, as though part of himself was missing; he tried to fill it with a memory of Magda that had amused him because it epitomized for him her quick and pragmatic mind.

' – When the news of your death hits the market, the bottom is going to drop out of Altmann stock.' He had realized this halfway through their final discussion that morning. 'I hadn't thought of that.' He was troubled by the complication.

'I had,' she smiled serenely. 'I estimate it will lose a hundred francs a share within the first week after the news breaks.'

'Doesn't that worry you?'

'Not really.' She gave that sudden wicked grin. 'I telexed a buying order to Zurich this morning. I expect to show a profit of not less than a hundred million francs when the stock bounces back.' Again the mischievous flash of green eyes. 'I do have to be recompensed for all this inconvenience, *tu ne penses pas?*'

And although he still smiled at the memory, the hollow place remained there inside him.

Pierre flew the Tahitian police out to Les Neuf Poissons in the Tri-Islander, and there followed two days of questions and statements. Nearly every member of the community wished to make a statement to the police, there had seldom been such entertainment and excitement available on the islands.

Nearly all of the statements were glowing eulogies to 'La Baronne' delivered to the accompaniment of lamentation and weeping. Only Hapiti had first-hand information and he made the most of this position of importance, embroidering and gilding the tale. He was even able to give a positive identification of the shark as a 'Dead White' – The English name startled Peter until he remembered that the movie *Jaws* was in the island's cassette video library and was undoubtedly the source of the big boatman's inspiration. Hapiti went on to describe its fangs as long and sharp as cane knives, and to give a gruesome imitation of the sound they made as they closed on 'La Baronne' – Peter would willingly have gagged him to prevent those flights of imagination, which were not supported by Peter's own statement, but the police sergeant was greatly impressed and encouraged Hapiti to further acts of creation with cries of astonishment.

On the last evening there was a funeral feast on the beach for Magda. It was a moving ritual, and Peter found himself curiously affected when the women of the island, swaying and wailing at the water's edge, cast wreaths of frangipani blooms onto the tide to be carried out beyond the reef.

Peter flew back to Tahiti-Faaa with the police the following morning, and they stayed with him, flanking him discreetly, on the drive to the headquarters of gendarmerie in the town. However, his interview with the Chief of Police was brief and courteous – clearly Magda had been there before him – and if there was no actual exchange of winks and nudges, the commissioner's handshake of farewell was firm and friendly.

'Any friend of La Baronne is a friend here.' And he used the present tense, then sent Peter back to the airport in an official car.

The UTA flight landed in California through that sulphurous eye-stinging layer of yellow air trapped between sea and mountains. Peter did not leave the airport, but after he had shaved and changed his shirt in the men's room he found a copy of the *Wall Street Journal* in the first-class Pan-Am Clipper lounge. It was dated the previous day, and the report of Magda Altmann's death was on Page Three. It was a full column, and Peter was surprised by the depth of the Altmann Industries involvement in the American financial scene. The complex of holdings was listed, followed by a résumé of Baron Aaron Altmann's career and that of his widow. The cause of death as given by the Tahitian police was 'Shark Attack' while scuba diving in the company of a friend – General Peter Stride – Peter was grimly satisfied that his name was mentioned. Caliph would read it, wherever he was, and draw the appropriate conclusion. Peter could expect something to happen now; he was not quite sure what, but he knew that he was being drawn closer to the centre like a fragment of iron to the magnet.

He managed to sleep for an hour, in one of the big armchairs, before the hostess roused him for the Pan-Am Polar flight to London's Heathrow.

He called Pat Stride, his sister-in-law, from Heathrow Airport. She was unaffectedly delighted to hear his voice.

' – Steven is in Spain, but I am expecting him home

tomorrow before lunch, that is if his meetings go the way he wants them. They want to build a thirty-six-hole golf course at San Istaban—' Steven's companies owned a complex of tourist hotels on the Spanish coast ' – and Steven had to go through the motions with the Spanish authorities. But, why don't you come down to Abbots Yew tonight? Alex and Priscilla are here, and there will be an amusing house party for the weekend—' He could hear the sudden calculating tone in Pat's voice as she began instinctively to run through the shortlist of potential mates for Peter.

After he had accepted and hung up, he dialled the Cambridge number and was relieved that Cynthia's husband, George Barrow, answered.

Give me a Bolshevik intellectual over a neurotic ex-wife any day, he thought as he greeted Melissa-Jane's stepfather warmly. Cynthia was at a meeting of the Faculty Wives Association, and Melissa-Jane was auditioning for a part in a production of Gilbert and Sullivan by the local drama society.

'How is she?' Peter wanted to know.

'I think she is well over it now, Peter. The hand is completely healed. She seems to have settled down—' They spoke for a few minutes more, then ran out of conversation. The two women were all they had in common.

'Give Melissa-Jane my very best love,' Peter told him, and picked up a copy of *The Financial Times* from a newsstand on his way to the Avis desk. He hired a compact and while waiting for it to be delivered he searched swiftly through the newspaper for mention of Magda Altmann. It was on an inside page, clearly a follow-up article to a previous report of her death. There had been a severe reaction on the London and European stock exchanges – the hundred-franc drop in Altmann stock that Magda had anticipated had already been exceeded on the Bourse – and again there was a brief mention of his own name in a repetition of the circumstances of her death. He was satisfied with the publicity, and with Magda's judgement in buying back her own stock. Indeed it all seemed to be going a little too smoothly. He became aware of the fateful prickle of apprehension down his spine, his own personal barometer of impending danger.

As always Abbots Yew was like coming home, and Pat met him on the gravel of the front drive, kissed him with sisterly affection and linked her arm through his to lead him into the gracious old house.

'Steven will be delighted,' she promised him. 'I expect he will telephone this evening. He always does when he is away.'

There was a buff cable envelope propped on the bedside table of the guest room overlooking the stables that was always reserved for Peter. The message originated at Ben-Gurion Airport, Tel Aviv, and was a single word – the code he had arranged with Magda to let him know that she arrived safely and without complication. The message gave him a sharp pang of wanting, and he lay in a deep hot bath and thought about her, remembering small details of conversation and shared experience that suddenly were of inflated value.

While he towelled himself he regarded his image in the steamed mirror with a critical eye. He was lean and hard and burned dark as a desert Arab by the Pacific sun. He watched the play of muscle under the tanned skin as he moved, and he knew that he was as fit and as mentally prepared for action as he had ever been, glad that Magda was safely beyond the reach of Caliph's talons so that he could concentrate all his energies on what his instincts told him must be the final stage of the hunt.

He went through to his bedroom with the towel around his waist and stretched out on the bed to wait for the cocktail hour in Pat Stride's rigidly run household.

He wondered what made him so certain that this was

the lead which would carry him to Caliph, it seemed so slim a chance and yet the certainty was like a steel thread, and the steel was in his heart.

That made him pause. Once again he went carefully over the changes which had taken place within him since his first exposure to Caliph's malignant influence; the fatal miasma of corruption that seemed to spread around Caliph like the poisonous mists from some evil swamp seemed to have engulfed Peter entirely.

He thought again of his execution of the blonde girl at Johannesburg what seemed like a thousand years before, but with mild surprise realized was months not years ago.

He thought of how he had been prepared to kill both Kingston Parker and Magda Altmann – and realized that contact with violence was brutalizing, capable of eroding the principles and convictions which he had believed inviolate after almost forty years of having lived with them.

If this was so, then after Caliph – if he succeeded in destroying him – what was there after Caliph? Would he ever be the same man again? Had he advanced too far beyond the frontiers of social behaviour and conscience? Would he ever go back? he wondered. Then he thought about Magda Altmann and realized she was his hope for the future, after Caliph there would be Magda.

These doubts were weakening, he told himself. There must be no distractions now, for once again he was in the arena with the adversary. No distraction, no doubts – only total concentration on the conflict ahead.

He stood up from the bed and began to dress.

Steven was delighted to have Peter at Abbots Yew again, as Pat had predicted.

He also was tanned from the short stay in Spain, but he had again put on weight, only a few pounds, but it would soon be a serious problem, good food and drink were two of the occupational hazards of success: the most evident but not the most dangerous temptations that face a man who has money enough to buy whatever idly engages his fancy.

Peter watched him covertly during the lunch, studying the handsome head which was so very much like his own, the same broad brow and straight aristocratic nose, and yet was so different in small but significant details, and it was not only Steven's thick dark moustache.

All right, it's easy to be wise afterwards, Peter told himself, as he watched his twin brother. Seeing again the little marks, which only now seemed to have meaning. The narrower set of eyes, slightly too close together, so that even when he laughed that deep bluff guffaw of his they seemed still to retain a cold cruel light, the mouth that even in laughter was still too hard, too determined, the mouth of a man who would brook no check to his ambitions, no thwarting of his desires. Or am I imagining it now? Peter wondered. It was so easy to see what you looked for expectantly.

The conversation at lunch dwelt almost exclusively on the prospects for the flat-racing season which had opened at Doncaster the previous weekend, and Peter joined it knowledgeably; but as he chatted he was casting back along the years, to the incidents that might have troubled him more if he had not immediately submerged them under an instinctive and unquestioning loyalty to his twin brother.

There was Sandhurst when Steven had been sent down, and Peter had known unquestioningly that it was unjust. No Stride was capable of what Steven had been accused of, and he had not even had to discuss it with his brother. He had affirmed his loyalty with a handshake and a few embarrassed muttered words.

'Thank you, Peter. I'll never forget that,' Steven had told him fervently, meeting Peter's gaze with steady clear eye.

Since then Steven's rise had been meteoric through the post-war years in which it seemed almost impossible for even the most able man to amass a great fortune, a man had to have special talents and take terrible risks to achieve what Steven had.

Now sitting at his brother's board, eating roast saddle of lamb and the first crisp white asparagus shoots of the season flown in from the Continent, Peter was at last covering forbidden ground, examining loyalties which until then had been unquestioned. Yet they were straws scattered by the winds of time, possibly without significance. Peter transferred his thoughts to the present.

'Stride,' Magda's control at Mossad in Tel-Aviv had said. Just the two names: 'Cactus Flower' and 'Stride'. That was fact and not conjecture.

Down the length of the luncheon table Sir Steven Stride caught his brother's eye.

'Wine with you, my dear fellow.' Steven lifted the glass of claret in the old salute.

'Enchanted, I'm sure.' Peter gave the correct reply, a little ritual between them, a hangover from Sandhurst days, and Peter was surprised at the depth of his regret. Perhaps Caliph has not yet succeeded in corrupting me entirely, Peter thought, as he drank the toast.

After lunch there was another of their brotherly rituals. Steven signalled it with a jerk of the head and Peter nodded agreement. Peter's old army duffle coat was in the cupboard below the back staircase with his Wellingtons, and he and Steven changed into rough clothing sitting side by side on the monk's bench in the rear entrance hall as they had so often before.

Then Steven went through into the gunroom, took down

a Purdey Royal shotgun from the rack, and thrust a handful of cartridges in his coat pocket.

'Damned vixen has a litter of cubs somewhere in the bottoms, playing merry hell with the pheasant chicks—' he explained as Peter asked a silent question. 'It goes against the grain a bit to shoot a fox but I must put a stop to her – haven't had a chance at her yet—' and he led the way out of the back door through the orchard towards the stream.

It was almost a formal beating of the bounds, the leisurely circuit of the estate boundaries that the two brothers always made on Peter's first day at Abbots Yew, another old comfortable tradition which allowed them time to have each other's news and reaffirm the bond between them

They sauntered along the riverbank, side by side, moving into single file with Steven leading when the path narrowed and turned away from the stream and went up through the woods.

Steven was elated by the success of his visit to Spain, and he boasted of his achievements in obtaining another parcel of prime seafront property on which to build the new golf course and to extend the hotel by another five hundred rooms.

'Now's the time to buy. Mark my words, Peter – we are on the verge of another explosion.'

'The cut-back in oil price is going to help, I'd expect,' Peter agreed.

'That's not the half of it, old boy.' Steven turned to glance back over his shoulder and he winked knowingly at Peter. 'You can expect another five per cent cut in six months, take my word on it. The Arabs and the Shah have come to their senses.' Steven went on swiftly, picking out those types of industry which would benefit most dramatically from the reduction in crude prices, then selecting the leading companies in those sectors. ' – If you have a few pounds lying idle, that's where to put it.' Steven's whole personality seemed to change when he spoke like this of power and great wealth. Then he came out from behind the façade of the English country squire which he was usually at such pains to cultivate; the glitter in his eyes was now undisguised and his bushy moustache bristled like the whiskers of some big dangerous predator.

He was still talking quickly and persuasively as they left the woods and began to cross the open fields towards the ruins of the Roman camp on the crest of the low hills.

' – These people have still to be told what to do, you know. Those damned shop stewards up in Westminster may have thrown the Empire away, but we still have our responsibilities.' Steven changed the Purdey shotgun from one arm to the other, carrying it in the crook of the arm, the gun broken open and the shining brass caps of the Eley Kynoch cartridges showing in the breeches. ' – Government only by those fit to govern.' Steven enlarged on that for a few minutes.

Then suddenly Steven fell silent, almost as though he had suddenly decided that he had spoken too much, even to somebody as trusted as his own younger twin. Peter was silent also, trudging up the curve of the hill with his boots squelching in the soft damp earth. There was something completely unreal about the moment, walking over well-remembered ground in the beautiful mellow sunlight of an English spring afternoon with a man he had known from the day of his birth – and yet perhaps had never known at all.

It was not the first time he had heard Steven talk like this, and yet perhaps it was the first time he had ever listened. He shivered and Steven glanced at him.

'Cold?'

'Goose walked over my grave,' Peter explained, and Steven nodded as they clambered up the shallow earth bank that marked the perimeter of the Roman camp.

They stood on the lip under the branches of a lovely copper beech, resplendent in its new spring growth of russet.

Steven was breathing hard from the pull up the hill, that extra weight was already beginning to tell. There was a spot of high unhealthy colour in each cheek, and little blisters of sweat speckled his chin.

He closed the breech of the shotgun with a metallic clash, and leaned the weapon against the trunk of the copper beech as he struggled to regain his breath.

Peter moved across casually and propped his shoulder against the copper beech, but his thumbs were hooked into the lapels of the duffle coat, not thrust into pockets, and he was still in balance, weight slightly forward on the balls of his feet. Although he seemed to be entirely relaxed and at rest he was in fact coiled like a spring, poised on the brink of violent action – and the shotgun was within easy reach of his right hand.

He had seen that Steven had loaded with number four shot. At ten paces it would disembowel a man. The safety catch on the top of the pistol grip of the butt engaged automatically when the breech was opened and closed again, but the right thumb would instinctively slip the catch forward as the hand closed on the grip.

Steven took a silver cigarette case from the side pocket of his coat and tapped down a cigarette on the lid.

'Damned shame about Magda Altmann,' he said gruffly, not meeting Peter's eyes.

'Yes,' Peter agreed softly.

'Glad they handled it in a civilized fashion. Could have made it awkward for you, you know.'

'I suppose they could have,' Peter agreed.

'What about your job at Narmco?'

'I don't know yet. I will not know until I get back to Brussels.'

'Well, my offer still stands, old boy. I could do with a bit of help. I really could. Somebody I could trust. You'd be doing me a favour.'

'Damned decent of you, Steven.'

'No, really, I mean it.' Steven lit the cigarette with a gold Dunhill lighter and inhaled with evident pleasure, and after a moment Peter asked him:

'I hope you were not in a heavy position in Altmann stock. I see it has taken an awful tumble.'

'Strange that.' Steven shook his head. 'Pulled out of Altmann's a few weeks ago, actually. Needed the money for San Istaban.'

'Lucky,' Peter murmured, or much more than luck. He wondered why Steven admitted the share transaction so readily. 'Of course,' he realized, 'it would have been very substantial and therefore easily traced.'

He studied his brother now, staring at him with a slight scowl of concentration. Was it possible? he asked himself. Could Steven really have masterminded something so complex, where ideology and self-interest and delusions of omnipotence seemed so inextricably snarled and entwined.

'What is it, old boy?' Steven asked, frowning slightly in sympathy.

'I was just thinking that the whole concept and execution has been incredible, Steven. I would never have suspected you were capable of it.'

'I'm sorry, Peter. I don't understand. What are you talking about?'

'Caliph,' Peter said softly.

It was there! Peter saw it instantly. The instant of utter stillness, like a startled jungle animal – but the flinch of the eyes, followed immediately by the effort of control.

The expression of Steven's face had not altered, the little frown of polite inquiry held perfectly, then turning slowly, deeper into puzzlement.

'I'm afraid you just lost me there, old chap.'

It was superbly done. Despite himself Peter was impressed. There were depths to his brother which he had never suspected – but that was his own omission. No matter which way you looked at it, it took an extraordinary ability to achieve what Steven had achieved in less than twenty years, against the most appalling odds. No matter how he had done it, it was the working of a particular type of genius.

He was capable of running Caliph, Peter accepted the fact at last – and immediately had a focal point for the corroding hatred he had carried within him for so long.

'Your only mistake so far, Steven, was to let Aaron Altmann know your name,' Peter went on quietly. 'I suspect you did not then know that he was a Mossad agent, and that your name would go straight onto the Israeli intelligence computer. Nobody, nothing, can ever wipe it from the memory rolls, Steven. You are known.'

Steven's eyes flickered down to the shotgun; it was instinctive, uncontrollable, the final confirmation if Peter needed one.

'No, Steven. That's not for you.' Peter shook his head. 'That's my work. You're fat and out of condition, and you have never had the training. You must stick to hiring others to do the actual killing. You wouldn't even get a hand on it.'

Steven's eyes darted back to his brother's face. Still the expression of his face had not altered.

'I think you've gone out of your head, old boy.'

Peter ignored it. 'You of all people should know that I am capable of killing anybody. You have conditioned me to that.'

'We are getting into an awful tangle now,' Steven protested. 'What on earth should you want to kill anybody for?'

'Steven, you are insulting both of us. I know. There is no point in going on with the act. We have to work out between us what we are going to do about it.'

He had phrased it carefully, offering the chance of

compromise. He saw the waver of doubt in Steven's eyes, the slight twist of his mouth, as he struggled to reach a decision.

' – But please do not underestimate the danger you are in, Steven.' As he spoke Peter produced an old worn pair of dark leather gloves from his pocket and began to pull them on. There was something infinitely menacing in that simple act, and again Steven's eyes were drawn irresistibly.

'Why are you doing that?' For the first time Steven's voice croaked slightly.

'I haven't yet touched the gun,' Peter explained reasonably. 'It has only your prints upon it.'

'Christ, you'd never get away with it, Peter.'

'Why, Steven? It is always dangerous to carry a loaded shotgun over muddy and uneven ground.'

'You couldn't do it, not in cold blood.' The edge of terror was in Steven's voice.

'Why not? You had no such qualms with Prince Hassied Abdel Hayek.'

'I am your brother – he was only a bloody wog—' Steven choked it off, staring now at Peter with stricken eyes, the expression of his face beginning at last to crack and crumble as he realized that he had made the fateful admission.

Peter reached for the shotgun without taking his eyes from his brother's.

'Wait!' Steven cried. 'Wait, Peter!'

'For what?'

'You've got to let me explain.'

'All right, go ahead.'

'You can't just say go ahead, like that. It's so complicated.'

'All right, Steven. Let's start at the beginning – with Flight 070. Tell me why?'

'We had to do it, Peter. Don't you see? There is over four billions of British investment in that country, another three billions of American money. It's the major world producer of gold and uranium, chrome and a dozen other strategic minerals. My God, Peter. Those ham-handed oafs in control now are on a suicide course. We had to take it away from them, and put in a controllable government. If we don't do that the Reds will have it all within ten years – probably much less.'

'You had an alternative government chosen?'

'Of course,' Steven told him urgently, persuasively, watching the shotgun that Peter still held low across his hips. 'It was planned in every detail. It took two years.'

'All right.' Peter nodded. 'Tell me about the murder of Prince Hassied.'

'It wasn't murder, for God's sake, man, it was absolutely essential. It was a matter of survival. They were destroying Western civilization with their childlike irresponsibility. Drunk with power, they were no longer amenable to reason, like spoiled children in a sweet shop – we had to put a stop to it, or face a breakdown of the capitalist system. They have probably done irreparable damage to the prestige of the dollar, they have taken sterling hostage and hold it in daily jeopardy with the threat of withdrawing those astronomic balances from London. We had to bring them to their senses, and look how small a price. We can reduce the price of crude oil gradually to its 1970 level. We can restore sanity to the currencies of the Western world and secure real growth and prosperity for hundreds of millions of peoples – all at the cost of a single life.'

'And anyway, he was only a bloody wog. Wasn't he?' Peter agreed reasonably.

'Look here, Peter. I said that but I didn't mean it. You are being unreasonable.'

'I will try not to be,' Peter assured him mildly. 'Tell me where it goes from here. Who do you bring under control next – the British Trade Union movement, perhaps?'

And Steven stared at him wordlessly for a moment.

'Damn it, Peter. That was a hell of a guess. But could

you imagine if we had a five-year wage freeze, and no industrial action during that time. It's them or us, Peter. We could get back to being one of the major industrial powers of the Western world. Great Britain! We could be that again.'

'You are very convincing, Steven,' Peter acknowledged. 'There are only a few details that worry me a little.'

'What are they, Peter?'

'Why was it necessary to arrange the murder of Kingston Parker and Magda Altmann—'

Steven stared at him, his jaw unhinging slightly and the hard line of his mouth going slack with astonishment. 'No,' he shook his head. 'That's not so.'

' – and why was it necessary to kill Baron Altmann, and torture him to death?'

'That was not my doing – all right, it was done. And I knew it was done – but I had nothing to do with it, Peter. Not the murder at least. Oh God, all right I knew it had to be done, but—' His voice tailed off, and he stared helplessly at Peter.

'From the beginning again, Steven. Let's hear it all—' Peter spoke almost gently.

'I cannot, Peter. You don't understand what might happen, what will happen if I tell you—'

Peter slid the safety catch off the Purdey shotgun. The click of the mechanism was unnaturally loud in the silence, and Steven Stride started and stepped back a pace, blinking at his brother, fastening all his attention on Peter's eyes.

'God,' he whispered. 'You would do it too.'

'Tell me about Aaron Altmann.'

'Can I have another cigarette?'

Peter nodded and Steven lit it with hands that trembled very slightly.

'You have to understand how it worked, before I can explain.'

'Tell me how it worked,' Peter invited.

'I was recruited—'

'Steven, don't lie to me – you are Caliph.'

'No, God, no, Peter. You have it all wrong,' Steven cried. 'It's a chain. I am only a link in Caliph's chain. I am not Caliph.'

'You are a part of Caliph, then?'

'Only a link in the chain,' Steven repeated vehemently.

'Tell me,' Peter invited with a small movement of the shotgun barrel that drew Steven's eyes immediately.

'There is a man I have known a long time. We have worked together before. A man with greater wealth and influence than I have. It was not an immediate thing. It grew out of many discussions and conversations over a long time, years, in which we both voiced our concern with the way that power had shifted to blocks of persons unfit to wield it—'

'All right,' Peter nodded grimly. 'I understand your political and ideological sentiments. Leave them out of the account.'

'Very well,' Steven agreed. ' – Well, finally this man asked me if I would be prepared to join an association of Western world political and industrial leaders dedicated to restoring power to the hands of those fitted by training and upbringing to govern.'

'Who was this man?'

'Peter, I cannot tell you.'

'You have no choice,' Peter told him, and there was a long moment as they locked eyes and wills; then Steven sighed in capitulation.

'It was—' The name was that of a mining magnate who controlled most of the free world supply of nuclear fuel and gold and precious stones.

'So he is the one who would have been in control of the new South African government with which you intended replacing the present regime in that country, if the taking of 070 had succeeded?' Peter demanded, and Steven nodded wordlessly.

'All right,' Peter nodded. 'Go on.'

'He had been recruited as I was,' Steven explained. 'But I was never to know by whom. In my turn I was to recruit another desirable member – but I would be the only one who knew who that was. It was how the security of the chain was to be maintained. Each link would know only the one above and below him, the man who had recruited him and the one who he recruited in his turn—'

'Caliph?' Peter demanded. 'What about Caliph?'

'Nobody knows who he is.'

'Yet he must know who you are.'

'Yes, of course.'

'Then there must be some way for you to get a message to Caliph,' Peter insisted. 'For instance, when you recruit a new member, you must be able to pass on the information? When he wants something from you, he must be able to contact you.'

'Yes.'

'How?'

'Christ, Peter. It's more than my life is worth.'

'We'll come back to it,' said Peter impatiently. 'Go on, tell me about Aaron Altmann.'

'That was a disaster. I chose Aaron as the man I would recruit. He seemed exactly the kind of man we needed. I had known him for years. I knew he could be very tough when it was necessary. So I approached him. He seemed very eager at first, leading me on. Getting me to explain the way Caliph would work. I was delighted to have recruited such an important man. He intimated that he would contribute twenty-five million dollars to the funds of the association, so I passed a message to Caliph. I told him that I had almost succeeded in recruiting Baron Altmann—'

Steven stopped nervously, and dropped the stub of his

cigarette onto the damp turf, grinding it out under his heel.

'What happened then?' Peter demanded.

'Caliph responded immediately. I was ordered to break off all contact with Aaron Altmann at once. I realized I must have chosen a potentially dangerous person. You tell me now he was Mossad. I did not know that – but Caliph must have known it. I did as I was told and dropped Aaron like a hot chestnut – and four days later he was abducted. I had nothing to do with it, Peter. I swear to you. I liked the man immensely. I admired him—'

'Yet he was abducted and horribly tortured. You must have known that Caliph had done it, and that you were responsible?'

'Yes.' Steven said the word flatly, without evasion. Peter felt a small stir of admiration for that.

'They tortured him to find out if he had passed the information you had given him about Caliph to Mossad,' Peter insisted.

'Yes. I expect so. I do not know.'

'If the picture I have of Aaron Altmann was correct they received no information from him.'

'No. He was like that. They must have lost patience with him in the end – to do what they did to him. It was my first moment of disillusionment with Caliph,' Steven muttered sombrely.

They were both silent now, until Peter burst out angrily. 'My God, Steven, can't you see what a disgusting business you are mixed up in?' And Steven was mute. 'Couldn't you see it?' Peter insisted, the anger raw in his voice. 'Couldn't you realize it from the beginning?'

'Not at the beginning.' Steven shook his head miserably. 'It seemed a brilliant solution for all the diseases of the Western world – and then once I began it was like being on board a speeding express train. It was just impossible to get off again.'

'All right. So then you tried to have me assassinated on the Rambouillet road?'

'Good God, no.' Steven was truly appalled. 'You're my brother, good God—'

'Caliph did it to stop me getting close to Aaron's widow who was out to avenge him.'

'I didn't know a thing about it, I swear to you. If Caliph did it, he knew better than to let me in on it.' Steven was pleading now. 'You must believe that.'

Peter felt a softening of his resolve, but forced back the knowledge that this man was his brother, someone who had been very dear over a lifetime.

'What was your next operation for Caliph then?' He asked without allowing the softness to reach his voice.

'There wasn't—'

'Damn you, Steven, don't lie to me.' Peter's voice cracked like a whiplash. 'You knew about Prince Hassied Abdel Hayek!'

'All right. I arranged that. Caliph told me what to do and I did it.'

'Then you kidnapped Melissa-Jane and had her mutilated—'

'Oh God! No!' Steven's voice was a sob.

' – To force me to assassinate Kingston Parker—'

'No, Peter. No!'

' – And then to kill Magda Altmann—'

'Peter, I swear to you. Not Melissa-Jane. I love her like one of my own daughters. You must know that. I had no idea it was Caliph.'

Steven was pleading wildly now.

' – You have to believe me. I would never have allowed that to happen. That is too horrible.'

Peter watched him with a steely merciless glint of blue in his eyes, cold and cutting as the edge of the executioner's blade.

'I will do anything to prove to you I had nothing to do

with Melissa-Jane. Anything you say, Peter. I'll take any chance to prove it to you. I swear it to you.'

Steven Stride's dismay and sincerity were beyond question. His face was drained of all colour and his lips were marble white and trembling with the strength of his denial.

Peter handed the shotgun to his brother without a word. Startled, Steven held it for a moment at arm's length.

'You are in bad trouble, Steven,' Peter said quietly. He knew that from now on he needed Steven's unreserved and whole-hearted commitment. He could not be forced to do what he must do at the point of a shotgun.

Steven recognized the gesture, and slowly lowered the gun. With his thumb he pushed across the breech-locking mechanism, and the weapon hinged open. He pulled the cartridges from the double eyes of the breeches and dropped them into the pocket of his shooting jacket.

'Let's get down to the house,' Steven said, his voice still unsteady with the trauma of the last minutes. 'I need a stiff whisky—'

There was a log fire burning in the deep walk-in fireplace of Steven's study. The portals were magnificently carved altar surrounds from a sixteenth-century German church, salvaged from the ruins of World War II Allied bombing and purchased by Steven from a Spanish dealer, after having been smuggled out through Switzerland.

Opposite the fireplace, bow windows with leaded panes and ancient wavy glass looked out over the rose garden. The other two walls housed Steven's collection of rare books, each boxed in its individual leather-bound container and lettered in gold leaf. The shelves reached from floor to the high moulded ceiling. It was a passion that the brothers shared.

Steven stood now in the fireplace with his back to the flames, one hand clasped in the small of his back, hoisting up the skirts of his tweed jacket to warm his backside. In the other hand he held a deep crystal tumbler, still half filled with whisky, hardly diluted by the soda he had dashed into it from the syphon.

Steven still looked shaken and pale, and every few minutes he shivered uncontrollably, although the room was oppressively heated by the blazing fire and all the windows were closed tightly.

Peter sprawled in the brocade-upholstered Louis Quatorze chair across the room, his legs thrust out straight and crossed at the ankles, hands thrust deeply into his pockets, and his chin lowered on his chest in deep thought.

'How much was your contribution to Caliph's war chest?' Peter asked abruptly.

'I was not in the same class as Aaron Altmann,' Steven answered quietly. 'I pledged five millions in sterling over five years.'

'So we must imagine a network extending across all international boundaries. Powerful men in every country, each contributing enormous sums of money – and almost unlimited information and influence—'

Steven nodded and took another swallow of his dark-toned whisky.

' – There is no reason to believe that it was only one man in each country. There may be a dozen in England, another dozen in Western Germany, fifty in the United States—'

'It's possible,' Steven agreed.

'So that Caliph could very easily have arranged the kidnapping of Melissa-Jane through another of his chain in this country.'

'You must believe I had nothing to do with it, Peter.'

Peter dismissed this new protestation impatiently, and went on thinking out aloud.

'It is still possible that Caliph is a committee of the founder members – not one man at all.'

'I don't think so—' Steven hesitated. ' – I had a very strong impression that it all was one man. I do not think a committee would be capable of such swift and determined action.' He shook his head, trying to cast his mind back for the exact words which had formed his impressions. ' – You must remember that I have only discussed Caliph with one other person, the man who recruited me. However, you can be certain that we discussed it in depth and over an extended period. I was not about to put out five million on something that didn't satisfy me entirely. No, it was one man who would make the decision for all of us – but the decisions would be in the interest of all.'

'Yet there was no guarantee that any individual member of the chain would be informed of every decision?'

'No. Of course not. That would have been madness. Security was the key to success.'

'You could trust somebody you had never met, whose identity was hidden from you – you could trust him with vast sums of money, and the destiny of the world as we know it?'

Steven hesitated again as if seeking the right words. 'Caliph has an aura that seems to envelop all of us. The man who recruited me—' Steven seemed reluctant to repeat the name again, proof to Peter of the influence that Caliph exerted ' – is a man whose judgement I respect tremendously. He was convinced, and this helped to convince me.'

'What do you think now?' Peter asked abruptly. 'Are you still convinced?'

Steven drained the whisky glass, and then smoothed his moustache with a little nervous gesture.

'Come on, Steven,' Peter encouraged him.

'I still think Caliph had the right idea—' he said reluctantly. ' – The rules have changed, Peter. We were fighting for survival of the world as we know it. We were merely playing to the new morality—'

He crossed to the silver tray on the corner of his desk and refilled the whisky glass.

' – Up to now we have had one hand tied behind our backs, while the Reds and the extreme left and the members of the Third World have had both hands to fight with and a dagger in each one. All Caliph did was to take off our shackles.'

'What has made you change your mind then?' Peter asked.

'I'm not sure that I have changed my mind.' Steven turned back to face him. 'I still think it was the right idea—'

' – But?' Peter insisted.

Steven shrugged. 'The murder of Aaron Altmann, the mutilation of Melissa-Jane—' He hesitated. ' – Other acts of which I suspect Caliph was the originator. They were not for the common good. They were merely to protect Caliph's personal safety, or to satisfy what I am beginning to believe is vaunted and unbridled lust for power.' Steven shook his head again. 'I believed Caliph to be noble and dedicated – but there is no nobility in some of the things he has done. He has acted like a common criminal. He has acted for personal advantage and glorification. I believe in the concept of Caliph – but I know now we have chosen the wrong man. He has been corrupted by the power that we placed in his hands.'

Peter listened to him carefully, his head cocked to one side, his blue eyes clear and quietly searching.

'All right, Steven. So we discover that Caliph is not a deity – but a man with a man's petty greed and self-interest.'

'Yes, I suppose I do.' Steven's handsome florid face was heavy with regret. 'Caliph is not what I believed he might be.'

'Do you accept now that he is evil – truly evil?'

'Yes, I accept that.' Then, fiercely, 'But God, how I wish Caliph had been what I believed he was at the beginning.'

Peter could understand that and he nodded.

'It was what this crazy world of ours needed—' Steven went on bitterly. ' – We need somebody, a strong man to tell us what to do. I thought it was Caliph. I wanted it so badly to be him.'

'So now, do you accept that Caliph was not that man?'

'Yes,' said Steven simply. 'But if there was a man like that I would follow him again, unquestioningly.'

'You said you would do anything to prove to me that you had nothing to do with Melissa-Jane – will you help me to destroy Caliph?'

'Yes.' Steven did not hesitate.

'There will be great personal risk,' Peter pointed out, and now Steven met his eyes steadily.

'I know that. I know Caliph better than you.'

Peter found that his affection for his brother was now reinforced with admiration. Steven lacked very few of the manly virtues, he thought. He had strength and courage and brains, perhaps his major vice was that he had too much of each.

'What do you want me to do, Peter?'

'I want you to arrange a meeting with Caliph – face to face.'

'Impossible.' Steven dismissed it immediately.

'You said that you had means of getting a message to him?'

'Yes, but Caliph would never agree to a meeting.'

'Steven, what is the single – the only weakness that Caliph has shown so far?'

'He has shown no weakness.'

'Yes, he has,' Peter denied.

'What is it?'

'He is obsessed with protecting his personal identity and safety,' Peter pointed out. 'As soon as that is threatened, he immediately reverts to abduction and torture and murder.'

'That isn't a weakness—' Steven pointed out. 'It's a strength.'

'If you can get a message to him – that his identity is in jeopardy. That somebody, an enemy, has penetrated his security screen and has managed to get close to him,' Peter suggested, and Steven considered it long and carefully.

'He would react very strongly,' Steven agreed. 'But it would not take him very long to find out that I was lying. That would immediately discredit me, and as you said earlier I would be at grave risk for no good reason.'

'It isn't a lie,' Peter told him grimly. 'There is a Mossad agent close to Caliph. Very close to him.'

'How do you know that?' Steven asked sharply.

'I cannot tell you,' Peter said. 'But the information is iron-clad. I even know the agent's code-name. I give you my word that the information is genuine.'

'In that case—' Steven thought it out again ' – Caliph would probably already be suspicious and would be prepared to accept my warning. However, all he would do would be to ask me to give him the name – pass it to him along his usual communications channel. That would be it.'

'You would refuse to pass the information – except face to face. You will protest that the information is much too sensitive. You would protest that your personal safety was at stake. What would be his reaction?'

'I would expect him to put pressure on me to divulge the name—'

'If you resisted?'

'I suppose he would have to agree to a meeting. As you have pointed out, it is his major obsession. But, if he met me face to face, his identity would be revealed anyway.'

'Think, Steven. You know how his mind works.'

It took a few seconds, then Steven's expression changed, consternation twisting his lips as though he was in pain.

'Good God – of course. If I forced him to a face-to-face meeting, I would be highly unlikely to survive it.'

'Exactly,' Peter nodded. 'If we baited it with something absolutely irresistible, Caliph would have to agree to meet you – but he would make arrangements to have you silenced immediately, before you had a chance to pass on his identity to anyone else.'

'Hell, Peter, this is creepy. As you told me earlier today, I am fat and out of condition. I wouldn't be much of a match against Caliph.'

'Caliph would take that into consideration when deciding whether to meet you or not,' Peter agreed.

'It sounds like suicide,' Steven persisted.

'You just signed on to be tough,' Peter reminded him.

'Tough is one thing, stupid is another.'

'You would be in no danger until you delivered the message. Caliph would not dare dispose of you until you delivered your message,' Peter pointed out. 'And I give you my word that I will never call on you to go to an assignation with Caliph.'

'I can't ask for more than that, I suppose.' Steven threw up his hands. 'When do you want me to contact him?'

'How do you do it – the contact?'

'Advert in the Personal column,' Steven told him, and Peter grinned with reluctant admiration. Neat, efficient and entirely untraceable.

'Do it as soon as you can,' Peter instructed.

'Monday morning,' Steven nodded, and went on studying his brother with a peculiarly intent expression.

'What is it, Steven?'

'I was just thinking. If only Caliph had been somebody like you, Peter.'

'Me?' For the first time Peter was truly startled.

'The warrior king – utterly ruthless in the pursuit of the vision of justice and rightness and duty.'

'I am not like that.' Peter denied it.

'Yes, you are,' Steven said positively. 'You are the type of man that I hoped Caliph might be. The type of man we needed.'

Peter had to presume that Caliph was watching him. After his murder of Baroness Altmann, Caliph's interest would be intense. Peter had to act predictably.

He caught the early Monday flight back to Brussels, and before midday was at his desk in Narmco headquarters. Here also he was the centre of much interest and power-play. Altmann Industries had lost its chief executive and there were strong undercurrents and court intrigues already afoot. Despite a number of subtle approaches Peter stayed aloof from the struggle.

On Tuesday evening Peter picked up the newspaper from the news-stand in the Hilton lobby. Steven's contact request was in the small-ads section.

> The children of Israel asked counsel of the Lord, saying, shall I go up again to battle? Judges. 20:23.

The quotation that Caliph had chosen seemed to epitomize his view of himself. He saw himself as godlike, set high above his fellow men.

Steven had explained to Peter that Caliph took up to forty-eight hours to answer.

Steven would wait each day after the appearance of the personal announcement at his desk in his office suite in Leadenhall Street, from noon until twenty minutes past the hour. He would have no visitors nor appointments for that time, and he would make certain that his direct unlisted telephone line was unengaged to receive the incoming contact.

There was no contact that Wednesday, but Steven had not expected one. On the Thursday Steven paced restlessly up and down the antique silk Kirman carpet as he waited for the call. He was already wearing the jacket of his suit, and his bowler and rolled umbrella were on the corner of the ornate French ormolu desk that squatted like some benign monster beneath the windows which looked across the street at Lloyds Exchange.

Steven Stride was afraid. He acknowledged the fact with direct self-honesty. Intrigue was part of his existence, had been for nearly all of his life – but always the game had been played to certain rules. He knew he was entering a new jungle, a savage wilderness where those few rules ceased entirely to exist. He was going in over his head; Peter had pointed out to him that this was not his way, and he knew Peter was right. Peter was right, and Steven was afraid as he had never been in his life. Yet he knew that he was going ahead with it. He had heard that it was the mark of true courage – to be able to meet and acknowledge fear, and yet control it sufficiently to be able to go ahead and do what duty dictated must be done.

He did not feel like a brave man.

The telephone rang once, too loud, too shrill – and every nerve in his body jumped taut and he found himself frozen, paralysed with fear in the centre of the beautiful and precious carpet.

The telephone rang again, the insistent double note sounded in his ears like the peal of doom, and he felt his bowels filled with the hot oily slime of fear, hardly to be contained.

The telephone rang the third time, and with an enormous effort he forced himself to make the three paces to his desk.

He lifted the telephone receiver, and heard the sharp chimes of the interference from the public telephone system.

'Stride,' he said. His voice was strained, high and almost shrill, and he heard the drop of the coin.

The voice terrified him. It was an electronic drone, inhuman, without gender, without the timbre of living emotion, without neither high nor low notes.

'Aldgate and Leadenhall Street,' said the voice.

Steven repeated the rendezvous and immediately the connection was broken.

Steven dropped the receiver onto its cradle and snatched up his bowler and umbrella as he hurried to the door.

His secretary looked up at him and smiled expectantly. She was a handsome grey-haired woman who had been with Steven for fifteen years.

'Sir?' She still called him that.

'I'm popping out for half an hour, May,' Steven told her. 'Look after the shop, there is a dear.' And he stepped into his private elevator and rode down swiftly to the underground garage where his Rolls was kept, together with the private vehicles of his senior executives.

In the elevator mirror he checked the exact angle of his bowler, a slightly raffish tilt over the right eye, and rearranged the bloom of the crimson carnation in the buttonhole of the dark blue Savile Row suit with its faint and elegant chalk stripe. It was important that he looked and acted entirely naturally during the next few minutes. His staff would remark on any departure from the normal.

In the garage he did not approach the dark-maroon Rolls-Royce which glowed in the subdued lighting like some precious gem. Instead he went towards the wicket gate in the steel roll-up garage door, and the doorman in his little glassed cubicle beside the door looked up from his football pools coupons, recognized the master and leaped to his feet.

'Afternoon, guv.'

'Good day, Harold. I won't be taking the car. Just stepping out for a few minutes.'

He stepped over the threshold of the gate, into the street and turned left, down towards the junction of Leadenhall Street and Aldgate. He walked fast, without seeming to hurry. Caliph spaced his intervals very tight, to make it difficult for the subject to pass a message to a surveillance unit. Steven knew he had only minutes to get from his office to the call box on the corner. Caliph seemed to know exactly how long it would take him.

The telephone in the red-framed and glass call box started to ring when he was still twenty paces away. Steven ran the distance.

'Stride,' he said, his voice slightly puffed with exertion, and immediately the coin dropped and the same electronic droning voice gave him the next contact point. It was the public call box at the High Street entrance to Aldgate tube station. Steven confirmed and the voice troubled him deeply, it sounded like that of a robot from some science fiction movie. It would not have been so bad if he had felt human contact.

The two receiving stations, neither of which was predictable, and the distances between them, had been carefully calculated to make it only just possible to reach them in time, to make it impossible for the call to be traced while the line was still open. Caliph or his agent was clearly moving from one call box to the next in another part of the city. Tracing them even a minute after he had left would be of no possible use in trying to establish identity.

The voice distorter that Caliph was using was a simple device no bigger than a small pocket calculator. Peter had told Steven that it could be purchased from a number of firms specializing in electronic surveillance, security and counter-measure equipment. It cost less than fifty dollars, and so altered the human voice – phasing out all sound outside the middle range – that even the most sophisticated recording device would not be able to lift a useable voice-print to compare with a computer bank memory. It would not even be able to determine whether the speaker was a man, a woman or a child.

Steven had an unusually clear path to the station, and found himself waiting outside the call box in the crowded entrance to the station while a young man in paint-speckled overalls, with long greasy blond hair, finished his conversation. Caliph's system allowed for prior use of the chosen public telephone, and as soon as the scruffy youth finished his leisurely chat, Steven pushed into the booth and made a show of consulting the directory.

The phone rang, and even though he was expecting it, Steven jumped with shock. He was perspiring now, with the walk and the tension, and his voice was ragged as he snatched the receiver.

'Stride,' he gulped.

The coin dropped and Caliph's impersonal tones chilled him again.

'Yes?'

'I have a message.'

'Yes?'

'There is danger for Caliph.'

'Yes?'

'A government intelligence agency has put an agent close to him, close enough to be extremely dangerous.'

'Say the source of your information.'

'My brother. General Peter Stride.' Peter had instructed him to tell the truth, as much as was possible.

'Say the government agency involved.'

'Negative. The information is too sensitive. I must have assurance that Caliph receives it personally.'

'Say the name or position of the enemy agent.'

'Negative. For the same reasons.'

Steven glanced at his gold Cartier tank watch with its black alligator strap. They had been speaking for fifteen seconds – he knew the contact would not last longer than thirty seconds. Caliph would not risk exposure beyond that time. He did not wait for the next question or instruction.

'I will pass the information only to Caliph, and I must be certain it is him, not one of his agents. I request a personal meeting.'

'That is not possible,' droned the inhuman voice.

'Then Caliph will be in great personal danger.' Steven found courage to say it.

'I repeat, say the name and position of enemy agent.'

Twenty-five seconds had passed.

'I say again, negative. You must arrange a face-to-face meeting for transfer of this information.'

A single droplet of sweat broke from the hairline of Steven's temple and ran down his cheek. He felt as though he were suffocating in the claustrophobic little telephone box.

'You will be contacted,' droned the voice and the line clicked dead.

Steven took the white silk handkerchief from his top pocket and dabbed at his face. Then he carefully rearranged the scrap of silk in his pocket, not folded into neat spikes but with a deliberately casual drape.

He squared his shoulders, lifted his chin and left the booth. Now for the first time he felt like a brave man. It was a feeling he relished, and he stepped out boldly swinging the rolled umbrella with a small flourish at each pace.

Peter had been within call of the telephone all that week, during the hours of involvement with the series of Narmco projects which he had put in train before his departure for Tahiti, and which all seemed to be maturing simultaneously. There were meetings that began in the morning and lasted until after dark, there were two separate day journeys, one to Oslo and another to Frankfurt, catching the early businessman's plane and back in the Narmco office before evening. Always he was within reach of a telephone and Steven Stride knew the number; even when he was in the NATO Officers Club gymnasium, sharpening his body to peak physical condition, or practising until after midnight in the underground pistol range until the 9-mm Cobra was an extension of his hands – either hand, left or right, equally capable of grouping the X circle at fifty metres, from any position, standing, kneeling or prone, always he was within reach of the telephone.

Peter felt like a prize fighter in training camp, concentrating all his attention on the preparations for the confrontation he knew lay ahead.

At last the weekend loomed, with the prospect of being boring and frustrating. He refused invitations to visit the country home of one of his Narmco colleagues, another to fly down to Paris for the Saturday racing – and he stayed alone in the Hilton suite, waiting for the call from Steven.

On Sunday morning he had all the papers sent up to his room, English and American and French – German which he could read better than he spoke, and even the Dutch and Italian papers which he could stumble through haltingly, missing every third word or so.

He went through them carefully, trying to find a hint of Caliph's activity. New abductions, hijackings or other acts which might give him a lead to some new Caliph-dominated pressures.

Italy was in a political uproar. The confusion so great that he could only guess at how much of it was from the left and how much from the right. There had been an assassination in Naples of five known members of the Terrorist Red Brigade, all five taken out neatly with a single grenade. The grenade type had been determined as standard NATO issue, and the execution had been in the kitchen of a Red

Brigade safe apartment in a slum area of the city. The police had no leads. It sounded like Caliph. There was no reason to believe that his 'chain' did not include prominent Italian businessmen. A millionaire Italian living in his own country had to be the earth's most endangered species after the blue whale, Peter thought wryly, and they might have called on Caliph to go on the offensive.

Peter finished the continental papers, and turned with relief to the English and American. It was a little before Sunday noon, and he wondered how he could live out the desolate hours until Monday morning. He was certain that there would be no reply to Steven's request for a meeting before then.

He started on the English-language newspapers, spinning them out to cover the blank time ahead.

The British Leyland Motor Company strike was in its fifteenth week – with no prospect of settlement. Now there was a case for Caliph, Peter smiled wryly, remembering his discussion with Steven. Knock a few heads together for their own good.

There was only one other item of interest in his morning's reading. The President of the United States had appointed a special negotiator in another attempt to find a solution to the Israeli occupation of the disputed territories in the Middle East. The man he had chosen was Dr Kingston Parker, who was described as a personal friend of the President and one of the senior members of his inner circle of advisors, a man well thought of by all parties in the dispute, and an ideal choice for the difficult job. Again Peter found himself in agreement. Kingston Parker's energies and resources seemed bottomless.

Peter dropped the last paper and found himself facing a void of boredom that would extend through until the following day. There were three books he should read beside his bed, and the Hermes crocodile case was half-filled with

Narmco material, yet he knew that he would not be able to concentrate – not with the prospect of the confrontation with Caliph over-shadowing all else.

He went through into the mirrored bathroom of the suite, and found the package that he had purchased the previous day in the cosmetic section of Galéries Anspach, one of the city's largest departmental stores.

The wig was of good-quality human hair, not the obviously shiny nylon substitute. It was in his own natural colour, but much longer than Peter wore his hair. He arranged it carefully along his own hairline, and then set to work with a pair of scissors, trimming and tidying it. When he had it as close to his liking as possible, he began to tint the temples with 'Italian Boy' hair silvering.

It took him most of the afternoon, for he was in no hurry, and he was critical of his own work. Every few minutes he consulted the snapshot which Melissa-Jane had taken with her new Polaroid camera, Peter's Christmas present to her, at Abbots Yew on New Year's Day. It was a good likeness of both the Stride brothers, Peter and Steven, standing full face and smiling indulgently at Melissa-Jane's command to do so.

It highlighted the resemblances of the two brothers, and also pointed out their physical differences. The natural hair colouring was identical but Steven's was fashionably longer, curling on his collar at the back, and appreciably greyer at the temples and streaked at the front.

Steven's face was heavier, with the first trace of jowls, and his colour was higher, perhaps the first ruddy warnings of heart malfunction or merely the banner of good living in his cheeks. Yet with the wig on his head, Peter's own face seemed much fuller.

Next Peter shaped the moustache, trimming it down into the infantry officer model that Steven favoured. There had been a good selection of artificial moustaches to choose from in the cosmetic section, amongst a display of artificial eyelashes and eyebrows, but none had been exactly right. Peter had to work on it carefully with the scissors, and then tint it with a little silver.

When he fastened it in place with the special adhesive gum, the result was quite startling. The moustache filled out his face even further, and of course the eyes of the twins were almost exactly the same shape and colour. Their noses were both straight and bony. Peter's mouth was a little more generous, and did not have the same hard relentless line of lip – but the moustache concealed much of that.

Peter stood back and examined himself in the full-length mirror. He and Steven were within a quarter of an inch in height, they had the same breadth of shoulder. Steven was heavier in the gut, and his neck was thickening, giving him a thrusting bull-like set to his head and shoulders. Peter altered his stance slightly. It worked. He doubted that anybody who did not know both of them intimately would be able to detect the substitution. There was no reason to believe that Caliph or any of his closest lieutenants would have seen either Steven or Peter in the flesh.

He spent an hour practising Steven's gait, watching himself in the mirror, trying to capture the buoyant cockiness of Steven's movements, searching for little personal mannerisms, the way Steven stood with both hands clasped under the skirts of his jacket; the way he brushed his moustache with one finger, from the parting under his nose – left and right.

Clothing was not a serious problem. Both brothers had used the same tailor since Sandhurst days, and Steven's dress habits were invariable and inviolable. Peter's knew exactly what he would wear in any given situation.

Peter stripped off wig and moustache and repacked them carefully in their Galéries Anspach plastic packets, then buttoned them into one of the interior divisions of the Hermes case.

Next he removed the Cobra parabellum from another

division. It was still in the chamois leather holster, and he bounced the familiar weight of the weapon in the palm of his hand. Reluctantly he decided he could not take it with him. The meeting would almost certainly be in England. The contact that Steven had had on Thursday had clearly originated in London. He had to believe the next contact would be in that same city. He could not take the chance of walking through British customs with a deadly weapon on his person. If he was stopped, there would be publicity. It would instantly alert Caliph. He would be able to get another weapon from Thor Command once he was in England. Colin Noble would supply him, just as soon as Peter explained the need, he was certain of that.

Peter went down and checked the Cobra pistol into the safe deposit box of the hotel reception office, and returned to his room to face the wearying and indefinite wait. It was one of a soldier's duties to which he had never entirely accustomed himself – he always hated the waiting.

However, he settled down to read Robert Asprey's *War in the Shadows*, that definitive tome on the history and practice of guerrilla warfare down the ages. He managed to lose himself sufficiently to be mildly surprised when he glanced at his watch and saw it was after eight o'clock. He ordered an omelette to be sent up by room service, and ten seconds after he replaced the receiver, the telephone rang. He thought it might be a query from the kitchen about his dinner order.

'Yes, what is it?' he demanded irritably.

'Peter?'

'Steven?'

'He has agreed to a meeting.'

Peter felt his heart lunge wildly.

'When? Where?'

'I don't know. I have to fly to Orly tomorrow. There will be instructions for me at the airport.'

Caliph covering and backtracking. Peter should have

expected it. Desperately he cast his mind back to the layout of Orly Airport. He had to find a private place to meet Steven and make the change-over. He discarded swiftly the idea of meeting in one of the lounges or washrooms. That left one other location.

'What time will you be there?' Peter demanded.

'Cooks have got me onto the early flight. I'll be there at eleven fifteen.'

'I'll be there before you,' Peter told him. He knew the Sabena timetable by heart and all senior Narmco executives had special VIP cards which assured a seat on any flight.

'I will book a room at the Air Hotel on the fourth floor of Orly South terminal in your name,' he told Steven now. 'I'll wait in the lobby. Go directly to the reception desk and ask for your key. I will check behind you to make certain you are not followed. Do not acknowledge me in any way. Have you got that, Steven?'

'Yes.'

'Until tomorrow, then.'

Peter broke the connection, and went through into the bathroom. He studied his own face in the mirror.

'Well, that takes care of getting a weapon from Thor.' Caliph had not set the meeting in England. It was clear now that Paris was only a staging point, and that in his usual careful fashion Caliph would move the subject on from there – perhaps through one or more staging points, to the final rendezvous.

The subject would go in unarmed, and unsupported – and Peter was certain that afterwards Caliph would take his usual pains to ensure that the subject would be unable to carry back a report of the meeting.

I am drawing two cards inside for a straight flush, and Caliph is the dealer from a pack that he has had plenty of time to prepare, Peter thought coldly, but at least the waiting was over. He began to pack his toilet articles into the waterproof Gucci bag.

Sir Steven Stride marched into the lobby of Orly South Air Hotel at five minutes past noon, and Peter smiled to himself in self-congratulation. Steven was wearing a blue double-breasted blazer, white shirt and cricket-club tie, above grey woollen slacks and black English handmade shoes – none of your fancy Italian footwear for Steven.

It was Steven's standard informal dress, and Peter had only been wrong about the tie – he had guessed that it would be an I Zingari pattern. Peter himself wore a double-breaster and grey slacks under his trench coat and his shoes were black Barkers.

Steven's eyes flickered around the lobby, passing over Peter sitting in a far corner with a copy of *Le Monde*, then Steven moved authoritively to the reception desk.

'My name is Stride, do you have a reservation for me?' Steven spoke slowly, in rich plummy tones, for very few of these damned people spoke English. The clerk checked swiftly, nodded, murmured a welcome and gave Steven the form and the key.

'Four One Six.' Steven checked the number loudly enough for Peter to hear. Peter had been watching the entrance carefully; fortunately there had been very few guests entering the lobby during the few minutes since Steven's arrival, and none of those could possibly have been Caliph surveillance. Of course, if this was a staging point, as Peter was certain it was, then Caliph would have no reason to put surveillance on Steven – not until he got much closer to the ultimate destination.

Steven moved to the elevator with a porter carrying his single small valise, and Peter drifted across and joined the small cluster of guests waiting at the elevators.

He rode up shoulder to shoulder with Steven in the crowded elevator, neither of them acknowledging the other's existence, and when Steven and the porter left at the fourth stage Peter rode on up three floors, walked the length of the corridor and back, then took the descending elevator to Steven's floor.

Steven had left the door to 416 off the catch, and Peter pushed it open and slipped in without knocking.

'My dear boy.' Steven was in his shirt sleeves. He had switched on the television, but now he turned down the sound volume and hurried to greet him with both affection and vast relief.

'No problems?' Peter asked.

'Like clockwork,' Steven told him. 'Would you like a drink? I got a bottle in the duty-free.'

While he hunted for glasses in the bathroom, Peter checked the room swiftly. A view down towards the square functional buildings of the market that had replaced the picturesque Les Halles in central Paris, matching curtains and covers on the twin beds, television and radio sets, between the beds, modern soulless furniture – it was a room, that was the most and the least that could be said for it.

Steven carried in the glasses and handed one to Peter.

'Cheers!'

Peter tasted his whisky. It was too strong and the Parisian tap water tasted of chlorine. He put it aside.

'How is Caliph going to get instructions to you?'

'Got them already.' Steven went to his blazer, hanging over the back of the chair, and found a long white envelope in the inside pocket. 'This was left at the Air France Information Desk.'

Peter took the envelope and as he split the flap he sank onto one of the armchairs. There were three items in the envelope.

A first-class Air France airline ticket, a voucher for a chauffeur-driven limousine and a hotel reservation voucher.

The air ticket could have been purchased for cash at any Air France outlet or agency, the limousine and hotel bookings could have been made equally anonymously. There was no possibility of a trace back from any of these documents.

Peter opened the Air France ticket and read the destination. Something began to crawl against his skin, like the loathsome touch of body vermin. He closed the ticket and checked the two vouchers; now the sick feeling of betrayal and evil spread through his entire body, numbing his fingertips and coating the back of his tongue with a bitter metallic taste like copper salts.

The air ticket was for this evening's flight from Orly to Ben-Gurion Airport in Israel, the hired-car voucher was good for a single journey from there to Jerusalem, the hotel voucher was for a room in the King David Hotel in that ancient and holy city.

'What is it, Peter?'

'Nothing,' said Peter, only then aware that the sickness must have shown on his face. 'Jerusalem,' he went on. 'Caliph wants you in Jerusalem.'

There was one person in Jerusalem at that moment. Somebody who had been in his thoughts almost unceasingly since last he had embraced her in the darkness of Bora-Bora Island – so very long ago.

Caliph was in Jerusalem, and Magda Altmann was in Jerusalem – and the sickness was heavy in the pit of his stomach.

The deviousness of Caliph.

No, he told himself firmly. I have travelled that road already. It cannot be Magda.

The genius of Caliph, evil and effortless.

It is possible. He had to admit it then. With Caliph, anything is possible. Every time Caliph shook the dice box the numbers changed, different numbers, making different totals – but always completely plausible, always completely believable.

It was one of the basic proven theorems of his trade that

a man, any man, was blinded and deafened and rendered senseless by love. Peter was in love, and he knew it.

All right. So now I have to try and free my mind and think it all over again, as though I were not besotted.

'Peter, are you all right?' Steven demanded again, now with real concern. It was impossible to think with Steven hovering over him. He would have to put it aside.

'I am going to Jerusalem in your place,' Peter said.

'Come again, old boy?'

'We are changing places – you and I.'

'You won't get away with it.' Steven shook his head decidedly. 'Caliph will take you on the full toss.'

Peter picked up his Hermes case and went through into the bathroom. He worked quickly with the wig and artificial moustache and then called.

'Steven, come here.'

They stood side by side and stared at themselves in the mirror.

'Good God!' Steven grunted. Peter altered his stance slightly, conforming more closely to his brother.

'That's incredible. Never knew you were such a good-looking blighter,' Steven chuckled, and wagged his head wonderingly. Peter imitated the gesture perfectly.

'Damn it, Peter.' The chuckle dried on Steven's lips. 'That's enough. You're giving me the creeps.'

Peter pulled the wig off his head. 'It will work.'

'Yes,' Steven conceded. 'It will work – but how the hell did you know I would be wearing a blazer and greys?'

'Trick of the trade,' Peter told him. 'Don't worry about it. Let's go through the paperwork now.'

In the bedroom they laid out their personal documents in two piles, and went swiftly through them.

The passport photographs would pass readily enough.

'You have to shave your soup-strainer,' Peter told him, and Steven stroked his moustache with one finger, left and right – lingeringly, regretfully.

'Is that absolutely necessary? I'd feel like I was walking around in public with no trousers on.'

Peter took the slim gold ball-point from his inside pocket and a sheaf of hotel stationery from the drawer. He studied Steven's signature in the passport for a minute, and then dashed it off on the top sheet.

'No.' He shook his head, and tried again. It was like Steven's walk, cocky and confident, the 'T' was crossed with a flourishing sword stroke of the pen.

In sixty seconds he had it perfected.

'With that wig on your head you could walk into my bank any day and sign for the whole damned bundle,' Steven muttered uneasily. 'Then go home and climb into bed with Pat.'

'Now, *there* is an idea.' Peter looked thoughtful.

'Don't joke about it,' Steven pleaded.

'Who's joking?' Peter went through the credit cards, club membership cards, driver's licence and all the other clutter of civilized existence.

Steven's mastery of his brother's signature was not nearly as effective, but after twenty minutes' practice was just adequate for hotel registration purposes.

'Here is the address of a hotel on the left bank. Magnificent restaurant, and the management are very understanding if you should want to invite a young lady up to your room for a drink.'

'Perish the thought.' Steven looked smug at the prospect.

'It should only be for a few days, Steven. Just keep very low. Pay cash for everything. Keep clear of the George V or the Meurice, Le Doyen and Maxim's – all the places where they know you.'

They went carefully over the last details of the exchange of identity, while Steven shaved off the moustache and anointed the bare patch tenderly with Eau de Sauvage.

'You'd better move now,' Peter told him at last. 'Wear

this—' It was Peter's buff trenchcoat that would cover his blazer. ' – And let's change ties.'

Steven was ready, and he stood rather awkwardly by the door, in the tightly fitting trenchcoat.

'Steven, can I ask you a question?' Peter did not know why he had to know now, it had been buried so deeply for so long and yet at this moment it was deadly important to know.

'Of course, old boy.' Steven seemed to welcome the postponement of the moment of parting.

'Sandhurst.' Peter tried to keep the embarrassment out of his voice. 'I never asked you before – but you didn't do it, did you, Steven?'

Steven met his eyes calmly, steadily. 'No, Peter. I did not do it. My word on it.'

Peter took his brother's proffered right hand and squeezed it hard. It was ridiculous to feel so relieved.

'I'm glad, Steven.'

'Take care of yourself, old boy.'

'I will,' Peter nodded. 'But if anything happens,' Peter hesitated, ' – Melissa-Jane—'

'Don't worry. I'll take care of it.'

Why do Englishmen have such difficulty talking to each other, Peter wondered, let alone communicating affection and gratitude?

'Well, I'll be getting along then,' said Steven.

'Take a guard on your middle stump, and don't be caught in the slips,' Peter cautioned him with the old inanity.

'Count on it,' said Steven, and went out into the passage, closing the door behind him firmly, leaving his brother to think about Jerusalem.

Only the name had changed from Lod to Ben-Gurion – otherwise the Arrivals Hall was as Peter remembered it. One of the few airports on the globe which has sufficient luggage trolleys, so that the passengers do not have to fight for possession.

In the Arrivals Hall there was a young Israeli driver with the name:

Sir Steven Stride

printed in white chalk on a schoolboy's black slate.

The driver wore a navy-blue cap with a black patent-leather peak. It was his only item of uniform, otherwise he was dressed in sandals and a white cotton shirt. His English had the usual strong American turn to it, and his attitude was casual and friendly – he might be driving the limousine today, but tomorrow he could be at the controls of a Centurion tank, and he was as good a man as his passenger any day.

'Shalom, Shalom,' he greeted Peter. 'Is that all your luggage?'

'Yes.'

'*Beserder*. Let's go.' He did not offer to push Peter's trolley, but chatted amicably as he led him out to the limousine.

It was a stretched-out 240 D Mercedes Benz – almost brand new, lovingly polished – but somebody had painted a pair of squinting eyes on each side of the chrome three-pointed star on the boot of the vehicle.

They had hardly pulled out through the airport gates when one of the characteristic aromas of Israel filled the cab of the Mercedes – the smell of orange blossom from the citrus orchards that lined each side of the road.

For some reason the smell made Peter feel uneasy, a sensation of having missed something, of having neglected some vital aspect. He tried to think it all out again, from the beginning, but the driver kept up a running commentary as they pulled up the new double highway, over the hills through the pine forests towards Jerusalem, and the voice distracted him.

Peter wished he had kept the list that he had drawn up in the hotel room at Orly instead of destroying it. He tried to reconstruct it in his mind.

There were a dozen items on the plus side. The third was:

Magda told me about Cactus Flower. Would she have done so if she was Caliph?

And then directly opposite, in the 'minus' column:

If Magda is Caliph, then 'Cactus Flower' does not exist. It was an invention for some undisclosed reason.

This was the item that pricked him like a burr in a woollen sock. He kept coming back to it; there was a link missing from the logic of it and he tried to tease it loose. It was there just below the surface of his mind, and he knew instinctively that if he missed it the consequences would be dire.

The driver kept chatting, turning to glance back at him every few minutes with a cheerful demand for recognition.

'That's right, isn't it?'

Peter grunted. The man was irritating him – the missing item was there, just beginning to surface. He could see the shape of it. Why had the smell of orange blossom worried him? The smell of flowers? Cactus flower? There was something there, something missing from the list.

If Magda is not Caliph then— Was that it? He was not certain. ' – Will that be all right, then?' The driver was insisting again.

'I'm sorry – what was that?'

'I said, I had to drop a parcel off at my mother-in-law,' the driver explained again. 'It's from my wife.'

'Can't you do that on your way back?'

'I'm not going back tonight—' The driver grinned

winningly over his shoulder. ' – My mother-in-law lives right on our way. It won't take five minutes. I promised my wife I'd get it to her mother today.'

'Oh, very well then,' Peter snapped. There was something about the man he did not like, and he had lost track of the item that had been worrying him.

He felt as though he was in a chess game with a vastly superior opponent, and he had overlooked a castle on an open file, or a knight in a position to fork simultaneous check on his king and queen.

'We turn off here,' the driver explained, and swung off into a section of new apartment blocks, all of them built of the custard-yellow Jerusalem stone, row upon row of them, Israel's desperate attempt to house its new citizens. At this time of evening the streets were deserted, as families gathered for the evening meal.

The driver jinked through the maze of identical-seeming streets with garrulous confidence and then braked and parked in front of one of the square, boxlike, yellow buildings.

'Two minutes,' he promised, and jumped out of the Mercedes, scampered around to the rear and opened the boot. There was a scratching sound, a small bump and then the lid of the boot slammed and the driver came back into Peter's line of vision – carrying a brown paper parcel.

He grinned at Peter, with the ridiculous cap pushed onto the back of his head, mouthed another assurance through the closed window: 'Two minutes—' and went into the main door of the apartment.

Peter hoped he might be longer. The silence was precious. He closed his eyes, and concentrated.

If Magda is not Caliph then – then— There was the ticking sound of the engine cooling, or was it the dashboard clock? Peter thrust the sound to the back of his mind.

– then – then Cactus Flower exists. Yes, that was it!

Cactus Flower exists, and if he exists he is close enough to Caliph to know of Sir Steven Stride's threat to expose him—

Peter sat upright, rigid in his seat. He had believed that Steven Stride would be perfectly safe – until after the meeting with Caliph. That was the terrible mistake.

– Cactus Flower must stop Steven Stride reaching Caliph! Yes, of course. Christ, how had he not seen it before. Cactus Flower was Mossad, and Peter was sitting in a street of Jerusalem – Mossad's front yard – dressed as Steven Stride.

Christ! He felt the certainty of mortal danger. Cactus Flower probably made the arrangements himself. If Magda Altmann is not Caliph, then I am walking right into Cactus Flower's sucker punch!

The damned clock kept ticking, a sound as nerve-racking as a leaky faucet.

I am in Cactus Flower's city – in Cactus Flower's limo—

The ticking. Oh God! It was not coming from the dashboard. Peter turned his head. It was coming from *behind him*; from the boot which the driver had opened and in which he had moved something. Something that was now ticking away quietly.

Peter wrenched the door handle and hit the door with his shoulder, instinctively grabbing the Hermes case with his other hand.

They would have stripped out the metal partition between the boot and the back seat to allow the blast to cut through. There was probably only the leather upholstery between him and whatever was ticking. That was why he had heard it so clearly.

Time seemed to have slowed, so he was free to think it out as the seconds dropped as lingeringly as spilled honey.

Infernal machine, he thought. Why that ridiculously nineteenth-century term should occur to him now, he could not guess, a relic from the childhood days when he read *Boy's Own Paper*, perhaps.

He was out of the Mercedes now, almost losing his balance as his feet hit the unsurfaced and broken sidewalk.

It is probably plastic explosive with a clockwork timer on the detonator, he thought, as he started to run. What delay would they use? Thirty seconds? No, the driver had to get well away. He had said two minutes, said it twice –

The thoughts raced through his mind, but his legs seemed to be shackled, dragging against an enormous weight. Like trying to run waist deep in the sucking surf of a sandy beach.

– It will be two minutes, and he has been gone that long—

Ten paces ahead of him there was a low wall that had been built as a flower box around the apartment block. It was knee high, a double brick wall with the cavity filled with dry yellow earth and precariously sustaining the life of a few wizened oleander bushes.

Peter dived head first over the wall, breaking his fall with shoulder and forearm, and rolling back hard under the protection of the low wall.

Above his head were the large windows of the ground-floor apartments. Lying on his side, peering up at them, Peter saw the reflection of the parked Mercedes as though in a mirror.

He covered his ears with the palms of both hands. The Mercedes was only fifty feet away. He watched it in the glass, his body braced, his mouth wide open to absorb blast shock in his sinuses.

The Mercedes erupted. It seemed to open quite sedately, like one of those time-elapse movies of a rose blooming. The shining metal spread and distorted like grotesque black petals, and bright white flame shot through it – that was all Peter saw, for the row of apartment windows disappeared, blown away in a million glittering shards by the blast wave, leaving the windows gaping like the toothless mouths of old decrepit men, and at the same moment the blast smashed into Peter.

Even though it was muted by the thick wall of the flower box, it crushed him, seemed to drive in his ribs, and the air whooshed from his lungs. The fearsome din of the explosion clamoured in his head, filling his skull with little bright chips of rainbow light.

He thought he must have lost consciousness for a moment, then there was the patter of falling debris raining down around him and something struck him a painful blow in the small of his back. It spurred him.

He dragged himself to his feet, struggling to refill his empty lungs. He knew he had to get away before the security forces arrived, or he could expect intensive interrogation which would certainly disclose the fact that he was not Sir Steven.

He started to run. The street was still deserted, although he could hear the beginning of the uproar which must follow. The cries of anguish and of fear.

He reached the corner and stopped running. He walked quickly to the next alley behind an apartment block. There were no street lights and he paused in the shadows. By now a dozen figures shouting questions and conjecture were hurrying towards the smoke and dust of the explosion.

Peter recovered his breath and dusted down his blazer and slacks, waiting until the confusion and shouting were at their peak. Then he walked quietly away.

On the main road he joined a short queue at the bus stop. The bus dropped him off in the Jaffa Road.

He found a café opposite the bus stop and went through into the men's room. He was unmarked, but pale and strained; his hands still shook from the shock of the blast as he combed his hair.

He went back into the café, found a corner seat and ordered falafel and pitta bread with coffee.

He sat there for half an hour, considering his next move.

If Magda Altmann is not Caliph— he repeated the conundrum which he had solved just in time to save his life.

Magda Altmann is not Caliph! He knew it then with utter certainty. Cactus Flower had tried to stop Sir Steven Stride reaching Caliph with his denunciation. Therefore Magda had told him the truth. His relief flooded his body with a great warm glow – and his first instinct was to telephone her at the Mossad number she had given him. Then he saw the danger. Cactus Flower was Mossad. He dared not go near her – not yet.

What must he do then? And he knew the answer without having to search for it. He must do what he had come to do. He must find Caliph, and the only fragile thread he had to follow was the trail that Caliph had laid for him.

He left the café and found a taxi at the rank on the corner.

'King David Hotel,' Peter said, and sank back in the seat.

At least I know the danger of Cactus Flower now, he thought grimly. I won't walk into the next one blind.

Peter took one glance around the room that had been reserved for him. It was in the back of the hotel and across the road the tall bell tower of the Y.M.C.A. made a fine stance from which a sniper could command the two windows.

'I ordered a suite,' Peter snapped at the reception clerk who had led him up.

'I'm sorry, Sir Steven.' The man was immediately flustered. 'There must have been a mistake.'

Another glance around the room and Peter had noted half a dozen sites at which Cactus Flower might have laid another explosive charge to back up the one that had failed in the back of the Mercedes. He would prefer to spend a night in a pit full of cobras rather than accept the quarters that Cactus Flower had prepared for him.

Peter stepped back into the passage and fixed the clerk with his most imperious gaze. The man scampered and returned within five minutes – looking mightily relieved.

'We have one of our best suites for you.'

Number 122 commanded a magnificent view across the valley to the Jaffa Gate in the wall of the Old City, and in the centre of this vista towered the Church of the Last Supper.

The gardens of the hotel were lush with lawns and tall graceful palms, children shrieked gleefully around the swimming pool while a cool light breeze broke the heat.

The suite abutted onto the long open terrace, and the moment he was alone, Peter lowered the heavy roller shutters across the terrace door. Cactus Flower could too easily send a man in that way. Then Peter stepped out onto the private balcony.

On the tall stone battlements of the French Consulate adjoining the gardens they were lowering the Tricolour against the flaming backdrop of the sunset. Peter watched it for a moment – then concentrated again on the security of the suite.

There was possible access from the room next door, an easy step across from window to balcony. Peter hesitated – then decided to leave the balcony unshuttered. He could not bring himself to accept the claustrophobic effect of a completely shuttered room.

Instead he drew the curtains and ordered a large whisky and soda from room service. He needed it. It had been a long hard day.

Then he stripped off tie and shirt, wig and moustache and washed away some of the tensions. He was towelling himself when there was a tap on the door.

'Damned quick service,' he muttered, and clapped the wig on his head and stepped into the lounge, just as a key rattled in the lock and the door swung open. Peter lifted the towel and pretended to be still drying his face to cover the lack of moustache on his lip.

'Come in,' he gruffed through the towel, and then froze in the doorway, and a vice seemed to close around his heart and restrict his breathing.

She wore a man's open-neck shirt, with patch pockets on the breasts, and khaki combat breeches hugged her narrow hips. The long legs were thrust into soft-soled canvas boots. Yet she carried herself with the same unforced chic as if she had been dressed in the height of Parisian fashion.

'Sir Steven.' She closed the door swiftly behind her, and Peter saw her palm the slim metal pick with which she had turned the lock. 'I'm Magda Altmann, we have met before. I have come to warn you that you are in very grave danger.'

The abundant short curls formed a dark halo around her head, and her eyes were huge and green with concern.

'You must immediately leave this country. I have my private executive jet aircraft at an airfield near here—'

Peter lowered the towel enough to allow himself to speak.

'Why are you telling me this?' he interrupted her brusquely. 'And why should I believe you?'

He saw the quick roses of anger bloom in her cheeks.

'You are dabbling in things you do not understand.'

'Why should you want to warn me?' Peter insisted.

'Because—' she hesitated and then went on sharply, ' – because you are Peter Stride's brother. For that reason and no other I would not want you killed.'

Peter tossed the towel back into the bathroom and with the same movement pulled off the wig and dropped it onto the chair beside him.

'Peter!' Astonishment riveted her and she stared at him, the colour that anger had painted in her cheeks fled and her eyes turned a deep luminous green. He had forgotten once again how beautiful she was.

'Well, don't just stand there,' he said, and she ran to him on those long, graceful legs and flung her arms around his neck.

They strained together silently, neither of them found words necessary for many minutes. Then she broke away.

'Peter, darling – I cannot stay long. I took a terrible chance coming here at all. They are watching the hotel and the girls on the switchboard are Mossad. That is why I could not telephone—'

'Tell me everything you can,' he ordered.

'All right, but hold me, *chéri.* I do not wish to waste a minute of this little time we have together.'

She hid in the bathroom when the waiter brought the whisky, then joined Peter on the couch.

'Cactus Flower reported to control that Steven had requested a meeting with Caliph, and that he intended to denounce him. That was all I knew until yesterday – but I could build on that. First of all I was amazed that Steven was the subject of the first Cactus Flower report and not you, Peter—' She caressed the smooth hard brown muscle of his chest as she spoke. ' – It had never occured to me, even when we discussed the fact that the report mentioned no Christian name.'

'It didn't occur to me either, not until I'd already left Les Neuf Poissons.'

'Then, of course, I guessed that you had taxed Steven with it, and told him the source of your information. It would have been a crazy thing to do – not your usual style, at all. But I thought that being your brother—' She trailed off.

'That is exactly what I did—'

'Peter, we could still talk if we were on the bed,' she murmured. 'I have been without you for so long.'

Her bare skin felt like hot satin, and they lay entwined with the hard smooth plain of her belly pressed to his. Her mouth was against his ear.

' – Steven's request for a meeting went directly to Caliph through a channel other than Cactus Flower. He had no chance to head it off—'

'Who is Cactus Flower, have you found that out?'

'No.' She shook her head. 'I still do not know.' And she raked her long fingernails lightly down across his belly.

'If you do that – I cannot think clearly,' he protested.

'I am sorry.' She brought her hand up to his cheek. 'Anyway, Caliph instructed Cactus Flower to arrange the meeting with Steven. I did not know what arrangements were being made – until I saw Sir Steven's name on the immigration lists this evening. I was not particularly looking for his name, but as soon as I saw it I guessed what was happening. I guessed that Cactus Flower had enticed him here to make his interception easier. It took me three hours to find where Sir Steven would be staying.'

They were both silent now, and she lowered her face and pressed it into the soft of his neck, sighing with happiness.

'Oh God, Peter. How I missed you.'

'Listen, my darling. You must tell me everything else you have.' Peter lifted her chin tenderly so he could see her face and her eyes came back into focus.

'Did you know that there was to be an assassination attempt on Steven?'

'No – but it was the logical step for Mossad to protect Cactus Flower.'

'What else?'

'Nothing.'

'You don't know if actual arrangements have been made for a meeting between Caliph and Steven?'

'No, I don't know,' she admitted.

'You still have no indication at all of Caliph's identity?'

'No, none at all.'

They were silent again, but now she propped herself on one elbow and watched his face as he spoke.

'Cactus Flower would have to make the arrangements for the meeting as Caliph instructed. He would not be able to take the chance of faking it – not with Caliph.'

Magda nodded in silent agreement.

'Therefore we have to believe that at this moment Caliph is close, very close.'

'Yes.' She nodded again, but reluctantly.

'That means that I have to go on impersonating Steven.'

'Peter, no. They will kill you.'

'They have already tried—' Peter told her grimly, and quietly outlined the destruction of the Mercedes. She touched the bruise in the small of his back where he had been struck by flying debris from the explosion.

'They won't let you get close to Caliph.'

'They may have no choice,' Peter told her. 'Caliph is so concerned for his own safety – he is going to insist on the meeting.'

'They will try and kill you again,' she implored him.

'Perhaps, but I'm betting the meeting with Caliph is arranged to take place very soon. They won't have much opportunity to set up another elaborate trap like the Mercedes, and I'll be expecting it – I've got to go ahead with it, Magda.'

'Oh, Peter—' But he touched her lips, silencing the protest, and he was thinking aloud again.

'Let's suppose Mossad knew that I was not Steven Stride, that my real purpose was not to denounce Cactus Flower? What difference would that make to the thinking at Mossad?'

She considered that. 'I'm not certain.'

'If they knew it was Peter Stride impersonating Steven Stride,' he insisted, 'would that make them curious enough to let the meeting go ahead?'

'Peter, are you suggesting I turn in a report to my control at Mossad – ?'

'Would you do that?'

'Sweet merciful God,' she whispered. 'I could be signing your death warrant, Peter my darling.'

' – or you could be saving my life.'

'I don't know.' She sat up erect in the bed and ran the fingers of both hands through the short dark curls, the lamplight glowed on her skin with a pale, smooth opalescence and the small fine breasts changed shape as she moved her arms. 'Oh, Peter, I don't know.'

'It could be our only chance to ever get close to Caliph,' he insisted, and the lovely face was racked with indecision.

'Caliph believes I have killed you, he believes that I have transmitted a warning to him through my brother. He will have his guard as low as ever it will be. We will never have a chance again like this.'

'I am so afraid for you, Peter. I am so afraid for myself without you—' She did not finish it, but pulled up her long naked legs and hugged her knees to her breasts. It was a defensive foetal position.

'Will you do it?' he asked gently.

'You want me to tell my control your real identity, to tell him that I believe your real purpose is not to denounce Cactus Flower – but some other unknown—'

'That is right.'

She turned her head and looked at him.

'I will do it in exchange for your promise,' she decided.

'What is that?'

'If I judge from my control at Mossad that you are still in danger, and that they still intend intercepting you before you reach Caliph – then I want your promise that you will abandon the attempt. That you will immediately go to where the Lear is waiting and that you will allow Pierre to fly you out of here to a safe place.'

'You will be honest with me?' he asked. 'You will judge Mossad's reaction fairly – and even if there is a half-decent chance of me reaching Caliph you will allow me to take that chance?'

She nodded, but he went on grimly, making certain of it. 'Swear it to me!'

'I would not try to prevent you – just as long as there is a chance of success.'

'Swear it to me, Magda.'

'On my love for you, I swear it,' she said quietly, and he relaxed slightly.

'And I in turn swear to you that if there is no chance of meeting Caliph – I will leave on the Lear.'

She turned against his chest, wrapping both her arms around his neck.

'Make love to me, Peter. Now! Quickly! I have to have that at least.'

As she dressed she went over the arrangements for communicating.

'I cannot come through the switchboard here – I explained why,' she told him as she laced the canvas boots. 'You must stay here, in this room where I can reach you. If there is danger I will send someone to you. It will be somebody I trust. He will say simply. "Magda sent me," and you must go with him. He will take you to Pierre and the Lear jet.'

She stood up and belted the khaki breeches around her narrow waist, crossing to the mirror to comb out the dark damp tangle of her curls.

'If you hear nothing from me it will mean that I judge there is still a chance of reaching Caliph—' Then she paused and her expression altered. ' – Are you armed, Peter?' She was watching him in the mirror as she worked with her hair. He shook his head.

'I could get a weapon to you – a knife, a pistol?'

And again he shook his head. 'They will search me before I am allowed near Caliph. If they find a weapon—' He did not have to finish it.

'You are right,' she agreed.

She turned back to him from the mirror, buttoning the shirt over the nipples of her breasts, which were still swollen and dark rosy red from their loving.

'It will all happen very quickly now, Peter. One way or the other it will be over by tomorrow night. I have a feeling here—' She touched herself between the small breasts that pushed out the cotton of her shirt. 'Now kiss me. I have stayed too long already – for the safety of both of us.'

Peter slept very little after Magda left him, even though he was very tired. A dozen times he started awake during the night with every nerve strung tightly, rigid and sweating in his bed.

He was up before first light, and ordered one of those strange Israeli breakfasts of salads and hard-boiled eggs with pale green centres to be sent up to his room.

Then he settled down once more to wait.

He waited the morning out, and when there had been no message from Magda by noon, the certainty increased that Mossad had decided not to prevent the meeting with Caliph. If there had been any doubt in Magda's mind she would have sent for him. He had a light lunch sent up to the room.

The flat bright glare of noon gradually mellowed into warm butter-yellow, the shadows crept out timidly from the foot of the palm trees in the garden as the sun wheeled across a sky of clear high aching blue, and still Peter waited.

When there was an hour left of daylight, the telephone rang again. It startled him, but he reached for it quickly.

'Good evening, Sir Steven. Your driver is here to fetch you,' said the girl at the reception desk.

'Thank you. Please tell him I will be down directly,' said Peter.

He was fully dressed, had been ready all that day to move immediately. He needed only to place the crocodile skin case in the cupboard and lock it, then he left the room and strode down the corridor to the elevators.

He had no way of knowing if he was going to meet Caliph, or if he was about to be spirited out of Israel in Magda's Lear jet.

'Your limousine is waiting outside,' the pretty girl at the desk told him. 'Have a nice evening.'

'I hope so,' Peter agreed. 'Thank you.'

The car was a small Japanese compact, and the driver was a woman, plump and grey-haired with a friendly, ugly face like Golda Meir, Peter thought.

He let himself into the back seat, and waited expectantly for the message, 'Magda sent me.'

Instead, the woman bade him 'Shalom Shalom' politely, started the engine, switched on the headlights and drove serenely out of the hotel grounds.

They swept sedately around the outer walls of the old city in the gathering dusk, and dropped down in the valley of Kidron. Glancing back Peter saw the elegant new buildings of the Jewish quarter rising above the tops of the walls.

When last he had been in Jerusalem that area had been a deserted ruin, deliberately devastated by the Arabs.

The resurrection of that holy quarter of Judaism seemed to epitomize the spirit of these extraordinary people, Peter thought.

It was a good conversational opening, and he remarked on the new development to his driver.

She replied in Hebrew, clearly denying the ability to speak English. Peter tried her in French with the same result.

The lady has been ordered to keep her mouth tight shut, he decided.

The night came down upon them as they skirted the lower slopes of the Mount of Olives, and left the last straggling buildings of the Arab settlements. The lady driver settled down to a comfortable speed, and the road was almost deserted. It dropped gently down through a dark shallow valley, with the crests of a desolate desert landscape humped up on each side of the wide metalled road.

The sky was empty of cloud or haze, and the stars were brighter white and clearer, as the last of the day faded from the western sky behind them.

The road had been well sign-posted, ever since they had left the city. Their direction was eastward towards the Jordan, the Dead Sea and Jericho – and twenty-five minutes after leaving the King David, Peter glimpsed in the headlights the signpost on the right-hand side of the road, declaring in English, Arabic and Hebrew that they were now descending below sea level into the valley of the Dead Sea.

Once again Peter attempted to engage the driver in conversation, but her reply was monosyllabic. Anyway, Peter decided, there was nothing she would be able to tell him. The car was from a hire company. There was a plastic nameplate fastened onto the dashboard giving the company's name, address and hire rates. All she would know was their final destination – and he would know that soon enough himself.

Peter made no further attempt to speak to her, but remained completely alert; without detectable movement he performed the pre-jump paratrooper exercises, pitting muscle against muscle so that his body would not stiffen with long inactivity but would be tuned to explode from stillness into instant violent action.

Ahead of them the warning signals of the crossroads caught the headlights, and the driver slowed and signalled the left turn. As the headlights caught the signpost, Peter saw that they had taken the Jericho road, turning away from the Dead Sea, and heading up the valley of the Jordan towards Galilee in the north.

Now the bull's horns of the new moon rose slowly over the harsh mountain peaks across the valley, and gave enough light to pick out small features in the dry blasted desert around them.

Again the driver slowed, this time for the town of Jericho itself, the oldest site of human communal habitation on this earth – for six thousand years men had lived here and their wastes had raised a mountainous tell hundreds of feet above the desert floor. Archaeologists had already excavated the collapsed walls that Joshua had brought crashing down with a blast of his ram's horns.

'A hell of a trick.' Peter grinned in the darkness. 'Better than the nuke bomb.'

Just before they reached the tell, the driver swung off the main road. She took the narrow secondary road between the clustered buildings – souvenir stalls, Arab cafés, antique dealers – and slowed for the twisting uneven surface.

They ground up onto higher dry hills in low gear, and at the crest the driver turned again onto a dirt track. Now fine talcum dust filled the interior and Peter sneezed once at the tickle of it.

Half a mile along the track a noticeboard stood on trestle legs, blocking the right of way.

'Military Zone,' it proclaimed. 'No access beyond this point.'

The driver had to pull out onto the rocky verge to avoid the notice, and there were no sentries to enforce the printed order.

Quite suddenly Peter became aware of the great black cliff face that rose sheer into the starry night ahead of them – blotting out half the sky.

Something stirred in Peter's memory – the high cliffs above Jericho, looking out across the valley of the Dead Sea; of course, he remembered then – this was the scene of the temptation of Christ. How did Matthew record it? Peter cast for the exact quotation:

> Again, the devil taketh him up into an exceeding high mountain, and sheweth him all the kingdoms of the world, and the glory of them –

Had Caliph deliberately chosen this place for its mystical association, was it all part of the quasi-religious image that Caliph had of himself?

> He shall give his angels charge concerning thee: and in their hands they shall bear thee up –

Did Caliph truly see himself as the heir to ultimate power over all the kingdoms of the world – that power that the ancient chroniclers had referred to as 'The Sixth Order of Angels'?

Peter felt his spirits quail in the face of such monumental madness, such immense and menacing vision, compared to which he felt insignificant and ineffectual. Fear fell over him like a gladiator's net, enmeshing his resolve, weakening him. He struggled with it silently, fighting himself clear of its mesh before it could render him helpless in Caliph's all-embracing power.

The driver stopped abruptly, turned in the seat and switched on the cab light. She studied him for a moment.

Was there a touch of pity in her old and ugly face, Peter wondered?

'Here,' she said gently.

Peter drew his wallet from the inner pocket of his blazer.

'No,' she shook her head. 'No, you owe nothing.'

'*Toda raba.*' Peter thanked her in his fragmentary Hebrew, and opened the side door.

The desert air was still and cold, and there was the sagey smell of the low thorny scrub.

'Shalom,' said the woman through the open window; then she swung the vehicle in a tight turn. The headlights swept the grove of date palms ahead of them, and then turned back towards the open desert. Slowly the small car pitched and wove along the track in the direction from which they had come.

Peter turned his back on it, allowing his eyes to become accustomed to the muted light of the yellow horned moon and the whiter light of the fat desert stars.

After a few minutes he picked his way carefully into the palm grove. There was the smell of smoke from a dung fire, and the fine blue mist of smoke hung amongst the trees.

Somewhere in the grove he heard a goat bleat plaintively, and then the high thin wail of a child – there must be a Bedouin encampment in the oasis. He moved towards it, and came abruptly into an opening surrounded by the palms. The earth had been churned by the hooves of many beasts, and Peter stumbled slightly in the loose footing and then caught his balance.

In the centre of the opening was the stone parapet which guarded a deep fresh-water well. There was a primitive windlass set above the parapet and another dark object which Peter could not immediately identify, dark and shapeless, crouching upon the parapet.

He went towards it cautiously, and felt his heart tumble within him as it moved.

It was a human figure, in some long voluminous robe

that swept the sandy earth, so that it seemed to float towards him in the gloom.

The figure stopped five paces from him, and he saw that the head was covered by a monk's cowl of the same dark woollen cloth, so that the face was in a forbidding black hole beneath the cowl.

'Who are you?' Peter demanded, and his voice rasped in his own ears. The monk did not reply, but shook one hand free of the wide sleeve and beckoned to him to follow, then turned and glided away into the palm grove.

Peter went after him, and within a hundred yards was stepping out hard to keep the monk in sight. His light city shoes were not made for this heavy going, loose sand with scattered outcrops of shattered rock.

They left the palm grove and directly ahead of them, less than a quarter of a mile away, the cliff fell from the sky like a vast cascade of black stone.

The monk led him along a rough but well-used footpath, and though Peter tried to narrow the distance between them, he found that he would have to break into a trot to do so – for although the monk appeared to be a broad and heavy man beneath the billowing robe, yet he moved lithely and lightly.

They reached the cliff, and the path zig-zagged up it, at such a gradient that they had to lean forward into it. The surface was loose with shale and dry earth – becoming progressively steeper. Then underfoot the path was paved, the worn steps of solid rock.

On one hand the drop away into the valley was deeper always and the sheer cliff on the other seemed to lean out as though to press him over the edge.

Always the monk was ahead of him, tireless and quick, his feet silent on the worn steps, and there was no sound of labouring breath. Peter realized that a man of that stamina and bulk must be immensely powerful. He did not move as you might expect a man of God and prayer to move. There was the awareness and balance of a fighting man about him, the unconscious pride and force of the warrior. With Caliph nothing was ever as it seemed, he thought.

The higher they climbed, so the moonlit panorama below them became more magnificent, a soaring vista of desert and mountain with the great shield of the Dead Sea a brilliant beaten silver beneath the stars.

– All the kingdoms of the world, and the glory of them, Peter thought.

They had not paused to rest once on the climb. How high was it, Peter wondered – a thousand feet, fifteen hundred perhaps? His own breathing was deep and steady, he was not yet fully extended and the light sweat that dewed his forehead cooled in the night air.

Something nudged his memory, and he sniffed at the faintly perfumed aroma on the air. It was not steady, but he had caught it faintly once or twice during the climb.

Peter was plagued by the non-smoker's acute sense of smell; perfumes and odours always had special significance for him – and this smell was important, but he could not quite place it now. It nagged at him, but then it was lost in a host of other more powerful odours – the smell of human beings in community.

The smell of cooking smoke, of food and the underlying sickly taint of rotting garbage and primitive sewage disposal.

Somewhere long ago he had seen photographs of the ancient monastery built into the top of these spectacular cliffs, the caves and subterranean chambers honeycombed the crest of the rock face, and walls of hewn rock had been built above them by men dead these thousand years.

Yet the memory of that faint perfumed aroma lingered with Peter, as they climbed the last hundred feet of that terrifying drop and came out suddenly against the stone tower and thick fortification, into which was set a heavy timber door twelve feet high and studded with iron bolts.

At their approach the door swung open. There was a

narrow stone passageway ahead of them lit by a single storm lantern in a niche at the corner of the passageway.

As Peter stepped through the gate, two other figures closed on each side of him out of the darkness and he moved instinctively to defend himself, but checked the movement and stood quiescent with his hand half raised as they searched him with painstaking expertise for a weapon.

Both these men were dressed in single-piece combat suits, and they wore canvas paratrooper boots. Their heads were covered by coarse woollen scarves wound over mouth and nose so only their eyes showed. Each of them carried the ubiquitous Uzi sub-machine guns, loaded and cocked and slung on shoulder straps.

At last they stood back satisfied, and the monk led Peter on through a maze of narrow passages. Somewhere there was the sound of monks at their devotions, the harsh chanting of the Greek Orthodox service. The sound of it, and the smoky cedarwood aroma of burning incense, became stronger, until the monk led Peter into a cavernous, dimly lit church nave hewn from the living rock of the cliff.

In the gloom the old Greek monks sat like long embalmed mummies in their tall dark wooden pews. Their time-worn faces masked by the great black bushes of their beards. Only their eyes glittered, alive as the jewels and precious metals that gilded the ancient religious icons on the stone walls.

The reek of incense was overpowering, and the hoarse chant of the office missed not a single beat as Peter and the robed monk passed swiftly amongst them.

In the impenetrable shadows at the rear of the church, the monk seemed abruptly to disappear, but when Peter reached the spot he discovered that one of the carved pews had been swung aside to reveal a dark secret opening in the rock.

Peter went into it cautiously. It was totally dark – but his feet found shallow stone steps, and he climbed a twisting stairway through the rock – counting the steps to five hundred, each step approximately six inches high.

Abruptly he stepped out into the cool desert night again. He was in a paved open courtyard, with the brilliant panoply of the stars overhead, the cliff rising straight ahead and a low stone parapet protecting the sheer drop into the valley behind him.

Peter realized that this must be one of the remotest and most easily defensible rendezvous that Caliph could have chosen – and there were more guards here.

Again they came forward, two of them, and searched him once again even more thoroughly than at the monastery gate.

While they worked Peter looked around him swiftly. The level courtyard was perched like an eagle's eyrie on the brink of the precipice, the parapet wall was five feet high. Across the courtyard were the oblong entrances to caves carved into the cliff face. They would probably be the retreats of the monks seeking solitude.

There were other men in the courtyard, wearing the same uniform with heads hidden by the Arab shawl headgear. Two of them were setting out flashlight beacons in the shape of a pyramid.

Peter realized they were beacons for an aircraft. – Not an aircraft. A helicopter was the only vehicle which would be able to get into this precarious perch on the side of the precipice.

All right then, the beacons would serve to direct a helicopter down into the level paved courtyard.

One of the armed guards ended his body search by checking the buckle of Peter's belt, tugging it experimentally to make certain it was not the handle of a concealed blade.

He stood back and motioned Peter forward. Across the courtyard the big monk waited patiently at the entrance to one of the stone cells that opened onto the courtyard.

Peter stooped through the low entrance. The cell was dimly lit by a stinking kerosene lamp set in a stone niche above the narrow cot. There was a crude wooden table against one wall, a plain crucifix above it and no other ornamentation.

Hewn from the rock wall was a ledge which acted as a shelf for a dozen heavy battered leather-bound books and a few basic eating utensils. It was also a primitive seat.

The monk motioned him towards it, but himself remained standing by the entrance to the cell with his hands thrust into the wide sleeves of his cassock, his face turned away and still masked completely by the deep hood.

There was utter silence from the courtyard beyond the doorway, but it was an electric waiting silence.

Suddenly Peter was aware of the perfumed aroma again, here in the crude stone cell, and then with a small tingling shock he recognized it. The smell came from the monk.

He knew instantly who the big man in the monk's cowl was, and the knowledge confused him utterly, for long stricken moments.

Then like the click of a well-oiled lock slipping home it all came together. He knew – oh God – he knew at last.

The aroma he had recognized was the faint trace of the perfumed smoke of expensive Dutch cheroots, and he stared fixedly at the big hooded monk.

Now there was a sound on the air, a faint flutter like moth's wings against the glass of the lantern, and the monk cocked his head slightly, listening intently.

Peter was balancing distances and times and odds in his head.

The monk, the five armed men in the courtyard, the approaching helicopter –

The monk was the most dangerous factor. Now that Peter knew who he was, he knew also that he was one of the most highly trained fighting men against whom he could ever match himself.

The five men in the yard – Peter blinked with sudden realization. *They would not be there any longer.* It was as simple as that. Caliph would never allow himself to be seen by any but his most trusted lieutenants, and by those about to die. The monk would have sent them away. They would be waiting close by, but it would take them time to get back into action.

There were only the monk and Caliph. For he knew that the dinning of rotor and engine was bringing Caliph in to the rendezvous. The helicopter sounded as though it were already directly overhead. The monk's attention was on it. Peter could see how he held his head under the cowl, he was off-guard for the first time.

Peter heard the sound of the spinning rotors change as the pilot altered pitch for the vertical descent into the tiny courtyard. The cell was lit through the doorway by the reflection of the helicopter's landing lights beating down into the courtyard with a relentless white glare.

Dust began to swirl from the down-draught of the rotors, it smoked in pale wisps into the cell and the monk moved.

He stepped to the doorway, the empty dark hole in the cowl which was his face turned briefly away from Peter as he glanced out through the entrance of the cell.

It was the moment for which Peter had waited, his whole body was charged, like the S in an adder's neck before it strikes. At the instant that the monk turned his head away, Peter launched himself across the cell.

He had ten feet to go, and the thunder of the helicopter's engines covered all sound – yet still some instinct of the fighting man warned the huge monk, and he spun into the arc of Peter's attack. The head under the cowl dropped defensively, so that Peter had to change his stroke. He could no longer go for the kill at the neck, and he chose the right shoulder for a crippling blow. His hand was stiff as a headman's blade and it slogged into the monk's shoulder between the neck and the humerus joint of the upper arm.

Peter heard the collar bone break with a sharp brittle crack, high above even the roar of the helicopter's engines.

With his left hand Peter caught the monk's crippled arm at the elbow and yanked it up savagely, driving the one edge of shattered bone against the other so it grated harshly, twisting it so the bone shards were razor cutting edges in their own living flesh – and the monk screamed, doubling from the waist to try and relieve the intolerable agony in his shoulder.

Shock had paralysed him, [illegible] big powerful body went slack in Peter's grasp.

Peter used all his weight and the impetus of his rush to drive the monk's head into the doorjamb of the cell; skull met stone with a solid clunk and the big man dropped face-down to the paved floor.

Peter rolled him swiftly and pulled up the skirts of the cassock. Under it the man wore paratrooper boots and the blue full-length overalls of Thor Command. On his webbing belt was the blue steel and polished walnut butt of the Browning Hi-power .45 pistol in its quick-release holster. Peter sprang it from its steel retaining clamp and cocked the pistol with a sweep of the left hand. It would be loaded with Velex explosives.

The woollen folds of the cowl had fallen back from Colin Noble's head, the wide generous mouth now hanging open slackly, the burned-toffee eyes glazed with concussion, the big crooked prize-fighter's nose – all the well-remembered features, once so dearly cherished in comradeship.

Blood was streaming from Colin's thick curling hairline, running down his forehead and under his ear – but he was still conscious.

Peter put the muzzle of the Browning against the bridge of his nose. The Velex bullet would cut the top off his skull. Peter had lost his wig in those desperate seconds, and he saw recognition spark in Colin's stunned eyes.

'Peter! No!' croaked Colin desperately. ' – I'm Cactus Flower!'

The shock of it hit Peter solidly, and he released the pressure on the Browning's trigger. It held him for only a moment and then he turned and ducked through the low doorway leaving Colin sprawling on the stone floor of the cell.

The helicopter had settled into the courtyard. It was a five-seater Bell Jet Ranger, painted in the blue and gold colours of Thor Command – and on its side was the Thor emblem and the words:

THOR COMMUNICATIONS

There was a pilot still at the controls, and one other man who had already left the cabin of the machine and was coming towards the entrance of the cell.

Even though he was doubled over to avoid the swirling rotor blades, there was no mistaking the tall powerful frame. The high wind of the rotors tumbled the thick greying leonine curls about the noble head, and the landing lights lit him starkly like the central character in some Shakespearian tragedy – a towering presence that transcended his mere physical stature.

Kingston Parker straightened as he came out from under the swinging rotor, and for an earth-stopping instant of time he stared at Peter across the stone-paved courtyard. Without the wig he recognized Peter instantly.

Kingston Parker stood for that instant like an old lion brought to bay.

'Caliph!' Peter called harshly, and the last doubt was gone as Kingston Parker whirled, incredibly swiftly for such a big man. He had almost reached the cabin door of the Jet Ranger before Peter had the Browning up.

The first shot hit Parker in the back, and flung him

forward through the open door, but the gun had thrown high and right. It was not a killing shot, Peter knew it, and now the helicopter was rising swiftly, turning on its own axis, rising out over the edge of the precipice.

Peter ran twenty feet and jumped to the parapet of the hewn stone wall. The Jet Ranger soared above him, its belly white and bloated like that of a man-eating shark, the landing lights blazing down, half dazzling Peter. It swung out over the edge of the cliff.

Peter took the Browning double-handed, shooting directly upwards, judging the exact position of the fuel tank in the rear of the fuselage, where it joined the long stalk-like tail – and he pumped the big heavy explosive shells out of the gun, the recoil pounding down his outflung arms and jolting into his shoulders.

He saw the Velex bullets biting into the thin metal skin of the underbelly, the tiny wink of each bullet as it burst, but still the machine reared away above him – and he had been counting his shots. The Browning was almost empty.

Seven, eight – then suddenly the sky above him filled with flame, and the great whooshing concussion of air jarred the stone under his feet.

The Jet Ranger turned over on her back, a bright bouquet of flame, the engine howling its death cry, and it toppled beyond the edge of the precipice and plunged, burning savagely, into the dark void below where Peter stood.

Peter began to turn back towards the courtyard, and he saw the armed men pouring in through the stone gateway.

They were Thor men, picked fighting men, men he had trained himself. There was one bullet left in the Browning. He knew he was not going to make it – but he made a try for the entrance to the stairway, his only escape route.

He ran along the top of the stone wall like a tightrope artist, and he snapped the single remaining bullet at the running men to distract them.

The crackle of passing shot dinned in his head, and he

flinched and missed his footing. He began to fall, twisting sideways away from the edge of the precipice – but then the bullets thumped into his flesh.

He heard the bullets going into his body with the rubbery socking sound of a heavyweight boxer hitting the heavy punch bag, and then he was flung out over the wall into the bottomless night.

He expected to fall for ever, a thousand feet to the desert floor below, where already the helicopter was shooting a hundred-foot fountain of fire into the air to mark Caliph's funeral pyre.

There was a narrow ledge ten feet below the parapet where a thorny wreath of desert scrub had found a precarious hold. Peter fell into it, and the curved thorns hooked into his clothing and into his flesh.

He hung there over the drop, and his senses began to fade.

His last clear memory was Colin Noble's bull bellow of command to the five Thor guards.

'Cease fire! Don't shoot again!' And then the darkness filled Peter's head.

In the darkness there were lucid moments, each disconnected from the other by eternities of pain and confused nightmare distortions of the mind.

He remembered being lifted up through the hatchway of an aircraft, lying in one of the light body-fitting Thor stretchers, strapped to it tightly, helpless as a newborn infant.

There was the memory of the inside cabin of Magda Altmann's Lear jet. He recognized the hand-painted decoration of the curved cabin roof. There were plasma bottles suspended above him; the whole blood was the beautiful ruby colour of fine claret in a crystal glass, and when he rolled his eyes downwards he saw the tubes connected to the thick bright needles driven into his arms – but he was terribly tired, an utter weariness that seemed to have bruised and crushed his soul – and he closed his eyes.

When he opened his eyes again, there was the roof of a long brightly lit corridor passing swiftly in front of his eyes. The feeling of motion, and the scratchy squeak of the wheels of a theatre trolley.

Quiet voices were speaking in French, and the bottle of beautiful bright blood was held above him by long slim hands that he knew so well.

He rolled his head slightly and he saw Magda's beloved face swimming on the periphery of his vision.

'I love you,' he said, but there was no sound and he realized that his lips had not moved. He could no longer support the weariness and he let his eyelids droop closed.

'How bad is it?' he heard Magda's voice speaking in that beautiful rippling French, and a man replied.

'One bullet is lying very close to the heart – we must remove it immediately.'

Then the prick of something into his flesh searching for the vein, and the sudden musty taste of Pentothal on his tongue, followed by the abrupt singing plunge back into the darkness.

He came back very slowly out of the darkness, conscious first of the bandages that swathed his chest and restricted his breathing.

The next thing he was aware of was Magda Altmann, and how beautiful she was. It seemed that she must have been there all along while he was in the darkness. He watched the joy bloom in her face as she saw that he was conscious.

'Thank you,' she whispered. 'Thank you for coming back to me, my darling.'

Then there was the room at La Pierre Bénite, with its high gilded ceilings and the view through the tall sash windows across the terraced lawns down to the lake. The trees along the edge of the water were in full leaf, and the very air seemed charged with spring and the promise of new life. Magda had filled the room with banks of flowers, and she was with him during most of each day.

'What happened when you walked back into the boardroom at Altmann Industries?' was one of the first questions he asked her.

'Consternation, *chéri*.' She chuckled, that husky little laugh of hers. 'They had already divided the spoils.'

The visitor came when Peter had been at La Pierre Bénite for eight days, and was able to sit in one of the brocaded chairs by the window.

Magda was standing beside Peter's chair, ready to protect him from over-exertion – physically or emotionally.

Colin Noble came into the room like a sheepish St Bernard dog. His right arm was strapped and carried in a sling across his chest. He touched it with his good hand.

'If I'd known it was you – and not Sir Steven – I'd never have turned my back on you,' he told Peter, and grinned placatingly.

Peter had stiffened, his face had transformed into a white rigid mask. Magda laid her hand upon his shoulder.

'Gently, Peter,' she whispered.

'Tell me one thing,' Peter hissed. 'Did you arrange the kidnapping of Melissa-Jane?'

Colin shook his head. 'My word on it. Parker used one of his other agents. I did not know it was going to happen.'

Peter stared at him, hard and unforgiving.

'Only after we had recovered Melissa-Jane, only then I knew that Caliph had planned it. If I had known – I would never have let it happen. Caliph must have known that. That is why he did not make me do it.' Colin was speaking quickly, urgently.

'What was Parker's object?' Peter's voice was still a vicious hiss.

'He had three separate objects. Firstly, to convince you that he was not Caliph. That's why his first order was to have you kill Parker himself. Of course, you never would have got near him. Then you were allowed to recover your daughter. It was Caliph himself who gave us O'Shaughnessy's name and where to find him. Then you were turned onto Magda Altmann—' Colin glanced at her apologetically. ' – Once you had killed her, you would have been bound to Caliph by guilt.'

'When did you learn this?' Peter demanded.

'The day after we found Melissa-Jane. By then there was nothing I could do that would not expose me as Cactus Flower – all I could do was to pass a warning to Magda through Mossad.'

'It's true, Peter,' said Magda quietly.

Slowly the rigidity went out of Peter's shoulders.

'When did Caliph recruit you as his Chief Lieutenant?' he asked, his voice also had altered, softened.

'As soon as I took over Thor Command from you. He was never certain of you, Peter, that was why he opposed your appointment to head of Thor – and why he jumped at the first chance to have you fired. That was why he tried to have you killed on the Rambouillet road. Only after the attempt failed did he realize your potential value to him.'

'Are the other Atlas unit commanders Caliph's lieutenants – Tanner at Mercury Command, Peterson at Diana?'

'All three of us. Yes!' Colin nodded, and there was a long silence.

'What else do you want to know, Peter?' Colin asked softly. 'Are there any other questions?'

'Not now.' Peter shook his head wearily. 'There will be many others later.'

Colin looked up at Magda Altmann inquiringly. 'Is he strong enough yet?' he asked. 'Can I tell him the rest of it?'

She hesitated a moment. 'Yes,' she decided. 'Tell him now.'

'Atlas was to be the secret dagger in the sleeve of Western civilization – a civilization which had emasculated itself and abased itself before its enemies. For once we would be able to meet naked violence and piracy with raw force. Atlas is a chain of powerful men of many nations banded together, and Caliph was to be its executive chief. Atlas is the only agency which transcends all national boundaries, and has as its object the survival of Western society as we know it. Atlas still exists, its structure is complete – only Caliph is dead. He died in a most unfortunate air accident over the Jordan valley – but Atlas still exists. It has to go on, once that part which Caliph has perverted is rooted out. It is our hope for the future in a world gone mad.'

Peter had never heard him speak so articulately, so persuasively.

'You know, of course, Peter, that you were the original choice to command Atlas. However, the wrong man superseded you – although nobody could know he was the wrong man at that time. Kingston Parker seemed to have all the qualities needed for the task – but there were hidden defects which only became apparent much later.' Colin began enumerating them, holding up the fingers of his uninjured arm.

'Firstly, he lacked physical courage. He became obsessed with his own physical safety – grossly abusing his powers to protect himself.

'Secondly, he was a man of unsuspected and overbearing ambition, with an ungoverned lust for raw power. Atlas swiftly became the vehicle to carry him to glory. His first goal was the Presidency of the United States. He was using Atlas to destroy his political opponents. Had he succeeded in achieving the presidency, no man can tell what his next goal would have been.'

Colin dropped his hand and balled it into a fist.

'The decision to allow you to reach the rendezvous with Kingston Parker on the cliffs above Jericho was made by more than one man – in more than one country.'

Colin grinned again, boyishly, disarmingly.

'I did not even know it was you. I believed it was Steven Stride, right up until the moment I turned my back on you!'

'Tell him,' said Magda quietly, 'Get it over with, Colin. He is still very weak.'

'Yes,' Colin agreed. 'I'll do it now. Yesterday at noon, your appointment to succeed Doctor Kingston Parker as head of Atlas Command was secretly confirmed.'

For Peter it was as though a door had at last opened, a door so long closed and locked, but through it now he could see his destiny stretching out ahead of him; clearly he could see it for the first time.

'You are the man best suited by nature and by training to fill the void which Kingston Parker has left.'

Even through the weakness of his abused body, Peter could feel a deep well of strength and determination within himself which he had never before suspected. It was as though it had been reserved expressly for this time, for this task.

'Will you accept the command of Atlas?' Colin asked. 'What answer must I take back with me?'

Magda's long fingers tightened on his shoulder, and they waited while he made his decision. It came almost immediately. There was no alternative open to him, Peter knew that – it was his destiny.

'Yes,' he said clearly. 'Tell them I accept the responsibility.'

It was a solemn moment, nobody smiled nor spoke for long seconds, and then:

'Caliph is dead,' Magda whispered. 'Long live Caliph.'

Peter Stride raised his head to look at her, but his voice when he replied was so cold that it seemed to frost upon his lips.

'Never,' he said, 'call me that again, ever.'

Magda made a small gesture of acquiescence, of total accord, then she stooped to kiss him on the mouth.

# HUNGRY AS THE SEA

This book is for my wife Danielle

Nicholas Berg stepped out of the taxi on to the floodlit dock and paused to look up at the *Warlock*. At this state of the tide she rode high against the stone quay, so that even though the cranes towered above her, they did not dwarf her.

Despite the exhaustion that fogged his mind and cramped his muscles until they ached, Nicholas felt a stir of the old pride, the old sense of value achieved, as he looked at her. She looked like a warship, sleek and deadly, with the high flared bows and good lines that combined to make her safe in any seaway.

The superstructure was moulded steel and glittering armoured glass, behind which her lights burned in carnival array. The wings of her navigation bridge swept back elegantly and were covered to protect the men who must work her in the cruellest weather and most murderous seas.

Overlooking the wide stern deck was the second navigation bridge, from which a skilled seaman could operate the great winches and drums of cable, could catch and control the hawser on the hydraulically operated rising fairleads, could baby a wallowing oil rig or a mortally wounded liner in a gale or a silky calm.

Against the night sky high above it all, the twin towers replaced the squat single funnel of the old-fashioned salvage tugs – and the illusion of a man-of-war was heightened by the fire cannons on the upper platforms from which the *Warlock* could throw fifteen hundred tons of sea water an hour on to a burning vessel. From the towers themselves could be swung the boarding ladders over which men could be sent aboard a hulk, and between them was painted the small circular target that marked the miniature heliport. The whole of it, hull and upper decks, was fireproofed so she could survive in the inferno of burning petroleum from a holed tanker or the flaming chemical from a bulk carrier.

Nicholas Berg felt a little of the despondency and spiritual exhaustion slough away, although his body still ached and his legs carried him stiffly, like those of an old man, as he started towards the gangplank.

'The hell with them all,' he thought. 'I built her and she is strong and good.'

Although it was an hour before midnight, the crew of the *Warlock* watched him from every vantage point they could find; even the oilers had come up from the engine room when the word reached them, and now loafed unobtrusively on the stern working deck.

David Allen, the First Officer, had placed a hand at the main harbour gates with a photograph of Nicholas Berg and a five-cent piece for the telephone call box beside the gate, and the whole ship was alerted now.

David Allen stood with the Chief Engineer in the glassed wing of the main navigation bridge and they watched the solitary figure pick his way across the shadowy dock, carrying his own case.

'So that's him.' David's voice was husky with awe and respect. He looked like a schoolboy under his shaggy bush of sun-bleached hair.

'He's a bloody film star.' Vinny Baker, the Chief Engineer, hitched up his sagging trousers with both elbows, and his spectacles slid down the long thin nose, as he snorted. 'A bloody film star,' he repeated the term with utmost scorn.

'He was first to Jules Levoisin,' David pointed out, and again the note of awe as he intoned that name, 'and he is a tug man from way back.'

'That was fifteen years ago.' Vinny Baker released his

elbow grip on his trousers and pushed his spectacles up on to the bridge of his nose. Immediately his trousers began their slow but inexorable slide deckwards. 'Since then he's become a bloody glamour boy – and an owner.'

'Yes,' David Allen agreed, and his baby face crumpled a little at the thought of those two legendary animals, master and owner, combined in one monster. A monster which was on the point of mounting his gangway to the deck of *Warlock*.

'You'd better go down and kiss him on the soft spot,' Vinny grunted comfortably, and drifted away. Two decks down was the sanctuary of his control room where neither masters nor owners could touch him. He was going there now.

David Allen was breathless and flushed when he reached the entry port. The new Master was halfway up the gangway, and he lifted his head and looked steadily at the mate as he stepped aboard.

Though he was only a little above average, Nicholas Berg gave the impression of towering height, and the shoulders beneath the blue cashmere of his jacket were wide and powerful. He wore no hat and his hair was very dark, very thick and brushed back from a wide unlined forehead. The head was big-nosed and gaunt-boned, with a heavy jaw, blue now with new beard, and the eyes were set deep in the cages of their bony sockets, underlined with dark plum-coloured smears, as though they were bruised.

But what shocked David Allen was the man's pallor. His face was drained, as though he had been bled from the jugular. It was the pallor of mortal illness or of exhaustion close to death itself, and it was emphasized by the dark eye-sockets. This was not what David had expected of the legendary Golden Prince of Christy Marine. It was not the face he had seen so often pictured in newspapers and magazines around the world. Surprise made him mute and the man stopped and looked down at him.

'Allen?' asked Nicholas Berg quietly. His voice was low and level, without accent, but with a surprising timbre and resonance.

'Yes, sir. Welcome aboard, sir.'

When Nicholas Berg smiled, the edges of sickness and exhaustion smoothed away at his brow and at the corners of his mouth. His hand was smooth and cool, but his grip was firm enough to make David blink.

'I'll show you your quarters, sir.' David took the Louis Vuitton suitcase from his grip.

'I know the way,' said Nick Berg. 'I designed her.'

He stood in the centre of the Master's day cabin, and felt the deck tilt under his feet, although the *Warlock* was fast to the stone dock, and the muscles in his thighs trembled.

'The funeral went off all right?' Nick asked.

'He was cremated, sir,' David said. 'That's the way he wanted it. I have made the arrangements for the ashes to be sent home to Mary. Mary is his wife, sir,' he explained quickly.

'Yes,' said Nick Berg. 'I know. I saw her before I left London. Mac and I were shipmates once.'

'He told me. He used to boast about that.'

'Have you cleared all his gear?' Nick asked, and glanced around the Master's suite.

'Yes sir, we've packed it all up. There is nothing of his left in here.'

'He was a good man.' Nick swayed again on his feet and looked longingly at the day couch, but instead he crossed to the port and looked out on to the dock. 'How did it happen?'

'My report—'

'Tell me!' said Nicholas Berg, and his voice cracked like a whip.

'The main tow-cable parted, sir. He was on the after-deck. It took his head off like a bullwhip.'

Nick stood quietly for a moment, thinking about that terse description of tragedy. He had seen a tow part under stress once before. That time it had killed three men.

'All right.' Nick hesitated a moment, the exhaustion had slowed and softened him so that for a moment he was on the point of explaining why he had come to take command of *Warlock* himself, rather than sending another hired man to replace Mac.

It might help to have somebody to talk to now, when he was right down on his knees, beaten and broken and tired to the very depths of his soul. He swayed again, then caught himself and forced aside the temptation. He had never whined for sympathy in his life before.

'All right,' he repeated. 'Please give my apologies to your officers. I have not had much sleep in the last two weeks, and the flight out from Heathrow was murder, as always. I'll meet them in the morning. Ask the cook to send a tray with my dinner.'

The cook was a huge man who moved like a dancer in a snowy apron and a theatrical chef's cap. Nick Berg stared at him as he placed the tray on the table at his elbow. The cook wore his hair in a shiny carefully coiffured bob that fell to his right shoulder, but was drawn back from the left cheek to display a small diamond earring in the pierced lobe of that ear.

He lifted the cloth off the tray with a hand as hairy as that of a bull gorilla, but his voice was as lyrical as a girl's, and his eyelashes curled soft and dark on to his cheek.

'There's a lovely bowl of soup, and a *pot-au-feu*. It's one of my little special things. You will adore it,' he said, and stepped back. He surveyed Nick Berg with those huge hands on his hips. 'But I took one look at you as you came aboard and I just knew what you really needed.' With a magician's flourish, he produced a half-bottle of Pinch Haig from the deep pocket of his apron. 'Take a nip of that with your dinner, and then straight into bed with you, you poor dear.'

No man had ever called Nicholas Berg 'dear' before, but his tongue was too thick and slow for the retort. He stared after the cook as he disappeared with a sweep of his white apron and the twinkle of the diamond, and then he grinned weakly and shook his head, weighing the bottle in his hand.

'Damned if I don't need it,' he muttered, and went to find a glass. He poured it half full, and sipped as he came back to the couch and lifted the lid of the soup pot. The steaming aroma made the little saliva glands under his tongue spurt.

The hot food and whisky in his belly taxed his last reserves, and Nicholas Berg kicked off his shoes as he staggered into his night cabin.

He awoke with the anger on him. He had not been angry in two weeks which was a measure of his despondency.

But when he shaved, the mirrored face was that of a stranger still, too pale and gaunt and set. The lines that framed his mouth were too deeply chiselled, and the early sunlight through the port caught the dark hair at his temple and he saw the frosty glitter there and leaned closer to the mirror. It was the first time he had noticed the flash of silver hair – perhaps he had never looked hard enough, or perhaps it was something new.

'Forty,' he thought. 'I'll be forty years old next June.'

He had always believed that if a man never caught the big one before he was forty, he was doomed never to do so. So what were the rules for the man who caught the big wave before he was thirty, and rode it fast and hard and high, then lost it again before he was forty and was washed out into the trough of boiling white water. Was he doomed also? Nick stared at himself in the mirror and felt the anger in him change its form, becoming directed and functional.

He stepped into the shower, and let the needles of hot water sting his chest. Through the tiredness and disillusion, he was aware, for the first time in weeks, of the underlying strength which he had begun to doubt was still there. He felt it rising to the surface in him, and he thought again of what an extraordinary sea creature he was, how it needed only a deck under him and the smell of the sea in his throat.

He stepped from the shower and dried quickly. This was the right place to be now. This was the place to recuperate – and he realized that his decision not to replace Mac with a hired skipper had been a gut decision. He needed to be here himself.

Always he had known that if you wanted to ride the big wave, you must first be at the place where it begins to peak. It's an instinctive thing, a man just knows where that place is. Nick Berg knew deep in his being that this was the place now, and, with his rising strength, he felt the old excitement, the old 'I'll show the bastards who is beaten' excitement, and he dressed swiftly and went up the Master's private companionway to the upper deck.

Immediately, the wind flew at him and flicked his dark wet hair into his face. It was force five from the south-east, and it came boiling over the great flat-topped mountain which crouched above the city and harbour. Nick looked up at it and saw the thick white cloud they called the 'table-cloth' spilling off the heights, and swirling along the grey rock cliffs.

'The Cape of Storms,' he murmured. Even the water in the protected dock leaped and peaked into white crests which blew away like wisps of smoke.

The tip of Africa thrust southwards into one of the most treacherous seas on all the globe. Here two oceans swept turbulently together off the rocky cliffs of Cape Point, and then roiled over the shallows of the Agulhas bank.

Here wind opposed current in eternal conflict. This was the breeding ground of the freak wave, the one that mariners called the 'hundred-year wave', because statistically that was how often it should occur.

But off the Agulhas bank, it was always lurking, waiting only for the right combination of wind and current, waiting for the inphase wave sequence to send its crest rearing a hundred feet high and steep as those grey rock cliffs of Table Mountain itself.

Nick had read the accounts of seamen who had survived that wave, and, at a loss for words, they had written only of a great hole in the sea into which a ship fell helplessly. When the hole closed, the force of breaking water would bury her completely. Perhaps the *Waratah Castle* was one which had fallen into that trough. Nobody would ever know – a great ship of 9,000 tons burden, she and her crew of 211 had disappeared without trace in these seas.

Yet here was one of the busiest sea lanes on the globe, as a procession of giant tankers ploughed ponderously around that rocky Cape on their endless shuttle between the Western world and the oil Gulf of Persia. Despite their bulk, those supertankers were perhaps some of the most vulnerable vehicles yet designed by man.

Now Nick turned and looked across the wind-ripped waters of Duncan Dock at one of them. He could read her name on the stern that rose like a five-storied apartment block. She was owned by Shell Oil, 250,000 dead weight tons, and, out of ballast, she showed much of her rust-red bottom. She was in for repairs, while out in the roadstead of Table Bay, two other monsters waited patiently for their turn in the hospital dock.

So big and ponderous and vulnerable – and valuable. Nick licked his lips involuntarily – hull and cargo together, she was thirty million dollars, piled up like a mountain.

That was why he had stationed the *Warlock* here at Cape Town on the southernmost tip of Africa. He felt the strength and excitement surging upwards in him.

All right, so he had lost his wave. He was no longer cresting and racing. He was down and smothered in white water. But he could feel his head breaking the surface, and he was still on the breakline. He knew there was another big wave racing down on him. It was just beginning to peak and he knew he still had the strength to catch her, to get up high and race again.

'I did it once – I'll damned well do it again,' he said aloud, and went down for breakfast.

He stepped into the saloon, and for a long moment nobody realized he was there. There was an excited buzz of comment and speculation that absorbed them all.

The Chief Engineer had an old copy of *Lloyd's List* folded at the front page and held above a plate of eggs as he read aloud. Nicholas wondered where he had found the ancient copy.

His spectacles had slid right to the end of his nose, so he had to tilt his head far backwards to see through them, and his Australian accent twanged like a guitar.

'In a joint statement issued by the new Chairman and incoming members of the Board, a tribute was paid to the fifteen years of loyal service that Mr Nicholas Berg had given to Christy Marine.'

The five officers listened avidly, ignoring their breakfasts, until David Allen glanced up at the figure in the doorway.

'Captain, sir,' he shouted, and leapt to his feet, while with the other hand, he snatched the newspaper out of Vinny Baker's hands and bundled it under the table.

'Sir, may I present the officers of *Warlock*.'

Shuffling, embarrassed, the younger officers shook hands hurriedly and then applied themselves silently to their congealing breakfasts with a total dedication that precluded any conversation, while Nick Berg took the Master's seat at the head of the long table in the heavy silence and David Allen sat down again on the crumpled sheets of newsprint.

The steward offered the menu to the new Captain, and returned almost immediately with a dish of stewed fruit.

'I ordered a boiled egg,' said Nick mildly, and an apparition in snowy white appeared from the galley, with the chef's cap at a jaunty angle.

'The sailor's curse is constipation, Skipper. I look after my officers – that fruit is delicious and good for you. I'm doing you your eggs now, dear, but eat your fruit first.' And the diamond twinkled again as he vanished.

Nick stared after him in the appalled silence.

'Fantastic cook,' blurted David Allen, his fair skin flushed pinkly and the *Lloyd's List* rustled under his backside. 'Could get a job on any passenger liner, could Angel.'

'If he ever left the *Warlock*, half the crew would go with him,' growled the Chief Engineer darkly, and hauled at his pants with elbows below the level of the table. 'And I'd be one of them.'

Nick Berg turned his head politely to follow the conversation.

'He's almost a doctor,' David Allen went on, addressing the Chief Engineer.

'Five years at Edinburgh Medical School,' agreed the Chief solemnly.

'Do you remember how he set the Second's leg? Terribly useful to have a doctor aboard.'

Nick picked up his spoon, and tentatively lifted a little of the fruit to his mouth. Every officer watched him intently as he chewed. Nick took another spoonful.

'You should taste his jams, sir,' David Allen addressed Nick directly at last. 'Absolutely Cordon Bleu stuff.'

'Thank you, gentlemen, for the advice,' said Nick. The

smile did not touch his mouth, but crinkled his eyes slightly. 'But would somebody convey a private message to Angel that if he ever calls me "dear" again I'll beat that ridiculous cap down about his ears.'

In the relieved laughter that followed, Nick turned to David Allen and sent colour flying to his cheeks again by asking, 'You seem to have finished with that old copy of the *List*, Number One. Do you mind if I glance at it again?'

Reluctantly, David lifted himself and produced the newspaper, and there was another tense silence as Nick Berg rearranged the rumpled sheets and studied the old headlines without any apparent emotion.

THE GOLDEN PRINCE OF CHRISTY MARINE DEPOSED

Nicholas hated that name. It had been old Arthur Christy's quirk to name all of his vessels with the prefix 'Golden' and twelve years ago, when Nick had rocketed to head of operations at Christy Marine, some wag had stuck that label on him.

ALEXANDER TO HEAD THE CHRISTY
BOARD OF DIRECTORS

Nicholas was surprised by the force of his hatred for the man. They had fought like a pair of bulls for dominance of the herd and the tactics that Duncan Alexander had used had won. Arthur Christy had said once, 'Nobody gives a damn these days whether it is moral or fair, all that counts is, will it work and can you get away with it?' For Duncan it had worked, and he had got away with it in the grandest possible style.

As Managing Director in charge of operations, Mr Nicholas Berg helped to build Christy Marine from a

> small coasting and salvage company into one of the five largest owners of cargo shipping operating anywhere in the world.
>
> After the death of Arthur Christy in 1968, Mr Nicholas Berg succeeded him as Chairman, and continued the company's spectacular expansion.
>
> At present, Christy Marine has in commission eleven bulk carriers and tankers in excess of 250,000 dead weight tons, and is building the 1,000,000 ton giant ultra-tanker *Golden Dawn*. It will be the largest vessel ever launched.

There it was, stated in the baldest possible terms, the labour of a man's lifetime. Over a billion dollars of shipping, designed, financed and built almost entirely with the energy and enthusiasm and faith of Nicholas Berg.

> Mr Nicholas Berg married Miss Chantelle Christy, the only child of Mr Arthur Christy. However, the marriage ended in divorce in September of last year and the former Mrs Berg has subsequently married Mr Duncan Alexander, the new Chairman of Christy Marine.

He felt the hollow nauseous feeling in his stomach again, and in his head the vivid image of the woman. He did not want to think of her now, but could not thrust the image aside. She was bright and beautiful as a flame – and, like a flame, you could not hold her. When she went, she took everything with her, everything. He should hate her also, he really should. Everything, he thought again, the company, his life's work, and the child. When he thought of the child, he nearly succeeded in hating her, and the newsprint shook in his hand.

He became aware again that five men were watching him, and without surprise he realized that not a flicker of his emotions had shown on his face. To be a player for fifteen years in one of the world's highest games of chance, inscrutability was a minimum requirement.

> In a joint statement issued by the new Chairman and incoming members of the Board, a tribute was paid.

Duncan Alexander paid the tribute for one reason, Nick thought grimly. He wanted the 100,000 Christy Marine shares that Nick owned. Those shares were very far from a controlling interest. Chantelle had a million shares in her own name, and there were another million in the Christy Trust, but insignificant as it was, Nick's holding gave him a voice in and an entry to the company's affairs. Nick had bought and paid for every one of those shares. Nobody had given him a thing, not once in his life. He had taken advantage of every stock option in his contract, had bartered bonus and salary for those options, and now those 100,000 shares were worth three million dollars, meagre reward for the labour which had built up a fortune of sixty million dollars for the Christy father and daughter.

It had taken Duncan Alexander almost a year to get those shares. He and Nicholas had bargained with cold loathing. They had hated each other from the first day that Duncan had walked into the Christy Building on Leadenhall Street. He had come as old Arthur Christy's latest *Wunderkind*, the financial genius fresh from his triumphs as financial controller of International Electronics, and the hatred had been instant and deep and mutual, a fierce smouldering chemical reaction between them.

In the end Duncan Alexander had won, he had won it all, except the shares, and he had bargained for those from overwhelming strength. He had bargained with patience and skill, wearing his man down over the months. Using all Christy Marine's reserves to block and frustrate Nicholas, forcing him back step by step, taxing even his strength to its limits, driving such a bargain that at the end Nicholas was forced to bow and accept a dangerous price for his shares. He had taken as full payment the subsidiary of Christy Marine, Christy Towage and Salvage, all its assets and all its debts. Nick had felt like a fighter who had been battered for fifteen rounds, and was now hanging desperately to the ropes with his legs gone, blinded by his own sweat and blood and swollen flesh; so he could not see from whence the next punch would come. But he had held on just long enough. He had got Christy Towage and Salvage – he had walked away with something that was completely and entirely his.

Nicholas Berg lowered the newspaper, and immediately his officers attacked their breakfasts ravenously and there was the clatter of cutlery.

'There is an officer missing,' he said.

'It's only the Trog, sir,' Dave Allen explained.

'The Trog?'

'The Radio Officer, sir. Speirs, sir. We call him the Troglodyte.'

'I'd like all the officers present.'

'He never comes out of his cave,' Vinny Baker explained helpfully.

'All right,' Nick nodded. 'I will speak to him later.'

They waited now, five eager young men, even Vin Baker could not completely hide his interest behind the smeared lenses of his spectacles and the tough Aussie veneer.

'I wanted to explain to you the new set-up. The Chief has kindly read to you this article, presumably for the benefit of those who were unable to do so for themselves a year ago.'

Nobody said anything, but Vin Baker fiddled with his porridge spoon.

'So you are aware that I am no longer connected in any way with Christy Marine. I have now acquired Christy Towage and Salvage. It becomes a completely independent company. The name is being changed.' Nicholas had resisted the vanity of calling it Berg Towage and Salvage. 'It will be known as Ocean Towage and Salvage.'

He had paid dearly for it, perhaps too dearly. He had given up his three million dollars' worth of Christy shares for God alone knew what. But he had been tired unto death.

'We own two vessels. The *Golden Warlock* and her sister ship which is almost ready for her sea trials, the *Golden Witch*.'

He knew exactly how much the company owed on those two ships, he had agonized over the figures through long and sleepless nights. On paper the net worth of the company was around four million dollars; he had made a paper profit of a million dollars on his bargain with Duncan Alexander. But it was paper profit only, the company had debts of nearly four million more. If he missed just one month's interest payments on those debts – he dismissed the thought quickly, for on a forced sale his residue in the company would be worth nothing. He would be completely wiped out.

'The names of both ships have been changed also. They will become simply *Warlock* and *Sea Witch*. From now onwards "Golden" is a dirty word around Ocean Salvage.'

They laughed then, a release of tension, and Nick smiled with them, and lit a thin black cheroot from the crocodile-skin case while they settled down.

'I will be running this ship until *Sea Witch* is commissioned. It won't be long, and there will be promotions then.'

Nick superstitiously tapped the mahogany mess table as he said it. The dockyard strike had been simmering for a long time. *Sea Witch* was still on the ways, but costing interest, and further delay would prove him mortal.

'I have got a long oil-rig tow. Bight of Australia to

South America. It will give us all time to shake the ship down. You are all tug men, I don't have to tell you when the big one comes up, there will be no warning.'

They stirred, and the eagerness was on them again. Even the oblique reference to prize money had roused them.

'Chief?' Nick looked across at him, and the Engineer snorted, as though the question was an insult.

'In all respects ready for sea,' he said, and tried simultaneously to adjust his trousers and his spectacles.

'Number One?' Nick looked at David Allen. He had not yet become accustomed to the Mate's boyishness. He knew that he had held a master mariner's ticket for ten years, that he was over thirty years of age and that MacDonald had hand-picked him – he had to be good. Yet that fair unlined face and quick high colour under the unruly mop of blond hair made him look like an undergraduate.

'I'm waiting on some stores yet, sir,' David answered quickly. 'The chandlers have promised for today, but none of it is vital. I could sail in an hour, if it is necessary.'

'All right.' Nick stood up. 'I will inspect the ship at 0900 hours. You'd best get the ladies off the ship.' During the meal there had been the faint tinkle of female voices and laughter from the crew's quarters.

Nick stepped out of the saloon and Vin Baker's voice was pitched to reach him. It was a truly dreadful imitation of what the Chief believed to be a Royal Naval accent.

'0900, chaps. Jolly good show, what?'

Nick did not miss a step, and he grinned tightly to himself. It's an old Aussie custom; you needle and needle until something happens. There is no malice in it, it's just a way of getting to know your man. And once the boots and fists have stopped flying, you can be friends or enemies on a permanent basis. It was so long since he had been in elemental contact with tough physical men, straight hard men who shunned all subterfuge and sham, and he found the novelty stimulating. Perhaps that was what he really needed now, the sea and the company of real men. He felt his step quicken and the anticipation of physical confrontation lift his spirits off the bottom.

He went up the companionway to the navigation deck, taking the steps three at a time, and the doorway opposite his suite opened. From it emerged the solid grey stench of cheap Dutch cigars and a head that could have belonged to some prehistoric reptile. It too was pale grey and lined and wrinkled, the head of a sea-turtle or an iguana lizard, with the same small dark glittery eyes.

The door was that of the radio room. It had direct access to the main navigation bridge and was merely two paces from the Master's day cabin.

Despite appearances, the head was human, and Nick recalled clearly how Mac had once described his radio officer. 'He is the most anti-social bastard I've ever sailed with, but he can scan eight different frequencies simultaneously, in clear and Morse, even while he is asleep. He is a mean, joyless, constipated son of a bitch – and probably the best radio man afloat.'

'Captain,' said the Trog, in a reedy petulant voice. Nick did not ponder the fact that the Trog recognized him instantly as the new Master. The air of command on some men is unmistakable. 'Captain, I have an "all ships signify".'

Nick felt the heat at the base of his spine, and the electric prickle on the back of his neck. It is not sufficient merely to be on the break line when the big wave peaks, it is also necessary to recognize your wave from the hundred others that sweep by.

'Coordinates?' he snapped, as he strode down the passageway to the radio room.

'72° 16′ south 32° 12′ west.'

Nick felt the jump in his chest and the heat mount up along his spine. The high latitudes down there in the vast and lonely wastes. There was something sinister and menacing in the mere figures. What ship could be down there?

The longitudinal coordinates fitted neatly in the chart that Nick carried in his mind, like a war chart in a military operations room. She was south and west of the Cape of Good Hope – down deep, beyond Gough and Bouvet Island, in the Weddell Sea.

He followed the Trog into the radio room. On this bright, sunny and windy morning, the room was dark and gloomy as a cave, the thick green blinds drawn across the ports; the only source of light was the glowing dials of the banked communication equipment, the most sophisticated equipment that all the wealth of Christy Marine could pack into her, a hundred thousand dollars' worth of electronic magic, but the stink of cheap cigars was overpowering.

Beyond the radio room was the operator's cabin, the bunk unmade, a tray of soiled dishes on the deck beside it.

The Trog hopped up into the swivel seat, and elbowed aside a brass shell-casing that acted as an ashtray and spilled grey flakes of ash and a couple of cold wet chewed cigar butts on to the desk.

Like a wizened gnome, the Trog tended his dials; there was a cacophony of static and electronic trash blurred with the sharp howl of Morse.

'The copy?' Nick asked, and the Trog pushed a pad at him. Nick read off quickly.

> CTMZ. 0603 GMT. 72° 16′ S. 32° 12′ W. All ships in a position to render assistance, please signify. CTMZ.

He did not need to consult the RT Handbook to recognize that call sign 'CTMZ'.

With an effort of will he controlled the pressure that caught him in the chest like a giant fist. It was as though he had lived this moment before. It was too neat. He forced himself to distrust his instinct, forced himself to think with his head and not his guts.

Beyond him he heard his officers' voices on the navigation bridge, quiet voices – but charged with tension. They were up from the saloon already.

'Christ!' he thought savagely. 'How do they know? So quickly?' It was as though the ship itself had come awake beneath his feet and trembled with anticipation.

The door from the bridge slid aside and David Allen stood in the opening with a copy of *Lloyd's Register* in his hands.

'CTMZ, sir, is the call sign of the *Golden Adventurer*. Twenty-two thousand tons, registered Bermuda 1975. Owners Christy Marine.'

'Thank you, Number One,' Nick nodded. Nicholas knew her well; he personally had ordered her construction before the collapse of the great liner traffic. Nick had planned to use her on the Europe-to-Australia run.

Her finished cost had come in at sixty-two million dollars, and she was a beautiful and graceful ship under her tall light alloy superstructure. Her accommodation was luxurious, in the same class as the *France* or the *United States*, but she had been one of Nick's few miscalculations.

When the feasibility of operation on the planned run had shown up prohibitive in the face of rising costs and diminishing trade, Nick had switched her usage. It was this type of flexible and intuitive planning and improvisation that had built Christy Marine into the Goliath she was now.

Nick had innovated the idea of adventure cruises – and changed the ship's name to *Golden Adventurer*. Now she carried rich passengers to the wild and exotic corners of the globe, from the Galapagos Islands to the Amazon, from the remote Pacific islands to the Antarctic, in search of the unusual.

She carried guest lecturers with her, experts on the environments and ecology of the areas she was to visit, and she was equipped to take her passengers ashore to study the monoliths of Easter Island or to watch the mating displays of the wandering albatross on the Falkland Islands.

She was probably one of the very few cruise liners that was still profitable, and now she stood in need of assistance.

Nicholas turned back from the Trog. 'Has she been transmitting prior to this signify request?'

'She's been sending in company code since midnight. Her traffic was so heavy that I was watching her.'

The green glow of the sets gave the little man a bilious cast, and made his teeth black, so that he looked like an actor from a horror movie.

'You recorded?' Nick demanded, and the Trog switched on the automatic playback of his tape monitors, recapitulating every message the distressed ship had sent or received since the previous midnight. The jumbled blocks of code poured into the room, and the paper strip printed out with the clatter of its keys.

Had Duncan Alexander changed the Christy Marine code? Nick wondered. It would be the natural procedure, completely logical to any operations man. You lose a man who has the code, you change immediately. It was that simple. Duncan had lost Nick Berg; he should change. But Duncan was not an operations man. He was a figures and paper man, he thought in numbers, not in steel and salt water.

If Duncan had changed, they would never break it. Not even with the Decca. Nick had devised the basis of the code. It was a projection that expressed the alphabet as a mathematical function based on a random six-figure master, changing the value of each letter on a progression that was impossible to monitor.

Nick hurried out of the stinking gloom of the radio room with the printout in his hands.

The navigation bridge of *Warlock* was gleaming chrome and glass, as bright and functional as a modern surgical theatre, or a futuristic kitchen layout.

The primary control console stretched the full width of the bridge, beneath the huge armoured windows. The old-fashioned wheel was replaced by a single steel lever, and the remote control could be carried out on to the wings of the bridge on its long extension cable, like the remote on a television set, so that the helmsman could con the ship from any position he chose.

Illuminated digital displays informed the master instantly of every condition of his ship: speed across the bottom at bows and stern, speed through the water at bows and stern, wind direction and strength, together with all the other technical information of function and malfunction. Nick had built the ship with Christy money, and stinted not at all.

The rear of the bridge was thc navigational area, and the chart-table divided it neatly with its overhead racks containing the 106 big blue volumes of the *Global Pilot* and as many other volumes of maritime publications. Below the table were the multiple drawers, wide and flat to contain the spread Admiralty charts that covered every corner of navigable water on the globe.

Against the rear bulkhead stood the battery of electronic navigational aids, like a row of fruit machines in a Vegas gambling hall.

Nick switched the big Decca Satellite Navaid into its computer mode and the display lights flashed and faded and relit in scarlet.

He fed it the six-figure control, numbers governed by the moon phase and date of dispatch. The computer digested this instantaneously, and Nick gave it the last arithmetical proportion known to him. The Decca was ready to decode and Nick gave it the block of garbled transmission – and waited for it to throw back gibberish at him. Duncan *must* have altered the code. He stared at the printout.

Christy Marine from Master of *Adventurer*. 2216 GMT. 72° 16′ S. 32° 05′ W. Underwater ice damage sustained midships starboard. Precautionary shutdown mains. Auxiliary generators activated during damage survey. Stand by.

So Duncan had let the code stand then. Nick groped for the croc-skin case of cheroots, and his hand was steady and firm as he held the flame to the top of the thin black tube. He felt the intense desire to shout aloud, but instead, he drew the fragrant smoke into his lungs.

'Plotted,' said David Allen from behind him. Already on the spread chart of the Antarctic he had marked in the reported position. The transformation was complete, the First Officer had become a grimly competent professional. There remained no trace of the high-coloured undergraduate.

Nick glanced at the plot, saw the dotted ice line far above the *Adventurer*'s position, saw the outline of the forbidding continent of Antarctica groping for the ship with merciless fingers of ice and rock.

The Decca printed out the reply:

Master of *Adventurer* from Christy Marine. 2222 GMT. Standing by.

The next message from the recording tape was flagged nearly two hours later, but was printed out almost continuously from the Trog's recording.

Christy Marine from Master of *Adventurer*. 0005 GMT. 72° 18′ S. 32° 05′ W. Water contained. Restarted mains. New course CAPE TOWN direct. Speed 8 knots. Stand by.

Dave Allen worked swiftly with parallel rulers and protractor.

'While she was without power she drifted thirty-four nautical miles, south-south-east – there is a hell of a wind or big current setting down there,' he said, and the other deck officers were silent and strained. Although none of them would dare crowd the Master at the Decca, yet in order of seniority they had taken up vantage points around the bridge best suited to follow the drama of a great ship in distress.

The next message ran straight out from the computer, despite the fact that it had been dispatched many hours later.

Christy Marine from Master of *Adventurer*. 0546 GMT. 72° 16′ S. 32° 12′ W. Explosion in flooded area. Emergency shutdown all. Water gaining. Request your clearance to issue 'all ships signify'. Standing by.

Master of *Adventurer* from Christy Marine. 0547 GMT. You are cleared to issue signify. Break. Break. Break. You are expressly forbidden to contract tow or salvage without reference Christy Marine. Acknowledge.

Duncan was not even putting in the old chestnut, 'except in the event of danger to human life'.

The reason was too apparent. Christy Marine underwrote most of its own bottoms through another of its subsidiaries, the London and European Insurance and Finance Company. The self-insurance scheme had been the brainchild of Alexander Duncan himself when first he arrived at Christy Marine. Nick Berg had opposed the scheme bitterly, and now he might live to see his reasoning being justified.

'Are we going to signify?' David Allen asked quietly.

'Radio silence,' snapped Nick irritably, and began to pace the bridge, the crack of his heels muted by the cork coating on the deck.

'Is this my wave?' Nick demanded of himself, applying the old rule he had set for himself long ago, the rule of deliberate thought first, action after.

The *Golden Adventurer* was drifting in the ice-fields two thousand and more miles south of Cape Town, five days and nights of hard running for the *Warlock*. If he made the go decision, by the time he reached her, she might have effected repairs and restarted, she might be under her own command again. Again, even if she was still helpless, *Warlock* might reach her to find another salvage tug had beaten her to the scene. So now it was time to call the roll.

He stopped his pacing at the door to the radio room and spoke quietly to the Trog.

'Open the telex line and send to Bach Wackie in Bermuda quote call the roll unquote.'

As he turned away, Nick was satisfied with his own forethought in installing the satellite telex system which enabled him to communicate with his agent in Bermuda, or with any other selected telex station, without his message being broadcast over the open frequencies and monitored by a competitor or any other interested party. His signals were bounced through the high stratosphere where they could not be intercepted.

While he waited, Nicholas worried. The decision to go would mean abandoning the Esso oil-rig tow. The tow fee had been a vital consideration in his cash-flow situation. Two hundred and twenty thousand sterling, without which he could not meet the quarterly interest payment due in sixty days' time – unless, unless . . . He juggled figures in his head, but the magnitude of the risk involved was growing momentarily more apparent – and the figures did not add up. He needed the Esso tow. God, how badly he needed it!

'Bach Wackie are replying,' called the Trog above the chatter of the telex receiver, and Nick spun on his heel.

He had appointed Bach Wackie as the agents for Ocean Salvage because of their proven record of quick and aggressive efficiency. He glanced at his Rolex Oyster and calculated that it was about two o'clock in the morning local time in Bermuda, and yet his request for information on the disposition of all his major competitors was now being answered within minutes of receipt.

> For Master *Warlock* from Bach Wackie latest reported positions. *John Ross* dry dock Durban. *Woltema Wolteraad* Esso tow Torres Straits to Alaska Shelf –

That took care of the two giant Safmarine tugs; half of the top opposition was out of the race.

> *Wittezee* Shell exploration tow Galveston to North Sea. *Grootezee* lying Brest –

That was the two Dutchmen out of it. The names and positions of the other big salvage tugs, each of them a direct and dire threat to *Warlock*, ran swiftly from the telex and Nicholas chewed his cheroot ragged as he watched, his eyes slitted against the spiralling blue smoke, feeling the relief rise in him as each report put another of his competitors in some distant waters, far beyond range of the stricken ship.

'*La Mouette*,' Nick's hands balled into fists as the name sprang on to the white paper sheet, '*La Mouette* discharged Brazgas tow Golfo San Jorge on 14th reported en route Buenos Aires.'

Nick grunted like a boxer taking a low blow, and turned

away from the machine. He walked out on to the open wing of the bridge and the wind tore at his hair and clothing.

*La Mouette*, the seagull, a fanciful name for that black squat hull, the old-fashioned high box of superstructure, the traditional single stack; Nick could see it clearly when he closed his eyes.

There was no doubt in his mind at all. Jules Levoisin was already running hard for the south, running like a hunting dog with the scent hot in its nostrils.

Jules had discharged in the southern Atlantic three days ago. He would certainly have bunkered at Comodoro. Nick knew how Jules' mind worked, he was never happy unless his bunkers were bulging.

Nick flicked the stub of his cigar away, and it was whisked far out into the harbour by the wind.

He knew that *La Mouette* had refitted and installed new engines eighteen months before. With a nostalgic twinge, he had read a snippet in *Lloyd's List*. But even nine thousand horsepower couldn't push that tubby hull at better than eighteen knots, Nick was certain of that. Yet even with *Warlock*'s superior speed, *La Mouette* was better placed by a thousand miles. There was no room for complacency. And what if *La Mouette* had set out to double Cape Horn instead of driving north up the Atlantic? If that had happened, and with Jules Levoisin's luck it might just have happened, then *La Mouette* was a long way inside him already.

Anybody else but Jules Levoisin, he thought, why did it have to be him? And oh God, why now? Why now when I am so vulnerable – emotionally, physically and financially vulnerable. Oh God, why did it come now?

He felt the false sense of cheer and well-being, with which he had buoyed himself that morning, fall away from him like a cloak, leaving him naked and sick and tired again.

I am not ready yet, he thought; and then realized that it was probably the first time in his adult life he had ever said that to himself. He had always been ready, good and ready, for anything. But not now, not this time.

Suddenly Nicholas Berg was afraid, as he had never been before. He was empty, he realized, there was nothing in him, no strength, no confidence, no resolve. The depth of his defeat by Duncan Alexander, the despair of his rejection by the woman he loved, had broken him. He felt his fear turn to terror, knowing that his wave had come, and would sweep by him now, for he did not have the strength to ride it.

Some deep instinct warned him that it would be the last wave, there would be nothing after it. The choice was go now, or never go again. And he knew he could not go, he could not go against Jules Levoisin, he could not challenge the old master. He could not go – he could not reject the certainty of the Esso tow, he did not have the nerve now to risk all that he had left on a single throw. He had just lost a big one, he couldn't go at risk again.

The risk was too great, he was not ready for it, he did not have the strength for it.

He wanted to go to his cabin and throw himself on his bunk and sleep – and sleep. He felt his knees buckling with the great weight of his despair, and he hungered for the oblivion of sleep.

He turned back into the bridge, out of the wind. He was broken, defeated, he had given up. As he went towards the sanctuary of his day cabin, he passed the long command console and stopped involuntarily.

His officers watched him in a tense, electric silence.

His right hand went out and touched the engine telegraph, sliding the pointer from 'off' to 'stand by'.

'Engine Room,' he heard a voice speak in calm and level tones, so it could not be his own. 'Start main engines,' said the voice.

Seemingly from a great distance he watched the faces of his deck officers bloom with unholy joy, like old-time pirates savouring the prospect of a prize.

The strange voice went on, echoing oddly in his ears, 'Number One, ask the Harbour Master for permission to clear harbour immediately – and, Pilot, course to steer for the last reported position of *Golden Adventurer*, please.'

From the corner of his eye, he saw David Allen punch the Third Officer lightly but gleefully on the shoulder before he hurried to the radio telephone.

Nicholas Berg felt suddenly the urge to vomit. So he stood very still and erect at the navigation console and fought back the waves of nausea that swept over him, while his officers bustled to their seagoing stations.

'Bridge. This is the Chief Engineer,' said a disembodied voice from the speaker above Nick's head. 'Main engines running.' A pause and then that word of special Aussie approbation. 'Beauty!' – but the Chief pronounced it in three distinct syllables, 'Be-yew-dy!'

*Warlock*'s wide-flared bows were designed to cleave and push the waters open ahead of her and in those waters below latitude 40° she ran like an old bull otter, slick and wet and fast for the south.

Uninterrupted by any landmass, the cycle of great atmospheric depressions swept endlessly across those cold open seas, and the wave patterns built up into a succession of marching mountain ranges.

*Warlock* was taking them on her starboard shoulder, bursting through each crest in a white explosion that leapt from her bows like a torpedo strike, the water coming aboard green and clear over her high foredeck, and sweeping her from stern to stern as she twisted and broke out, dropping sheer into the valley that opened ahead of her.

Her twin ferro-bronze propellers broke clear of the surface, the slamming vibration instantly controlled by the sophisticated variable-pitch gear, until she swooped forward and the propellers bit deeply again, the thrust of the twin Mirrlees diesels hurtling her towards the slope of the next swell.

Each time it seemed that she could not rise in time to meet the cliff of water that bore down on her. The water was black under the grey sunless sky. Nick had lived through typhoon and Caribbean hurricane, but had never seen water as menacing and cruel as this. It glittered like the molten slag that pours down the dump of an iron foundry and cools to the same iridescent blackness.

In the deep valleys between the crests, the wind was blanketed so they fell into an unnatural stillness, an eerie silence that only enhanced the menace of that towering slope of water.

In the trough, *Warlock* heeled and threw her head up, climbing the slope in a gut-swooping lift, that buckled the knees of the watch. As she went up, so the angle of her bridge tilted back, and that sombre cheerless sky filled the forward bridge windows with a vista of low scudding cloud.

The wind tore at the crest of the wave ahead of her, ripping it away like white cotton from the burst seams of a black mattress, splattering custard-thick spume against the armoured glass. Then *Warlock* put her sharp steel nose deeply into it. Gouging a fat wedge of racing green over her head, twisting violently at the jarring impact, dropping sideways over the crest, and breaking out to fall free and repeat the cycle again.

Nick was wedged into the canvas Master's seat in the corner of the bridge. He swayed like a camel-driver to the thrust of the sea and smoked his black cheroots quietly, his head turning every few minutes to the west, as though he expected at any moment to see the black ugly hull of *La*

*Mouette* come up on top of the next swell. But he knew she was a thousand miles away still, racing down the far leg of the triangle which had at its apex the stricken liner.

'If she *is* running,' Nick thought, and knew that there was no doubt. *La Mouette* was running as frantically as was *Warlock* – and as silently. Jules Levoisin had taught Nick the trick of silence. He would not use his radio until he had the liner on his radar scan. Then he would come through in clear, 'I will be in a position to put a line aboard you in two hours. Do you accept "Lloyd's Open Form"?'

The Master of the distressed vessel, having believed himself abandoned without succour, would overreact to the promise of salvation, and when *La Mouette* came bustling up over the horizon, flying all her bunting and with every light blazing in as theatrical a display as Jules could put up, the relieved Master would probably leap at the offer of 'Lloyd's Open Form' – a decision that would surely be regretted by the ship's owners in the cold and unemotional precincts of an arbitration court.

When Nick had supervised the design of *Warlock*, he had insisted that she look good as well as being able to perform. The master of a disabled ship was usually a man in a highly emotional state. Mere physical appearance might sway him in the choice between two salvage tugs coming up on him. *Warlock* looked magnificent; even in this cold and cheerless ocean, she looked like a warship. The trick would be to show her to the master of *Golden Adventurer* before he struck a bargain with *La Mouette*.

Nick could no longer sit inactive in his canvas seat. He judged the next towering swell and, with half a dozen quick strides, crossed the bridge deck in those fleeting moments as *Warlock* steadied in the trough. He grabbed the chrome handrail above the Decca computer.

On the keyboard he typed the function code that would set the machine in navigational mode, coordinating the transmissions she was receiving from the circling satellite stations high above the earth. From these were calculated *Warlock*'s exact position over the earth's surface, accurate to within twenty-five yards.

Nick entered the ship's position and the computer compared this with the plot that Nick had requested four hours previously. It printed out quickly the distance run and the ship's speed made good. Nick frowned angrily and swung round to watch the helmsman.

In this fiercely running cross sea, a good man could hold *Warlock* on course more efficiently than any automatic steering device. He could anticipate each trough and crest and prevent the ship paying off across the direction of the swells, and then kicking back violently as she went over, wasting critical time and distance.

Nick watched the helmsman work, judging each sea as it came aboard, checking the ship's heading on the big repeating compass above the man's head. After ten minutes, Nick realized that there was no wastage; *Warlock* was making as good a course as was possible in these conditions.

The engine telegraph was pulled back to her maximum safe power-setting, the course was good and yet *Warlock* was not delivering those few extra knots of speed that Nick Berg had relied on when he had made the critical decision to race *La Mouette* for the prize.

Nick had relied on twenty-eight knots against the Frenchman's eighteen, and he was not getting it. Involuntarily, he glanced out to the west as *Warlock* came up on the top of the next crest. Through the streaming windows, from which the spinning wipers cleared circular areas of clean glass, Nick looked out across a wilderness of black water, forbidding and cold and devoid of other human presence.

Abruptly Nick crossed to the R/T microphone.

'Engine Room confirm we are top of the green.'

'Top of the green, it is, Skipper.'

The Chief's casual tones floated in above the crash of the next sea coming aboard.

'Top of the green' was the maximum safe power-setting recommended by the manufacturers for those gigantic Mirrlees diesels. It was a far higher setting than top economical power, and they were burning fuel at a prodigious rate. Nick was pushing her as high as he could without going into the 'red' danger area above eighty per cent of full power, which at prolonged running might permanently damage her engines.

Nick turned away to his seat, and wedged himself into it. He groped for his cheroot case, and then checked himself, the lighter in his hand. His tongue and mouth felt furred over and dry. He had smoked without a break every waking minute since leaving Cape Town, and God knows he had slept little enough since then. He ran his tongue around his mouth with distaste before he returned the cheroot to his case, and crouched in his seat staring ahead, trying to work out why *Warlock* was running slow.

Suddenly he straightened and considered a possibility that brought a metallic green gleam of anger into Nick's eyes.

He slid out of his seat, nodded to the Third Officer who had the deck and ducked through the doorway in the back of the bridge into his day cabin. It was a ploy. He didn't want his visit below decks announced, and from his own suite he darted into the companionway.

The engine control room was as modern and gleaming as *Warlock*'s navigation bridge. It was completely enclosed with double glass to cut down the thunder of her engines. The control console was banked below the windows, and all the ship's functions were displayed in green and red digital figures.

The view beyond the windows into the main engine

room was impressive, even for Nick who had designed and supervised each foot of the layout.

The two Mirrlees diesel engines filled the white-painted cavern with only walking space between, each as long as four Cadillac Eldorados parked bumper to bumper and as deep as if another four Cadillacs had been piled on top of them.

The thirty-six cylinders of each block were crowned with a moving forest of valve stems and con-rod ends, each enormous powerhouse capable of pouring out eleven thousand usable horsepower.

It was only custom that made it necessary for any visitor, including the Master, to announce his arrival in the engine room to the Chief Engineer. Ignoring custom, Nick slipped quietly through the glass sliding doors, out of the hot burned-oil stench of the engine room into the cooler and sweeter conditioned air of the control room.

Vin Baker was deep in conversation with one of his electricians, both of them kneeling before the open doors of one of the tall grey steel cabinets which housed a teeming mass of coloured cables and transistor switches. Nick had reached the control console before the Chief Engineer uncoiled his lanky body from the floor and spun round to face him.

When Nick was very angry, his lips compressed in a single thin white line, the thick dark eyebrows seemed to meet above the snapping green eyes and large slightly beaked nose.

'You pulled the override on me,' he accused in a flat, passionless voice that did not betray his fury. 'You're governing her out at seventy per cent of power.'

'That's top of the green in my book,' Vin Baker told him. 'I'm not running my engines at eighty per cent in this sea. She'll shake the guts out of herself.' He paused and the stern was flung up violently as *Warlock* crashed over the top of another sea. The control room shuddered with the vibration of the screws breaking out of the surface, spinning wildly in the air before they could bite again.

'Listen to her, man. You want me to pour on more of it?'

'She's built to take it.'

'Nothing's built to run that hard, and live in this sea.'

'I want the override out,' said Nick flatly, indicating the chrome handle and pointer with which the engineer could cancel the power settings asked for by the bridge. 'I don't care when you do it – just as long as it's any time within the next five seconds.'

'You get out of my engine room – and go play with your toys.'

'All right,' Nick nodded, 'I'll do it myself.' And he reached for the override gear.

'You take your hands off my engines,' howled Vin Baker, and picked up the iron locking handle off the deck. 'You touch my engines and I'll break your teeth out of your head, you ice-cold Pommy bastard.'

Even in his own anger, Nick blinked at the epithet. When he thought about the blazing passions and emotions that seethed within him, he nearly laughed aloud. *Ice-cold*, he thought, so that's how he sees me.

'You stupid Bundaberg-swilling galah,' he said quietly, as he reached for the override. 'I don't really care if I have to kill you first, but we are going to eighty per cent.'

It was Vin Baker's turn to blink behind his smeared glasses, he had not expected to be insulted in the colloquial. He dropped the heavy steel handle to the deck. It fell with a clang.

'I don't need it,' he announced, and tucked his spectacles into his back pocket and hoisted his trousers with both elbows. 'It will be more fun to take you to pieces by hand.'

It was only then that Nick realized how tall the engineer was. His arms were ridged with the lean wiry taut muscle of hard physical labour. His fists, as he balled them, were lumpy with scar tissue across the knuckles and the size of a pair of nine-pound hammers. He went down into a fighter's crouch, and rode the plunging deck with an easy flexing of the long powerful legs.

As Nicholas touched the chrome override handle, the first punch came from the level of Baker's knees, but it came so fast that Nick only just had time to sway away from it. It whistled up past his jaw and scraped the skin from the outside corner of his eye, but he counter-punched instinctively, swaying back and slamming it in under the armpit, feeling the blow land so solidly that his teeth jarred his own head. The Chief's breath hissed, but he swung left-handed and a bony fist crushed the pad of muscle on the point of Nick's shoulder, bounced off and caught him high on the temple.

Even though it was a glancing blow, it felt as though a door had slammed in Nick's head, and resounding darkness closed behind his eyes. He fell forward into a clinch to ride the darkness, grabbing the lean hard body and smothering it in a bear hug as he tried to clear the singing darkness in his head.

He felt the Chief shift his weight, and was shocked at the power in that wiry frame, it took all his own strength to hold him. Suddenly and clearly he knew what was going to happen next. There were little white ridges of scar tissue half hidden by the widow's peak of flopping sandy hair on the Chief's forehead. Those scars from previous conflicts warned Nick.

Vin Baker reared back, like a cobra flaring for the strike, and then flung his head forward; it was the classic butt aimed for Nick's face and, had it landed squarely, it would have crushed in his nose and broken his teeth off level to the gums – but Nick anticipated, and dropped his own chin, tucking it down hard so that their foreheads met with a crack like a breaking oak branch.

The impact broke Nick's grip, and both of them reeled apart across the heaving deck, Vin Baker howling like a moon-sick dog and clutching his own head.

'Fight fair, you Pommy bastard!' he howled in outrage, and he came up short against the steel cabinets that lined the far side of the control room. The astonished electrician dived for cover under the control console, scattering tools across the deck.

Vin Baker lay for a moment gathering his lanky frame, and then, as *Warlock* swung hard over, rolling viciously in the cross sea, he used her momentum to hurl himself down the steeply tilting deck, dropping his head again like a battering ram to crush in Nick's ribs as he charged.

Nick turned like a cattle man working an unruly steer. He whipped one arm round Vin Baker's neck and ran with him, holding his head down and building up speed across the full length of the control room. They reached the armoured glass wall at the far end, and the top of Vin Baker's head was the point of impact with the weight of both their bodies behind it.

The Chief Engineer came round at the prick of the needle that Angel forced through the thick flap of open flesh on top of his head. He came round fighting drunkenly, but the cook held him down with one huge hairy arm.

'Easy, love.' Angel pulled the needle through the torn red weeping scalp and tied the stitch.

'Where is he, where is the bastard?' slurred the Chief.

'It's all over, Chiefie,' Angel told him gently. 'And you

are lucky he bashed you on the head – otherwise he might have hurt you.' He took another stitch.

The Chief winced as Angel pulled the thread up tight and knotted it. 'He tried to mess with my engines. I taught the bastard a lesson.'

'You've terrified him,' Angel agreed sweetly. 'Now you take a swig of this and lie still. I want you in this bunk for twelve hours – and I might come and tuck you in.'

'I'm going back to my engines,' announced the Chief, and drained the medicine glass of brown spirit, then whistled at the bite of the fumes.

Angel left him and crossed to the telephone. He spoke quickly into it, and as the Chief lumbered off the bunk, Nick Berg stepped into the cabin, and nodded to the cook.

'Thank you, Angel.'

Angel ducked out of the cabin and left them facing each other. The Chief opened his mouth to snarl at Nick.

'Jules Levoisin in *La Mouette* has probably made five hundred miles on us while you have been playing prima donna,' said Nick quietly, and Vin Baker's mouth stayed open, although no sound came out of it.

'I built this ship to run fast and hard in just this kind of contest, and now you are trying to do all of us out of prize money.'

Nick turned on his heel and went back up the companionway to his navigation deck. He settled into his canvas chair and fingered the big purple swelling on his forehead tenderly. His head felt as though a rope had been knotted around it and twisted up tight. He wanted to go to his cabin and take something for the pain, but he did not want to miss the call when it came.

He lit another cheroot, and it tasted like burned tarred rope. He dropped it into the sandbox and the telephone at his shoulder rang once.

'Bridge, this is the Engine Room.'

'Go ahead, Chief.'

'We are going to eighty per cent now.'

Nick did not reply, but he felt the change in the engine vibration and the more powerful rush of the hull beneath him.

'Nobody told me *La Mouette* was running against us. No way that frog-eating bastard's going to get a line on her first,' announced Vin Baker grimly, and there was a silence between them. Something more had to be said.

'I bet you a pound to a pinch of kangaroo dung,' challenged the Chief, 'that you don't know what a galah is, and that you've never tasted a Bundaberg rum in your life.'

Nick found himself smiling, even through the blinding pain in his head.

'Be-yew-dy!' Nick said, making three syllables of it and keeping the laughter out of his voice, as he hung up the receiver.

Dave Allen's voice was apologetic. 'Sorry to wake you, sir, but the *Golden Adventurer* is reporting.'

'I'm coming,' mumbled Nick, and swung his legs off the bunk. He had been in that black death-sleep of exhaustion, but it took him only seconds to pull back the dark curtains from his mind. It was his old training as a watch-keeping officer.

He rubbed away the last traces of sleep, feeling the rasping black stubble of his beard under his fingers as he crossed quickly to his bathroom. He spent forty seconds in bathing his face and combing his tousled hair, and regretfully decided there was no time to shave. Another rule of his was to look good in a world which so often judged a man by his appearance.

When he went out on to the navigation bridge, he knew at once that the wind had increased its velocity. He guessed it was rising force six now, and *Warlock*'s motion was more violent and abandoned. Beyond the warm, dimly lit capsule of the bridge, all those elements of cold water and vicious racing winds turned the black night to a howling tumult.

The Trog was crouched over his machines, grey and wizened and sleepless. He hardly turned his head to hand Nick the message flimsy.

'Master of *Golden Adventurer* to Christy Marine,' the Decca decoded swiftly, and Nick grunted as he saw the new position report. Something had altered drastically in the liner's circumstances. 'Main engines still unserviceable. Current setting easterly and increasing to eight knots. Wind rising force six from north-west. Critical ice danger to the ship. What assistance can I expect?'

There was a panicky note to that last line, and Nick saw why when he compared the liner's new position on the spread chart.

'She's going down sharply on the lee shore,' David muttered as he worked quickly over the chart. 'The current and wind are working together – they are driving her down on to the land.'

He touched the ugly broken points of Coatsland's shoreline with the tip of one finger.

'She is eighty miles offshore now. At the rate she is drifting, it will take her only another ten hours before she goes aground.'

'If she doesn't hit an iceberg first,' said Nick. 'From the Master's last message, it sounds as though they are into big ice.'

'That's a cheerful thought,' agreed David, and straightened up from the chart.

'What's our time to reach her?'

'Another forty hours, sir,' David hesitated and pushed

the thick white-gold lock of hair off his forehead, 'if we can make good this speed – but we may have to reduce when we reach the ice.'

Nick turned away to his canvas chair. He felt the need to pace back and forward, to release the pent-up forces within him. However, any movement in this heavy pounding sea was not only difficult but downright dangerous, so he groped his way to the chair and wedged himself in, staring ahead into the clamorous black night.

He thought about the terrible predicament of the liner's Captain. His ship was at deadly risk, and the lives of his crew and passengers with it.

How many lives? Nick cast his mind back and came up with the figures. The *Golden Adventurer*'s full complement of officers and crew was 235, and there was accommodation for 375 passengers, a possible total of over six hundred souls. If the ship was lost, *Warlock* would be hard put to take aboard that huge press of human life.

'Well, sir, they signed on for adventure,' David Allen spoke into his thoughts as though he had heard them, 'and they are getting their money's worth.'

Nick glanced at him, and nodded. 'Most of them will be elderly. A berth on that cruise costs a fortune, and it's usually only the oldsters who have that sort of gold. If she goes aground, we are going to lose life.'

'With respect, Captain,' David hesitated, and blushed again for the first time since leaving port, 'if her Captain knows that assistance is on the way, it may prevent him doing something crazy.'

Nick was silent. The Mate was right, of course. It was cruel to leave them in the despair of believing they were alone down there in those terrible icefields. The *Adventurer*'s Captain could make a panic decision, one that could be averted if he knew how close succour was.

'The air temperature out there is minus five degrees, and if the wind is at thirty miles an hour, that will make it a lethal chill factor. If they take to the boats in that—' David was interrupted by the Trog calling from the radio room.

'The owners are replying.'

It was a long message that Christy Marine were sending to their Captain. It was filled with those same hollow assurances that a surgeon gives to a cancer patient, but one paragraph had relevance for Nick:

'All efforts being made to contact salvage tugs reported operating South Atlantic.'

David Allen looked at him expectantly. It was the right humane thing to do. To tell them he was only eight hundred miles away, and closing swiftly.

Nervous energy fizzed in Nick's blood, making him restless and angry. On an impulse he left his chair and carefully crossed the heaving deck to the starboard wing of the bridge.

He slid open the door and stepped out into the gale. The shock of that icy air took his breath away and he gasped like a drowning man. He felt tears streaming from his eyes across his cheeks and the frozen spray struck into his face like steel darts.

Carefully he filled his lungs, and his nostrils flared as he smelt the ice. It was that unmistakeable dank smell, he remembered so well from the northern Arctic seas. It was like the body smell of some gigantic reptilian sea monster – and it struck the mariner's chill into his soul.

He could endure only a few seconds more of the gale, but when he stepped back into the cosy green-lit warmth of the bridge, his mind was clear, and he was thinking crisply.

'Mr Allen, there is ice ahead.'

'I have a watch on the radar, sir.'

'Very good,' Nick nodded, 'but we'll reduce to fifty per cent of power.' He hesitated, and then went on, 'and maintain radio silence.'

The decision was hard made, and Nick saw the

accusation in David Allen's eyes before he turned away to give the orders for the reduction in power. Nick felt a sudden and uncharacteristic urge to explain the decision to him. He did not know why – perhaps he needed the Mate's understanding and sympathy. Instantly Nick saw that as a symptom of his weakness and vulnerability. He had never needed sympathy before, and he steeled himself against it now.

His decision to maintain radio silence was correct. He was dealing with two hard men. He knew he could not afford to give an inch of sea room to Jules Levoisin. He would force him to open radio contact first. He needed that advantage.

The other man with whom he had to deal was Duncan Alexander, and he was a hating man, dangerous and vindictive. He had tried once to destroy Nick – and perhaps he had already succeeded. Nick had to guard himself now, he must pick with care his moment to open negotiations with Christy Marine and the man who had displaced him at its head. Nick must be in a position of utmost strength when he did so.

Jules Levoisin must be forced to declare himself first, Nick decided. The Captain of the *Golden Adventurer* would have to be left in the agonies of doubt a little longer, and Nick consoled himself with the thought that any further drastic change in the liner's circumstances or a decision by the Master to abandon his ship and commit his company to the lifeboats would be announced on the open radio channels and would give him a chance to intervene.

Nick was about to caution the Trog to keep a particular watch on Channel 16 for *La Mouette*'s first transmission, then he checked himself. That was another thing he never did – issue unnecessary orders. The Trog's grey wrinkled head was wreathed in clouds of reeking cigar smoke but was bowed to his mass of electronic equipment, and he adjusted a dial with careful lover's fingers; his little eyes were bright and sleepless as those of an ancient sea turtle.

Nick went to his chair and settled down to wait out the few remaining hours of the short Antarctic summer night.

The radar screen had shown strange and alien capes and headlands above the sea clutter of the storm, strange islands, anomalies which did not relate to the Admiralty charts. Between these alien masses shone myriad other smaller contacts, bright as fireflies, any one of which could have been the echo of a stricken ocean liner – but which was not.

As *Warlock* nosed cautiously down into this enchanted sea, the dawn that had never been far from the horizon flushed out, timorous as a bride, decked in colours of gold and pink that struck splendorous splinters of light off the icebergs.

The horizon ahead of them was cluttered with ice, some of the fragments were but the size of a billiard table and they bumped and scraped down the *Warlock*'s side, then swung and bobbed in her wake as she passed. There were others the size of a city block, weird and fanciful structures of honeycombed white ice, that stood as tall as *Warlock*'s upperworks as she passed.

'White ice is soft ice,' Nick murmured to David Allen beside him, and then caught himself. It was an unnecessary speech, inviting familiarity, and before the Mate could answer, Nick turned quickly away to the radar-repeater and lowered his face to the eyepiece in the coned hood. For a minute he studied the images of the surrounding ice in the darkened body of the instrument, then went back to his seat and stared ahead impatiently.

*Warlock* was running too fast, Nick knew it; he was

relying on the vigilance of his deck officers to carry her through the ice. Yet still this speed was too slow for his seething impatience.

Above their horizon rose another shoreline, a great unbroken sweep of towering cliff which caught the low sun, and glowed in emerald and amethyst, a drifting tableland of solid hard ice, forty miles across and two hundred feet high.

As they closed with that massive translucent island, so the colours that glowed through it became more hauntingly beautiful. The cliffs were rent by deep bays, and split by crevasses whose shadowy depths were dark sapphire, blue and mysterious, paling out to a thousand shades of green.

'My God, it's beautiful!' said David Allen with the reverence of a man kneeling in a cathedral.

The crests of the ice cliffs blazed in clearest ruby; to windward, the big sea piled in and crashed against those cliffs, surging up them in explosive bursts of white spray. Yet the iceberg did not dip nor swing or work, even in that murderous sea.

'Look at the lee she is making.' Dave Allen pointed. 'You could ride out a force twelve behind her.'

On the leeward side, the waters were protected from the wind by that mountain of sheer ice. Green and docile, they lapped those mysterious blue cliffs, and *Warlock* went into the lee, passing in a ship's length from the plunging rearing action of a wild horse into the tranquillity of a mountain lake, calm, windless and unnatural.

In the calm, Angel brought trays piled with crisp brown-baked Cornish pasties and steaming mugs of thick creamy cocoa, and they ate breakfast at three in the morning, marvelling at the fine pale sunlight and the towers of incredible beauty, the younger officers shouting and laughing when a school of five black killer whales passed so close that they could see their white cheek patterns and wide grinning mouths through the icy clear waters.

The great mammals circled the ship, then ducked beneath her hull, surging up on the far side with their huge black triangular fins shearing the surface as they blew through the vents in the top of their heads. The fishy stink of their breath pervaded the bridge, and then they were gone, and *Warlock* motored calmly along in the lee of the ice, like a holiday launch of day-trippers.

Nicholas Berg did not join the spontaneous gaiety. He munched one of Angel's delicious pies full of meat and thick gravy, but he could not finish it. His stomach was too tense. He found himself resenting the high spirits of his officers. The laughter offended him, now when his whole life hung in precarious balance. He felt the temptation to quell them with a few harsh words, conscious of the power he had to plunge them into instant consternation.

Nick listened to their carefree banter and felt old enough to be their father, despite the few years' difference in their ages. He was impatient with them, irritated that they should be able to laugh like this when so much was at stake – six hundred human lives, a great ship, tens of millions of dollars, his whole future. They would probably never themselves know what it felt like to put a lifetime's work at risk on a single flip of the coin – and then suddenly, unaccountably, he envied them.

He could not understand the sensation, could not fathom why suddenly he longed to laugh with them, to share the companionship of the moment, to be free of pressure for just a little while. For fifteen years, he had not known that sort of hiatus, had never wanted it.

He stood up abruptly, and immediately the bridge was silent. Every officer concentrating on his appointed task, not one of them glancing at him as he paced once, slowly, across the wide bridge. It did not need a word to change the mood, and suddenly Nick felt guilty. It was too easy, too cheap.

Carefully Nick steeled himself, shutting out the weakness,

building up his resolve and determination, bringing all his concentration to bear on the Herculean task ahead of him, and he paused at the door of the radio room. The Trog looked up from his machines, and they exchanged a single glance of understanding. Two completely dedicated men, with no time for frivolity.

Nick nodded and paced on, the strong handsome face stern and uncompromising, his step firm and measured – but when he stopped again by the side windows of the bridge and looked up at the magnificent cliff of ice, he felt the doubts surging up again within him.

How much had he sacrificed for what he had gained, how much joy and laughter had he spurned to follow the high road of challenge, how much beauty had he passed along the way without seeing it in his haste, how much love and warmth and companionship? He thought with a fierce pang of the woman who had been his wife, and who had gone now with the child who was his son. Why had they gone, and what had they left him with – after all his strivings?

Behind him, the radio crackled and hummed as the carrier beam opened Channel 16, then it pitched higher as a human voice came through clearly.

> 'Mayday. Mayday. Mayday. This is the *Golden Adventurer*.'

Nick spun and ran to the radio room as the calm masculine voice read out the coordinates of the ship's position.

> 'We are in imminent danger of striking. We are preparing to abandon ship. Can any vessel render assistance? Repeat, can any vessel render assistance?'

'Good God,' David Allen's voice was harsh with anxiety, 'the current's got them, they're going down on Cape Alarm at nine knots – she's only fifty miles offshore and we are still two hundred and twenty miles from that position.'

'Where is *La Mouette?*' growled Nick Berg. 'Where the hell is she?'

'We'll have to open contact now, sir,' David Allen looked up from the chart. 'You cannot let them go down into the boats – not in this weather, sir. It would be murder.'

'Thank you, Number One,' said Nick quietly. 'Your advice is always welcome.' David flushed, but there was anger and not embarrassment beneath the colour. Even in the stress of the moment, Nick noted that, and adjusted his opinion of his First Officer. He had guts as well as brains.

The Mate was right, of course. There was only one thing to consider now, the conservation of human life.

Nick looked up at the top of the ice cliff and saw the low cloud tearing off it, roiling and swirling in the wind, pouring down over the edge like boiling milk frothing from the lip of a great pot.

He had to send now. *La Mouette* had won the contest of silence. Nick stared up at the cloud and composed the message he would send. He must reassure the Master, urge him to delay his decision to abandon ship and give *Warlock* the time to close the gap, perhaps even reach her before she struck on Cape Alarm.

The silence on the bridge was deepened by the absence of wind. They were all watching him now, waiting for the decision, and in that silence the carrier beam of Channel 16 hummed and throbbed.

Then suddenly a rich Gallic accent poured into the silent bridge, a full fruity voice that Nick remembered so clearly, even after all the years.

> 'Master of *Golden Adventurer*, this is the Master of salvage tug *La Mouette*. I am proceeding at best speed

your assistance. Do you accept Lloyd's Open Form "No cure no pay"?'

Nick kept his face from showing any emotion, but his heart barged wildly against his ribs. Jules Levoisin had broken silence.

'Plot his position report,' he said quietly.

'God! She's inside us.' David Allen's face was stricken as he marked *La Mouette*'s reported position on the chart. 'She's a hundred miles ahead of us.'

'No.' Nick shook his head. 'He's lying.'

'Sir?'

'He's lying. He always lies.' Nick lit a cheroot and when it was drawing evenly, he spoke again to his radio officer.

'Did you get a bearing?' and the Trog looked up from his radio direction-finding compass on which he was tracing *La Mouette*'s transmissions.

'I have only one coordinate, you won't get a fix—'

But Nick interrupted him, 'We'll use his best course from Golfo San Jorge for a fix.' He turned back to David Allen. 'Plot that.'

'There's a difference of over three hundred nautical miles.'

'Yes.' Nick nodded. 'That old pirate wouldn't broadcast an accurate position to all the world. We are inside him and running five knots better, we'll put a line over *Golden Adventurer* before he's in radar contact.'

'Are you going to open contact with Christy Marine now, sir?'

'No, Mr Allen.'

'But they will do a deal with *La Mouette* – unless we bid now.'

'I don't think so,' Nick murmured, and almost went on to say, 'Duncan Alexander won't settle for Lloyd's Open Form while he is the underwriter, and his ship is free and floating. He'll fight for daily hire and bonus, and Jules

Levoisin won't buy that package. He'll hold out for the big plum. They won't do a deal until the two ships are in visual contact – and by that time I'll have her in tow and I'll fight the bastard in the awards court for twenty-five per cent of her value—' But he did not say it. 'Steady as she goes, Mr Allen,' was all he said, as he left the bridge.

He closed the door of his day cabin and leaned back against it, shutting his eyes tightly as he gathered himself. It had been so very close, a matter of seconds and he would have declared himself and given the advantage to *La Mouette*.

Through the door behind him, he heard David Allen's voice. 'Did you see him? He didn't feel a thing – not a bloody thing. He was going to let those poor bastards go into the boats. He must piss ice-water.' The voice was muffled, but the outrage in it was tempered by awe.

Nick kept his eyes shut a moment longer, then he straightened up and pushed himself away from the door. He wanted it to begin now. It was the waiting and the uncertainty which was eroding what was left of his strength.

'Please God, let me reach them in time.' And he was not certain whether it was for the lives or for the salvage award that he was praying.

Captain Basil Reilly, the Master of the *Golden Adventurer*, was a tall man, with a lean and wiry frame that promised reserves of strength and endurance. His face was very darkly tanned and splotched with the dark patches of benign sun cancer. His heavy moustache was silvered like the pelt of a snow fox, and though his eyes were set in webs of finely wrinkled and pouchy skin, they were bright and calm and intelligent.

He stood on the windward wing of his navigation bridge and watched the huge black seas tumbling in to batter his helpless ship. He was taking them broadside now, and each time they struck, the hull shuddered and heeled with a sick dead motion, giving reluctantly to the swells that rose up and broke over her rails, sweeping her decks from side to side, and then cascading off her again in a tumble of white that smoked in the wind.

He adjusted the life jacket he wore, settling the rough canvas more comfortably around his shoulders as he reviewed his position once more.

*Golden Adventurer* had taken the ice in that eight-to-midnight watch traditionally allotted to the most junior of the navigating officers. The impact had hardly been noticeable, yet it had awoken the Master from deep sleep – just a slight check and jar that had touched some deep chord in the mariner's instinct.

The ice had been a growler, one of the most deadly of all hazards. The big bergs standing high and solid to catch the radar beams, or the eye of even the most inattentive deck watch, were easily avoided. However, the low ice lying awash, with its great bulk and weight almost completely hidden by the dark and turbulent waters, was as deadly as a predator in ambush.

The growler showed itself only in the depths of each wave trough, or in the swirl of the current around it, as though a massive sea-monster lurked there. At night, these indications would pass unnoticed by even the sharpest eyes, and below the surface, the wave action eroded the body of the growler, turning it into a horizontal blade that lay ten feet or more below the water level and reached out two or three hundred feet from the visible surface indications.

With the Third Officer on watch, and steaming at cautionary speed of a mere twelve knots, the *Golden Adventurer* had brushed against one of these monsters, and although the actual impact had gone almost unnoticed on board, the ice had opened her like the knife stroke which splits a herring for the smoking rack.

It was classic *Titanic* damage, a fourteen-foot rent through her side, twelve feet below the Plimsoll line, shearing two of her watertight compartments, one of which was her main engine-room section.

They had held the water easily until the electrical explosion, and since then, the Master had battled to keep her afloat. Slowly, step by step, fighting all the way, he had yielded to the sea. All the bilge pumps were running still, but the water was steadily gaining.

Three days ago he had brought all his passengers up from below the main deck, and he had battened down all the watertight bulkheads. The crew and passengers were accommodated now in the lounges and smoking rooms. The ship's luxury and opulence had been transformed into the crowded, unhygienic and deteriorating conditions of a city under siege.

It reminded him of the catacombs of the London underground converted to air-raid shelters during the blitz. He had been a lieutenant on shore-leave and he had passed one night there that he would remember for the rest of his life.

There was the same atmosphere on board now. The sanitary arrangements were inadequate. Fourteen toilet bowls for six hundred, many of them seasick and suffering from diarrhoea. There were no baths nor showers, and insufficient power for the heating of water in the hand-basins. The emergency generators delivered barely sufficient power to work the ship, to run the pumps, to supply minimal lighting, and to keep the communicational and navigational equipment running. There was no heating in the ship and the outside air temperature had fallen to minus twenty degrees now.

The cold in the spacious public lounges was brutal. The passengers huddled in their fur coats and bulky life jackets under mounds of blankets. There were limited cooking facilities on the gas stoves usually reserved for adventure tours ashore. There was no baking or grilling, and most of the food was eaten cold and congealed from cans; only the soup and beverages steamed in the cold clammy air, like the breaths of the waiting and helpless multitude.

The desalination plants had not been in use since the ice collision and now the supply of fresh water was critical; even hot drinks were rationed.

Of the 368 paying passengers, only forty-eight were below the age of fifty, and yet the morale was extraordinary. Men and women who before the emergency could and did complain bitterly at a dress shirt not ironed to crisp perfection or a wine served a few degrees too cold, now accepted a mug of beef tea as though it were a vintage Château Margaux, and laughed and chatted animatedly in the cold, shaming with their fortitude the few that might have complained. These were an unusual sample of humanity, men and women of achievement and resilience, who had come here to this outlandish corner of the globe in search of new experience. They were mentally prepared for adventure and even danger, and seemed almost to welcome this as part of the entertainment provided by the tour.

Yet, standing on his bridge, the Master was under no illusion as to the gravity of their situation. Peering through the streaming glass, he watched a work party, led by his First Officer, toiling heroically in the bows. Four men in glistening yellow plastic suits and hoods, drenched by the icy seas, working with the slow cold-numbed movements of automatons as they struggled to stream a sea anchor and bring the ship's head up into the sea, so that she might ride more easily, and perhaps slow her precipitous rush down onto the rocky coast. Twice in the preceding days, the anchors they had rigged had been torn away by sea and wind and the ship's dead weight.

Three hours before, he had called his engineering

officers up from below, where the risk to their lives had become too great to chance against the remote possibility of restoring power to his main engines. He had conceded the battle to the sea and now he was planning the final moves when he must abandon his command and attempt to remove six hundred human beings from this helpless hulk to the even greater dangers and hardships of Cape Alarm's barren and storm-rent shores.

Cape Alarm was one of those few pinnacles of barren black rock which thrust out from beneath the thick white mantle of the Antarctic cap, pounded free of ice like an anvil beneath the eternal hammering assault of storm and sea and wind.

The long straight ridge protruded almost fifty miles into the eastern extremity of the Weddell Sea, was fifty miles across at its widest point, and terminated in a pair of bull's horns which formed a small protected bay named after the polar explorer Sir Ernest Shackleton.

Shackleton Bay, with its steep purple-black beaches of round polished pebbles, was the nesting ground of a huge colony of chin-strap penguin, and for this reason was one of *Golden Adventurer*'s regular ports of call.

On each tour, the ship would anchor in the deep and calm waters of the bay, while her passengers went ashore to study and photograph the breeding birds and the extraordinary geological formations, sculptured by ice and wind into weird and grotesque shapes.

Only ten days earlier, *Golden Adventurer* had weighed anchor in Shackleton Bay and stood out into the Weddell Sea. The weather had been mild and still, with a slow oily swell and a bright clear sun. Now, before a force seven gale, in temperatures forty-five degrees colder, and borne on the wild dark sweep of the current, she was being carried back to that same black and rocky shore.

There was no doubt in Captain Reilly's mind – they

were going to go aground on Cape Alarm, there was no avoiding that fate with this set of sea and wind, unless the French salvage tug reached them first.

*La Mouette* should have been in radar contact already, if the tug's reported position was correct, and Basil Reilly let a little frown of worry crease the brown parchment skin of his forehead and shadows were in his eyes.

'Another message from head office, sir.' His Second Officer was beside him now, a young man with the shape of a teddy bear swathed in thick woollen jerseys and marine blue top coat. Basil Reilly's strict dress regulations had long ago been abandoned and their breaths steamed in the frigid air of the navigation bridge.

'Very well.' Reilly glanced at the flimsy. 'Send that to the tug master.' The contempt was clear in his voice, his disdain for this haggling between owners and salvors, when a great ship and six hundred lives were at risk in the cold sea.

He knew what he would do if the salvage tug made contact before *Golden Adventurer* struck the waiting fangs of rock, he would override his owner's express orders and exercise his rights as Master by immediately accepting the offer of assistance under Lloyd's Open Form.

'But let him come,' he murmured to himself. 'Please God, let him come,' and he raised his binoculars and slowly swept a long jagged horizon where the peaks of the swells seemed black and substantial as rock. He paused with a leap of his pulse when something white blinked in the field of the glasses and then, with a little sick slide, realized that it was only a random ray of sunlight catching a pinnacle of ice from one of the floating bergs.

He lowered the glasses and crossed from the windward wing of the bridge to the lee. He did not need the glasses now, Cape Alarm was black and menacing against the sow's-belly grey of the sky. Its ridges and valleys picked out with gleaming ice and banked snow, and against her steep shore, the sea creamed and leapt high in explosions of purest white.

'Sixteen miles, sir,' said the First Officer, coming to stand beside him. 'And the current seems to be setting a little more northerly now.' They were both silent, as they balanced automatically against the violent pitch and roll of the deck.

Then the Mate spoke again with a bitter edge to his voice, 'Where is that bloody frog?' And they watched the night of Antarctica begin to shroud the cruel lee shore in funereal cloaks of purple and sable, picked out with the ermine collars and cuffs of ice.

She was very young, probably not yet twenty-five years of age, and even the layers of heavy clothing topped by a man's anorak three sizes too big could not disguise the slimness of her body, that almost coltish elegance of long fine limbs and muscle toned by youth and hard exercise.

Her head was set jauntily on the long graceful stem of her neck, like a golden sunflower, and the profuse mane of long hair was sun-bleached, streaked with silver and platinum and copper gold, twisted up carelessly into a rope almost as thick as a man's wrist and piled on top of her head. Yet loose strands floated down on to her forehead and tickled her nose so that she pursed her lips and puffed them away.

Her hands were both occupied with the heavy tray she carried, and she balanced like a skilled horsewoman against the ship's extravagant plunging as she offered it.

'Come on, Mrs Goldberg,' she wheedled. 'It will warm the cockles of your tum.'

'I don't think so, my dear,' the white-haired woman faltered.

'Just for me, then,' the girl wheedled.

'Well,' the woman took one of the mugs and sipped it tentatively. 'It's good,' she said, and then quickly and furtively, 'Samantha, has the tug come yet?'

'It will be here any minute now, and the Captain is a dashing Frenchman, just the right age for you, with a lovely tickly moustache. I'm going to introduce you first thing.'

The woman was a widow in her late fifties, a little overweight and more than a little afraid, but she smiled and sat up a little straighter.

'You naughty thing,' she smiled.

'Just as soon as I've finished with this,' Samantha indicated the tray, 'I'll come and sit with you. We'll play some klabrias, okay?' When Samantha Silver smiled, her teeth were very straight and white against the peach of her tanned cheeks and the freckles that powdered her nose like gold dust. She moved on.

They welcomed her, each of them, men and women, competing for her attention, for she was one of those rare creatures that radiate such warmth, a sort of shining innocence, like a kitten or a beautiful child, and she laughed and chided and teased them in return and left them grinning and heartened, but jealous of her going, so they followed her with their eyes. Most of them felt she belonged to them personally, and they wanted all of her time and presence, making up questions or little stories to detain her for a few extra moments.

'There was an albatross following us a little while ago, Sam.'

'Yes, I saw it through the galley window—'

'It was a wandering albatross, wasn't it, Sam?'

'Oh, come on, Mr Stewart! You know better than that. It was *Diomedea melanophris*, the black-browed albatross, but still it's good luck. All albatrosses are good luck – that's a scientifically proven fact.'

Samantha had a doctorate in biology and was one of the

ship's specialist guides. She was on sabbatical leave from the University of Miami where she held a research fellowship in marine ecology.

Passengers thirty years her senior treated her like a favourite daughter most of the time. However, in even the mildest crisis they became childlike in their appeal to her and in their reliance on her natural strength which they recognized and sought instinctively. She was to them a combination of beloved pet and den-mother.

While a ship's steward refilled her tray with mugs, Samantha paused at the entrance to the temporary galley they had set up in the cocktail room and looked back into the densely packed lounge.

The stink of unwashed humanity and tobacco smoke was almost a solid blue thing, but she felt a rush of affection for them. They were behaving so very well, she thought, and she was proud of them.

'Well done, team,' she thought, and grinned. It was not often that she could find affection in herself for a mass of human beings. Often she had pondered how a creature so fine and noble and worthwhile as the human individual could, in its massed state, become so unattractive.

She thought briefly of the human multitudes of the crowded cities. She hated zoos and animals in cages, remembering as a little girl crying for a bear that danced endlessly against its bars, driven mad by its confinement. The concrete cages of the cities drove their captives into similar strange and bizarre behaviour. All creatures should be free to move and live and breathe, she believed, and yet man, the super-predator, who had denied that right to so many other creatures, was now destroying himself with the same single-mindedness, poisoning and imprisoning himself in an orgy that made the madness of the lemmings seem logical in comparison. It was only when she saw human beings like these in circumstances like these that she could be truly proud of them – and afraid for them.

She felt her own fear deep down, at the very periphery of her awareness, for she was a sea-creature who loved and understood the sea – and knew its monumental might. She knew what awaited them out there in the storm, and she was afraid. With a deliberate effort she lifted the slump of her shoulders, and set the smile brightly on her lips and picked up the heavy tray.

At that moment the speakers of the public-address system gave a preliminary squawk, and then filtered the Captain's cultured and measured tones into the suddenly silent ship.

'Ladies and gentlemen, this is your Captain speaking. I regret to inform you that we have not yet established radar contact with the salvage tug *La Mouette*, and that I now deem it necessary to transfer the ship's company to the lifeboats.'

There was a sigh and stir in the crowded lounges, heard even above the storm. Samantha saw one of her favourite passengers reach for his wife and press her silvery-grey head to his shoulder.

'You have all practised the lifeboat drill many times and you know your teams and stations. I am sure I do not have to impress upon you the necessity to go to your stations in orderly fashion, and to obey explicitly the orders of the ship's officers.'

Samantha set down her tray and crossed quickly to Mrs Goldberg. The woman was weeping, softly and quietly, lost and bewildered, and Samantha slipped her arm around her shoulder.

'Come now,' she whispered. 'Don't let the others see you cry.'

'Will you stay with me, Samantha?'

'Of course I will.' She lifted the woman to her feet. 'It will be all right – you'll see. Just think of the story you'll be able to tell your grandchildren when you get home.'

Captain Reilly reviewed his preparations for leaving the ship, going over them item by item in his mind. He now knew by heart the considerable list he had compiled days previously from his own vast experience of Antarctic conditions and the sea.

The single most important consideration was that no person should be immersed, or even drenched by sea water during the transfer. Life expectation in these waters was four minutes. Even if the victim were immediately pulled from the water, it was still four minutes, unless the sodden clothing could be removed and heating provided. With this wind blowing, rising eight of the Beaufort scale at forty miles an hour and an air temperature of minus twenty degrees, the chill factor was at the extreme of stage seven, which, translated into physical terms, meant that a few minutes' exposure would numb and exhaust a man, and that mere survival was a matter of planning and precaution.

The second most important consideration was the physiological crisis of his passengers, when they left the comparative warmth and comfort and security of the ship for the shrieking cold and the violent discomfort of a life-raft afloat in an Antarctic storm.

They had been briefed, and mentally prepared as much as was possible. An officer had checked each passenger's clothing and survival equipment, they had been fed high-sugar tablets to ward off the cold, and the life-raft allocations had been carefully worked out to provide balanced complements, each with a competent crew member in command. It was as much as he could do for them, and he turned his attention to the logistics of the transfer.

The lifeboats would go first – six of them, slung three on each side of the ship, each crewed by a navigation officer and five seamen. While the great drogue of the sea-anchor held the ship's head into the wind and the sea, they would be swung outboard on their hydraulic derricks and the winches would lower them swiftly to the surface of a sea temporarily smoothed by the oil sprayed from the pumps in the bows.

Although they were decked-in, powered, and equipped with radio, the lifeboats were not the ideal vehicles for survival in these conditions. Within hours, the men aboard them would be exhausted by the cold. For this reason, none of the passengers would be aboard them. Instead, they would go into the big inflatable life-rafts, self-righting even in the worst seas and enclosed with a double skin of insulation. Equipped with emergency rations and battery-powered locator beacons, they would ride the big black seas more easily and each provide shelter for twenty human beings, whose body warmth would keep the interior habitable, at least for the time it took to tow the rafts to land.

The motor lifeboats were merely the shepherds for the rafts. They would herd them together and then tow them in tandem to the sheltering arms of Shackleton Bay.

Even in these blustering conditions, the tow should not take more than twelve hours. Each boat would tow five rafts, and though the crews of the motor boats would have to change, brought into the canopy of the rafts and rested, there should be no insurmountable difficulties; Captain Reilly was hoping for a tow-speed of between three and four knots.

The lifeboats were packed with equipment and fuel and food sufficient to keep the shipwrecked party for a month, perhaps two on reduced rations, and once the calmer shores of the bay had been reached, the rafts would be carried ashore, the canopies reinforced with slabs of packed snow and transformed into igloo-type huts to shelter the survivors. They might be in Shackleton Bay a long time, for even when the French tug reached them, it could not take aboard six hundred persons; some would have to remain and await another rescue ship.

Captain Reilly took one more look at the land. It was very close now, and even in the gloom of the onrushing night, the peaks of ice and snow glittered like the fangs of some terrible and avaricious monster.

'All right,' he nodded to his First Officer, 'we will begin.'

The Mate lifted the small two-way radio to his lips. 'Foredeck. Bridge. You may commence laying the oil now.'

From each side of the bows, the hoses threw up silver dragonfly wings of sprayed diesel oil, pumped directly from the ship's bunkers; its viscous weight resisted the wind's efforts to tear it away, and it fell in a thick coating across the surface of the sea, broken by the floodlights into the colour spectrum of the rainbow.

Immediately, the sea was soothed, the wind-riven surface flattened by the weight of oil, so the swells passed in smooth and weighty majesty beneath the ship's hull.

The two officers on the wing of the bridge could feel the sick, waterlogged response of the hull. She was heavy with the water in her, no longer light and quick and alive.

'Send the boats away,' said the Captain, and the mate passed the order over the radio in quiet conversational tones.

The hydraulic arms of the derricks lifted the six boats off their chocks and swung them out over the ship's side, suspended one moment high above the surface; then, as the ship fell through the trough, the oil-streaked crest raced by only feet below their keels. The officer of each lifeboat must judge the sea, and operate the winch so as to drop neatly onto the back slope of a passing swell – then instantly detach the automatic clamps and stand away from the threatening steel cliff of the ship's side.

In the floodlights, the little boats shone wetly with spray, brilliant electric yellow in colour, and decorated with garlands of ice like Christmas toys. In the small armoured-glass windows the officers' faces also glistened whitely with the strain and concentration of these terrifying moments, as each tried to judge the rushing black seas.

Suddenly the heavy nylon rope that held the cone-shaped drogue of the sea-anchor snapped with a report like a cannon shot, and the rope snaked and hissed in the air, a vicious whiplash which could have sliced a man in half.

It was like slipping the head halter from a wild stallion. *Golden Adventurer* threw up her bows, joyous to be freed of restraint. She slewed back across the scend of the sea, and was immediately pinned helplessly broadside, her starboard side into the wind, and the three yellow lifeboats still dangling.

A huge wave reared up out of the darkness. As it rushed down on the ship, one of the lifeboats sheared her cables and fell heavily to the surface, the tiny propeller churning frantically, trying to bring her round to meet the wave – but the wave caught her and dashed her back against the steel side of the ship.

She burst like a ripe melon and the guts spilled out of her; from the bridge they saw the crew swirled helplessly away into the darkness. The little locator lamps on their lifejackets burned feebly as fireflies in the darkness and then blinked out in the storm.

The forward lifeboard was swung like a door-knocker against the ship, her forward cable jammed so she dangled stern upmost, and as each wave punched into her, she was smashed against the hull. They could hear the men in her screaming, a thin pitiful sound on the wind, that went on for many minutes as the sea slowly beat the boat into a tangle of wreckage.

The third boat was also swung viciously against the hull. The releases on her clamps opened, and she dropped twenty feet into the boil and surge of water, submerging completely and then bobbing free like a yellow fishing float after the strike. Leaking and settling swiftly, she limped away into the clamorous night.

'Oh, my God,' whispered Captain Reilly, and in the harsh lights of the bridge, his face was suddenly old and haggard. In a single stroke he had lost half his boats. As yet he did not mourn the men taken by the sea, that would come later – now it was the loss of the boats that appalled him, for it threatened the lives of nearly six hundred others.

'The other boats' – the First Officer's voice was ragged with shock – 'the others got away safely, sir.'

In the lee of the towering hull, protected from both wind and sea, the other three boats had dropped smoothly to the surface and detached swiftly. Now they circled out in the dark night, with their spotlights probing like long white fingers. One of them staggered over the wildly plunging crests to take off the crew of the stricken life-boat, and they left the cracked hull to drift away and sink.

'Three boats,' whispered the Captain, 'for thirty rafts.' He knew that there were insufficient shepherds for his flock – and yet he had to send them out, for even above the wind, he thought he could hear the booming artillery barrage of high surf breaking on a rocky shore. Cape Alarm was waiting hungrily for his ship. 'Send the rafts away,' he said quietly, and then again under his breath, 'And God have mercy on us all.'

'Come on, Number 16,' called Samantha. 'Here we are, Number 16.' She gathered them to her, the eighteen passengers who made up the complement of her allotted life-raft. 'Here we are – all together now. No stragglers.'

They were gathered at the heavy mahogany doors that opened on to the open forward deck.

'Be ready,' she told them. 'When we get the word, we have to move fast.'

With the broadsiding seas sweeping the deck and cascading down over the lee, it would be impossible to embark from landing-nets into a raft bobbing alongside.

The rafts were being inflated on the open deck, the passengers hustled across to them and into the canopied interior between waves and then the laden rafts were lifted over the side by the clattering winches and dropped into the quieter waters afforded by the tall bulk of the ship. Immediately, one of the lifeboats picked up the tow and took each raft out to form the pitiful little convoy.

'Right!' the Third Officer burst in through the mahogany doors and held them wide. 'Quickly!' he shouted. 'All together.'

'Let's go, gang!' sang out Samantha, and there was an awkward rush out on to the wet and slippery deck. It was only thirty paces to where the raft crouched like a monstrous yellow bullfrog, gaping its ugly dark mouth, but the wind struck like an axe and Samantha heard them cry out in dismay. Some of them faltered in the sudden merciless cold.

'Come on,' Samantha shouted, pushing those ahead of her, half-supporting Mrs Goldberg's plump body that suddenly felt as heavy and unco-operative as a full sack of wheat. 'Keep going.'

'Let me have her,' shouted the Third Officer, and he grabbed Mrs Goldberg's other arm. Between them they tumbled her through the entrance of the raft.

'Good on you, love,' the officer grinned at Samantha briefly. His smile was attractive and warm, very masculine and likeable. His name was Ken and he was five years her senior. They would probably have become lovers fairly soon, Samantha knew, for he had pursued her furiously since she stepped aboard in New York. Although she knew she did not love him, yet he had succeeded in arousing her and she was slowly succumbing to his obvious charms and her own passionate nature. She had made the decision to have him, and had been merely savouring it up until then. Now, with a pang, she realized that the moment might never come.

'I'll help you with the others.' She raised her voice above the hysterical shriek of the wind.

'Get in,' he shouted back, and swung her brusquely towards the raft. She crept into the crowded interior and looked back at the brightly lit deck that glistened in the arc lamps.

Ken had started back to where one of the women had slipped and fallen. She sprawled helplessly on the wet deck, while her husband stooped over her, trying to lift her back to her feet.

Ken reached them and lifted the woman easily; the three of them were the only ones out on the open deck now, and the two men supported thc woman between them, staggering against the heavy sullen roll of the waterlogged hull.

Samantha saw the wave come aboard and she shrieked a warning.

'Go back, Ken! For God's sake go back!' But he seemed not to hear her. The wave came aboard; over the windward rail like some huge black slippery sea-monster, it came with a deep silent rush.

'Ken!' she screamed, and he looked over his shoulder an instant before it reached them. Its crest was higher than his head. They could reach neither the raft, nor the shelter of the mahogany doors. She heard the clatter of the donkey-winch and the raft lifted swiftly off the deck, with a swooping tug in her guts. The operator could not let the rushing power of the wave crash into the helpless raft, throwing it against the superstructure or tearing its belly out on the ship's railing, for the frail plastic skin would rupture and it would collapse immediately.

Samantha hurled herself to the entrance and peered down. She saw the sea take the three figures in a black glittering rush. It cut them down, and swept them away. For a moment, she saw Ken clinging to the railing while the waters poured over him, burying his head in a tumbling fall of white and furious water. He disappeared and when the ship rolled sullenly back, shaking herself clear of the water, her decks were empty of any human shape.

With the next roll of the ship, the winch-operator high up in his glassed cabin swung the dangling raft outboard and lowered it swiftly and dexterously to the surface of the sea where one of the lifeboats circled anxiously, ready to take them in tow.

Samantha closed and secured the plastic door-cover, then she groped her way through the press of packed and terrified bodies until she found Mrs Goldberg.

'Are you crying, dear?' the elderly woman quavered, clinging to her desperately.

'No,' said Samantha, and placed one arm around her shoulders. 'No, I'm not crying.' And with her free hand, she wiped away the icy tears that streamed down her cheeks.

The Trog lifted his headset and looked at Nick through the reeking clouds of cigar smoke.

'Their radio operator has screwed down the key of his set. He's sending a single unbroken homing beam.'

Nick knew what that meant – they had abandoned *Golden Adventurer*. He nodded once but remained silent. He had wedged himself into the doorway from the bridge. The restless impatience that consumed him would not allow him to sit or be still for more than a few moments at a time. He was slowly facing up to the reality of disaster. The dice had fallen against him and his gamble had been with very survival. It was absolutely certain that *Golden Adventurer* would go aground and be beaten into a total wreck by this storm. He could expect a charter from Christy Marine to assist *La Mouette* in ferrying the survivors back to Cape Town, but the fee would be a small fraction of the Esso tow fee that he had forsaken for this wild and desperate dash south.

The gamble had failed and he was a broken man. Of course, it would take months still for the effects of his folly to become apparent, but the repayments of his loans and the construction bills for the other tug still building would slowly throttle and bring him down.

'We might still reach her before she goes aground,' said David Allen sturdily, and nobody else on the bridge spoke. 'I mean there could be a backlash of the current close inshore which could hold her off long enough to give us a chance—' His voice trailed off as Nick looked across at him and frowned.

'We are still ten hours away from her, and for Reilly to make the decision to abandon ship, she must have been very close indeed. Reilly is a good man.' Nick had personally selected him to command the *Golden Adventurer*. 'He was a destroyer captain on the North Atlantic run, the youngest in the navy, and then he was ten years with P & O. They pick only the best—' He stopped talking abruptly. He was becoming garrulous. He crossed to the radarscope and adjusted it for maximum range and illumination before looking down into the eyepiece. There was much fuzz and sea clutter, but on the extreme southern edge of the circular screen there showed the solid luminous glow of the cliffs and peaks of Cape Alarm. In good weather they were a mere five hours' steaming away, but now they had left the shelter of that giant iceberg and were staggering and plunging wildly through the angry night. She could have taken more speed, for *Warlock* was built for big seas, but always there was the deadly menace of ice, and Nick had to hold her at this cautionary speed, which meant ten hours more before they were in sight of *Golden Adventurer* – if she was still afloat.

Behind him, the Trog's voice crackled rustily with excitement. 'I'm getting voice – it's only strength one, weak and intermittent. One of the lifeboats is sending on a battery-powered transmitter.' He held his earphones pressed to his head with both hands as he listened.

'They are towing a batch of life-rafts with all survivors aboard to Shackleton Bay. But they've lost a life-raft,' he said. 'It's broken away from their towline, and they haven't got enough boats to search for it. They are asking *La Mouette* to keep a watch for it.'

'Is *La Mouette* acknowledging?'

The Trog shook his head. 'She's probably still out of range of this transmission.'

'Very well.' Nick turned back into the bridge. He had still not broken radio silence, and could feel his officers' disapproval, silent but strong. Again he felt the need for human contact, for the warmth and comfort of human conversation and friendly encouragement. He didn't yet have the strength to bear his failure alone.

He stopped beside David Allen and said, 'I have been studying the Admiralty sailing directions for Cape Alarm, David,' and pretended not to notice that the use of his Christian name had brought a startled look and quick colour to the mate's features. He went on evenly, 'the shore is very steep-to and she is exposed to this westerly weather, but there are beaches of pebble and the glass is going up sharply again.'

'Yes, sir,' David nodded enthusiastically. 'I have been watching it.'

'Instead of hoping for a cross-current to hold her off, I suggest you offer a prayer that she goes up on one of those beaches and that the weather moderates before she is beaten to pieces. There is still a chance we can put ground tackle on her before she starts breaking up.'

'I'll say ten Hail Marys, sir,' grinned David. Clearly he was overwhelmed by this sudden friendliness from his silent and forbidding Captain.

'And say another ten that we hold our lead on *La Mouette*,' said Nick, and smiled. It was one of the few times that David Allen had seen him smile, and he was amazed at the change it made to the stern features. They lightened with a charm and warmth and he had not before noticed the clear green of Nick Berg's eyes and how white and even were his teeth.

'Steady as she goes,' said Nick. 'Call me if anything changes,' and he turned away to his cabin.

'Steady as she goes, it is, sir,' said David Allen with a new friendliness in his voice.

The strange and marvellous lights of the aurora australis quivered and flickered in running streams of red and green fire along the horizon, and formed an incredible backdrop for the death agonies of a great ship.

Captain Reilly looked back through the small portholes of the leading lifeboat and watched her going to her fate. It seemed to him she had never been so tall and beautiful as in these terrible last moments. He had loved many ships, as if each had been a wonderful living creature, but he had loved no other ship more than *Golden Adventurer*, and he felt something of himself dying with her.

He saw her change her action. The sea was feeling the land now, the steep bank of Cape Alarm, and the ship seemed to panic at the new onslaught of wave and wind, as though she knew what fate awaited her there.

She was rolling through thirty degrees, showing the dull red streak of her belly paint as she came up short at the limit of each huge penduluming arc. There was a headland, tall black cliffs dropping sheer into the turbulent waters and it seemed that *Golden Adventurer* must go full on to them, but in the last impossible moments she slipped by, borne on the backlash of the current, avoiding the cliffs and swinging her bows on into the shallow bay beyond where she was hidden from Captain Reilly's view.

He stood for many minutes more, staring back across the leaping wave-tops and in the strange unnatural light of the heavens his face was greenish grey and heavily furrowed with the marks of grief.

Then he sighed once, very deeply, and turned away, devoting all his attention to guiding his pathetic limping little convoy to the safety of Shackleton Bay.

Almost immediately it was apparent that the fates had relented, and given them a favourable inshore current to carry them up on to the coast. The lifeboats were strung out over a distance of three miles, each of them with its string of bloated and clumsy rafts lumbering along in its wake. Captain Reilly had two-way VHF radio contact with each of them, and despite the brutal cold, they were all in good shape and making steady and unexpectedly rapid progress. Three or four hours would be sufficient, he began to hope. They had lost so much life already, and he could not be certain that there would be no further losses until he had the whole party ashore and encamped.

Perhaps the tragic run of bad luck had changed at last, he thought, and he picked up the small VHF radio. Perhaps the French tug was in range at last and he began to call her.

'*La Mouette*, do you read me? Come in, *La Mouette* . . .'

The lifeboat was low down on the water and the output of the little set was feeble in the vastness of sea and ice, yet he kept on calling.

They had accustomed themselves to the extravagant action of the disabled liner, her majestic roll and pitch, as regular as a gigantic metronome. They had adjusted to the cold of the unheated interior of the great ship, and the discomfort of her crowded and unsanitary conditions.

They had steeled themselves and tried to prepare themselves mentally for further danger and greater hardship, but not one of the survivors in life-raft Number 16 had imagined anything like this. Even Samantha, the youngest, probably physically the toughest and certainly the one most prepared by her training and her knowledge and love of the sea, had not imagined what it would be like in the raft.

It was utterly dark, not the faintest glimmer of light penetrated the insulated domed canopy, once its entrance was secured against the sea and the wind.

Samantha realized almost immediately how the darkness would crush their morale and, more dangerously, would induce disorientation and vertigo, so she ordered two of them at a time to switch on the tiny locator bulbs on their life jackets. It gave just a glimmering of light, enough to let them see each others' faces and take a little comfort in the proximity of other humans.

Then she arranged their seating, making them form a circle around the sides with all their legs pointing inwards, to give the raft better balance and to ensure that each of them had space to stretch out.

Now that Ken had gone, she had naturally taken command, and, as naturally, the others had turned to her for guidance and comfort. It was Samantha who had gone out through the opening into the brutal exposure of the night to take aboard and secure the tow rope from the lifeboat. She had come in again half-frozen, shaking in a palsy of cold, with her hands and face numbed. It had taken nearly half an hour of hard massage before feeling returned and she was certain that she had avoided frostbite.

Then the tow began, and if the movement of the light raft had been wild before, it now became a nightmare of uncoordinated movement. Each whim of sea and wind was transmitted directly to the huddling circle of survivors, and each time the raft pulled away or sheered off, the tow rope brought it up with a violent lurch and jerk. The wave crests whipped up by the wind and feeling the press of the land were up to twenty feet high, and the raft swooped over them and dropped heavily into the troughs. She did not have the lateral stability of a keel, so she spun on her axis until the tow rope jerked her up and she spun the other way. The first of them to start vomiting was Mrs Goldberg and it spurted in a warm jet down the side of Samantha's anorak.

The canopy was almost airtight, except for the small ventilation holes near the apex of the roof, and immediately the sweetish acrid stench of vomit permeated the raft. Within minutes, half a dozen of the other survivors were vomiting also.

It was the cold, however, that frightened Samantha. The cold was the killer. It came up even through the flexible insulated double skin of the deck, and was transferred into their buttocks and legs. It came in through the plastic canopy and froze the condensation of their breaths, it even froze the vomit on their clothing and on the deck.

'Sing!' Samantha told them. 'Come on, sing! Let's do "Yankee Doodle Dandy", first. You start, Mr Stewart, come on. Clap your hands, clap hands with your neighbour.' She hectored them relentlessly, not allowing any of them to fall into that paralytic state which is not true sleep but the trance caused by rapidly dropping body temperature. She crawled among them, prodding them awake, popping barley sugar from the emergency rations into their mouths.

'Suck and sing!' she commanded them, the sugar would

combat the cold and the seasickness. 'Clap your hands. Keep moving, we'll be there soon.'

When they could sing no more, she told them stories – and whenever she mentioned the word 'dog' they must all bark and clap their hands, or crow like the rooster, or bray like the donkey.

Samantha's throat was scratchy with singing and talking, and she was dizzy with fatigue and sick with cold, recognizing in herself the first symptoms of disinterest and lethargy, the prelude to giving up. She roused herself, struggling up into the sitting position from where she had slumped.

'I'm going to try and light the stove and get us a hot drink.' she sang out brightly. Around her there was only a mild stir and somebody retched painfully.

'Who's for a mug of beef tea—' she stopped abruptly. Something had changed. It took her a long moment to realize what it was. The sound of the wind had muted and the raft was riding more easily now, it was moving into a more regular rhythm of sweep and fall, without the dreadful jerk of the tow rope snapping it back.

Frantically she crawled to the entrance of the raft, and with cold crippled fingers she tore at the fastenings.

Outside the dawn had broken into a clear cold sky of palest ethereal pinks and mauves. Although the wind had dropped to a faint whisper, the seas were still big and unruly, and the waters had changed from black to the deep bottle green of molten glass.

The tow rope had torn away at the connecting shackle, leaving only a dangling flap of plastic. Number 16 had been the last raft in the line being towed by number three, but of the convoy, Samantha could now see no sign – though she crawled out through the entrance and clung precariously to the side of the raft, scanning the wave-caps about her desperately.

There was no sign of a lifeboat, no sight even of the

rocky, ice-capped shores of Cape Alarm. They had drifted away, during the night, into the vast and lonely reaches of the Weddell Sea.

Despair cramped her belly muscles, and she wanted to cry out in protest against this further cruelty of fate, but she prevented herself doing so, and stayed out in the clear and frosty air, drawing it in carefully for she knew that it could freeze her lung tissue. She searched and searched until her eyes streamed with the cold and the wind and concentration. Then at last the cold drove her back into the dark and stinking interior of the raft. She fell wearily among the supine and quiescent bodies, and pulled the hood of her anorak more tightly around her head. She knew it would not take long for them to start dying now, and somehow she did not care. Her despair was too intense, she let herself begin sinking into the morass of despondency which gripped all the others, and the cold crept up her legs and arms. She closed her eyes, and then opened them again with a huge effort.

'I'm not going to die,' she told herself firmly. 'I refuse to just lie down and die,' and she struggled up onto her knees. It felt as though she wore a rucksack filled with lead, such was the physical weight of her despair.

She crawled to the central locker that held all their emergency rations and equipment.

The emergency locator transmitter was packed in polyurethane and her fingers were clumsy with cold and the thick mittens, but at last she brought it out. It was the size of a cigar-box, and the instructions were printed on the side of it. She did not need to read them, but switched on the set and replaced it in its slot. Now for forty-eight hours, or until the battery ran out, it would transmit a DF homing-signal on 121,5 megahertz.

It was possible, just possible, that the French tug might pick up that feeble little beam, and track it down to its source. She set it out of her mind, and devoted herself to the Herculean task of trying to heat half a mug of water on the small solid-fuel stove without scalding herself as she held the stove in her lap and balanced it against the raft's motion. While she worked, she searched for the courage and the words to tell the others of their predicament.

The *Golden Adventurer*, deserted of all human beings, her engines dead, but with her deck lights still burning, her wheel locked hard over, and the Morse key in the radio room screwed down to transmit a single unbroken pulse, drifted swiftly down on the black rock of Cape Alarm.

The rock was of so hard a type of formation that the cliffs were almost vertical, and even exposed as they were to the eternal onslaught of this mad sea, they had weathered very little. They still retained the sharp vertical edges and the glossy polished planes of cleanly fractured faults.

The sea ran in and hit the cliff without any check. The impact seemed to jar the very air, like the concussion of bursting high explosive, and the sea shot high in a white fury against the unyielding rock of the cliff, before rolling back and forming a reverse swell.

It was these returning echoes from the cliff that held *Golden Adventurer* off the cliff. The shore was so steep-to that it dropped to forty fathoms directly below the cliffs. There was no bottom on which the ship could gut herself.

The wind was blanketed by the cliff and in the eerie stillness of air, she drifted in closer and closer, rolling almost to her limits as the swells took her broadside. Once she actually touched the rock with her superstructure on one of those rolls, but then the echo-wave nudged her away. The next wave pushed her closer, and its smaller weaker offspring pushed back at her. A man could have jumped from a ledge on the cliff on to her deck as she drifted slowly, parallel to the rock.

The cliff ended in an abrupt and vertical headland, where it had calved into three tall pillars of serpentine, as graceful as the sculptured columns of a temple of Olympian Zeus.

Again, *Golden Adventurer* touched one of those pillars, she bumped it lightly with her stern. It scraped paint from her side and crushed in her rail, but then she was past.

The light bump was just sufficient to push her stern round, and she pointed her bows directly into the wide shallow bay beyond the cliffs.

Here a softer, more malleable rock-formation had been eroded by the weather, forming a wide beach of purple-black pebbles, each the size of a man's head and water-worn as round as cannon balls.

Each time the waves rushed up this stony beach, the pebbles struck against each other with a rattling roar, and the brash of rotten and mushy sea ice that filled the bay susurrated and clinked, as it rose and fell with the sea.

Now *Golden Adventurer* was clear of the cliff, she was more fully in the grip of the wind. Although the wind was dying, it still had force enough to move her steadily deeper into the bay, her bows pointed directly at the beach.

Unlike the cliff shore, the bay sloped up gently to the beach and this allowed the big waves to build up into rounded sliding humps. They did not curl and break into white water because the thick layer of brash ice weighted and flattened them, so that these swells joined with the wind to throw the ship at the beach with smoothly gathering impetus.

She took the ground with a great metallic groan of her straining plates and canted over slowly, but the moving pebble beach moulded itself quickly to her hull, giving gradually, as the waves and wind thrust her higher and higher until she was firmly aground; then, as the short night ended so the wind fell further, and in sympathy the swells moderated also and the tide drew back, letting the ship settle more heavily.

By noon of that day, *Golden Adventurer* was held firmly by the bows on the curved purple beach, canted over at an angle of 10°. Only her after end was still floating, rising and falling like a see-saw on the swell patterns which still pushed in steadily, but the plummeting air temperature was rapidly freezing the brash ice around her stern into a solid sheet.

The ship stood very tall above the glistening wet beach. Her upperworks were festooned with rime and long rapier-like stalactites of shining translucent ice hung from her scuppers and from the anchor fair-leads.

Her emergency generator was still running, and although there was no human being aboard her, her lights burned gaily and piped music played softly through her deserted public rooms.

Apart from the rent in her side, through which the sea still washed and swirled, there was no external evidence of damage, and beyond her the peaks and valleys of Cape Alarm, so wild and fierce, seemed merely to emphasize her graceful lines and to underline how rich a prize she was, a luscious ripe plum ready for the picking.

Down in her radio room, the transmitting key continued to send out an unbroken beam that could be picked up for 500 miles around.

Two hours of deathlike sleep – and then Nick Berg woke with a wild start, knowing that something of direct consequence was about to happen. But it took fully ten seconds for him to realize where he was.

He stumbled from his bunk, and he knew he had not slept long enough. His skull was stuffed with the cotton-wool of fatigue, and he swayed on his feet as he shaved in the shower, trying to steam himself awake with the scalding water.

When he went out on to the bridge, the Trog was still at his equipment. He looked up at Nick for a moment with his little rheumy pink eyes, and it was clear that he had not slept at all. Nick felt a prick of shame at his own indulgence.

'We are still inside *La Mouette*,' said the Trog, and turned back to his set. 'I reckon we have an edge of almost a hundred miles.'

Angel appeared on the bridge, bearing a huge tray, and the saliva jetted from under Nick's tongue as he smelled it.

'I did a little special for your brekker, Skipper,' said Angel. 'I call it "Eggs on Angel's Wings".'

'I'm buying,' said Nick, and turned back to the Trog with his mouth full and chewing. 'What of the *Adventurer?*'

'She's still sending a DF, but her position has not altered in almost three hours.'

'What do you mean?' Nick demanded, and swallowed heavily.

'No change in position.'

'Then she's aground,' Nick muttered, the food in his hand forgotten, and at that moment David Allen hurried on to the bridge still shrugging on his pea-jacket. His eyes were puffy and his hair was hastily wetted and combed, but spiky at the back from contact with his pillow. It had not taken him long to hear that the Captain was on the bridge. 'And in one piece, if her transmitter is still sending.'

'It looks like those Hail Marys worked, David.' Nick

flashed his rare smile and David slapped the polished teak top of the chart table.

'Touch wood, and don't dare the devil.'

Nick felt his early despair slipping away with his fatigue, and he took another big mouthful and savoured it as he strode to the front windows and stared ahead.

The sea had flattened dramatically, but a weak and butter-yellow sun low on the horizon gave no warmth, and Nick glanced up at the thermometer and read the outside air temperature at minus thirty degrees.

Down here below 60° south, the weather was so unstable, caught up on the wheel of endlessly circling atmospheric depressions, that a gale could rise in minutes and drop to a flat calm almost as swiftly. Yet foul weather was the rule. For a hundred days and more each year, the wind was at galeforce or above. The photographs of Antarctica always gave a completely false impression of fine days with the sun sparkling on pristine snow fields and lovely towering icebergs. The truth was that you cannot take photographs in a blizzard or a white-out.

Nick distrusted this calm, and yet found himself praying that it would hold. He wanted to increase speed again, and was on the point of taking that chance, when the officer of the watch called a sharp alteration of course.

Ahead of them, Nick made out the sullen swirl of hidden ice below the surface, like a lurking monster, and as *Warlock* altered course to avoid it, the ice broke the surface. Black ice, striated with bands of glacial mud, ugly and deadly. Nick did not pass the order for the increase in speed.

'We should be raising Cape Alarm within the hour,' David Allen gloated beside him. 'If this visibility holds.'

'It won't,' said Nick. 'We'll have fog pretty soon,' and he indicated the surface of the sea, which was beginning to steam, emitting ghostly tendrils and eddies of seafret, as the difference between sea and air temperature widened.

'We'll be at the *Golden Adventurer* in four hours more.' David was bubbling with renewed excitement, and he slapped the teak table again. 'With your permission, sir, I'll go down and double-check the rocket-lines and tow equipment.'

While the air around them thickened into a ghostly white soup, and blotted out all visibility to a few hundred yards, Nick paced the bridge like a caged lion, his hands clasped behind his back and a black unlit cheroot clamped between his teeth. He broke his pacing every time that the Trog intercepted another transmission from either Christy Marine, Jules Levoisin or Captain Reilly on his VHF radio.

At mid-morning, Reilly reported that he and his slow convoy had reached Shackleton Bay without further losses, that they were taking full advantage of the moderating weather to set up an encampment, and he ended by urging *La Mouette* to keep a watch on 121,5 megahertz to try and locate the missing life-raft that had broken away during the night. *La Mouette* did not acknowledge.

'They aren't reading on the VHF,' grunted the Trog.

Nick thought briefly of the hapless souls adrift in this cold, and decided that they would probably not last out the day unless the temperature rose abruptly. Then he dismissed the thought and concentrated on the exchanges between Christy Marine and *La Mouette*.

The two parties had diametrically changed their bargaining standpoints.

While *Golden Adventurer* was adrift on the open sea, and any salvage efforts would mean that the tug should merely put a rocket-line across her, pass a messenger wire to carry the big steel hawser and then take her in tow, Jules Levoisin had pressed for Lloyd's Open Form 'No cure no pay' contract.

Since the 'cure' was almost certain, 'pay' would follow as a matter of course. The amount of payment would be fixed by the arbitration of the committee of Lloyd's in

London under the principles of international maritime law, and would be a percentage of the salved value of the vessel. The percentage decided upon by the arbitrator would depend upon the difficulties and dangers that the salvor had overcome. A clever salvor in an arbitration court could paint a picture of such daring and ingenuity that the award would be in millions of dollars.

Christy Marine had been desperately trying to avoid a 'No cure no pay' contract. They had been trying to wheedle Levoisin into a daily hire and bonus contract, since this would limit the total cost of the operation, but they had been met by a Gallic acquisitiveness – right up to the moment when it became clear that *Golden Adventurer* had gone aground.

When that happened, the roles were completely reversed. Jules Levoisin, with a note of panic in his transmission, had immediately withdrawn his offer to go Lloyd's Open Form. For now the 'cure' was far from certain, and the *Adventurer* might already be a total wreck, beaten to death on the rocks of Cape Alarm, in which case there would be 'no pay'.

Now Levoisin was desperately eager to strike a daily hire contract, including the run from South America and the ferrying of survivors back to civilization. He was offering his services at $10,000 a day, plus a bonus of 2½per cent of any salved value of the vessel. They were fair terms, for Jules Levoisin had given up the shining dream of millions and he had returned to reality.

However, Christy Marine, who had previously been offering a princely sum for daily hire, had just as rapidly withdrawn that offer.

'We will accept Lloyd's Open Form, including ferrying of survivors,' they declared on Channel 16.

'Conditions on site have changed,' Jules Levoisin sent back, and the Trog got another good fix on him.

'We are head-reaching on him handsomely,' he

announced with satisfaction, blinking his pink eyes rapidly while Nick marked the new relative positions on the chart.

The bridge of *Warlock* was once again crowded with every officer who had an excuse to be there. They were all in working rig, thick blue boiler suits and heavy sea boots, bulked up with jerseys and balaclava helmets, and they watched the plot with total fascination, arguing quietly among themselves.

David Allen came in carrying a bundle of clothing. 'I've got working rig for you, sir. I borrowed it from the Chief Engineer. You are about the same size.'

'Does the Chief know?' Nick asked.

'Not exactly, I just borrowed it from his cabin—'

'Well done, David,' Nick chuckled. 'Please put it in my day cabin.' He felt himself warming more and more to the younger man.

'Captain, sir,' the Trog sang out suddenly. 'I'm getting another transmission. It's only strength one, and it's on 121,5 megahertz.'

'Oh, shit!' David Allen paused in the entrance to the Captain's day cabin. 'Oh, shit!' he repeated, and his expression was stricken. 'It's that bloody missing life-raft.'

'Relative bearing!' snapped Nick angrily.

'She bears 280° relative and 045° magnetic,' the Trog answered instantly, and Nick felt his anger flare again.

The life-raft was somewhere out on their port beam, eighty degrees off their direct course to the *Golden Adventurer*.

The consternation on the bridge was carried in a babble of voices, that Nick silenced with a single black glance – and they stared at the plot in dismayed hush.

The position of each of the tugs was flagged with a coloured pin – and there was another, a red flag, for the position of the *Golden Adventurer*. It was so close ahead of them now, and their lead over *La Mouette* so slender, that one of the younger officers could not remain silent.

'If we go to the raft, we'll be handing it to the bloody frog on a plate.'

The words ended the restraint and they began to argue again, but in soft controlled tones. Nick Berg did not look up at them, but remained bowed over the chart, with his fist on the tabletop bunched so fiercely that the knuckles were ivory white.

'Christ, they have probably all had it by now. We'd be throwing it all away for a bunch of frozen stiffs.'

'There is no telling how far off course they are, those sets have a range of a hundred miles.'

'*La Mouette* will waltz away with it.'

'We could pick them up later – after we put a line on *Golden Adventurer*.'

Nick straightened slowly and took the cheroot out of his mouth. He looked across at David Allen and spoke levelly, without change of expression.

'Number One, will you please instruct your junior officers in the rule of the sea.'

David Allen was silent for a moment, then he answered softly 'The preservation of human life at sea takes precedent over all other considerations.'

'Very well, Mr Allen,' Nick nodded. 'Alter 80° to port and maintain a homing course on the emergency transmission.'

He turned away to his cabin. He could control his anger until he was alone, and then he turned and crashed his fist into the panel above his desk.

Out on the navigation bridge behind him nobody spoke nor moved for fully thirty seconds, then the Third Officer protested weakly.

'But we are so close!'

David Allen roused himself, and spoke angrily to the helmsman.

'New course 045° magnetic.'

And as *Warlock* heeled to the change, he flung the

armful of clothing bitterly on to the chart-table and went to stand beside the Trog.

'Corrections for course to intercept?' he asked.

'Bring her on to 050°,' the Trog instructed, and then cackled without mirth. 'First you call him an ice-water pisser – now you squeal like a baby because he answers a mayday.'

And David Allen was silent as the *Warlock* turned away into the fog, every revolution of her big variable-pitch propellers carrying her directly away from her prize, and *La Mouette*'s triumphant transmissions taunted them as the Frenchman raced across the last of the open water that separated her from Cape Alarm, bargaining furiously with the owners in London.

The fog seemed so thick that it could be chopped into chunks like cheese. From the bridge it was not possible to see *Warlock*'s tall bows. Nick groped his way into it like a blind man in an unfamiliar room, and all around him the ice pressed closely.

They were in the area of huge tabular icebergs again. The echoes of the great ice islands flared green and malevolently on the radar screen and the awful smell and taste of the ice was on every breath they drew.

'Radio Officer?' Nick asked tensely, without taking his eyes from the swirling fog curtains ahead.

'Still no contact,' the Trog answered, and Nick shuffled on his feet. The fog had mesmerized him, and he felt the shift of vertigo in his head. For a moment he had the illusion that his ship was listing heavily to one side, almost as though it were a space vehicle. He forcibly rejected the hallucination and stared fixedly ahead, tensing himself for the first green loom of ice through the fog.

'No contact for nearly an hour now,' David muttered beside him.

'Either the battery on the DF has run down, or they have snagged ice and sunk—' volunteered the Third Officer, raising his voice just enough for Nick to hear.

' – or else their transmitter is blanketed by an iceberg,' Nick finished for him, and there was silence on the bridge for another ten minutes, except for the quietly requested changes of course that kept *Warlock* zigzagging between the unseen but omnipresent icebergs.

'All right,' Nick made the decision at last. 'We'll have to accept that the raft has floundered and break off the search.' And there was a stir of reawakening interest and enthusiasm. 'Pilot, new course to *Golden Adventurer*, please, and we'll increase to fifty per cent power.'

'We could still beat the frog.' Again speculation and rising hope buoyed the young officers. 'She could run into ice and have to reduce—' They wished misfortune on *La Mouette* and her Captain, and even the ship beneath Nick's feet seemed to regain its lightness and vibrancy as she turned back for a last desperate run for the prize.

'All right, David,' Nick spoke quietly. 'One thing is certain now, we aren't going to reach the prize ahead of Levoisin. So we are going to play our ace now—' he was about to elaborate, when the Trog's voice squeaked with excitement.

'New contact, on 121,5,' he cried, and the dismay on the bridge was a tangible thing.

'Christ!' said the Third Officer. 'Why won't they just lie down and die!'

'The transmission was blanked by that big berg north of us,' the Trog guessed. 'They are close now. It won't take long.'

'Just long enough to make certain we miss the prize.'

The berg was so big that it formed its own weather

system about it, causing eddies and currents of both air and water, enough to stir the fog.

The fog opened like a theatre curtain, and directly ahead there was a heart-stopping vista of green and blue ice, with darker strata of glacial mud banding cliffs which disappeared into the higher layers of fog above as though reaching to the very heavens. The sea had carved majestic arches of ice and deep caverns from the foot of the cliff.

'There they are!'

Nick snatched the binoculars from the canvas bin and focused on the dark specks that stood out so clearly against the backdrop of glowing ice.

'No,' he grunted. Fifty emperor penguins formed a tight bunch on one of the flat floes, big black birds standing nearly as tall as a man's shoulder; even in the lens, they were deceptively humanoid.

*Warlock* passed them closely, and with sudden fright they dropped on to their bellies and used their stubby wings to skid themselves across the floe, and drop into the still and steaming waters below the cliff. The floe eddied and swung on the disturbance of *Warlock*'s passing.

*Warlock* nosed on through solid standing banks of fog and into abrupt holes of clear air where the mirages and optical illusions of Antarctica's flawed air maddened them with their inconsistencies, transforming flocks of penguins into herds of elephants or bands of waving men, and placing in their path phantom rocks and bergs which disappeared again swiftly as they approached.

The emergency transmissions from the raft faded and silenced, then beeped again loudly into the silence of the bridge, and seconds later were silent again.

'God damn them,' David swore quietly and bitterly, his cheeks pink with frustration. 'Where the hell are they? Why don't they put up a flare or a rocket?' And nobody answered as another white fog monster enveloped the ship, muting all sound aboard her.

'I'd like to try shaking them up with the horn, sir,' he said, as *Warlock* burst once more into sparkling and blinding sunlight. Nick grunted acquiescence without lowering his binoculars.

David reached up for the red-painted foghorn handle above his head, and the deep booming blast of sound, the characteristic voice of an ocean-going salvage tug, reverberated through the fog, seeming to make it quiver with the volume of the sound. The echoes came crashing back off the ice cliffs of the bergs like the thunder of the skies.

Samantha held the solid-fuel stove in her lap using the detachable fibreglass lid of the locker as a tray. She was heating half a pint of water in the aluminium pannikin, balancing carefully against the wallowing motion of the raft.

The blue flame of the stove lit the dim cavern of plastic and radiated a feeble glow of warmth insufficient to sustain life. They were dying already.

Gavin Stewart held his wife's head against his chest, and bowed his own silver head over it. She had been dead for nearly two hours now, and her body had already cooled, the face peaceful and waxen.

Samantha could not bear to look across at them, she crouched over the stove and dropped a cube of beef into the water, stirring it slowly and blinking against the tears of penetrating cold. She felt thin watery mucus run down her nostrils and it required an effort to lift her arm and wipe it away on her sleeve. The beef tea was only a little above blood warmth, but she could not waste time and fuel on heating it further.

The metal pannikin passed slowly from mittened hand to numbed and clumsy hand. They slurped the warm liquid and passed it on reluctantly, though there were some who had neither the strength nor the interest to take it.

'Come on, Mrs Goldberg,' Samantha whispered painfully. The cold seemed to have closed her throat, and the foul air under the canopy made her head ache with grinding, throbbing pain. 'You must drink—' Samantha touched the woman's face, and cut herself off. The flesh had a putty-like texture and was cooling swiftly. It took long lingering minutes for the shock to pass, then carefully Samantha pulled the hood of the old woman's parka down over her face. Nobody else seemed to have noticed. They were all too far sunk into lethargy.

'Here,' whispered Samantha to the man beside her – and she pressed the pannikin into his hands, folding his stiff fingers around the metal to make certain he had hold of it. 'Drink it before it cools.'

The air around her seemed to tremble suddenly with a great burst of sound, like the bellow of a dying bull, or the rumble of cannon balls across the roof of the sky. For long moments, Samantha thought her mind was playing tricks with her, and only when it came again did she raise her head.

'Oh God,' she whispered. 'They've come. It's going to be all right. They've come to save us.'

She crawled to the locker, slowly and stiffly as an old woman.

'They've come. It's all right, gang, it's going to be all right,' she mumbled, and she lit the globe on her life jacket. In its pale glow, she found the packet of phosphorus flares.

'Come on now, gang. Let's hear it for Number 16.' She tried to rouse them as she struggled with the fastenings of the canopy. 'One more cheer,' she whispered, but they were still and unresponsive, and as she fumbled her way out into the freezing fog, the tears that ran down her cheeks were not from the cold.

She looked up uncomprehendingly, it seemed that from the sky around her tumbled gigantic cascades of ice, sheer sheets of translucent menacing green ice. It took her moments to realize that the life-raft had drifted in close beneath the precipitous lee of a tabular berg. She felt tiny and inconsequential beneath that ponderous mountain of brittle glassy ice.

For what seemed an eternity, she stood, with her face lifted, staring upwards – then again the air resonated with the deep gut-shaking bellow of the siren. It filled the swirling fog-banks with solid sound that struck the cliff of ice above her and shattered into booming echoes, that bounded from wall to wall and rang through the icy caverns and crevices that split the surface of the great berg.

Samantha held aloft one of the phosphorus flares, and it required all the strength of her frozen arm to rip the igniter tab. The flare spluttered and streamed acrid white smoke, then burst into the dazzling crimson fire that denotes distress at sea. She stood like a tiny statue of liberty, holding the flare aloft in one hand and peering with streaming eyes into the sullen fog-banks.

Again the animal bellow of the siren boomed through the milky, frosted air; it was so close that it shook Samantha's body the way the wind moves the wheat on the hillside, then it went on to collide solidly with the cliff of ice that hung above her.

The working of sea and wind, and the natural erosion of changing temperatures had set tremendous forces at work within the glittering body of the berg. Those forces had found a weak point, a vertical fault line, that ran like an axe-stroke from the flattened tableland of the summit, five hundred feet down to the moulded bottom of the berg far below the surface.

The booming sound waves of *Warlock*'s horn found a sympathetic resonance with the body of the mountain that set the ice on each side of the fault vibrating in different frequencies.

Then the fault sheared, with a brittle cracking explosion of glass bursting under pressure, and the fault opened. One hundred million tons of ice began to move as it broke away from the mother berg. The block of ice that the berg calved was in itself a mountain, a slab of solid ice twice the size of Saint Paul's Cathedral – and as it swung out and twisted free, new pressures and forces came into play within it, finding smaller faults and flaws so that ice burst within ice and tore itself apart, as though dynamited with tons of high explosive.

The air itself was filled with hurtling ice, some pieces the size of a locomotive and others as small and as sharp and as deadly as steel swords; and below this plunging toppling mass, the tiny yellow plastic raft bobbed helplessly.

'There,' called Nick. 'On the starboard beam.' The phosphorus distress flare lit the fog-banks internally with a fiery cherry red and threw grotesque patterns of light against the belly of lurking cloud. David Allen blew one last triumphant blast on the siren.

'New heading 150°,' Nick told the helmsman and *Warlock* came around handily, and almost instantly burst from the enveloping bank of fog into another arena of open air.

Half a mile away, the life-raft bobbed like a fat yellow toad beneath a glassy green wall of ice. The top of the iceberg was lost in the fog high above, and the tiny human figure that stood erect on the raft and held aloft the brilliant crimson flare was an insignificant speck in this vast wilderness of fog and sea and ice.

'Prepare to pick up survivors, David,' said Nick, and the mate hurried away while Nick moved to the wing of the bridge from where he could watch the rescue.

Suddenly Nick stopped and lifted his head in bewilderment. For a moment he thought it was gunfire, then the explosive crackling of sound changed to a rending shriek as of the tearing of living fibre when a giant redwood tree is falling to the axes. The volume of sound mounted into a rumbling roar, the unmistakeable roar of a mountain in avalanche.

'Good Christ!' whispered Nick, as he saw the cliff of ice begin to change shape. Slowly sagging outwards, it seemed to fold down upon itself. Faster and still faster it fell, and the hissing splinters of bursting ice formed a dense swirling cloud, while the cliff leaned further and further beyond its point of equilibrium and at last collapsed and lifted pressure waves from the green waters that raced out one behind the other, flinging *Warlock*'s bows high as she rode them and then nosed down into the troughs between.

Since Nick's oath, nobody had spoken on the bridge. They clutched for balance at the nearest support and stared in awe at that incredible display of careless might, while the water still churned and creamed with the disturbance and pieces of broken jagged ice, some the size of a country house, bobbed to the surface and revolved slowly, finding their balance as they swirled and bumped against each other.

'Closer,' snapped Nick. 'Get as close as you can.'

Of the yellow life-raft there was no longer any sign. Jagged shards of ice had ripped open its fragile skin and the grinding, tumbling lumps had trodden it and its pitiful human cargo deep beneath the surface.

'Closer,' urged Nick. If by a miracle anybody had survived that avalanche, then they had four minutes left of life, and Nick pushed *Warlock* into the still rolling and roiling mass of broken ice – pushing it open with ice-strengthened bows.

Nick flung open the bridge doors beside him and stepped out into the freezing air of the open wing. He ignored the cold, buoyed up by new anger and frustration. He had paid the highest price to make this rescue, he had given up his chance at *Golden Adventurer* for the lives of a handful of strangers, and now, at this last moment, they had been snatched away from him. His sacrifice had been in vain, and the terrible waste of it all appalled him. Because there was no other outlet for his feelings, he let waves of anger sweep over him and he shouted at David Allen's little group on the foredeck.

'Keep your eyes open. I want those people—'

Red caught his eye, a flash of vivid red, seen through the green water, becoming brighter and more hectic as it rose to the surface.

'Both engines half astern!' he screamed. And *Warlock* stopped dead as the twin propellers changed pitch and bit into the water, pulling her up in less than her own length.

In a small open area of green water the red object broke out. Nick saw a human head in a red anorak hood, supported by the thick inflated life jacket. The head was thrown back, exposing a face as white and glistening with wetness as the deadly ice that surrounded it. The face was that of a young boy, smooth and beardless, and quite incredibly beautiful.

'Get him,' Nick yelled, and at the sound of his voice the eyes in that beautiful face opened. Nick saw they were a misty green and unnaturally large in the glistening pale oval framed by the crimson hood.

David Allen was racing back, carrying life-ring and line.

'Hurry. God damn you.' The boy was still alive, and Nick wanted him. He wanted him as fiercely as he had wanted anything in his life, he wanted at least this one young life in return for all he had sacrificed. He saw that the boy was watching him. 'Come on, David,' he shouted again.

'Here!' called David, bracing himself at the ship's rail and he threw the life-ring. He threw it with an expert round arm motion that sent it skimming forty feet to where the hooded head bobbed on the agitated water. He threw it so accurately that it hit the bobbing figure a glancing blow on the shoulder and then plopped into the water alongside, almost nudging the boy.

'Grab it,' yelled Nick. 'Grab hold!'

The face turned slowly, and the boy lifted a gloved hand clear of the surface, but the movement was blunderingly uncoordinated.

'There. It's right next to you,' David encouraged. 'Grab it, man!'

The boy had been in the water for almost two minutes already, he had lost control of his body and limbs; he made two inconclusive movements with the raised hand, one actually bumped the ring but he could not hold it and slowly the life-ring bobbed away from him.

'You bloody idiot,' stormed Nick. 'Grab it!' And those huge green eyes turned back to him, looking up at him with the total resignation of defeat, one stiff arm still raised – almost a farewell salute.

Nick did not realize what he was going to do until he had shrugged off his coat and kicked away his shoes; then he realized that if he stopped to think about it, he would not go.

He jumped feet first, throwing himself far out to miss the rail below him, and as the water closed over his head he experienced a terrified sense of disbelief at the cold.

It seized his chest in a vice that choked the air from his lungs, it drove needles of agony deep into his forehead, and blinded him with the pain as he rose to the surface again. The cold rushed through his light clothing, it crushed his testicles and his stomach was filled with nausea. The marrow in the bones of his legs and arms ached so that he found it difficult to force his limbs to respond, but he struck out for the floating figure.

It was only forty feet, but halfway there he was seized by a panic that he was not going to make it. He clenched his teeth and fought the icy water as though it was a mortal enemy, but it sapped away his strength with the heat of his body.

He struck the floating figure with one outflung arm before he realized he had reached him, and he clung desperately to him, peering up at *Warlock*'s deck.

David Allen had retrieved the ring by its line and he threw it again. The cold had slowed Nick down so that he could not avoid the ring and it struck him on the forehead, but he felt no pain, there was no feeling in his face or feet or hands.

The fleeting seconds counted out the life left to them as he struggled with the inert figure, slowly losing command of his own limbs as he tried to fit the ring over the boy's body. He did not accomplish it. He got the boy's head and one arm through, and he knew he could do no more.

'Pull,' he screamed in rising panic, and his voice was remote and echoed strangely in his own ears.

He took a twist of line around his arm, for his fingers could no longer hold, and he clung with the remains of his strength as they dragged them in.

Jagged ice brushed and snatched at them, but he held the boy with his free arm.

'Pull,' he whispered. 'Oh, for God's sake, pull!' And then they were bumping against *Warlock*'s steel side, were being lifted free of the water, the twist of line smearing the wet skin from his forearm, staining his sleeve with blood that was instantly dissolved to pink by sea water. He felt no pain.

With the other arm, he hung on to the boy, holding him from slipping out of the life-ring. He did not feel the hands that grabbed at him. There was no feeling in his legs and he collapsed face forward, but David caught him before he struck the deck and they hustled him into the steaming warmth of Angel's galley, his legs dragging behind him.

'Are you okay, Skipper?' David kept demanding, and when Nick tried to reply, his jaw was locked in a frozen rictus and great shuddering spasms shook his whole body.

'Get their clothes off,' grated Angel, and, with an easy swing of his heavily muscled shoulders, lifted the boy's body on to the galley table and laid it out face upwards. With a single sweep of a Solingen steel butcher's knife he split the crimson anorak from neck to crutch and stripped it away.

Nick found his voice, it was ragged and broken by the convulsions of frozen muscles.

'What the hell are you doing, David? Get your arse on deck and get this ship on course for *Golden Adventurer*,' he grated, and would have added something a little more forceful, but the next convulsion caught him, and anyway David Allen had already left.

'You'll be all right.' Angel did not even glance up at Nick as he worked with the knife, ripping away layer after layer of the boy's clothing. 'A tough old dog like you – but I think we've got a ripe case of hypothermia here.'

Two of the seamen were helping Nick out of his sodden clothing, the cloth crackled with the thin film of ice that had already formed. Nick winced with the pain of returning circulation to half-frozen hands and feet.

'Okay,' he said, standing naked in the middle of the galley and scrubbing at himself with a rough towel. 'I'll be all right now, return to your stations.' He crossed to the kitchen range, tottering like a drunk, and welcomed the blast of heat from it, rubbing warmth into himself, still shaking and shuddering, his body mottled puce and purple with cold and his genitals shrunken and drawn up into the dense black bush at his crotch.

'Coffee's boiling. Get yourself a hot drink, Skip,' Angel

told him, glancing up at Nick from his work. He ran a quick appreciative glance over Nick's body, taking in the wide rangy shoulders, the dark curls of damp hair that covered his chest, and the trim lines of hard muscle that moulded his belly and waist.

'Put lots of sugar in it – it will warm you the best possible way,' Angel instructed him, and returned his attention to the slim young body on the table.

Angel had put aside his camp airs, and worked with the brusque efficiency of a man who had been trained at his task.

Then suddenly he stopped and stood back for a moment. 'Would you believe! No fun gun!' Angel sighed.

Nick turned just as Angel spread a thick woollen blanket over the pale naked body on the table and began to massage it vigorously.

'You better leave us girls alone together, Skipper,' said Angel with a sweet smile and a twinkle of his diamond earrings, and Nick was left with the memory of a single fleeting glimpse of the stunningly lovely body of a young woman below the pale face and the thick sodden head of copper and gold hair.

Nick Berg was swaddled in a grey woollen blanket, over the boiler suit and bulk jerseys. His feet were in thick Norwegian trawlerman's socks and heavy rubber working boots. He held a china mug of almost boiling coffee in both hands, bending over it to savour the aroma of the steam. It was the third cup he had drunk in the last hour – and yet the shivering spasms still shook him every few minutes.

David Allen had moved his canvas chair across the bridge so he could watch the Trog and work the ship at the same time. Nick could see the loom of the black rock cliffs of Cape Alarm close on their port beam.

The Morse beam squealed suddenly, a long sequence of code to which every man on the bridge listened with complete attention, but it needed the Trog to say it for them.

'*La Mouette* has reached the prize.' He seemed to take a perverse relish in seeing their expressions. 'She's beaten us to it, lads. 12½ per cent salvage to her crew—'

'I want it word for word,' snapped Nick irritably, and the Trog grinned spitefully at him before bowing over his pad.

'*La Mouette* to Christy Marine. *Golden Adventurer* is hard aground, held by ice and receding tides. Stop. Ice damage to plating appears to be below surface. Stop. Hull is flooded and open to sea. Stop. Under no circumstances will Lloyd's Open Form be acceptable. Emphasize importance of beginning salvage work immediately. Stop. Worsening weather and sea conditions. My final hire offer of $8,000 *per diem* plus 2½ per cent of salvaged value open until 1435 GMT. Standing by.'

Nick lit one of his cheroots and irrelevantly decided he must conserve them in future. He had opened his last box that morning. He frowned through the blue smoke and pulled the blanket closer around his shoulders.

Jules Levoisin was playing it touch and hard now. He was dictating terms and setting ultimatums. Nick's own policy of silence was paying off. Probably by now, Jules felt completely safe that he was the only salvage tug within two thousand miles, and he was holding a big-calibre gun to Christy Marine's head.

Jules had seen the situation of the *Golden Adventurer*'s hull. If he had been certain of effecting salvage – no, even if there had been a fifty-fifty chance of a good salvage, Jules would have gone Open Form.

So Jules was not happy with his chances, and he had the shrewdest and most appraising eye in the salvage business. It was a tough one then. *Golden Adventurer* was probably held fast by the quicksand effect of beach and ice, and *La Mouette* could build up a mere nine thousand horsepower.

It would mean throwing out ground-tackle, putting power on *Adventurer*'s pumps – the problems and solutions passed in review through Nick's mind. It was going to be a tough one, but *Warlock* had twenty-two thousand rated horsepower and a dozen other high cards.

He glanced at his gold Rolex Oyster, and he saw that Jules had set a two-hour ultimatum.

'Radio Officer,' he said quietly, and every man on the bridge stiffened and swayed closer, so as not to miss a word.

'Open the telex line direct to Christy Marine, London, and send quote "Personal for Duncan Alexander from Nicholas Berg Master of *Warlock*. Stop. I will be alongside *Golden Adventurer* in one hour forty minutes. Stop. I make firm offer Lloyd's Open Form Contract Salvage. Stop. Offer closes 1300 GMT".'

The Trog looked up at him startled, and blinked his pink eyes swiftly.

'Read it back,' snapped Nick, and the Trog did it in a high penetrating voice and when he finished, waited quizzically, as if expecting Nick to cancel.

'Send it,' said Nick, and rose to his feet. 'Mr Allen,' he turned to David, 'I want you and the Chief Engineer in my day cabin right away.'

The buzz of excitement and speculation began before Nick had closed the door behind him.

David knocked and followed him three minutes later, and Nick looked up from the notes he was making.

'What are they saying?' Nick asked. 'That I am crazy?'

'They're just kids,' shrugged David. 'What do they know?'

'They know plenty, and they're right. I am crazy to go Open Form on a site unseen! But it's the craziness of a man with no other option. Sit down, David.

'When I made the decision to leave Cape Town on the chance of this job – that was when I did the crazy thing.' Nick could no longer keep the steely silence. He had to say it, to talk it out. 'I was throwing dice for my whole bundle. When I turned down the Esso tow, that was when I went on the line for the whole company, *Warlock* and her sister, the whole thing depended on the cash from the Esso tow—'

'I see,' muttered David, and his colour was pink and high, embarrassed by this confidence from Nick Berg.

'What I am doing now is risking nothing. If I lose now, if I fail to pull *Golden Adventurer* out of there, I have lost nothing that is not already forfeit.'

'We could have offered daily hire at a better rate than *La Mouette*,' David suggested.

'No. Duncan Alexander is my enemy. The only way I can get the contract is to make it so attractive that he has no alternative. If he refuses my offer of Open Form, I will take him up before Lloyd's Committee and his own shareholders. I will make a rope of his own guts and hoist it around his neck. He has to go with me – whereas, if I had offered daily hire at a few thousand dollars less than *La Mouette*—' Nick broke off, reached for the box of cheroots on the corner of his desk, then arrested the gesture and swivelled in his chair at the heavy knock on the cabin door.

'Come!'

Vin Baker's overalls were pristine blue, but the bandage around his head was smeared with engine grease, and he had recovered all the bounce and swagger that Nick had banged out of him against the engine-room windows.

'Jesus!' he said. 'I hear you just flipped. I hear you blew your mind and jumped overboard – and when they fished you out, you up and went Open Form on a bomber that's beating herself to death on Cape Alarm.'

'I'd explain it to you,' offered Nick solemnly, 'only I don't know enough words of one syllable.' The Chief Engineer grinned wickedly at that and Nick went on quickly, 'Just believe me when I tell you that I'm playing with someone else's chips. I'm not risking anything I haven't lost already.'

'That's good business,' the Australian agreed handsomely, and helped himself to one of Nick's precious cheroots.

'Your share of 12½ per cent of daily hire is peanuts and apple jelly,' Nick went on.

'Too right,' Vin Baker agreed, and hoisted at his waistline with his elbows.

'But if we snatch *Golden Adventurer* and if we can plug her and pump her out, and if we can keep her afloat for three thousand miles, there will be a couple of big "M's" – and that's beef and potatoes.'

'You know something,' Vin Baker grunted. 'For a Pommy, I'm beginning to like the sound of your voice.' He said it reluctantly and shook his head, as if he didn't really believe it.

'All I want from you now,' Nick told him, 'are your plans for getting power on to *Golden Adventurer*'s pumps and anchor-winch. If she's up on the beach, we will have to kedge her off and we won't have much time.'

Kedging off was the technique of using a ship's own anchor and power winch to assist the pull of the tug in dragging her off a stranding.

Vin Baker waved the cheroot airily. 'Don't worry about that, I'm here.' And at that moment the Trog put his head through the doorway again, this time without knocking.

'I have an urgent and personal for you, Skipper.' He brandished the telex flimsy like a royal flush in spades.

Nick glanced through it once, then read it aloud:

'Master of *Warlock* from Christy Marine. Your offer Lloyd's Open Form "No cure no pay" accepted. Stop. You are hereby appointed main salvage contractor for wreck of *Golden Adventurer*. ENDS.'

Nick grinned with that rare wide irresistible flash of very white teeth. 'And so, gentlemen, it looks as though we are still in business – but the devil knows for just how much longer.'

*Warlock* rounded the headland, where the three black pillars of serpentine rock stood into a lazy green sea, across which low oily swells marched in orderly ranks to push in gently against the black cliffs.

They came round to the sudden vista of the wide, ice-choked bay. The abandoned hulk of *Golden Adventurer* was so majestic, so tall and beautiful that not even the savage mountains could belittle her. She looked like an illustration from a child's book of fairy tales, a lovely ice ship, glistening and glittering in the yellow sunlight.

'She's a beauty,' whispered the Chief Engineer, and his voice captured the sorrow they all felt for a great ship in mortal distress. To every single man on the bridge of *Warlock*, a ship was a living thing for which at best they could feel love and admiration; even the dirtiest old tramp roused a grudging affection. But *Golden Adventurer* was like a lovely woman. She was something rare and special, and all of them felt it.

For Nick Berg, the bond was much more deeply felt. She was child of his inspiration, he had watched her lines take shape on the naval architect's drawingboard, he had seen her keel laid and her bare skeleton fleshed out with lovingly worked steel, and he had watched the woman who had once been his wife speak the blessing and then smash the bottle against her bows, laughing in the sunlight while the wine spurted and frothed.

She was his ship, and now, as he would never have believed possible, his destiny depended upon her.

He looked away from her at last to where *La Mouette* waited in the mouth of the bay at the edge of the ice. In contrast to the liner, she was small and squat and ugly, like a wrestler with all the weight in his shoulders. Greasy black smoke rose straight into the pale sky from her single stack, and her hull seemed to be painted the same greasy black.

Through his glasses, Nick saw the sudden bustle of activity on her bridge as *Warlock* burst into view. The headland would have blanketed *La Mouette*'s radar and, with Nick's strict radio silence, this would be the first that Jules Levoisin knew of *Warlock*'s presence. Nick could imagine the consternation on her navigation bridge, and he noted wryly that Jules Levoisin had not even gone through the motions of putting a line on to *Golden Adventurer*. He must have been completely sure of himself, of his unopposed presence. In maritime law, a line on to a prize's hull bestowed certain rights, and Jules should have made the gesture.

'Get *La Mouette* in clear,' he instructed, and picked up the hand microphone as the Trog nodded to him.

'*Salut Jules, ca va?* You pot-bellied little pirate, haven't they caught and hung you yet?' Nick asked kindly in French, and there was a long disbelieving silence on Channel 16 before the fruity Gallic tones boomed from the overhead speaker.

'Admiral James Bond, I think?' and Jules chuckled, but unconvincingly. 'Is that a battleship or a floating whore-house? You always were a fancy boy, Nicholas, but what kept you so long? I expected to get a better run for my money.'

'Three things you taught me, *mon brave:* the first was to

take nothing for granted; the second was to keep your big yap shut tight when running for a prize; and the third was to put a line on it when you got there – you've broken your own rules, Jules.'

'The line is nothing. I am arrived.'

'And I, old friend, am arrived also. But the difference is that I am Christy Marine's contractor.'

'*Tu rigoles!* You are joking!' Jules was shocked. 'I heard nothing of this!'

'I am not joking,' Nick told him. 'My James Bond equipment lets me talk in private. But go ahead, call Christy Marine and ask them – and while you are doing it, move that dirty old greaser of yours out of the way. I've got work to do.' Nick tossed the microphone back to the Trog. 'Tape everything he sends,' he instructed, and then to David Allen, 'We are going to smash up that ice before it grabs too tight a hold on *Golden Adventurer*. Put your best man on the wheel.'

Nick was a man transformed, no longer the brooding, moody recluse, agonizing over each decision, uncertain of himself and reacting to each check with frustrated and undirected anger.

'When he starts moving – he really burns it up,' thought David Allen, as he listened to Nick on the engine-room intercom.

'I want flank power on both, Chief. We are going to break ice. Then I want you in full immersion with helmet, we are going on board her to take a peek at her engine room.' He swung back to David Allen. 'Number One, you can stand by to take command.' The man of action glorying in the end to inactivity, he almost seemed to dance upon his feet, like a fighter at the first bell. 'Tell Angel I want a hot meal for us before we go into the cold, plenty of sugar in it.'

'I'll ask the steward,' said David, 'Angel is no good at

the moment. He's playing dolls with the lass you pulled out the water. God, he'll be dressing her up and wheeling her around in a pram—'

'You tell Angel, I want food – and good food,' growled Nick, and turned away to the window to study the ice that blocked the bay, 'or I'll go down personally and kick his backside.'

'He'd probably enjoy that,' muttered David, and Nick rounded on him.

'How many times have you checked out the salvage gear since we left Cape Town?'

'Four times.'

'Make it five. Do it again. I want all the diesel auxiliaries started and run up, then shut down for freezing and rigged to be swung out. I want to have power on *Adventurer* by noon tomorrow.'

'Sir.'

But before he could go, Nick asked, 'What is the barometric reading?'

'I don't know—'

'From now until the end of this salvage, you will know, at any given moment, the exact pressure and you will inform me immediately of any variation over one millibar.'

'Reading is 1018,' David checked hastily.

'It's too high,' said Nick. 'And it's too bloody calm. Watch it. We are going to have a pressure bounce. Watch it like an eagle scout.'

'Sir.'

'I thought I asked you to check the gear.'

The Trog called out, 'Christy Marine has just called *La Mouette* and confirmed that we are the main contractor – but Levoisin has accepted daily hire to pick up a full load of survivors from Shackleton Bay and ferry them to Cape Town. Now he wants to speak to you again.'

'Tell him I'm busy.' Nick did not take his attention from

the ice-packed bay, then he changed his mind. 'No, I'll talk to him.' He took the hand microphone. 'Jules?'

'You don't play fair, Nicholas. You go behind the back of an old friend, a man who loves you like a brother.'

'I'm a busy man. Did you truly call to tell me that?'

'I think you made a mistake, Nicholas. I think your'e crazy to go Lloyd's Open on this one. That ship is stuck fast – and the weather! Did you read the met from Gough Island? You got yourself a screaming bastard there, Nicholas. You listen to an old man.'

'Jules I've got twenty-two thousand horses running for me—'

'I still think you made a mistake, Nicholas. I think you're going to burn more than just your fingers.'

'*Au revoir*, Jules. Come and watch me in the awards court.'

'I still think that's a whorehouse, not a tug, you are sailing. You can send over a couple of blondes and a bottle of wine—'

'Goodbye, Jules.'

'Good luck, *mon vieux*.'

'Hey, Jules – you say "good luck" and it's the worst possible luck. You taught me that.'

'*Oui*, I know.'

'Then good luck to you also, Jules.' For a minute Nick looked after the departing tug. It waddled away over the oily swells, small and fat-bottomed and cheeky, for all the world like its Master – and yet there was something dejected and crestfallen about her going.

He felt a prick of affection for the little Frenchman, he had been a true and good friend as well as a teacher, and Nick felt his triumph softening to regret.

He crushed it down ruthlessly. It had been a straight, hard but fair run, and Jules had been careless. Long ago, Nick had taught himself that anybody in opposition was an enemy, to be hated and beaten, and when you had done so, you despised them. You did not feel compassion, it weakened your own resolve.

He could not quite bring himself to despise Jules Levoisin. The Frenchman would bounce back, probably snatching the next job out from under Nick's nose, and anyway he had the lucrative contract to ferry the survivors from Shackleton Bay. It would pay the costs of his long run southwards and leave some useful change over.

Nick's own dilemma was not as easily resolved. He put Jules Levoisin out of his mind, turning away before the French tug had rounded the headland and he studied the ice-choked bay before him with narrow eyes and a growing feeling of concern. Jules had been right – this was going to be a screaming bastard of a job.

The high seas that had thrown *Golden Adventurer* ashore had been made even higher by the equinoctial spring tides. Both had now abated and she was fast.

The liner's hull had swung also, so she was not aligned neatly at right angles to the beach. *Warlock* would not be able to throw a straight pull on to her. She would have to drag her sideways. Nick could see that now as he closed.

Still closer, he could see how the heavy steel hull, half filled with water, had burrowed itself into the yielding shingle. She would stick like toffee to a baby's blanket.

Then he looked at the ice, it was not only brash and pancake ice, but there were big chunks, bergie bits, from rotten and weathered icebergs, which the wind had driven into the bay, like a sheepdog with its flock.

The plunging temperatures had welded this mass of ice into a whole; like a monstrous octopus, it was wrapping thick glistening tentacles around *Adventurer*'s stern. The ice had not yet had sufficient time to become impenetrable, and *Warlock*'s bows were ice-strengthened for just such an emergency – yet Nick knew enough not to underestimate the hardness of ice. 'White ice is soft ice' was the old adage, and yet here there were big lumps and hummocks of green and striated glacial ice in the mass, like fat plums in a pudding, any one of which could punch a hole through *Warlock*'s hull.

Nick grimaced at the thought of having to send Jules Levoisin a mayday.

He spoke to the helmsman quietly. 'Starboard five – midships,' lining *Warlock* up for a fracture-line in the ice-pack. It was vital to come in at a right angle, to take the ice fully on the stem; a glancing blow could throw the bows off line and bring the vulnerable hull in contact with razor ice.

'Stand by, engine room,' he alerted them, and *Warlock* bore down on the ice at a full ten knots and Nick judged the moment of impact finely. Half a ship's length clear, he gave a crisp order.

'Both half back.'

*Warlock* checked, going up on to the ice as she decelerated, but still with a horrid rasping roar that echoed through the ship. Her bows rose, riding up over the ice. It gave with a rending crackle, huge slabs of ice upending and tumbling together.

'Both full back.'

The huge twin propellers changed their pitch smoothly into reverse thrust, and the wash boiled into the broken ice, sweeping it clear, as *Warlock* drew back into open water and Nick steadied her and lined her up again.

'Both ahead full.'

*Warlock* charged forward, checking at the last moment, and again thick slabs of white ice broke away, and grated along the ship's side. Nick swung her stern first starboard then port, deftly using the twin screws to wash the broken ice free, then he pulled *Warlock* out and lined up again.

Butting and smashing and pivoting, *Warlock* worked her way deeper into the bay, opening a spreading web of cracks across the white sheet of ice.

David Allen was breathless, as he burst on to the bridge.

'All gear checked and ready, sir.'

'Take her,' said Nick. 'She's broken it up now – just keep it stirred up.' He wanted to add a warning that the big variable-pitch propellers were *Warlock*'s most vulnerable parts, but he had a high enough opinion now of his Mate's ability, so he went on instead, 'I'm going down now to kit up.'

Vin Baker was in the aft salvage hold ahead of him, he had already half finished the tray of rich food and Angel hovered over him, but, as Nick came down the steel ladder, he lifted the cover off another steaming tray.

'It's good,' said Nick, although he could hardly force himself to swallow. The nerves in his stomach were bunched up too tightly. Yet food was one of the best defences against the cold.

'Samantha wants to talk to you, Skip.'

'Who the hell is Samantha?'

'The girl – she wants to thank you.'

'Use your head, Angel, can't you see I have other things on my mind?'

Nick was already pulling on the rubber immersion suit over a full-length woollen undersuit. He needed the assistance of a seaman to enter the opening in the chest of the suit.

He had already forgotten about the girl as they closed the chest opening of the suit with a double ring seal, and then over the watertight bootees and mittens went another full suit of polyurethane. Nick and Vin Baker looked like a pair of fat Michelin men, as their dressers helped them into the full helmets, with wraparound visors, built-in radio microphones and breathing valves.

'Okay, Chief?' Nick asked, and Vin Baker's voice squawked too loudly into his headphones.

'Clear to roll.'

Nick adjusted the volume, and then shrugged into the oxygen rebreathing set. They were not going deeper than thirty feet, so Nick had decided to use oxygen rather than the bulky steel compressed-air cylinders.

'Let's go,' he said, and waddled to the ladder.

The Zodiac sixteen-foot inflatable dinghy swung overboard with the four of them in it, two divers and two picked seamen to handle the boat. Vin pushed one of them aside and primed the outboard himself.

'Come on, beauty,' he told it sternly, and the big Johnson Seahorse fired at the first kick. Gingerly, they began to feel their way through an open lead in the ice, with the two seamen poling away small sharp pieces that would have ripped the fabric of the Zodiac.

In Nick's radio headset, David Allen's voice spoke suddenly.

'Captain, this is the First Officer. Barometric pressure is 1021 – it looks like it's going through the roof.'

The pressure was bouncing, as Nick had predicted. What goes up, must come down – and the higher she goes, the lower she falls.

Jules Levoisin had warned him it was going to be a screamer.

'Did you read the last met from Gough Island?'

'They have 1005 falling, and the wind at 320° and thirty-five knots.'

'Lovely,' said Nick. 'We've got a big blow coming.' And through the visor of his helmet he looked up at the pale and beautiful sun. It was not bright enough to pain the eye, and now it wore a fine golden halo like the head of a saint in a medieval painting.

'Skipper, this is as close as we can get,' Vin Baker told

him, and slipped the motor into neutral. The Zodiac coasted gently into a small open pool in the ice pack, fifty yards from *Golden Adventurer*'s stern.

A solid sheet of compacted ice separated them, and Nick studied it carefully. He had not taken the chance of working *Warlock* in closer until he could get a look at the bottom here. He wanted to know what depth of water he had to manoeuvre in, and if there were hidden snags, jagged rock to rip through the *Warlock*'s hull, or flat shingle on which he could risk a bump.

He wanted to know the slope of the bottom, and if there was good holding for his ground-tackle, but most of all, he wanted to inspect the underwater damage to *Golden Adventurer*'s hull.

'Okay, Chief?' he asked, and Vin Baker grinned at him through the visor.

'Hey, I just remembered – my mommy told me not to get my feet wet. I'm going home.'

Nick knew just how he felt. There was thick sheet ice between them and *Adventurer*, they had to go down and swim below it. God alone knew what currents were running under the ice, and what visibility was like down there. A man in trouble could not surface immediately, but must find his way back to open water. Nick felt a claustrophobic tightening of his belly muscles, and he worked swiftly, checking out his gear, cracking the valve on his oxygen tank to inflate the breathing bag, checking the compass and Rolex Oyster on his wrist and clipping his buddy line on to the Zodiac, a line to return along, like Theseus in the labyrinth of the Minotaur.

'Let's go,' he said, and flipped backwards into the water. The cold struck through the multiple layers of rubber and cloth and polyurethane almost instantly, and Nick waited only for the Chief Engineer to break through the surface beside him in a cloud of swirling silver bubbles.

'God,' Vin Baker's voice was distorted by the earphones,

'it's cold enough to crack the gooseberries off a plaster saint.'

Paying out the line behind him, Nick sank down into the hazy green depths, looking for bottom. It came up dimly, heavy shingle and pebble, and he checked his depth gauge – almost six fathoms – and he moved in towards the beach.

The light from the surface was filtered through thick ice, green and ghostly in the icy depths, and Nick felt unreasonable panic stirring deep in him. He tried to thrust it aside and concentrate on the job, but it flickered there, ready to burst into flame.

There was a current working under the ice, churning the sediment so that the visibility was further reduced, and they had to fin hard to make headway across the bottom, always with the hostile ceiling of sombre green ice above them, cutting them off from the real world.

Suddenly the *Golden Adventurer*'s hull loomed ahead of them, the twin propellers glinting like gigantic bronze wings in the gloom.

They moved in within arm's length of the steel hull and swam slowly along it. It was like flying along the outer wall of a tall apartment block, a sheer cliff of riveted steel plate – but the hull was moving.

The *Golden Adventurer* was hogging on the bottom, the stern dipping and swaying to the pulse of the sea, the heaving groundswell that came in under the ice; her stern bumped heavily on the pebbly bottom, like a great hammer beating time to the ocean.

Nick knew that she was settling herself in. Every hour now was making his task more difficult and he drove harder with his swim fins, pulling slightly ahead of Vin Baker. He knew exactly where to look for the damage. Reilly had reported it in minute detail to Christy Marine, but he came across it without warning.

It looked as though a monstrous axe had been swung

horizontally at the hull, a clean slash, the shape of an elongated teardrop. The metal around it had been depressed, and the paint smeared away so that the steel gleamed as though it had been scoured and polished.

At its widest, the lips of the fifteen-foot rent gaped open by three feet or a little more, and it breathed like a living mouth – for the force of the groundswell pushing into the gap built up pressure within the hull, then as the swell subsided the trapped water was forcibly expelled, sucking in and out with tremendous pressure.

'It's a clean hole,' Vin Baker's voice squawked harshly. 'But it's too long to pump with cement.'

He was right, of course, Nick had seen that at once. Liquid cement would not plug that wicked gash, and anyway, there wasn't time to use cement, not with weather coming. An idea began forming in his mind.

'I'm going to penetrate.' Nick made the decision aloud, and beside him the Chief was silent for long incredulous seconds, then he covered the edge of fear in his voice with,

'Listen, cobber, every time I've ever been into an orifice shaped like that, it's always meant big trouble. Reminds me of my first wife—'

'Cover for me,' Nick interrupted him. 'If I'm not out in five minutes—'

'I'm coming with you,' said the Chief. 'I've got to take a look at her engine room. This is as good a time as any.'

Nick did not argue with him.

'I'll go first,' he said and tapped the Chief's shoulder. 'Do what I do.'

Nick hung four feet from the gash, finning to hold himself there against the current.

He watched the swirl of water rushing into the opening, and then gushing out again in a rash of silver bubbles. Then, as she began to breathe again, he darted forward.

The current caught him and he was hurled at the gap,

with only time to duck his helmeted head and cover the fragile oxygen bag on his chest with both arms.

Raw steel snagged at his leg; there was no pain, but almost instantly he felt the leak of sea water into his suit. The cold stung like a razor cut, but he was through into the total darkness of the cavernous hull. He was flung into a tangle of steel piping, and he anchored himself with one arm and groped for the underwater lantern on his belt.

'You okay?' The Chief's voice boomed in his headphones.

'Fine.'

Vin Baker's lantern glowed eerily in the dark waters ahead of him.

'Work fast,' instructed Nick. 'I've got a tear in my suit.'

Each of them knew exactly what to do and where to go. Vin Baker swam first to the watertight bulkheads and checked all the seals. He was working in darkness in a totally unfamiliar engine room, but he went unerringly to the pump system, and checked the valve settings; then he rose to the surface, feeling his way up the massive blocks of the main engines.

Nick was there ahead of him. The engine room was flooded almost to the deck above and the surface was a thick stinking scum of oil and diesel, in which floated a mass of loose articles, most of them undefinable, but in the beam of his lantern Nick recognized a gumboot and a grease pot floating beside his head. The whole thick stinking soup rose and fell and agitated with the push of the current through the rent.

The lenses of their lanterns were smeared with the oily filth and threw grotesque shadows into the cavernous depths, but Nick could just make out the deck above him, and the dark opening of the vertical ventilation shaft. He wiped the filth from his visor and saw what he wanted to see and the cold was spreading up his leg. He asked brusquely, 'Okay, Chief?'

'Let's get the hell out of here.'

There were sickening moments of panic when Nick thought they had lost the line to the opening. It had sagged and wrapped around a steam pipe. Nick freed it and then sank down to the glimmer of light through the gash.

He judged his moment carefully, the return was more dangerous than the entry, for the raw bright metal had been driven in by the ice, like the petals of a sunflower – or the fangs in a shark's maw. He used the suck of water and shot through without a touch, turning and finning to wait for Vin Baker.

The Australian came through in the next rush of water, but Nick saw him flicked sideways by the current, and he struck the jagged opening a touching blow. There was instantly a roaring rush of escaping oxygen from his breathing bag, as the steel split it wide, and for a moment the Chief was obscured in the silver cloud of gas that was his life's breath.

'Oh God, I'm snagged,' he shouted, clutching helplessly at his empty bag, plummeting sharply into the green depths at the drastic change in his buoyance. The heavily leaded belt around his waist had been weighted to counter the flotation of the oxygen bag, and he went down like a gannet diving on a shoal of sardine.

Nick saw instantly what was about to happen. The current had him – it was dragging him down under the hull, sucking him under that hammering steel bottom, where he would be crushed against the stony beach by twenty-two thousand tons of pounding steel.

Nick went head down, finning desperately to catch the swirling body which tumbled like a leaf in high wind. He had a fleeting glimpse of Baker's face, contorted with terror and lack of breath, the glass visor of his helmet already swamping with icy water as the pressure spurted through the non-return valve. The Chief's headset microphone squealed once and then went dead as the water shorted it out.

'Drop your belt,' yelled Nick, but Baker did not respond; he had not heard, his headset had gone and instead he fought ineffectually in the swirling current, drawn inexorably down to brutal death.

Nick got a hand to him and threw back with all his strength on his fins to check their downward plunge, but still they went down and Nick's right hand was clumsy with cold and the double thickness of his mittens as he groped for the quick-release on the Chief's belt.

He hit the rounded bottom of the great hull with his shoulder, and felt them dragged under to where clouds of sediment blew like smoke from the working of the keel. Locked together like a couple of waltzing dancers, they swung around and he saw the keel, like the blade of a guillotine, rise up high above them. He could not reach the Chief's release toggle.

There were only microseconds in which to go for his one other chance. He hit his own release and the thick belt with thirty-five pounds of lead fell away from Nick's waist; with it went the buddy line that would guide them back to the waiting Zodiac, for it had been clipped into the back of the belt.

The abrupt loss of weight checked their downward plunge, and fighting with all the strength of his legs, Nick was just able to hold them clear of the great keel as it came swinging downwards.

Within ten feet of them, steel struck stone with a force that rang in Nick's eardrum like a bronze gong but he had an armlock on the Chief's struggling body, and now at last his right hand found the release toggle on the other man's belt.

He hit it, and another thirty-five pounds of lead dropped away. They began to rise, up along the hogging steel hull, faster and faster as the oxygen in Nick's bag expanded with the release of pressure. Now their plight was every bit as desperate, for they were racing upwards to a roof of solid ice with enough speed to break bone or crack a skull.

Nick emptied his lungs, exhaling on a single continuous breath, and at the same time opened the valve to vent his bag, blowing away the precious life-giving gas in an attempt to check their rise – yet still they went into the ice with a force that would have stunned them both, had Nick not twisted over and caught it on his shoulder and outflung arm. They were pinned there under the ice by the cork-like buoyancy of their rubber suits and the remaining gas in Nick's bag.

With mild and detached surprise Nick saw that the lower side of the ice pack was not a smooth sheet, but was worked into ridges and pinnacles, into weird flowing shapes like some abstract sculpture in pale green glass. It was only a fleeting moment that he looked at it, for beside him Baker was drowning.

His helmet was flooded with icy water and his face was empurpled and his mouth contorted into a horrible rictus; already his movements were becoming spasmodic and uncoordinated, as he struggled for breath.

Nick realized that haste would kill them both now. He had to work fast but deliberately – and he held Baker to him as he cracked the valve on his steel oxygen bottle, reinflating his chest bag.

With his right hand, he began to unscrew the breathing pipe connection into the side of Baker's helmet. It was slow, too slow. He needed touch for this delicate work.

He thought, 'This could cost me my right hand,' and he stripped off the thick mitten in a single angry gesture. Now he could feel – for the few seconds until the cold paralysed his fingers. The connection came free and while he worked, Nick was pumping his lungs like a bellows, hyper-ventilating, washing his blood with pure oxygen until he felt light-headed and dizzy.

One last sweet breath, and then he unscrewed his own hose connection; icy water flooded through the valve but he held his head at an angle to trap oxygen in the top of his helmet, keeping his nose and eyes clear, and he rescrewed his own hose into Baker's helmet with fingers that no longer had feeling.

He held the Chief's body close to his chest, embracing like lovers, and he cracked the last of the oxygen from his bottle. There was just sufficient pressure of gas left to expunge the water from Baker's helmet. It blew out with an explosive hiss through the valve, and Nick watched carefully with his face only inches from Baker's.

The Chief was choking and coughing, gulping and gasping at the rush of cold oxygen, his eyes watery and unseeing, his spectacles blown awry and the lenses obscured by sea water, but then Nick felt his chest begin to swell and subside. Baker was breathing again, 'which is more than I am doing,' Nick thought grimly – and then suddenly he realized for the first time that he had lost the guide line with his weight belt.

He did not know in which direction was the shore, nor which way to swim to reach the Zodiac. He was utterly disorientated, and desperately he peered through his half-flooded visor for sight of the *Golden Adventurer*'s hull to align himself. She was not there, gone in the misty green gloom – and he felt the first heave of his lungs as they demanded air. And as he denied his body the driving need to breathe, he felt the fear that had flickered deep within him flare up into true terror, swiftly becoming cold driving panic.

A suicidal urge to tear at the green ice roof of this watery tomb almost overwhelmed him. He wanted to try and rip his way through it with bare freezing hands to reach the precious air.

Then, just before panic completely obliterated his reason, he remembered the compass on his wrist. Even then his brain was sluggish, beginning to starve for oxygen, and it took precious seconds working out the reciprocal of his original bearing.

As he leaned forward to read the compass, more sea water spurted into his helmet, spiking needles of icy cold agony into the sinuses of his cheeks and forehead, making the teeth ache in his jaws, so he gasped involuntarily and immediately choked.

Still holding Baker to him, linked by the thick black umbilical cord of his oxygen hose, Nick began to swim out on the reciprocal compass heading. Immediately his lungs began to pump, convulsing in involuntary spasms, like those of childbirth, craving air, and he swam on.

With his head thrown back slightly he saw that the sheet of ice moved slowly above him; at times, when the current held them, it moved not at all, and it required all his self-control to keep finning doggedly, then the current relaxed its grip and they moved forward again, but achingly slowly.

He had time then to realize how exquisitely beautiful was the ice roof; translucent, wondrously carved and sculptured – and suddenly he remembered standing hand in hand with Chantelle beneath the arched roof of Chartres Cathedral, staring up in awe. The pain in his chest subsided, the need to breathe passed, but he did not recognize that as the sign of mortal danger, nor the images that formed before his eyes as the fantasy of a brain deprived of oxygen and slowly dying.

Chantelle's face was before him then, glowing hair soft and thick and glossy as a butterfly's wing, huge dark eyes and that wide mouth so full of the promise of delight and warmth and love.

'I loved you,' he thought. 'I really loved you.'

And again the image changed. He saw again the

incredible slippery explosive liquid burst with which his son was born, heard the first querulous cry as he dangled pink and wet and hairless from the rubber-gloved hand, and felt again the soul-consuming wonder and joy.

'A drowning man—' Nick recognized at last what was happening to him. He knew then he was dying, but the panic had passed, as the cold had passed also, and the terror. He swam on, dreamlike, into the green mists. Then he realized that his own legs were no longer moving; he lay relaxed not breathing, not feeling, and it was Baker's body that was thrusting and working against him.

Nick peered into the glass visor still only inches from his eyes, and he saw that Baker's face was set and determined. He was gulping the pure sweet oxygen and gaining strength with each breath, driving on strongly.

'You beauty,' whispered Nick dreamily, and felt the water shoot into his throat, but there was no pain.

Another image formed before him, an Arrowhead-class yacht with spinnaker set, running free across a bright Mediterranean sea, and his son at the tiller, the dense tumble of curls that covered his small neat head fluttering in the wind, and the same velvety dark eyes as his mother's in the suntanned oval of his face as he laughed.

'Don't let her run by the lee, Peter,' Nicholas wanted to shout to his son, but the image faded into blackness. He thought for a moment that he had passed into unconsciousness, but then he realized suddenly that it was the black rubber bottom of the Zodiac only inches from his eyes, and that the rough hands that dragged him upwards, lifting him and tearing loose the fastening of his helmet, were not part of the fantasy.

Propped against the pillowed gunwale of the Zodiac, held by the two boatmen from falling backwards, the first breaths of sub-zero air were too rich for his starved lungs, and Nick coughed and vomited weakly down the front of his suit.

Nick came out of the shower cabinet. The cabin was thick with steam, and his body glowed dull angry red from the almost boiling water. He wrapped the towel around his waist as he stepped through into his night cabin.

Baker slouched in the armchair at the foot of his bunk. He wore fresh overalls, his hair stood up in little damp spikes around the shaven spot where Angel's catgut stitches still held the scabbed wound closed. One of the side frames of his spectacles had snapped during those desperate minutes below *Golden Adventurer*'s stern, and Baker had repaired it with black insulating tape.

He held two glasses in his left hand, and a big flat brown bottle of liquor in the other. He poured two heavy slugs into the glasses as Nick paused in the bathroom door, and the sweet, rich aroma smelled like the sugar-cane fields of northern Queensland.

Baker passed a glass to Nick, and then showed him the bottle's yellow label.

'Bundaberg rum,' he announced, 'the dinky die stuff, sport.'

Nick recognized both the offer of liquor and the salutation as probably the highest accolade the Chief would ever give another human being.

Nick sniffed the dark honey-brown liquor and then took it in a single toss, swirled it once around his mouth, swallowed, shuddered like a spaniel shaking off water droplets, exhaled harshly and said: 'It's still the finest rum in the world.' Dutifully he said what was expected of him, and held out his glass.

'The Mate asked me to give you a message,' said Baker as he poured another shot for each of them. 'Glass hit 1035 and now it's diving like a dingo into its hole – back to 1020 already. It's going to blow – is it ever going to blow!'

They regarded each other over the rims of the glasses.

'We've wasted almost two hours, Beauty,' Nick told

him, and Baker blinked at the unlikely name, then grinned crookedly as he accepted it.

'How are you going to plug that hull?'

'I've got ten men at work already. We are going to fother a sail into a collision mat.'

Baker blinked again, then shook his head in disbelief. 'That's Hornblower stuff—'

'The *Witch of Endor*,' Nick agreed. 'So you can read?'

'You haven't got pressure to drive it home,' Baker objected. 'The trapped air from the engine room will blow it out.'

'I'm going to run a wire down the ventilation shaft of the engine room and out through the gash. We'll fix the collision mat outside the hull and winch it home with the wire.'

Baker stared at him for five seconds while he examined the proposition. A sail was fothered by threading the thick canvas with thousands of strands of unravelled oakum until it resembled a huge shaggy doormat. When this was placed over an aperture below a ship's waterline, the pressure of water forced it into the hole, and the water swelled the mass of fibre until it formed an almost watertight plug.

However, in *Golden Adventurer*'s case the damage was extensive and as the hull was already flooded, there was no pressure differential to drive home the plug. Nick proposed to beat that by using an internal wire to haul the plug into the gash.

'It might work.' Beauty Baker was noncommittal.

Nick took the second rum at a gulp, dropped the towel and reached for his working gear laid out on the bunk.

'Let's get power on her before the blow hits us,' he suggested mildly, and Baker lumbered to his feet and stuffed the Bundaberg bottle into his back pocket.

'Listen, sport,' he said. 'All that guff about you being a Pommy, don't take it too seriously.'

'I won't,' said Nick. 'Actually, I was born and educated

in Blighty, but my father's an American. So that makes me one also.'

'Christ.' Beauty hitched disgustedly at his waist with both elbows. 'If there's anything worse than a bloody Pom, it's a goddamned Yank.'

Now that Nick was certain that the bottom of the bay was clean and free of underwater snags, he handled *Warlock* boldly but with a delicately skilful touch which David Allen watched with awe.

Like a fighting cock, the *Warlock* attacked the thicker ice line along the shore, smashing free huge lumps and slabs, then washing them clear with the propellers, giving herself space to work about *Golden Adventurer*'s stern.

The ominous calm of both sea and air made the work easier, although the vicious little current working below *Adventurer*'s stern complicated the transfer of the big alternator.

Nick had two Yokohama fenders slung from *Warlock*'s side, and the bloated plastic balloons cushioned the contact of steel against steel as Nick laid *Warlock* alongside the stranded liner, holding her there with delicate adjustments of power and rudder and screw pitch.

Beauty Baker and his working party, swaddled in heavy Antarctic gear, were already up on the catwalk of *Warlock*'s forward gantry, seventy feet above the bridge and overlooking *Adventurer*'s sharply canted deck.

As Nick nudged *Warlock* in, they dropped the steel boarding-ladder across the gap between the two ships and Beauty led them across in single file, like a troop of monkeys across the limb of a forest tree.

'All across,' the Third Officer confirmed for Nick, and then added, 'Glass has dropped again, sir. Down to 1005.'

'Very well,' Nick drew *Warlock* gently away from the liner's stern, and held her fifty feet off. Only then did he flick his eyes up at the sky. The midnight sun had turned into a malevolent jaundiced yellow, while the sun itself was a ball of dark satanic red above the peaks of Cape Alarm, and it seemed that the snowfields and glaciers were washed with blood.

'It's beautiful.' Suddenly the girl was beside him. The top of her head was on a level with his shoulder, and in the ruddy light, her thick roped hair glowed like newly minted sovereigns in red gold. Her voice was low and a little husky with shyness, and touched a chord of response in Nick, but when she lifted her face to him he saw how young she was.

'I came to thank you,' she said softly. 'It's the first chance I've had.'

She wore baggy, borrowed men's clothing that made her look like a little girl dressing up, and her face, free of cosmetics, had that waxy plastic glow of youth, like the polished skin of a ripe apple.

Her expression was solemn and there were traces of her recent ordeal beneath her eyes and at the corners of her mouth. Nick sensed the tension and nervousness in her.

'Angel wouldn't let me come before,' she said, and suddenly she smiled. The nervousness vanished and it was the direct warm unselfconscious smile of a beautiful child that has never known rejection. Nick was shocked by the strength of his sudden physical desire for her, his body moved, clenching like a fist in his groin, and he felt his heart pound furiously in the cage of his ribs.

His shock turned to anger, for she looked but fourteen or fifteen years of age; almost she seemed as young as his own son, and he was shamed by the perversity of his attraction. Since the good bright times with Chantelle, he had not experienced such direct and instant involvement with a woman. At the thought of Chantelle, his emotions collapsed in a disordered tangle, from which only his lust and his anger emerged clearly.

He cupped the anger to him, like a match in a high wind, it gave him strength again. Strength to thrust this aside, for he knew how vulnerable he still was and how dangerous a course had opened before him, to be led by this child-woman. Suddenly he was aware that he had swayed bodily towards the girl and had been staring into her face for many long seconds, that she was meeting his gaze steadily and that something was beginning to move in her eyes like cloud shadow across the sunlit surface of a green mountain lake. Something was happening which he could not afford, could not chance – and then he realized also that the two young deck officers were watching them with undisguised curiosity, and he turned his anger on her.

'Young lady,' he said. 'You have an absolute genius for being in the wrong place at the wrong time.' And his tone was colder and more remote than even he had intended it.

Before he turned away from her, he saw the moment of her disbelief turn to chagrin, and the green eyes misted slightly. He stood stiffly staring down the foredeck where David Allen's team was opening the forward salvage hold.

Nick's anger evaporated almost at once, to be replaced by dismay. He realized clearly that he had completely alienated the girl and he wanted to turn back to her and say something gracious that might retrieve the situation, but he could think of nothing and instead lifted the hand microphone to his lips and spoke to Baker over the VHF radio.

'How's it going, Chief?'

There were ten seconds of delay, and Nick was very conscious of the girl's presence near him.

'Their emergency generator has burned out, it will need two days' work to get it running again. We'll have to take on the alternator,' Beauty told him.

'We are ready to give it to you,' Nick told him, and then called David Allen on the foredeck.

'Ready, David?'

'All set.'

Nick began edging *Warlock* back towards the liner's towering stern, and now at last he turned back to the girl. Unaccountably, he now wanted her approbation, so his smile was ready – but she had already gone, taking with her that special aura of brightness.

Nick's voice had a jagged edge to it as he told David Allen, 'Let's do this fast and right, Number One.'

*Warlock* nuzzled *Adventurer*'s stern, the big black Yokohama fenders gentling her touch, and on her foredeck the winch whined shrilly, the lines squealing in their blocks and from the open salvage hatch the four-ton alternator swung out. It was mounted on a sledge for easy handling. The diesel tanks were charged and the big motor primed and ready to start.

It rose swiftly, dangling from the tall gantry, and a dozen men synchronized their efforts, in those critical moments when it hung out over *Warlock*'s bows. A nasty freaky little swell lifted the tug and pushed her across, for the dangling burden was already putting a slight list on her, and it would have crashed into the steel side of the liner had not Nick thrown the screws into reverse thrust and given her a burst of power to hold her off.

The instant the swell subsided, he closed down and slid the pitch to fine forward, pressing the cushioned bows lightly back against *Adventurer*'s side.

'He's good!' David Allen watched Nicholas work. 'He's better than old Mac ever was.' Mackintosh, *Warlock*'s previous skipper, had been careful and experienced, but Nicholas Berg handled the ship with the flair and intuitive touch that even Mac's vast experience could never have matched.

David Allen pushed the thought aside and signalled the

winchman. The huge dangling machine dropped with the control of a roosting seagull on to the liner's deck. Baker's crew leapt on it immediately, releasing the winch cable and throwing out the tackle, to drag it away on its sledge.

*Warlock* drew off, and when Baker's crew was ready, she went in to drop another burden, this time one of the high-speed centrifugal pumps which would augment *Golden Adventurer*'s own machinery – if Baker could get that functioning. It went up out of *Warlock*'s forward hold, followed ten minutes later by its twin.

'Both pumps secured.' Baker's voice had a spark of jubilation in it, but at that moment a shadow passed over the ship, as though a vulture wheeled above on widespread pinions, and as Nick glanced up he saw the men on the foredeck lift their heads also.

It was a single cloud seeming no bigger than a man's fist, a thousand or fifteen hundred feet above them, but it had momentarily obscured the lowering sun, before scuttling on furtively down the peaks of Cape Alarm.

'There is still much to do,' Nick thought, and he opened the bridge door and stepped out on to the exposed wing. There was no movement of air, and the cold seemed less intense although a glance at the glass confirmed that there were thirty degrees still of frost. No wind here, but high up it was beginning.

'Number One,' Nick snapped into the microphone. 'What's going on down there – do you think this is your daddy's yacht?'

And David Allen's team leapt to the task of closing down the forward hatch, and then tramped back to the double salvage holds on the long stern quarter.

'I am transferring command to the stern bridge.' Nick told his deck officers and hurried back through the accommodation area to the second enclosed bridge, where every control and navigational aid was duplicated, a unique feature of salvage-tug construction where so much of the work took place on the afterdeck.

This time from the aft gantries, they lifted the loaded pallets of salvage gear on to the liner's deck, another eight tons of equipment went aboard *Golden Adventurer*. Then they pulled away and David Allen battened down again. When he came on to the bridge stamping and slapping his own shoulders, red-cheeked and gasping from the cold, Nick told him immediately.

'Take command, David, I'm going on board.' Nick could not bring himself to wait out the uncertain period while Beauty Baker put power and pumps into action.

Anything mechanical was Baker's responsibility, as seamanship was strictly Nick's, but it could take many hours yet, and Nick could not remain idle that long.

From high on the forward gantry, Nick looked out across that satiny ominous sea. It was a little after midnight now and thc sun was halfway down behind the mountains, a two-dimensional disc of metal heated to furious crimson. The sea was sombre purple and the icebergs were sparks of brighter cherry red. From this height he could see that the surface of the sea was crenellated, a small regular swell spreading across it like ripples across a pond, from some disturbance far out beyond the horizon.

Nick could feel the fresh movement of *Warlock*'s hull as she rode this swell, and suddenly a puff of wind hit Nick in the face like the flit of a bat's wing, and the metallic sheen of the sea was scoured by a cat's-paw of wind that scratched at the surface as it passed.

He pulled the drawstring of the hood of his anorak up more tightly under his chin and stepped out on to the open boarding-ladder, like a steeplejack, walking upright and balancing lightly seventy feet above *Warlock*'s slowly rolling foredeck.

He jumped down on to *Golden Adventurer*'s steeply

canted, ice-glazed deck and saluted *Warlock*'s bridge far below in a gesture of dismissal.

'I tried to warn you, dearie,' said Angel gently, as she entered the steamy galley, for with a single glance he was aware of Samantha's crestfallen air. 'He tore you up, didn't he?'

'What are you talking about?' She lifted her chin, and the smile was too bright and too quick. 'What do you want me to do?'

'You can separate that bowl of eggs,' Angel told her, and stooped again over twenty pounds of red beef, with his sleeves rolled to the elbows about his thick and hairy arms, clutching a butcher's knife in a fist like that of Rocky Marciano.

They worked in silence for five minutes, before Samantha spoke again.

'I only tried to thank him—' And again there was a grey mist in her eyes.

'He's a lower-deck pig,' Angel agreed.

'He is not,' Samantha came in hotly. 'He's not a pig.'

'Well, then, he's a selfish, heartless bastard – with jumped-up ideas.'

'How *can* you say that!' Samantha's eyes flashed now. 'He is not selfish – he went into the water to get me—'

Then she saw the smile on Angel's lips and the mocking quizzical expression in his eyes, and she stopped in confusion and concentrated on cracking the eggshells and slopping the contents into the mixing basin.

'He's old enough to be your father,' Angel needled her, and now she was really angry; a ruddy flush under the smooth gloss of her skin made the freckles shine like gold dust.

'You talk the most awful crap, Angel.'

'God, dearie, where did you learn that language?'

'Well, you're making me mad.' She broke an egg with such force that it exploded down the front of her pants. 'Oh, shit!' she said, and stared at him defiantly. Angel tossed her a dishcloth, she wiped herself violently and they went on working again.

'How old is he?' she demanded at last. 'A hundred and fifty?'

'He's thirty-eight,' Angel thought for a moment, 'or thirty-nine.'

'Well, smart arse,' she said tartly, 'the ideal age is half the man's age, plus seven.'

'You aren't twenty-six, dearie,' Angel said gently.

'I will be in two years' time,' she told him.

'You really want him badly, hey? A fever of lust and desire?'

'That's nonsense, Angel, and you know it. I just happen to owe him a rather large debt – he saved my life – but as for wanting him, ha!' She dismissed the idea with a snort of disdain and a toss of her head.

'I'm glad,' Angel nodded. 'He's not a very nice person, you can see by those ferrety eyes of his—'

'He has beautiful eyes—' she flared at him, and then stopped abruptly, saw the cunning in his grin, faltered and then collapsed weakly on the bench beside him, with a cracked egg in one hand.

'Oh, Angel, you are a horrible man and I hate you. How can you make fun of me now?'

He saw how close she was to tears, and became brisk and businesslike.

'First of all, you better know something about him—' and he began to tell her, giving her a waspish biography of Nicholas Berg, embellished by a vivid imagination and a wicked sense of humour, together with a quasi-feminine love of gossip, to which Samantha listened avidly, making an occasional exclamation of surprise.

'His wife ran away with another man, she could be out of her mind, don't you think?'

'Dearie, a change is like two weeks at the seaside.'

Or asking a question. 'He owns this ship, actually owns it? Not just Master?'

'He owns this ship, and its sister, and the company. They used to call him the Golden Prince. He's a high flyer, dearie, didn't you recognize it?'

'I didn't—'

'Of course you did. You're too much woman not to. There is no more powerful aphrodisiac than success and power, nothing like the clink of gold to get a girl's hormones revving up, is there?'

'That's unfair, Angel. I didn't know a thing about him. I didn't know he was rich and famous. I don't give a damn for money—'

'Ho! Ho!' Angel shook his curls and the diamond studs flashed in his ears. But he saw her anger flare again. 'All right, dearie, I'm teasing. But what really attracts you is his strength and air of purpose. The way other men obey, and follow and fear him. The air of command, of power and with it, success.'

'I didn't—'

'Oh, be honest with yourself, love. It was not the fact he saved your life, it wasn't his beautiful eyes nor the lump in his jeans—'

'You're crude, Angel.'

'You're bright and beautiful, and you just can't help yourself. You're like a nubile little gazelle, all skittish and ready, and you have just spotted the herd bull. You can't help yourself, dearie, you're just a woman.'

'What am I going to do, Angel?'

'We'll make a plan, love, but one thing is certain, you're not going to trail around behind him, dressed like an escapee from a junk shop, breathing adoration and hero-worship. He's doing a job. He doesn't need to trip over you every time he turns. Play hard to get.'

Samantha thought about it for a moment. 'Angel, I don't want to play it that hard that I never get around to being got – if you follow me.'

Beauty Baker had the work in hand, well organized and going ahead as fast as even Nick, in his overwhelming impatience, could expect.

The alternator had been manhandled through the double doors into the superstructure on B deck, and it had been secured against a steel bulkhead and lashed down.

'As soon as I have power, we'll drill the deck and bolt her down,' he explained to Nick.

'Have you got the lines in?'

'I'll bypass the main junction box on C deck, and I will select from the temporary box—'

'But you've identified the foredeck winch circuit, and the pumps?'

'Jesus, sport, why don't you go sail your little boat and leave me to do my work?'

On the upper deck one of Baker's gangs was already at work with the gas welding equipment. They were opening access to the ventilation shaft of the main engine room. The gas cutter hissed viciously and red sparks showered from the steel plate of the tall dummy smokestack. The stack was merely to give the *Golden Adventurer* the traditional rakish lines, and now the welder cut the last few inches of steel plating. It fell away into the deep, dark cavern, leaving a roughly square opening six feet by six feet which gave direct access into the half-flooded engine room fifty feet below.

Despite Baker's advice, Nick took command here,

directing the rigging of the winch blocks and steel wire cable that would enable a cable to be taken down into the flooded engine room and out again through that long, viciously fanged gash in the ship's side. When he looked at his Rolex Oyster again, almost an hour had passed. The sun had gone and a luminous green sky filled with the marvellous pyrotechnics of the *Aurora Australis* turned the night eerie and mysterious.

'All right, bosun, that's all we can do now. Bring your team up to the bows.'

As they hurried forward along the open foredeck, the wind caught them, a single shrieking gust that had them reeling and staggering and grabbing for support; then it was past and the wind settled down to nag and whine and pry at their clothing as Nick directed the work at the two huge anchor winches; but he heard the rising sea starting to push and stir the pack-ice, making it growl and whisper menacingly.

They catted the twin sea-anchors and with two men working over *Adventurer*'s side they secured collars of heavy chain to the crown of each anchor. *Warlock* would now be able to drag those anchors out, letting them bump along the bottom, but in the opposite direction to that in which they had been designed to drag, so that the pointed flukes would not be able to dig in and hold.

Then, when the anchors were out to the full reach of their own chains, *Warlock* would drop them, the flukes would dig in and hold. This was the ground-tackle which might resist the efforts of even a force twelve wind to throw *Golden Adventurer* further ashore.

When Baker had power on the ship, the anchor winches would be used to kedge *Golden Adventurer* off the bank. Nick placed much reliance on these enormously powerful winches to assist *Warlock*'s own engines, for even as they worked, he could feel through the soles of his feet how heavily grounded the liner was.

It was a tense and heavy labour, for they were working with enormous weights of dead-weight steel chain and shackles. The securing shackle, which held the chain collar on the anchor crown, alone weighed three hundred pounds and had to be manhandled by six men using complicated tackle.

By the time they had the work finished, the wind was rising force six, and wailing in the superstructure. The men were chilled and tired, and tempers were flashing.

Nick led them back to the shelter of the main superstructure. His boots seemed to be made of lead, and his lungs pumped for the solace of cheroot smoke, and he realized irrelevantly that he had not slept now for over fifty hours – since he had fished that disturbing little girl from the water. Quickly he pushed the thought of her aside, for it distracted him from his purpose, and, as he stepped over the door-sill into the liner's cold but wind-protected main accommodation, he reached for his cheroot-case.

Then he arrested the movement and blinked with surprise as suddenly garish light blazed throughout the shipdeck lights and internal lights, so that instantly a festival air enveloped her and from the loudspeakers on the deck above Nicholas' head wafted soft music as the broadcasting equipment switched itself in. It was the voice of Donna Summer, as limpid and ringing clear as fine-leaded crystal. The sound was utterly incongruous in this place and in these circumstances.

'Power is on!'

Nick let out a whoop and ran through to B deck. Beauty Baker was standing beside his roaring alternator and hugging himself with glee.

'Howzat, sport?' he demanded. Nick punched his shoulder.

'Right on, Beauty.' He wasted a few moments and a cheroot by placing one of the precious black tubes between Baker's lips and flashing his lighter. The two of them smoked for twenty seconds in close and companionable silence.

'Okay,' Nick ended it. 'Pumps and winches.'

'The two emergency portables are ready to start, and I'm on my way to check the ship's main pumps.'

'The only thing left is to get the collision mat into place.'

'That is your trick,' Baker told him flatly. 'You're not getting me into the water again, ever. I've even given up bathing.'

'Yeah, did you notice I'm standing upwind?' Nick told him. 'But somebody has got to go down again to pass the wire.'

'Why don't you send Angel?' Baker grinned evilly. 'Excuse me, cobber – I've got work to do.' He inspected the cheroot. 'After we've pulled this dog off the ground, I hope you will be able to afford decent gaspers.' And he was gone into the depths of the liner, leaving Nick with the one task he had been avoiding even thinking about. Somebody had to go down into that engine room. He could call for volunteers, of course, but then it was another of his own rules never to ask another man to do what you are afraid to do yourself.

'I can leave David to lay out the ground-tackle, but I can't let anybody else put the collision mat in.' He faced it now. He would have to go down again, into the cold and darkness and mortal danger of the flooded engine room.

The ground-tackle that David Allen had laid was holding *Golden Adventurer* handsomely, even in the aggravated swell which was by now pouring into the open mouth of the bay, driven on by the rising wind that was inciting it to wilder abandon.

David had justified Nick's confidence in the seamanlike

manner in which he had taken the *Golden Adventurer*'s twin anchors out and dropped them a cable's length offshore, at a finely judged angle to give the best purchase and hold.

Beauty Baker had installed and test-run the two big centrifugals and he had even resuscitated two of the liner's own forward pump assemblies which had been protected by the watertight bulkhead from the sea break-in. He was ready now to throw the switch on this considerable arsenal of pumps, and he had calculated that if Nick could close that gaping rent in the hull, he would be able to pump the liner's hull dry and clean in just under four hours.

Nick was in full immersion kit again, but this time he had opted for a single-bottle Drager diving-set; he was off oxygen sets for life, he decided wryly.

Before going down, he paused on the open deck with the diving helmet under his arm. The wind must be rising seven now, he decided, for it was kicking off the tops of the waves in bursts of spray and a low scudding sky of dirty grey cloud had blotted out the rising sun and the peaks of Cape Alarm. It was a cold dark dawn, with the promise of a wilder day to follow.

Nick took one glance across at *Warlock*. David Allen was holding her nicely in position, and his own team was ready, grouped around that ugly black, freshly burned opening in *Adventurer*'s stack. He lifted the helmet on to his head, and while his helpers closed the fastenings and screwed down the hose connections, he checked the radio.

'*Warlock*, do you read me?'

Allen's voice came back immediately, acknowledging and confirming his readiness, then he went on, 'The glass just went through the floor, Skipper, she's 996 and going down. Wind's force six rising seven and backing. It looks like we are fair in the dangerous quadrant of whatever is coming.'

'Thank you, David,' Nick replied. 'You warm my heart.'

He stepped forward, and they helped him into the canvas bosun's chair. Nick checked the tackle and rigging, that 'once-more-for-luck' check, and then he nodded.

The interior of the engine room was no longer dark, for Baker had rigged floodlights high above in the ventilation shaft, but the water was black with engine oil, and as Nick was lowered slowly down, with legs dangling from the bosun's chair, it surged furiously back and across like some panic-stricken monster trying to break out of its steel cage. That wind-driven swell was crashing into *Golden Adventurer*'s side and boiling in through the opening, setting up its own wave action, forming its own currents and eddies which broke and leaped angrily against the steel bulkheads.

'Slower,' Nick spoke into the microphone. 'Stop!'

His downward progress was halted ten feet above the starboard main engine block, but the confined surge of water broke over the engine as though it were a coral reef, covering it entirely at one instant, and then sucking back and exposing it again at the next.

The rush of water could throw a man against that machinery with force enough to break every bone in his body, and Nick hung above it and studied the purchases for his blocks.

'Send down the main block,' he ordered, and the huge steel block came down out of the shadows and dangled in the floodlights.

'Stop.' Nick began directing the block into position. 'Down two feet. Stop!'

Now waist-deep in the oily, churning water, he struggled to drive the shackle pin and secure the block to one of the main frames of the hull. Every few minutes a stronger surge would hurl the water over his head, forcing him to cling helplessly, until it relinquished its grip, and his visor cleared sufficiently to allow him to continue his task.

He had to pull out and rest after forty minutes of it. He

sat as close as he could to the heat-exchangers of the running diesel engine of the alternator, taking warmth from them and drinking Angel's strong sweet Thermos coffee. He felt like a fighter between rounds, his body aching, every muscle strained and chilled by the efforts of fighting that filthy churned emulsion of sea water and oil, his flanks and ribs bruised from harsh contact with the submerged machinery. But after twenty minutes, he stood up again.

'Let's go,' he said and resettled the helmet. The hiatus had given him a chance to replan the operation, thinking his way around the problems he had found down there; now the work seemed to fall more readily into place, though he had lost all sense of time alone in the infernal resounding cavern of steel and he was not sure of the hour, or the phase of the day, when at last he was ready to carry the messenger out through the gap.

'Send it down,' he ordered into his headset, and the reel of light line came down, swinging and circling under the glaring floodlights to the ship's motion and throwing grotesque shadows into the far corners of the engine room.

The line was of finely plaited Dacron, with enormous strength and elasticity in relation to its thinness and lightness. One end was secured on the deck high above, and Nick threaded it into the sheave blocks carefully, so that it was free to run.

Then he clamped the reel of line on to his belt, riding it on his hip where it could be protected from snagging when he made the passage of the gap.

He realized then how close to final exhaustion he was, and he considered breaking off the work to rest again, but the heightened action of the sea into the hull warned him against further delay. An hour from now the task might be impossible, he had to go, and he reached for the reserve of strength and purpose deep inside himself, surprised to find that it was still there – for the icy chill of the water seemed to have penetrated his suit and entered his soul, dulling every sense and turning his very bones brittle and heavy.

It must be day outside, he realized, for light came through the gash of steel, pale light further obscured by the filthy muck of mixed oil and water contained in the hull.

He clung to one of the engine-room stringers, his head seven feet from the opening, breathing in the slow, even rhythm of the experienced scuba diver, feeling the ebb and flow through the hull, and trying to find some pattern in the action of the water. But it seemed entirely random, a hissing, bubbling ingestion followed by three or four irregular and weak inflows, then three vicious exhalations of such power that they would have windmilled a swimming man end over into those daggers of splayed steel. He had to choose and ride a middling-sized swell, strong enough to take him through smoothly, without the dangerous power and turbulence of those viciously large swells.

'I'm ready to go now, David,' he said into his helmet. 'Confirm that the work boat is standing by for the pick-up outside the hull.'

'We are all ready.' David Allen's voice was tense and sharp.

'Here we go,' said Nick, this was his wave now. There was no point in waiting longer.

He checked the reel on his belt, ensuring that the line was free to run, and watched the gash suck in clean green water, filled with tiny bright bubbles, little diamond chips that flew past his head to warn him of the lethal speed and power of that flood.

The inflow slowed and stopped as the hull filled to capacity, building up great pressures of air and water, and then the flow reversed abruptly as the swell on the far side subsided, and trapped water began to rush out again.

Nick released his grip on the stringer and instantly the water caught him. There was no question of being able to swim in that mill-race, all he could hope for was to keep his arms at his sides and his legs straight together to give himself a smoother profile, and to steer with his fins.

The accelerating speed appalled him as he was flung head first at that murderous steel mouth, he could feel the nylon line streaming out against his leg, the reel on his belt racing as though a giant marlin had struck and hooked upon the other end.

The rush of his progress seemed to leave his guts behind him as though he rode a fairground rollercoaster, and then a flick of the current turned him, he felt himself beginning to roll – and he fought wildly for control just as he hit.

He hit with a numbing shock, so his vision starred in flashing colour and light. The shock was in his shoulders and left arm, and he thought it might have been severed by that razor steel.

Then he was swirling, end over end, completely disorientated so he did not know which direction was up. He did not know if he was still inside *Golden Adventurer*'s hull, and the nylon line was wrapping itself around his throat and chest, around the precious air tubes and cutting off his air supply like a stillborn infant strangled by its own umbilical cord.

Again he hit something, this time with the back of his head, and only the cushioning of his helmet saved his skull from cracking. He flung out his arms and found the rough irregular shape of ice above him.

Terror wrapped him again, and he screamed soundlessly into his mask, but suddenly he broke out into light and air, into the loose scum of slush and rotten ice mixed with bigger, harder chunks, one of which had hit him.

Above him towered the endless steel cliff of the liner's side and beyond that, the low bruised wind-sky, and as he struggled to disentangle himself from the coils of nylon, he realized two things. The first was that both his arms were still attached to his body, and still functioning, and the second was that *Warlock*'s work boat was only twenty feet away and butting itself busily through the brash of rotten broken ice towards him.

The collision mat looked like a five-ton Airedale terrier curled up to sleep in the bows of the work boat, just as shaggy and shapeless, and of the same wiry, furry brown colour.

Nick had shed his helmet and pulled an Arctic cloak and hood over his bare head and suited torso. He was balanced in the stern of the work boat as she plunged and rolled and porpoised in the big swells; chunks of ice crashed against her hull, knocking loose chips off her paintwork, but she was steel-hulled, wide and sea-kindly. The helmsman knew his job, working her with calm efficiency to Nick's handsignals, bringing her in close through the brash ice, under the tall sheer of *Golden Adventurer*'s stern.

The thin white nylon line was the only physical contact with the men on the liner's towering stack of decks, the messenger which would carry heavier tackle. However it was vulnerable to any jagged piece of pancake ice, or the fangs of that voracious underwater steel jaw.

Nick paid out the line through his own numbed hands, feeling for the slightest check or jerk which could mean a snag and a break-off.

With handsignals, he kept the work boat positioned so that the line ran cleanly into the pierced hull, around the sheave blocks he had placed with such heart-breaking labour in the engine room, from there up the tall ventilation shaft, out of the burned square opening in the stack and around the winch, beside which Beauty Baker was supervising the recovery of the messenger.

The gusts tore at Nick's head so that he had to crouch

to shield the small two-way radio on his chest, and Baker's voice was tinny and thin in the buffeting boom of wind.

'Line running free.'

'Right, we are running the wire now,' Nick told him. The second line was as thick as a man's index finger, and it was of the finest Scandinavian steel cable. Nick checked the connection between nylon and steel cable himself, the nylon messenger was strong enough to carry the weight of steel, but the connection was the weakest point.

He nodded to the crew, and they let it go over the side; the white nylon disappeared into the cold green water and now the black steel cable ran out slowly from the revolving drum.

Nick felt the check as the connection hit the sheave block in the engine room. He felt his heart jump. If it caught now, they would lose it all; no man could penetrate that hull again, the sea was now too vicious. They would lose the tackle, and they would lose *Golden Adventurer*; she would break up in the seas that were coming.

'Please God, let it run,' Nick whispered in the boom and burst of sea wind. The drum halted, made a half turn and jammed. Somewhere down there, the cable had snagged and Nick signalled to the helmsman to take the work boat in closer, to change the angle of the line into the hull.

He could almost feel the strain along his nerves as the winch took up the pull, and he could imagine the fibres of the nylon messenger stretching and creaking.

'Let it run! Let it run!' prayed Nick, and then suddenly he saw the drum begin to revolve again, the cable feeding out smoothly, and streaming down into the sea.

Nick felt light-headed, almost dizzy with relief, as he heard Baker's voice over the VHF, strident with triumph.

'Wire secured.'

'Stand by,' Nick told him. 'We are connecting the two-inch wire now.'

Again, the whole laborious, touchy, nerve-scouring process as the massive two-inch steel cable was drawn out by its thinner, weaker forerunner – and it was a further forty vital minutes, with the wind and sea rising every moment, before Baker shouted, 'Main cable secured, we are ready to haul!'

'Negative,' Nick told him urgently. 'Take the strain and hold.' If the collision mat in the bows hooked and held on the work boat's gunwale, Baker would pull the bows under and swamp her.

Nick signalled to his crew and the five of them shambled up into the bows, bulky and clumsy in their electric-yellow oilskins and work boots. With handsignals, Nick positioned them around the shaggy head-high pile of the collision mat before he signalled to the helmsman to throw the gear in reverse and pull back from *Golden Adventurer*'s side.

The mass of unravelled oakum quivered and shook as the two-inch cable came up taut and they struggled to heave the whole untidy mass overboard.

There was nearly five tons of it and the weight would have been impossible to handle were it not for the reverse pull of the work boat against the cable. Slowly, they heaved the mat forward and outward, and the work boat took on a dangerous list under the transfer of weight. She was down at the bows and canting at an angle of twenty degrees, the diesel motor screaming angrily and her single propeller threshing frantically, trying to pull her out from under her cumbersome burden.

The mat slid forward another foot, and snagged on the gunwale, sea water slopped inboard, ankle-deep around their rubber boots as they strained and heaved at the reluctant mass of coarse fibre.

Some instinct of danger made Nick look up and out to sea. *Warlock* was lying a quarter of a mile farther out in the bay, at the edge of the ice, and beyond her, Nick saw the rearing shape of a big wave alter the line of the horizon. It was merely a forerunner of the truly big waves that the storm was running before her, like hounds before the hunter, but it was big enough to make *Warlock* throw up her stern sharply, and even then the sea creamed over the tug's bows and streamed from her scuppers.

It would hit the exposed and hampered work boat in twenty-five seconds, it would hit her broadside while her bows were held down and anchored by mat and cable. When she swamped, the five men who made up her crew would die within minutes, pulled down by their bulky clothing, frozen by the icy green water.

'Beauty,' Nick's voice was a scream in the microphone, 'heave all – pull, damn you, pull.'

Almost instantly the cable began to run, drawn in by the powerful winch on *Golden Adventurer*'s deck; the strain pulled the work boat down sharply and water cascaded over her gunwale.

Nick seized one of the oaken oars and thrust it under the mat at the point where it was snagged, and using it as a lever he threw all his weight upon it.

'Lend a hand,' he yelled at the man beside him, and he strained until he felt his vision darkening and the fibres of his back muscles creaking and popping.

The work boat was swamping, they were almost knee-deep now and the wave raced down on them. It came with a great silent rush of irresistible power, lifting the mass of broken ice and tossing it carelessly aside without a check.

Suddenly, the snag cleared and the whole lumpy massive weight of oakum slid overboard. The work boat bounded away, relieved of her intolerable burden, and Nick windmilled frantically with both arms to get the helmsman to bring her bows round to the wave.

They went up the wave with a gut-swooping rush that threw them down on to the floorboards of the half-flooded work boat, and then crashed over the crest.

Behind them the wave slogged into *Golden Adventurer*'s stern, and shot up it with an explosion of white and furious water that turned to white driven spray in the wind.

The helmsman already had the work boat pushing heavily through the pack-ice, back towards the waiting *Warlock*.

'Stop,' Nick signalled him. 'Back up.'

Already he was struggling out of his hood and oilskins, as he staggered back to the stern.

He shouted in the helmsman's face, 'I'm going down to check,' and he saw the disbelieving, almost pleading, expression on the man's face. He wanted to get out of there now, back to the safety of *Warlock*, but relentlessly Nick resettled the diving helmet and connected his air hose.

The collision mat was floating hard against *Golden Adventurer*'s side, buoyant with trapped air among the mass of wiry fibre.

Nick positioned himself beneath it, twenty feet from the maelstrom created by the gashed steel.

It took him only a few seconds to ensure that the cable was free, and he blessed Beauty Baker silently for stopping the winch immediately it had pulled the mat free of the work boat. Now he could direct the final task.

'She's looking good,' he told Baker. 'But take her up slowly, fifty feet a minute on the winch.'

'Fifty feet, it is,' Baker confirmed.

And slowly the bobbing mat was drawn down below the surface.

'Good, keep it at that.'

It was like pressing a field-dressing into an open bleeding wound. The outside pressure of water drove it deep into the gash, while from the inside the two-inch cable plugged it deeper into place. The wound was staunched almost instantly and Nick finned down, and swam carefully over it.

The deadly suck and blow of high pressure through the gap was killed now, and he detected only the lightest movement of water around the edges of the mat; but the oakum fibres would swell now they were submerged and, within hours, the plug would be watertight.

'It's done,' said Nick into his microphone. 'Hold a twenty-ton pull on the cable – and you can start your pumps and suck the bitch clean.'

It was a measure of his stress and relief and fatigue that Nick called that beautiful ship a bitch, and he regretted the word as soon as it was spoken.

Nick craved sleep, every nerve, every muscle shrieked for surcease, and in his bathroom mirror his eyes were inflamed, angry with salt and wind and cold; the smears of exhaustion that underlined them were as lurid as the fresh bruises and abrasions that covered his shoulders and thighs and ribs.

His hands shook in a mild palsy with the need for rest and his legs could hardly carry him as he forced himself back to *Warlock*'s navigation bridge.

'Congratulations, sir,' said David Allen, and his admiration was transparent.

'How's the glass, David?' Nick asked, trying to keep the weariness from showing.

'994 and dropping, sir.'

Nick looked across at *Golden Adventurer*. Below that dingy low sky, she stood like a pier, unmoved by the big swells that marched on her in endless ranks, and she shrugged aside each burst of spray, hard aground and heavy with the water in her womb. However, that water was being flung from her, in solid white sheets.

Baker's big centrifugals were running at full power, and from both her port and starboard quarters the water poured. It looked as though the floodgates had been opened on a concrete dam, so powerful was the rush of expelled water.

The oil and diesel mixed with that discharge formed a sullen, iridescent slick around her, sullying the ice and the pebble beach on which she lay. The wind caught the jets from the pump outlets and tore them away in glistening plumes, like great ostrich feathers of spray.

'Chief,' Nick called the ship. 'What's your discharge rate?'

'We are moving nigh on five hundred thousand gallons an hour.'

'Call me as soon as she alters her trim,' he said, and then glanced up at the pointer of the anemometer above the control panel. The wind force was riding eight now, but he had to blink his stinging swollen eyes to read the scale.

'David,' he said, and he could hear the hoarseness in his voice, the flat dead tone. 'It will be four hours before she will be light enough to make an attempt to haul her off, but I want you to put the main towing cable on board her and make fast, so we will be ready when she is.'

'Sir.'

'Use a rocket-line,' said Nick, and then stood dumbly, trying to think of the other orders he must give, but his brain was blank.

'Are you all right, sir?' David asked with quick concern, and immediately Nick felt the prick of annoyance. He had never wanted sympathy in his life, and he found his voice again. But he stopped the sharp words that came so quickly to his lips.

'You know what to do, David. I won't give you any other advice.' He turned like a drunkard towards his quarters. 'Call me when you've done it, or if Baker reports alteration of trim – or if anything else changes, anything, anything at all, you understand.'

He made it to the cabin before his knees buckled and he dropped his terry robe as he toppled backwards on to his bunk.

At 60° south latitude, there runs the only sea lane that circumnavigates the entire globe, unbroken by any land mass. This wide girdle of open water runs south of Cape Horn and Australasia and the Cape of Good Hope, and it has the fearsome reputation of breeding the wildest weather on earth. It is the meeting-ground of two vast air masses, the cold slumping Antarctic air, and the warmer, more buoyant airs of the subtropics. These are flung together by the centrifugal forces generated by the earth as it revolves on its own axis, and their movement is further complicated by the enormous torque of the Coriolis force. As they strike each other, the opposing air masses split into smaller fragments that retain their individual characteristics. They begin to revolve upon themselves, gigantic whirlpools of tortured air, and as they advance, so they gain in strength and power and velocity.

The high-pressure system which had brought that ominously calm and silken weather to Cape Alarm, had bounced the pressure right up to 1035 millibars, while the great depression which pursued it so closely and swiftly had a centre pressure as low as 985 millibars. Such a sharp contrast meant that the winds along the pressure gradient were ferocious.

The depression itself was almost fifteen hundred miles across its circumference, and it reached up to the high troposphere, thirty thousand feet above the level of the sea. The mighty winds it contained reached right off the maximum of the Beaufort scale of force twelve, gusting 120 miles an hour and more. They roared unfettered upon a terrible sea, unchecked by the bulwark of any land mass, nothing in their path, but the sudden jagged barrier of Cape Alarm.

While Nicholas Berg slept the deathlike sleep of utter exhaustion, and Beauty Baker tended his machines, driving them to their limits in an effort to pump *Golden Adventurer* free of her burden of salt water, the storm rushed down upon them.

When her knock was unanswered, Samantha stood uncertainly, balancing the heavy tray against the *Warlock*'s extravagant action as she rode the rising swells at the entrance to the bay.

Her uncertainty lasted not more than three seconds, for she was a lady given to swift decisions. She tried the door-latch and when it turned, she pushed it open slowly enough to warn anybody on the far side, and stepped into the Captain's day cabin.

'He ordered food,' she justified her intrusion, and closed the door behind her, glancing swiftly around the empty cabin. It had been furnished in the high style of the old White Star liners. Real rosewood panelling and the couch and chairs were in rich brown calf hide, polished and buttoned, while the deck was carpeted in thick shaggy wool, the colour of tropical forest leaves.

Samantha placed the tray on the table that ran below the starboard portholes, and she called softly. There was no reply, and she stepped to the open doorway into the night cabin.

A white terry robe lay in a heap in the centre of the deck, and she thought for one disturbing moment that the body on the bed was naked, but then she saw he wore a thin pair of white silk boxer shorts.

'Captain Berg,' she called again, but softly enough not to disturb him, and with a completely feminine gesture picked up the robe from the floor, folded it and dropped it over a chair, moving forward at the same time until she stood beside his bunk.

She felt a quick flare of concern when she saw the bruises which stood out so vividly on the smooth pale skin, and concern turned to dismay when she realized how he lay like a dead man, his legs trailing over the edge of the bunk and his body twisted awkwardly, one arm thrown back over his shoulder and his head lolling from side to side as *Warlock* rolled.

She reached out quickly and touched his cheek, experiencing a lift of real relief as she felt the warmth of his flesh and saw his eyelids quiver at her touch.

Gently she lifted his legs and he rolled easily on to his side, exposing the sickening abrasion that wrapped itself angrily across back and shoulder. She touched it with a light exploring fingertip and knew that it needed attention, but she sensed that rest was what he needed more.

She stood back and for long seconds gave herself over to the pleasure of looking at him. His body was fined down, he carried no fat on his belly or flanks; clearly she could see the rack of his ribs below the skin, and the muscles of his arms and legs were smooth but well defined, a body that had been cared for and honed by hard exercise. Yet there was a certain denseness to it, that thickening of shoulder and neck, and the distinctive hair patterns of the mature man.

It might not have the grace and delicacy of the boys she had known, yet it was more powerful than that of even the strongest of the young men who had until then filled her world. She thought of one of them whom she had believed she loved. They had spent two months in Tahiti together on the same field expedition. She had surfed with him, danced and drunk wine, worked and slept sixty consecutive days and nights with him; in the same period they had become engaged to marry, and had argued, and parted, with surprisingly little regret on her part – but he had had the most beautifully tanned and sculptured body she had ever known. Now, looking at the sleeping figure on the bunk, she knew that even he would not have been able to match this man in physical determination and strength.

Angel had been right. It was the power that attracted her so strongly. The powerful, rangy body with the dark coarse hair covering his chest and exploding in flak bursts in his armpits – this, together with the power of his presence.

She had never known a man like this, he filled her with a sense of awe. It was not only the legend that surrounded him, nor the formidable list of his accomplishments that Angel had recounted for her, nor yet was it only the physical strength which he had just demonstrated while the entire crew of *Warlock*, she among them, had watched and listened avidly over the VHF relay. She leaned over him again, and she saw that even in repose, his jawline was hard and uncompromising, and the little creases and lines and marks that life had chiselled into his face, around the eyes at the corners of the mouth, heightened the effect of power and determination, the face of a man who dictated his own terms to life.

She wanted him. Angel was right, oh God, how she wanted him! They said there was no love at first sight – they had to be mad.

She turned away and unfolded the eiderdown from the foot of the bunk, spreading it over him, and then once again she stooped and gently lifted the fall of thick dark hair from his forehead, smoothing it back with a maternally protective gesture.

Although he had slept on while she lifted and covered him, strangely this lightest of touches brought him to the edge of consciousness and he sighed and twisted, then whispered hoarsely, 'Chantelle, is that you?'

Samantha recoiled at the bitter sharp pang of jealousy with which another woman's name stabbed her. She turned away and left him, but in the day cabin she paused again beside his desk.

There were a few small personal items thrown carelessly on the leather-bound blotter – a gold money clip holding a mixed sheath of currency notes, five pounds sterling, fifty US dollars, Deutschmarks and francs, a gold Rolex Oyster perpetual watch, a gold Dunhill lighter with a single white diamond set in it, and a billfold of the smoothest finest calf leather. They described clearly the man who owned them and, feeling like a thief, she picked up the billfold and opened it.

There were a dozen cards in their little plastic envelopes, American Express, Diners, Bank American, Carte Blanche, Hertz No. 1, Pan Am VIP and the rest. But opposite them was a colour photograph. Three people: a man, Nicholas in a cable-stitch jersey, his face bronzed, his hair windruffled; a small boy in a yachting jacket with a mop of curly hair and solemn eyes above a smiling mouth – and a woman. She was probably one of the most beautiful women Samantha had ever seen, and she closed the billfold, replaced it carefully, and quietly left the cabin.

David Allen called the Captain's suite for three minutes without an answer, slapping his open palm on the mahogany chart table with impatience and staring through the navigation windows at the spectacle of a world gone mad.

For almost two hours, the wind had blown steadily from

the north-west at a little over thirty knots, and although the big lumpy seas still tumbled into the mouth of the bay, *Warlock* had ridden them easily, even connected, as she was, to *Golden Adventurer* by the main tow-cable.

David had put a messenger over the liner's stern, firing the nylon line from a rocket gun, and Baker's men had retrieved the line and winched across first the carrier wire and then the main cable itself.

*Warlock* had let the main cable be drawn out of her by *Adventurer*'s winches, slowly revolving off the great winch drums in the compartment under the tug's stern deck, out through the cable ports below the after navigation bridge where David stood controlling each inch of run and play with light touches on the controls.

A good man could work that massive cable like a fly-fisherman playing a big salmon in the turbulent water of a mountain torrent, letting it slip against the clutchplates, or run free, or recover slack, bringing it up hard and fast under a pull of five hundred tons – or, in dire emergency, he could hit the shear button, and snip through the flexible steel fibre, instantaneously relinquishing the tow, possibly saving the tug itself from being pulled under or being rushed by the vessel it was towing.

It had taken an hour of delicate work, but now the tow was in place, a double yoke made fast to *Golden Adventurer*'s main deck bollards, one on her starboard and one on her port stern quarters.

The yoke was Y-shaped, drooping over the high stern to join at the white nylon spring, three times the thickness of a man's thigh and with the elasticity to absorb sudden shock which might have snapped rigid steel cable. From the yoke connection, the single main cable looped back to the tug.

David Allen was lying back a thousand yards from the shore, holding enough strain on the tow-cable to prevent it from sagging to touch and possibly snag on the unknown bottom. He was holding his station with gentle play on the pitch and power of the twin screws, and checking his exact position against the electronic dials which gave him his speed across the ground in both directions, accurate to within a foot a minute.

It was all nicely under control, and every time he glanced up at the liner, the discharge of water still boiled from her pump outlets.

Half an hour previously, he had been unable to contain his impatience, for he knew with a seaman's deep instinct what was coming down upon them out of the dangerous quadrant of the wind. He had called Baker to ask how the work on the liner was progressing. It had been a mistake.

'You've got nothing better to do than call me out of the engine room to ask about my piles, and the FA Cup final? I'll tell you when I'm ready, believe me, sonny, I'll call you. If you are bored, go down and give Angel a kiss, but for God's sake, leave me alone.'

Beauty Baker was working with two of his men in that filthy, freezing steel box deep down in the liner's stern that housed the emergency steering-gear. The rudder was right across at full port lock. Unless he could get power on the steering machinery, she would be almost unmanageable, once she was under tow, especially if she was pulled off stern first. It was vital that the big ship was responding to her helm when *Warlock* tried to haul her off.

Baker cursed and cajoled the greasy machinery, knocking loose a flap of thick white skin from his knuckles when a spanner slipped, but working on grimly without even bothering to lift the injury to his mouth to suck away the welling blood. He let it drop on to the spanner and thicken into a sticky jelly, swearing softly but viciously as he concentrated all his skills on the obdurate steel mass of the steering gear. He knew every bit as well as the First Officer what was coming down upon them.

The wind had dropped to a gentle force four, a moderate

steady breeze that blew for twenty minutes, just long enough for the crests of the waves to stop breaking over on themselves. Then slowly, it veered north – and without any further warning, it was upon them.

It came roaring like a ravening beast, lifting the surface of the sea away in white sheets of spray that looked as though red-hot steel had been quenched in it. It laid *Warlock* right over, so that her port rail went under and she was flung up so harshly on her main cable that her stern was pulled down sharply, water pouring in through her stern scuppers.

It took David by surprise, so that she paid off dangerously before he could slam open the port throttle and throw the starboard screw into full reverse thrust. As she came up, he hit the call to the Captain's suite, watching with rising disbelief as the mad world dissolved around him.

Nick heard the call from far away, it only just penetrated to his fatigue-drugged brain, and he tried to respond, but it felt as though his body was crushed under an enormous weight and that his brain was slow and sluggish as a hibernating reptile.

The buzzer insisted, a tinny, nagging whine and he tried to force his eyes open, but they would not respond. Then dimly, but deeply, he felt the wild anguished action of his ship and the tumult that he believed at first was in his own ears, but was the violent uproar of the storm about the tug's superstructure.

He forced himself up on one elbow, and his body ached in every joint. He still could not open his eyes but he groped for the handset.

'Captain to the after bridge!' He could hear something in David Allen's voice that forced him to his feet.

When Nick staggered on to the after navigation bridge, the First Officer turned gratefully to him.

'Thank God you've come, sir.'

The wind had taken the surface off the sea, had stripped it away, tearing each wave to a shrieking fog of white spray and mingling it with the sleet and snow that drove horizontally across the bay.

Nick glanced once at the dial of the wind anemometer, and then discounted the reading. The needle was stuck at the top of the scale. It made no sense, a wind speed of 120 miles an hour was too much to accept, the instrument had been damaged by the initial gusts of this wind, and he refused to believe it; to do so now would be to admit disaster, for nobody could salvage an ocean-going liner in wind velocities right off the Beaufort scale.

*Warlock* stood on her tail, like a performing dolphin begging for a meal, as the cable brought her up short and the bridge deck became a vertical cliff down which Nick was hurled. He crashed into the control panel and clung for purchase to the foul-weather rail.

'We'll have to shear the cable and stand out to sea.' David Allen's voice was pitched too high and too loud, even for the tumult of the wind and the storm.

There were men on board *Golden Adventurer*; Baker and sixteen others, Nick thought swiftly, and even her twin anchors could not be trusted to hold in this.

Nick clung to the rail and peered out into the storm. Frozen spray and sleet and impacted snow drove on the wind, coming in with the force of buckshot fired at point-blank range, cracking into the armoured glass of the bridge and building up in thick clots and lumps that defeated the efforts of the spinning 'clear vision' panels.

He looked across a thousand yards and the hull of the liner was just visible, a denser area in the howling, swirling, white wilderness.

'Baker?' he asked into the hand microphone. 'What is your position?'

'The wind's got her, she's slewing. The starboard anchor is dragging.' And then, while Nick thought swiftly, 'You'll not be able to take us off in this.' It was a flat statement, an acceptance of the fact that the destinies of Baker and his sixteen men were inexorably linked to that of the doomed ship.

'No,' Nick agreed. 'We won't be able to get you off.' To approach the stricken ship was certain disaster for all of them.

'Shear the cable and stand off,' Baker advised. 'We'll try to get ashore as she breaks up.' Then, with a hangman's chuckle, he went on, 'Just don't forget to come and fetch us when the weather moderates – that is if there is anybody to fetch.'

Abruptly Nick's anger came to the surface through the layers of fatigue, anger at the knowledge that all he had risked and suffered was now to be in vain, that he was to lose *Golden Adventurer*, and probably with her sixteen men, one of whom had become a friend.

'Are you ready to heave on the anchor winches?' he asked. 'We are going to pull the bitch off.'

'Jesus!' said Baker. 'She's still half flooded—'

'We will have a lash at it, cobber,' said Nick quietly.

'The steering-gear is locked, you won't be able to control her. You'll lose *Warlock* as well as—' but Nicholas cut Baker short.

'Listen, you stupid Queensland sheep-shagger, get on to those winches.' As he said it, *Golden Adventurer* disappeared, her bulk blotted out completely by the solid, white curtains of the blizzard.

'Engine room,' Nick spoke crisply to the Second Engineer. 'Disengage the override, and give me direct control of both power and pitch.'

'Control transferred to bridge, sir,' the Engineer confirmed, and Nick touched the shining stainless-steel levers with fingers as sensitive as those of a concert pianist. *Warlock*'s response was instantaneous. She pivoted, shrugging aside a green slithering burst of water which came in over her shoulder and thundered down the side of her superstructure.

'Anchor winches manned.' Beauty Baker's tone was almost casual.

'Stand by,' said Nick, and felt his way through that white inferno. It was impossible to maintain visual reference, the entire world was white and swirling, even the surface of the sea was gone in torn streamers of white; the very pull of gravity, that should have defined even a simple up or down, was confused by the violent pitch and roll of the deck.

Nick felt his exhausted brain begin to lurch dizzily in the first attacks of vertigo. Swiftly he switched his attention to the big compass and the heading indicator.

'David,' he said, 'take the wheel.' He wanted somebody swift and bright at the helm now.

*Warlock* plunged suddenly, so viciously that Nick's bruised ribs were brought in brutal contact with the edge of the control console. He grunted involuntarily with the pain. *Warlock* was feeling her cable, she had come up hard.

'Starboard ten,' said Nick to David, bringing her bows up into that hideous wind.

'Chief,' he spoke into the microphone, his voice still ragged with the pain in his chest. 'Haul starboard winch, full power.'

'Full power starboard.'

Nick slid pitch control to fully fine, and then slowly nudged open the throttles, bringing in twenty-two thousand horse-power.

Held by her tail, driven by the great wind, and tortured by the sea, lashed by her own enormous propellers, *Warlock* went berserk. She corkscrewed and porpoised to her very limits, every frame in her hull shook with the vibration of her screws as her propellers burst out of the surface and spun wildly in the air.

Nick had to clench his jaws as the vibration threatened to crack his teeth, and when he glanced across at the forward and lateral speed-indicators, he saw that David Allen's face was icy white and set like that of a corpse.

*Warlock* was slewing down on the wind, describing a slow left-hand circle at the limit of the cable as the engine torque and the wind took her around.

'Starboard twenty,' Nick snapped, correcting the turn, and despite the rigour of his features, David Allen's response was instantaneous.

'Twenty degrees of starboard wheel on, sir.'

Nick saw the lateral drift stop on the ground speed-indicator, and then with a wild lurch of elation he saw the forward speed-indicator flicked into green. Its electronic digital read out, changing swiftly – they were moving forward at 150 feet a minute.

'We are moving her,' Nick cried aloud, and he snatched up the microphone.

'Full power both winches.'

'Both full and holding,' answered Baker immediately.

And Nick glanced back at the forward speed across the ground, 150, 110, 75 feet a minute, *Warlock*'s forward impetus slowed, and Nick realized with a slide of dismay that it was merely the elasticity of the nylon spring that had given them that reading. The spring was stretching out to its limit.

For two or three seconds, the dial recorded a zero rate of speed. *Warlock* was standing still, the cable drawn out to the full limit of her strength, then abruptly the dial flicked into vivid red; they were going backwards, as the nylon spring exerted pressures beyond that of the twin diesels and the big bronze screws – *Warlock* was being dragged back towards that dreadful shore.

For another five minutes, Nick kept both clenched fists on the control levers, pressing them with all his strength to the limit of their travel, sending the great engines shrieking, driving the needles up around the dials, deep into the red 'never exceed' sectors.

He felt tears of anger and frustration scalding his swollen eyelids, and the ship shuddered and shook and screamed under him, her torment transmitted through the soles of his feet and the palms of his hands.

*Warlock* was held down by cable and power, so she could not rise to meet the seas that came out of the roaring whiteness. They tumbled aboard her, piling up on each other, so she burrowed deeper and more dangerously.

'For God's sake, sir,' David Allen was no longer able to contain himself. His eyes looked huge in his bone-white face. 'You'll drive her clean under.'

'Baker,' Nick ignored his Mate, 'Are you gaining?'

'No recovery either winch,' Beauty told him. 'She is not moving.'

Nick pulled back the stainless steel levers, the needles sank swiftly back around their dials, and *Warlock* reacted gratefully, shaking herself free of the piled waters.

'You'll have to shear the tow.' Baker's disembodied voice was muted by the clamour of the storm. 'We'll take our chances, sport.'

Beside him, David Allen reached for the red-painted steel box that housed the shear button. It was protected by the box from accidental usage; David Allen opened the box and looked expectantly, almost pleadingly, at Nick.

'Belay that!' Nick snarled at him, and then to Baker, 'I'm shortening tow. Be ready to haul again, when I am in position.'

David Allen stared at him, his right hand still on the open lid of the red box.

'Close that bloody thing,' Nick said, and turned to the main cable controls. He moved the green lever to reverse, and felt the vibration in the deck as below him in the main cable room the big drums began to revolve, drawing the thick ice-encrusted cable up over *Warlock*'s stern.

Fighting every inch of the way like a wild horse on a head halter, *Warlock* was drawn in cautiously by her own winches, and the officers watched in mounting horror as out of the white terror of the blizzard emerged the mountainous ice-covered bulk of *Golden Adventurer*.

She was so close that the main cable no longer dipped below the surface of the sea, but ran directly from the liner's stern to the tug's massive fairleads on her stern quarter.

'Now we can see what we are doing,' Nick told them grimly. He could see now that much of *Warlock*'s power had been wasted by not exerting a pull on exactly the same plane as *Golden Adventurer*'s keel. He had been disoriented in the white-out of the blizzard, and had allowed *Warlock* to pull at an angle. It would not happen now.

'Chief,' he said. 'Pull, pull all, pull until she bursts her guts!' And again he slid the throttle handles fully home.

*Warlock* flung up against the elastic yoke, and Nick saw the water spurt from the woven fibres and turn instantly to ice crystals as it was whipped away on the shrieking wind.

'She's not moving, sir,' David cried beside him.

'No recovery either winch,' Baker confirmed almost immediately. 'She's solid!'

'Too much water still in her,' said David, and Nick turned on him as though to strike him to the deck.

'Give me the wheel,' he said, his voice cracking with his anger and frustration.

With both engines boiling the sea to white foam, and roaring like dying bulls, Nick swung the wheel to full port lock.

Wildly *Warlock* dug her shoulder in, water pouring on board her as she rolled, instantly Nick spun the wheel to full starboard lock and she lurched against the tow, throwing an extra ton of pressure on to it.

Even above the storm, they heard *Golden Adventurer* groan, the steel of her hull protesting at the weight of water in her and the intolerable pressure of the anchor winches and *Warlock*'s tow cable.

The groan became a crackling hiss as the pebble bottom gave and moved under her.

'Christ, she's coming!' shrieked Baker, and Nick swung her to full port lock again, swinging *Warlock* into a deep trough between waves, then a solid ridge of steaming water buried her, and Nick was not certain she could survive that press of furious sea. It came green and slick over the superstructure and she shuddered wearily, gone slow and unwieldy. Then she lifted her bows and, like a spaniel, shook herself free, becoming again quick and light.

'Pull, my darling, pull,' Nick pleaded with her.

With a slow reluctant rumble, *Golden Adventurer*'s hull began to slide over the holding, clinging bottom.

'Both winches recovering,' Baker howled gleefully, and *Warlock*'s ground speed-indicator flicked into the green, its little angular figures changing in twinkling electronic progression as *Warlock* gathered way.

They all saw *Golden Adventurer*'s stern swinging to meet the next great ridge of water as it burst around her. She was floating, and for moments Nick was paralysed by the wonder of seeing that great and beautiful ship come to life again, become a living, vital sea creature as she took the seas and rose to meet them.

'We've done it, Christ, we've done it!' howled Baker, but it was too soon for self-congratulation. As *Golden Adventurer* came free of the ground and gathered sternway under *Warlock*'s tow, so her rudder bit and swung her tall stern across the wind.

She swung, exposing the enormous windage of her starboard side to the full force of the storm. It was like setting a mainsail, and the wind took her down swiftly on the rocky headland with its sentinel columns that guarded the entrance to the bay.

Nick's first instinct was to try and hold her off, to oppose the force of the wind directly, and he flung *Warlock* into the task, relying on her great diesels and the two anchors to keep the liner from going ashore again – but the wind toyed with them, it ripped the anchors out of the pebble bottom and *Warlock* was drawn stern first through the water, straight down on the jagged rock of the headland.

'Chief, get those anchors up,' Nick snapped into the microphone. 'They'll never hold in this.'

Twenty years earlier, bathing off a lonely beach in the Seychelles, Nick had been caught out of his depth by one of those killer currents that flow around the headlands of oceanic islands, and it had sped him out into the open sea so that within minutes the silhouette of the land was low and indistinct on his watery horizon. He had fought that current, swimming directly against it, and it had nearly killed him. Only in the last stages of exhaustion had he begun to think, and instead of battling it, he had ridden the current, angling slowly across it, using its impetus rather than opposing it.

The lesson he had learned that day was well remembered, and as he watched Baker bring *Golden Adventurer*'s dripping anchors out of the wild water he was driving *Warlock* hard, bringing her around on her cable so the wind was no longer in her teeth, but over her stern quarter.

Now the wind and *Warlock*'s screws were no longer opposed, but *Warlock* was pulling two points off the wind, as fine a course as Nick could judge barely to clear the most seaward of the rocky sentinels; now the liner's locked rudder was holding her steady into the wind – but opposing *Warlock*'s attempt to angle her away from the land.

It was a problem of simple vectors of force, that Nick tried to work out in his head and prove in physical terms, as he delicately judged the angle of his tow and the direction of the wind, balancing them against the tremendous leverage of the liner's locked rudder, the rudder which was dragging her suicidally down upon the land.

Grimly, he stared ahead to where the black rock cliffs were still hidden in the white nothingness. They were invisible, but their presence was recorded on the cluttered screen of the radar repeater. With both wind and engines driving them, their speed was too high, and if *Golden Adventurer* went on to the cliffs like this, her hull would shatter like a watermelon hurled against a brick wall.

It was another five minutes before Nick was absolutely certain they would not make it. They were only two miles off the cliffs now, he glanced again at the radar screen, and they would have to drag *Golden Adventurer* at least half a mile across the wind to clear the land. They were just not going to make it.

Helplessly, Nick stood and peered into the storm, waiting for the first glimpse of black rock through the swirling eddies of snow and frozen spray, and he had never felt more tired and unmanned in his entire life as he moved to the shear button, ready to cut *Golden Adventurer* loose and let her go to her doom.

His officers were silent and tense around him, while under his feet *Warlock* shuddered and buffeted wildly, driven to her mortal limits by the sea and her own engines, but still the land sucked at them.

'Look!' David Allen shouted suddenly, and Nick spun to the urgency in his voice.

For a moment he did not understand what was happening. He knew only that the shape of *Golden Adventurer*'s stern was altered subtly.

'The rudder,' shouted David Allen again. And Nick saw it revolving slowly on its stock as the ship lifted on another big sea.

Almost immediately, he felt *Warlock* making offing from under that lee shore, and he swung her up another point into the wind, *Golden Adventurer* answering her tow with a more docile air, and still the rudder revolved slowly.

'I've got power on the emergency steering gear now,' said Baker.

'Rudder amidships,' Nick ordered.

'Amidships it is,' Baker repeated, and now he was pulling her out stern first, almost at right angles across the wind.

Through the white inferno appeared the dim snow-blurred outline of the rock sentinels, and the sea broke upon them like the thunder of the heavens.

'God, they are close,' whispered David Allen. So close that they could feel the backlash of the gale as it rebounded from the tall rock walls, moderating the tremendous force that was bearing them down – moderating just enough to allow them to slide past the three hungry rocks, and before them lay three thousand miles of wild and tumultuous water, all of it open sea room.

'We made it. This time we really made it,' said Baker, as though he did not believe it was true, and Nick pulled back the throttle controls taking the intolerable strain off her engines before they tore themselves to pieces.

'Anchors and all,' Nick replied. It was a point of honour to retrieve even the anchors. They had taken her off clean and intact – anchors and all.

'Chief,' he said, 'instead of sitting there hugging yourself, how about pumping her full of Tannerax?' The anti-corrosive chemical would save her engines and much of her vital equipment from further sea-water damage, adding enormously to her salvaged value.

'You just never let up, do you?' Baker answered accusingly.

'Don't you believe it,' said Nick. He felt stupid and frivolous with exhaustion and triumph. Even the storm that still roared about them seemed to have lost its murderous intensity. 'Right now I'm going down to my bunk to sleep for twelve hours – and I'll kill anybody who tries to wake me.'

He hung the handmike on its bracket and put his hand on David Allen's shoulder. He squeezed once, and said:

'You did well – you all did very well. Now take her, Number One, and look after her.'

Then he stumbled from the bridge.

It was eight days before they saw the land again. They rode out the storm in the open sea, eight days of unrelenting tension and heart-breaking labour.

The first task was to move the two-cable to *Golden Adventurer*'s bows. In that sea, the transfer took almost 24 hours, and three abortive attempts before they had her head-on to the wind. Now she rode more easily, and *Warlock* had merely to hang on like a drogue, using full power only when one of the big icebergs came within dangerous range, and it was necessary to draw her off.

However, the tension was always there and Nick spent most of those days on the bridge, watchful and worried, nagged by the fear that the plug in the gashed hull would not hold. Baker used timbers from the ship's store to shore up the temporary patch, but he could not put steel in place while *Golden Adventurer* plunged and rolled in the heavy seas, and Nick could not go aboard to check and supervise the work.

Slowly, the great wheel of low pressure revolved over them, the winds changed direction, backing steadily into the west, as the epicentre marched on down the sea lane towards Australasia – and at last it had passed.

Now *Warlock* could work up towing speed. Even in those towering glassy swells of black water that the storm had left them as a legacy, she was able to make four knots.

Then one clear and windy morning under a cold yellow sun, she brought *Golden Adventurer* into the sheltered waters of Shackleton Bay. It was like a diminutive guide-dog leading a blinded colossus.

As the two ships came up into the still waters under the sheltering arm of the bay, the survivors came down from their encampment to the water's edge, lining the steep black pebble beach, and their cheers and shouts of welcome and relief carried thinly on the wind to the officers on *Warlock*'s bridge.

Even before the liner's twin anchors splashed into the clear green water, Captain Reilly's boat was puttering out to *Warlock*, and when he came aboard, his eyes were haunted by the hardship and difficulties of these last days, by the disaster of a lot command and the lives that had been ended with it. But when he shook hands with Nick, his grasp was firm.

'My thanks and congratulations, sir!'

He had known Nicholas Berg as Chairman of Christy Marine, and, as no other, he was aware of the magnitude of this most recent accomplishment. His respect was apparent.

'It's good to see you again,' Nick told him. 'Naturally you have access to my ship's communications to report to your owners.'

Immediately he turned back to the task of manoeuvring *Warlock* alongside, so that steel plate could be swung up from her salvage holds to the liner's deck; it was another hour before Captain Reilly emerged from the radio room.

'Can I offer you a drink, Captain?' Nick led him to his day cabin, and began with tact to deal with the hundred details which had to be settled between them. It was a delicate situation, for Reilly was no longer Master of his own ship. Command had passed to Nicholas as salvage master.

'The accommodation aboard *Golden Adventurer* is still quite serviceable, and, I imagine, a great deal warmer and more comfortable than that occupied by your passengers at present—' Nick made it easier for him while never for a moment letting him lose sight of his command position, and Reilly responded gratefully.

Within half an hour, they had made all the necessary arrangements to transfer the survivors aboard the liner. Levoisin on *La Mouette* had been able to take only one hundred and twenty supernumeraries on board his little tug. The oldest and weakest of them had gone and Christy Marine was negotiating for a charter from Cape Town to Shackleton Bay to take off the rest of them. Now that charter was unnecessary, but the cost of it would form part of Nick's claim for salvage award.

'I won't take up more of your time.' Reilly drained his glass and stood. 'You have much to do.'

There were another four days and nights of hard work. Nick went aboard *Golden Adventurer* and saw the cavernous engine room lit by the eye-scorching blue glare of the electric welding flames, as Baker placed his steel over the wound and welded it into place. Even then, neither he nor Nick was satisfied until the new patches had been shored and stiffened with baulks of heavy timber. There was a hard passage through the roaring forties ahead of them, and until they had *Golden Adventurer* safely moored in Cape Town docks, the salvage was incomplete.

They sat side by side among the greasy machinery and the stink of the anti-corrosives, and drank steaming Thermos coffee laced with Bundaberg rum.

'We get this beauty into Duncan Docks – and you are going to be a rich man,' Nick said.

'I've been rich before. With me it never lasts long – and it's always a relief when I've spent the stuff.' Beauty gargled the rum and coffee appreciatively, before he went on, shrewdly. 'So you don't have to worry about losing the best goddamned engineer afloat.'

Nick laughed with delight. Baker had read him accurately. He did not want to lose this man.

Nick left him and went to see to the trim of the liner, studying her carefully and using the experience of the last days to determine her best points of tow, before giving his orders to David Allen to raise her slightly by the head.

Then there was the transfer from the liner's bunkers of sufficient bunker oil to top up *Warlock*'s own tanks against the long tow ahead, and Bach Wackie in Bermuda kept the telex clattering with relays from underwriters and Lloyd's, with the first tentative advances from Christy Marine; already Duncan Alexander was trying out the angles, manoeuvring for a liberal settlement of Nick's claims, without, as he put it, the expense of the arbitration court.

'Tell him I'm going to roast him,' Nick answered with grim relish. 'Remind him that as Chairman of Christy Marine I advised against underwriting our own bottoms – and now I'm going to rub his nose in it.'

The days and nights blurred together, the illusion made complete by the imbalance of time down here in the high latitudes, so that Nick could often believe neither his senses nor his watch when he had been working eighteen hours straight and yet the sun still burned, and his watch told him it was three o'clock in the morning.

Then again, it did not seem part of reality when his senior officers, gathered around the mahogany table in his day cabin, reported that the work was completed – the repairs and preparation, the loading of fuel, the embarkation of passengers and the hundred other details had all been attended to, and *Warlock* was ready to drag her massive charge out into the unpredictable sea, thousands of miles to the southernmost tip of Africa.

Nick passed the cheroot-box around the circle and while the blue smoke clouded the cabin, he allowed them all a few minutes to luxuriate in the feeling of work done, and done well.

'We'll rest the ship's company for twenty-four hours,' he

announced in a rush of generosity. 'And take in tow at 0800 hours Monday. I'm hoping for a two speed of six knots – twenty-one days to Cape Town, gentlemen.'

When they rose to leave, David Allen lingered self-consciously. 'The wardroom is arranging a little Christmas celebration tonight, sir, and we would like you to be our guest.'

The wardroom was the junior officers' club from which, traditionally, the Master was excluded. He could enter the small panelled cabin only as an invited guest, but there was no doubt at all about the genuine warmth of the welcome they gave him. Even the Trog was there. They stood and applauded him when he entered, and it was clear that most of them had made an early start on the gin. David Allen made a speech which he read haltingly from a scrap of paper which he tried to conceal in the palm of one hand. It was a speech full of hyperbole, clichés and superlatives, and he was clearly mightily relieved once it was over.

Then Angel brought in a cake he had baked for the occasion. It was iced in the shape of *Golden Adventurer*, a minor work of art, with the figures '12½%' picked out in gold on its hull, and they applauded him. That 12½ per cent had significance to set them all grinning and exclaiming.

Then they called on Nick to speak, and his style was relaxed and easy. He had them hooting with glee within minutes – a mere mention of the prize money that would be due to them once they brought *Golden Adventurer* into Cape Town had them in ecstasy.

The girl was wedged into a corner, almost swallowed in the knot of young officers who found it necessary to press as closely around her as was possible without actually smothering her.

She laughed with a clear unaffected exuberance, her voice ringing high above the growl of masculine mirth, so that Nick found it difficult not to keep looking across at her.

She wore a dress of green clinging material, and Nick wondered where it had come from, until he remembered that *Golden Adventurer*'s passenger accommodation was intact and that earlier that morning, he had noticed the girl standing beside David Allen in the stern of the work boat as it returned from the liner, with a large suitcase at her feet. She had been to fetch her gear and she probably should have stayed aboard the liner. Nick was pleased she had not.

Nick finished his little speech, having mentioned every one of his officers by name and given to each the praise they deserved, and David Allen pressed another large whisky into his one hand and an inelegant wedge of cake into the other, and then left hurriedly to join the tight circle around the girl. It opened reluctantly, yielding to his seniority and Nick found himself almost deserted.

He watched with indulgence the open competition for her attention. She was shorter than any of them, so Nick saw only the top of that magnificent mane of sun-streaked hair, hair the colour of precious metal that shone as she nodded and tilted her head, catching the overhead lights.

Beauty Baker was on one side of her, dressed in a ready-made suit of shiny imitation sharkskin that made a startling contrast to his plaid shirt and acid-yellow tie; the trousers of the suit needed hoisting every few minutes and his spectacles glittered lustfully as he hung over the girl.

David Allen was close on her other side, blushing pinkly every time she turned to speak to him, plying her with cake and liquor – and Nick found his indulgence turning to irritation.

He was irritated by the presence of a tongue-tied fourth

officer who had clearly been delegated to entertain him, and was completely awed by the responsibility. He was irritated by the antics of his senior officers. They were behaving like a troupe of performing seals in their competition for the girl's attention.

For a few moments, the tight circle around her opened, and Nick was left with a few vivid impressions. The green of her dress matched exactly the brilliant sparkling green of her eyes. Her teeth were very white, and her tongue as pink as a cat's when she laughed. She was not the child he had imagined from their earlier encounters; with colour touched to her lips and pearls at her throat, he realized she was in her twenties, early twenties perhaps, but a full woman, nevertheless.

She looked across the wardroom and their eyes met. The laughter stilled on her lips, and she returned his gaze. It was a solemn enigmatic gaze, and he found himself once again regretting his previous rudeness to her. He dropped his gaze from hers and saw now that under the clinging green material, her body was slim and beautifully formed, with a lithe athletic grace. He remembered vividly that one nude glimpse he had been given.

Although the green dress was high-necked, he saw that her breasts were large and pointed, and that they were not trussed by any undergarments; the young shapely flesh was as strikingly arresting as if it had been naked.

It made him angry to see her body displayed in this manner. It did not matter that every young girl in the streets of New York or London went so uncorseted, here it made him angry to see her do the same, and he looked back into her eyes. Something charged there, a challenge perhaps, his own anger reflected? He was not sure. She tilted her head slightly, now it was an invitation – or was it? He had known and handled easily so many, many women. Yet this one left him with a feeling of uncertainty, perhaps it was merely her youth, or was it some special quality she possessed? Nicholas Berg was uncertain and he did not relish the feeling.

David Allen hurried to her with another offering, and cut off the gaze that passed between them, and Nick found himself staring at the Chief Officer's slim, boyish back, and listening to the girl's laughter again, sweet and high. But somehow it seemed to be directed tauntingly at Nick, and he said to the young officer beside him,

'Please ask Mr Allen for a moment of his time.' Patently relieved the officer went to fetch him.

'Thank you for your hospitality, David,' said Nick, when he came.

'You aren't going yet, sir?' Nick took a small sadistic pleasure in the Mate's obvious dismay.

He sat at the desk in his day cabin and tried to concentrate. It was the first opportunity he had had to consider the paperwork that awaited him. The muted sounds of revelry from the deck below distracted him, and he found himself listening for the sounds of her laughter while he should have been composing his submissions to his London attorneys, which would be taken to the arbitrators of Lloyd's, a document and record of vital importance, the whole basis of his claim against *Golden Adventurer*'s underwriters. And yet he could not concentrate.

He swung his chair away from the desk and began to pace the thick, sound-deadening carpet, stopping once to listen again as he heard the girl's voice calling gaily, the words unintelligible, but the tone unmistakable. They were dancing, or playing some raucous game which consisted of a great deal of bumping and thumping and shrieks of laughter.

He began to pace again, and suddenly Nick realized he was lonely. The thought stopped him dead again. He was lonely, and completely alone. It was a disturbing realization, especially for a man who had travelled much of life's journey as a loner. Before it had never troubled him, but now he felt desperately the need for somebody to share his triumph. Triumph it was, of course. Against the most improbable odds, he had snatched spectacular victory, and he crossed slowly to the cabin portholes and looked across the darkened bay to where *Golden Adventurer* lay at anchor, all her lights burning, a gay and festive air about her.

He had been knocked off his perch at the top of the tree, deprived of a life's work, a wife and a son – yet it had taken him only a few short months to clamber back to the top.

With this simple operation, he had transformed Ocean Salvage from a dangerously insecure venture, a tottering cash-starved, problem-hounded long chance, into something of real value. He was off and running again now, with a place to go and the means of getting there. Then why did it suddenly seem of so little worth? He toyed with the idea of returning to the revelry in the wardroom, and grimaced as he imagined the dismay of his officers at the Master's inhibiting intrusion.

He turned away from the porthole and poured whisky into a glass, lit a cheroot and dropped into the chair. The whisky tasted like toothpaste and the cheroot was bitter. He left the glass on his desk and stubbed the cheroot before he went through on to the navigation bridge.

The night lights were so dim after his brightly lit cabin that he did not notice Graham, the Third Officer, until his eyes adjusted to the ruby glow.

'Good evening, Mr Graham.' He moved to the chart-table and checked the log. Graham was hovering anxiously, and Nick searched for something to say.

'Missing the party?' he asked at last.

'Sir.'

It was not a promising conversational opening, and despite his loneliness of a few minutes previously, Nick suddenly wanted to be alone again.

'I will stand the rest of your watch. Go off and enjoy yourself.'

The Third Officer gawped at him.

'You've got three seconds before I change my mind.'

'That's jolly decent of you, sir,' called Graham over his shoulder as he fled.

The party in the wardroom had by now degenerated into open competition for Samantha's attention and approbation.

David Allen, wearing a lampshade on his head and, for some unaccountable reason, with his right hand thrust into his jacket in a Napoleonic gesture, was standing on the wardroom bar counter and declaiming Henry's speech before Agincourt, glossing over the passages which he had forgotten with a 'dum-de-dum'. However, when Tim Graham entered, he became immediately the First Officer. He removed the lampshade and inquired frostily.

'Mr Graham, am I correct in believing that you are officer of the watch? Your station at this moment is on the bridge—'

'The old man came and offered to stand my watch,' said Tim Graham.

'Good Lord!' David replaced his lampshade, and poured a large gin for his Third Officer. 'The old bastard must have come over all soft suddenly.'

Beauty Baker, who was hanging off the wall like a gibbon ape, dropped to his feet and drew himself up with rather unsteady dignity, hitched his trousers and announced ominously,

'If anybody calls the old bastard a bastard, I will personally kick his teeth down his throat.' He swept the wardroom with an eye that was belligerent and truculent, until it alighted on Samantha. Immediately it softened. 'That one doesn't count, Sammy!' he said.

'Of course not,' Samantha agreed. 'You can start again.'

Beauty returned to the starting point of the obstacle course, fortified himself with a draught of rum, pushed up his spectacles with a thumb and spat on his palms.

'One to get ready, two to get steady – and three to be off,' sang out Samantha, and clicked the stopwatch. Beauty Baker swung dizzily from the roof, clawing his way around the wardroom without touching the deck, cheered on by the entire company.

'Eight point six seconds!' Samantha clicked the watch, as he ended up on the bar counter, the finishing post. 'A new world record.'

'A drink for the new world champion.'

'I'm next, time me, Sammy!'

They were like schoolboys. 'Hey, watch me, Sammy!' But after another ten minutes, she handed the stopwatch to Tim Graham, who as a late arrival was still sober.

'I'll be back,' she lied, picked up a plate with a large untouched hunk of Angel's cake upon it and was gone before any of them realized it was happening.

Nick Berg was working over the chart-table, so intently that he was not aware of her for many seconds. In the dramatic lighting of the single overhead lamp, the strength of his features was emphasized. She saw the hard line of his jawbone, the heavy brow and the alert, widely spaced set of his eyes. His nose was large and slightly hooked, like that of a plains Indian or a desert Bedouin, and there were lines at the corners of his mouth and around his eyes that were picked out in dark shadow. In his complete absorption with the charts and *Admiralty Pilot*, he had relaxed his mouth from its usual severe line.

She saw now that the lips were full without being fleshy, and there was a certain sensitivity and voluptuousness there that she had not noticed before.

She stood quietly, enchanted with him, until he looked up suddenly, catching the rapt expression upon her face.

She tried not to appear flustered, but even in her own ears her voice was breathless.

'I'm sorry to disturb you. I brought some cake for Timmy Graham.'

'I sent him below to join the party.'

'Oh, I didn't notice him. I thought he was here.'

She made no move to leave, holding the plate in one hand, and they were silent a moment longer.

'I don't suppose I could interest you in a slice? It's going begging.'

'Share it,' he suggested, and she came to the chart-table.

'I owe you an apology,' he said, and was immediately aware of the harshness in his own voice. He hated to apologize, and she sensed it.

'I picked a bad moment,' she said, and broke off a piece of the cake. 'But this seems a better time. Thank you again, and I'm sorry for all the trouble I caused. I understand now that it nearly cost you the *Golden Adventurer*.'

They both turned to look out of the big armoured glass windows to where she lay.

'She is beautiful, isn't she?' said Nick, and his voice had lost its edge.

'Yes, she's beautiful,' Samantha agreed, and suddenly they were very close in the intimate ruddy glow of the night lights.

He began to talk, stiffly and self-consciously at first, but she drew him on, and with secret joy, she sensed him warming and relaxing. Only then did she begin to put her own ideas forward.

Nick was surprised and a little disconcerted at the depth

of her view, and at her easy coherent expression of ideas, for he was still very much aware of her youth. He had expected the giddiness and the giggle, the shallowness and uninformed self-interest of immaturity, but it was not there, and suddenly the difference in their ages was of no importance. They were very close in the night, touching only with their minds, but becoming each minute so much more closely involved in their ideas that time had no significance.

They spoke about the sea, for they were both creatures of that element and as they discovered this, so their mutual delight in each other grew.

From below came the faint unmelodious strains of Beauty Baker leading the ship's officers in a chorus of:

*'—The working class can kiss my arse*
*I've got my 12½ per cent at last!'*

And at another stage in the evening, a very worried Tim Graham appeared on the bridge and blurted out,

'Captain, sir, Doctor Silver is missing. She's not in her cabin and we have searched—' He saw her then, sitting in the Captain's chair and his worry turned to consternation. 'Oh, I see. We didn't know – I mean we didn't expect – I'm sorry, sir. Excuse me, sir. Goodnight, sir.' And again he fled the bridge.

'Doctor?' Nick asked.

'I'm afraid so,' she smiled, and then went on to talk about the university, explaining her research project, and the other work she had in mind. Nicholas listened silently, for like all highly competitive and successful men, he respected achievement and ambition.

The chasm that he imagined existed between them shrank rapidly, so that it was an intrusion when the eight-to-twelve watch ended, and the relief brought other human presence to the bridge, shattering the fragile mood they had created around themselves, and denying them further excuse for remaining together.

'Goodnight, Captain Berg,' she said.

'Goodnight, Doctor Silver,' he answered reluctantly. Until that night, he had not even known her name, and there was so much more he wanted to know now, but she was gone from the bridge. As he entered his own suite, Nick's earlier loneliness returned, but with even more poignancy.

During the long day of getting *Golden Adventurer* under tow, the hours of trim and accommodation to the sea, until she was following meekly settling down to the long journey ahead, Nick thought of the girl at unlikely moments; but when he changed his usual routine and dined in the saloon rather than his own cabin, she was surrounded by a solidly attentive phalanx of young men and, with a small shock of self-honesty, Nick realized that he was actually jealous of them. Twice during the meal, he had to suppress the sharp jibes that came to his lips, and would have plunged the unfortunate recipient into uncomprehending confusion.

Nick ate no desert and took coffee alone in his day cabin. He might have relished Beauty Baker's company, but the Australian was aboard *Golden Adventurer*, working on her main engines. Then, despite the tensions and endeavours of the day, his bunk had no attractions for him. He glanced at the clock on the panelled bulkhead above his desk and saw that it was a few minutes after eight o'clock.

On impulse he went through to the navigation bridge, and Tim Graham leapt guiltily to his feet. He had been sitting in the Master's chair, a liberty which deserved at the least a sharp reprimand, but Nick pretended not to notice and made a slow round of the bridge, checking every detail from the cable tensions of the tow and power settings of *Warlock*'s engines, to the riding lights on both ships and the last log entry.

'Mr Graham,' he said, and the young officer stiffened to attention like the victim before a firing squad, 'I will stand this watch – you may go and get some dinner.'

The Third Officer was so thunderstruck that he needed a large gin before he could bring himself to tell the wardroom of his good fortune.

Samantha did not look up from the board but moved a bishop flauntingly across the front of David Allen's queen, and when David pounced on it with a gurgle of glee, she unleashed her rook from the rear file and said, 'Mate in three, David.'

'One more, Sam, give me my revenge,' pleaded David, but she shook her head and slipped out of the wardroom.

Nicholas became aware of the waft of her perfume. It was an inexpensive but exuberant fragrance – 'Babe', that was it, the one advertised by Hemingway's granddaughter. It suited Samantha perfectly. He turned to her, and it was only then that he was honest enough to admit to himself that he had relieved his Third Officer with the express intention of luring the girl up to the bridge.

'There are whales ahead,' he told her, and smiled one of those rare, irresistible smiles that she had come to treasure. 'I hoped you might come up.'

'Where? Where are they?' she asked with unfeigned excitement, and then they both saw the spout, a golden feather of spray in the low night sunlight two miles ahead.

'*Balaenoptera musculus!*' she exclaimed.

'I'll take your word for it, Doctor Silver, but to me it's still a blue whale.' Nick was still smiling, and she looked abashed for a moment.

'Sorry, I wasn't trying to dazzle you with science.' Then she looked back at the humpy, uninviting cold sea as the whale blew again, a far and ethereal column of lonely spray.

'One,' she said, 'only one.' And the excitement in her voice cooled. 'There are so few of them left now – that might be the last one we will ever see.'

'So few that they cannot find each other in the vastness of the ocean to breed.' Nick's smile was gone also, and again they talked of the sea, of their own involvement with it, their mutual concern at what man had done to it, and what he was still doing to it.

'When the Marxist government of Mozambique took over from the Portuguese colonists, it allowed the Soviets to send in dredgers – not trawlers, but dredgers – and they dredged the weed beds of Delagoa Bay. They actually *dredged* the breeding grounds of the Mozambique prawn. They took out a thousand tons of prawn, and destroyed the grounds for ever – and they drove an entire species into extinction in six short months.' Her outrage was in her voice as she told it.

'Two months ago the Australians arrested a Japanese trawler in their territorial waters. She had in her freezers the meat of 120,000 giant clams that her crew had torn from the barrier reef with crowbars. The calm population of a single coral reef would not exceed 20,000. That means they had denuded six oceanic reefs in one expedition – and they fined the Captain a thousand pounds.'

'It was the Japanese who perfected the "long line",' Nick agreed, 'the endless floating line, armed with specially designed hooks, and laid across the lanes of migration of the big pelagic surface-feeding fish, the tuna and the marlin. They wipe out the shoals as they advance – wipe them out to the last fish.'

'You cannot reduce any animal population beyond a certain point.' Samantha seemed much older as she turned her face up to Nick. 'Look what they did to the whales.'

Together they turned back to the windows, gazing out in hope of another glimpse of that gentle monster, doomed now to extinction, one last look at another creature that would disappear from the seas.

'The Japanese and the Russians again,' said Nick. 'They would not sign the whaling treaty until there were not enough blues left in the seas to make their killing an economic proposition. Then they signed it. When there were two or three thousand blue whales left in all the oceans, that is when they signed.'

'Now they will hunt the fin and the sei and the minke to extinction.'

As they stood side by side staring into the bizarre sun-lit night, searching vainly for that spark of life in the watery wilderness, without thinking Nick lifted his arm; he would have placed it around her shoulders, the age-old protective attitude of man to his woman, but he caught himself at the last moment before he actually touched her. She had felt his movement and tensed for it, swaying slightly towards him in anticipation, but he stepped away, letting his arm fall and stooped over the radarscope. She only realized then how much she had wanted him to touch her, but for the rest of that evening he stayed within the physical limits which he seemed to have set for himself.

The next evening she declined the wardroom's importunate invitations, and after dinner waited in her own cabin, the door an inch ajar so she heard Tim Graham leave the bridge, clattering down the companionway with exuberance, relieved once more of his watch. The moment he entered the wardroom, Samantha slipped from her cabin and ran lightly up to the bridge.

She was with him only minutes after he had assumed the watch and Nick was amused by the strength of his pleasure. They grinned at each other like schoolchildren in a successful piece of mischief.

Before the light went, they passed close by one of the big tabular bergs, and she pointed out the line of filth that marked the white ice like the ring around a bathtub that had been used by a chimney sweep.

'Paraffin wax,' she said,' and undissolved hydrocarbons.'

'No,' he said, 'that's only glacial striation.'

'It's crude oil,' she answered him. 'I've sampled it. It was one of the reasons I took the guide job on *Golden Adventurer*, I wanted first-hand knowledge of these seas.'

'But we are two thousand miles south of the tanker lanes.'

'The beach at Shackleton Bay is thick with wax balls and crude droplets. We found oil-soaked penguins on Cape Alarm, dead and dying. They hit an oil slick within fifty miles of that isolated shore.'

'I can hardly believe—' Nick started, but she cut across him.

'That's just it!' she said. 'Nobody wants to believe it. Just walk on by, as though it's another mugging victim lying on the sidewalk.'

'You're right,' Nick admitted grudgingly. 'Very few people really care.'

'A few dead penguins, a few little black tar balls sticking to your feet on the beach. It doesn't seem much to shout about, but it's what we cannot see that should terrify us. Those millions of tons of poisonous hydrocarbons that dissolve into the sea, that kill slowly and insidiously, but surely. That's what should really terrify us, Nicholas!'

She had used his given name for the first time, and they were both acutely aware of it. They were silent again, staring intently at the big iceberg as it passed slowly. The sun had touched it with ethereal pinks and dreaming amethyst, but that dark line of poisonous filth was still there.

'The world has to use fossil fuels, and we sailors have to transport them,' he said at last.

'But not at such appalling risks, not with an eye only to the profits. Not in the same greedy thoughtless grabbing petty way as man wiped out the whale, not at the cost of turning the sea into a stinking festering cesspool.'

'There are unscrupulous owners—' he agreed, and she cut across him angrily.

'Sailing under flags of convenience, without control, ships built to dangerous standards, equipped with a single boiler—' she reeled out the charges and he was silent.

'Then they waived the winter load-line for tankers rounding the Cape of Good Hope in the southern winter, to enable them to carry that extra fifty thousand tons of crude. The Agulhas Bank, the most dangerous winter sea in the world, and they send overloaded tankers into it.'

'That was criminal,' he agreed.

'Yet you were Chairman of Christy Marine, you had a representative on the Board of Control.'

She saw that she had made a mistake. His expression was suddenly ferocious. His anger seemed to crackle like electricity in the ruby gloom of the bridge. She felt an unaccountable flutter of real fear. She had forgotten what kind of man he was.

But he turned away and made a slow circuit of the bridge, elaborately checking each of the gauges and instruments, and then he paused at the far wing and lit a cheroot. She ached to offer some token of reconciliation, but instinctively she knew not to do so. He was not the kind of man who respected compromise or retreat.

He came back to her at last, and the glow of the cheroot lit his features so that she could see the anger had passed.

'Christy Marine seems like another existence to me now,' he said softly, and she could sense the deep pain of unhealed wounds. 'Forgive me, your reference to it took me off balance. I did not realize that you know of my past history.'

'Everybody on board knows.'

'Of course,' he nodded, and drew deeply on the cheroot before he spoke again. 'When I ran Christy Marine, I insisted on the highest standards of safety and seamanship for every one of our vessels. We opposed the Cape winter-line decision, and none of my tankers loaded to their summer-line on the Good Hope passage. None of my tankers made do with only one boiler, the design and engineering of every Christy Marine vessel was of the same standard as that ship there,' he pointed back at *Golden Adventurer*, 'or this one here,' and he stamped once on the deck.

'Even the *Golden Dawn?*' she asked softly, braving his anger again – but he merely nodded.

'*Golden Dawn*,' he repeated softly. 'It sounds such an absurdly presumptuous name, doesn't it? But I really thought of her as that, when I conceived her. The first million-ton tanker, with every refinement and safety feature that man has so far tested and proved. From inert gas scrubbers to independently articulated main tanks, not one boiler but four, just like one of the old White Star liners – she was really to be the golden dawn of crude oil transportation.

'However, I am no longer Chairman of Christy Marine, and I am no longer in control of *Golden Dawn*, neither her design nor her construction.' His voice was hollow, and in the dim light his eyes seemed shrunken into their cavities like those of a skull. 'Nor yet am I in control of her operation.'

It was all turning out so badly; she did not want to argue with him, nor make him unhappy. However, she had stirred memories and regrets within him, and she wished vainly that she had not disturbed him so. Her instinct warned her she should leave him now.

'Goodnight, Doctor Silver,' he nodded non-committally at her sudden plea of tiredness.

'My name is Sam,' she told him, wishing that she could comfort him in some way, any way, 'or Samantha, if you prefer it.'

'I do prefer it,' he said, without smiling. 'Goodnight, Samantha.'

She was angry with both herself and him, angry that the good feeling between them had been destroyed, so she flashed at him:

'You really are old-fashioned, aren't you?' and hurried from the bridge.

The following evening she almost did not go up to him, for she was ashamed of those parting words, for having pointed up their age difference so offensively. She knew he was sufficiently aware of their differences, without being reminded. She had done herself harm, and she did not want to face him again.

While she was in the shower of the guest cabin, she heard Tim Graham come clattering down the stairs on the other side of the thin bulkhead. She knew that Nicholas had relieved him.

'I'm not going up,' she told herself firmly, and took her time drying and talcuming and brushing out her hair before she clambered naked and still pink from the hot water into her bunk.

She read for half an hour, a western that Beauty Baker had lent her, and it required all her concentration to follow the print, for her mind kept trying to wander. At last she gave an exclamation of self-disgust, threw back the blankets and began dressing.

His relief and pleasure, when she appeared beside him, were transparent, and his smile was a princely welcome for her. She was suddenly very glad she had come, and this night she effortlessly steered past all the pitfalls.

She asked him to explain how the Lloyd's Open Form contract worked, and she followed his explanations swiftly.

'If they take into consideration the danger and difficulties involved in the salvage,' she mused, 'you should be able to claim an enormous award.'

'I'm going to ask for twenty per cent of the hull value—'

'What is the hull value of *Golden Adventurer?*'

And he told her. She was silent a moment as she checked his mental arithmetic.

'That's six million dollars,' she whispered in awe.

'Give or take a few cents,' he agreed.

'But there isn't that much money in the world!' She turned and stared back at the liner.

'Duncan Alexander is going to agree with you.' Nick smiled a little grimly.

'But,' she shook her head, 'what would anybody do with that much money?'

'I'm asking for six – but I won't get it. I'll walk away with three or four million.'

'Still, that's too much. Nobody could spend that much, not if they tried for a lifetime.'

'It's spent already. It will just about enable me to pay off my loans, launch my other tug, and to keep Ocean Salvage going for another few months.'

'You owe three or four million dollars?' She stared at him now in open wonder. 'I'd never sleep, not one minute would I be able to sleep—'

'Money isn't for spending,' he explained. 'There is a limit to the amount of food you can eat, or clothes you can wear. Money is a game, the biggest most exciting game in town.'

She listened attentively to it all, happy because tonight he was gay and excited with grand designs and further plans, and because he shared them with her.

'What we will do is this, we'll come down here with both tugs and catch an iceberg.'

She laughed. 'Oh, come on!'

'I'm not joking,' he assured her, but laughing also. 'We'll put tow-lines on a big berg. It may take a week to build up tow speed, but once we get it moving nothing will stop it.

We will guide it up into the middle forties, catch the roaring forties and, just like the old wool clippers on the Australian passage, we will run our eastings down.' He moved to the chart-table, selected a large-scale chart of the Indian Ocean and beckoned her to join him.

'You're serious.' She stopped laughing, and stared at him again. 'You really are serious, aren't you?'

He nodded, still smiling, and traced it out with his finger. 'Then we'll swing northwards, up into the Western Australian current, letting the flow carry us north in a great circle, until we hit the easterly monsoon and the north equatorial current.' He described the circle, but she watched his face. They stood very close, but still not touching and she felt herself stirred by the timbre of his voice, as though to the touch of fingers. 'We will cross the Indian Ocean to the east coast of Africa with the current pushing all the way, just in time to catch the south-westerly monsoon drift – right into the Persian Gulf.' He straightened up and smiled again.

'A hundred billion tons of fresh water delivered right into the driest and richest corner of the globe.'

'But – but—' she shook her head, 'it would melt!'

'From a helicopter we spray it with a reflective polyurethane skin to lessen the effect of the sun, and we moor it in a shallow specially prepared dock where it will cool its own surrounds. Sure, it will melt, but not for a year or two and then we'll just go out and catch another one and bring it in, like roping wild horses.'

'How would you handle it?' she objected. 'It's too big.'

'My two tugs hustle forty-four thousand horses – we could pull in Everest, if we wanted.'

'Yes, but once you get it to the Persian Gulf?'

'We cut it into manageable hunks with a laser lance, and lift the hunks into a melting dam with an overhead crane.'

She thought about it. 'It could work,' she admitted.

'It will work,' he told her. 'I've sold the idea to the Saudis already. They are already building the dock and the dams. We'll give them water at one hundredth the cost of using nuclear condensers on sea water, and without the risk of radioactive contamination.'

She was absorbed with his vision, and he with hers. As they talked deep into the long watches of the night, they drew closer in spirit only.

Although each of them treasured those shared hours, somehow neither could bridge the narrow chasm between friendliness and real intimacy. She was instinctively aware of his reserves, that he was a man who had considered life and established his code by which to live it. She guessed that he did nothing unless it was deeply felt, and that a casual physical relationship would offer no attraction to him; she knew of the turmoil to which his life had so recently been reduced, and that he was pulling himself out of that by main strength, but that he was now wary of further hurt. There was time, she told herself, plenty of time – but *Warlock* bore steadily north by north-east, dragging her crippled ward up through the roaring forties; those notorious winds treated her kindly and she made good the six knots that Nick had hoped for.

On board *Warlock*, the attitude of the officers towards Samantha Silver changed from fawning adulation to wistful respect. Every one of them knew of the nightly ritual of the eight-to-midnight watch.

'Bloody cradle-snatcher,' groused Tim Graham.

'Mr Graham, it is fortunate I did not hear that remark,' David Allen warned him with glacial coldness – but they all resented Nicholas Berg, it was unfair competition, yet they kept a new respectful distance from the girl, not one of them daring to challenge the herd bull.

The time that Samantha had looked upon as endless was running out now, and she closed her mind to it. Even when David Allen showed her the fuzzy luminescence of the African continent on the extreme range of the radar screen, she pretended to herself that it would go on like this – if not for ever, at least until something special happened.

During the long voyage up from Shackleton Bay, Samantha had streamed a very fine-meshed net from *Warlock*'s stern, collecting an incredible variety of krill and plankton and other microscopic marine life. Angel had grudgingly given her a small corner of his scullery in return for her services as honorary assistant under-chef and unpaid waitress, and she spent many absorbed hours there each day, identifying and preserving her specimens.

She was working there when the helicopter came out to *Warlock*. She looked up at the buffeting of the machine's rotors as they changed into fine pitch for the landing on *Warlock*'s heli-deck, and she was tempted to go up like every idle and curious hand on board, but she was in the middle of staining a slide, and somehow she resented the encroachment on this little island of her happiness. She worked on, but now her pleasure was spoiled, and she cocked her head when she heard the roar of the rotors as the helicopter rose from the deck again and she was left with a sense of foreboding.

Angel came in from the deck, wiping his hands on his apron and he paused in the doorway.

'You didn't tell me he was going, dearie.'

'What do you mean?' Samantha looked up at him, startled.

'Your boyfriend, darling. Socks and toothbrush and all.' Angel watched her shrewdly. 'Don't tell me he didn't even kiss you goodbye.'

She dropped the glass slide into the stainless steel sink and it snapped in half. She was panting as she gripped the rail of the upper deck and stared after the cumbersome yellow machine.

It flew low across the green wind-chopped sea, hump-backed and nose low, still close enough to read the operating company's name 'COURT' emblazoned on its fuselage, but it dwindled swiftly towards the far blue line of mountains.

Nick Berg sat in the jump seat between the two pilots of the big S. 58T Sikorsky and looked ahead towards the flat silhouette of Table Mountain. It was overlaid by a thick mattress of snowy cloud, at the south-easterly wind swirled across its summit.

From their altitude of a mere thousand feet, there were still five big tankers in sight, ploughing stolidly through the green sea on their endless odyssey, seeming to be alien to their element, not designed to live in harmony with it, but to oppose every movement of the waters. Even in this low sea, they wore thick garlands of white at their stubby rounded bows, and Nick watched one of them dip suddenly and take spray as high as her foremast. In any sort of blow, she would be like a pier with pylons set on solid ground. The seas would break right over her. It was not the way a ship should be, and now he twisted in his seat and looked back.

Far behind them, *Warlock* was still visible. Even at this distance, and despite the fact that she was dwarfed by her charge, her lines pleased the seaman in him. She looked good, but that backward glance invoked a pang of regret that he had been so stubbornly trying to ignore – and he had a vivid image of green eyes and hair of platinum and gold.

His regret was spiced by the persistent notion that he

had been cowardly. He had left *Warlock* without being able to bring himself to say goodbye to the girl, and he knew why he had done so. He would not take the chance of making a fool of himself. He grimaced with distaste as he remembered her exact words, 'You really are old-fashioned, aren't you?'

There was something vaguely repulsive in a middle-aged man lusting after young flesh – and he supposed he must now look upon himself as middle-aged. In six months he would be forty years of age, and he did not really expect to live to eighty. So he was in the middle of the road.

He had always scorned those grey, lined, balding, unattractive little men with big cigars, sitting in expensive restaurants with pretty young girls beside them, the young thing pretending to hang on every pearl-like word, while her eyes focused beyond his shoulder – on some younger man.

But still, it had been cowardice. She had become a friend during those weeks, and she could hardly have been aware of the emotions that she had aroused in him during those long dark hours on *Warlock*'s bridge. She was not to blame for his unruly passions, in no way had she encouraged him to believe that he was more than just an older man, not even a father figure, but just someone with whom to pass an otherwise empty hour. She had been as friendly and cheerful to everyone else on board *Warlock*, from the Mate to the cook.

He really had owed her the common courtesy of a handshake and an assurance of the pleasure he had taken from her company, but he had not been certain he could restrict it to that.

He winced again as he imagined her horror as he blurted out some sort of declaration, some proposal to prolong their relationship or alter its structure into something more intimate, her disenchantment when she realized that behind the façade of the mature and cultured man, he was just as grimy an old lecher as the furtive drooling browsers in the porno-shops of Times Square.

'Let it go,' he had decided. No matter that he was probably in better physical shape now than he had been at twenty-five, to Dr Samantha Silver he was an old man – and he had a frightening vision of an episode from his own youth.

A woman, a friend of his mother's, had trapped the nineteen-year-old Nicholas alone one rainy day in the old beach house at Martha's Vineyard. He remembered his own revulsion at the sagging white flesh, the wrinkles, the lines of stria across her belly and breasts, and the *oldness* of her. She would then have been a woman of forty, the same age as he was now, and he had done her the service she required out of some obligation of pity, but afterwards he had scrubbed his teeth until the gums bled and he had stood under the shower for almost an hour.

It was one of the cruel deceits of life that a person aged from the outside inwards. He had thought of himself in the fullness of his physical and mental powers, especially now after bringing in *Golden Adventurer*. He was ready for them to lead on the dragons and he would tear out their jugulars with his bare hands – then she had called him an old-fashioned thing, and he had realized that the sexual fantasy which was slowly becoming an obsession must be associated with the male menopause, a sorry symptom of the ageing process of which he had not been conscious until then. He grinned wryly at the thought.

The girl would probably hardly notice that he had left the ship, at the worst might be a little piqued by his lack of manners, but in a week would have forgotten his name. As for himself, there was enough, and more than enough to fill the days ahead, so that the image of a slim young body and that precious mane of silver and gold would fade until it became the fairy tale it really was.

Resolutely he turned in the jump seat and looked ahead. Always look ahead, there are never regrets in that direction.

They clattered in over False Bay, crossing the narrow isthmus of the Cape Peninsula under the bulk of the cloud-capped mountain, from the Indian Ocean to the Atlantic in under ten minutes.

He saw the gathering, like vultures at the lion kill, as the Sikorsky lowered to her roost on the helipad within the main harbour area of Table Bay.

As Nick jumped down, ducking instinctively under the still-turning rotors, they surged forward, ignoring the efforts of the Courtline dispatcher to keep the pad clear; they were led by a big red-faced man with a scorched-looking bald head and the furry arms of a tame bear.

'Larry Fry, Mr Berg,' he growled. 'You remember me?'

'Hello, Larry.' He was the local manager for Bach Wackie & Co, Nick's agents.

'I thought you might say a few words to the Press.' But the journalists swarmed around Nick now, demanding, importuning, jostling each other, their minions firing flash bulbs.

Nick felt his irritation flare, and he needed a deep breath and a conscious effort to control his anger.

'All right, lads and ladies.' He held up both hands, and grinned that special boyish grin. They were doing a tough job, he reminded himself. It couldn't be easy to be forced daily into the company of rich and successful men, grabbing for tidbits, and being grossly underpaid for your efforts with the long-term expectation of ulcers and cirrhosis of the liver.

'Play the game with me and I'll play it with you,' he promised, and thought for a moment how it would be if they *didn't* want to speak with him, how it would be if they didn't know who he was, and didn't care.

'Where have you booked me?' he asked Larry Fry now,

and turned back to them. 'In two hours' time I'll be in my suite at the Mount Nelson Hotel. You're invited, and there'll be whisky.'

They laughed and tried a few more half-hearted questions, but they had accepted the compromise – at least they had got the pictures.

As they went up the palm-lined drive to the gracious old hotel, built in the days when space included five acres of carefully groomed gardens, Nick felt the stir of memory, but he suppressed that and listened intently to the list of appointments and matters of urgency from which Larry Fry read. The change in the big man's attitude was dramatic. When Nick had first arrived to take command of *Warlock*, Larry Fry had given him ten minutes of his time and sent a deputy to complete the business.

Then Nick had been touched by the mark of the beast, a man on his way down, with as much appeal as a leper. Larry Fry had accorded him the minimum courtesy due the master of a small vessel, but now he was treating him like visiting royalty, limousine and fawning attention.

'We have chartered a 707 from South African Airways to fly *Golden Adventurer*'s passengers to London, and they will take scheduled commercial flights to their separate destinations from there.'

'What about berthing for *Golden Adventurer?*'

'The Harbour Master is sending out an inspector to check the hull before he lets her enter harbour.'

'You have made the arrangements?' Nick asked sharply. He had not completed the salvage until the liner was officially handed over to the company commissioned to undertake the repairs.

'Court are flying him out now,' Larry Fry assured him. 'We'll have a decision before nightfall.'

'Have the underwriters appointed a contractor for the repairs?'

'They've called for tenders.'

The hotel manager himself met Nicholas under the entrance portico.

'Good to see you again, Mr Berg.' He waived the registration procedures. 'We can do that when Mr Berg has settled in.' And then he assured Nick, 'We have given you the same suite.'

Nick would have protested, but already they were ushering him into the sitting room. If it had been a room lacking completely in character or taste, the memories might not have been so poignant. However, unlike one of those soulless plastic and vinyl coops built by the big chains and so often offered to travellers under the misnomer of 'inns', this room was furnished with antique furniture, oil-paintings and flowers. The memories were as fresh as those flowers, but not as pleasing.

The telephone was ringing as they entered, and Larry Fry seized it immediately, while Nick stood in the centre of the room. It had been two years since last he stood here, but it seemed as many days, so clear was the memory.

'The Harbour Master has given permission for *Golden Adventurer* to enter harbour.' Larry Fry grinned triumphantly at Nick, and gave him the thumbs-up signal.

Nick nodded, the news was an anti-climax after the draining endeavours of the last weeks. Nick walked through to the bedroom. The wallpaper was a quietly tasteful floral design with matching curtains.

From the four-poster bed, Nick remembered, you could look out over the lawns. He remembered Chantelle sitting under that canopy, with a gossamer-sheer bed-robe over her creamy shoulders, eating thin strips of marmaladed toast and then delicately and carefully licking each slim tapered finger with a pink pointed tongue.

Nicholas had come out to negotiate the transportation of South African coal from Richards Bay, and iron ore from

Saldanha Bay to Japan. He had insisted that Chantelle accompany him. Perhaps he had the premonition of imminent loss, but he had overridden her objections.

'But Africa is such a primitive place, Nicky, they have things that bite.'

And she had in the end gone with him. He had been rewarded with four days of rare happiness. The last four days ever, for though he did not then even suspect it, he was already sharing her bed and body with Duncan Alexander. He had never tired in thirteen years of that lovely smooth creamy body; rather, he had delighted in its slow luscious ripening into full womanhood, believing without question that it belonged to him.

Chantelle was one of those unusual women who grew more beautiful with time; it had always been one of his pleasures to watch her enter a room filled with other internationally acclaimed beauties, and see them pale beside his wife. And suddenly, for no good reason, he imagined Samantha Silver beside Chantelle – the girl's coltish grace would be transmuted to gawkiness beside Chantelle's poise, her manner as gauche as a schoolgirl's beside Chantelle's mature control, a warm lovable little bunny beside the sleekly beautiful mink—

'Mr Berg, London.' Larry Fry called from the sitting room interrupting him, and with relief Nick picked up the telephone. 'Just keep going forward,' he reminded himself, and before he spoke, he thought again of the two women, and wondered suddenly how much that thick rich golden mane of Samantha's hair would pale beside Chantelle's lustrous sable, and just how much of the mother-of-pearl glow would fade from that young, clear skin—

'Berg,' he said abruptly into the telephone.

'Mr Berg, good morning. Will you speak to Mr Duncan Alexander of Christy Marine?'

Nick was silent for five full seconds. He needed that long to adjust to the name, but Duncan Alexander was the natural extension of his previous thoughts. In the silence he heard the banging of doors and rising clamour of voices, as the journalists converged on the liquor cabinet next door.

'Mr Berg, are you there?'

'Yes,' he said, and his voice was steady and cool. 'Put him on.'

'Nicholas, my dear fellow.' The voice was glossy as satin, slow as honey, Eton and King's College, a hundred thousand pound accent, impossible to imitate, not quite foppish nor indolent; razor steel in a scabbard of velvet encrusted with golden filigree and precious stones – and Nicholas had seen the steel bared. 'It seems that it is impossible to hold a good man down.'

'But you tried, young Duncan,' Nick answered lightly. 'Don't feel bad about it, indeed you tried.'

'Come, Nicholas. Life is too short for recriminations. This is a new deck of cards, we start equal again.' Duncan chuckled softly. 'At least be gracious enough to accept my congratulations.'

'Accepted,' Nicholas agreed. 'Now what do we talk about?'

'Is *Golden Adventurer* in dock yet?'

'She has been cleared to enter. She'll be tied up within twenty-four hours – and you'd better have your cheque book ready.'

'I hoped that we might avoid going up before the Committee. There has been too much bitterness already. Let's try and keep it in the family, Nicholas.'

'The family?'

'Christy Marine is the family – you, Chantelle, old Arthur Christy – and Peter.'

It was the very dirtiest form of fighting, and Nick found suddenly that he was shaking like a man in fever and that his fist around the receiver was white with the force of his grip. It was the mention of his son that had affected him so.

'I'm not in that family any more.'

'In a way you will always be part of it. It is as much your achievement as any man's, and your son—'

Nick cut across him brusquely, his voice gravelly.

'You and Chantelle made me a stranger. Now treat me like one.'

'Nicholas—'

'Ocean Salvage as main contractor for the recovery of *Golden Adventurer* is open to an offer.'

'Nicholas—'

'Make an offer.'

'As bluntly as that?'

'I'm waiting.'

'Well now. My Board has considered the whole operation in depth, and I am empowered to make you an outright settlement of three-quarters of a million dollars.'

Nick's tone did not alter. 'We have been set down for a hearing at Lloyd's on the 27th of next month.'

'Nicholas, the offer is negotiable within reasonable limits—'

'You are speaking a foreign language,' Nick cut him off. 'We are so far apart that we are wasting each other's time.'

'Nicholas, I know how you feel about Christy Marine, you know the company is underwriting its own—'

'Now you are really wasting my time.'

'Nicholas, it's not a third party, it's not some big insurance consortium, it's Christy Marine—'

He used his name again, though it scalded his tongue.

'Duncan, you're breaking my heart. I'll see you on the 27th of next month, at the arbitration court.' He dropped the receiver on to its bracket, and moved across to the mirror, swiftly combing his hair and composing his features, startled to see how hard and bleak his expression was, and how fierce his eyes.

However, when he went through to the lounge of the suite, he was relaxed and urbane and smiling.

'All right, ladies and gentlemen. I'm all yours,' and one of the ladies of the press, blonde, pretty and not yet thirty but with eyes as old as life itself, took another sip of her whisky as she studied him, then murmured huskily, 'I wouldn't mind at all, duckie.'

Golden *Adventurer* stood tall and very beautiful against the wharf of Cape Town harbour, waiting her turn to go into the dry dock.

Globe Engineering, the contractors who had been appointed to repair her, had signed for her and legally taken over responsibility from *Warlock*'s First Officer. But David Allen still felt an immense proprietary pride in her.

From *Warlock*'s navigation bridge, he could look across the main harbour basin and see the tall, snowy superstructure glistening in the bright hot summer sunshine, towering as high as the giraffe-necked steel wharf cranes; and in gloating self-indulgence, David dwelt on a picture of the liner, wreathed in snow, half obscured by driving sleet and sea fume, staggering in the mountainous black seas off Antarctica. It gave him a solid feeling of achievement, and he thrust his hands deeply into his pockets and whistled softly to himself, smiling and watching the liner.

The Trog thrust his wrinkled head from the radio room.

'There's a call for you on the landline,' he said, and David picked up the handset.

'David?'

'Yessir.' He drew himself to his full height as he recognized Nicholas Berg's voice.

'Are you ready for sea?'

David gulped, then glanced at the bulkhead clock. 'We discharged tow an hour and ten minutes ago.'

'Yes, I know. How soon?'

David was tempted to lie, estimate short, and then fake it for the extra time he needed. Instinct warned him against lying deliberately to Nicholas Berg.

'Twelve hours,' he said.

'It's an oil-rig tow, Rio to the North Sea, a semi-submersible rig.'

'Yessir,' David adjusted quickly, thank God he had not yet let any of his crew ashore. He had arranged for bunkering at 1300 hours. He could make it. 'When are you coming aboard, sir?'

'I'm not,' said Nick. 'You're the new Master. I'm leaving for London on the five o'clock flight. I won't even get down to shout at you. She's all yours, David.'

'Thank you, sir,' David stuttered, feeling himself flush hot scarlet.

'Bach Wackie will telex you full details of the tow at sea, and you and I will work out your own contract later. But I want you running at top economic power for Rio by dawn tomorrow.'

'Yessir.'

'I've watched you carefully, David.' Nick's voice changed, becoming personal, warmer. 'You're a damn good tug-man. Just keep telling yourself that.'

'Thank you, Mr Berg.'

Samantha had spent half the afternoon helping with the arrangements for taking off the remaining passengers from *Golden Adventurer* and embarking them in the waiting fleet of tourist buses which would distribute them to hotels throughout the city while they waited for the London charter flight.

It had been a sad occasion, farewell to many who had become friends, and remembering those who had not come back from Cape Alarm with them – Ken, who might have been her lover, and the crew of raft Number 16 who had been her special charges.

Once the final bus had left, with the occupants waving for the last time to Samantha, 'Take care, honey!' 'You come and visit with us now, you hear?' she was as lonely and forlorn as the silent ship. She stood for a long time staring up the liner's high side, examining the damage where sea and ice had battered her – then she turned and picked her way dejectedly along the edge of the basin, ignoring the occasional whistle or ribald invitation from the fishermen and crew members of the freighters on their moorings.

*Warlock* seemed as welcoming as home, rakish and gallant, wearing her new scars with high panache, already thrusting and impatient at the restraint of her mooring lines. And then Samantha remembered that Nicholas Berg was no longer aboard her, and her spirits sagged again.

'God,' Tim Graham met her at the gangplank. 'I'm glad you got back. I didn't know what to do with your gear.'

'What do you mean?' Samantha demanded. 'Are you throwing me off the ship?'

'Unless you want to come with us to Rio.' He thought about that for a moment, and then he grinned, 'Hey, that's not a bad idea, how about it, old girl? Rio in Carnival time, you and me—'

'Don't get carried away, Timothy,' she warned him. 'Why Rio?'

'The Captain—'

'Captain Berg?'

'No, David Allen, he's the new skipper,' and she lost interest.

'When are you sailing?'

'Midnight.'

'I'd best go pack up.' She left him on the quarterdeck, and Angel pounced on her as she passed the galley.

'Where have you been?' He was in a flutter, all wrists and tossing hair, 'I've been beside myself, darling.'

'What is it, Angel?'

'It's probably too late already.'

'What is it?' She caught his urgency. 'Tell me.'

'He's still in town.'

'Who?' But she knew, they spoke of only one person in these emotional terms.

'Don't be dense, luv. Your crumpet.' She hated it when he referred to Nick like that, but now she let him go on. 'But he won't be very much longer. His plane leaves at five o'clock, he is making the local flight to Johannesburg, and connecting there for London.'

She stared at him.

'Well what are you waiting for?' Angel keened. 'It's almost four o'clock now, and it will take you at least half an hour to reach the airport.'

She did not move. 'But, Angel,' she almost wrung her hands in anguish, 'but what do I do when I get there?'

Angel shook his head and twinkled his diamonds in exasperation. 'Sweet merciful heavens, duckie.' Then he sighed. 'When I was a boy I had two guinea pigs, and they also refused to get it on. I think they were retarded, or something. I tried everything, even hormones, but neither of them survived the shots. Alas, their love was never consummated—'

'Be serious, Angel.'

'You could hold him down while I give him a hormone shot—'

'I hate you, Angel.' She had to laugh, even in her anxiety.

'Dearie, every night for the past month you have tried to set him on fire with your dulcet silvery voice – and we haven't even passed "GO" and collected our first $200—'

'I know, Angel. I know.'

'It seems to me, sweetie, that it's time now to cut out the jawing and to ignite him with that magic little tinderbox of yours.'

'You mean right there in the departure lounge of the airport?' She clapped her hands with delight, then struck a lascivious pose. 'I'm Sam – fly me!'

'Hop, poppet there is a taxi on the wharf – he's been waiting an hour, with his meter running.'

There is no first-class lounge in Cape Town's DF Malan Airport, so Nicholas sat in the snake-pit, amongst the distraught mothers and their whining, sticky offspring, the harassed tourists loaded like camels with souvenirs and the florid-faced commercial travellers, but he was alone in a multitude; with unconscious deference they allowed him a little circle of privacy and he used the Louis Vuitton briefcase on his knee as a desk.

It occurred to him suddenly how dramatically the balance had swung in the last mere forty days, since he had recognized his wave peaking, but had almost not been able to find the strength for it.

A shadow passed across his eyes, and the little creased crow's foot appeared between them as he remembered the physical and emotional effort that it had taken to make the 'Go' decision on *Golden Adventurer*, and he shivered slightly in fear of what might have happened if he had not gone. He would have missed his wave, and there would never have been another.

With a small firm movement of his head, he pushed that memory of fear behind him. He had caught his wave, and he was riding high and fast. Now it seemed that the fates were intent on smothering him with largesse: the oil-rig for *Warlock*, Rio to the Bravo Sierra field off Norway – then a back-to-back tow from the North Sea through Suez to the new South Australian field, would keep *Warlock* fully employed for the next six months. That was not all, the threatening dockyard strike at Construction Navale

Atlantique had been smoothed over and the delivery date for the new tug had come forward by two months. At midnight the night before, a telephone call from Bach Wackie had awakened him to let him know Kuwait and Qatar were now also studying the iceberg-to-water project with a view to commissioning similar schemes; he would have to build himself another two vessels if they decided to go.

'All I need now is to hear that I have won the football pools,' he thought, and turned his head, started and caught his breath with a hiss, as though he had been punched in the ribs.

She stood by the automatic doors, and the wind had caught her hair and torn it loose from its thick twisted knot so that fine gold tendrils floated down on to her cheeks – cheeks that were flushed as though she had run fast, and her chest heaved so that she held one hand upon it, fingers spread like a star between those fine pointed breasts. She was poised like a forest animal that has scented the leopard, fearful, tremulous, but not yet certain in which direction to run. Her agitation was so apparent that he thrust aside his briefcase and stood up.

She saw him instantly, and her face lit with an expression of such unutterable joy, that he was halted in his intention of going towards her, while she in contrast wheeled and started to run towards him.

She collided with a portly, sweating tourist, nearly flooring him and shaking loose a rain of carved native curios and anonymous packets which clattered to the floor around him like ripe fruit.

He snarled angrily, then his expression changed as he looked at her. 'Sorry!' She stooped swiftly, picked up a packet, thrust it into his arms, hit him with her smile, and left him beaming bemusedly after her.

However, now she was more restrained, her precipitous rush calmed to that long-legged, thrusting, hip-swinging walk of hers, and the smile was a little uncertain as she pushed vainly at the loose streamers of golden hair, trying to tuck them up into the twisted rope on top of her head.

'I thought I'd missed you.' She stopped a little in front of him.

'Is something wrong?' he asked quickly, still alarmed by her behaviour.

'Oh no,' she assured him hurriedly. 'Not any more,' and suddenly she was awkward and coltish again. 'I thought,' her voice hushed, 'it was just that I thought I'd missed you.' And her eyes slid away from him. 'You didn't say goodbye—'

'I thought it was better that way.' And now her eyes flew back to his face, sparkling with green fire.

'Why?' she demanded, and he had no answer to give her.

'I didn't want to—' How could he say it to her, without making the kind of statement that would embarrass them both?

Above them, the public address system squawked into life.

> 'South African Airways announces the departure of their Airbus flight 235 to Johannesburg. Will passengers please board at Gate Number Two.'

She had run out of time. 'I'm Sam – Fly Me! Please!' she thought, and felt the urge to giggle, but instead she said:

'Nicholas, tomorrow you'll be in London – in midwinter.'

'It's a sobering thought,' he agreed, and for the first time smiled; his smile closed like a fist around her heart and her legs felt suddenly weak.

'Tomorrow or at least the day after, I'll be riding the long sea at Cape St Francis,' she said. They had spoken of that, on those enchanted nights. He had told her how he had first ridden the surf at Waikiki Beach long ago before the sport had become a craze, and it had been part of their shared experience, part of their love of the sea, drawing them closer together.

'I hope the surf's up for you,' he said. Cape St Francis was three hundred and fifty miles north of Cape Town, simply another beach and headland in a shoreline that stretched in unbroken splendour for six thousand miles, and yet it was unique in all the world. The young and the young-at-heart came in almost religious pilgrimage to ride the long sea at Cape St Francis. They came from Hawaii and California, from Tahiti and Queensland, for there was no other wave quite like it.

At the departure gate, the shuffling queue was shortening, and Nick stooped to pick up his briefcase, but she reached out and laid her hand on his biceps, and he froze.

It was the first time she had deliberately touched him, and the shock of it spread through his body like ripples on a quiet lake. All the emotions and passions which he had so strenuously denied came tumbling back upon him, and it seemed that their strength had grown a hundredfold while under restraint. He ached for her, with a deep, yearning, wanting ache.

'Come with me, Nicholas,' she whispered, and his own throat closed so he could not answer. He stared at her, and already the ground hostesses at the gate were peering around irritably for their missing passenger.

She had to convince him and she shook his arm urgently, startled at the hardness of the muscle under her fingers.

'Nicholas, I really want,' she began, intending to finish, 'you to,' but her tongue played a Freudian trick on her, and she said, 'I really want you.'

'Oh God,' she thought, as she heard herself say it, 'I sound like a whore,' and in panic she corrected herself.

'I really want you to,' and she flushed, the blood came

up from her neck, dark under the peach of her tan so the freckles glowed on her skin like flakes of gold-dust.

'Which one is it?' he asked, and then smiled again.

'There isn't time to argue.' She stamped her foot, feigning impatience, hiding her confusion, then added, 'Damn you!' for no good reason.

'Who is arguing?' he asked quietly, and suddenly, like magic, she was in his arms, trying to burrow herself deeper and deeper into his embrace, trying to draw all the man smell of him into her lungs, amazed at the softness and warmth of his mouth and the hard rasp of new beard on his chin and cheek, making little soft mewing sounds of comfort deep in her throat as she clung to him.

'Passenger Berg. Will passenger Berg please report to the departure gate,' chanted the public address.

'They're calling me,' Nicholas murmured.

'They can go right to the back of the queue,' she mumbled into his lips.

Sunlight was made for Samantha. She wore it like a cloak that had been woven especially for her. She wore it in her hair, sparkling like jewellery, she used it to paint her face and body in lustrous shades of burnt honey and polished amber, she wore it glowing in golden freckles on her cheeks and nose.

She moved in sunlight with wondrous grace, barefooted in the white sand, so that her hips and buttocks roistered brazenly under the thin green stuff of her bikini.

She sprawled in the sunlight like a sleeping cat, offering her face and her naked belly to it, so he felt that if he laid his hands against her throat he would feel her purr deep inside her chest.

She ran in the sunlight, light as a gull in flight, along the hard wet sand at the water's edge, and he ran beside her, tirelessly, mile after mile, the two of them alone in a world of green sea and sun and tall pale hot skies. The beach curved away in both directions to the limit of the eye, smooth and white as the snows of Antarctica, devoid of human life or the scars of man's petty endeavours, and she laughed beside him in the sunlight, holding his hand as they ran together.

They found a deep, clear rock pool in a far and secret place. The sunlight off the water dappled her body, exploding silently upon it like the reflections of light from a gigantic diamond, as she cast aside the two green wisps of her bikini, let down the thick rope of her hair and stepped into the pool, turning, knee-deep, to look back at him. Her hair hung almost to her waist, springing and thick and trying to curl in the salt and wind, it cloaked her shoulders and her breasts peeped through the thick curtains of it. Her breasts, untouched by the sun, were rich as cream and tipped in rose, so big and full and exuberant that he wondered that he had ever thought her a child; they bounced and swung as she moved, and she pulled back her shoulders and laughed at him shamelessly when she saw the direction of his eyes.

She turned back to the pool and her buttocks were white with the pinkish sheen of a deep-sea pearl, round and tight and deeply divided, and, as she bent forward to dive, a tiny twist of copper gold curls peeped briefly and coyly from the wedge where the deep cleft split into her tanned smooth thighs.

Through the cool water, her body was warm as bread fresh from the oven, cold and heat together, and when he told her this, she entwined her arms around his neck.

'I'm Sam the baked Alaska, eat me!' she laughed, and the droplets clung to her eyelashes like diamond chips in the sunlight.

Even in the presence of others, they walked alone; for

them, nobody else really existed. Among those who had come from all over the world to ride the long sea at Cape St Francis were many who knew Samantha, from Florida and California, from Australia and Hawaii, where her field trips and her preoccupation with the sea and the life of the sea had taken her.

'Hey, Sam!' they shouted, dropping their boards in the sand and running to her, tall muscular men, burned dark as chestnuts in the sun. She smiled at them vaguely, holding Nicholas' hand a little tighter, and replied to their chatter absentmindedly, drifting away at the first opportunity.

'Who was that?'

'It's terrible, but I can't remember – I'm not even sure where I met him or when.' And it was true, she could concentrate on nothing but Nicholas, and the others sensed it swiftly and left them alone.

Nicholas had not been in the sun for over a year, his body was the colour of old ivory, in sharp contrast to the thick dark body hair which covered his chest and belly. At the end of that first day in the sun, the ivory colour had turned to a dull angry red.

'You'll suffer,' she told him, but the next morning his body and limbs had gone the colour of mahogany and she drew back the sheets and marvelled at it, touching him exploringly with the tip of her fingers.

'I'm lucky, I've got a hide like a buffalo,' he told her.

Each day he turned darker, until he was the weathered bronze of an American Indian, and his high cheekbones heightened the resemblance.

'You must have Indian blood,' she told him, tracing his nose with her fingertip.

'I only know two generations back,' he smiled at her. 'I've always been terrified to look further than that.'

She sat over him, cross-legged in the big bed and touched him, exploring him with her hands, touching his lips and the lobes of his ears, smoothing the thick dark curve of his eyebrows, the little black mole on his cheek, and exclaiming at each new discovery.

She touched him when they walked, reaching for his hand, pressing her hip against him when they stood, on the beach sitting between his spread knees and leaning back against his chest, her head tucked into his shoulder – it was as if she needed constant physical assurance of his presence.

When they sat astride their boards, waiting far out beyond the three-mile reef for the set of the wave, she reached across to touch his shoulder, balancing the board under her like a skilled horsewoman, the two of them close and spiritually isolated from the loose assembly of thirty or forty surf-riders strung out along the line of the long set.

This far out, the shore was a low dark green rind, above the shaded green and limpid blues of the water. In the blue distance, the mountains were blue on the blue of the sky and above them, the thunderheads piled dazzling silver, tall and arrogant enough to dwarf the very earth.

'This must be the most beautiful land in the world,' she said, moving her board so that her knee lay against his thigh.

'Because you are here,' he told her.

Under them, the green water breathed like a living thing, rising and falling, the swells long and glassy, sliding away towards the land.

Growing impatient, one of the inexperienced riders would move to catch a bad swell, kneeling on the board and paddling with both hands, coming up unsteadily on to his feet and then toppling and falling as the water left him, and the taunts and friendly catcalls of his peers greeted him as he surfaced, grinning sheepishly, and crawled back on to his board.

Then the ripple of excitement, and a voice calling, 'A three set!' the boards quickly rearranging themselves, sculled by cupped bare hands, spacing out for running room, the riders peering back eagerly over their dark burned shoulders, laughing and kidding each other as the wave set bumped up on the horizon, still four miles out at sea, but big enough so that they could count the individual swells that made up the set.

Running at fifty miles an hour, the swells took nearly five minutes, from the moment when they were sighted, to reach the line, and during that time Samantha had a little ritual of preparation. First, she hoisted the bottom of her bikini which had usually slipped down to expose a pair of dimples and a little of the deep cleft of her buttocks, then she tightened her top hamper, pulling open the brassière of her costume and cupping each breast in turn, settling it firmly in its sheath of thin green cloth, grinning at Nick as she did it.

'You're not supposed to watch.'

'I know, it's bad for my heart.'

Then she plucked out a pair of hairpins and held them in her mouth as she twisted the wrist-thick plait of hair tighter until it hung down between her shoulder blades and pinned back the wisps over her ears.

'All set?' he called, and she nodded and answered,

'Ride three?'

The third wave in the set was traditionally the big one, and they let the first one swing them high and drop them again into its trough. Half the other riders were up and away, only their heads still visible above the peak of the wave, the land obscured by the moving wall of water.

The second wave came through, bigger, more powerful, but swooping up and over the crest and most of the other riders went on it, two or three tumbling on the steep front of water, losing their boards, dragged under as the ankle lines came up taut.

'Here we go!' exulted Samantha, and three came rustling, green and peaking, and in the transparent wall of water four big bottle-nosed porpoises were framed, in perfect motion, racing in the wave, pumping their flat delta-shaped tails and grinning that fixed porpoise grin of delight.

'Oh look!' sang Samantha. 'Just look at them, Nicholas!'

Then the wave was upon them and they sculled frantically, weight high on the board, the heart-stopping moment when it seemed the water would sweep away and leave them, then suddenly the boards coming alive under them and starting to run, tipping steeply forward, with the hiss of the waxed fibreglass through the water.

Then they were both up and laughing in the sunlight, dancing the intricate steps that balanced and controlled the boards, lifted high on the crest, so they could see the sweep of the beach three miles ahead, and the ranks of other riders on the twin waves that had gone before them.

One of the porpoises frolicked with them on the racing crest, ducking under the flying boards, turning on its side to grin up at Samantha, so she stooped and stretched out a hand to touch him, lost her balance, and almost fell while the porpoise grinned at her mischievously and flipped away to rise fin up on her far side.

Now, out on their right hand, the wave was feeling the reef and starting to curl over on itself, the crest arching forwards, holding that lovely shape for long moments, then slowly collapsing.

'Go left,' Nick called urgently to her, and they kicked the boards around and danced up on to the stubby prows, bending at the knees to ride the hurtling craft, their speed rocketing as they cut across the green face of the wave, but behind them the arching wave spread rapidly towards them, faster than they could run before it.

Now at their left shoulders, the water formed a steep vertical wall, and, glancing at it, Samantha found the porpoise swimming head-high beside her, his great tail pumping powerfully, and she was afraid, for the majesty and strength of that wave belittled her.

'Nicholas!' she screamed, and the wave fanned out over her head, arcing across the sky, cutting out the sunlight, and now they flew down a long, perfectly rounded tunnel of roaring water. The sides were smooth as blown glass, and the light was green and luminous and weird as though they sped through a deep submarine cavern, only ahead of them was the perfect round opening at the mouth of the tunnel – while behind her, close behind her, the tunnel was collapsing in a furious thunder of murderous white water, and she was as terrified and as exulted as she had ever been in her life.

He yelled at her, 'We must beat the curl,' and his voice was far away and almost lost in the roar of water, but obediently she went forward on her board until all her bare toes were curled over the leading edge.

For long moments they held their own, then slowly they began to gain, and at last they shot out through the open mouth of the tunnel into the sunlight again, and she laughed wildly, still high on the exultation of fresh terror.

Then they were past the reef and the wave firmed up, leaving the white water like lace on the surface far behind.

'Let's go right!' Samantha sang out to stay within the good structure of the wave, and they turned and went back, swinging across the steep face. The splatter of flung water sparkled on her belly and thighs, and the plait of her hair stood out behind her head like the tail of an angry lioness, her arms were extended and her hands held open, unconsciously making the delicate finger gestures of a Balinese temple dancer as she balanced; and miraculously the porpoise swam, fin up, beside her, following like a trained dog.

Then at last, the wave felt the beach and ran berserk, tumbling wildly upon itself, booming angrily, and churning the sand like gruel, and they kicked out of the wave, falling back over the crest and dropping into the sea beside the bobbing boards, laughing and panting at each other with the excitement and terror and the joy of it.

Samantha was a sea-creature with a huge appetite for the fruits of the sea, cracking open the crayfish legs in her fingers and sucking the white sticks of flesh into her mouth with a noisy sensuality, while her lips were polished with butter sauce, not taking her eyes from his face as she ate.

Samantha in the candlelight gulping those huge Knysna oysters, and then slurping the juice out of the shells.

'You're talking with your mouth full.'

'It's just that I've still got so much to tell you,' she explained.

Samantha was laughter, laughter in fifty different tones and intensities, from the sleepy morning chortle when she awoke and found him beside her, to the wild laughter yelled from the crest of a racing wave.

Samantha was loving. With a face of thundering innocence and the virginal, guileless green eyes of a child, she combined hands and a mouth whose wiles and wicked cunning left Nick stunned and disbelieving.

'The reason I ran away without a word was that I did not want to have your ravishment and violation on my conscience,' he shook his head at her disbelievingly.

'I wrote my PhD thesis in those subjects,' she told him blithely, using her forefinger to twist spit-curls in his sweat-dampened chest hairs. 'And what's more, buster, that was just the introductory offer – now we sign you up for a full course of treatment.'

Her delight in his body was endless, she must touch and examine every inch of it, exclaiming and revelling in it without a trace of self-consciousness, holding his hand in her lap and bending her head studiously over it, tracing the lines of his palm with her fingernail.

'You are going to meet a beautiful wanton blonde, give her fifteen babies and live to be a hundred and fifty.'

She touched the little chiselled lines around his eyes and at the corners of his mouth with the tip of her tongue, leaving cool damp smears of saliva on his skin.

'I always wanted a real craggy man all for myself.'

Then, when her examination became more intimate and clinical and he demurred, she told him severely, 'Hold still, this is a private thing between me and himself.'

Then a little later.

'Oh wow! He's real poison!'

'Poison?' he demanded, his manhood denigrated.

'Poison,' she sighed. 'Because he just slays me!'

In fairness, she offered herself for his touch and scrutiny, guiding his hands, displaying herself eagerly.

'Look, touch, it's yours – all yours,' wanting his approval, not able to give him sufficient to satisfy her own need to give. 'Do you like it, Nicholas? Is this good for you? Is there anything else you want, Nicholas, anything at all that I can give you?'

And when he told her how beautiful she was, when he told her how much he wanted her, when he touched and marvelled over the gifts she brought to him, she glowed and stretched and purred like a great golden cat so that when he learned that the zodiacal sign of her birthday was Leo, he was not at all surprised.

Samantha was loving in the early slippery grey-pearl light of dawn, soft sleepy loving, with small gasps and murmurs and chuckles of deep contentment.

Samantha was loving in the sunlight, spread like a beautiful starfish in the fierce reflected sunlight of the sculptured dunes. The sand coated her body like crystals of sugar, and their cries rose together, high and ecstatic as those of the curious seagulls that floated above them on motionless white wings.

Samantha was loving in the green cool water, their two heads bobbing beyond the first line of breakers, his toes only just touching the sandy bottom and she twined about him like sea kelp about a submerged rock, clutching both their swimsuits in one hand and gurgling merrily.

'What's good enough for a lady blue whale is good enough for Samantha Silver! Thar blows Moby Dick!'

And Samantha was loving in the night, with her hair brushed out carefully and spread over him, lustrous and fragrant, a canopy of gold in the lamplight, and she kneeling astride him in almost religious awe, like a temple maid making the sacrifice.

But more than anything else, Samantha was vibrant, bursting life – and youth eternal.

Through her, Nicholas recaptured those emotions which he had believed long atrophied by cynicism and the pragmatism of living. He shared her childlike delight in the small wonders of nature, the flight of a gull, the presence of the porpoise, the discovery of the perfect translucent fan of papery nautilus shell washed up on the white sand with the rare tentacled creature still alive within the convoluted interior.

He shared her outrage when even those remote and lonely beaches were invaded by an oil slick, tank washings from a VLCC out on the Agulhas current, and the filthy clinging globules of spilled crude oil stuck to the soles of their feet, smeared the rocks and smothered the carcasses of the jackass penguins they found at the water's edge.

Samantha was life itself, just to touch the warmth of her and to drink the sound of her laughter was to be rejuvenated. To walk beside her was to feel vital and strong.

Strong enough for the long days in the sea and sun, strong enough to dance to the loud wild music half the night, and then strong enough to lift her when she faltered and carry her down to their bungalow above the beach, she in his arms like a sleepy child, her skin tingling with the memory of the sun, her muscles aching deliciously with fatigue, and her belly crammed with rich food.

'Oh Nicholas, Nicholas – I'm so happy I want to cry.'

Then Larry Fry arrived; he arrived on a cloud of indignation, red-faced and accusing as a cuckolded husband.

'Two weeks,' he blared. 'London and Bermuda and St Nazaire have been driving me mad for two weeks!' And he brandished a sheath of telex flimsies that looked like the galley proofs for the *Encyclopaedia Britannica*.

'Nobody knew what had happened to you. You just disappeared.' He ordered a large gin and tonic from the white-jacketed bartender and sank wearily on to the stool beside Nick. 'You nearly cost me my job, Mr Berg, and that's the truth. You'd have thought I'd bumped you off personally and dumped your body in the bay. I had to hire a private detective to check every hotel register in the country.' He took a long, soothing draught of the gin.

At that moment, Samantha drifted into the cocktail lounge. She wore a loose, floating dress the same green as her eyes, and a respectful hush fell on the pre-luncheon drinkers as they watched her cross the room. Larry Fry forgot his indignation and gaped at her, his bald scorched head growing shining under a thin film of perspiration.

'Godstrewth,' he muttered. 'I'd rather feel that, than feel sick.' And then his admiration turned to consternation when she came directly to Nicholas, laid her hand on his shoulder and in full view of the entire room kissed him lingeringly on the mouth.

There was a soft collective sigh from the watchers and Larry Fry knocked over his gin.

'We must go now, today,' Samantha decided. 'We mustn't stay even another hour, Nicholas, or we will spoil it. It was perfect, but now we must go.'

Nicholas understood. Like him she had the compulsion to keep moving forward. Within the hour, he had chartered a twin-engined Beechcraft Baron. It picked them up at the little earth strip near the hotel and put them down at Johannesburg's Jan Smuts Airport an hour before the departure of the UTA flight for Paris.

'I always rode in the back of the bus before,' said Samantha, as she looked around the first-class cabin appraisingly. 'Is it true that up this end you can eat and drink as much as you like, for free?'

'Yes.' Then Nick added hastily, 'But you don't have to take that as a personal challenge.' Nicholas had come to stand in awe of Samantha's appetites.

They stayed overnight at the Georges V in Paris and caught the mid-morning TAT flight down to Nantes, the nearest airfield to the shipyards at St Nazaire, and Jules Levoisin was there to meet them at the Château Bougon field.

'Nicholas!' he shouted joyfully, and stood on tiptoe to buss both his cheeks, enveloping him in a fragrant cloud of eau de Cologne and pomade. 'You are a pirate, Nicholas, you stole that ship from under my nose. I hate you.' He held Nicholas at arm's length. 'I warned you not to take the job, didn't I?'

'You did, Jules, you did.'

'So why do you make a fool of me?' he demanded, and twirled his moustaches. He was wearing expensive cashmere and an Yves St Laurent necktie; ashore, Jules was always the dandy.

'Jules, I am going to buy lunch for you at La Rôtisserie,' Nicholas promised.

'I forgive you,' said Jules, it was one of his favourite

eating-places – but at that moment Jules became aware that Nicholas was not travelling alone.

He stood back, took one long look at Samantha and it seemed that tricolours unfurled around him and brass bands burst into the opening bars of 'La Marseillaise'. For if dalliance was the national sport, Jules Levoisin considered himself veteran champion of all France.

He bowed over her hand, and tickled the back of it with his still black moustache. Then he told Nicholas, 'She is too good for you, *mon petit*, I am going to take her away from you.'

'The same way you did *Golden Adventurer?*' Nick asked innocently.

Jules had his ancient Citroën in the car park. It was lovingly waxed and fitted with shiny gewgaws and dangling mascots. He handed Samantha into the front seat as though it was a Rolls Camargue.

'He's beautiful,' she whispered, as he scampered around to the driver's door.

Jules could not devote attention to both the road ahead and to Samantha, so he concentrated solely upon her, without deviating from the Citroën's top speed, only occasionally turning to shout, '*Cochon!*' at another driver or jerk his fist at them with the second finger pointed stiffly upwards in ribald salutation.

'Jules' great-grandfather charged with the Emperor's cavalry at Quatre Bras,' Nick explained. 'He is a man without fear.'

'You will enjoy La Rôtisserie,' Jules told Samantha. 'I can only afford to eat there when I find somebody rich who wishes a favour of me.'

'How do you know I want a favour?' Nick asked from the back seat, clinging to the door-handle.

'Three telegrams, a telephone call from Bermuda – another from Johannesburg,' Jules chuckled fruitily and winked at Samantha. 'You think I believe Nicholas Berg wants to discuss old times? You think I believe he feels so deeply for his old friend, who taught him everything he knows? A man who treated him like a son, and whom he blatantly robbed—' Jules sped across the Loire bridge and plunged into that tangled web of narrow one-way streets and teeming traffic which is Nantes; a way opened for him miraculously.

In the Place Briand, he handed Samantha gallantly from the Citroën, and in the restaurant he puffed out his cheeks and made little anxious clucking and tut-tutting noises, as Nicholas discussed the wine list with the *sommelier* – but he nodded reluctant approval when they settled on a Chablis Moutonne and a Chambertin-Clos-de-Bèze, then he applied himself with equal gusto to the food, the wine and Samantha.

'You can tell a woman who is made for life and love, by the way she eats,' and when Samantha made wide lascivious eyes at him over her trout, Nicholas expected him to crow like a cockerel.

Only when the cognac was in front of them, and both he and Nick had lit cheroots, did he demand abruptly:

'So, now, Nicholas, I am in a good mood. Ask me.'

'I need a Master for my new tug,' said Nick, and Jules veiled his face behind a thick blue curtain of cigar smoke.

They fenced like masters of épée all the way from Nantes to St Nazaire.

'Those ships you build, Nicholas, are not tugs. They are fancy toys, floating bordellos – all those gimmicks and gadgets—'

'Those gimmicks and gadgets enabled me to deal with Christy Marine while you still hadn't realized that I was within a thousand miles.' Jules blew out his cheeks and muttered to himself.

'Twenty-two thousand horsepower, *c'est ridicule!* They are over-powered—'

'I needed every single one of those horses when I pulled *Golden Adventurer* off Cape Alarm.'

'Nicholas, do not keep reminding me of that shameful episode.' He turned to Samantha. 'I am hungry, *ma petite*, and in the next village there is a *pâtisserie*,' he sighed and kissed his bunched fingers, 'you will adore the pastry.'

'Try me,' she invited, and Jules had found a soulmate.

'Those fancy propellers – variable pitch – ouf!' Jules spoke through a mouthful of pastry, and there was whipped cream on his moustache.

'I can make twenty-five knots and then slam *Warlock* into reverse thrust and stop her within her own length.'

Jules changed pace, and attacked from a new direction.

'You'll never find full employment for two big expensive ships like that.'

'I'm going to need four, not two,' Nick contradicted him. 'We are going to catch icebergs,' and Jules forgot to chew, as he listened intently for the next ten minutes. 'One of the beauties of the iceberg scheme is that all my ships will be operating right on the tanker lanes, the busiest shipping lanes in all the oceans—'

'Nicholas,' Jules shook his head in admiration, 'you move too fast for me. I am an old man, old-fashioned—'

'You're not old,' Samantha told him firmly. 'You're only just in your prime.' And Jules threw up both hands theatrically.

'Now you have a pretty girl heaping flattery on my bowed grey head,' he looked at Nicholas; 'is no trick too deceitful for you?'

It was snowing the next morning, a slow sparse sprinkling from a grey woollen sky, when they drove into St Nazaire from the little seaside resort of La Baule twenty-five kilometres up the Atlantic coast.

Jules had a small flat in one of the apartment blocks. It was a convenient arrangement, for *La Mouette*, his command, was owned by a Breton company and St Nazaire was her home port. It was a mere twenty-minute drive before they made out the elegant arch of the suspension bridge which crosses the estuarine mouth of the Loire river at St Nazaire.

Jules drove through the narrow streets of that area of the docks just below the bridge which comprises the sprawling shipbuilding yard of Construction Navale Atlantique, one of the three largest shipbuilding companies in Europe.

The slipways for the larger vessels, the bulk carriers and naval craft, faced directly on to the wide smooth reach of the river; but the ways for the small vessels backed on to the inner harbour.

So Jules parked the Citroën at the security gates nearest the inner harbour, and they walked through to where Charles Gras was waiting for them in his offices overlooking the inner basin.

'Nicholas, it is good to see you again.' Gras was one of Atlantique's top engineers, a tall stooped man with a pale face and lank black hair that fell to his eyebrows, but he had the sharp foxy Parisian features and quick bright eyes that belied the morose unsmiling manner.

He and Nicholas had known each other many years, and they used the familiar 'tu' form of address.

Charles Gras changed to heavily accented English when he was introduced to Samantha, and back to French when he asked Nicholas,

'If I know you, you will want to go directly to see your ship now, *n'est-ce pas?*'

*Sea Witch* stood high on her ways, and although she

was an identical twin to *Warlock*, she seemed almost twice her size with her underwater hull exposed. Despite the fact that the superstructure was incomplete and she was painted in the drab oxide red of marine primer, yet it was impossible to disguise the symmetrically functional beauty of her lines.

Jules puffed, and muttered '*Bordello*' and made remarks about 'Admiral Berg and his battleship', but he could not hide the gleam in his eye as he strutted about the incomplete navigation bridge, or listened intently as Charles Gras explained the electronic equipment and the other refinements that made the ship so fast, efficient and manoeuvrable.

Nick realized that the two experts should be left alone now to convince each other; it was clear that although this was their first meeting the two of them had established an immediate rapport.

'Come.' Nick quietly took Samantha's arm and they stepped carefully around the scaffolding and loose equipment, picking their way through groups of workmen to the upper deck.

The snow had stopped, but a razor of a wind snickered in from the Atlantic. They found a sheltered corner, and Samantha pressed close to Nick, snuggling into the circle of his arm.

High on her ways, *Sea Witch* gave them a sweeping view, through the forest of construction cranes, over the roofs of the warehouses and offices to the river slipways where the keels of the truly big hulls were laid down.

'You spoke about *Golden Dawn*,' Nick said. 'There she is.'

It took some moments for Samantha to realize she was looking at a ship.

'My God,' she breathed. 'It's so big.'

'They don't come bigger,' he agreed.

The structure of steel was almost a mile and a half long,

three city blocks, and the hull was as tall as a five-storey building, while the navigation tower was another 100 feet higher than that.

Samantha shook her head. 'It's beyond belief. It looks like – like a city! It's terrifying to think of that thing afloat.'

'That is only the main hull, the tank pods have been constructed in Japan. The last I heard is that they are under tow direct to the Persian Gulf.'

Nick stared solemnly across the ship, blinking his eyes against the stinging wind.

'I must have been out of my mind,' he whispered, 'to dream up a monster like that.' But there was a touch of defiant pride in his tone.

'It's so big – beyond imagination,' she encouraged him to talk about it. 'How big *is* it?'

'It's not a single vessel,' he explained. 'No harbour in the world could take a ship that size, it could not even approach the continental United States, for that matter, there is just not enough water to float it.'

'Yes?' She loved to listen to him expound his vision, she loved to hear the force and power of his convictions.

'What you're seeing is the carrying platform, the accommodation and the main power source.' He held her closer. 'On to that, we attach the four tank pods, each one of them capable of carrying a quarter of a million tons of crude oil, each tank almost as large as the biggest ship afloat.'

He was still explaining the concept while they sat at lunch, and Charles Gras and Jules Levoisin listened as avidly as she did.

'A single rigid hull of those dimensions would crack and break up in heavy seas,' he took the cruet set and used it to demonstrate, 'but the four individual pods have been designed so that they can move independently of each other. This gives them the ability to ride and absorb the movement of heavy seas. It is the most important principle of ship construction, a hull must ride the water – not try to oppose it.'

Across the table, Charles Gras nodded lugubrious agreement.

'The tank pods hive on to the main hull, and are carried upon it like remora on the body of a shark, not using their own propulsion systems, but relying on the multiple boilers and quadruple screws of the main hull to carry them across the oceans.' He pushed the cruet set around the table and they all watched it with fascination. 'Then, when it reaches the continental shelf opposite the shore discharge site, the main hull anchors, forty or fifty, even a hundred miles offshore, detaches one or two or all of its pod tanks, and they make those last few miles under their own propulsion. In protected water and in chosen weather conditions, their propulsion systems will handle them safely. Then the empty pod ballasts itself and returns to hook on to the main hull.'

As he spoke, Nicholas detached the salt cellar from the cruet and docked it against Samantha's plate. The two Frenchmen were silent, staring at the silver salt cellar, but Samantha watched Nick's face. It was burned dark by the sun now, lean and handsome, and he seemed charged and vital, like a thoroughbred horse in the peak of training, and she was proud of him, proud of the force of his personality that made other men listen when he spoke, proud of the imagination and the courage it took to conceive and then put into operation a project of this magnitude. Even though it were no longer his – yet his had been the vision.

Now Nicholas was talking again. 'Civilization is addicted to liquid fossil fuels. Without them, it would be forced into a withdrawal trauma too horrible to contemplate. If then we have to use crude, let's pipe it out of the earth, transport and ship it with all possible precautions to protect ourselves from its side effects—'

'Nicholas,' Charles Gras interrupted him abruptly. 'When last did you inspect the drawings of *Golden Dawn?*'

Nick paused, taken in full stride and a little off balance. He frowned as he cast back, 'I walked out of Christy Marine just over a year ago.' And the darkness of those days settled upon him, making his eyes bleak.

'A year ago we had not even been awarded the contract for the construction of *Golden Dawn*.' Charles Gras twisted the stem of his wineglass between his fingers, and thrust out his bottom lip. 'The ship you have just described to us is very different from the ship we are building out there.'

'In what way, Charles?' Nick's concern was immediate, a father hearing of radical surgery upon his first-born.

'The concept is the same. The mother vessel and the four tank pods, but—' Charles shrugged, that eloquent Gallic gesture, 'it would be easier to show it to you. Immediately after lunch.'

'*D'accord*,' Jules Levoisin nodded. 'But on the condition that it does not interfere with the further enjoyment of this fine meal.' He nudged Nicholas. 'If you eat with a scowl on your face, *mon vieux*, you will grow yourself ulcers like a bunch of Loire grapes.'

Standing beneath the bulk of *Golden Dawn*, she seemed to reach up into that low grey snow-sky, like a mighty alp of steel. The men working on the giddy heights of her scaffolding were small as insects, and quite unbelievably, as Samantha stared up at them, a little torn streamer of wet grey cloud, coming up the Loire basin from the sea, blew over the ship, obscuring the top of her navigation bridge for a few moments.

'She reaches up to the clouds,' said Nick beside her, and the pride was in his voice as he turned back to Charles Gras. 'She looks good?' It was a question, not a statement. 'She looks like the ship I planned—'

'Come, Nicholas.'

The little party picked its way through the chaos of the yard. The squeal of power cranes and the rumble of heavy steel transporters, the electric hissing crackle of the huge automatic running welders combined with the roaring gunfire barrage of the riveters into a cacophony that numbed the senses. The scaffolding and hoist systems formed an almost impenetrable forest about the mountainous hull, and steel and concrete were glistening wet and rimmed with thin clear ice.

It was a long walk through the crowded yard, almost twenty minutes merely to round the tanker's stern – and suddenly Nicholas stopped so abruptly that Samantha collided with him and might have fallen on the icy concrete, but he caught her arm and held her as he stared up at the bulbous stern.

It formed a great overhanging roof like that of a medieval cathedral, so that Nick's head was flung back, and the grip on her arm tightened so fiercely that she protested. He seemed not to hear, but went on staring upwards.

'Yes,' Charles Gras nodded, and the lank black hair flopped against his forehead. 'That is one difference from the ship you designed.'

The propeller was in lustrous ferro-bronze, six-bladed, each shaped with the beauty and symmetry of a butterfly's wing, but so enormous as to make the comparison laughable. It was so big that not even the bulk of *Golden Dawn*'s own hull could dwarf it, each separate blade was longer and broader than the full wingspan of a jumbo-jet airliner, a gargantuan sculpture in gleaming metal.

'One!' whispered Nick. 'One only.'

'Yes,' Charles Gras agreed. 'Not four – but one propeller only. Also, Nicholas, it is fixed pitch.'

They were all silent as they rode up in the cage of the hoist. The hoist ran up the outside of the hull to the level of the main deck, and though the wind searched for them remorselessly through the open mesh of the cage, it was not the cold that kept them silent.

The engine compartment was an echoing cavern,

harshly lit by the overhead floodlights, and they stood high on one of the overhead steel catwalks looking down fifty feet on to the boiler and condensers of the main engine.

Nick stared down for almost five minutes. He asked no questions, made no judgements, but at last he turned to Charles Gras and nodded once curtly.

'All right. I've seen enough,' he said, and the engineer led them to the elevator station. Again they rode upwards. It was like being in a modern office block – the polished chrome and wood panelling of the elevator, the carpeted passageways high in the navigation tower along which Charles Gras led them to the Master's suite and unlocked the carved mahogany doorway with a key from his watch chain.

Jules Levoisin looked slowly about the suite and shook his head wonderingly. 'Ah, this is the way to live,' he breathed. 'Nicholas, I absolutely insist that the Master's quarters of *Sea Witch* be decorated like this.'

Nick did not smile, but crossed to the view windows that looked forward along the tanker's main deck to her round, blunt, unlovely prow a mile and a quarter away. He stood with his hands clasped behind his back, legs apart, chin thrust out angrily and nobody else spoke while Charles Gras opened the elaborate bar and poured cognac into the crystal brandy balloons. He carried a glass to Nick who turned away from the window.

'Thank you, Charles. I need something to warm the chill in my guts.' Nick sipped the cognac and rolled it on his tongue as he looked slowly around the opulent cabin.

It occupied almost half the width of the navigation bridge, and was large enough to house a diplomatic reception. Duncan Alexander had picked a good decorator to do the job, and without the view from the window it might have been an elegant Fifth Avenue New York apartment, or one of those penthouses high on the cliffs above Monte Carlo, overlooking the harbour.

Slowly Nick crossed the thick green carpet, woven with the house device, the entwined letters C and M for Christy Marine, and he stopped before the Degas in its place of honour above the marble fireplace.

He remembered Chantelle's bubbling joy at the purchase of that painting. It was one of Degas' ballet pieces, soft, almost luminous light on the limbs of the dancers, and, remembering the unfailing delight that Chantelle had taken in it during the years, he was amazed that she had allowed it to be used on board one of the company ships, and that it was left here virtually unguarded and vulnerable. That painting was worth a quarter of a million pounds.

He leaned closer to it, and only then did he realize how clever a copy of the original it was. He shook his head in dismissal.

'The owners were advised that the sea air may damage the original,' Charles Gras shrugged, and spread his hands deprecatingly, 'and not many people would know the difference.'

That was typical of Duncan Alexander, Nicholas thought savagely. It could only be his idea, the sharp accountant's brain. The conviction that it was possible to fool all of the people all of the time.

Everybody knew that Chantelle owned that work, therefore nobody would doubt its authenticity. That's the way Duncan Alexander would reason it. It could not be Chantelle's idea. She had never been one to accept anything that was sham or dross; it was a measure of the power that he exerted over her, for her to go along with this cheap little fraud.

Nicholas indicated the forgery with his glass and spoke directly to Charles Gras.

'This is a cheat,' he spoke quietly, his anger contained and controlled, 'but it is harmless.' Now he turned away from it and, with a wider gesture that embraced the whole ship, went on, 'But this other cheat, this enormous fraud,' he paused to control the metallic edge that had entered his tone, going on quietly again, 'this is a vicious, murderous gamble he is taking. He has bastardized the entire concept of the scheme. One propeller instead of four – it cannot manoeuvre a hull of these dimensions with safety in any hazardous situation, it cannot deliver sufficient thrust to avoid collision, to fight her off a lee shore, to handle heavy seas.' Nick stopped, and his voice dropped even lower, yet somehow it was more compelling. 'This ship cannot, by all moral and natural laws, be operated on a single boiler. My design called for eight separate boilers and condensers, the standard set for the old White Star and Cunard Lines. But Duncan Alexander has installed a single boiler system. There is no back-up, no fail-safe – a few gallons of sea water in the system could disable this monster.'

Nicholas stopped suddenly as a new thought struck him. 'Charles,' his voice sharper still, 'the pod tanks, the design of the pod tanks. He hasn't altered that, has he? He hasn't cut the corners there? Tell me, old friend, they are still self-propelled, are they not?'

Charles Gras brought the Courvoisier bottle to where Nicholas stood, and when Nick would have refused the addition to his glass, Charles told him sorrowfully, 'Come, Nicholas, you will need it for what I have to tell you now.'

As he poured, he said, 'The pod tankers, their design has been altered also.' He drew a breath to tell it with a rush. 'They no longer have their own propulsion units. They are now only dumb barges that must be docked and undocked from the main hull and manoeuvred only by attendant tugs.'

Nicholas stared at him, his lips blanched to thin white lines. 'No. I do not believe it. Not even Duncan—'

'Duncan Alexander has saved forty-two million dollars by redesigning *Golden Dawn* and equipping her with only a single boiler and propeller.' Charles Gras shrugged again. 'And forty-two million dollars is a lot of money.'

There was a pale gleam of wintry sunlight that flickered through the low grey cloud and lit the fields not far from the River Thames with that incredibly vivid shade of English green.

Samantha and Nicholas stood in a thin line of miserably cold parents and watched the pile of struggling boys across the field in their coloured jerseys; the light blue and black of Eton, the black and white of St Paul's, were so muddied as to be barely distinguishable.

'What are they doing?' Samantha demanded, holding the collar of her coat around her ears.

'It's called a scrum,' Nick told her. 'That's how they decide which team gets the ball.'

'Wow. There must be an easier way.'

There was a flurry of sudden movement and the slippery egg-shaped ball flew back in a lazy curve that was snapped up by a boy in the Etonian colours. He started to run.

'It's Peter, isn't it?' cried Samantha.

'Go it, Peter boy!' Nick roared, and the child ran with the ball clutched to his chest and his head thrown back. He ran strongly with the reaching coordinated stride of an older boy, swerving round a knot of his opponents, leaving them floundering in the churned mud, and angling across the lush thick grass towards the white-painted goal line, trying to reach the corner before a taller, more powerfully built lad who was pounding across the field to intercept him.

Samantha began to leap up and down on the same spot, shrieking wildly, completely uncertain of what was happening, but wild with excitement that infected Nicholas.

The two runners converged at an angle which would bring them to the white line at the same moment, at a point directly in front of where Nick and Samantha stood.

Nick saw the contortion of his son's face, and realized that this was a total effort. He felt a physical constriction of his own chest as he watched the boy drive himself to his utmost limits, the sinews standing out in his throat, his lips drawn back in a frozen rictus of endeavour that exposed the teeth clenched in his jaw.

From infancy, Peter Berg had brought to any task that faced him the same complete focus of all his capabilities. Like his grandfather, old Arthur Christy, and his own father, he would be one of life's winners. Nick knew this instinctively, as he watched him run. He had inherited the intelligence, the comeliness and the charisma, but he bolstered all that with this unquenchable desire to succeed in all he did. The single-minded determination to focus all his talents on the immediate project. Nick felt the pressure in his chest swell. The boy was all right, more than all right, and pride threatened to choke him.

Sheer force of will had driven Peter Berg a pace ahead of his bigger, longer-legged adversary, and now he leaned forward with the ball held in both hands, arms fully extended, reaching for the line to make the touchdown.

He was ten feet from where Nick stood, a mere instant from success, but he was unbalanced, and the St Paul's boy dived at him, crashing into the side of his chest, the impact jarring and brutal, hurling Peter out of the field of play with the ball spinning from his hands and bouncing away loosely, while Peter smashed into the earth on both knees, then rolled forward head over heels, and sprawled face down on the soggy turf.

'It's a touchdown!' Samantha was still leaping up and down.

'No,' said Nick. 'No, it isn't.'

Peter Berg dragged himself upright. His cheek was

streaked with chocolate mud and both his knees were running blood, the skin smeared open by the coarse grass.

He did not glance down at his injuries, and he shrugged away the St Paul boy's patronizing hand, holding himself erect against the pain as he limped back on to the field. He did not look at his father, and the moisture that filled his eyes and threatened to flood over the thick dark lashes were not tears of pain, but of humiliation and failure. With an overwhelming feeling of kinship, Nick knew that for his son those feelings were harder to bear than any physical agony.

When the game ended he came to Nicholas, all bloodied and mud-smeared, and shook hands solemnly.

'I am so glad you came, sir,' he said. 'I wish you could have watched us win.'

Nick wanted to say: 'It doesn't matter, Peter, it's only a game.' But he did not. To Peter Berg, it mattered very deeply, so Nicholas nodded agreement and then he introduced Samantha.

Again Peter shook hands solemnly and startled her by calling her, 'M'am.' But when she told him, 'Hi, Pete. A great game, you deserved to slam them,' he smiled, that sudden dazzling irresistible flash that reminded her so of Nicholas that she felt her heart squeezed. Then when the boy hurried away to shower and change, she took Nick's arm.

'He's a beautiful boy, but does he always call you "sir"?'

'I haven't seen him in three months. It takes us both a little while to relax.'

'Three months is a long time—'

'It's all tied up by the lawyers. Access and visiting rights – what's good for the child, not what's good for the parents. Today was a special concession from Chantelle, but I still have to deliver him to her at five o'clock. Not five past five, five o'clock.'

They went to the Cockpit teashop and Peter startled

Samantha again by pulling out her chair and seating her formally. While they waited for the best muffins in Britain to be brought to the table, Nicholas and Peter engaged each other in conversation that was stiff with self-consciousness.

'Your mother sent me a copy of your report, Peter. I cannot tell you how delighted I was.'

'I had hoped to do better, sir. There are still three others ahead of me.'

And Samantha ached for them. Peter Berg was twelve years of age. She wished he could just throw his arms around Nicholas' neck and say, 'Daddy, I love you,' for the love was transparent, even through the veneer of public-school manners. It shone behind the thick dark lashes that fringed the boy's golden brown eyes, and glowed on the cheeks still as creamy and smooth as a girl's.

She wanted desperately to help them both, and on inspiration she launched into an account of *Warlock*'s salvage of *Golden Adventurer*, a tale with emphasis on the derring-do of *Warlock*'s Master, not forgetting his rescue of Samantha Silver from the icy seas of Antarctica.

Peter's eyes grew enormous as he listened, never leaving her face except to demand of Nicholas, 'Is that true, Dad?' And when the story was told, he was silent for a long moment before announcing, 'I'm going to be a tug captain when I'm big.'

Then he showed Samantha how to spread strawberry jam on her muffins in the correct way, and chewing together heartily with cream on their lips the two of them became fast friends, and Nicholas joined their chatter more easily, smiling his thanks to Samantha and reaching under the table to squeeze her hand.

He had to end it at last. 'Listen, Peter, if we are to make Lynwood by five—' and the boy sobered instantly.

'Dad, couldn't you telephone Mother? She might just let me spend the weekend in London with you.'

'I already tried that.' Nick shook his head. 'It didn't work,' and Peter stood up, his feeling choked by an expression of stoic resignation.

From the back of Nick's Mercedes 450 Coupé the boy leaned forward into the space between the two bucket seats, and the three of them were very close in the snug interior of the speeding car, their laughter that of old friends.

It was almost dark when Nicholas turned in through Lynwood's stone gateway, and he glanced at the luminous dial of his Rolex. 'We'll just make it.'

The drive climbed the hill in a series of broad, even curves through the carefully tended woods, and the three-storied Georgian country house on the crest was ablaze with light in every window.

Nick never came here without that strange hollow feeling in the bottom of his stomach. Once this had been his home, every room, every acre of the grounds had its memories, and now, as he parked under the white columned portico, they came crowding back.

'I have finished the model Spitfire you sent me for Christmas, Dad.' Peter was playing desperately for time now. 'Won't you come up and see it?'

'I don't think so—' Nicholas began, and Peter blurted out before he could finish.

'It's all right, Uncle Duncan won't be here. He always comes down late from London on Friday nights, and his Rolls isn't in the garage yet.' Then, in a tone that tore at Nick like thorns, 'Please . . . I won't see you again until Easter.'

'Go,' said Samantha. 'I'll wait here.' And Peter turned on her, 'You come too, Sam, please.'

Samantha felt herself infected by that fatal curiosity, the desire to see, to know more of Nick's past life; she knew he was going to demur further, but she forestalled him, slipping quickly out of the Mercedes.

'Okay, Pete, let's go.'

Nick must follow them up the broad steps to the double oaken doors, and he felt himself carried along on a tide of events over which he had no control. It was a sensation that he never relished.

In the entrance hall Samantha looked around her quickly, feeling herself overcome by awe. It was so grand, there was no other word to describe the house. The stairwell reached up the full height of the three storeys, and the broad staircase was in white marble with a marble balustrade, while on each side of the hall, glass doors opened on to long reception rooms. But she did not have a chance to look further, for Peter seized her hand and raced her up the staircase, while Nick followed them up to Peter's room at a more sedate pace.

The Spitfire had place of honour on the shelf above Peter's bed. He brought it down proudly, and they examined it with suitable expressions of admiration. Peter responded to their praise like a flower to the sun.

When at last they descended the staircase, the sadness and restraint of parting was on them all, but they were stopped in the centre of the hall by the voice from the drawing-room door on the left.

'Peter, darling.' A woman stood in the open doorway, and she was even more beautiful than the photograph that Samantha had seen of her.

Dutifully Peter crossed to her. 'Good evening, Mother.'

She stooped over him, cupping his face in her hands, and she kissed him tenderly, then she straightened, holding his hand so he was ranged at her side, a subtle drawing of boundaries.

'Nicholas,' she tilted her head, 'you look marvellous – so brown and fit.'

Chantelle Alexander was only a few inches taller than her son, but she seemed to fill and light the huge house with a shimmering presence, the way a single beautiful bird can light a dim forest.

Her hair was dark and soft and glowing, and her skin and the huge dark sloe eyes were a legacy from the beautiful Persian noblewoman that old Arthur Christy had married for her fortune, and come to love with an obsessive passion.

She was dainty. Her tiny, narrow feet peeped from below the long, dark green silk skirt, and the exquisite little hand that held Peter's was emphasized by a single deep throbbing green emerald the size of a ripe acorn.

Now she turned her head on the long graceful neck, and her eyes took the slightly oriental slant of a modern-day Nefertiti as she looked at Samantha.

For seconds only, the two women studied each other, and Samantha's chin came up firmly as she looked into those deep dark gazelle eyes, touched with all the mystery and intrigue of the East. They understood each other instantly. It was an intuitive flash, like a discharge of static electricity, then Chantelle smiled, and when she smiled the impossible happened – she became more beautiful than before.

'May I present Dr Silver?' Nick began, but Peter tugged at his mother's hand.

'I asked Sam to see my model. She's a marine biologist, and she's a professor at Miami University—'

'Not yet, Pete,' Samantha corrected him, 'but give me time.'

'Good evening, Dr Silver. It seems you have made a conquest.' Chantelle let the statement hang ambiguously as she turned back to Nick. 'I was waiting for you, Nicholas, and I'm so glad to have a chance to speak to you.' She glanced again at Samantha. 'I do hope you will excuse us for a few minutes, Dr Silver. It is a matter of some urgency. Peter will be delighted to entertain you. As a biologist, you will find his guinea pigs of interest, I'm sure.'

The commands were given so graciously, by a lady in such control of her situation, that Peter went to take Samantha's hand and lead her away.

It was one of the customs of Lynwood that all serious discussion took place in the study. Chantelle led the way, and went immediately to the false-fronted bookcase that concealed the liquor cabinet, and commenced the ritual of preparing a drink for Nicholas. He wanted to stop her. It was something from long ago, recalling too much that was painful, but instead, he watched the delicate but precise movements of her hands pouring exactly the correct measure of Chivas Royal Salute into the crystal glass, adding the soda and the single cube of ice.

'What a pretty young girl, Nicholas.'

He said nothing. On the ornate Louis Quatorze desk was a silver-framed photograph of Duncan Alexander and Chantelle together, and he looked away and moved to the fireplace, standing with his back to the blaze as he had done on a thousand other evenings.

Chantelle brought the glass to him, and stood close, looking up at him – and her fragrance touched a deep nostalgic chord. He had first bought *Calèche* for her on a spring morning in Paris; with an effort he forced the memory aside.

'What did you want to speak to me about, is it Peter?'

'No. Peter is doing as well as we can hope for, in the circumstances. He still resents Duncan – but—' she shrugged, and moved away. He had almost forgotten how narrow was her waist, he would still be able to span it with both hands.

'It's hard to explain, but it's Christy Marine, Nicholas. I desperately need the advice of someone I can trust.'

'You can trust me?' he asked.

'Isn't it strange? I would still trust you with my life.' She came back to him, standing disconcertingly close, enveloping him with her scent and heady beauty. He sipped at the whisky to distract himself.

'Even though I have no right to ask you, Nicholas, still I know you won't refuse me, will you?'

She wove spells, he could feel the mesh falling like gossamer around him.

'I always was a sucker, wasn't I?'

Now she touched his arm. 'No, Nicholas, please don't be bitter.' She held his gaze directly.

'How can I help you?' Her touch on his arm disturbed him, and, sensing this, she increased the pressure of her fingers for a moment, then lifted her hand and glanced at the slim white gold Piaget on her wrist.

'Duncan will be home soon – and what I have to tell you is long and complicated. Can we meet in London early next week?'

'Chantelle,' he began.

'Nicky, please.' *Nicky*, she was the only one who ever called him that. It was too familiar, too intimate.

'When?'

'You are meeting Duncan on Tuesday morning to discuss the arbitration of *Golden Adventurer*.'

'Yes.'

'Will you call me at Eaton Square when you finish? I'll wait by the telephone.'

'Chantelle—'

'Nicky, I have nobody else to turn to.'

He had never been able to refuse her – which was part of the reason he had lost her, he thought wryly.

There was no engine noise, just the low rush of air past the body of the Mercedes.

'Damn these seats, they weren't made for lovers,' Samantha said.

'We'll be home in an hour.'

'I don't know if I can wait that long,' Samantha whispered huskily. 'I want to be closer to you.'

And they were silent again, until they slowed for the weekend traffic through Hammersmith.

'Peter is a knockout. If only I were ten years old, I'd cash in my dolls.'

'My guess is he would swop his Spitfire.'

'How much longer?'

'Another half-hour.'

'Nicholas, I feel threatened,' her voice had a sudden panicky edge to it. 'I have this terrible foreboding—'

'That's nonsense.'

'It's been too good – for too long.'

James Teacher was the head of Salmon, Peters and Teacher, the lawyers that Nick had retained for Ocean Salvage. He was a man with a formidable reputation in the City, a leading expert on maritime law – and a tough bargainer. He was florid and bald, and so short that his feet did not touch the floorboards of the Bentley when he sat on the back seat.

He and Nick had discussed in detail where this preliminary meeting with Christy Marine should be held, and at last they had agreed to go to the mountain, but James Teacher had insisted on arriving in his chocolate-coloured Bentley, rather than a cab.

'Smoked salmon, Mr Berg, not fish and chips – that's what we are after.'

Christy House was one of those conservative smoke-stained stone buildings fronted on to Leadenhall Street, the centre of Britain's shipping industry. Almost directly opposite was Trafalgar House, and a hundred yards further was Lloyd's of London. The doorman crossed the pavement to open Nicholas' door.

'Good to see you again, Mr Berg sir.'

'Hello, Alfred. You taking good care of the shop?'

'Indeed, sir.'

The following cab, containing James Teacher's two juniors and their bulky briefcases, pulled up behind the Bentley and they assembled on the pavement like a party of raiding Vikings before the gates of a medieval city. The three lawyers settled their bowler hats firmly and then moved forward determinedly in spearhead formation.

In the lobby, the doorman passed them on to a senior clerk who was waiting by the desk.

'Good morning, Mr Berg. You are looking very well, sir.'

They rode up at a sedate pace in the elevator with its antique steel concertina doors. Nicholas had never brought himself to exchange them for those swift modern boxes. And the clerk ushered them out on to the top-floor landing.

'Will you follow me, please, gentlemen?'

There was an antechamber that opened on to the board room, a large room, panelled and hung with a single portrait of old Arthur Christy on the entrance wall – fighting jaw and sharp black eyes under beetling white eyebrows. A log fire burned in the open grate, and there was sherry and Madeira in crystal decanters on the central table – another one of the old man's little traditions – that both James Teacher and Nick refused curtly.

They waited quietly, standing facing the door into the Chairman's suite. They waited for exactly four minutes before the door was thrown open and Duncan Alexander stepped through it.

His eyes flicked across the room and settled instantly on Nick, locking with his, like the horns of two great bull buffalo, and the room was very still.

The lawyers around Nick seemed to shrink back and the men behind Duncan Alexander waited, not yet following him into the antechamber, but all of them watched and waited avidly; this meeting would be the gossip of the City for weeks to come. It was a classic confrontation, and they wanted to miss not a moment of it.

Duncan Alexander was a strikingly good-looking man, very tall, two inches taller than Nick, but slim as a dancer, and he carried his body with a dancer's control. His face also was narrow, with the long lantern jaw of a young Lincoln, already chiselled by life around the eyes and at the corners of the mouth.

His hair was very dense and a metallic blond; though he wore it fashionably long over the ears, yet it was so carefully groomed that each gleaming wave seemed to have been sculptured.

His skin was smooth and tanned darker than his hair, sunlamp or skiing at Chantelle's lodge at Gstaad perhaps, and now when he smiled his teeth were dazzlingly white, perfect large teeth in the wide friendly mouth – but the eyes did not smile though they crinkled at the corners. Duncan Alexander watched from behind the handsome face like a sniper in ambush.

'Nicholas,' he said, without moving forward or offering a hand.

'Duncan,' said Nick quietly, not answering the smile, and Duncan Alexander adjusted the hang of his lapel. His clothes were beautifully cut, and the cloth was the finest, softest wool, but there were foppish little touches: the hacking slits in the tails of the jacket, the double-flapped pockets, and the waistcoat in plum-coloured velvet. Now he touched the buttons with his fingertips, another little distracting gesture, the only evidence of any discomfort.

Nicholas stared at him steadily, trying to measure him dispassionately, and now for the first time he began to see how it might have happened. There was a sense of excitement about the man, a wicked air of danger, the fascination of the leopard – or some other powerful predator. Nick could understand the almost irresistible attraction he had for women, especially for a spoiled and bored lady, a matron of thirteen years who believed there was still excitement and adventure in life that she was missing. Duncan had done his cobra dance, and Chantelle had watched like a mesmerized bird of paradise – until she had toppled from the branch – or that's how Nicholas liked to think it had happened. He was wiser now, much wiser and more cynical.

'Before we begin,' Nick knew that anger was seething to his still surface, must soon bubble through unless he could give it release, 'I should like five minutes in private.'

'Of course.' Duncan inclined his head, and there was a hurried scampering as his minions cleared the doorway into the Chairman's suite. 'Come through.'

Duncan stood aside, and Nick walked through. The offices had been completely redecorated, and Nick blinked with surprise, white carpets and furniture in chrome and perspex, stark abstract geometrical art in solid primary colours on the walls; the ceiling had been lowered by an eggcrate design in chrome steel and free-swivelling studio spotlights gave selected light patterns on wall and ceiling. It was no improvement, Nick decided.

'I was in St Nazaire last week.' Nicholas turned in the centre of the wide snowy floor and faced Duncan Alexander as he closed the door.

'Yes, I know.'

'I went over *Golden Dawn*.'

Duncan Alexander snapped open a gold cigarette case and offered it to Nick, then when he shook his head in refusal, selected one himself. They were a special blend, custom-made for him by Benson and Hedges.

'Charles Gras exceeded his authority,' Duncan nodded. 'Visitors are not allowed on *Golden Dawn*.'

'I am not surprised you are ashamed of that death-trap you are building.'

'But you do surprise me, Nicholas.' Duncan showed his teeth again. 'It was your design.'

'You know it was not. You took the idea, and bastardized it. Duncan, you cannot send that,' Nick sought the word, 'monster on to the open sea. Not with one propulsion unit, and a single screw. The risk is too appalling.'

'I tell you this for no good reason, except perhaps that this was once your office,' Duncan made a gesture that embraced the room, 'and because it amuses me to point out to you the faults in your original planning. The concept was sound, but you soured the cream by adding those preposterous, shall we call them Bergean, touches. Five separate propulsion units, and a forest of boilers. It wasn't viable, Nicholas.'

'It was good, the figures were right.'

'The whole tanker market has changed since you left Christy Marine. I had to rework it.'

'You should have dropped the whole concept if the cost-structure changed.'

'Oh no, Nicholas, I restructured. My way, even in these hard times, I will recover capital in a year, and with a five-year life on the hull there is two hundred million dollars' profit in it.'

'I was going to build a ship that would last for thirty years,' Nick told him. 'Something of which we could be proud—'

'Pride is an expensive commodity. We aren't building dynasties any more, we are in the game of selling tanker space.' Duncan's tone was patronizing, that impeccable accent drawn out, emphasizing the difference in their backgrounds. 'I'm aiming at a five-year life, two hundred million profit, and then we sell the hull to the Greeks or Japs. It's a one-time thing.'

'You always were a smash-and-grab artist,' Nick agreed. 'But it isn't like dealing in commodities. Ships aren't wheat and bacon, and the oceans aren't the orderly market floors.'

'I disagree, I'm afraid. The principles are the same – one buys, one sells.'

'Ships are living things, the ocean is a battleground of all the elements.'

'Come, Nicholas, you don't really believe that romantic nonsense.' Duncan drew a gold Hunter from his waist pocket, and snapped open the lid to read the dial, another of his affectations which irritated Nicholas. 'Those are very expensive gentlemen waiting next door.'

'You will be risking human life, the men who sail her.'

'Seamen are well paid—'

'You will be taking a monstrous risk with the life of the oceans. Wherever she goes *Golden Dawn* will be a potential—'

'For God's sake, Nicholas, two hundred million dollars is worth some kind of risk.'

'All right,' Nick nodded. 'Let's forget the environment, and the human life, and consider the important aspects – the money.'

Duncan sighed, and wagged that fine head, smiling as at a recalcitrant child.

'I have considered the money – in detail.'

'You will not get an A1 rating at Lloyd's. You will not get insurance on that hull – unless you underwrite yourself, the same way you did with *Golden Adventurer*, and if you think that's wise, just wait until I've finished with my salvage claim.'

Duncan Alexander's smile twisted slowly, and blood darkened his cheeks under the snow-tan. 'I do not need a Lloyd's rating, though I am sure I could get one if I wanted it. I have arranged continental and oriental underwriters. She will be fully insured.'

'Against pollution claims, also? If you burst that bag of crude on the continental shelf of America, or Europe, they'll hit you for half a billion dollars. Nobody would underwrite that.'

'*Golden Dawn* is registered in Venezuela, and she has no sister ships for the authorities to seize, like they did with the *Torrey Canyon*. To whom will they address the pollution bill? A defunct South American Company? No, Nicholas, Christy Marine will not be paying any pollution bills.'

'I cannot believe it, even of you.' Nick stared at him. 'You are cold-bloodedly talking about the possibility – no, the probability – of dumping a million tons of crude oil into the sea.'

'Your moral indignation is touching. It really is. However, Nicholas, may I remind you that this is family and house business – and you are no longer either family or house.'

'I fought you every time you cut a corner,' Nick reminded him. 'I tried to teach you that cheap is always expensive in the long run.'

'You taught me?' For the first time Duncan taunted him openly. 'What could you ever teach me about ships or money,' and he rolled his tongue gloating around the next words, 'or women?'

Nick made the first movement of lunging at him, but he caught himself, and forced himself to unclench his fists at his sides. The blood sang in his ears.

'I'm going to fight you,' he said quietly. 'I'm going to fight you from here to the maritime conference, and beyond.' He made the decision in that moment, he hadn't realized he was going to do it until then.

'A maritime conference has never taken less than five years to reach a decision restricting one of its members. By that time *Golden Dawn* will belong to some Japanese, Hong-Kong-based company – and Christy Marine will have banked two hundred million.'

'I'll have the oil ports closed to you—'

'By whom? Oil-thirsty governments, with lobbies of the big oil companies?' Duncan laughed lightly, he had replaced the urbane mask. 'You really are out of your depth again. We have bumped heads a dozen times before, Nicholas – and I'm still on my feet. I'm not about to fold up to your fine threats now.'

After that, there was no hope that the meeting in the panelled boardroom would lead to conciliation. The atmosphere crackled and smouldered with the antagonism of the two leading characters, so that they seemed to be the only persons on the stage.

They sat opposite each other, separated by the glossy surface of the rosewood table top, and their gazes seldom disengaged. They leaned forward in their chairs, and when they smiled at each other, it was like the silent snarl of two old dog wolves circling with hackles erect.

It took an enormous effort of self-control for Nicholas to force back his anger far enough to be able to think clearly, and to allow his intuition to pick up the gut-impressions, the subtle hints of the thinking and planning that were taking place across the table behind Duncan Alexander's handsome mask of a face.

It was half an hour before he was convinced that something other than personal rivalry and antagonism was motivating the man before him. His counter-offer was too low to have any hope of being accepted, so low that it became clear that he did not want to settle. Duncan Alexander wanted to go to arbitration – and yet there was nothing he could gain by that. It must be obvious to everyone at the table, beyond any doubt whatsoever, that Nicholas' claim was worth four million dollars. Nicholas would have settled for four, even in his anger he would have gone for four – risking that an arbitration board might have awarded six, and knowing the delay and costs of going to litigation might amount to another million. He would have settled.

Duncan Alexander was offering two and a half. It was a frivolous offer. Duncan was going through the motions only. There was no serious attempt at finding a settlement. He didn't want to come to terms, and it seemed to Nicholas that by refusing to settle he was gaining nothing, and risking a great deal. He was a big enough boy to know that you never, but never, go to litigation if there is another way out. It was a rule that Nicholas had graven on his heart in letters of fire. Litigation makes only lawyers fat.

Why was Duncan baulking, what was he to gain by this obstruction? Nicholas crushed down the temptation to stand up and walk out of the room with an exclamation of disgust. Instead, he lit another cheroot and leaned forward again, staring into Duncan Alexander's steely grey eyes, trying to fathom him, needling, probing for the soft rotten spot – and thinking hard.

What had Duncan Alexander to gain from not settling now? Why did he not try with a low, but realistic offer – what was he to gain?

Then quite suddenly he knew what it was. Chantelle's enigmatic appeal for help and advice flashed back to him, and he knew what it was. Duncan Alexander wanted time. It was as simple as that. Duncan Alexander needed time.

'All right.' Satisfied at last, Nicholas leaned back in the deep leather-padded chair, and veiled his eyes. 'We are still a hundred miles apart. There will be only one meeting-ground. That's in the upper room at Lloyd's. It's set down for the 27th. Are we at least agreed on that date?'

'Of course.' Duncan leaned back also and Nicholas saw

the shift of his eyes, the little jump of nerves in the point of his clenched jaws, the tightening of the long pianist's fingers that lay before him on the leather-bound blotter. 'Of course,' Duncan repeated, and began to stand up, a gesture of dismissal. He lied beautifully; had Nicholas not known he would lie, he might have missed the little tell-tale signs.

In the ancient lift, James Teacher was jubilant, rubbing his little fat hands together. 'We'll give him a go!' Nicholas glanced at him sourly. Win, lose or draw, James Teacher would still draw his fee, and Duncan Alexander's refusal to settle had quadrupled that fee. There was something almost obscene about the little lawyer's exultation.

'They are going to duck,' Nick said grimly, and James Teacher sobered slightly.

'Before noon tomorrow, Christy Marine will have lodged for postponement of hearing,' Nick prophesied. 'You'll have to use *Warlock* with full power on both to pull them before the arbitration board.'

'Yes, you're right,' James Teacher nodded. 'They had me puzzled, I sensed something—'

'I'm not paying you to be puzzled,' Nick's voice was low and hard. 'I'm paying you to out-guess and out-jump them. I want them at the hearing on the 27th, get them there, Mr Teacher.' He did not have to voice the threat, and in a moment, the exultation on James Teacher's rotund features had changed to apprehension and deep concern.

The drawing-room in Eaton Square was decorated in cream and pale gold, cleverly designed as a frame for the single exquisite work of art which it contained, the original of the group of Degas ballet-dancers whose copy hung in *Golden Dawn*'s stateroom. It was the room's centrepiece; cunningly lit by a hidden spotlight, it glowed like a precious jewel. Even the flowers on the ivory grand piano were cream and white roses and carnations, whose pale ethereal blossoms put the painting into stronger contrast.

The only other flash of brightness was worn by Chantelle. She had the oriental knack of carrying vivid colour without it seeming gaudy. She wore a flaming Pucci that could not pale her beauty, and as she rose from the huge shaggy white sofa and came to Nicholas, he felt the soft warm melting sensation in his stomach spreading slowly through his body like a draught of some powerful aphrodisiac. He knew he would never be immune to her.

'Dear Nicky, I knew I could rely upon you.' She took his hand and looked up at him, and still holding his hand she led him to the sofa, and then she settled beside him, like a bright, lovely bird alighting. She drew her legs up under her, her calves and ankles flashed like carved and polished ivory before she tucked the brilliant skirt around them, and lifted the Wedgwood porcelain teapot.

'Orange pekoe,' she smiled at him. 'No lemon and no sugar.'

He had to smile back at her. 'You never forget,' and he took the cup.

'I told you that you looked well,' she said, slowly and unself-consciously studying him. 'And you really do, Nicholas. When you came down to Lynwood for Peter's birthday in June I was so worried about you. You looked terribly ill and tired – but now,' she tilted her head critically, 'you look absolutely marvellous.'

Now he should tell her that she was beautiful as ever, he thought grimly, and then they would start talking about Peter and their old mutual friends.

'What did you want to talk to me about?' he asked quietly, and there was a passing shadow of hurt in her dark eyes.

'Nicholas, you can be so remote, so—' she hesitated, seeking the correct word, 'so detached.'

'Recently someone called me an ice-cold Pommy bastard,' he agreed, but she shook her head.

'No. I know you are not, but if only—'

'The three most dangerous and inflammatory phrases in the English language,' he stopped her. 'They are "you always" and "you never" and "if only". Chantelle, I came here to help you with a problem. Let's discuss that – only.'

She stood up quickly, and he knew her well enough to recognize the fury in the snapping dark eyes and the quick dancing steps that carried her to the mantelpiece, and she stood looking up at the Degas with her small fists clenched at her sides.

'Are you sleeping with that child?' she asked, and now the fury was raw in her voice.

Nicholas stood up from the sofa.

'Goodbye, Chantelle.'

She turned and flew to him, taking his arm.

'Oh, Nicholas, that was unforgivable, I don't know what possessed me. Please don't go.' And when he tried to dislodge her hand. 'I beg you, for the first time ever, I beg you, Nicholas. Please don't go.'

He was still stiff with anger when he sank back on the sofa, and they were silent for nearly a minute while she regained her composure.

'This is all going so terribly badly. I didn't want this to happen.'

'All right, let's get on to safer ground.'

'Nicholas,' she started, 'you and Daddy created Christy Marine. If anything, it was more yours than his. The great days were the last ten years when you were Chairman, all the tremendous achievements of those years—'

He made a gesture of denial and impatience, but she went on softly.

'Too much of your life is locked up in Christy Marine, you are still deeply involved, Nicholas.'

'There are only two things I am involved with now,' he told her harshly. 'Ocean Salvage and Nicholas Berg.'

'We both know that is not true,' she whispered. 'You are a special type of man.' She sighed. 'It took me so long to recognize that. I thought all men were like you. I believed strength and nobility of mind were common goods on the market—' she shrugged. 'Some people learn the hard way,' and she smiled, but it was an uncertain, twisted little smile.

He said nothing for a moment, thinking of all that was revealed by those words, then he replied.

'If you believe that, then tell me what is worrying you.'

'Nicholas, something is terribly wrong with Christy Marine. There is something happening there that I don't understand.'

'Tell me.'

She turned her head away for a moment, and then looked back at him. Her eyes seemed to change shape and colour, growing darker and sadder. 'It is so difficult not to be disloyal, so difficult to find expression for vague doubts and fears,' she stopped and bit her lower lip softly. 'Nicholas, I have transferred my shares in Christy Marine to Duncan as my nominee, with voting rights.'

Nicholas felt the shock of it jump down his nerves and string them tight. He shifted restlessly on the sofa and stared at her, and she nodded.

'I know it was madness. The madness of those crazy days a year ago. I would have given him anything he asked for.'

He felt the premonition that she had not yet told him all and he waited while she rose and went to the window, looked out guiltily and then turned back to him.

'May I get you a drink?'

He glanced at his Rolex. 'The sun is over the yardarm, what about Duncan?'

'These days he is never home before eight or nine.' She went to the decanter on the silver tray and poured the whisky with her back to him, and now her voice was so low that he barely caught the words.

'A year ago I resigned as executrix of the Trust.'

He did not answer, it was what he had been waiting for, he had known there was something else. The Trust that old Arthur Christy had set up was the backbone and sinews of Christy Marine. One million voting shares administered by three executors: a banker, a lawyer and a member of the Christy family.

Chantelle turned and brought the drink to him.

'Did you hear what I said?' she asked, and he nodded and sipped the drink before he asked,

'The other executors? Pickstone of Lloyd's and Rollo still?'

She shook her head and again bit her lip.

'No, it's not Lloyd's any more, it's Cyril Forbes.'

'Who is he?' Nick demanded.

'He is the head of London and European.'

'But that's Duncan's own bank,' Nick protested.

'It's still a registered bank.'

'And Rollo?'

'Rollo had a heart attack six months ago. He resigned, and Duncan put in another younger man. You don't know him.'

'My God, three men and each of them is Duncan Alexander – he has had a free hand with Christy Marine for over a year, Chantelle, there is no check on him.'

'I know,' she whispered. 'It was a madness. I just cannot explain it.'

'It's the oldest madness in the world.' Nick pitied her then; for the first time, he realized and accepted that she had been under a compulsion, driven by forces over which she had no control, and he pitied her.

'I am so afraid, Nicholas. I'm afraid to find out what I have done. Deep down I know there is something terribly wrong, but I'm afraid of the truth.'

'All right, tell me everything.'

'There isn't anything else.'

'If you lie to me, I cannot help you,' he pointed out gently.

'I have tried to follow the new structuring of the company, it's all so complicated, Nicholas. London and European is the new holding company, and – and—' her voice trailed off. 'It just goes round and round in circles, and I cannot pry too deep or ask too many questions.'

'Why not?' he demanded.

'You don't know Duncan.'

'I am beginning to,' he answered her grimly. 'But, Chantelle, you have every right to ask and get answers.'

'Let me get you another drink.' She jumped up lightly.

'I haven't finished this one.'

'The ice has melted, I know you don't like that.' She took the glass and emptied the diluted spirit, refilled it and brought it back to him.

'All right,' he said. 'What else?'

Suddenly she was weeping. Smiling at him wistfully and weeping. There was no sobbing or sniffing, the tears merely welled up slowly as oil or blood from the huge dark eyes, broke from the thick, arched lashes and rolled softly down her cheeks. Yet she still smiled.

'The madness is over, Nicholas. It didn't last very long – but it was a holocaust while it did.'

'He comes home at nine o'clock now,' Nicholas said.

'Yes, he comes home at nine o'clock.'

He took the linen handkerchief from his inner pocket and handed it to her.

'Thank you.'

She dabbed away the tears, still smiling softly.

'What must I do, Nicholas?'

'Call in a team of auditors,' he began, but she shook her head and cut him short.

'You don't know Duncan,' she repeated.

'There is nothing he could do.'

'He could do anything,' she contradicted him. 'He is capable of anything. I am afraid, Nicholas, terribly afraid, not only for myself, but for Peter also.'

Nicholas sat erect then.

'Peter. Do you mean you are afraid of something physical?'

'I don't know, Nicholas. I'm so confused and alone. You are the only person in the world I can trust.'

He could no longer remain seated. He stood up and began to pace about the room, frowning heavily, looking down at the glass in his hand and swirling the ice so that it tinkled softly.

'All right,' he said at last. 'I will do what I can. The first thing is to find out just how much substance there is to your fears.'

'How will you do that?'

'It's best you don't know, yet.'

He drained his glass and she stood up, quick with alarm.

'You aren't going, are you?'

'There is nothing else to discuss now. I will contact you when or if I learn anything.'

'I'll see you down.'

In the hall she dismissed the uniformed West Indian maid with a shake of her head, and fetched Nicholas' top-coat from the closet herself.

'Shall I send for the car? You'll not get a cab at five o'clock.'

'I'll walk,' he said.

'Nicholas, I cannot tell you how grateful I am. I had forgotten how safe and secure it is to be with you.' Now she was standing very close to him, her head lifted, and her lips were soft and glossy and ripe, her eyes still flooded and bright. He knew he should leave immediately. 'I know it's going to be all right now.'

She placed one of those dainty ivory hands on his lapel, adjusting it unnecessarily with that proprietary feminine gesture, and she moistened her lips.

'We are all fools, Nicholas, every one of us. We all complicate our lives – when it's so easy to be happy.'

'The trick is to recognize happiness when you stumble on it, I suppose.'

'I'm sorry, Nicholas. That's the first time I've ever apologized to you. It's a day of many first times, isn't it? But I am truly sorry for everything I have ever done to hurt you. I wish with all my heart that it were possible to wipe it all out and begin again.'

'Unfortunately, it doesn't work that way.' With a major effort of will he broke the spell, and stepped back. In another moment he would have stooped to those soft red lips.

'I'll call you if I learn anything,' he said, as he buttoned the top of his coat and opened the front door.

Nicholas stepped out furiously with the cold striking colour into his cheeks, but her presence kept pace with him and his blood raced not from physical exertion alone.

He knew then, beyond all doubt, that he was not a man who could switch love on and off at will.

'You old-fashioned thing.' Samantha's words came back to him clearly – and she was right, of course. He was cursed by a constancy of loyalty and emotion that restricted his freedom of action. He was breaking one of his own rules now, he was no longer moving ahead. He was circling back.

He had loved Chantelle Christy to the limits of his soul, and had devoted almost half of his life to Christy Marine. He realized then that those things could never change, not for him, not for Nicholas Berg, prisoner of his own conscience.

Suddenly he found himself opposite the Kensington Natural History Museum in the Cromwell Road, and swiftly he crossed to the main gates – but it was a quarter to six and they were closed already. Samantha would not have been in the public rooms anyway, but in those labyrinthine vaults below the great stone building. In a few short days, she had made half a dozen cronies among the museum staff. He felt a stab of jealousy, that she was with other human beings, revelling in their companionship, delighting in the pleasures of the mind – had probably forgotten he existed.

Then suddenly the unfairness of it occurred to him, how his emotions of a minute previously had been stirring and boiling with the memories of another woman. Only then did he realize that it was possible to be in love with two different people, in two entirely different ways, at exactly the same time.

Troubled, torn by conflicting loves, conflicting loyalties, he turned away from the barred iron gates of the museum.

Nicholas' apartment was on the fifth floor of one of those renovated and redecorated buildings in Queen's Gate.

It looked as though a party of gypsies were passing through. He had not hung the paintings, nor had he arranged his books on the shelves. The paintings were stacked against the wall in the hallway, and his books were pyramided at unlikely spots around the lounge floor, the carpet still rolled and pushed aside, two chairs facing the television set, and another two drawn up to the dining-room table.

It was an eating and sleeping place, sustaining the bare minima of existence; in two years he had probably slept here on sixty nights, few of them consecutive. It was impersonal, it contained no memories, no warmth.

He poured a whisky and carried it through into the bedroom, slipping the knot of his tie and shrugging out of his jacket. Here it was different, for evidence of Samantha's presence was everywhere. Though she had remade the bed that morning before leaving, still she had left a pair of shoes abandoned at the foot of it, a booby trap to break the ankles of the unwary; her simple jewellery was strewn on the bedside table, together with a book, Noel Mostert's *Supership*, opened face down and in dire danger of a broken spine; the cupboard door was open and his suits had been bunched up in one corner to give hanging space to her slacks and dresses; two very erotic and transparent pairs of panties hung over the bath to dry; her talcum powder still dusted the tiled floor and her special fragrance pervaded the entire apartment.

He missed her with a physical ache in the chest, so that when the front door banged and she arrived like a high wind, shouting for him, 'Nicholas, it's me!' as though it could possibly have been anyone else, her hair tangled and wild with the wind and high colour under the golden tan of her cheeks, he almost ran to her and seized her with a suppressed violence.

'Wow,' she whispered huskily. 'Who is a hungry baby, then.' And they tumbled on to the bed clinging to each other with a need that was almost desperation.

Afterwards they did not turn the light on in the room that had gone dark except for the dim light of the street lamps filtered by the curtains and reflected off the ceiling.

'What was that all about?' she asked, then snuggled against his chest, 'not that I'm complaining, mind you.'

'I've had a hell of a day. I needed you, badly.'

'You saw Duncan Alexander?'

'I saw Duncan.'

'Did you settle?'

'No. There was never really any chance.'

'I'm hungry,' she said. 'Your loving always makes me hungry.'

So he put on his pants and went down to the Italian restaurant at the corner for pizzas. They ate them in bed with a white Chianti from whisky tumblers, and when she was finished, she sighed and said:

'Nicholas, I have to go home.'

'You can't go,' he protested instantly.

'I have work to do – also.'

'But,' he felt a physical nausea at the thought of losing her, 'but you can't go before the hearing.'

'Why not?'

'It would be the worst possible luck, you are my fortune.'

'A sort of good-luck charm?' She pulled a face. 'Is that all I'm good for?'

'You are good for many things. May I demonstrate one of them?'

'Oh, yes please.'

An hour later Nick went for more pizzas.

'You have to stay until the 27th,' he said with his mouth full.

'Darling Nicholas, I just don't know—'

'You can ring them, tell them your aunt died, that you are getting married.'

'Even if I were getting married, it wouldn't lessen the importance of my work. I think you know that is something I will never give up.'

'Yes, I do know, but it's only a couple of days more.'

'All right, I'll call Tom Parker tomorrow.' Then she grinned at him. 'Don't look like that. I'll be just across the Atlantic, we'll be virtually next-door neighbours.'

'Call him now. It's lunchtime in Florida.'

She spoke for twenty minutes, wheedling and charming, while the blood-curdling transatlantic rumblings on the receiver slowly muted to reluctant and resigned mutterings.

'You're going to get me into trouble one of these days, Nicholas Berg,' she told him primly as she hung up.

'Now *there* is a happy thought,' Nick agreed, and she hit him with her pillow.

The telephone rang at two minutes past nine the next morning. They were in the bath together and Nicholas swore and went through naked and steaming and dripping suds.

'Mr Berg?' James Teacher's voice was sharp and businesslike. 'You were right, Christy Marine petitioned for postponement of hearing late yesterday afternoon.'

'How long?' Nicholas snapped.

'Ninety days.'

'The bastard,' grunted Nick. 'What grounds?'

'They want time to prepare their submission.'

'Block them,' Nick instructed.

'I have a meeting with the Secretary at eleven. I'm going to ask for an immediate preliminary hearing to set down and confirm the return date.'

'Get him before the arbitrators,' said Nick.

'We'll get him.'

Samantha welcomed him back to the tub by drawing her knees up under her chin. Her hair was piled on top of her head, but damp wisps hung down her neck and on to her cheeks. She looked pink and dewy as a little girl.

'Careful where you put your toes, sir,' she cautioned him, and he felt the tension along his nerves easing. She had that effect on him.

'I'll buy you lunch at Les A if you can tear yourself away from your microscope and fishy-smelling specimens for an hour or two.'

'Les Ambassadeurs? I've heard about it! For lunch there I'd walk across London on freshly amputated stumps.'

'That won't be necessary, but you will have to charm a tribe of wild desert Sheikhs. I understand they are very sympathetic towards blondes.'

'Are you going to sell me into a harem – sounds fun, I've always fancied myself in baggy, transparent bloomers.'

'You, I'm not selling – icebergs, I am. I'll pick you up at the front gate of the museum at one o'clock sharp.'

She went with laughter and a great clatter and banging of doors and Nicholas settled at the telephone.

'I'd like to speak to Sir Richard personally, it's Nicholas Berg.' Sir Richard was at Lloyd's, an old and good friend.

Then he called and spoke to Charles Gras.

There were no new delays or threats to *Sea Witch*'s completion date.

'I am sorry for any trouble you had with Alexander.'

'*Cą ne fait rien*, Nicholas. Good luck at the hearing. I will be watching the *Lloyd's List*.' Nicholas felt a sense of relief. Charles Gras had risked his career to show him *Golden Dawn*. It could have been serious.

Then Nick spoke for nearly half an hour to Bernard Wackie of Bach Wackie in Bermuda. *Warlock* had reported on the telex two hours previously; she was making good passage with her oil-rig tow, would drop off at Bravo II on schedule and pick up her next tow as soon as she had anchored.

'David Allen is a good youngster,' Bernard told Nick. 'But have you got Levoisin for *Sea Witch?*'

'Jules is playing the prima donna, he has not said yes, but he'll come.'

'You'll have a good team, then. What's the latest date for *Sea Witch?*'

'End March.'

'The sooner the better, I've got contacts to keep both tugs running hard until the iceberg project matures.'

'I'm having lunch with the Sheikhs today.'

'I know. There's a lot of interest. I've got a good feeling.

There is something big brewing, but they are a cagey bunch. The inscrutable smile on the face of the sphinx – when do we see you?'

'I'll come across just as soon as I've got Duncan Alexander into the arbitration court – end of the month, hopefully.'

'We've got a lot to talk about, Nicholas.'

Nick hesitated for the time it took to smoke the first cheroot of the day before he called Monte Carlo – for the call would cost him at least fifty thousand dollars, probably closer to seventy-five. The best is always the cheapest, he reminded himself, picked up the receiver and spoke to a secretary in Monte Carlo, giving his name.

While he waited for the connection he thought how his life was complicating itself once more. Very soon Bach Wackie would not be enough, there would have to be a London branch of Ocean Salvage, offices, secretaries, files, accounts, and then a New York branch, a branch in Saudi, the whole cycle again. He thought suddenly of Samantha, uncluttered and simple happiness, life without its wearisome trappings – then the connection was made and he heard the thin, high, almost feminine voice.

'Mr Berg – Claud Lazarus.' No other greeting, no expressions of pleasure at the renewal of contact. Nick imagined him sitting at his desk in the suite high above the harbour, like a human foetus – preserved in spirits, bottled on the museum shelf. The huge bald, domed head, the soft, putty-coloured rudimentary features, the nose hardly large enough to support the thick spectacles. The eyes distorted and startled by the lens, changing shape like those of a fish in an aquarium as the light moved. The body underdeveloped, as that of a foetus, narrow shoulders, seemingly tapering away to the bowed question mark of a body.

'Mr Lazarus. Are you in a position to undertake an indepth study for me?' It was the euphemism for financial and industrial espionage; Claud Lazarus' network was not limited by frontiers or continents; it spanned the globe with delicately probing tentacles.

'Of course,' he piped softly.

'I want the financial structuring, the lines of control and management, the names of the nominees and their principals, the location and inter-relationship of all the elements of the Christy Marine Group and London European Insurance and Banking Co. Group, with particular reference to any changes in structure during the previous fourteen months. Do you have that?'

'This is being recorded, Mr Berg.'

'Of course. Further, I want the country of registration, the insurers and underwriters of all bottoms traceable to their holdings.'

'Please continue.'

'I want an accurate estimate of the reserves of London and European Insurance in relations to their potential liability.'

'Continue.'

'I am particularly interested in the vessel *Golden Dawn* presently building at the yards of Construction Navale Atlantique at St Nazaire. I want to know if she has been chartered or has contracted with any oil company for carriage of crude and, if so, on what routes and at what rates.'

'Yes?' Lazarus squeaked softly.

'Time is of the essence – and, as always, so is discretion.'

'You need not have mentioned that, Mr Berg.'

'My contact, when you are ready to pass information, is Back Wackie in Bermuda.'

'I will keep you informed of progress.'

'Thank you, Mr Lazarus.'

'Good day, Mr Berg.'

It was refreshing not to have to pretend to be the bosom comrade of somebody who supplied essentials but nonetheless revolted him, Nick thought, and comforting to know he had the best man in the world for the job.

He looked at his watch. It was lunchtime, and he felt the quick lift of his spirits at the thought of being with Samantha.

Lime Street is a narrow alleyway, with tall buildings down each side of it, which opens off Leadenhall Street. A few yards from the junction, on the left-hand side as you leave the street of shipping, is the covered entrance to Lloyd's of London.

Nicholas stepped out of James Teacher's Bentley and took Samantha on his arm. He paused a moment, with a feeling of certain reverence.

As a seaman, the history of this remarkable institution touched him intimately. Not that the building itself was particularly old or venerable. Nothing now remained of the original coffee house, except some of the traditions: the caller who intoned the brokers' names like the offertory in the temple of some exotic religion, the stalls in which the underwriters conducted their business and the name and uniform of the institution's servants, the 'waiters' with brass buttons and red collar tabs.

Rather it was the tradition of concern that was enshrined here, the concern for ships and for all men who went down to the sea in those ships and did their business in great waters.

Perhaps later, Nicholas would find time to take Samantha through the Nelson rooms and show her the displays of memorabilia associated with the greatest of Britain's sailors, the plate and letters and awards. Certainly he would have her as lunch guest in the big dining room, at the table set aside specifically for visiting sea captains.

But now there were more important considerations to

demand all his attention. He had come to hear the verdict given on his future – within a few hours he would know just how high and how fast the wave of his fortune had carried him.

'Come,' he said to Samantha, and led her up the short flight of steps into the lobby, where there was a waiter alerted to receive them.

'We will be using the Committee Room today, sir.'

The earlier submissions by both parties had been heard in one of the smaller offices, leading off the high gallery above the vast floor of the exchange with its rows of underwriters' stalls. However, due to the extraordinary nature of this action, the Committee of Lloyd's had made a unique decision – to have their arbitrators give their findings and make their award in surroundings more in keeping with the importance of the occasion.

They rode up in silence, all of them too tense to make the effort of smalltalk. and the waiter led them down the wide corridor, past the Chairman's suite of offices and through the double doors into the grandeur of the room designed by Adam for Bowood House, the country home of the Marquess of Lansdowne. It had been taken to pieces, panel by panel, floor, ceiling, fireplace and plaster mouldings, transported to London and re-erected in its entirety with such care and attention that when Lord Lansdowne inspected it, he found that the floorboards squeaked in exactly the same places as they had before.

At the long table, under the massive glittering pyramids of the three chandeliers, the two arbitrators were already seated. Both of them were master mariners, selected for their deep knowledge and experience of the sea, and their faces were toughened and leathery from the effects of sea and salt water. They talked quietly together, without acknowledging in any way the rows of quietly attentive faces in the rows of chairs facing them – until the minute hand of the antique clock on the Adam fireplace touched its zenith. Then the President of the Court looked across at the waiter who obediently closed the double doors and stood to attention before them.

'This Arbitration Court has been set up under the Committee of Lloyd's and empowered to receive evidence in the matter between the Christy Marine Steamship Co. Ltd. and the Ocean Salvage and Towage Co. Ltd. This Court finds common ground in the following areas:

'Firstly, a contract of salvage under Lloyd's Open Form "No cure no pay" for the recovery of the passenger liner *Golden Adventurer*, a ship of 22,000 tons gross burden and registered at Southampton, exists between the parties.

'Secondly, that the Master of the *Golden Adventurer* while steaming on a south-westerly heading during the night of December 16th at or near 72° 16′ south and 32° 12′ west—'

The President let no dramatics intrude on his assembly of the facts. He recounted it all in the driest possible terms, succeeding in making *Golden Adventurer*'s plight and the desperate endeavours of her rescuers sound boring. Indeed, his colleague seemed to descend into a condition of coma at the telling of it. His eyes slowly closed, and his head sagged gently sideways, his lips vibrating slightly at each breath – a volume not quite sufficient to make it a snore.

It took nearly an hour, with the occasional consultation of the ship's logbooks and a loose volume of handwritten and typed notes, before the President was satisfied that he had recounted all the facts, and now he rocked back in his chair and hooked his thumbs into his waistcoat. His expression became decisive, and while he surveyed the crowded room, his colleague stirred, opened his eyes, took out a white linen handkerchief and blew two sharp blasts, one for each nostril, like the herald angel sounding the crack of doom.

There was a stir of reawakened interest, they all recognized the moment of decision, and for the first time Duncan Alexander and Nicholas Berg looked directly at each other over the heads of the lawyers and company men. Neither of them changed expression, no smile nor scowl, but something implacable and clearly understood passed between them. They did not unlock their gaze, until the President began to speak again.

'Taking into consideration the foregoing, this Court is of the firm opinion that a fair and good salvage of the vessel was effected by the salvors, and that therefore, they are entitled to salvage awards commensurate with the services rendered to the owners and underwriters.'

Nicholas felt Samantha's fingers groping for his. He took her hand, and it was slim and cold and dry; he interlocked their fingers and laid their hands upon his upper thigh.

'This Court, in arriving at the value of the salvor's services, has taken into consideration, firstly, the situation and conditions existing on the site of operations. We have heard evidence that much of the work was carried out in extreme weather conditions. Temperatures of thirty degrees below freezing, wind forces exceeding twelve on the Beaufort scale, and extreme icing.

'We have also considered that the vessel *Golden Adventurer* was no longer under command. That she had been abandoned by her passengers, her crew and her Master. She was aground on a remote and hostile coast.

'We have further noted that the salvors undertook a voyage of many thousands of miles, without any guarantee of recompense, but merely in order to be in a position to offer assistance, should that have become necessary.'

Nicholas glanced across the aisle at Duncan Alexander. He sat at ease, as though he were in his box at Ascot. His suit was of sombre gunmetal grey, but on him it seemed flamboyant and the I Zingari tie as rakish as any of Cardin's fantasies.

Duncan turned that fine leonine head and looked directly at Nicholas again. This time Nicholas saw the deep angry glow in his eyes as when a vagrant breeze fans the coals of an open fire. Then Duncan turned his face back towards the President, and he balanced his thrusting square chin on the clenched, carefully manicured fingers of his right fist.

'Furthermore, we have taken into consideration the transportation of the survivors from the site of the striking, to the nearest port of succour, Cape Town in the Republic of South Africa.'

The President was summing up strongly in favour of Ocean Salvage. It was a dangerous sign; so often a judge about to deliver an unfavourable decision prefaced it by building a strong case for the loser and then tearing it down again.

Nicholas steeled himself; anything below three million dollars would not be sufficient to keep Ocean Salvage alive. That was the barest minimum he needed to keep *Warlock* afloat, and to put *Sea Witch* on the water for the first time. He felt the spasm of his stomach muscles as he contemplated his commitments – even with three million he would be at the mercy of the Sheikhs, unable to manoeuvre, a slave to any conditions they wished to set. He would not be off his knees even.

Nicholas squeezed Samantha's hand for luck, and she pressed her shoulder against his.

Four million dollars would give him a fighting chance, a slim margin of choice – but he would still be fighting hard, pressed on all sides. Yet he would have settled for four million, if Duncan Alexander had made the offer. Perhaps Duncan had been wise after all, perhaps he might yet see Nicholas broken at a single stroke.

‘Three.’ Nicholas held the figure in his head. ‘Let it be three, at least let it be three.’

‘This Court has considered the written reports of the Globe Engineering Co., the contractors charged with the repairing and refurbishing of *Golden Adventurer*, together with those of two independent marine engineering experts commissioned separately by the owners and the salvors to report on the condition of the vessel. We have also had the benefit of a survey carried out by a senior inspector of Lloyd's of London. From all of this, it seems apparent that the vessel sustained remarkably light damage. There was no loss of equipment, the salvors recovering even the main anchors and chains—’

Strange how that impressed a salvage court. ‘We took her off, anchors and all,’ Nick thought, with a stir of pride.

‘Prompt anti-corrosion precautions by the salvors resulted in minimal damage to the main engines and ancillary equipment—’

It went on and on. Why cannot he come to it now? I cannot wait much longer, Nicholas thought.

‘This Court has heard expert opinion and readily accepts that the residual value of the *Golden Adventurer*'s hull, as delivered to the contractors in Cape Town can be fairly set at twenty-six million US dollars or fifteen million, three hundred thousand pounds sterling, and in consideration of the foregoing, we are further of the firm opinion that the salvors are entitled to an award of twenty per cent of the residual hull value—’

For long cold seconds Nicholas doubted his hearing, and then he felt the flush of exultation burning on his cheeks.

‘In addition, it was necessary to compute the value of the passage provided to the survivors of the vessel—’

It was six – six million dollars! He was clear and running free as a wild albatross sweeping across the oceans on wide pinions.

Nicholas turned his head and looked at Duncan Alexander, and he smiled. He had never felt so strong and vital and alive in his life before. He felt like a giant, immortal, and at his side was the vibrant young body pressing to him, endowing him with eternal youth.

Across the aisle, Duncan Alexander tossed his head, a gesture of dismissal and turned to speak briefly with his counsel who sat beside him. He did not look at Nicholas, however, and there was a waxen cast to his skin now as though it had a fine sheen of perspiration laid upon it, and the blood had drained away beneath the tan.

'Anyway, another few days and you'd probably have started to find me a boring dolly-bird, or one of us would have had a heart attack.' Samantha smiled at him, a pathetic, lopsided little grin, nothing like her usual brilliant golden flashing smile. 'I like to quit while I'm still ahead.'

They sat close on the couch in the Pan Am Clipper Lounge at Heathrow.

Nicholas was shocked by the extent of his own desolation. It felt as though he were about to be deprived of the vital force of life itself, he felt the youth and strength draining away as he looked at her and knew that in a few minutes she would be gone.

'Samantha,' he said. 'Stay here with me.'

'Nicholas,' she whispered huskily, 'I have to go, my darling. It's not for very long but I have to go.'

'Why?' he demanded.

'Because it's my life.'

'Make me your life.'

She touched his cheek, as she countered his offer.

'I have a better idea, give up *Warlock* and *Sea Witch* – forget your icebergs and come with me.'

'You know I cannot do that.'

'No,' she agreed, 'you could not, and I would not want you to. But, Nicholas, my love, no more can I give up my life.'

'All right, then, marry me,' he said.

'Why, Nicholas?'

'So I don't lose my lucky charm, so that you'd damn well have to do what I tell you.'

And she laughed delightedly and snuggled against his chest. 'It doesn't work like that any more, my fine Victorian gentleman. There is only one good reason for marrying, Nicholas, and that's to have babies. Do you want to give me a baby?'

'What a splendid idea.'

'So that I can warm the bottles and wash the nappies while you go off to the ends of the oceans – and we'll have lunch together once a month?' She shook her head. 'We might have a baby together one day – but not now, there is still too much to do, there is still too much life to live.'

'Damn it.' He shook his head. 'I don't like to let you run around loose. Next thing you'll take off with some twenty-five-year-old oaf, bulging with muscles and—'

'You have given me a taste for vintage wine,' she laughed in denial. 'Come as soon as you can, Nicholas. As soon as you have done your work here, come to Florida and I'll show you my life.'

The hostess crossed the lounge towards them, a pretty smiling girl in the neat blue Pan Am uniform.

'Dr Silver? They are calling Flight 432 now.'

They stood and looked at each other, awkward as strangers.

'Come soon,' she said, and then she stood on tiptoe and placed her arms around his shoulders. 'Come as soon as you can.'

Nicholas had protested vigorously as soon as James Teacher advanced the proposition. 'I don't want to speak to him, Mr Teacher. The only thing I want from Duncan Alexander is his cheque for six million dollars, preferably guaranteed by a reputable bank – and I want it before the 10th of next month.'

The lawyer had wheedled and jollied Nicholas along. 'Think of the pleasure of watching his face – indulge yourself, Mr Berg, gloat on him a little.'

'I will obtain no pleasure by watching his face, offhand I can think of a thousand faces I'd rather watch.' But in the end Nicholas had agreed, stipulating only that this time the meeting should be at a place of Nicholas' choice, an unsubtle reminder of whose hand now held the whip.

James Teacher's rooms were in one of those picturesque, stone buildings in the Inns of Court covered with ivy, surrounded by small velvety lawns, bisected with paved walkways that connected the numerous blocks, the entire complex reeking of history and tradition and totally devoid of modern comforts. Its austerity was calculated to instil confidence in the clients.

Teacher's rooms were on the third floor. There was no elevator and the stairs were narrow, steep and dangerous. Duncan Alexander arrived slightly out of breath and flushed under his tan. Teacher's clerk surveyed him discouragingly from his cubicle.

'Mr who?' he asked, cupping his hand to one ear. The clerk was a man as old, grey and picturesque as the building. He even affected a black alpaca suit, shiny and greenish with age, together with a butterfly collar and a black string tie like that last worn by Neville Chamberlain as he promised peace in our time.

'Mr who?' and Duncan Alexander flushed deeper. He was not accustomed to having to repeat his name.

'Do you have an appointment, Mr Arbuthnot?' the clerk

enquired frostily, and laboriously consulted his diary before at last waving Duncan Alexander through into the spartan waiting room.

Nicholas kept him there exactly eight minutes, twice as long as he himself had waited in the board room of Christy Marine, and he stood by the small electric fire in the fireplace, not answering Duncan's brilliant smile as he entered.

James Teacher sat at his desk under the windows, out of the direct line of confrontation, like the umpire at Wimbledon, and Duncan Alexander barely glanced at him.

'Congratulations, Nicholas,' Duncan shook that magnificent head and the smile faded to a rueful grin. 'You turned one up for the books, you truly did.'

'Thank you, Duncan. However, I must warn you that today I have an impossible schedule to meet, I can give you only ten minutes.' Nicholas glanced at his watch. 'Fortunately I can imagine only one thing that you and I have to discuss. The tenth of next month, either a transfer to the Bermuda account of Ocean Salvage, or a guaranteed draft by registered airmail to Bach Wackie.'

Duncan held up his hand in mock protest. 'Come now, Nicholas – the salvage money will be there, on the due date set by the Court.'

'That's fine,' Nicholas told him, still smiling. 'I have no taste for another brawl in the debtors' court.'

'I wanted to remind you of something that old Arthur Christy once said—'

'Ah, of course, our mutual father-in-law.' Nicholas said softly, and Duncan pretended not to hear; instead he went on unruffled.

'He said, with Berg and Alexander I have put together one of the finest teams in the world of shipping.'

'The old man was getting senile towards the end.' Nicholas had still not smiled.

'He was right, of course. We just never got into step.

My God, Nicholas, can you imagine if we had been working together, instead of against each other. You the best salt and steel man in the business, and I—'

'I'm touched, Duncan, deeply touched by this new and gratifying esteem in which I find myself held.'

'You rubbed my nose in it, Nicholas. Just as you said you would. And I'm the kind of man who learns by his mistakes, turning disaster to triumph is a trick of mine.'

'Play your trick now,' Nicholas invited. 'Let's see you turn six million dollars into a flock of butterflies.'

'Six million dollars and Ocean Salvage would buy you back into Christy Marine. We'd be on equal terms.'

The surprise did not show on Nicholas' face, not a flicker of an eyelid, not even a tightening of the lips, but his mind raced to get ahead of the man.

'Together we would be unstoppable. We would build Christy Marine into a giant that controlled the oceans, we'd diversify out into ocean oil exploration, chemical containers.' The man had immense presence and charm, he was almost – but not quite – irresistible, his enthusiasm brimming and overflowing, his fire flaring and spreading to light the dingy room, and Nicholas studied him carefully, learning more about him every second.

'Good God, Nicholas, you are the type of man who can conceive of a venture like the *Golden Dawn* or salvage a giant liner in a sub-zero gale, and I am the man who can put together a billion dollars on a wink and whistle. Nothing could stand before us, there would be no frontiers we could not cross,' He paused now and returned Nicholas' scrutiny as boldly, studying the effect of his words. Nicholas lit the cheroot he was holding, but his eyes watched shrewdly through the fine blue veil of smoke.

'I understand what you are thinking,' Duncan went on, his voice dropping confidentially. 'I know that you are stretched out, I know that you need those six big Ms to keep Ocean Salvage floating. Christy Marine will guarantee

Ocean Salvage outstandings, that's a minor detail. The important thing is us together, like old Arthur Christy saw it, Berg and Alexander.'

Nicholas took the cheroot from his mouth and inspected the tip briefly before he looked back at him.

'Tell me, Duncan,' he asked mildly, 'in this great sharing you envisage, do we put our women into the kitty also?'

Duncan's mouth tightened, and the flesh wrinkled at the corners of his eyes.

'Nicholas,' he began, but Nicholas silenced him with a gesture.

'You said that I need that six million badly, and you were right. I need three million of it for Ocean Salvage and the other three to stop you running that monster you have built. Even if I don't get it, I will still use it to stop you. I'll slap a garnishee order on you by ten minutes past nine on the morning of the eleventh. I told you I would fight you and *Golden Dawn*. The warning still stands.'

'You are being petty,' Duncan said. 'I never expected to see you join the lunatic fringe.'

'There are many things you do not know about me, Duncan. But, by God, you are going to learn – the hard way.'

Chantelle had chosen San Lorenzo in Beauchamp Place when Nicholas had refused to go again to Eaton Square. He had learned that it was dangerous to be alone with her, but San Lorenzo was also a bad choice of meeting-ground.

It carried too many memories from the golden days. It had been a family ritual, Sunday lunch whenever they were in town. Chantelle, Peter and Nicholas laughing together at the corner table. Mara had given them the corner table again.

'Will you have the *osso bucco?*' Chantelle asked, peeping at him over the top of her menu.

Nicholas always had the *osso bucco*, and Peter always had the *lasagne*, it was part of the ritual.

'I'm going to have a sole.' Nicholas turned to the waiter who was hovering solicitously. 'And we'll drink the house white.' Always the wine had been a Sancerre; Nicholas was deliberately downgrading the occasion by ordering the carafe.

'It's good.' Chantelle sipped it and then set the glass aside. 'I spoke to Peter last night, he is in the san with flu, but he will be up today, and he sent you his love.'

'Thank you,' he spoke stiffly, stilted by the curious glances from some of the other tables where they had been recognized. The scandal would fly around London like the plague.

'I want to take Peter to Bermuda with me for part of the Easter holidays,' Nicholas told her.

'I shall miss him – he's such a delight.'

Nicholas waited for the main course to be served before he asked bluntly, 'What did you want to speak to me about?'

Chantelle leaned towards him, and her perfume was light and subtle and evocative.

'Did you find out anything, Nicholas?'

'No,' he thought to himself. 'That's not what she wants.' It was the Persian in her blood, the love of secrecy, the intrigue. There was something else here.

'I have learned nothing,' he said. 'If I had, I would have called you.' His eyes bored into hers, green and hard and searching. 'That is not what you wanted,' he told her flatly.

She smiled and dropped her eyes from his. 'No,' she admitted, 'it wasn't.'

She had surprising breasts, they seemed small, but really they were too big for her dainty body. It was only their perfect proportions and the springy elasticity of the creamy flesh that created the illusion. She wore a flimsy silk blouse with a low lacy front, which exposed the deep cleft between them. Nicholas knew them so well, and he found himself staring at them now.

She looked up suddenly and caught his eyes, and the huge eyes slanted with a sly heart-stopping sexuality. Her lips pouted softly and she moistened them with the tip of her tongue.

Nick felt himself sway in his seat, it was a tell-tale mannerism of hers. That set of lips and movement of tongue were the heralds of her arousal, and instantly he felt the response of his own body, too powerful to deny, although he tried desperately.

'What was it?' He did not hear the husk in his voice, but she did and recognized it as readily as he had the flicker of her tongue. She reached across the table and took his wrist, and she felt the leap of his pulse under her fingers.

'Duncan wants you to come back into Christy Marine,' she said. 'And so do I.'

'Duncan sent you to me.' And when she nodded, he asked, 'Why does he want me back? God knows what pains the two of you took to get rid of me.' And he gently pulled his wrist from her fingers and dropped both hands into his lap.

'I don't know why Duncan wants it. He says that he needs your expertise.' She shrugged, and her breasts moved under the silk. He felt the tense ache of his groin, it confused his thinking. 'It isn't the true reason, I'm sure of that. But he wants you.'

'Did he ask you to tell me that?'

'Of course not.' She fiddled with the stem of her glass; her fingers were long and perfectly tapered, the painted nails set upon them with the brilliance of butterflies' wings. 'It was to come from me alone.'

'Why do you think he wants me?'

'There are two possibilities that I can imagine.' She

surprised him sometimes with her almost masculine appraisal. That was what made her lapse so amazing; as he listened to her now, Nicholas wondered again how she could ever have let control of Christy Marine pass to Duncan Alexander – then he remembered what a wild and passionate creature she could be. 'The first possibility is that Christy Marine owes you six million dollars, and he has thought up some scheme to avoid having to pay you out.'

'Yes,' Nicholas nodded. 'And the other possibility?'

'There are strange and exciting rumours in the City about you and Ocean Salvage – they say that you are on the brink of something big. Something in Saudi Arabia. Perhaps Duncan wants a share of that.'

Nicholas blinked. The iceberg project was something between the Sheikhs and himself, then he remembered that others knew. Bernard Wackie in Bermuda, Samantha Silver, James Teacher – there had been a leak somewhere then.

'And you? What are your reasons?'

'I have two reasons, Nicholas,' she answered. 'I want control back from Duncan. I want the voting rights in my shares, and I want my rightful place on the Trust. I didn't know what I was doing, it was madness when I made Duncan my nominee. I want it back now, and I want you to get it for me.'

Nicholas smiled, a bitter wintry smile. 'You're hiring yourself a gunman, just the way they do in the Western serials. Duncan and I alone on the deserted street, spurs clinking.' The smile turned to a chuckle, but he was thinking hard, watching her – was she lying? It was almost impossible to tell, she was so mysterious and unfathomable. Then he saw tears well in the depths of those huge eyes, and he stopped laughing. Were the tears genuine, or all part of the intrigue?

'You said you had two reasons.' And now his voice was

gentler. She did not answer immediately, but he could see her agitation, the rapid rise and fall of those lovely breasts under the silk, then she caught her breath with a little hiss of decision and she spoke so softly that he barely caught the words.

'I want you back. That's the other reason, Nicholas.' And he stared at her while she went on. 'It was all part of the madness. I didn't realize what I was doing. But the madness is over now. Sweet merciful God, you'll never know how much I've missed you. You'll never know how I've suffered.' She stopped and fluttered one small hand. 'I'll make it up to you, Nicholas, I swear it to you. But Peter and I need you, we both need you desperately.'

He could not answer for a moment, she had taken him by surprise and he felt his whole life shaken again and the separate parts of it tumbled like dice from the cup of chance.

'There is no road back, Chantelle. We can only go forward.'

'I always get what I want, Nicholas, you know that,' she warned him.

'Not this time, Chantelle.' He shook his head, but he knew her words would wear away at him.

Duncan Alexander slumped on the luxurious calf-hide seat of the Rolls, and he spoke into the telephone extension that connected him directly with his office in Leadenhall Street.

'Were you able to reach Kurt Streicher?' he asked.

'I'm sorry, Mr Alexander. His office was unable to contact him. He is in Africa on a hunting safari. They did not know when to expect him back in Geneva.'

'Thank you, Myrtle.' Duncan's smile was completely lacking in humour. Streicher was suddenly one of the world's most industrious sportsmen – last week he had been skiing and was out of contact, this week he was in Africa slaughtering elephant, perhaps next week he would be chasing polar bears in the Arctic. And by then, it would be too late, of course.

Streicher was not alone. Since the salvage award on *Golden Adventurer*, so many of his financial contacts had become elusive, veritable will-o'-the-wisps skipping ahead of him with their chequebooks firmly buttoned into their pockets.

'I shall not be back at the office again today,' he told his secretary. 'Please have my pending tray sent round to Eaton Square. I will work on it tonight, and do you think you could get in an hour earlier tomorrow morning?'

'Of course, Mr Alexander.'

He replaced the handset and glanced out of the window. The Rolls was passing Regent's Park, heading in the direction of St John's Wood; three times in the last six months he had taken this route, and suddenly Duncan felt that hot scalding lump deep under his ribs. He straightened up in his seat but the pain persisted, and he sighed and opened the rosewood liquor cabinet, spilled a spoonful of the powder into a glass and topped it with soda water.

He considered the turbid draught with distaste, then drank it at a gulp. It left an aftertaste of peppermint on his tongue, but the relief was almost immediate. He felt the acid burn subside, and he belched softly.

He did not need a doctor to tell him that it was a duodenal ulcer, probably a whole bunch of them – or was that the correct collective noun, a tribe of ulcers, a convocation? He smiled again, and carefully combed his brazen waves of hair, watching himself in the mirror.

The strain did not show on his face, he was sure of that. The façade was intact, devoid of cracks. He had always had the strength, the courage to ride with his decisions. This had been a hard ride, however, the hardest of his life.

He closed his eyes briefly, and saw *Golden Dawn* standing on her ways. Like a mountain. The vision gave him strength, he felt it rising deep within him, welling up to fill his soul.

They thought of him only as a money man, a paper man. There was no salt in his blood nor steel in his guts – that was what they said of him in the City. When he had ousted Berg from Christy Marine, they had shied off, watching him shrewdly, standing aside and waiting for him to show his guts, forcing him to live upon the fat of Christy Marine, devouring himself like a camel in the desert, running him thin.

'The bastards,' he thought, but it was without rancour. They had done merely what he would have done, they had played by the hard rules which Duncan knew and respected, and by those same rules, once he had shown his guts to be of steel, they would ply him with largesse. This was the testing time. It was so close now, two months still to live through – yet those sixty days seemed as daunting as the hard year through which he had lived already.

The stranding of *Golden Adventurer* had been a disaster. Her hull value had formed part of the collateral on which he had borrowed; the cash she generated with her luxury cruises was budgeted carefully to carry him through the dangerous times before *Golden Dawn* was launched. Now all that had altered drastically. The flow of cash had been switched off, and he had to find six million in real hard money – and find it before the 10th of the month. Today was the 6th, and time was running through his fingers like quicksilver.

If only he had been able to stall Berg. He felt a corrosive welling up of hatred again; if only he had been able to stall him. The bogus offer of partnership might have held him just long enough, but Berg had brushed it aside contemptuously. Duncan had been forced to scurry about in undignified haste, trying to pull together the money. Kurt

Streicher was not the only one suddenly unavailable, it was strange how they could smell it on a man, he had the same gift of detecting vulnerability or weakness in others so he understood how it worked. It was almost as though the silver blotches showed on his hands and face and he walked the city pavements chanting the old leper's cry, 'Unclean. Beware. Unclean.'

With so much at stake, it was a piddling amount, six million for two months, the insignificance of it was an insult, and he felt the tension in his belly muscles again and the rising hot acid sting of his digestive juices. He forced himself to relax, glancing again from the window to find that the Rolls was turning into the cul-de-sac of yellow-face brick apartments piled upon each other like hen-coops, angular and unimaginatively lower middle class.

He squared his shoulders and watched himself in the mirror, practising the smile. It was only six million, and for only two months, he reminded himself, as the Rolls slid to a halt before one of the anonymous buildings.

Duncan nodded to his chauffeur as he held the door open and handed Duncan the pigskin briefcase.

'Thank you, Edward. I should not be very long.'

Duncan took the case and he crossed the pavement with the long, confident stride of an athlete, his shoulders thrown back, wearing his topcoat like an opera cloak, the sleeves empty and the tails swirling about his legs, and even in the grey overcast of a March afternoon, his head shone like a beacon fire.

The man who opened the door to him seemed only half Duncan's height, despite the tall black Homburg hat that he wore squarely over his ears.

'Mr Alexander, shalom, shalom.' His beard was so dense and bushy black that it covered the starched white collar and white tie, regulation dress of the strict Hasidic Jew. 'Even though you come to me last, you still bring honour on my house,' and his eyes twinkled, a mischievous sparkling black under thick brows.

'That is because you have a heart of stone and blood like iced water,' said Duncan, and the man laughed delightedly, as though he had been paid the highest compliment.

'Come,' he said, taking Duncan's arm. 'Come in, let us drink a little tea together and let us talk.' He led Duncan down the narrow corridor, and halfway they collided with two boys wearing yamulka on their curly heads coming at speed in the opposite direction.

'Ruffians,' cried the man, stooping to embrace them briefly and then send them on their way with a fond slap on their backsides. Still beaming and shaking the ringlets that dangled out from under the black Homburg, he ushered Duncan into a small crowded bedroom that had been converted to an office. A tall old-fashioned pigeonholed desk filled one wall and against the other stood an overstuffed horsehair sofa on which were piled ledgers and box files.

The man swept the books aside, making room for Duncan. 'Be seated,' he ordered, and stood aside while a jolly little woman his size brought in the teatray.

'I saw the award court's arbitration on *Golden Adventurer* in *Lloyd's List*,' the Jew said when they were alone. 'Nicholas Berg is an amazing man, a hard act to follow – I think that is the expression.' He pondered, watching the sudden bloom of anger on Duncan's cheeks and the murderous expression in the pale eyes.

Duncan controlled his anger with an effort, but each time that somebody spoke that way of Nicholas Berg, he found it more difficult. There was always the comparison, the snide remarks, and Duncan wanted to stand up and leave this cluttered little room and the veiled taunts, but he knew he could not afford to, nor could he speak just yet for his anger was very close to the surface. They sat in silence for what seemed a long time.

'How much?' The man broke the silence at last, and Duncan could not bring himself to name the figure for it was too closely related to the subject that had just infuriated him.

'It is not a large amount, and for a short period – sixty days only.'

'How much?'

'Six million,' Duncan said. 'Dollars.'

'Six million is not an impossibly large amount of money, when you have it – but it is a great fortune when you do not.' The man tugged at the thick black bush of his beard. 'And sixty days can be an eternity.'

'I have a charter for *Golden Dawn*,' Duncan said softly. 'A ten-year charter.' He slipped the nine-carat gold catches on the slim, finely grained pigskin briefcase and brought out a batch of xeroxed sheets. 'As you see, it is signed by both parties already.'

'Ten years?' asked the man, watching the papers in Duncan's hand.

'Ten years, at ten cents a hundred ton miles and a guaranteed minimum annual of 75,000 miles.'

The hand on the man's thick black beard stilled. '*Golden Dawn* has a burden of a million tons – that will gross a minimum of seventy-five million dollars a year.' With an effort he managed to disguise his awe, and the hand resumed its gentle tugging at the beard. 'Who is the charterer?' The thick eyebrows formed two thick black question marks.

'Orient Amex,' said Duncan, and handed him the xeroxed papers.

'The El Barras field.' The man's eyebrows stayed up as he read swiftly. 'You are a brave man, Mr Alexander. But I never once doubted that.' He read on in silence for another minute, shaking his head slowly so that the ringlets danced on his cheeks. 'The El Barras field.' He folded the papers and looked up at Duncan. 'I think Christy Marine may have found a worthy successor to Nicholas Berg – perhaps the shoes are even a little small, maybe they will begin to pinch your toes soon, Mr Alexander.' He squirmed down in his chair thinking furiously, and Duncan watched him, hiding his trepidation behind a remotely amused half-smile.

'What about the environmentalists, Mr Alexander? The new American administration, this man Carter is very conscious of environmental dangers.'

'The lunatic fringe,' said Duncan. 'There is too much invested already. Orient Amex have nearly a billion in the new cadmium cracking plants at Galveston, and three of the other oil giants are in it. Let them fuss, we'll still carry in the new cad-rich crudes.'

Duncan spoke with the force of complete conviction. 'There is too much at stake, the potential profits are too large and the opposition is too weak. The whole world is sick of the doom-merchants, the woolly-headed sentimentalists,' he dismissed them with a short abrupt gesture. 'Man has already adjusted to a little oil on the beaches, a little smoke in the air, a few less fish in the sea or birds in the sky, and he will go on adjusting.'

The man nodded, listening avidly. 'Yes,' he nodded. 'You are a brave man. The world needs men like you.'

'The important thing is a cadmium catalyst cracking system which breaks down the high carbon atoms of crude and gives back a 90 per cent yield in low carbon instead of the 40 per cent we hope for now. 90 per cent yield, double-double profits, double efficiency—'

' – and double danger.' The man smiled behind his beard.

'There is danger in taking a bath. You might slip and crack your skull, and we haven't invested a billion dollars in bathing.'

'Cadmium in concentrations of 100 parts to the million is more poisonous than cyanide or arsenic; the cad-rich crudes of the El Barras field are concentrated 2,000 parts to the million.'

'That's what makes them so valuable,' Duncan nodded. 'To enrich crude artificially with cadmium would make the whole cracking process hopelessly uneconomic. We've turned what appeared to be a hopelessly contaminated oilfield into one of the most brilliant advances in oil refining.'

'I hope you have not underestimated the resistance to the transportation of—'

Duncan cut him short. 'There will be no publicity. The loading and unloading of the crude will be conducted with the utmost discretion, and the world will not know the difference. Just another ultra-tanker moving across the oceans with nothing to suggest that she is carrying cad-rich.'

'But, just suppose the news did leak?'

Duncan shrugged. 'The world is conditioned to accept anything, from DDT to Concorde, nobody really cares any more. Come hell and high water, we'll carry the El Barras oil. Nobody is strong enough to stop us.'

Duncan gathered his papers and went on softly, 'I need six million dollars for sixty days – and I need it by noon tomorrow.'

'You are a brave man,' the man repeated softly. 'But you are finely stretched out. Already my brothers and I have made a considerable investment in your courage. To be blunt, Mr Alexander, Christy Marine has exhausted its collateral. Even *Golden Dawn* is pawned down to her last rivet – and the charter for Orient Amex does not change that.'

Duncan took another sheaf of papers, bound in a brown folder, and the man lifted an eyebrow in question.

'My personal assets,' Duncan explained, and the man skimmed swiftly through the typed lists.

'Paper values, Mr Alexander. Actual values are 50 per cent of those you list, and that is not six million dollars of collateral.' He handed the folder back to Duncan. 'They will do for a start, but we'll need more than that.'

'What more is there?'

'Share options, stock options in Christy Marine. If we are to share risk, then we must have a share of the winnings.'

'Do you want my soul also?' Duncan demanded harshly, and the man laughed.

'We'll take a slice of that as well,' he agreed amiably.

It was two hours later that Duncan sank wearily into the leather-work of the Rolls. The muscles in his thighs trembled as though he had run a long way and there was a nerve in the corner of his eye that jumped as though a cricket was trapped beneath the skin. He had made the gamble, everything – Christy Marine, his personal fortune, his very soul. It was all at risk now.

'Eaton Square, sir?' the chauffeur asked.

'No,' Duncan told him. He knew what he needed now to smooth away the grinding, destroying tension that wracked his body, but he needed it quickly without fuss and, like the peppermint-tasting powder, like a medicine.

'The Senator Club in Frith Street,' he told the chauffeur.

Duncan lay face down on the massage table in the small green-curtained cubicle. He was naked, except for the towel, and his body was smooth and lean. The girl worked up his spine with strong skilled fingers, finding the little knots of tension in the sleek muscle and unravelling them.

'Do you want the soft massage, sir?' she asked.

'Yes,' he said and rolled on to his back. She lifted away the towel from around his waist. She was a pretty blonde girl in a short green tunic with the golden laurel leaf club insignia on the pocket, and her manner was brisk and business-like.

'Do you want any extras, sir?' Her tone was neutral, and she began to unbutton the green tunic automatically.

'No,' Duncan said. 'No extras,' and closed his eyes, surrendering himself completely to the touch of her expert fingers.

He thought of Chantelle, feeling the sneaking guilt of the moment, but it was so seldom these days that he had the energy for her smouldering, demanding Persian passions. He did not have the strength for her, he was drained and weary, and all he wanted was the release, swift and simple. In two months' time it would be different, he would have the strength and energy to pick the world up in his bare hands and shake it like a toy.

His mind was separated from his body, and odd disconnected images flitted across the red darkness of his closed eyelids. He thought again how long it had been since last he and Chantelle had made love together, and he wondered what the world would say if they knew of it.

'Nicholas Berg left a big empty place in his bed also,' they would say.

'The hell with them,' Duncan thought, but without the energy for real anger.

'The hell with all of them.' And he gave himself up to the explosion of light that burst against his eyelids and the dark, but too fleeting, peace that followed it.

Nicholas lay back in the rather tatty old brown leather armchair which was one of James Teacher's concessions to creature comfort and he stared at the cheap hunting prints on the faded wallpaper through a thin fug of cheroot smoke. Teacher could have afforded a decent Gauguin or a Turner, but such vulgar display was frowned on in the Inns of Court. It might lead prospective clients to ponder the amount of the fees that they were to be charged.

James Teacher replaced the telephone and stood up behind his desk. It did not make much difference to his height.

'Well, I think we have covered all the entrances to the warren,' he announced cheerfully, and he began to tick off the items on his fingers. 'The sheriff of the South African supreme court will serve notice of attachment on the hull of *Golden Adventurer* at noon local time tomorrow. Our French correspondent will do the same on *Golden Dawn*—' He spoke for three minutes more, and, listening to him, Nicholas reluctantly admitted to himself that he earned the greater proportion of his enormous fees.

'Well, there it is, Mr Berg. If your hunch is correct—'

'It's not a hunch, Mr Teacher. It's a certainty. Duncan Alexander has his backside pinched in the doorway. He's been rushing round the City like a demented man looking for money. My God, he even tried to stall me with that incredible offer of a partnership. No, Mr Teacher, it's not a hunch. Christy Marine is going to default.'

'I cannot understand that. Six millions is peanuts,' said James Teacher. 'At least it's peanuts to a company like Christy Marine, one of the healthiest shipping owners.'

'It was, a year ago,' Nicholas agreed grimly. 'But since then, Alexander has had a clear run, no checks, it's not a public company, he administers the shares in the Trust.' He drew on his cheroot. 'I'm going to use this to force a full investigation of the company's affairs. I'm going to have Alexander under the microscope and we'll have a close look at all his pimples and warts.'

Teacher chuckled and picked up the telephone at the first ring. 'Teacher,' he chuckled, and then laughed out loud, nodding, 'Yes,' and 'Yes!' again. He hung up and turned to Nicholas, his face bright red with mirth, fat and round as the setting sun.

'I have a disappointment for you, Mr Berg.' He guffawed. 'An hour ago a transfer was made to the credit of Ocean Salvage in Bermuda by Christy Marine.'

'How much?'

'Every penny, Mr Berg. In full and final payment. Six million and some odd dollars in the legal currency of the United States of America.'

Nicholas stared at him, uncertain as to which of his emotions prevailed – relief at having the money, or disappointment at being prevented from tearing Duncan Alexander to shreds.

'He's a high roller and very fast on his feet,' said Teacher. 'It wouldn't pay to underestimate a man like Duncan Alexander.'

'No, it would not,' Nicholas agreed quietly, knowing that he had done so more than once and each time it had cost him dearly.

'I wonder if your clerk could find out from British Airways when the next flight leaves for Bermuda?'

'You are leaving so soon? Will it be in order to mark my brief and send it direct to Bach Wackie in Bermuda?' Teacher asked delicately.

Bernard Wackie was waiting in person for Nicholas beyond the customs barrier. He was tall and lean and alert, burned dark as a stick of chew tobacco by the sun, and dressed in open-neck shirt and cotton trousers.

'Nicholas, it's good to see you.' His handshake was hard and dry and cool. He was under sixty and over forty; it was impossible to get nearer to his age. 'I'm taking you directly to the office, there is too much to discuss. I don't want to waste time.' And he took Nicholas' arm and hurried him through burning sunlight into the shivery cold of the Rolls's air-conditioning.

The car was too big for the island's narrow winding roads. Here ownership of automobiles was restricted to one per family unit, but Bernard made the most of his rights.

He was one of those men whose combination of energy and brilliance made it impossible for him to live in England and to subject himself to the punitive taxes of envy.

'It's hard to be a winner, in a society dedicated to the glorification of the losers,' he had told Nicholas, and had moved his whole operation to this taxless haven.

To a lesser man it would have been suicide, but Bernard had taken over the top floor of the Bank of Bermuda building, with a magnificent view across Hamilton Harbour, and had fitted it out with a marine operations room and a communications system the equal of NATO Command.

From it, he offered a service so efficient, so personally involved, so orientated to every single facet of ship ownership and operation, that not only had his old clients followed him, but others had come flocking.

'No taxes, Nicholas,' he smiled. 'And look at the view.' The picturesque buildings of Hamilton town were painted in candy colours, strawberries and limes, plum and lemon – and across the bay the cedar trees stood tall in the sunlight, and the yachts from the pink-painted clubhouse spread multicoloured sails across green waters. 'It's better than London in winter, isn't it?'

'The same temperature,' said Nicholas, and glanced up at the air-conditioning.

'I'm a hot-blooded man,' Bernard explained, and when his tall nubile secretary entered to his ring, bearing the Ocean Salvage files like a high priestess carrying the sacrament, Bernard fell into an awed silence, concentrating all his attention on her pneumatic bosoms; they bounced and strained against the laws of gravity as though filled with helium.

She flashed a dazzling, painted smile at Nicholas as she placed the files on Bernard's desk, and then she left with her perfectly rounded buttocks under the tightly tailored skirt, swinging and dancing to a distant music. 'She can type too,' Bernard assured Nick with a sigh, and shook his head as if to clear it. He opened the top file.

'Right,' he began. 'The deposit from Christy Marine—'

The money had come in, and only just in time. The next instalment on *Sea Witch* was already forty-eight hours overdue and Atlantique were becoming highly agitated.

'Son of a gun,' said Bernard. 'You would not think six million was an easy sum of money to get rid of, would you?'

'You don't even have to try,' Nick agreed. 'It just spends itself.' Then with a scowl, 'What's this?'

'They've invoked the escalation clause again, another 3 + 106 per cent.' *Sea Witch's* builders had included a clause that related the contract price to the index cost of steel and the Union labour rates. They had avoided the threatened dockyard strike by capitulating to Union demands, and now the figures came back to Nicholas. They were big fat ugly figures. The clause was a festering canker to Nicholas, draining his strength and money.

They worked on through the afternoon, paying, paying and paying. Bunkers and the other running costs of *Warlock*, interest and capital repayments on the debts of Ocean

Salvage, lawyers' fees, agents' fees, the six million whittled away. One of the few payments that gave Nicholas any pleasure was the 12½ per cent salvage money to the crew of *Warlock*. David Allen's share was almost thirty thousand dollars; Beauty Baker another twenty-five thousand – Nick included a note with that cheque, 'Have a Bundaberg on me!'

'Is that all the payments?' Nicholas asked at last.

'Isn't it enough?'

'It's enough.' Nick felt groggy with jetlag and from juggling with figures. 'What's next?'

'Good news, next.' Bernard picked up the second file. 'I think I've squared Esso. They hate you, they have threatened never to use your tugs again, but they are not going to sue.' Nicholas had breached contract when he deserted the Esso tow and ran south for *Golden Adventurer*; the breach of contract suit had been hanging since then. It was a relief to have it aside. Bernard Wackie was worth every penny of his hire.

'Okay. Next?'

It went on for another six unbroken hours, piled on top of the jetlag that Nicholas had accumulated across the Atlantic.

'You okay?' Bernard asked at last. Nicholas nodded, though his eyes felt like hard-boiled eggs, and his chin was dark and raspy with beard.

'You want something to eat?' Bernard asked, and then Nick shook his head and realized that it was dark outside. 'Drink? You'll need one for what comes next.'

'Scotch,' Nicholas agreed, and the secretary brought the tray through, and poured the drinks in another respectful hush.

'That will be all, Mr Wackie?'

'For now, honey.' Bernard watched her go, and then saluted Nicholas with his glass.

'I give you the Golden Prince!' And when Nicholas

scowled, he went on swiftly, 'No, Nicholas, I'm not shafting you. It's for real. You've done it again. The sheikhs are fixing to make you an offer. They want to buy you out, clean, take over the whole show, liabilities, everything. Of course, they'll want you to run it for them – two years, while you train one of their own men. A hell of a salary,' he went on crisply, and Nicholas stared at him.

'How much?'

'Two hundred grand, plus 2½ per cent profits.'

'Not the salary,' Nicholas told him. 'How much are they offering for the company?'

'They are Arabs. The first offer is just to stir the pot a little.'

'How much?' Nicholas asked impatiently.

'The sum of five was delicately mentioned.'

'What do you think they'll go to?'

'Seven, seven and half – eight, perhaps.'

Through the fuzz of fatigue, far off like a lantern in the window on a winter's night, Nicholas saw the vision of a new life, a life such as Samantha had shown him. A life uncluttered, uncomplicated, shorn of all but joy and purpose.

'Eight million dollars clear?' Nicholas' voice was husky, and he tried to wipe away the fatigue from his stinging eyelids with thumb and forefinger.

'Maybe only seven,' Bernard demurred, 'but I'd try for eight.'

'I'll have another drink,' Nicholas said.

'That's a splendid idea,' Bernard agreed, and rang for his secretary with an anticipatory sparkle in his eyes.

Samantha wore her hair in twin braids down her back, and hacked-off denim pants which left her long brown legs bare and exposed a pale sliver of tight round buttock at each step as she walked away. She had sandals on her feet and sunglasses pushed up on top of her head.

'I thought you were never coming,' she challenged Nick as he stepped through the barrier at Miami International. He dropped his bag and fielded her rush against his chest. She clung to him and he had forgotten the clean, sun-drenched smell of her hair.

She was trembling with a suppressed eagerness like a puppy, and it was only when a small quivering sob shook her shoulders that he realized she was weeping.

'Hey now!' He lifted her chin, and her eyes were flooded. She snuffled once loudly.

'What's the trouble, little one?'

'I'm just so happy,' Samantha told him, and Nicholas deeply envied the ability to live so near the surface. To be able to cry with joy seemed to him at that moment to be the supreme human accomplishment. He kissed her and she tasted salty with tears. With surprise he felt a choke deep in his own throat.

The jaded airport crowds had to open and trickle around the two of them like water around a rock, and they were oblivious to it all.

Even when they came out of the building into the Florida sunlight, she had both arms around his waist, hampering his stride, as she led him to her vehicle.

'Good God!' exclaimed Nicholas, and he shied when he saw it. It was a Chevy van, but its paintwork had been restyled. 'What's that?'

'It's a masterpiece,' she laughed. 'Isn't it?' It was rainbowed, in layers of vibrant colour and panels of fantastic landscapes and seascapes.

'You did that?' Nick asked, and he took his dark glasses

from his breast pocket, and inspected the seagulls and palm trees and flowers through them.

'It's not that bad,' she protested. 'I was bored and depressed without you. I needed something to brighten my life.'

One of the panels depicted the translucent green of a curling wave, and on the face of the wave a pair of human figures on Hawaii boards and a graceful dolphin shape flew in formation together. Nick leaned closer and barely recognized the male figure as himself; each detail of the features had been rendered with loving attention, and he came out of it looking like something between Clark Gable and Superman – only a little more glamorous.

'From memory,' she said proudly.

'It's tremendous,' he told her. 'But I've got bigger biceps, and I'm more beautiful.'

Despite the wild choice of colour and the romantic style, he realized she had real talent.

'You don't expect me to ride in that – what if one of my creditors saw me!'

'Get your mind out of its stiff collar and blue suit, mister. You have just signed on for the voyage to Never-Never land by way of the moon.'

Before she started the engine she looked at him seriously out of those great shining green eyes.

'How long, Nicholas?' she asked. 'How long have we got together this time?'

'Ten days,' he told her. 'Sorry, but I must be back in London by the 25th. There is a big one coming up, *the* big one. I'll tell you about it.'

'No.' She covered her ears with both hands. 'I don't want to hear about it, not yet.'

She drove the Chevy with careless unforced skill, very fast and efficiently, acknowledging the homage of other male drivers with a grin and a shake of her braids.

When she slipped off Highway 95 and parked in the lot of a supermarket, Nicholas raised an eyebrow.

'Food,' she explained, and then with a lascivious roll of her eyes, 'I reckon to get mighty hungry later.'

She chose steaks, a bag full of groceries and a jug of California Riesling, and would not let him pay. 'In this town, you are my guest.'

Then she paid the toll and took the Rickenbacker causeway across the water to Virginia Key.

'That's the marine division of the University of Miami and that's my lab at the top of the jetty, just beyond that white fishing boat – see it?'

The low buildings were crowded into a corner of the island, between the seaquarium and the wharves and jetties of the University's own little harbour.

'We aren't stopping,' Nicholas observed.

'Are you kidding?' she laughed at him. 'I don't need a controlled scientific environment for the experiment I am about to conduct.'

And with no diminution of speed, the Chevy flew across the long bridge between Virginia Key and Key Biscayne, and three miles on she turned off sharply left on a narrow dirt track that twisted through a lush tropical maritime forest of banyan and palmetta and palm, and ended at a clapboard shack just above the water.

'I live close to the shop,' Samantha explained, as she clattered up on to the screened porch, her arms full of groceries.

'This is yours?' Nicholas asked. He could just make out the tops of big blocks of condominiums on each side; they were incompletely screened by the palms.

'Pa left it to me. He bought it the year I was born,' Samantha explained proudly. 'My ground stretches from there to there.'

A few hundred yards, but Nicholas realized the value of

it. Everybody in the world wants to live on the water, and those condominiums were pressing in closely.

'It must be worth a million.'

'There is no price on it,' she said firmly. 'That's what I tell those awful sweaty little men with their big cigars. Pa left it to me and it's not for sale.'

She had the door open now, bumping it with her denim-clad backside.

'Don't just stand there, Nicholas,' she implored him. 'We've only got ten days.'

He followed her into the kitchen as she dumped her load into the sink, and whirled back to him.

'Welcome to my house, Nicholas,' and then as she slid her arms around his waist, jerked his shirt tails out of his belt and slid her hands up his bare back, 'You'll never know just how welcome. Come, let me show you around – this is the living room.'

It had spartan furniture, with Indian rugs and pottery, and Samantha's chopped-off denims were discarded in the centre of the floor along with Nicholas' shirt.

'And this – surprise! surprise! – is the bedroom.' She dragged him by one hand, and under the short tee-shirt her bottom reminded him of a chipmunk with its cheeks stuffed with nuts, chewing vigorously.

The tiny bedroom overlooked the beach. The sea breeze fluffed out the curtains and the sound of the low surf breathed like a sleeping giant, a deep regular hiss and sigh that filled the air around them.

The bed was too big for the room, all ornate antique brass, with a cloudy soft mattress and an old-fashioned patchwork quilt in a hundred coloured and patterned squares.

'I don't think I could have lived another day without you,' she said, and unwound the thick plaits of her hair. 'You came like the cavalry, in the very nick of time.'

He reached up and took the golden tresses of hair,

winding them thickly around his wrist, twining them in his fingers, and he pulled her gently down beside him.

Suddenly Nick's life was uncluttered and simple again. Suddenly he was young and utterly carefree again. The petty strivings, the subterfuge, the lies and the cheating did not exist in this little universe that encompassed a tiny wooden shack on the edge of the ocean, and a huge brass bed that clanged and rattled and banged and squeaked with the wholesale, the completely abandoned happiness that was the special miracle called Samantha Silver.

Samantha's laboratory was a square room, built on piles over the water, and the soft hum of the electric pumps blended with the slap of the wavelets below and the burble and blurp of the tanks.

'This is my kingdom,' she told him. 'And these are my subjects.'

There were almost a hundred tanks, like the small glass-sided aquaria for goldfish, and suspended over each of them was a complicated arrangement of coils and bottles and electric wiring.

Nick sauntered across to the nearest of the tanks and peered into it. It contained a single large salt-water clam; the animal was feeding with the double shells agape, the pink soft flesh and frilly gills rippling and undulating in the gentle flow of pumped and filtered sea water. To each half of the shell, thin copper wires were attached with blobs of polyurethane cement.

Samantha came to stand beside him, touching, and he asked her, 'What's happening?'

She touched a switch and immediately the cylindrical scroll above the tank began to revolve slowly and a stylus, after a few preliminary jerks and quivers, began to trace out a regular pattern on the paper scroll, a trough and double peak, the second a fraction lower than the first, and then the trough again.

She said, 'He's wired and bugged.'

'You're a member of the CIA,' he accused.

And she laughed. 'His heartbeat. I'm passing an electric impulse through the heart – the heart is only a millimetre across – but each spasm changes the resistance and moves the stylus.' She studied the curve for a moment. 'This fellow is one very healthy cheerful *Spisula solidissima*.'

'Is that his name?' Nick asked. 'I thought he was a clam.'

'One of fifteen thousand bivalves who use that common generic,' she corrected.

'I had to pick an egghead,' said Nicholas ruefully. 'But what's so interesting about his heart?'

'It's the closest and cheapest thing to a pollution metre that we have discovered so far – or rather,' she corrected herself without false modesty, 'that I have discovered.'

She took his hand and led him down the long rows of tanks. 'They are sensitive, incredibly sensitive to any contamination of their environment, and the heartbeat will register almost immediately any foreign element or chemical, organic or otherwise, in such low concentrate that it would take a highly trained specialist with a spectroscope to detect otherwise.'

Nicholas felt his mild attention changing and growing into real interest as Samantha began to prepare samples of common pollutants on the single bench against the forewall of the cluttered little laboratory.

'Here,' she held up one test tube, 'aromatic carbons, the more poisonous elements of crude petroleum – and here,' she indicated the next tube, 'mercury in a concentration of 100 parts to the million. Did you see the photographs of the human vegetables and the Japanese children with the flesh falling off their bones at Kiojo? That was mercury. Lovely stuff.'

She picked up another tube. 'PCB, a by-product of the electrical industry, the Hudson River is thick with it. And these, tetrahydrofurane, cyclohexane, methylbenzene – all industrial by-products but don't let the fancy names throw you. One day they will come back to haunt us, in newspaper headlines, as THF or CMB – one day there will be other human cabbages and babies born without arms or legs.' She touched the other tubes. 'Arsenic, old-fashioned Agatha Christie vintage poison. And then here is the real living and breathing bastard daddy of them all – this is cadmium; as a sulphide so it's easily absorbed. In 100 parts to the million it's as lethal as a neutron bomb.'

While he watched, she carried the tray of tubes across to the tanks and set the ECG monitors running. Each began to record the normal double-peaked heartbeat of a healthy clam.

'Now,' she said, 'watch this.'

Under controlled conditions, she began to drip the weak poisoned solutions into the reticulated water systems, a different solution to each of the tanks.

'These concentrations are so low that the animals will not even be aware of trauma, they will continue to feed and breed without any but long-term indications of systemic poisoning.'

Samantha was a different person, a cool quick-thinking professional. Even the white dust-coat that she had slipped over her tee-shirt altered her image and she had aged twenty years in poise and authority as she passed back and forth along the row of tanks.

'There,' she said, with grim satisfaction as the stylus on one recording drum made a slightly double beat at its peak and then just detectably flattened the second peak. 'Typical aromatic carbon reaction.'

The distorted heartbeat was repeated endlessly on the slowly turning drum, and she passed on to the next tank.

'See the pulse in the trough, see the fractional speeding

up of the heart spasm? That's cadmium in ten parts to the million, at 100 parts it will kill all sea life, at five hundred it will kill man slowly, at seven hundred parts in air or solution it will kill him very quickly indeed.'

Nicholas' interest became total fascination, as he helped Samantha record the experiments and control the flow and concentration in the tanks. Slowly they increased the dosage of each substance and the moving stylus dispassionately recorded the increasing distress and the final convulsions and spasmodic throes that preceded death.

Nicholas voiced the tickle of horror and revulsion he felt at watching the process of degeneration.

'It's macabre.'

'Yes.' She stood back from the tanks. 'Death always is. But these organisms have such rudimentary nervous systems that they don't experience pain as we know it.' She shuddered slightly herself and went on. 'But imagine an entire ocean poisoned like one of these tanks, imagine the incredible agonies of tens of millions of seabirds, of the mammals, seals and porpoises and whales. Then think of what would happen to man himself—' Samantha shrugged off her white dust-coat.

'Now I'm hungry,' she announced, and then looking up at the fibreglass panels in the roof, 'No wonder! It's dark already!'

While they cleaned and tidied the laboratory, and made a last check of the pumps and running equipment, Samantha told him, 'In five hours we have tested over a hundred and fifty samples of contaminated water and got accurate indications of nearly fifty dangerous substances – at a probable cost of fifty cents a sample.' She switched out the lights. 'To do the same with a gas spectroscope would have cost almost ten thousand dollars and taken a highly specialized team two weeks of hard work.'

'It's a hell of a trick,' Nicholas told her. 'You're a clever lady – I'm impressed, I really am.'

At the psychedelic Chevy van she stopped him, and in the light of the street lamp, she looked up at him guiltily.

'Do you mind if I show you off, Nicholas?'

'What does that mean?' he asked suspiciously.

'The gang are eating shrimps tonight. Then they'll sleep over on the boat and have the first shot at fish tagging tomorrow – but we don't have to go. We could just get some more steaks and another jug of wine.' But he could see she really wanted to go.

She was fifty-five foot, an old purse-seiner with the ungainly wheelhouse forward looking like a sentry box or an old-fashioned pit latrine. Even with her coat of new paint, she had an old-fashioned look.

She was tied up at the end of the University jetty, and as they walked out to her, so they could hear the voices and the laughter coming up from below decks.

'*Tricky Dicky*,' Nicholas read her name on the high ugly rounded stern.

'But we love her,' Samantha said, and led him across the narrow, rickety gangplank. 'She belongs to the University. She's only one of our four research vessels. The others are all fancy modern ships, two-hundred-footers, but the *Dicky* is our boat for short field trips to the Gulf or down the Keys, and she's also the faculty clubhouse.'

The main cabin was monastically furnished, bare planking and hard benches, a single long table, but it was as crowded as a fashionable discotheque, packed solid with sunburned young people, girls and boys all in faded jeans and tee-shirts, impossible to judge sexes by clothing or by the length of their sun-tortured and wind-tangled hair.

The air was thick with the rich smell of broiling Gulf shrimps and molten butter, and there were gallon jugs of California wine on the table.

'Hey!' Samantha shouted above the uproar of voices raised in heated dispute and jovial repartee. 'This is Nicholas.'

A comparative silence descended on the gathering, and they looked him over with the curious veiled group hostility of any tribe for an interloper, an intruder in a closed and carefully guarded group. Nick returned the scrutiny calmly, met each pair of eyes, while realizing that despite the affected informality of their dress and some of the wildly unkempt hairstyles and the impressive profusion of beards, they were an élite group. There was not a face that was not intelligent, not a pair of eyes that was not alert and quick, and there was that special feeling of pride and self-confidence in all of them.

At the head of the table sat a big impressive figure, the oldest man in the cabin, perhaps Nick's age or a little older, for there were silver strands in his beard and his face was lined and beaten by sun and wind and time.

'Hi, Nick,' he boomed. 'I won't pretend we've never heard of you. Sam has given us all cauliflower ears—'

'You cut that out, Tom Parker,' Samantha stopped him sharply, and there was a ripple of laughter, a relaxation of tension and a casual round of greetings.

'Hi, Nick, I'm Sally-Anne.' A pretty girl with china-blue eyes behind wire-framed spectacles put a heavy tumbler of wine into his hand.

'We are short of glasses, guess you and Sam will have to share.'

She slid up along the bench and gave them a few inches of space and Samantha perched on Nicholas' lap. The wine was a rough fighting red, and it galloped, booted and spurred across his palate but Samantha sipped her share with the same relish as if it had been a '53 Château Lafitte, and she nuzzled Nicholas' ear and whispered:

'Tom is prof of the Biology Department. He's a honey. After you – he's my most favourite man in the world.'

A woman came through from the galley, carrying a huge platter piled high with bright pink shrimps and a bowl of molten butter. There was a roar of applause for her as she placed the dishes in the centre of the table, and they fell upon the food with unashamed gusto.

The woman was tall with dark hair in braids and a strong capable face, lean and supple in tight breeches, but she was older than the other women and she paused beside Tom Parker and draped one arm across his shoulders in a comfortable gesture of long-established affection.

'That's Antoinette, his wife.' The woman heard her name and smiled across at them, and with dark gentle eyes she studied Nicholas and then nodded and made the continental 'O' of thumb and forefinger at Samantha, before slipping back into the galley.

The food did not inhibit the talk, the lively contentious flow of discussion that swung swiftly from banter to deadly seriousness and back again, bright, trained, informed minds clicking and cannoning off each other with the crispness of ivory billiard balls, while at the same time buttery fingers ripped the whiskered heads off the shrimps, delving for the crescent of sweet white flesh, then leaving greasy fingerprints on the wine tumblers.

As each of them spoke, Samantha whispered their names and credentials. 'Hank Petersen, he's doing a PhD on the bluefin tuna – spawning and a trace of its migratory routes. He's the one running the tagging tomorrow.

'That's Michelle Rand, she's on loan from UCLA, and she's porpoises and whales.'

Then suddenly they were all discussing indignantly a rogue tanker captain who the week before had scrubbed his tanks in the middle of the Florida straits and left a thirty-mile slick down the Gulf Stream. He had done it under cover of night, and changed course as soon as he was into the Atlantic proper.

'We fingerprinted him,' Tom Parker spoke like an angry

bear, 'we had him made, dead in the cross-hairs.' Nick knew he was talking of the finger-printing of oil residues, the breakdown of samples of the slick under gas spectroscopy which could match them exactly to the samples taken by the Coast Guard from the offender's tanks. The identification was good enough to bear up in an international court of law. 'But the trick is getting the son-of-a-bitch into court.' Tom Parker went on. 'He was fifty miles outside our territorial waters by the time the Coast Guard got to him, and he's registered in Liberia.'

'We tried to cover cases like that in the set of proposals I put up to the last maritime conference.'

Nick joined the conversation for the first time. He told them of the difficulties of legislating on an international scale, of policing and bringing to justice the blatant transgressors; then he listed for them what had been done so far, what was in process and finally what he believed should still be done to protect the seas.

He spoke quietly, succinctly, and Samantha noticed again, with a swell of pride, how all the men listened when Nicholas Berg talked. The moment he paused, they came at him from every direction, using their bright young minds like scalpels, tearing into him with sharp lancing questions. He answered them in the same fashion, sharp and hard, armed with total knowledge of his subject, and he saw the shift in the group attitude, the blooming of respect, the subtle opening of ranks to admit him, for he had spoken the correct passwords and they recognized him as one of their own number, as one of the élite.

At the head of the table, Tom Parker sat and listened, nodding and frowning, sitting in judgement with his arm around Antoinette's slim waist and she stood beside him and played idly with a curl of thick wiry hair on the top of his head.

Tom Parker found fish forty miles offshore where the Gulf Stream was setting blue and warm and fast into the north. The birds were working, falling on folded wings down the backdrop of cumulonimbus storm clouds that bruised the horizon. The birds were bright, white pinpoints of light as they fell, and they struck the dark blue water with tiny explosions of white spray, and went deep. Seconds later they popped to the surface, stretching their necks to force down another morsel into their distended crops, before launching into flight again, climbing in steep circles against the sky to join the hunt again. There were hundreds of them and they swirled and fell like snowflakes.

'Anchovy,' grunted Tom Parker, and they could see the agitated surface of the water under the bird flock where the frenzied bait-fish churned. 'Could be bonito working under them.'

'No,' said Nick. 'They are blues.'

'You sure?' Tom grinned a challenge.

'The way they are bunching and holding the bait-fish, it's tuna,' Nick repeated.

'Five bucks?' Tom asked, as he swung the wheel over, and *Tricky Dicky*'s big diesel engine boomed as she went on to the top of her speed.

'You're on,' Nick grinned back at him, and at that moment, they both saw a fish jump clear. It was a brilliant shimmering torpedo, as long as a man's arm. It went six feet into the air, turned in flight and hit the water again with a smack they heard clearly above the diesel.

'Blues,' said Nick flatly. 'Shoal blues – they'll go twenty pounds each.'

'Five bucks,' Tom grunted with disgust. 'Son of a gun, I don't think I can afford you, man,' and he delivered a playful punch to the shoulder which rattled Nick's teeth, then he turned to the open window of the wheelhouse and bellowed out on to the deck, 'Okay, kids, they are blues'.

There was a scramble and chatter of excitement as they rushed for lines and tagging poles. It was Hank's show: he was the bluefin tunny expert; he knew as much about their sex habits, their migratory routes and food chains as any man living, but when it came to catching them, Nick observed drily, he could probably do a better job as a blacksmith.

Tom Parker was no fisherman either. He ran down the shoal, charging *Tricky Dicky* through the centre of it, scattering birds and fish in panic – but by sheer chance one of the gang in the stern hooked in, and after a great deal of heaving and huffing and shouted encouragement from his peers, dragged a single luckless baby bluefin tuna over the rail. It skittered and jumped around the deck, its tail hammering against the planking, pursued by a shrieking band of scientists who slid and slipped in the fish slime, knocked each other down and finally cornered the fish against the rail. The first three attempts to affix the plastic tag were unsuccessful, Hank's lunges with the dart pole becoming wilder as his frustration mounted. He almost succeeded in tagging Samantha's raised backside as she knelt on the deck trying to cradle the fish in both arms.

'You do this often?' Nicholas asked mildly.

'First time with this gang,' Tom Parker admitted sheepishly. 'Thought you'd never guess.'

By now the triumphant band was solicitously returning the fish to the sea, the barbed dart of the plastic tag embedded dangerously near its vitals; and if that didn't eventually kill it, the rough handling probably would. It had pounded its head on the deck so heavily that blood oozed from the gill covers. It floated away, belly up on the stream, oblivious of Samantha's anguished cries of:

'Swim, fish, get in there and swim!'

'Mind if we try it my way?' Nick asked, and Tom relinquished command without a struggle.

Nicholas picked the four strongest and best co-ordinated

of the young men, and gave them a quick demonstration and lecture on how to handle the heavy handlines with the Japanese feather lures, showing them how to throw the bait, and the recovery with an underhand flick that recoiled the line between the feet. Then he gave each a station along the starboard rail, with the second member of each team ready with a tagging pole and Hank Petersen on the roof of the wheelhouse to record the fish taken and the numbers of the tags.

They found another shoal within the hour and Nicholas circled up on it, closing steadily at good trolling speed, helping the feeding tuna bunch the shoal of frenzied anchovy on the surface, until he could lock *Tricky Dicky*'s wheel hard down starboard and leave her to describe her own sedate circles around the shoal. Then he hurried out on to the deck.

The trapped and surrounded fish thrashed the surface until it boiled like a porridge of molten, flashing silver; through it drove the fast dark torpedoes of the hungry tuna.

Within minutes Nick had his four fishermen working to the steady rhythm of throwing the lures into the frothing water, almost instantly striking back on the line as a tuna snatched the feathers, and then swinging hand over head, recovering and coiling line fast with minimum effort, swinging the fish out and up with both hands and then catching its streamlined body under the left armpit like a quarterback picking up a long pass, clamping it there firmly, although the cold, firm, silver bullet shape juddered and quivered and the tail beat in a blur of movement. Then he taught them to slip the hook from the jaw, careful not to damage the vulnerable gills, holding the fish firmly but gently while the assistant pressed the barbed dart into the thick muscle at the back of the dorsal fin. When the fish was dropped back over the side, there were so few after-effects that it almost immediately began feeding again on the packed masses of tiny anchovies.

Each plastic tag was numbered and imprinted with a request in five languages to mail it back to the University of Miami with details of the date and place of capture, providing a valuable trace of the movements of the shoals in their annual circumnavigation of the globe. From their spawning grounds somewhere in the Caribbean they worked the Gulf Stream north and east across the Atlantic, then south down and around the Cape of Good Hope with an occasional foray down the length of the Mediterranean Sea – although now the dangerous pollution of that landlocked water was changing their habits. From Good Hope east again south of Australia to take a gigantic swing up and around the Pacific, running the gauntlet of the Japanese long-liners and the California tunny men before ducking down under the terrible icy seas of the Horn and back to their spawning grounds in the Caribbean.

They sat up on the wheelhouse as the *Dicky* ran home in the sunset, drinking beer and talking. Nicholas studied them casually and saw that they possessed so many of the qualities he valued in his fellow humans; they were intelligent and motivated, they were dedicated and free of that particular avarice that mars so many others.

Tom Parker crumpled the empty beer can in a huge fist as easily as if it had been a paper packet, fished two more from the pack beside him and tossed one across to Nick. The gesture seemed to have some special significance and Nicholas saluted him with the can before he drank.

Samantha was snuggled down in luxurious weariness against his shoulder, and the sunset was a magnificence of purple and hot molten crimson. Nicholas thought idly how pleasant it would be to spend the rest of his life doing things like this with people like these.

Tom Parker's office had shelves to the ceiling, and they were sagging with hundreds of bottled specimens and rows of scientific papers and publications.

He sat well back in his swivel chair with ankles crossed neatly in the centre of the cluttered desk.

'I ran a check on you, Nicholas. Damned nerve, wasn't it? You have my apology.'

'Was it an interesting exercise?' Nicholas asked mildly.

'It wasn't difficult. You have left a trail behind you like a—' Tom sought for a comparison, 'like a grizzly bear through a honey farm. Son of a gun, Nicholas, that's a hell of a track record you've got yourself.'

'I've kept busy,' Nicholas admitted.

'Beer?' Tom crossed to the refrigerator in the corner that was labelled 'Zoological Specimens. DO NOT OPEN.'

'It's too early for me.'

'Never too early,' said Tom and pulled the tag on a dewy can of Millers and then picked up Nicholas' statement. 'Yes, you have kept busy. Strange, isn't it, that around some men things just happen.'

Nicholas did not reply, and Tom went on. 'We need a man around here who can *do*. It's all right thinking it out, then you need the catalyst to transform thought and intention into action.' Tom sucked at the can and then licked the froth off his moustache. 'I know what you have done. I've heard you speak, I've seen you move, and those things count. But most important of all, I know you care. I've been watching you carefully, Nick, and you really care, down deep in your guts, the way we do.'

'It sounds as though you're offering me a job, Tom.'

'I'm not going to horse around, Nick, I *am* offering you a job.' He waved a huge paw, like a bunch of broiled pork sausages. 'Hell, I know you're a busy man, but I'd like to romance you into an associate professorship. We'd want a little of your time when it came to hassling and negotiating up in Washington, we'd call for you when we needed real muscle to put our case, when we need the right contacts, somebody with a big reputation to open doors, when we need a man who knows the practical side of the oceans and the men that use them and abuse them.

'We need a man who is a hard-headed businessman, who knows the economics of sea trade, who has built and run tankers, who knows that human need is of paramount importance, but who can balance the human need for protein and fossil fuels against the greater danger of turning the oceans into watery deserts.' Tom lubricated his throat with beer, watching shrewdly for some reaction from Nicholas, and when he received no encouragement, he went on more persuasively. 'We are specialists, perhaps we have the specialist's narrow view; God knows, they think of us as sentimentalists, the lunatic fringe of doomsayers, long-haired intellectual hippies. What we need is a man with real clout in the establishment – shit, Nicholas, if you walked into a Congressional committee they'd really jerk out of their geriatric trance and switch on their hearing-aids.' Nicholas was silent still and Tom was becoming desperate. 'What can we offer in return? I know you aren't short of cash, and it would be a lousy 12,000 a year, but an associate professorship is a nice title. We start out holding hands with that. Then we might start going steady, a full professorship – chair of applied oceanology, or some juicy title like that which we'd think up. I don't know what else we can offer you, Nick, except perhaps the warm good feeling in your guts when you're doing a tough job that has to be done.' He stopped again, running out of words, and he wagged his big shaggy head sadly.

'You aren't interested, are you?' he asked.

Nick stirred himself. 'When do I start?' he asked, and as Tom's face split into a great beaming grin, Nick held out his hand. 'I think I'll take that beer now.'

The water was cool enough to be invigorating. Nick and Samantha swam so far out that the land was almost lost in the lowering gloom of dusk, and then they turned and swam back side by side. The beach was deserted; in their mood, the lights of the nearest condominiums were no more intrusive than the stars, the faint sound of music and laughter no more intrusive than the cry of gulls.

It was the right time to tell her, and he did it in detail beginning with the offer by the Sheikhs to buy out Ocean Salvage and Towage.

'Will you sell?' she asked quietly. 'You won't, will you?'

'For seven million dollars clear?' he asked. 'Do you know how much money that is?'

'I can't count that far,' she admitted. 'But what would you do if you sold? I cannot imagine you playing bowls or golf for the rest of your life.'

'Part of the deal is that I run Ocean Salvage for them for two years, and then I've been offered a part-time assignment which will fill any spare time I've got left over.'

'What is it?'

'Associate Professor at Miami University.'

She stopped dead and dragged him around to face her.

'You're having me on!' she accused.

'That's a start only,' he admitted. 'In two years or so, when I've finished with Ocean Salvage, there may be a full chair of applied oceanology.'

'It's not true!' she said, and took him by the arms, shaking him with surprising strength.

'Tom wants me to ramrod the applied aspects of the environmental research. I'll troubleshoot with legislators and the maritime conference, a sort of hired gun for the Greenpeacers—'

'Oh Nicholas, Nicholas!'

'Sweet Christ!' he accused. 'You're crying again.'

'I just can't help it.' She was in his arms still wet and

cold and gritty with beach sand. She clung to him, quivering with joy. 'Do you know what this means, Nicholas? You don't, do you? You just don't realize what this means.'

'Tell me,' he invited. 'What does it mean?'

'What it means is that, in future, we can do everything together, not just munch food and go boom in bed – but everything, work and play and, and *live* together like a man and woman should!' She sounded stunned and frightened by the magnitude of the vision.

'The prospect daunts me not at all,' he murmured gently, and lifted her chin.

They washed off the salt and the sand, crowding together into the thick, perfumed steam of the shower cubicle and afterwards they lay together on the patchwork quilt in the darkness with the sound of the sea as background music to the plans and dreams they wove together.

Every time they both descended to the very frontiers of sleep, one of them would think of something vitally important and prod the other awake to say it.

'I've got to be in London on Tuesday.'

'Don't spoil it all, now,' she murmured sleepily.

'And then we're launching *Sea Witch* on the 7th April.'

'I'm not listening,' she whispered. 'I've got my fingers in my ears.'

'Will you launch her – I mean break the bottle of bubbly and bless her?'

'I've just taken my fingers out again.'

'Jules would love it.'

'Nicholas, I cannot spend my life commuting across the Atlantic, not even for you. I've got work to do.'

'Peter will be there, I'll work that as a bribe.'

'That's unfair pressure,' she protested.

'Will you come?'

'You know I will, you sexy bastard. I wouldn't miss it for

all the world.' She moved across the quilt and found his ear with her lips. 'I am honoured.'

'Both of you are sea witches,' Nick told her.

'And you are my warlock.'

'Sea witch and warlock,' he chuckled. 'Together we will work miracles.'

'Look, I know it's terribly forward of me, but seeing that we are both wide awake, and it's only two o'clock in the morning, I would be super ultra-grateful if you could work one of your little miracles for me right now.'

'It will be a great pleasure,' Nick told her.

Nicholas was early, he saw as he came out of the American Consulate and glanced at his Rolex, so he moderated his pace across the Place de la Concorde, despite the gentle misty rain that settled in minute droplets on the shoulders of his trench coat.

Lazarus was at the rendezvous ahead of him, standing under one of the statues in the corner of the square closest to the French naval headquarters.

He was heavily muffled against the cold, dressed all in sombre blue with a long cashmere scarf wound around his throat and a dark blue hat pulled down so low as to conceal the pale smooth bulge of his forehead.

'Let's find a warm place,' Nick suggested, without greeting the little man.

'No,' said Lazarus, looking up at him through the thick distorting lenses of his spectacles. 'Let us walk.' And he led the way through the underpass on to the promenade above the embankment of the Seine, and set off in the direction of the Petit Palais.

In the middle of such an inclement afternoon they were the only strollers, and they walked in silence three or four hundred yards while Lazarus satisfied himself absolutely of this, and while he adjusted his mincing little steps to Nick's stride. It was like taking Toulouse-Lautrec for a stroll, Nick smiled to himself. Even when Lazarus began speaking, he kept glancing back over his shoulder, and once when two bearded Algerian students in combat jackets overtook them, he let them get well ahead before he went on.

'You know there will be nothing in writing?' he piped.

'I have a recorder in my pocket,' Nick assured him.

'Very well, you are entitled to that.'

'Thank you,' murmured Nick dryly.

Lazarus paused, it was almost as though a new reel was being fitted into the computer, and when he began talking again, his voice had a different timbre, a monotonous, almost electronic tone, as though he was indeed an automaton.

First, there was a recital of share movements in the thirty-three companies which make up the Christy Marine complex, every movement in the previous eighteen months.

The little man reeled them off steadily, as though he were actually reading from the share registers of the companies. He must have had access, Nicholas realized, to achieve such accuracy. He had the date, the number of the shares, the transferor and transferee, even the transfer of shares in Ocean Salvage and Towage to Nicholas himself, and the reciprocal transfer of Christy Marine stock was faithfully detailed, confirming the accuracy of Lazarus' other information. It was all an impressive exhibition of total knowledge and total recall, but much too complicated for Nicholas to make any sense of it. He would have to study it carefully. All that he would hazard was that somebody was putting up a smokescreen.

Lazarus stopped on the corner of the Champs Elysées and the rue de la Boétie. Nicholas glanced down at him and saw his shapeless blob of a nose was an unhealthy purplish pink in the cold, and that his breathing had coarsened and laboured with the exertion of walking. Nick realized suddenly that the little man was probably asthmatic, and as if to confirm this, he took a little silver and turquoise pill-box from his pocket and slipped a single pink capsule into his mouth before leading Nicholas into the foyer of a movie house and buying two tickets.

It was a porno movie, a French version of *Deep Throat* entitled *Gorge Profonde*. The print was scratched and the French dubbing was out of synchronization. The cinema was almost empty, so they found two seats in isolation at the rear of the stalls.

Lazarus stared unblinkingly at the screen, as he began the second part of his report. This was a detailed breakdown of cash movements within the Christy Marine Group, and Nick was again amazed at the man's penetration.

He drew a verbal picture of the assemblage of enormous sums of money, marshalled and channelled into orderly flows by a master tactician. The genius of Duncan Alexander was as clearly identifiable as that flourishing signature with the flamboyant 'A' and 'X' which Nicholas had seen him dash off with studied panache. Then suddenly the cashflow was not so steady and untroubled, there were eddies and breaks, little gaps and inconsistencies that nagged at Nicholas like the false chimes of a broken clock. Lazarus finished this section of his report with a brief summation of the Group's cash and credit position as at a date four days previously and Nicholas realized that the doubts were justified. Duncan had run the Group out along a knife-edge.

Nicholas sat hunched down in the threadbare velvet seat, both hands thrust into the pockets of his trenchcoat, watching the incredible feats of Miss Lovelace on the screen, without really seeing them, while beside him

Lazarus took an aerosol can from his pocket, screwed a nozzle on to it and noisily sprayed a fine mist down his own throat. It seemed to relieve him almost immediately.

'Insurance and marine underwriting of vessels owned by the Christy Marine Group of companies.' He began again with names and figures and dates, and Nicholas picked up the trend. Duncan was using his own captive company, London and European Insurance and Banking, to lead the risk on all his vessels, and then he was reinsuring in the marketplace, spreading part of the risk, but carrying a whacking deductible himself, the principle of self-insurance that Nicholas had opposed so vigorously, and which had rebounded so seriously upon Duncan's head with the salvage of *Golden Adventurer*.

The last of the vessels in Lazarus' recital was *Golden Dawn*, and Nicholas shifted restlessly in his seat at the mention of the name, and almost immediately he realized that something strange was taking place.

'Christy Marine did not apply for a Lloyd's survey of this vessel.' Nicholas knew that already. 'But she has been rated first class by the continental surveyors.' It was a much easier rating to obtain, and consequently less acceptable than the prestigious A1 at Lloyd's.

Lazarus went on, lowering his voice slightly as another patron entered the almost deserted cinema and took a seat two rows in front of them.

'And insurance has been effected outside Lloyd's.' The risk was led by London and European Insurance. Again, Duncan was self-insuring, Nicholas noted grimly, but not all of it. 'And further lines were written by—' Lazarus listed the other companies which carried a part of the risk, with whom Duncan had reinsured. But it was all too thin, too nebulous. Again, only careful study of the figures would enable Nicholas to analyse what Duncan was doing, how much was real insurance and how much was bluff to convince his financiers that the risk was truly covered, and their investment protected.

Some of the names of the reinsurers were familiar; they had been on the list of transferees who had taken stock positions in Christy Marine.

'Is Duncan buying insurance with capital?' Nicholas pondered. Was he buying at desperate prices? He must have cover, of course. Without insurance the finance houses, the banks and institutions which had loaned the money to Christy Marine to build the monstrous tanker, would dig in against Duncan. His own shareholders would raise such hell – No, Duncan Alexander had to have cover, even if it was paper only, without substance, a mere incestuous circle, a snake eating itself tail first.

Oh, but the trail was so cleverly confused, so carefully swept and tied up, only Nicholas' intimate knowledge of Christy Marine made him suspicious, and it might take a team of investigators years to unravel the tortured tapestry of deceit. In the first instant, it had occurred to Nicholas that the easiest way to stop Duncan Alexander was to leak his freshly gleaned suspicions to Duncan's major creditors, to those who had financed the building of *Golden Dawn*. But immediately he realized that this was not enough. There were no hard facts, it was all inference and innuendo. By the time the facts could be exhumed and laid out in all their putrefaction for autopsy, *Golden Dawn* would be on the high seas, carrying a million tons of crude. Duncan might have won sufficient time to make his profit and sell out to some completely uncontrollable Greek or Chinaman, as he had boasted he would do. It would not be so simple to stop Duncan Alexander; it was folly to have believed that for one moment. Even if his creditors were made aware of the flimsy insurance cover over *Golden Dawn*, were they too deeply in already? Would they not then accept the risks, spreading them where they could, and simply twist the financial rope a little tighter around Duncan's throat? No, it was not the way to stop him. Duncan had to be forced to remodify the giant tanker's hull, forced to make her an acceptable moral risk, forced to accept the standard Nicholas had originally stipulated for the vessel.

Lazarus had finished the insurance portion of his report and he stood up abruptly, just as Miss Lovelace was about to attempt the impossible. With relief, Nick followed him down the aisle and into the chill of a Parisian evening, and they breathed the fumes that the teeming city exhaled as Lazarus led him back eastwards through the VIII[e] Arrondissement with those little dancing steps, while he recited the details of the charters of all Christy Marine's vessels, the charterer, the rates, the dates of expiry of contract; and Nicholas recognized most of them, contracts that he himself had negotiated, or those that had been renewed on expiry with minor alterations to the terms. He was relying on the recorder in his pocket, listening only with the surface layer of his mind, pondering all he had heard so far from this extraordinary little man – so that when it came he almost did not realize what he was hearing.

'On 10th January Christy Marine entered a contract of carriage with Orient Amex. The tenure is ten years. The vessel to be employed is the *Golden Dawn*. The rate is 10 cents US per hundred ton miles with a minimum annual guaranteed usage of 75,000 nautical miles.'

Nicholas registered the trigger word *Golden Dawn* and then he assimilated it all. The price, ten cents per hundred ton miles, that was wrong, high, much too high, ridiculously high in this depressed market. Then the name, Orient Amex – what was there about it that jarred his memory?

He stopped dead, and a following pedestrian bumped him. Nicholas shouldered him aside thoughtlessly and stood thinking, ransacking his mind for buried items of information. Lazarus had stopped also and was waiting patiently, and now Nicholas laid a hand on the little man's shoulder.

'I need a drink.'

He drew him into a brasserie which was thick with steam from the coffee machine and the smoke of Caporal and Disque Bleu, and sat him at a tiny table by the window overlooking the sidewalk.

Primly, Lazarus asked for a Vittel water and sipped it with an air of virtue, while Nicholas poured soda into his whisky.

'Orient Amex,' Nicholas asked, as soon as the waiter had left. 'Tell me about it.'

'That is outside my original terms of reference,' Lazarus demurred delicately.

'Charge me for it,' Nicholas invited, and Lazarus paused as the computer reels clicked in his mind, then he began to speak.

'Orient Amex is an American-registered company, with an issued capital of twenty-five million shares at a par value of ten dollars—' Lazarus recited the dry statistics. 'The company is presently undertaking substantial dry-land exploration in Western Australia and Ethiopia, and offshore exploration within the territorial waters of Norway and Chile. It has erected a refinery at Galveston in Texas to operate under the new atomic catalyst-cracking process, first employed at its pilot plant on the same site. The plant is projected for initial operation in June this year, and full production in five years.'

It was all vaguely familiar to Nicholas, the names, the process of cracking the low-value high-carbon molecules, breaking up the carbon atoms and reassembling them in volatile low-carbon molecules of high value.

'The company operates producing wells in Texas, and in the Santa Barbara offshore field, in Southern Nigeria, and has proven crude reserves in the El Barras field of

Kuwait, which will be utilized by the new cracking plant in Galveston.'

'Good God,' Nicholas stared at him. 'The El Barras field – but it's cadmium-contaminated, it's been condemned by—'

'The El Barras field is a high cadmium field, naturally enriched with the catalyst necessary for the new process.'

'What are the cadmium elements?' Nicholas demanded.

'The western area of the El Barras field has sampled at 2,000 parts per million, and the north and eastern anticline have sampled as high as 42,000 parts per million.' Lazarus recited the figures pedantically. 'The American and Nigerian crudes will be blended with the El Barras crudes during the revolutionary cracking process. It is projected that the yield of low-carbon volatiles will be increased from 40 per cent to 85 per cent by this process, making it five to eight times more profitable, and extending the life of the world's known reserves of crude petroleum by between ten and fifteen years.'

As he listened, Nicholas had a vivid mental image of the stylus in Samantha's laboratory recording the death throes of a cadmium-poisoned clam. Lazarus was talking on dispassionately. 'During the cracking process, the cadmium sulphide will be reduced to its pure metallic, non-toxic form, and will be a valuable by-product, reducing the costs of refining.'

Nicholas shook his head in disbelief, and he spoke aloud. 'Duncan is going to do it. Across two oceans, a million tons at a time, in that vulnerable jerry-built monster of his, Duncan is going to do what no other shipowner has ever dared to do – he's going to carry the cad-rich crudes of El Barras!'

From the balcony windows of his suite in the Ritz, Nicholas could look out across the Place Vendôme at the column in the centre of the square with its spiral bas-relief made from the Russian and Austrian guns and commemorating the little Corsican's feats of arms against those two nations. While he studied the column and waited for his connection, he did a quick calculation and realized that it would be three o'clock in the morning on the eastern seaboard of North America. At least he would find her at home. Then he smiled to himself. If she wasn't at home, he'd want to know the reason why.

The telephone rang and he picked it up without turning away from the window.

There was a confused mumbling and Nicholas asked, 'Who is this?'

'It's Sam Silver – what's the time? Who is it? Good God, it's three o'clock. What do you want?'

'Tell that other guy to put his pants on and go home.'

'Nicholas!' There was a joyous squeal, followed immediately by a crash and clatter that made Nicholas wince and lift the receiver well away from his ear.

'Oh damn it to hell, I've knocked the table over. Nicholas, are you there? Speak to me, for God's sake!'

'I love you.'

'Say that again, please. Where are you?'

'Paris. I love you.'

'Oh,' her tone drooped miserably. 'You sound so close. I thought—' Then she rallied gamely. 'I love you too – how's himself?'

'On the dole.'

'Who is she?'

'Dole is unemployment insurance – welfare—' He sought the American equivalent. 'I mean he is temporarily unemployed.'

'Great. Keep him that way. Did I tell you I love you, I forget?'

'Wake up. Shake yourself. I've got something to tell you.'

'I'm awake – well, almost anyway.'

'Samantha, what would happen if somebody dumped a million tons of 40,000 parts concentration of cadmium sulphide in an emulsion of aromatic Arabian crude into the Gulf Stream, say thirty nautical miles off Key West?'

'That's a freaky question, Nicholas. For three in the morning, that's a bomber.'

'What would happen?' he insisted.

'The crude would act as a transporting medium,' she was struggling to project a scenario through her sleepiness, 'it would spread out on the surface to a thickness of a quarter of an inch or so, so you'd end up with a slick of a few thousand miles long and four or five hundred wide, and it would keep going.'

'What would be the results?'

'It would wipe out most of the marine life on the Bahamas and on the eastern seaboard of the States, no, correct that – it would wipe out all marine life, that includes the spawning grounds of the tuna, the freshwater eels and the sperm whale, and it would contaminate—' she was coming fully awake now, and a stirring horror altered her tone. 'You're macabre, Nicholas, what a sick thing to think about, especially at three in the morning.'

'Human life?' he asked.

'Yes, there would be heavy loss,' she said. 'As sulphide, it would be readily absorbed and in that concentration it would be poisonous on contact, fishermen, vacationers, anybody who walked on a contaminated beach.' She was truly beginning to realize the enormity of it. 'A large part of the population of the cities on the east coast – Nicholas, it could amount to hundreds of thousands of human beings, and if it was carried beyond America on the Gulf Stream, the Newfoundland Banks, Iceland, the North Sea, it would poison the cod fisheries, it would kill everything, man, fish, bird and animal. Then the tail of the Gulf Stream twists around the British Isles and the north continent of Europe – but why are you asking me this, what kind of crazy guessing game is this, Nicholas?'

'Christy Marine has signed a ten-year contract to carry one million ton loads of crude from the El Barras field on the South Arabian Gulf to the Orient Amex refinery in Galveston. The El Barras crude has a cadmium sulphide constituent of between 2,000 and 40,000 parts per million.'

Now there was trembling outrage in her voice as she whispered, 'A million tons! That's some sort of genocide, Nicholas, there has probably never been a more deadly cargo in the history of seafaring.'

'In a few weeks' time *Golden Dawn* will run down her ways at St Nazaire – and when she does, the seeds of catastrophe will be sewn upon the oceans.'

'Her route from the Arabian Gulf takes her around Good Hope.'

'One of the most dangerous seas in the world, the home of the hundred-year wave,' Nicholas agreed.

'Then across the southern Atlantic—'

' – and into the bottleneck of the Gulf Stream between Key West and Cuba, into the Devil's Triangle, the breeding ground of the hurricanes—'

'You can't let them do it, Nicholas,' she said quietly. 'You just have to stop them.'

'It won't be easy, but I'll be working hard on it this side, there are a dozen tricks I am going to try, but you have to take over on your side,' he told her. 'Samantha, you go get Tom Parker. Get him out of bed, if necessary. He has to hit Washington with the news, hit all the media – television, radio and the press. A confrontation with Orient Amex, challenge them to make a statement.'

Samantha picked up the line he was taking. 'We'll get the Greenpeacers to picket the Orient Amex refinery in Galveston, the one which will process the cadmium crudes.

We'll have every environmental agency in the country at work – we'll raise a stink like that of a million corpses,' she promised.

'Fine,' he said. 'You do all that, but don't forget to get your chubby little backside across here for the launching of *Sea Witch*.'

'Chubby obese, or chubby nice?' she demanded.

'Chubby beautiful,' he grinned. 'And I'll have room service ready to send up the food, in a front-end loader.'

Nicholas sat over the telephone for the rest of the day, having his meals brought up to the suite, while he worked systematically down the long list of names he had drawn up with the help of the tape recording of Lazarus' report.

The list began with all those who it seemed had loaned capital to Christy Marine for the construction of *Golden Dawn*, and then went on to those who had written lines of insurance on the hull, and on the pollution cover for the tanker.

Nicholas dared not be too specific in the summation he gave to each of them, he did not want to give Duncan Alexander an opportunity to throw out a smokescreen of libel actions against him. But in each case, Nicholas spoke to the top men, mostly men he knew well enough to use their Christian names, and he said just enough to show that he knew the exact amount of their involvement with Christy Marine, to suggest they re-examine the whole project, especially with regard to *Golden Dawn*'s underwriting and to her contract of carriage with Orient Amex.

In the quiet intervals between each telephone call, or while a name was tracked down by a secretary, Nicholas sat over the Place Vendôme and carefully re-examined himself and his reasons for what he was doing.

It is so very easy for a man to attribute to himself the most noble motives. The sea had given Nicholas a wonderful life, and had rewarded him in wealth, reputation and achievement. Now it was time to repay part of that debt, to use some of that wealth to protect and guard the oceans, the way a prudent farmer cherishes his soil. It was a fine thought, but when he looked below its shining surface, he saw the shape and movement of less savoury creatures, like the shadows of shark and barracuda in the depths.

There was pride. *Golden Dawn* had been his creation, the culmination of a lifetime's work, it was going to be the laurel crown on his career. But it had been taken from him, and bastardized – and when it failed, when the whole marvellous concept collapsed in disaster and misery, Nicholas Berg's name would still be on it. The world would remember then that the whole grandiose design had originated with him.

There was pride, and then there was hatred. Duncan Alexander had taken his woman and child. Duncan Alexander had wrested his very life from him. Duncan Alexander was the enemy, and by Nicholas' rules, he must be fought with the same single-mindedness, with the same ruthlessness, as he did everything in his life.

Nicholas poured himself another cup of coffee and lit a cheroot; brooding alone in the magnificence of his suite, he asked himself the question:

'If it had been another man in another ship who was going to transport the El Barras crudes – would I have opposed him so bitterly?'

The question needed no formal reply. Duncan Alexander was the enemy.

Nicholas picked up the telephone, and placed the call he had been delaying. He did not need to look in the red calf-bound notebook for the number of the house in Eaton Square.

'Mrs Chantelle Alexander, please.'

'I am sorry, sir. Mrs Alexander is at Cap Ferrat.'

'Of course,' he muttered. 'Thank you.'

'Do you want the number?'

'That's all right, I have it.' He had lost track of time. He dialled again, this time down to the Mediterranean coast.

'This is the residence of Mrs Alexander. Her son Peter Berg speaking.'

Nicholas felt the rush of emotion through his blood, so that it burned his cheeks and stung his eyes.

'Hello, my boy.' Even in his own ears his voice sounded stilted, perhaps pompous.

'Father,' undisguised delight. 'Dad, how are you – sir? Did you get my letters?'

'No, I didn't, where did you send them?'

'The flat – in Queen's Gate.'

'I haven't been back there for,' Nicholas thought, 'for nearly a month.'

'I got your cards, Dad, the one from Bermuda and the one from Florida. I just wrote to tell you—' and there was a recital of schoolboy triumphs and disasters.

'That's tremendous, Peter. I'm really proud.'

Nicholas imagined the face of his son as he listened, and his heart was squeezed – by guilt, that he could do so little, could give him so little of his time, squeezed by longing for what he had lost. For it was only at times such as these that he could admit how much he missed his son.

'That's great, Peter—' The boy was trying to tell it all at the same time, gabbling out the news he had stored so carefully, flitting from subject to subject, as one thing reminded him of another. Then, of course, the inevitable question:

'When can I come to you, Dad?'

'I'll have to arrange that with your mother, Peter. But it will be soon. I promise you that.' Let's get away from that, Nick thought, desperately. 'How is *Apache?* Have you raced her yet these holidays?'

'Oh yes, Mother let me have a new set of Terylene sails, in red and yellow. I raced her yesterday.' *Apache* had not actually been placed first in the event, but Nicholas gained the impression that the blame lay not with her skipper but rather on the vagaries of the wind, the unsporting behaviour of the other competitors who bumped when they had the weather gauge, and finally the starter who had wanted to disqualify *Apache* for beating the gun. 'But,' Peter went on, 'I'm racing again on Saturday morning—'

'Peter, where is your mother?'

'She's down at the boathouse.'

'Can you put this call through there? I must speak to her, Peter.'

'Of course.' The disappointment in the child's voice was almost completely disguised. 'Hey, Dad. You promised, didn't you? It will be soon?'

'I promised.'

'Cheerio, sir.'

There was a clicking and humming on the line and then suddenly her voice, with its marvellous timbre and serenity.

'*C'est Chantelle Alexander qui parle*.'

'*C'est Nicholas ici*.'

'Oh, my dear. How good to hear your voice. How are you?'

'Are you alone?'

'No, I have friends lunching with me. The Contessa is here with his new boyfriend, a matador no less!'

The 'Contessa' was an outrageously camp and wealthy homosexual who danced at Chantelle's court. Nicholas could imagine the scene on the wide paved terrace, screened from the cliffs above by the sighing pines and the rococo pink boathouse with its turrets and rusty-coloured tiles. There would be gay and brilliant company under the colourful umbrellas.

'Pierre and Mimi sailed across from Cannes for the day.'

Pierre was the son of the largest manufacturer of civil and military jet aircraft in Europe. 'And Robert—'

Below the terrace was the private jetty and small beautifully equipped yacht basin. Her visitors would have moored their craft there, the bare masts nodding lazily against the sky and the small Mediterranean-blue wavelets lapping the stone jetty. Nicholas could hear the laughter and the tinkle of glasses in the background, and he cut short the recital of the guest list.

'Is Duncan there?'

'No, he's still in London – he won't be out until next week.'

'I have news. Can you get up to Paris?'

'It's impossible, Nicky.' Strange how the pet name did not jar from her. 'I must be at Monte Carlo tomorrow, I'm helping Grace with the Spring Charity—'

'It's important, Chantelle.'

'Then there's Peter. I don't like to leave him. Can't you come here? There is a direct flight at nine tomorrow. I'll get rid of the house guests so we can talk in private.'

He thought quickly, then, 'All right, will you book me a suite at the Negresco?'

'Don't be silly, Nicky. We've thirteen perfectly good bedrooms here – we are both civilized people and Peter would love to see you, you know that.'

The Côte d'Azur was revelling in a freakish burst of early spring weather when Nicholas came down the boarding ladder at Nice Airport, and Peter was waiting for him at the boundary fence, hopping up and down and waving both hands above his head like a semaphore signaller. But when Nicholas came through the gate he regained his composure and shook hands formally.

'It's jolly good to see you, Dad.'

'I swear you've grown six inches,' said Nicholas, and on impulse stooped and hugged the child. For a moment they clung to each other, and it was Peter who pulled away first. Both of them were embarrassed by that display of affection for a moment, then quite deliberately Nicholas placed his hand on Peter's shoulder and squeezed.

'Where is the car?'

He kept his hand on the child's shoulder as they crossed the airport foyer, and as Peter became more accustomed to this unusual gesture of affection, so he pressed closer to his father, and seemed to swell with pride.

Characteristically, Nicholas wondered what had changed about him that made it easier for him to act naturally towards those he loved. The answer was obvious, it was Samantha Silver who had taught him to let go.

'Let go, Nicholas.' He could almost hear her voice now.

The chauffeur was new, a silent unobtrusive man, and there were only the two of them in the back seat of the Rolls on the drive back through Nice, and along the coast road.

'Mother has gone across to the Palace. She won't be back until dinner time.'

'Yes, she told me. We've got the day to ourselves,' Nicholas grinned, as the chauffeur turned in through the electric gates and white columns that guarded the entrance to the estate. 'What are we going to do?'

They swam and they played tennis and took Peter's Arrowhead-class yacht *Apache* on a long reach up the coast as far as Menton and then raced back, gull-winged and spinnaker set on the wind with the spray kicking up over the bows and flicking into their faces. They laughed a lot and they talked even more, and while Nicholas changed for dinner, he found himself caught up in the almost postcoital melancholy of too much happiness – happiness that was transitory and soon must end. He tried to push the sadness aside, but it persisted as he dressed in a white silk rollneck and double-breasted blazer and went down to the terrace room.

Peter was there before him, early as a child on Christmas morning, his hair still wet and slicked down from the shower and his face glowing pinkly from the sun and happiness.

'Can I pour you a drink, Dad?' he asked eagerly, already hovering over the silver drinks tray.

'Leave a little in the bottle,' Nicholas cautioned him, not wanting to deny him the pleasure of performing this grown-up service, but with a healthy respect for the elephantine tots that Peter dispensed in a sense of misplaced generosity.

He tasted the drink cautiously, gasped, and added more soda. 'That's fine,' he said, Peter looked proud, and at that moment Chantelle came down the wide staircase into the room.

Nicholas found it impossible not to stare. Was it possible she had grown more lovely since their last meeting, or had she merely taken special pains this evening?

She was dressed in ivory silk, woven gossamer fine, so it floated about her body as she moved, and as she crossed the last ruddy glow of the dying day that came in from the French windows of the terrace, the light struck through the sheer material and put the dainty line of her legs into momentary silhouette. Closer to him, he saw the silk was embroidered with the same thread, ivory on ivory, a marvellous understatement of elegance, and under it the shadowy outline of her breasts, those fine shapely breasts that he remembered so well, and the faint dusky rose suggestion of her nipples. He looked away quickly and she smiled.

'Nicky,' she said, 'I'm so sorry to have left you alone.'

'Peter and I have had a high old time,' he said.

She had emphasized the shape and size of her eyes, and the planes of the bone structure of her cheeks and jawline, with a subtlety that made it appear she wore no make-up, and her hair had a springing electrical fire to it, a rich glowing sable cloud about the small head. The honeyed ivory of her skin had tanned to the velvety texture of a cream-coloured rose petal across her bare shoulders and arms.

He had forgotten how relaxed and gracious she could be, and this magnificent building filled with its treasures standing in its pine forest high above the darkening ocean and the fairy lights of the coast was her natural setting. She filled the huge room with a special glow and gaiety, and she and Peter shared an impish sense of fun that had them all laughing at the old well-remembered jokes.

Nicholas could not sustain his resentment, could not bring himself to dwell on her betrayal in this environment, so the laughter was easy and the warmth uncontrived. When they went through to the small informal dining room, they sat at the table as they had done so often before; they seemed to be transported back in time to those happy almost forgotten years.

There were moments which might have jarred, but Chantelle's instinct was so certain that she could skirt delicately around these. She treated Nicholas as an honoured guest, not as the master of the house; instead she made Peter the host. 'Peter darling, will you carve for us?' and the boy's pride and importance was almost overwhelming, although the bird looked as though it had been caught in a combine harvester by the time he had finished with it. Chantelle served food and wine, a chicken stuffed in Creole style and a petit Chablis, that had no special associations from the past; and the choice of music was Peter's. 'Music to develop ulcers by,' as Nicholas remarked aside, to Chantelle.

Peter fought a valiant rearguard action to delay the passage of time, but finally resigned himself when Nicholas told him, 'I'll come and see you up to bed.'

He waited while Peter cleaned his teeth with an impressive vigour that might have continued beyond midnight if Nicholas had not protested mildly. When at last he was installed between the sheets, Nicholas stooped over him and the boy wrapped both arms around his neck with a quiet desperation.

'I'm so happy,' he whispered against Nicholas' neck and when they kissed he crushed Nicholas' lips painfully with his mouth – then, 'Wouldn't it be fabulous if we could be like this always?' he asked. 'If you didn't have to go away again, Dad?'

Chantelle had changed the wild music to the muted haunting melodies of Liszt, and as he came back into the room she was pouring cognac into a thin crystal balloon.

'Did he settle down?' she asked, and then answered herself immediately. 'He's exhausted, although he doesn't know it.'

She brought him the cognac and then turned away and went out through the doors on to the terrace. He followed her out, and they stood at the stone balustrade side by side. The air was clear but chill.

'It's beautiful,' she said. The moon paved a wide silver path across the surface of the sea. 'I always thought that the highway to my dreams.'

'Duncan,' he said. 'Let's talk about Duncan Alexander,' and she shivered slightly, folding her arms across her breasts and grasping her own naked shoulders.

'What do you want to know?'

'In what terms did you give him control of your shares?'

'As an agent, my personal agent.'

'With full discretion?'

She nodded, and he asked next, 'Did you have an escape clause? In what circumstances can you reclaim control?'

'The dissolution of marriage,' she said, and then shook her head. 'But I think I knew that no court would uphold the agreement if I wanted to change it. It's too Victorian. Anytime I want to I could simply apply to have the appointment of Duncan as my agent set aside.'

'Yes, I think you're right,' Nicholas agreed. 'But it might take a year or more, unless you could prove malafides, unless you could prove he deliberately betrayed the trust of agency.'

'Can I prove that, Nicky?' She turned to him now, lifting her face to him. 'Has he betrayed that trust?'

'I don't know yet,' Nicholas told her cautiously, and she cut in.

'I've made a terrible fool of myself, haven't I?' He kept silent, and she went on tremulously, 'I know there is no way I can apologize to you for – for what I did. There is no way that I can make it up to you, but believe me, Nicholas – please believe me when I tell you, I have never regretted anything so much in all my life.'

'It's past, Chantelle. It's over. There is no profit in looking back.'

'I don't think there is another man in the world who would do what you are doing now, who would repay deceit and betrayal with help and comfort. I just wanted to say that.'

She was standing very close to him now, and in the cool night he could feel the warmth of her flesh across the inches that separated them, and her perfume had a subtly altered fragrance on that creamy skin. She always wore perfume so well, the same way she wore her clothes.

'It's getting cold,' he said brusquely, took her elbow and steered her back into the light, out of that dangerous intimacy. 'We still have a great deal to discuss.'

He paced the thick forest-green carpet, quickly establishing a beat as regular as that of a sentry, ten paces from the glass doors, passing in front of where she sat in the centre of the wide velvet couch, turning just before he reached the headless marble statue of a Greek athlete from antiquity that guarded the double oaken doors into the lobby, and then back in front of her again. As he paced, he told her in carefully prepared sequence all that he had learned from Lazarus.

She sat like a bird on the point of flight, turning her head to watch him, those huge dark eyes seeming to swell larger as she listened.

It was not necessary to explain it to her in layman's language, she was Arthur Christy's daughter, she understood when he told her how he suspected that Duncan Alexander had been forced to self-insure the hull of *Golden Dawn* and how he had used Christy stock to buy re-insurance, stock that he had probably already pledged to finance construction of the vessel.

Nicholas reconstructed the whole inverted pyramid of Duncan Alexander's machinations for her to examine, and almost immediately she saw how vulnerable, how unstable it was.

'Are you certain of all this?' she whispered, and her face was drained of all its lustrous rose tints.

He shook his head. 'I've reconstructed the Tyrannosaurus from a jawbone,' he admitted frankly. 'The shape of it might be a little different, but one thing I am certain of is that it's a big and dangerous beast.'

'Duncan could destroy Christy Marine,' she whispered again. 'Completely!' She looked around slowly, at the house – at the room and its treasures, the symbols of her life. 'He has risked everything that is mine, and Peter's.'

Nicholas did not reply, but he stopped in front of her and watched her carefully as she absorbed the enormity of it all.

He saw outrage turn slowly to confusion, to fear and finally to terror. He had never seen her even afraid before – but now, faced with the prospect of being stripped naked of the armour which had always protected her, she was like a lost animal, he could even see that flutter of her heart under the pale swelling flesh of her bosom, and she shivered again.

'Could he lose everything, Nicholas? He couldn't, could he?' She wanted assurance, but he could not give it to her, all he could give her was pity. Pity was the one emotion, probably the only one she had never aroused in him, not once in all the years he had known her.

'What can I do, Nicholas?' she pleaded. 'Please help me. Oh God, what must I do?'

'You can stop Duncan launching *Golden Dawn* – until the hull and propulsion has been modified, until it has been properly surveyed and underwritten – and until you have taken full control of Christy Marine out of his hands again.' And his voice was gentle, filled with his compassion as he told her.

'That's enough for one day, Chantelle. If we go on now, we will begin chasing our tails. Tonight you know what could happen, tomorrow we will discuss how we can prevent it. Have you a Valium?'

She shook her head. 'I've never used drugs to hide from things.' It was true, he knew, that she had never lacked courage. 'How much longer can you stay?'

'I have a seat on the eleven o'clock plane. I have to be back in London by tomorrow night – we'll have time tomorrow morning.'

The guest suite opened on to the second-floor balcony which ran along the entire front of the building overlooking the sea and the private harbour. The five main bedrooms all opened on to this balcony, an arrangement from fifty years previously when internal security against kidnapping and forcible entry had been of no importance.

Nicholas determined to speak to Chantelle about that in the morning. Peter was an obvious target for extortion, and he felt the goose bumps of horror rise on his arms as he imagined his son in the hands of those degenerate monsters who were everywhere allowed to strike and destroy with impunity. There was a price to pay these days for being rich and successful. The smell of it attracted the hyenas and vultures. Peter must be better protected, he decided.

In the sitting-room, there was a well-stocked liquor cabinet concealed behind mirrors, nothing so obvious and resoundingly middle-class as a private bar. The daily papers, in English, French and German were set out on the television table, *France-Soir*, *The Times*, *Allgemeine Zeitung*, with even an airmail version of the *New York Times*.

Nicholas flipped open *The Times* and glanced quickly at the closing prices. Christy Marine common stock was at £5.32p, up 15p on yesterday's prices. The market had not sniffed corruption – yet.

He pulled off his silk rollneck, and even though he had bathed three hours previously, the tension had left his skin feeling itchy and unclean. The bathroom had been lavishly redecorated in green onyx panels and the fittings were eighteen-carat gold, in the shape of dolphins. Steaming water gushed from their gaping mouths at a touch. It could have been vulgar, but Chantelle's unerring touch steered it into Persian opulence instead.

He showered, turning the setting high so that the stinging needles of water scalded away his fatigue and the feeling of being unclean. There were half a dozen thick white terry towelling robes in the glass-fronted warming cupboard, and he selected one and went through into the bedroom, belting it around his naked waist. In his briefcase there was a draft of the agreement of sale of Ocean Salvage and Towage to the Sheikhs. James Teacher and his gang of bright young lawyers had read it, and made a thick sheaf of notes. Nicholas must study these before tomorrow evening when he met them in London.

He took the papers from his case and carried them through into the sitting room, glancing at the top page before dropping them carelessly on to the low coffee table while he went to pour himself a small whisky, heavily diluted. He brought the drink back with him and sprawled into the deep leather armchair, picked up the papers and began to work.

He became aware of her perfume first, and felt his blood quicken uncontrollably at the fragrance, and the papers rustled in his hand.

Slowly he lifted his head. She had come in utter silence on small bare feet. She had removed all her jewellery and had let down her hair brushing it out on to her shoulders.

It made her seem younger, more vulnerable, and the gown she wore was cuffed and collared in fine soft lace. She moved slowly towards his chair, timorous and for once uncertain, the eyes huge and dark and haunted, and when he rose from the armchair, she stopped and one hand went to her throat.

'Nicholas,' she whispered, 'I'm so afraid, and so alone.' She moved a step closer, and saw his eyes shift, his lips harden, and she stopped instantly.

'Please,' she pleaded softly, 'don't send me away, Nicky. Not tonight, not yet. I'm afraid to be alone – please.'

He knew then that this had been going to happen, he had hidden the certainty of it from himself all that evening, but now it was upon him, and he could do nothing to avoid it. It was as though he had lost the will to resist, as though he stood mesmerized, his resolve softening and melting like wax in the candle flame of her beauty, of the passions which she commanded so skilfully, and his thoughts lost coherence, began to tumble and swirl like storm surf breaking on rock.

She recognized the exact instant when it happened to him, and she came forward silently, with small gliding footsteps, not making the mistake of speaking again and pressed her face to his bare chest framed in the collar of his robe. The thick curling hair was springing over hard flat muscle, and she flared her nostrils at the clean virile animal smell of his skin.

He was still resisting, standing stiffly with his hands hanging at his sides. Oh, she knew him so well. The terrible conflict he must suffer before he could be made to act against that iron code of his own. Oh, she knew him, knew that he was as sexual and physical an animal as she was herself, that he was the only man who had ever been able to match her appetites. She knew the defences he had erected about himself, the fortressing of his passions, the controls and repressions, but she knew so well how to subvert these elaborate defences, she knew exactly what to do and what to say, how to move and touch. As she began now, she found the deliberate act of breaking down his resistance excited her so swiftly that it was pain almost, agony almost, and it required all her own control not to advance too swiftly for him, to control the shaking of her legs and the pumping of her lungs, to play still the hurt and bewildered and frightened child, using his kindness, the sense of chivalry which would not allow him to send her away, in such obvious distress.

Oh God, how her body churned, her stomach cramped with the strength of her wanting, her breasts felt swollen and so sensitive that the contact of silk and lace was almost too painfully abrasive to bear.

'Oh, Nicky, please – just for a moment. Just once, hold me. Please, I cannot go on alone. Just for a moment, please.'

She felt him lift his hands, felt the fingers on her shoulders, and the terrible pain of wanting was too much to bear, she could not control it – she cried out, it was a soft little whimper, but the force of it shook her body, and immediately she felt his reaction. Her timing had been immaculate, her natural womanly cunning had guided her. His fingers on her shoulders had been gentle and kindly, but now they hooked cruelly into her flesh.

His back arched involuntarily, his breath drummed from his chest under her ear, a single agonized exhalation like that of a boxer taking a heavy body punch. She felt his every muscle become taut, and she knew again the frightening power, the delirious giddy power she could still wield. Then, at last, joyously, almost fearfully, she experienced the great lordly lift and thrust of his loins – as though the whole world had moved and shifted about her.

She cried out again, fiercely, for now she could slip the hounds she had held so short upon the leash, she could let them run and hunt again. They had been too long denied, but now there was no longer need for care and restraint.

She knew exactly how to hunt him beyond the frontiers of reason, to course him like a flying stag, and his fingers tangled frantically in the foaming lace at her throat as he tried to free her tight swollen breasts. She cried out a third time, and with a single movement jerked open the fastening at his waist, exposing the full hard lean length of his body, and her hands were as frantic as his.

'Oh, sweet God, you're so hard and strong – oh sweet God, I've missed you so.'

There was time later for all the refinements and nuances of love, but now her need was too cruel and demanding to be denied another moment. It had to happen this instant before she died of the lack.

Nicholas rose slowly towards the surface of sleep, aware of a brooding sense of regret. Just before he reached consciousness, a dream image formed in his sleep-starved brain, he relived a moment from the distant past. A fragment of time, recaptured so vividly as to seem whole and perfect. Long ago he had picked a deep-sea trumpet shell at five fathoms from the oceanic wall of the coral reef beyond the Anse Baudoin lagoon of Praslin Island. It was the size of a ripe coconut and once again he found himself holding the shell in both cupped hands, gazing into the narrow oval opening, around which the weed-furred and barnacle-encrusted exterior changed dramatically, flaring into the pouting lips and exposing the inner mother-of-pearl surfaces that were slippery to the touch, a glossy satin sheen, pale translucent pink, folded and convoluted upon themselves, shading darker into fleshy crimsons and wine purples as the passage narrowed and sank away into the mysterious lustrous depths of the shell.

Then abruptly, the dream image changed in his mind. The projected opening in the trumpet shell expanded, articulating on jaw-hinges and he was gaping into the deep and terrible maw of some great predatory sea-creature, lined with multiple rows of serrated triangular teeth – shark-like, terrifying, so he cried out in half-sleep, startling himself awake, and he rolled quickly on to his side and raised himself on one elbow. Her perfume still lingered on his skin, mingled with the smell of his own sweat, but the bed beside him was empty, though warm and redolent with the memory of her body.

Across the room, the early sun struck a long sliver of light through a narrow chink in the curtains. It looked like a blade, a golden blade. It reminded him instantly of Samantha Silver. He saw her again wearing sunlight like a cloak, barefoot in the sand – and it seemed that the blade of sunlight was being driven up slowly under his ribs.

He swung his feet off the wide bed and padded softly

across to the gold and onyx bathroom. There was a dull ache of sleeplessness and remorse behind his eyes and as he ran hot water from the dolphin's mouth into the basin, he looked at himself in the mirror although the steam slowly clouded the image of his own face. There were dark smears below his eyes and his features were gaunt, harsh angles of bone beneath drawn skin.

'You bastard,' he whispered at the shadowy face in the mirror. 'You bloody bastard.'

They were waiting breakfast for him, in the sunlight on the terrace under the gaily coloured umbrellas. Peter had preserved the mood of the previous evening, and he ran laughing to meet Nicholas.

'Dad, hey Dad.' He seized Nicholas' hand and led him to the table.

Chantelle wore a long loose housegown, and her hair was down on her shoulders, so soft that it stirred like spun silk in even that whisper of breeze. It was calculated, Chantelle did nothing by chance; the intimately elegant attire and the loose fall of her hair set the mood of domesticity – and Nicholas found himself resisting it fiercely.

Peter sensed his father's change of mood with an intuitive understanding beyond his years, and his dismay was a palpable thing, the hurt and reproach in his eyes as he looked at Nicholas; and then the chatter died on his lips and he bent his head studiously over his plate and ate in silence.

Nicholas deliberately refused the festival array of food, took only a cup of coffee, and lit a cheroot, without asking Chantelle's permission, knowing how she would resent that. He waited in silence and as soon as Peter had eaten he said:

'I'd like to speak to your mother, Peter.'

The boy stood up obediently.

'Will I see you before you leave, sir?'

'Yes.' Nicholas felt his heart wrung again. 'Of course.'

'We could sail again?'

'I'm sorry, my boy. We won't have time. Not today.'

'Very well, sir.' Peter walked to the end of the terrace, very erect and dignified, then suddenly he began to run, taking the steps down two at a time, and he fled into the pine forest beyond the boathouse as though pursued, feet flying and arms pumping wildly.

'He needs you, Nicky,' said Chantelle softly.

'You should have thought about that two years ago.'

She poured fresh coffee into his cup. 'Both of us have been stupid – all right, worse than that. We've been wicked. I have had my Duncan, and you have had that American child.'

'Don't make me angry now,' he warned her softly. 'You've done enough for one day.'

'It's as simple as this, Nicholas. I love you, I have always loved you – God, since I was a gawky schoolgirl.' She had never been that, but Nicholas let it pass. 'Since I saw you that first day on the bridge of old *Golden Eagle*, the dashing ship's captain—'

'Chantelle. All we have to discuss is *Golden Dawn* and Christy Marine.'

'No, Nicholas. We were born for each other. Daddy saw that immediately, we both knew it at the same time – it was only a madness, a crazy whim that made me doubt it for a moment.'

'Stop it, Chantelle.'

'Duncan was a stupid mistake. But it's unimportant—'

'No, it's not unimportant. It changed everything. It can never be the same again, besides—'

'Besides, what? Nicky, what were you going to say?'

'Besides, I am building myself another life now. With another very different person.'

'Oh God, Nicky, you aren't serious?' She laughed then, genuine amusement, clapping her hands delightedly. 'My dear, she's young enough to be your daughter. It's the forty syndrome, the Lolita complex.' Then she saw his real anger, and she was quick, retrieving the situation neatly, aware that she had carried it too far.

'I'm sorry, Nicky. I should never have said that.' She paused, and then went on. 'I will say she's a pretty little thing, and I'm sure she's sweet – Peter liked her.' She damned Samantha with light condescension, and then dismissed her as though she were merely a childlike prank of Nicholas', a light and passing folly of no real significance.

'I understand, Nicholas, truly I do. However, when you are ready, as you will be soon, then Peter and I and Christy Marine are waiting for you still. This is your world, Nicholas.' She made a gesture which embraced it all. 'This is your world; you will never really leave it.'

'You are wrong, Chantelle.'

'No.' She shook her head. 'I am very seldom wrong, and on this I cannot be wrong. Last night proved that, it is still there – every bit of it. But let's discuss the other thing now, *Golden Dawn* and Christy Marine.'

Chantelle Alexander lifted her face to the sky and watched the big silver bird fly. It climbed nose high, glinting in the sunlight, twin trails of dark unconsumed fuel spinning out behind it as the engines howled under the full thrust. With the wind in this quarter, the extended centreline of the main Nice runway brought it out over Cap Ferrat.

Beside Chantelle, only an inch or two shorter than she was, Peter stood and watched it also and she took his arm, tucking her small dainty hand into the crook of his elbow.

'He stayed such a short time,' Peter said, and overhead the big airbus turned steeply on to its crosswind leg.

'We will have him with us again soon,' Chantelle

promised, and then she went on. 'Where were you, Peter? We hunted all over when it was time for Daddy to go.'

'I was in the forest,' he said evasively. He had heard them calling, but Peter was hidden in the secret place, the smuggler's cleft in the yellow rock of the cliff; he would have killed himself rather than let Nicholas Berg see him weeping.

'Wouldn't it be lovely if it was like the old times again?' Chantelle asked softly, and the boy stirred beside her, but unable to take his gaze from the aircraft. 'Just the three of us again?'

'Without Uncle Duncan?' he asked incredulously, and high above them the aircraft, with a last twinkle of sunlight, drove deeply into the banks of cumulus cloud that buttressed the northern sky. Peter turned at last to face her.

'Without Uncle Duncan?' he demanded again. 'But that's impossible.'

'Not if you help me, darling.' She took his face in her cupped hands. 'You will help me, won't you?' she asked, and he nodded once, a sharply incisive gesture of assent; she leaned forward and kissed him tenderly on the forehead.

'That's my man,' she whispered.

'Mr Alexander is not available. May I take a message?'

'This is Mrs Alexander. Tell my husband that it's urgent.'

'Oh, I'm terribly sorry, Mrs Alexander.' The secretary's voice changed instantly, cool caution becoming effusive servility. 'I didn't recognize your voice. The line is dreadful. Mr Alexander will speak to you directly.'

Chantelle waited, staring impatiently from the study

windows. The weather had changed in the middle of the morning with the cold front sweeping down off the mountains, and now icy wind and rain battered at the windows.

'Chantelle, my dear,' said the rich glossy voice that had once so dazzled her. 'Is this my call to you?'

'It's mine, Duncan. I must speak to you urgently.'

'Good,' he agreed with her. 'I wanted to speak to you also. Things are happening swiftly here. It's necessary for you to come up to St Nazaire next Tuesday, instead of my joining you at Cap Ferrat.'

'Duncan—'

But he went on over her protest, his voice as full of self-confidence, as ebullient as she had not heard it in over a year.

'I have been able to save almost four weeks on *Golden Dawn*.'

'Duncan, listen to me.'

'We will be able to launch on Tuesday. It will be a makeshift ceremony, I'm afraid, at such short notice.' He was inordinately proud of his own achievement. It annoyed her to hear him. 'What I have arranged is that the pod tanks will be delivered direct to the Gulf from the Japanese yards. They are towing them in their ballast with four American tugs. I will launch the hull here, with workmen still aboard her, and they will finish her off at sea during the passage around Good Hope, in time for her to take on her tanks and cargo at El Barras. We'll save nearly seven and a half million—'

'Duncan!' Chantelle cried again, and this time something in her tone stopped him.

'What is it?'

'This can't wait until Tuesday, I want to see you right away.'

'That's impossible,' he laughed, lightly, confidently. 'It's only five days.'

'Five days is too long.'

'Tell me now,' he invited. 'What is it?'

'All right,' she said deliberately, and the vicious streak of Persian cruelty was in her voice. 'I'll tell you. I want a divorce, Duncan, and I want control of my shares in Christy Marine again.'

There was a long, hissing crackling silence on the line, and she waited, the way the cat waits for the first movement of the crippled mouse.

'This is very sudden.' His voice had changed completely, it was bleak and flat, lacking any timbre or resonance.

'We both know it is not,' she contradicted him.

'You have no grounds.' There was a thin edge of fear now. 'Divorce isn't quite as easy as that, Chantelle.'

'How is this for grounds, Duncan?' she asked, and there was a spiteful sting in her voice now. 'If you aren't here by noon tomorrow, then my auditors will be in Leadenhall Street and there will be an urgent order before the courts—'

She did not have to go on, he spoke across her and there was a note of panic in his voice. She had never heard it before. He said, 'You are right. We do have to talk right away.' Then he was silent again, collecting himself, and his voice was once more calm and careful when he went on, 'I can charter a Falcon and be at Nice before midday. Will that do?'

'I'll have the car meet you,' she said, and broke the connection with one finger. She held the bar down for a second, then lifted her finger.

'I want to place an international call,' she said in her fluent rippling French when the operator answered. 'I do not know the number, but it is person to person. Doctor Samantha Silver at the University of Miami.'

'There is a delay of more than two hours, madame.'

'*J'attendrai*,' she said, and replaced the receiver.

The Bank of the East is in Curzon Street, almost opposite the White Elephant Club. It has a narrow frontage of bronze and marble and glass, and Nicholas had been there, with his lawyers, since ten o'clock that morning. He was learning at first hand the leisurely age-old ritual of oriental bargaining.

He was selling Ocean Salvage, plus two years of his future labour – and even for seven million dollars he was beginning to wonder if it was worth it – and it was not a certain seven million either. The words tripped lightly, the figures seemed to have no substance in this setting. The only constant was the figure of the Prince himself, seated on the low couch, in a Savile Row suit but with the fine white cotton and gold-corded headdress framing his dark handsome features with theatrical dash.

Beyond him moved a shadowy, ever-changing background of unctuous whispering figures. Every time that Nicholas believed that a point had been definitely agreed, another rose-pink or acid-yellow Rolls-Royce with Arabic script numberplates would deposit three or four more dark-featured Arabs at the front doors and they would hurry through to kiss the Prince on his forehead, on the bridge of his nose and on the back of his hand, and the hushed discussion would begin all over again with the newcomers picking up at the point they had been an hour previously.

James Teacher showed no impatience, and he smiled and nodded and went through the ritual like an Arab born, sipping the little thimbles of treacly coffee and watching patiently for the interminable whisperings to be translated into English before making a measured counter proposal.

'We are doing fine, Mr Berg,' he assured Nicholas quietly. 'A few more days.'

Nicholas had a headache from the strong coffee and the Turkish tobacco smoke, and he found it difficult to concentrate. He kept worrying about Samantha. For four days he had tried to contact her. He had to get out for a while and he excused himself to the Prince, and went down to the Enquiries Desk in the Bank's entrance hall and the girl told him,

'I'm sorry, sir, there is no reply to either of those numbers.'

'There must be,' Nicholas told her. One number was Samantha's shack at Key Biscayne and the other was her private number in her laboratory.

She shook her head. 'I've tried every hour.'

'Can you send a cable for me?'

'Of course, sir.'

She gave him a pad of forms and he wrote out the message.

'Please phone me urgently, reverse charges to—' he gave the number of the Queen's Gate flat and James Teacher's rooms, then he thought with the pen poised, trying to find the words to express his concern, but there were none.

'I love you,' he wrote. 'I really do.'

Since Nicholas's midnight call to tell her of the carriage of cad-rich crude petroleum, Samantha Silver had been caught up in a kaleidoscope whirl of time and events.

After a series of meetings with the leaders of Greenpeace, and other conservation bodies in an effort to publicize and oppose this new threat to the oceans, she and Tom Parker had flown to Washington and met with a deputy director of the Environmental Protection Agency and with two young senators who spearheaded the conservation lobby – but their efforts to go further had been frustrated by the granite walls of big oil interest. Even usually cooperative sources had been wary of condemning or speaking out against Orient Amex's new carbon-cracking technology. As one thirty-year-old Democrat senator had pointed out, 'It's tough to try and take a shot at something that's going to increase the fossil fuel yield by fifty per cent.'

'That's not what we are shooting at,' Samantha had flared, bitter with fatigue and frustration. 'It's this irresponsible method of carrying the cad-rich through sensitive and highly vulnerable seaways we are trying to prevent.' But when she presented the scenario she had worked out, picturing the effects on the North Atlantic deluged with a million tons of toxic crude, she saw the disbelief in the man's eyes and the condescending smile of the sane for the slightly demented.

'Oh God, why is common sense the hardest thing in the world to sell?' she had lamented.

She and Tom had gone on to meet the leaders of Greenpeace in the north, and in the west, and they had given advice and promises of support. The Californian Chapter counselled physical intervention as a last resort, as some of their members had successfully interposed small craft between the Russian whalers and the breeding minkes they were hunting in the Californian Gulf.

In Galveston, they met the young Texans who would picket the Orient Amex refinery as soon as they were certain the ultra-tanker had entered the Gulf of Mexico.

However, none of their efforts were successful in provoking confrontation with Orient Amex. The big oil company simply ignored invitations to debate the charges on radio or television, and stonewalled questions from the media. It's hard to stir up interest in a one-sided argument, Samantha found.

They managed one local Texas television show, but without controversy to give it zip, the producer cut Samantha's time down to forty-five seconds, and then tried to date her for dinner.

The energy crisis, oil tankers and oil pollution were joyless subjects. Nobody had ever heard of cadmium pollution, the Cape of Good Hope was half a world away, a million tons was a meaningless figure, impossible to visualize, and it was all rather a bore.

The media let it drop flat on its face.

'We're just going to have to smoke those fat cats at Orient Amex out into the open,' Tom Parker growled angrily, 'and kick their arses blue for them. The only way we are going to do that is through Greenpeace.'

They had landed back at Miami International, exhausted and disappointed, but not yet despondent. 'Like the man said,' Samantha muttered grimly, as she threaded her gaudy van back into the city traffic flow, 'we have only just begun to fight.'

She had only a few hours to clean herself up and stretch out on the patchwork quilt before she had to dress again and race back to the airport. The Australian had already passed through customs and was looking lost and dejected in the terminal lobby.

'Hi, I'm Sam Silver.' She pushed away fatigue, and hoisted that brilliant golden smile like a flag.

His name was Mr Dennis O'Connor and he was the top man in his field, doing fascinating and important work on the reef populations of Eastern Australian waters, and he had come a long way to talk to her and see her experiments.

'I didn't expect you to be so young.' She had signed her correspondence 'Doctor Silver' and he gave the standard reaction to her. Samantha was just tired and angry enough not to take it.

'And I'm a woman. You didn't expect that either,' she agreed. 'It's a crying bastard, isn't it? But then, I bet some of your best friends are young females.'

He was a dinky-die Aussie, and he loved it. He burst into an appreciative grin, and as they shook hands, he said, 'You are not going to believe this, but I like you just the way you are.'

He was tall and lean, sunburned and just a little grizzled

at the temples, and within minutes they were friends, and the respect with which he viewed her work confirmed that.

The Australian had brought with him, in an oxygenated container, five thousand live specimens of *E. digitalis*, the common Australian water snail, for inclusion in Samantha's experimentation. He had selected these animals for their abundance and their importance in the ecology of the Australian inshore waters, and the two of them were soon so absorbed in the application of Samantha's techniques to this new creature that when her assistant stuck her head through and yelled, 'Hey, Sam, there's a call for you.' She shouted back, 'Take a message. If they're lucky I'll call them back.'

'It's international, person to person!' and Samantha's pulse raced; instantly forgotten was the host of spiral-coned sea snails.

'Nicholas!' she shouted happily, spilled half a pint of sea water down the Australian's trouser leg and ran wildly to the small cubicle at the end of the laboratory.

She was breathless with excitement as she snatched up the receiver and she pressed one hand against her heart to stop it thumping.

'Is that Doctor Silver?'

'Yes! It's me.' Then correcting her grammar, 'It is she!'

'Go ahead, please,' said the operator, and there was a click and pulse on the line as it came alive.

'Nicholas!' she exulted. 'Darling Nicholas, is that you?'

'No.' The voice was very clear and serene, as though the speaker stood beside her, and it was familiar, disconcertingly so, and for no good reason Samantha felt her heart shrink with dread.

'This is Chantelle Alexander, Peter's mother. We have met briefly.'

'Yes.' Samantha's voice was now small, and still breathless.

'I thought it would be kind to tell you in person, before

you hear from other sources – that Nicholas and I have decided to remarry.'

Samantha sat down jerkily on the office stool.

'Are you there?' Chantelle asked after a moment.

'I don't believe you,' whispered Samantha.

'I'm sorry,' Chantelle told her gently. 'But there is Peter, you see, and we have rediscovered each other – discovered that we had never stopped loving each other.'

'Nicholas wouldn't—' her voice broke, and she could not go on.

'You must understand and forgive him, my dear,' Chantelle explained. 'After our divorce he was hurt and lonely. I'm sure he did not mean to take advantage of you.'

'But, but – we were supposed to, we were going to—'

'I know. Please believe me, this has not been easy for any of us. For all our sakes—'

'We had planned a whole life together.' Samantha shook her head wildly, and a thick skein of golden hair came loose and flopped into her face, she pushed it back with a combing gesture. 'I don't believe it, why didn't Nicholas tell me himself? I won't believe it until he tells me.'

Chantelle's voice was compassionate, gentle. 'I so wanted not to make it ugly for you, my child, but now what can I do but tell you that Nicholas spent last night in my house, in my bed, in my arms, where he truly belongs.'

It was almost miraculous, a physical thing, but sitting hunched on the hard round stool Samantha Silver felt her youth fall away from her, sloughed off like a glittering reptilian skin. She was left with the sensation of timelessness, possessed of all the suffering and sorrow of every woman who had lived before. She felt very old and wise and sad, and she lifted her fingers and touched her own cheek, mildly surprised to feel that the skin was not dried and withered like that of some ancient crone.

'I have already made the arrangements for a divorce

from my present husband, and Nicholas will resume his position at the head of Christy Marine.'

It was true, Samantha knew then that it was true. There was no question, no doubt, and slowly she replaced the receiver of the telephone, and sat staring blankly at the bare wall of the cubicle. She did not cry, she felt as though she would never cry, nor laugh, again in her life.

Chantelle Alexander studied her husband carefully, trying to stand outside herself, and to see him dispassionately. She found it easier now that the giddy insanity had burned away.

He was a handsome man, tall and lean, with those carefully groomed metallic waves of coppery hair. Even the wrist that he shot from the crisp white cuff of his sleeve was covered with those fine gleaming hairs. She knew so well that even his lean chest was covered with thick golden curls, crisp and curly as fresh lettuce leaves. She had never been attracted by smooth hairless men.

'May I smoke?' he asked, and she inclined her head. His voice had also attracted her from the first, deep and resonant, but with those high-bred accents, the gentle softening of the vowel sounds, the lazy drawling of consonants. The voice and the patrician manner were things that she had been trained to appreciate – and yet, under the mannered cultivated exterior was the flash of exciting wickedness, that showed in the wolfish white gleam of smile, and the sharp glittering grey steel of his gaze.

He lit the custom-made cigarette with the gold lighter she had given him – her very first gift, the night they had become lovers. Even now, the memory of it was piquant, and for a moment she felt the soft melting warmth in her lower belly and she stirred restlessly in her chair. There had been reason, and good reason for that madness, and even now it was over, she would never regret it.

It had been a period in her life which she had not been able to deny herself. The grand sweeping illicit passion, the last flush of her youth, the final careless autumn that preceded middle age. Another ordinary woman might have had to content herself with sweaty sordid gropings and grapplings in anonymous hotel bedrooms, but not Chantelle Christy. Her world was shaped by her own whims and desires, and, as she had told Nicholas, whatever she desired was hers to take. Long ago, her father had taught her that there were special rules for Chantelle Christy, and the rules were those she made herself.

It had been marvellous, she shivered slightly at the lingering sensuality of those early days, but now it was over. During the past months she had been carefully comparing the two men. Her decision had not been lightly made.

She had watched Nicholas retrieve his life from the gulf of disaster. On his own, stripped naked of all but that invisible indefinable mantle of strength and determination, he had fought his way back out of the gulf. Strength and power had always moved her, but she had over the years grown accustomed to Nicholas. Familiarity had staled their relationship for her. But now her interlude with Duncan had freshened her view of him, and he had for her all the novel appeal of a new lover – yet with the proven values and qualities of long intimate acquaintance. Duncan Alexander was finished; Nicholas Berg was the future.

But, no, she would never regret this interlude in her life. It had been a time of rejuvenation. She would not even regret Nicholas' involvement with the pretty American child. Later, it would add a certain perverse spice to their own sexuality, she thought, and felt the shiver run down her thighs and the soft secret stirring of her flesh, like the opening of a petalled rosebud. Duncan had taught her many things, bizarre little tricks of arousal, made more poignant by being forbidden and wicked. Unfortunately Duncan relied almost entirely on the tricks, and not all of them had worked for her – the corners of her mouth turned down with distaste as she remembered; perhaps it was just that which had begun the curdling process.

No, Duncan Alexander had not been able to match her raw, elemental sexuality and soaring abandon. Only one man had ever been able to do that. Duncan had served a purpose, but now it was over. It might have dragged on a little longer, but Duncan Alexander had endangered Christy Marine. Never had she thought of that possibility; Christy Marine was a fact of her life, as vast and immutable as the heavens, but now the foundations of heaven were being shaken. His sexual attraction had staled. She might have forgiven him that, but not the other.

She became aware of Duncan's discomfort. He twisted sideways in his chair, crossing and uncrossing his long legs, and he rolled the cigarette between his fingers, studying the rising spiral of blue smoke to avoid the level, expressionless gaze of her dark fathomless eyes. She had been staring at him, but seeing the other man. Now, with an effort, she focused her attention on him.

'Thank you for coming so promptly,' she said.

'It did seem rather urgent.' He smiled for the first time, glossy and urbane – but with fear down there in the cool grey eyes, and his tension was betrayed by the clenched sinew in the point of his jaw.

Looking closely, as she had not done for many months, she saw how he was fined down. The long tapered fingers were bony, and never still. There were new harder lines to his mouth, and a frown to the set of his eyes. The skin at the corners cracked like oil paint into hundreds of fine wrinkles that the deep brown snow-tan hid from a casual glance. Now he returned her scrutiny directly.

'From what you told me yesterday—'

She lifted her hand to stop him. 'That can wait. I merely wanted to impress you with the seriousness of what is happening. What is really of prime importance now is what you have done with control of my shares and those of the Trust.'

His hands went very still. 'What does that mean?'

'I want auditors, my appointed auditors, sent in—'

He shrugged. 'All this will take time, Chantelle, and I'm not certain that I'm ready to relinquish control.' He was very cool, very casual now and the fear was gone.

She felt a stir of relief, perhaps the horror story that Nicholas had told her was untrue, perhaps the danger was imaginary only. Christy Marine was so big, so invulnerable.

'Not just at the moment, anyway. You'd have to prove to me that doing so was in the best interest of the company and of the Trust.'

'I don't have to prove anything, to anyone,' she said flatly.

'This time you do. You have appointed me—'

'No court of law would uphold that agreement.'

'Perhaps not, Chantelle, but do you want to drag all this through the courts – at a time like this?'

'I'm not afraid, Duncan.' She stood up quickly, light on her feet as a dancer, the lovely legs in loose black silk trousers, soft flat shoes making her seem still smaller, a slim gold chain emphasizing the narrowness of the tiny waist. 'You know I'm afraid of nothing.' She stood over him, and pointed the accuser's finger. The nails tipped in scarlet, the colour of fresh arterial blood. 'You should be the one to fear.'

'And precisely what is it you are accusing me of?'

And she told him, reeling off swiftly the lists of guarantees made by the Trust, the transfer of shares and the issues of new shares and guarantees within the Christy Marine group of subsidiaries, she listed the known layering of underwriting cover on *Golden Dawn* that Nicholas had unearthed.

'When my auditors have finished, Duncan darling, not only will the courts return control of Christy Marine to me, but they will probably sentence you to five years of hard labour. They take this sort of thing rather seriously, you know.'

He smiled. He actually smiled! She felt her fury seething to the surface and the set of her eyes altered, colour tinted the smooth pale olive of her cheeks.

'You dare to grin at me,' she hissed. 'I will break you for that.'

'No,' he shook his head. 'No, you won't.'

'Are you denying—' she snapped, but he cut her off with a raised hand, and a shake of that handsome arrogant head.

'I am denying nothing, my love. On the contrary, I am going to admit it – and more, much more.' He flicked the cigarette away, and it hissed sharply in the lapping blue wavelets of the yacht basin. While she stared at him, struck speechless, he let the silence play out like a skilled actor as he selected and lit another cigarette from the gold case.

'For some weeks now I have been fully aware that somebody was prying very deeply into my affairs and those of the company.' He blew a long blue feather of cigarette smoke, and cocked one eyebrow at her, a cynical mocking gesture which increased her fury, but left her feeling suddenly afraid and uncertain. 'It didn't take long to establish that the trace was coming from a little man in Monte Carlo who makes a living at financial and industrial espionage. Lazarus is good, excellent, the very best. I have used him myself, in fact it was I who introduced him to Nicholas Berg.' He chuckled then, shaking his head indulgently. 'The silly things we do sometimes. The connection was immediate. Berg and Lazarus. I have run my own check on what they have come up with and I estimate that even Lazarus could not have uncovered more than twenty-five per cent of the answers.' He leaned forward and suddenly his voice snapped with a new authority. 'You see, Chantelle dear, I am probably one of the best in the world myself. They could never have traced it all.'

'You are not denying then—' She heard the faltering tone in her own voice, and hated herself for it. He brushed her aside contemptuously.

'Be quiet, you silly little woman, and listen to me. I am going to tell you just how deeply you are in – I am going to explain to you, in terms that even you can understand, why you will not send in your auditors, why you will not fire me, and why you will do exactly what I tell you to do.'

He paused and stared into her eyes, a direct trial of strength which she could not meet. She was confused and uncertain, for once not in control of her own destiny. She dropped her eyes, and he nodded with satisfaction.

'Very well. Now listen. I have put it all – everything that is Christy Marine – it is all riding on *Golden Dawn*.'

Chantelle felt the earth turn giddily under her feet and the sudden roaring rush of blood in her ears. She stepped back and the stone parapet caught the back of her knees. She sat down heavily.

'What are you talking about?' she whispered. And he told her, in substantial detail, from the beginning, how it had worked out. From the laying of *Golden Dawn*'s keel in the times of vast tanker tonnage demand. 'My calculations were based on demand for tanker space two years ago, and on construction costs of that time.'

The energy crisis and collapse in demand for tankers had come with the vicious rise in inflation, bloating the costs of construction of *Golden Dawn* by more than double. Duncan had countered by altering the design of the gigantic tanker. He had reduced the four propulsion units to one, he had cut down the steel structuring of the hull reinforcement by twenty per cent, he had done away with elaborate safety functions and fail-safe systems designed by Nicholas Berg, and he had cut it too fine. He had forfeited the Al Lloyd's rating, the mark of approval from the inspectors of that venerable body; without the insurance backing of that huge underwriting market, he had been forced to look elsewhere to find the cover to satisfy his financiers. The premiums had been crippling. He had to pledge Christy Marine stock, the Trust stock. Then the spiralling cost of production had overtaken him again and he needed money and more money. He had taken it where he could find it, at rates of interest that were demanded, and used more Christy stock as collateral.

Then the insurance cover had been insufficient to cover the huge increase in the cost of the ultra-tanker's hull.

'When luck runs out—' Duncan shrugged eloquently, and went on. 'I had to pledge more Christy stock, all of it. It's all at risk, Chantelle, every single piece of paper, even the shares we retrieved from your Nicholas – and even that wasn't enough. I have had to write cover through front companies, cover that is worthless. Then,' Duncan smiled again, relaxed and unruffled, almost as though he was enjoying himself, 'then, there was that awful fiasco when *Golden Adventurer* went up on the ice, and I had to find six million dollars to pay the salvage award. That was the last of it, I went out for everything then, all of it. The Trust, the whole of Christy Marine.'

'I'll break you,' she whispered. 'I'll smash you. I swear before God—'

'You don't understand, do you?' He shook his head sorrowfully, as though at an obtuse child. 'You cannot break me, without breaking Christy Marine and yourself. You are in it, Chantelle, much much deeper than I am. You have everything, every penny, this house, that emerald on your finger, the future of your brat – all of it is riding on *Golden Dawn*'.

'No.' She closed her eyes very tightly, and there was no colour in her cheeks now.

'Yes. I'm afraid it's yes,' he contradicted. 'I didn't plan it that way. I saw a profit of 200 millions in it, but we have been caught up in circumstances, I'm afraid.'

They were both silent, and Chantelle swayed slightly as the full enormity of it overwhelmed her.

'If you whistle up your hounds now, if you call in your axemen, there will be plenty for them to work on,' he laughed again, 'buckets of dung for us all to wallow in. And my backers will line up to cancel out. *Golden Dawn* will never run down her ways – she is not fully covered, as I explained to you. It all hangs on a single thread, Chantelle. If the launching of *Golden Dawn* is delayed now, delayed by a month – no, by a week even, it will all come tumbling down.'

'I'm going to be sick,' she whispered thickly.

'No, you are not.' He stood up and crossed quickly to her. Coldly he slapped her face, two hard open-handed back and forth blows, that snapped her head from side to side, leaving the livid marks of his fingers on her pale cheeks. It was the first time ever that a man had struck her, but she could not find the indignation to protest. She merely stared at him.

'Pull yourself together,' he snarled at her, and gripped her shoulders fiercely, shaking her as he went on. 'Listen to me. I have told you the worst that can happen. Now, I will tell you the best. If we stand together now, if you obey me implicitly, without question, I will pull off one of the greatest financial coups of the century for you. All it needs is one successful voyage by *Golden Dawn* and we are home free – a single voyage, a few short weeks, and I will have doubled your fortune.' She was staring at him, sickened and shaken to the core of her existence. 'I have signed an agreement of charter with Orient Amex, that will pull us out from under a single voyage, and the day *Golden Dawn* anchors in Galveston roads and sends in her tank pods to discharge, I will have a dozen buyers for her.' He stepped back, and straightened the lapels of his jacket. 'Men are going to remember my name. In future when they talk of tankers, they are going to talk of Duncan Alexander.'

'I hate you,' she said softly. 'I truly hate you.'

'That is not important.' He waved it away. 'When it is over, I can afford to walk away – and you can afford to let me go. But not a moment before.'

'How much will you make from this, if it succeeds?' she asked, and she was recovering, her voice firmer.

'A great deal. A very great deal of money – but my real reward will be in reputation and achievement. After this, I will be a man who can write his own ticket.'

'For once, you will be able to stand comparison with Nicholas Berg. Is that it?' She saw she had scored immediately, and she pressed harder, trying to wound and destroy. 'But you and I both know it is not true. *Golden Dawn* was Nicholas' inspiration and he would not have had to descend to the cheat and sham—'

'My dear Chantelle—'

'You will never be, could never be the man Nicholas is.'

'Damn you.' Suddenly he was shaking with anger, and she was screaming at him.

'You're a cheat and a liar. For all your airs, you're still a cheap little barrow-boy at heart. You're small and shoddy—'

'I've beaten Nicholas Berg every time I've met him.'

'No, you haven't, Duncan. It was I who beat him for you—'

'I took you.'

'For a while,' she sneered. 'Just for a short fling, Duncan dear. But when he wanted me he took me right back again.'

'What do you mean by that?' he demanded.

'The night before last, Nicholas was here, and he loved me in a way you never could. I'm going back to him, and I'll tell the world why.'

'You bitch.'

'He is so strong, Duncan. Strong where you are weak.'

'And you are a whore.' He half turned away, and then paused. 'Just be at St Nazaire on Tuesday.' But she could see he was hurt, at last she had cut through the carapace and touched raw quick nerves.

'He loved me four times in one night, Duncan. Magnificent, soaring love. Did you ever do that?'

'I want you at St Nazaire, smiling at the creditors on Tuesday.'

'Even if you succeed with *Golden Dawn*, within six months Nicholas will have your job.'

'But until then you'll do exactly what I say.' Duncan braced himself, a visible effort, and began to walk away.

'You are going to be the loser, Duncan Alexander,' she screamed after him, her voice cracking shrilly with frustration and outrage. 'I will see to that – I swear it to you.'

He subdued the urge to run, and crossed the terrace, holding himself carefully erect, and the storm of her hatred and frustration burst around him.

'Go into the streets where you belong, into the gutter where I found you,' she screamed, and he went up the stone staircase and out of her sight. Now he could hurry, but he found his legs were trembling underneath him, his breath was ragged and broken, and there was a tight knot of anger and jealousy turning his guts into a ball.

'The bastard,' he spoke aloud. 'That bastard Berg.'

'Tom? Tom Parker?'

'That's right, who is this, please?' His voice was so clear and strong, although the Atlantic Ocean separated them.

'It's Nicholas, Nicholas Berg.'

'Nick, how are you?' the big voice boomed with genuine pleasure. 'God, I'm glad you called. I've been trying to reach you. I've got good news. The best.'

Nicholas felt a quick lift of relief.

'Samantha?'

'No, damn it,' Tom laughed. 'It's the job. Your job. It went up before the Board of Governors of the University yesterday. I had to sell it to them hard – I'll tell you that for free – but they okayed it. You're on, Nick, isn't that great?'

'It's terrific, Tom.'

'You're on the Biology faculty as an associate. It's the thin end of the wedge, Nicholas. We'll have you a chair by the end of next year, you wait and see.'

'I'm delighted.'

'Christ, you don't sound it,' Tom roared. 'What's bugging you, boy?'

'Tom, what the hell has happened to Samantha?'

And Nicholas sensed the mood change, the silence lasted a beat too long, and then Tom's tone was guileless.

'She went off on a field trip – down the Keys, didn't she tell you?'

'Down the Keys?' Nicholas' voice rose with his anger and frustration. 'Damn it, Tom. She was supposed to be here in France. She promised to come over for the launching of my new vessel. I've been trying to get in touch with her for a week now.'

'She left Sunday,' said Tom.

'What is she playing at?'

'That's a question she might want to ask you sometime.'

'What does that mean, Tom?'

'Well, before she took off, she came up here and had a good weep with Antoinette – you know, my wife. She plays den mother for every hysterical female within fifty miles, she does.'

Now it was Nicholas' turn to be silent, while the coldness settled on his chest, the coldness of formless dread.

'What was the trouble?'

'Good God, Nick, you don't expect me to follow the intimate details of the love life—'

'Can I speak to Antoinette?'

'She isn't here, Nick. She went up to Orlando for a meeting. She won't be back until the weekend.'

The silence again.

'All that heavy breathing is costing you a fortune, Nicholas. You're paying for this call.'

'I don't know what got into Sam.' But he did. Nicholas knew – and the guilt was strong upon him.

'Listen, Nick. A word to the wise. Get your ass across here, boy. Just as soon as you can. That girl needs talking to, badly. That is, if you care about it.'

'I care about it,' Nicholas said quickly. 'But hell, I am launching a tug in two days' time. I've got sea trials, and a meeting in London.'

Tom's voice had an air of finality. 'A man's got to do what he's got to do.'

'Tom, I'll be across there as soon as I possibly can.'

'I believe it.'

'If you see her, tell her that for me, will you?'

'I'll tell her.'

'Thanks, Tom.'

'The governors will want to meet you, Nicholas. Come as soon as you can.'

'It's a promise.'

Nicholas cradled the receiver, and stood staring out of the windows of the site office. The view across the inner harbour was completely blocked by the towering hull of his tug. She stood tall on her ways. Her hull already wore its final coat of glistening white and the wide flaring bows bore the name *Sea Witch* and below that the port of registration, 'Bermuda'.

She was beautiful, magnificent, but now Nicholas did not even see her. He was overwhelmed by a sense of imminent loss, the cold premonition of onrushing disaster. Until that moment when he faced the prospect of losing her, he had not truly known how large a part that lovely golden girl had come to play in his existence, and in his plans for the future.

There was no way that Samantha could have learned of that single night of weakness, the betrayal that still left Nicholas sickened with guilt – there must be something else that had come between them. He bunched his right fist and slammed it against the sill of the window. The skin on his knuckles smeared, but he did not feel the pain, only the bitter frustration of being tied down here in St Nazaire, weighed down by his responsibilities, when he should have been free to follow the jack-o'-lantern of happiness.

The loudspeaker above his head gave a preliminary squawk, and then crackled out the message, 'Monsieur Berg. Will Monsieur attend upon the bridge?'

It was a welcome distraction, and Nicholas hurried out into the spring sunshine. Looking upwards, he could see Jules Levoisin on the wing of the bridge. His portly figure foreshortened against the open sky, like a small pugnacious rooster. He stood facing the electronics engineer who was responsible for the installation of *Sea Witch*'s communications system, and Jules' cries of 'Sacré bleu' and 'Merde' and 'Imbécile' carried clearly above the cacophony of shipyard noises.

Nicholas started to run as he saw the engineer's arms begin to wave and his strident Gallic cries blended with those of *Sea Witch*'s new Master. It was only the third time that Jules Levoisin had become hysterical that day, however it was not yet noon. As the hour of launching came steadily closer, so the little Frenchman's nerves played him tricks. He was behaving like a prima ballerina awaiting the opening curtain. Unless Nicholas reached the bridge within the next few minutes, he would need either a new Master or a new electronics engineer.

Ten minutes later, Nicholas had a cheroot in each of their mouths. The atmosphere was still tense but no longer explosive, and gently Nick took the engineer by the elbow, placed his other arm around Jules Levoisin's shoulders and led them both back into the wheelhouse.

The bridge installation was complete, and Jules Levoisin was accepting delivery of the special equipment from the contractors, a negotiation every bit as traumatic as the Treaty of Versailles.

'I myself authorized the modification of the MK IV transponder,' Nicholas explained patiently. 'We had trouble with the same unit on *Warlock*. I should have told you, Jules.'

'You should have,' agreed the little Master huffily.

'But you were perceptive to notice the change from the specification,' Nicholas soothed him, and Jules puffed out his chest a little and rolled the cheroot in his mouth.

'I may be an old dog, but I know all the new tricks.' He removed the cheroot and smugly blew a perfect smoke ring.

When Nicholas at last left them chatting amiably over the massed array of sophisticated equipment that lined the navigation area at the back of the bridge, they were paging him from the site office.

'What is it?' he asked, as he came in through the door.

'It's a lady,' the foreman indicated the telephone lying on the littered desk below the window.

'Samantha,' Nick thought, and snatched up the receiver.

'Nicky.' He felt the shock of quick guilt at the voice.

'Chantelle, where are you?'

'In La Baule.' The fashionable resort town just up the Atlantic coast was a better setting for Chantelle Alexander than the grubby port with its sprawling dockyards. 'Staying at the Castille. God, it's too awful. I'd forgotten how awful it was.'

They had stayed there together, once long ago, in a different life it seemed now.

'But the restaurant is still quite cute, Nicholas. Have lunch with me. I must speak to you.'

'I can't leave here.' He would not walk into the trap again.

'It's important. I must see you.' He could hear that husky tone in her voice, imagine clearly the sensuous droop of the eyelids over those bold Persian eyes. 'For an hour, only an hour. You can spare that.' Despite himself, he felt the pull of temptation, the dull ache of it at the base of his belly – and he was angry at her for the power she could still exert over him.

'If it's important, then come here,' he said brusquely, and she sighed at his intransigence.

'All right, Nicholas. How will I find you?'

The Rolls was parked opposite the dockyard gates and Nicholas crossed the road and stepped through the door that the chauffeur held open for him.

Chantelle lifted her face to him. Her hair was cloudy dark and shot with light like a bolt of silk, her lips the colour of ripe fruit, moist and slightly parted. He ignored the invitation and touched her cheek with his lips before settling into the corner opposite her.

She made a little moue, and slanted her eyes at him in amusement. 'How chaste we are, Nicky.'

Nicholas touched the button on the control console and the glass soundproof partition slid up noiselessly between them and the chauffeur.

'Did you send in the auditors?' he asked.

'You look tired, darling, and harassed.'

'Have you blown the whistle on Duncan?' he avoided the distraction. 'The work on *Golden Dawn* is still going ahead. The arc lights were burning over her all night and the talk in the yards is that she is being launched at noon tomorrow, almost a month ahead of schedule. What happened, Chantelle?'

'There is a little bistro at Mindin, it's just across the bridge—'

'Damn it, Chantelle. I haven't time to fool around.'

But the Rolls was already gliding swiftly through the narrow streets of the port, between the high warehouse buildings.

'It will take five minutes, and the Lobster Armoricaine is the local speciality – not to be confused with Lobster Américaine. They do it in a cream sauce, it's superb,' she chatted archly, and the Rolls turned out on to the quay. Across the narrow waters of the inner harbour humped the ugly camouflaged mounds of the Nazi submarine pens, armoured concrete so thick as to resist the bombs of the RAF and the efforts of all demolition experts over the years since then.

'Peter asked me to give you his love. He has got his junior team colours. I'm so proud.'

Nicholas thrust his hands deep into his jacket pockets and slumped down resignedly against the soft leather seat.

'I am delighted to hear it,' he said.

And they were silent then until the chauffeur checked the Rolls at the toll barrier to pay before accelerating out on to the ramp of the St Nazaire bridge. The great span of the bridge rose in a regal curve, three hundred feet above the waters of the Loire river. The river was almost three miles wide here, and from the highest point of the bridge there was an aerial view over the dockyards of the town.

There were half a dozen vessels building along the banks of the broad muddy river, a mighty forest of steel scaffolding, tall gantries and half-assembled hulls, but all of it insignificant under the mountainous bulk of *Golden Dawn*. Without her pod tanks, she had an incomplete gutted appearance, as though the Eiffel Tower had toppled over and somebody had built a modernistic apartment block at one end. It seemed impossible that such a structure was capable of floating. God, she was ugly, Nick thought.

'They are still working on her,' he said. One of the gantries was moving ponderously along the length of the ship like an arthritic dinosaur, and at fifty paces the brilliant blue electric fires of the welding torches flickered; while upon the grotesquely riven hull crawled human figures reduced to ant-like insignificance by the sheer size of the vessel.

'They are still working,' he repeated it as an accusation.

'Nicholas, nothing in this life is simple—'

'Did you spell it out for Duncan?'

' – except for people like you.'

'You didn't confront Duncan, did you?' he accused her bitterly.

'It's easy for you to be strong. It's one of the things that first attracted me.'

And Nicholas almost laughed aloud. It was ludicrous to talk of strength, after his many displays of weakness with this very woman.

'Did you call Duncan's cards?' he insisted, but she put him off with a smile.

'Let's wait until we have a glass of wine—'

'Now,' he snapped. 'Tell me right now. Chantelle, I haven't time for games.'

'Yes, I spoke to him,' she nodded. 'I called him down to Cap Ferrat, and I accused him – of what you suspected.'

'He denied it? If he denies it, I now have further proof—'

'No, Nicholas. He didn't deny a thing. He told me that I knew only the half of it.' Her voice rose sharply, and suddenly it all spilled out in a torrent of tortured words.

Her composure was eroded swiftly away as she relived the enormity of her predicament. 'He's gambled with my fortune, Nicholas. He's risked the family share of Christy Marine, the Trust shares, my shares, it's all at risk. And he gloated as he told me, he truly gloried in his betrayal.'

'We've got him now.' Nicholas had straightened slowly in his seat as he listened. His voice was grimly satisfied and he nodded. 'That's it. We will stop the *Golden Dawn*, like that—' he hammered his bunched fist into the palm of the other hand with a sharp crack. 'We will get an urgent order before the courts.'

Nicholas stopped suddenly and stared at her. Chantelle was shaking her head slowly from side to side. Her eyes slowly filled, making them huge and glistening, a single tear spilled over the lid and clung in the thick dark lashes like a drop of morning dew.

The Rolls had stopped now outside the tiny bistro. It was on the river front, with a view across the water to the dockyards. To the west the river debouched into the open sea and in the east the beautiful arch of the bridge across the pale blue spring sky.

The chauffeur held open the door and Chantelle was gone with her swift birdlike grace, leaving Nicholas no choice but to follow her.

The proprietor came through from his kitchen and fussed over Chantelle, seating her at the window and lingering to discuss the menu.

'Oh, let's drink the Muscadet, Nicholas.' She had always had the most amazing powers of recovery, and now the tears were gone and she was brittle and gay and beautiful, smiling at him over the rim of her glass. The sunlight through the leaded window panes danced in the cool golden wine and rippled on the smoky dark fall of her hair.

'Here's to us, Nicholas darling. We are the last of the great.' It was a toast from long ago, from the other life, and it irritated him now but he drank it silently and then set down the glass.

'Chantelle, when and how are you going to stop Duncan?'

'Don't spoil the meal, darling.'

'In about thirty seconds I'm going to start becoming very angry.'

She studied him for a moment, and saw that it was true. 'All right then,' she agreed reluctantly.

'When are you going to stop him?'

'I'm not, darling.'

He stared at her. 'What did you say?' he asked quietly.

'I'm going to do everything in my power to help him launch and sail the *Golden Dawn*.'

'You don't understand, Chantelle. You're talking about risking a million tons of the most deadly poison—'

'Don't be silly, Nicky. Keep that heroic talk for the newspapers. I don't care if Duncan dumps a million tons of cadmium in the water supply of Greater London, just as long as he pulls the Trust and me out of the fire.'

'There is still time to make the modifications to *Golden Dawn*.'

'No, there isn't. You don't understand, darling. Duncan has put us so deeply into it that a delay of a few days even would bring us down. He has stripped the cupboard bare, Nicky. There is no money for modifications, no time for anything, except to get *Golden Dawn* under way.'

'There is always a way and a means.'

'Yes, and the way is to fill *Golden Dawn*'s pod tanks with crude.'

'He's frightened you by—'

'Yes,' she agreed. 'I am frightened. I have never been so frightened in my life, Nicky. I could lose everything – I am terrified. I could lose it all.' She shivered with the horror of it. 'I would kill myself if that happened.'

'I am still going to stop Duncan.'

'No, Nicky. Please leave it, for my sake – for Peter's sake. It's Peter's inheritance that we are talking about. Let *Golden Dawn* make one voyage, just one voyage – and I will be safe.'

'It's the risk to an ocean, to God alone knows how many human lives, we are talking about.'

'Don't shout, Nicky. People are looking.'

'Let them look. I'm going to stop that monster.'

'No, Nicholas. Without me, you cannot do a thing.'

'You best believe it.'

'Darling, I promise you, after her first voyage we will sell *Golden Dawn*. We'll be safe then, and I can rid myself of Duncan. It will be you and I again, Nicky. A few short weeks, that's all.'

It took all his self-control to prevent his anger showing. He clenched his fists on the starched white tablecloth, but his voice was cool and even.

'Just one more question, Chantelle. When did you telephone Samantha Silver?'

She looked puzzled for a moment as though she was trying to put a face to a name. 'Samantha, oh, your little friend. Why should I want to telephone her?' And then her expression changed. 'Oh, Nicky, you don't really believe I'd do that? You don't really believe I would tell anybody about it, about that wonderful—' Now she was stricken, again those huge eyes brimmed and she reached across and stroked the fine black hairs on the back of Nicholas' big square hand. 'You don't think that of me! I'm not that much of a bitch. I don't have to cheat to get the things I want. I don't have to inflict unnecessary hurt on people.'

'No,' Nicholas agreed quietly. 'You'd not murder more than a million or poison more than a single ocean at a time, would you?' He pushed back his chair.

'Sit down, Nicky. Eat your lobster.'

'Suddenly I'm not hungry.' He stripped two one-hundred-franc notes from his money clip and dropped them beside his plate.

'I forbid you to leave,' she hissed angrily. 'You are humiliating me, Nicholas.'

'I'll send your car back,' he said, and walked out into the sunlight. He found with surprise that he was trembling, and that his jaws were clenched so tightly that his teeth ached.

The wind turned during the night, and the morning was cold with drifts of low, grey, fast-flying cloud that threatened rain. Nicholas pulled up his collar against the wind and the tails of his coat flogged about his legs, for he was exposed on the highest point of the arched bridge of St Nazaire.

Thousands of others had braved the wind, and the guardrail was lined two and three deep, all the way across the curve of the northern span. The traffic had backed up and half a dozen gendarmes were trying to get it moving again; their whistles shrilled plaintively. Faintly the sound of a band floated up to them, rising and falling in volume as the wind caught it, and even with the naked eye Nicholas could make out the wreaths of gaily coloured bunting which fluttered on the high cumbersome stern tower of *Golden Dawn*.

He glanced at his wristwatch, and saw it was a few minutes before noon. A helicopter clattered noisily under the grey belly of cloud, and hovered about the yards of Construction Navale Atlantique on the gleaming silver coin of its rotor.

Nicholas lifted the binoculars and the eyepieces were

painfully cold against his skin. Through the lens, he could almost make out individual features among the small gathering on the rostrum under the tanker's stern.

The platform was decorated with a tricolour and a Union Jack, and as he watched the band fell silent and lowered their instruments.

'Speech time,' Nicholas murmured, and now he could make out Duncan Alexander, his bared head catching one of the fleeting rays of sun, a glimmer of coppery gold as he looked up at the towering stern of *Golden Dawn*.

His bulk almost obscured the tiny feminine figure beside him. Chantelle wore that particular shade of malachite green which she so dearly loved. There was confused activity around Chantelle, half a dozen gentlemen assisting in the ceremony she had performed so very often. Chantelle had broken the champagne on almost all of Christy Marine's fleet; the first time had been when she was Arthur Christy's fourteen-year-old darling – it was another of the company's many traditions.

Nicholas blinked, believing for an instant that his eyes had tricked him, for it seemed that the very earth had changed its shape and was moving.

Then he saw that the great hull of *Golden Dawn* had begun to slide forward. The band burst into the 'Marseillaise', the heroic strains watered down by wind and distance, while *Golden Dawn* gathered momentum.

It was an incredible, even a stirring sight, and despite himself, Nicholas felt the goosebumps rise upon his forearms and the hair lift on the back of his neck. He was a sailor, and he was watching the birthing of the mightiest vessel ever built.

She was grotesque, monstrous, but she was part of him. No matter that others had bastardized and perverted his grand design – still the original design was his and he found himself gripping the binoculars with hands that shook.

He watched the massive wooden-wedged arresters kick

out from under that great sliding mass of steel as they served to control her stern-first rush down the ways. Steel cable whipped and snaked upon itself like the Medusa's hair, and *Golden Dawn*'s stern struck the water.

The brown muddy water of the estuary opened before her, cleaved by the irresistible rush and weight, and the hull drove deep, opening white-capped rollers that spread out across the channel and broke upon the shores with a dull roar that carried clearly to where Nicholas stood.

The crowd that lined the bridge was cheering wildly. Beside him, a mother held her infant up to watch, both of them screaming with glee.

While *Golden Dawn*'s bows were still on the dockyard's ways her stern was thrusting irresistibly a mile out into the river; forced down by the raised bows it must now be almost touching the muddy bottom for the wave was breaking around her stern quarters.

God, she was huge! Nicholas shook his head in wonder. If only he had been able to build her the right way, what a ship she would have been. What a magnificent concept!

Now her bows left the end of the slips, and the waters burst about her, seething and leaping into swirling vortices.

Her stern started to rise, gathering speed as her own buoyancy caught her, and she burst out like a great whale rising to blow. The waters spilled from her, creaming and cascading through the steelwork of her open decks, boiling madly in the cavernous openings that would hold the pod tanks when she was fully loaded.

Now she came up short on the hundreds of retaining cables that prevented her from driving clear across the river and throwing herself ashore on the far bank.

She fought against this restraint, as though having felt the water she was now eager to run. She rolled and dipped and swung with a ponderous majesty that kept the crowds along the bridge cheering wildly. Then slowly she settled and floated quietly, seeming to fill the Loire river from bank to bank and to reach as high as the soaring spans of the bridge itself.

The four attendant harbour tugs moved in quickly to assist the ship to turn its prodigious length and to line up for the roads and the open sea.

They butted and backed, working as a highly skilled team, and slowly they coaxed *Golden Dawn* around. Her sideways motion left a mile-wide sweep of disturbed water across the estuary. Then suddenly there was a tremendous boil under her counter, and Nicholas saw the bronze flash of her single screw sweeping slowly through the brown water. Faster and still faster it turned, and despite himself Nicholas thrilled to see her come alive. A ripple formed under her bows, and almost imperceptibly she began to creep forward, overcoming the vast inertia of her weight, gathering steerage way, under command at last.

The harbour tugs fell back respectfully, and as the mighty bows lined up with the open sea she drove forward determinedly.

Silver spouts of steam from the sirens of the tugs shot high, and moments later, the booming bellow of their salute crashed against the skies.

The crowds had dispersed and Nicholas stood alone in the wind on the high bridge and watched the structured steel towers of *Golden Dawn*'s hull blending with the grey and misted horizon. He watched her turn, coming around on to her great circle course that would carry her six thousand miles southward to Good Hope, and even at this distance he sensed her change in mood as she steadied and her single screw began to push her up to top economic speed.

Nicholas checked his watch and murmured the age-old Master's command that commenced every voyage.

'Full away at 1700 hours,' he said, and turned to trudge back along the bridge to where he had left the hired Renault.

It was after six o'clock and the site office was empty by the time Nicholas got back to *Sea Witch*. He threw himself into a chair and lit a cheroot while he thumbed quickly through his address book. He found what he wanted, dialled the direct London code, and then the number.

'Good afternoon. This is the *Sunday Times*. May I help you?'

'Is Mr Herbstein available?' Nicholas asked.

'Hold on, please.'

While he waited, Nicholas checked his address book for his next most likely contact, should the journalist be climbing the Himalayas or visiting a guerrilla training camp in Central Africa, either of which were highly likely – but within seconds he heard his voice.

'Denis,' he said. 'This is Nicholas Berg. How are you? I've got a hell of a story for you.'

Nicholas tried to bear the indignity of it with stoicism, but the thick coating of pancake make-up seemed to clog the pores of his skin and he moved restlessly in the make-up chair.

'Please keep still, sir,' the make-up girl snapped irritably; there was a line of unfortunates awaiting her ministrations along the bench at the back of the narrow room. One of them was Duncan Alexander and he caught Nicholas' eye in the mirror and raised an eyebrow in a mocking salute.

In the chair beside him, the anchorman of *The Today and Tomorrow Show* lolled graciously; he was tall and elegant with dyed and permanently waved hair, a carnation in his buttonhole, a high camp manner and an ostentatiously liberal image.

'I've given you the first slot. If it gets interesting, I'll run you four minutes forty seconds, otherwise I'll cut it off at two.'

Denis Herbstein's Sunday article had been done with high professionalism, especially bearing in mind the very short time he had to put it together. It had included interviews with representatives of Lloyd's of London, the oil companies, environmental experts both in America and England, and even with the United States Coast Guard.

'Try to make it tight and hard,' advised the anchorman. 'Let's not pussyfoot around.' He wanted sensation, not too many facts or figures, good gory horror stuff – or a satisfying punch-up. The *Sunday Times* article had flushed them out at Orient Amex and Christy Marine; they had not been able to ignore the challenge for there was a question tabled for Thursday by a Labour member in the Commons, and ominous stirrings in the ranks of the American Coast Guard service.

There had been enough fuss to excite the interest of *The Today and Tomorrow Show*. They had invited the parties to meet their accuser, and both Christy Marine and Orient Amex had fielded their first teams. Duncan Alexander with all his charisma had come to speak for Christy Marine, and Orient Amex had selected one of their directors who looked like Gary Cooper. With his craggy honest face and the silver hairs at his temples he looked like the kind of man you wanted flying your airliner or looking after your money.

The make-up girl dusted Nicholas' face with powder.

'I'm going to invite you to speak first. Tell us about this stuff – what is it, cadmium?' the interviewer checked his script.

Nicholas nodded, he could not speak for he was suffering the ultimate indignity. The girl was painting his lips.

The television studio was the size of an aircraft hangar, the concrete floor strewn with thick black cables and the roof lost in the gloomy heights, but they had created the illusion of intimacy in the small shell of the stage around which the big mobile cameras cluttered like mechanical crabs around the carcass of a dead fish.

The egg-shaped chairs made it impossible either to loll or to sit upright, and the merciless white glare of the arc lamps fried the thick layer of greasy make-up on Nicholas' skin. It was small consolation that across the table Duncan looked like a Japanese Kabuki dancer in make-up too white for his coppery hair.

An assistant director in a sweatshirt and jeans clipped the small microphone into Nicholas' lapel and whispered,

'Give them hell, ducky.'

Somebody else in the darkness beyond the lights was intoning solemnly, 'Four, three, two, one – you're on!' and the red light lit on the middle camera.

'Welcome to *The Today and Tomorrow Show*,' the anchorman's voice was suddenly warm and intimate and mellifluous. 'Last week in the French shipbuilding port of St Nazaire, the largest ship in the world was launched—' In a dozen sentences he sketched out the facts, while on the repeating screens beyond the cameras Nicholas saw that they were running newsreel footage of *Golden Dawn*'s launching. He remembered the helicopter hovering over the dockyard, and he was so fascinated by the aerial views of the enormous vessel taking to the water that when the cameras switched suddenly to him, he was taken by surprise and saw himself start on the little screen as the interviewer began introducing him, swiftly running a thumbnail portrait and then going on:

'Mr Berg has some very definite views on this ship.'

'In her present design and construction, she is not safe to carry even regular crude petroleum oil,' Nicholas said. 'However, she will be employed in the carriage of crude oil that has been contaminated by cadmium sulphide in such concentrations as to make it one of the more toxic substances in nature.'

'Your first statement, Mr Berg, does anyone else share your doubts as to the safety of her design?'

'She does not carry the Al rating by the marine inspectors of Lloyd's of London,' said Nicholas.

'Now can you tell us about the cargo she will carry – the so-called cad-rich crudes?'

Nicholas knew he had perhaps fifteen seconds to draw a verbal picture of the Atlantic Ocean turned into a sterile poisoned desert; it was too short a time, and twice Duncan Alexander interjected, skilfully breaking up the logic of Nicholas' presentation and before he had finished, the anchor-man glanced at his watch and cut him short.

'Thank you, Mr Berg. Now Mr Kemp is a director of the oil company.'

'My company, Orient Amex, last year allocated the sum of two million U.S. dollars as grants to assist in the scientific study of world environmental problems. I can tell you folks, right now, that we at Orient Amex are very conscious of the problems of modern technology—' He was projecting the oil-company image, the benefactors of all humanity.

'Your company's profit last year, after taxation, was four hundred and twenty-five million dollars,' Nicholas cut in clearly. 'That makes point four seven per cent on environmental research – all of it tax deductible. Congratulations, Mr Kemp.'

The oil man looked pained and went on: 'Now we at Orient Amex,' plugging the company name again neatly, 'are working towards a better quality of life for all peoples. But we do realize that it is impossible to put back the clock a hundred years. We cannot allow ourselves to be blinded by the romantic wishful thinking of *amateur* environmentalists, the weekend scientists and the doomcriers who—'

'Cry *Torrey Canyon*,' Nicholas suggested helpfully, and the oil man suppressed a shudder and went on quickly.

' – who would have us discontinue such research as the

revolutionary cadmium cracking process, which could extend the world's utilization of fossil fuels by a staggering forty per cent and give the world's oil reserves an extended life of twenty years or more.'

Again the anchorman glanced at his watch, cut the oil man off in mid-flow and switched his attention to Duncan Alexander.

'Mr Alexander, your so-called ultra-tanker will carry the cad-rich crudes. How would you reply to Mr Berg?'

Duncan smiled, a deep secret smile. 'When Mr Berg had my job as head of Christy Marine, the *Golden Dawn* was the best idea in the world. Since he was fired, it's suddenly the worst.'

They laughed, even one of the cameramen out beyond the lights guffawed uncontrollably, and Nicholas felt the hot red rush of his anger.

'Is the *Golden Dawn* rated A1 at Lloyd's?' asked the anchorman.

'Christy Marine has not applied for a Lloyd's listing – we arranged our insurance in other markets.'

Even through his anger Nicholas had to concede how good he was. He had a mind like quicksilver.

'How safe is your ship, Mr Alexander?'

Now Duncan turned his head and looked directly across the table at Nicholas.

'I believe she is as safe as the world's leading marine architects and naval engineers can make her.' He paused, and there was a malevolent gleam in his eyes now, 'So safe, that I have decided to end this ridiculous controversy by a display of my personal confidence.'

'What form will this show of faith take, Mr Alexander?' The anchorman sensed the sensational line for which he had been groping and he leaned forward eagerly.

'On *Golden Dawn*'s maiden voyage, when she returns from the Persian Gulf fully laden with the El Barras crudes, I and my family, my wife and my stepson, will travel aboard her for the final six thousand miles of her voyage – from Cape Town on the Cape of Good Hope to Galveston in the Gulf of Mexico.' As Nicholas gaped at him wordlessly, he went on evenly, 'That's how convinced I am that *Golden Dawn* is capable of performing her task in perfect safety.'

'Thank you.' The anchorman recognized a good exit line, when he heard one. 'Thank you, Mr Alexander. You've convinced me – and I am sure you have convinced many of our viewers. We are now crossing to Washington via satellite where—'

The moment the red 'in use' light flickered out on the television camera, Nicholas was on his feet and facing Duncan Alexander. His anger was fanned by the realization that Duncan had easily grandstanded him with that adroit display of showmanship, and by the stabbing anxiety at the threat to take Peter aboard *Golden Dawn* on her hazardous maiden voyage.

'You're not taking Peter on that death trap of yours,' he snapped.

'That's his mother's decision,' said Duncan evenly. 'As the daughter of Arthur Christy, she's decided to give the company her full support,' he emphasized the word 'full'.

'I won't let either of you endanger my son's life for a wild public-relations stunt.'

'I'm sure you will try to prevent it,' Duncan nodded and smiled, 'and I'm sure your efforts will be as ineffectual as your attempts to stop *Golden Dawn*.' He deliberately turned his back on Nicholas and spoke to the oil man. 'I do think that went off rather well,' he said, 'don't you?'

James Teacher gave a graphic demonstration of why he could charge the highest fees in London and still have his desk piled high with important briefs. He had Nicholas' urgent application before a Judge-in-Chambers within seventy-two hours, petitioning for a writ to restrain Chantelle Alexander from allowing the son of their former marriage, one Peter Nicholas Berg, aged twelve years, to accompany her on an intended voyage from Cape Town in the Republic of South Africa to Galveston in the state of Texas aboard the bulk crude-carrier *Golden Dawn*, and/or to prevent the said Chantelle Alexander from allowing the child to undertake any other voyage aboard the said vessel.

The Judge heard the petition during a recess in the criminal trial of a young post-office worker standing accused of multiple rape. The judge's oak-panelled book-lined chambers were overcrowded by the two parties, their lawyers, the judge's registrar and the considerable bulk of the judge himself.

Still in his wig and robes from the public court, the judge read swiftly through the written submission of both sides, listened attentively to James Teacher's short address and the rebuttal by his opposite number, before turning sternly to Chantelle.

'Mrs Alexander.' The stern expression wavered slightly as he looked upon the devastating beauty which sat demurely before him. 'Do you love your son?'

'More than anything else in this life.' Chantelle looked at him steadily out of those vast dark eyes.

'And you are happy to take him on this journey with you?'

'I am the daughter of a sailor. If there was danger I would understand it. I am happy to go myself and take my son with me.'

The judge nodded, looked down at the papers on his desk for a moment.

'As I understand the circumstances, Mr Teacher, it is common ground that the mother has custody?'

'That is so, my lord. But the father is the child's guardian.'

'I'm fully aware of that, thank you,' he snapped acidly. He paused again before resuming in the measured tones of judgement, 'We are concerned here exclusively with the welfare and safety of the child. It has been shown that the proposed journey will be made during the holidays and that no loss of schooling will result. On the other hand, I do not believe that the petitioner has shown that reasonable doubts exist about the safety of the vessel on which the voyage will be made. It seems to be a modern and sophisticated ship. To grant the petition would, in my view, be placing unreasonable restraint on the child's mother.' He swivelled in his chair to face Nicholas and James Teacher. 'I regret, therefore, that I see insufficient grounds to accede to your petition.'

In the back seat of James Teacher's Bentley, the little lawyer murmured apologetically. 'He was right, of course, Nicholas. I would have done the same in his place. These domestic squabbles are always—'

Nicholas was not listening. 'What would happen if I picked up Peter and took him to Bermuda or the States?'

'Abduct him!' James Teacher's voice shot up an octave, and he caught Nicholas' arm with genuine alarm. 'I beg of you, dismiss the thought. They would have the police waiting for you – God!' Now he wriggled miserably in his seat. 'I can't bear to think of what might happen. Apart from getting you sent to gaol, your former wife might even get an order restraining you from seeing your boy again. She could get guardianship away from you. If you did that, you could lose the child, Nicholas. Don't do it. Please don't do it!'

Now he patted Nicholas' arm ingratiatingly. 'You'd be playing right into their hands.' And then with relief he switched his attention to the briefcase on his lap.

'Can we read through the latest draft of the agreement of sale again?' he asked. 'We haven't got much time, you know.' Then, without waiting for a reply, he began on the preamble to the agreement which would transfer all the assets and liabilities of Ocean Salvage and Towage to the Directors of the Bank of the East, as nominees for parties unnamed.

Nicholas slumped in the far corner of the seat, and stared thoughtfully out of the window as the Bentley crawled in the traffic stream out of the Strand, around Trafalgar Square with its wheeling clouds of pigeons and milling throngs of tourists, swung into the Mall and accelerated down the long straight towards the Palace.

'I want you to stall them,' Nicholas said suddenly, and Teacher broke off in the middle of a sentence and stared at him distractedly.

'I beg your pardon?'

'I want you to find a way to stall the Sheikhs.'

'Good God, man.' James Teacher was utterly astounded. 'It's taken me nearly a month – four hard weeks to get them ripe to sign,' his voice choked a little at the memory of the long hours of negotiation. 'I've written every line of the agreement in my own blood.'

'I need to have control of my tugs. I need to be free to act—'

'Nicholas, we are talking about seven million dollars.'

'We are talking about my son,' said Nicholas quietly. 'Can you stall them?'

'Yes, of course I can, if that's what you truly want.' Wearily James Teacher closed the file on his lap. 'How long?'

'Six weeks – long enough for *Golden Dawn* to finish her maiden voyage, one way or the other.'

'You realize that this may blow the whole deal, don't you?'

'Yes, I realize that.'

'And you realize also that there isn't another buyer?'

'Yes.'

They were silent then, until the Bentley pulled up before the Bank building in Curzon Street, and they stepped out on to the pavement.

'Are you absolutely certain?' Teacher asked softly.

'Just do it,' Nicholas replied, and the doorman held the bronze and glass doors open for them.

Bermuda asserted its calming influence over Nicholas the moment he stepped out of the aircraft into its comfortable warmth and clean, glittering sunlight. Bernard Wackie's gorgeous burnt-honey-coloured secretary was there to welcome him. She wore a thin cotton dress the colour of freshly cut pineapple and a flashing white smile.

'Mr Wackie's waiting for you at the Bank, sir.'

'Are you out of your mind, Nicholas?' Bernard greeted him. 'Jimmy Teacher tells me you blew the Arabs out of the window. Tell me it's not true, please tell me it's not true.'

'Oh, come on, Bernard,' Nicholas shook his head and patted him consolingly on the shoulder, 'your commission would only have been a lousy point seven million, anyway.'

'Then you did it!' Bernard wailed, and tried to pull his hand out of Nicholas' grip. 'You screwed it all up.'

'The Sheikhs have been screwing us up for over a month, Bernie baby. I just gave them a belt of the same medicine, and do you know what? They loved it. The

Prince sat up and showed real interest for the first time. For the first time we were speaking the same language. They'll still be around six weeks from now.'

'But why? I don't understand. Just explain to me why you did it.'

'Let's go into the plot, and I'll explain it to you.'

In the plot Nicholas stood over the perspex map of the oceans of the globe, and studied it carefully for fully five minutes without speaking.

'That's *Sea Witch*'s latest position. She's making good passage?'

The green plastic disc that bore the tug's number was set in mid-Atlantic.

'She reported two hours ago.' Bernie nodded, and then said with professional interest, 'How did her sea trials go off?'

'There were the usual wrinkles to iron out, that's what kept me in St Nazaire so long. But we got them straight – and Jules has fallen in love with her.'

'He's still the best skipper in the game.'

But already Nicholas' attention had switched halfway across the world.

'*Warlock*'s still in Mauritius,' his voice snapped like a whip.

'I had to fly out a new armature for the main generator. It was just bad luck that she broke down in that God-forsaken part of the world.'

'When will she be ready for sea?'

'Allen promises noon tomorrow. Do you want to telex him for an update on that?'

'Later.' Nicholas wet the tip of a cheroot carefully, without taking his eyes off the plot, calculating distances and currents and speeds.

'*Golden Dawn?*' he asked, and lit the cheroot while he listened to Bernard's reply.

'Her pod tanks arrived under tow at the new Orient Amex depot on El Barras three weeks ago.' Bernie picked up the pointer and touched the upper bight of the deep Persian Gulf. 'They took on their full cargoes of crude and lay inshore to await *Golden Dawn*'s arrival.'

For a moment, Nicholas contemplated the task of towing those four gigantic pod tanks from Japan to the Gulf, and then he discarded the thought and listened to Bernard.

'*Golden Dawn* arrived last Thursday and, according to my agent at El Barras, she coupled up with her pod tanks and made her turn around within three hours.' Bernard slid the tip of the pointer southwards down the eastern coast of the African continent. 'I have had no report of her since then, but if she makes good her twenty-two knots, then she'll be somewhere off the coast of Mozambique, or Maputo as they call it now, and she should double the Cape within the next few days. I will have a report on her then. She'll be taking on mail as she passes Cape Town.'

'And passengers,' said Nicholas grimly; he knew that Peter and Chantelle were in Cape Town already. He had telephoned the boy the night before and Peter had been wildly elated at the prospect of the voyage on the ultra-tanker.

'It's going to be tremendous fun, Dad,' his voice cracking with the onset of both excitement and puberty. 'We'll be flying out to the ship in a helicopter.'

Bernard Wackie changed the subject, now picking up a sheaf of telex flimsies and thumbing swiftly through them.

'Right, I've confirmed the standby contract for *Sea Witch*.' Nicholas nodded, the contract was for Jules Levoisin and the new tug to stand by three offshore working rigs, standard exploration rigs, that were drilling in the Florida Bay, that elbow of shallow water formed by the sweep of the Florida Keys and the low swampy morass of the Everglades. 'It's ridiculous to use a twenty-two-thousand-horsepower ocean-going tug as an oil-rig standby,' Bernard lowered the file, and could no longer contain his irritation.

'Jules is going to go bananas sitting around playing nurse-maid. You are going to have a mutiny on your hands – and you'll be losing money. The daily hire won't cover your direct costs.'

'She will be sitting exactly where I want her,' said Nicholas, and switched his attention back to the tiny dot of an island in the middle of the Indian Ocean. 'Now *Warlock*.'

'Right. *Warlock*.' Bernie picked up another file. 'I have tendered for a deep-sea tow.'

'Cancel it,' said Nicholas. 'Just as soon as Allen has repaired his generator, I want him running top of the green for Cape Town.'

'For Cape Town – top of the green?' Bernard stared at him. 'Christ, Nicholas. What for?'

'He won't be able to catch *Golden Dawn* before she rounds the Cape, but I want him to follow her.'

'Nicholas, you're out of your mind – do you know what that would cost?'

'If *Golden Dawn* gets into trouble he'll be only a day or two behind her. Tell Allen he is to shadow her all the way into Galveston roads.'

'Nicholas, you're letting this whole thing get out of all proportion. It's become an obsession with you, for God's sake!'

'With her superior speed, *Warlock* should be up with her before she enters the—'

'Listen to me, Nicholas. Let's think this all out carefully. What are the chances of *Golden Dawn* suffering structural failure or crippling breakdown on her maiden voyage – a hundred to one against it? It's that high?'

'That's about right.' Nicholas agreed. 'A hundred to one.'

'What is it going to cost to hold one ocean-going salvage tug on standby, at a lousy 1,500 dollars a day – and then to send another halfway around the world at top of the green?'

Bernard clasped his brow theatrically. 'It's going to cost you a quarter of a million dollars, if you take into consideration the loss of earnings on both vessels – that's the very least it's going to cost you. Don't you have respect for money any longer?'

'Now you understand why I had to stall the Sheikhs,' Nicholas smiled calmly. 'I couldn't shoot their money on a hundred-to-one chance – but it's not their money yet. It's mine. *Sea Witch* and *Warlock* aren't their tugs, they are mine. Peter isn't their son, he's mine.'

'You're serious,' said Bernard incredulously. 'I do believe you are serious.'

'Right,' Nicholas agreed. 'Damned right, I am. Now get a telex off to David Allen and ask him for his estimated time of arrival in Cape Town.'

Samantha Silver had one towel wrapped around her head like a turban. Her hair was still wet from the luxurious shampooing it had just received. She wore the other towel tucked under her armpits, making a short sarong of it. She still glowed all over from the steaming tub and she smelled of soap and talcum powder.

After a long field trip, it took two or three of these soakings and scrubbings to get the salt and the smell of the mangroves out of her pores, and the Everglades mud from under her nails.

She poured the batter into the pan, the oil spitting and crackling with the heat and she sang out, 'How many waffles can you eat?'

He came through from the bathroom, a wet towel wrapped around his waist, and he stood in the doorway and grinned at her. 'How many have you got?' he asked. She had still not accustomed her ear to the Australian twang.

He was burned and brown as she was, and his hair was bleached at the ends, hanging now, wet from the shower, into his face.

They had worked well together, and she had learned much from him. The drift into intimacy had been gradual, but inevitable. In her hurt, she had turned to him for comfort, and also in deliberate spite of Nicholas. But now, if she turned her head away, she would not really be able to remember his features clearly. It took an effort to remember his name – Dennis, of course, Doctor Dennis O'Connor.

She was detached from it all, as though a sheet of armoured glass separated her from the real world. She went through the motions of working and playing, of eating and sleeping, of laughing and loving, but it was all a sham.

Dennis was watching her from the doorway now, with that slightly puzzled expression, the helpless look of a person who watches another one drowning and is powerless to give aid.

Samantha turned away quickly. 'Ready in two minutes,' she said, and he turned back into the bedroom to finish dressing.

She flipped the waffles on to a plate and poured a fresh batch of batter.

Beside her, the telephone rang and she sucked her fingers clean and picked it up with her free hand.

'Sam Silver,' she said.

'Thank God. I've been going out of my mind. What happened to you, darling?'

Her knees went rubbery under her, and she had to sit down quickly on one of the stools.

'Samantha, can you hear me?'

She opened her mouth, but no sound came out.

'Tell me what's happening—' She could see his face before her, clearly, each detail of it so vividly remembered, the clear green eyes below the heavy brow, the line of cheekbone and jaw, and the sound of his voice made her shiver.

'Samantha.'

'How is your wife, Nicholas?' she asked softly – and he broke off. She held the receiver to her ear with both hands, and the silence lasted only a few beats of her heart, but it was long enough. Once or twice, in moments of weakness during the last two weeks, she had tried to convince herself that it was not true. That it had all been the viciousness of a lying woman. Now she knew beyond any question that her instinct had been correct. His silence was the admission, and she waited for the lie that she knew would come next.

'Would it help to tell you I love you?' he asked softly, and she could not answer. Even in her distress, the felt the rush of relief. He had not lied. At that moment it was the most important thing in her life. He had not lied. She felt it begin to tear painfully, deep in her chest. Her shoulders shook spasmodically.

'I'm coming to get you,' he said into the silence.

'I won't be here,' she whispered, but she felt it welling up into her throat, uncontrollably. She had not wept before, she had kept it all safely bottled away – but now, the first sob burst from her, and with both hands she slammed the telephone back on to its cradle.

She stood there still, shaking wildly, and the tears poured down her cheeks and dripped from her chin.

Dennis came into the kitchen behind her, tucking his shirt into the top of his trousers, his hair shiny and wet with the straight lines of the comb through it.

'Who was that?' he asked cheerfully, and then stopped aghast.

'What is it, love?' He started forward again, 'Come on now.'

'Don't touch me, please,' she whispered huskily, and he

stopped again uncertainly. 'We are fresh out of milk,' she said without turning. 'Will you take the van down to the shopping centre?'

By the time Dennis returned, she was dressed and she had rinsed her face and tied a scarf around her head like a gypsy. They chewed cold, unappetizing waffles in silence, until she spoke.

'Dennis, we've got to talk—'

'No,' he smiled at her. 'It's all right, Sam. You don't have to say it. I should have moved on days ago, anyway.'

'Thanks,' she said.

'It was Nicholas, wasn't it?'

She regretted having told him now, but at the time it had been vitally necessary to speak to somebody.

She nodded, and his voice had a sting to it as he went on.

'I'd like to bust that bastard in the mouth.'

'We levelled the score, didn't we?' She smiled, but it was an unconvincing smile, and she didn't try to hold it.

'Sam, I want you to know that for me it was not just another quick shack job.'

'I know that.' Impulsively she reached out and squeezed his hand. 'And thanks for understanding – but is it okay if we don't talk about it any more?'

Peter Berg had twisted round in his safety straps, so that he could press his face to the round perspex window in the fuselage of the big Sikorsky helicopter.

The night was completely, utterly black.

Across the cabin, the Flight Engineer stood in the open doorway, the wind ripping at his bright orange overalls, fluttering them around his body, and he turned and grinned across at the boy, then he made a windmilling gesture with his hand and stabbed downwards with his thumb. It was impossible to speak in the clattering, rushing roar of wind and engine and rotor.

The helicopter banked gently and Peter gasped with excitement as the ship came into view.

She was burning all her lights; tier upon tier, the brilliantly lit floors of her stern quarters rose above the altitude at which the Sikorsky was hovering, and, seeming to reach ahead to the black horizon, the tank deck was outlined with rows of hooded lamps, like the street lamps of a deserted city.

She was so huge that she looked like a city. There seemed to be no end to her, stretched to the horizon and towering into the sky.

The helicopter sank in a controlled sweep towards the white circular target on the heliport, guided down by the engineer in the open doorway. Skilfully the pilot matched his descent to the forward motion of the ultra-tanker, twenty-two knots at top economical – Peter had swotted the figures avidly – and the deck moved with grudging majesty to the scend of the tall Cape rollers pushing in unchecked from across the length of the Atlantic Ocean.

The pilot hovered, judging his approach against the brisk north-westerly crosswind, and from fifty feet Peter could see that the decks were almost level with the surface of the sea, pressed down deeply by the weight of her cargo. Every few seconds, one of the rollers that raced down her length would flip aboard and spread like spilled milk, white and frothy in the deck lights, before cascading back over the side.

Made arrogant and unyielding by her vast bulk, the *Golden Dawn* did not woo the ocean, as other ships do. Instead, her great blunt bows crushed the swells, churning them under or shouldering them contemptuously aside.

Peter had been around boats since before he could walk.

He too was a sea-creature. But though his eye was keen, it was as yet unschooled, so he did not notice the working of the long wide deck.

Sitting beside Peter on the bench seat, Duncan Alexander knew to look for the movement in the hull. He watched the hull twisting and hogging, but so slightly, so barely perceptibly, that Duncan blinked it away, and looked again. From bows to stern she was a mile and a half long, and in essence she was merely four steel pods held together by an elaborate flexible steel scaffolding and driven forward by the mighty propulsion unit in the stern. There was small independent movement of each of the tank pods, so the deck twisted as she rolled, and flexed like a longbow as she took the swells under her. The crest of these swells were a quarter of a mile apart. At any one time, there were four separate wave patterns beneath *Golden Dawn*'s hull, with the peaks thrusting up and the troughs allowing the tremendous dead weight of her cargo to push downwards; the elastic steel groaned and gave to meet these shearing forces.

No hull is ever completely rigid, and elasticity had been part of the ultra-tanker's original design, but those designs had been altered. Duncan Alexander had saved almost two thousand tons of steel, by reducing the stiffening of the central pillar that docked the four pods together, and he had dispensed with the double skins of the pods themselves. He had honed *Golden Dawn* down to the limits at which his own architects had baulked; then he had hired Japanese architects to rework the designs. They had expressed themselves satisfied that the hull was safe, but had also respectfully pointed out that nobody had ever carried a million tons of crude petroleum in a single cargo before.

The helicopter sank the last few feet and bumped gently on to the insulated green deck, with its thick coat of plasticized paint which prevented the striking of spark.

Even a grain of sand trodden between leather sole and bare steel could ignite an explosive air and petroleum gas mixture.

The ship's party swarmed forward, doubled under the swirling rotor. The luggage in its net beneath the fuselage was dragged away and strong hands swung Peter down on to the deck. He stood blinking in the glare of deck lamps and wrinkling his nose to the characteristic tanker stench. It is a smell that pervades everything aboard one of these ships: the food, the furniture, the crew's clothing – even their hair and skin.

It is the thin, acrid chemical stench of under-rich fumes vented off from the tanks. Oxygen and petroleum gas are only explosive in a mixture within narrow limits: too much oxygen makes the blend under-rich and too much petroleum gas makes it over-rich, either of which mixtures are non-explosive, non-combustible.

Chantelle Alexander was handed down next from the cabin of the helicopter, bringing an instant flash of elegance to the starkly lit scene of bleak steel and ugly functional machinery. She wore a catsuit of dark green with a bright Jean Patou scarf on her head. Two ship's officers closed in solicitously on each side of her and led her quickly away towards the towering stern quarters, out of the rude and blustering wind and the helicopter engine roar.

Duncan Alexander followed her down to the deck and shook hands quickly with the First Officer.

'Captain Randle's compliments, sir. He is unable to leave the bridge while the ship is in the inshore channel.'

'I understand.' Duncan flashed that marvellous smile. The great ship drew almost twenty fathoms fully laden and she had come in very close, as close as was prudent to the mountainous coastline of Good Hope with its notorious currents and wild winds. However, Chantelle Christy must not be exposed to the ear-numbing discomfort of the helicopter flight for a moment longer than was necessary, and so *Golden Dawn* had come in through the inner channel, perilously close to the guardian rocks of Robben Island that stood in the open mouth of Table Bay.

Even before the helicopter rose and circled away towards the distant glow of Cape Town city under its dark square mountain, the tanker's great blunt bows were swinging away towards the west, and Duncan imagined the relief of Captain Randle as he gave the order to make the offing into the open Atlantic with the oceanic depths under his cumbersome ship.

Duncan smiled again and reached for Peter Berg's hand.

'Come on, my boy.'

'I'm all right, sir.'

Skilfully Peter avoided the hand and the smile, containing his wild excitement so that he walked ahead like a man, without the skipping energy of a little boy. Duncan Alexander felt the customary flare of annoyance. No, more than that – bare anger at this further rejection by Berg's puppy. They went in single file along the steel catwalk with the child leading. He had never been able to get close to the boy and he had tried hard in the beginning. Now Duncan stopped his anger with the satisfying memory of how neatly he had used the child to slap Berg in the face, and draw the fangs of his opposition.

Berg would be worrying too much about his brat to have time for anything else. He followed Chantelle and the child into the gleaming chrome and plastic corridors of the stern quarters. It was difficult to think of decks and bulkheads rather than floors and walls in here. It was too much like a modern apartment block, even the elevator which bore them swiftly and silently five storeys up to the navigation bridge helped to dispel the feelings of being shipborne.

On the bridge itself, they were so high above the sea as to be divorced from it. The deck lights had been extinguished once the helicopter had gone, and the darkness of the night, silenced by the thick double-glazed windows, heightened the peace and isolation. The riding lights in the bows seemed remote as the very stars, and the gentle lulling movement of the immense hull was only just noticeable.

The Master was a man of Duncan Alexander's own choosing. The command of the flagship of Christy Marine should have gone to Basil Reilly, the senior captain of the fleet. However, Reilly was Berg's man, and Duncan had used the foundering of *Golden Adventurer* to force premature retirement on the old sailor.

Randle was young for the responsibility – just a little over thirty years of age – but his training and his credentials were impeccable, and he was an honours graduate of the tanker school in France. Here top men received realistic training in the specialized handling of these freakish giants in cunningly constructed lakes and scale-model harbours, working thirty-foot models of the bulk carriers that had all the handling characteristics of the real ships.

Since Duncan had given him the command, he had been a staunch ally, and he had stoutly defended the design and construction of his ship when the reporters, whipped up by Nicholas Berg, had questioned him. He was loyal, which weighed heavily, tipping the balance for Duncan against his youth and inexperience.

He hurried to meet his important visitors as they stepped out of the elevator into his spacious, gleaming modern bridge, a short stocky figure with a bull neck and the thrusting heavy jaw of great determination or great stubbornness. His greeting had just the right mixture of warmth and servility, and Duncan noted approvingly that he treated even the boy with careful respect. Randle was bright enough to realize that one day the child would be head of Christy Marine. Duncan liked a man who could think so clearly and so far ahead, but Randle was not quite prepared for Peter Berg.

'Can I see your engine room, Captain?'

'You mean right now?'

'Yes.' For Peter the question was superfluous. 'If you don't mind, sir,' he added quickly. Today was for doing things and tomorrow was lost in the mists of the future. Right now, would be just fine.

'Well now,' the Captain realized the request was deadly serious, and that this lad could not be put off very easily, 'we go on automatic during the night. There's nobody down there now – and it wouldn't be fair to wake the engineer, would it? It's been a hard day.'

'I suppose not.' Bitterly disappointed, but amenable to convincing argument, Peter nodded.

'But I am certain the Chief would be delighted to have you as his guest directly after breakfast.'

The Chief Engineer was a Scot with three sons of his own in Glasgow, the youngest of them almost exactly Peter's age. He was more than delighted. Within twenty-four hours, Peter was the ship's favourite, with his own blue company-issue overalls altered to fit him and his name embroidered across the back by the lascar steward, 'PETER BERG'. He wore his bright yellow plastic hard hat at the same jaunty angle as the Chief did, and carried a wad of cotton waste in his back pocket to wipe his greasy hands after helping one of the stokers clean the fuel filters – the messiest job on board, and the greatest fun.

Although the engine control room with its rough camaraderie, endless supplies of sandwiches and cocoa and satisfying grease and oil that made a man look like a professional, was Peter's favourite station, yet he stood other watches.

Every morning he joined the First Officer on his inspection. Starting in the bows, they worked their way back, checking each of the pod tanks, every valve, and every one of the heavy hydraulic docking clamps that held the pod tanks attached to the main frames of the hull. Most important of all they checked the gauges on each compartment which gave the precise indication of the gas mixtures contained in the air spaces under the main deck of the crude tanks.

*Golden Dawn* operated on the 'inert' system to keep the trapped fumes in an over-rich and safe condition. The exhaust fumes of the ship's engine were caught, passed through filters and scrubbers to remove the corrosive sulphur elements and then, as almost pure carbon dioxide and carbon monoxide, they were forced into the air spaces of the petroleum tanks. The evaporating fumes of the volatile elements of the crude mingled with the exhaust fumes to form an over-rich, oxygen-poor, and unexplosive gas.

However, a leak through one of the hundreds of valves and connections would allow air into the tanks, and the checks to detect this were elaborate, ranging from an unceasing electronic monitoring of each tank to the daily physical inspection, in which Peter now assisted.

Peter usually left the First Officer's party when it returned to the stern quarters, he might then pass the time of day with the two-man crew in the central pump room.

From here the tanks were monitored and controlled, loaded and offloaded, the flow of inert gas balanced, and the crude petroleum could be pushed through the giant centrifugal pumps and transferred from tank to tank to make alterations to the ship's trim, during partial discharge, or when one or more tanks were detached and taken inshore for discharge.

In the pump room was kept a display that always fascinated Peter. It was the sample cupboard with its rows of screw-topped bottles, each containing samples of the cargo taken during loading. As all four of *Golden Dawn*'s tanks had been filled at the same offshore loading point and all with crude from the same field, each of the bottles bore the identical label.

EL BARRAS CRUDE
BUNKERS 'C'
HIGH CADMIUM

Peter liked to take one of the bottles and hold it to the light. Somehow he had always expected the crude oil to be treacly and tar-like, but it was thin as human blood and when he shook the bottle, it coated the glass and the light through it was dark red, again like congealing blood.

'Some of the crudes are black, some yellow and the Nigerians are green,' the pump foreman told him. 'This is the first red that I've seen.'

'I suppose it's the cadmium in it,' Peter told him.

'Guess it is,' the foreman agreed seriously; all on board had very soon learned not to talk down to Peter Berg. He expected to be treated on equal terms.

By this time it was mid-morning and Peter had worked up enough appetite to visit the gallery, where he was greeted like visiting royalty. Within days, Peter knew his way unerringly through the labyrinthine and usually deserted passageways. It was characteristic of these great crude-carriers that you might wander through them for hours without meeting another human being. With their huge bulk and their tiny crews, the only place where there was always human presence was the navigation bridge on the top floor of the stern quarters.

The bridge was always one of Peter's obligatory stops.

'Good morning, Tug,' the officer of the watch would greet him. Peter had been christened with his nickname when he had announced at the breakfast table on his first morning:

'Tankers are great, but I'm going to be a tug captain, like my dad.'

On the bridge the ship might be taken out of automatic to allow Peter to spell the helmsman for a while, or he would assist the junior deck officers while they made a sun shot as an exercise to check against the satellite navigational Decca; then, after socializing with Captain Randle for a while, it was time to report to his true station in the engine.

'We were waiting on you, Tug,' growled the Chief. 'Get your overalls on, man, we're going down the propeller shaft tunnel.'

The only unpleasant period of the day was when Peter's mother insisted that he scrub off the top layers of grease and fuel oil, dress in his number ones, and act as an unpaid steward during the cocktail hour in the elaborate lounge of the owner's suite.

It was the only time that Chantelle Alexander fraternized with the ship's officers and it was a painfully stilted hour, with Peter one of the major sufferers – but the rest of the time he was successful in avoiding the clinging restrictive rulings of his mother and the fiercely hated but silently resented presence of Duncan Alexander, his stepfather.

Still, he was instinctively aware of the new and disturbing tensions between his mother and Duncan Alexander. In the night he heard the raised voices from the master cabin, and he strained to catch the words. Once, when he had heard the cries of his mother's distress, he had left his bunk and gone barefooted to knock on the cabin door. Duncan Alexander had opened it to him. He was in a silk dressing gown and his handsome features were swollen and flushed with anger.

'Go back to bed.'

'I want to see my mother,' Peter had told him quietly.

'You need a damned good hiding,' Duncan had flared. 'Now do as you are told.'

'I want to see my mother.' Peter had stood his ground, standing very straight in his pyjamas with both his tone and expression neutral, and Chantelle had come to him in her nightdress and knelt to embrace him.

'It's all right, darling. It's perfectly all right.' But she had been weeping. After that there had been no more loud voices in the night.

However, except for an hour in the afternoon, when the swimming pool was placed out of bounds to officers and crew, while Chantelle swam and sunbathed, she spent the rest of the time in the owner's suite, eating all her meals there, withdrawn and silent, sitting at the panoramic windows of her cabin, coming to life only for an hour in the evenings while she played the owner's wife to the ship's officers.

Duncan Alexander, on the other hand, was like a caged animal. He paced the open decks, composing long messages which were sent off regularly over the telex in company code to Christy Marine in Leadenhall Street.

Then he would stand out on the open wing of *Golden Dawn*'s bridge, staring fixedly ahead at the northern horizon, awaiting the reply to his last telex, chafing openly at having to conduct the company's business at such long remove, and goaded by the devils of doubt and impatience and fear.

Often it seemed as though he were trying to forge the mighty hull onwards, faster and faster into the north, by the sheer power of his will.

In the north-western corner of the Caribbean basin, there is an area of shallow warm water, hemmed in on one side by the island chain of the Great Antilles, the bulwark of Cuba and Hispaniola, while in the west the sweep of the Yucatan peninsula runs south through Panama into the great land-mass of South America – shallow, warm, trapped water and saturated tropical air, enclosed by land masses which can heat very rapidly in the high hot sun of the tropics. However, all of it is gently cooled and moderated by the benign influence of the north-easterly trade winds – winds so unvarying in strength and direction that over the centuries, seafaring men have placed their lives and their fortunes at risk upon their balmy wings, gambling on the constancy of that vast moving body of mild air.

But the wind does fail; for no apparent reason and without previous warning, it dies away, often merely for an hour or two, but occasionally – very occasionally – for days or weeks at a time.

Far to the south and east of this devil's spawning ground, the *Golden Dawn* ploughed massively on through the sweltering air and silken calm of the doldrums, northwards across the equator, changing course every few hours to maintain the great circle track that would carry her well clear of that glittering shield of islands that the Caribbean carries, like an armoured knight, on its shoulder.

The treacherous channels and passages through the islands were not for a vessel of *Golden Dawn*'s immense bulk, deep draught and limited manoeuvrability. She was to go high above the Tropic of Cancer, and just south of the island of Bermuda she would make her westings and enter the wider and safer waters of the Florida Straits above Grand Bahamas. On this course, she would be constricted by narrow and shallow seaways for only a few hundred miles before she was out into the open waters of the Gulf of Mexico again.

But while she ran on northwards, out of the area of

equatorial calm, she should have come out at last into the sweet cool airs of the trades, but she did not. Day after day, the calm persisted, and stifling still air pressed down on the ship. It did not in any way slow or affect her passage, but her Master remarked to Duncan Alexander:

'Another corker today, by the looks of it.'

When he received no reply from his brooding, silent Chairman, he retired discreetly, leaving Duncan alone on the open wing of the bridge, with only the breeze of the ship's passage ruffling his thick coppery hair.

However, the calm was not merely local. It extended westwards in a wide, hot belt across the thousand islands and the basin of shallow sea they enclosed.

The calm lay heavily on the oily waters, and the sun beat down on the enclosing land masses. Every hour the air heated and sucked up the evaporating waters; a fat bubble like a swelling blister began to rise, the first movement of air in many days. It was not a big bubble, only a hundred miles across, but as it rose, the rotation of the earth's surface began to twist the rising air, spinning it like a top, so that the satellite cameras, hundreds of miles above, recorded a creamy little spiral wisp like the decorative-icing flower on a wedding cake.

The cameras relayed the picture through many channels, until at last it reached the desk of the senior forecaster of the hurricane watch at the meteorological headquarters at Miami in southern Florida.

'Looks like a ripe one,' he grunted to his assistant, recognizing that all the favourable conditions for the formation of a revolving tropical storm were present. 'We'll ask air force for a fly-through.'

At forty-five thousand feet the pilot of the US Air Force B52 saw the rising dome of the storm from two hundred miles away. It had grown enormously in only six hours.

As the warm saturated air was forced upwards, so the icy cold of the upper troposphere condensed the water vapour into thick, puffed-up silver clouds. They boiled upwards, roiling and swirling upon themselves. Already the dome of cloud and ferociously turbulent air was higher than the aircraft.

Under it, a partial vacuum was formed, and the surrounding surface air tried to move in to fill it. But it was compelled into an anticlockwise track around the centre by the mysterious forces of the earth's rotation. Compelled to travel the long route, the velocity of the air mass accelerated ferociously, and the entire system became more unstable, more dangerous by the hour, turning faster, perpetuating itself by creating greater wind velocities and steeper pressure gradients.

The cloud at the top of the enormous rising dome reached an altitude where the temperature was thirty degrees below freezing and the droplets of rain turned to crystals of ice and were smeared away by upper-level jet-streams. Long, beautiful patterns of cirrus against the high blue sky were blown hundreds of miles ahead of the storm to serve as its heralds.

The US Air Force B52 hit the first clear-air turbulence one hundred and fifty miles from the storm's centre. It was as though an invisible predator had seized the fuselage and shaken it until the wings were almost torn from their roots, and in one surge, the aircraft was flung five thousand feet straight upwards.

'Very severe turbulence,' the pilot reported. 'We have vertical wind speeds of three hundred miles an hour plus.'

The senior forecaster in Miami picked up the telephone and called the computer programmer on the floor above him. 'Ask Charlie for a hurricane code name.'

And a minute later the programmer called him back. 'Charlie says to call the bitch "Lorna".'

Six hundred miles south-west of Miami the storm began to move forward, slowly at first but every hour gathering power, spiralling upon itself at unbelievable velocities, its high dome swelling upwards now through fifty thousand feet and still climbing. The centre of the storm opened like a flower, the calm eye extended upwards in a vertical tunnel with smooth walls of solid cloud rising to the very summit of the dome, now sixty thousand feet above the surface of the wind-tortured sea.

The entire mass began to move faster, back towards the east, in a directly contrary direction to the usual track of the gentle trade winds. Spinning and roaring upon itself, devouring everything in its path, the she-devil called Lorna launched itself across the Caribbean Sea.

Nicholas Berg turned his head to look down upon the impressive skyline of Miami Beach. The rampart of tall, elegant hotel buildings followed the curve of the beach into the north, and behind it lay the ugly sprawled tangle of urban development and snarled highways.

The Eastern Airlines direct flight from Bermuda turned on to its base leg and then on to the final approach, losing height over the beach and Biscayne Bay.

Nicholas felt uncomfortable, the nagging of guilt and uncertainty. His guilt was of two kinds. He felt guilty that he had deserted his post at the moment when he was likely to be desperately needed.

Ocean Salvage's two vessels were out there somewhere in the Atlantic, *Warlock* running hard up the length of the Atlantic in a desperate attempt to catch up with *Golden Dawn*, while Jules Levoisin in *Sea Witch* was now approaching the eastern seaboard of America where he would refuel before going on to his assignment as standby tug on the exploration field in the Gulf of Mexico. At any moment, the Master of either vessel might urgently need to have his instructions.

Then there was *Golden Dawn*. She had rounded the Cape of Good Hope almost three weeks ago. Since then, even Bernard Wackie had been unable to fix her position. She had not been reported by other craft, and any communications she had made with Christy Main must have been by satellite telex, for she had maintained strict silence on the radio channels. However, she must rapidly be nearing the most critical part of her voyage when she turned west and began her approach to the continental shelf of North America and the passage of the islands into the Gulf. Peter Berg was on board that monster, and Nicholas felt the chill of guilt. His place was at the centre, in the control room of Bach Wackie on the top floor of the Bank of Bermuda building in Hamilton town. His post was there where he could assess changing conditions and issue instant commands to coordinate his salvage tugs.

Now he had deserted his post, and even though he had made arrangements to maintain contact with Bernard Wackie, still it would take him hours, perhaps even days, to get back to where he was needed, if there was an emergency.

But then there was Samantha. His instincts warned him that every day, every hour he delayed in going to her would reduce his chances of having her again.

There was more guilt there, the guilt of betrayal. It was no help to tell himself that he had made no marriage vows to Samantha Silver, that his night of weakness with Chantelle had been forced upon him in circumstances almost impossible to resist, that any other man in his position would have done the same, and that in the end the episode had been a catharsis and a release that had left him free for ever of Chantelle.

To Samantha, it had been betrayal, and he knew that much was destroyed by it. He felt terrible aching guilt, not for the act – sexual intercourse without love is fleeting and insignificant – but for the betrayal and for the damage he had wrought.

Now he was uncertain, uncertain as to just how much he had destroyed, how much was left for him to build upon. All that he was certain of was that he needed her, more than he had needed anything in his life. She was still the promise of eternal youth and of the new life towards which he was groping so uncertainly. If love was needing, then he loved Samantha Silver with something close to desperation.

She had told him she would not be there when he came. He had to hope now that she had lied. He felt physically sick at the thought that she meant it.

He had only a single Louis Vuitton overnight valise as cabin luggage so he passed swiftly through customs, and as he went into the telephone booths, he checked his watch. It was after six o'clock; she'd be home by now.

He had dialled the first four digits of her number before he checked himself.

'What the hell am I phoning for?' he asked himself grimly. 'To tell her I'm here, so she can have a flying start when she runs for the bushes?'

There is nothing so doomed as a timid lover. He dropped the receiver back on its cradle, and went for the Hertz desk at the terminal doors.

'What's the smallest you've got?' he asked.

'A Cougar,' the pretty blonde in the yellow uniform told him. In America, 'small' is a relative term. He was just lucky she hadn't offered him a Sherman tank.

The brightly painted Chevy van was in the lean-to shelter under the spread branches of the ficus tree, and he parked the Cougar's nose almost touching its tailgate. There was no way she could escape now, unless she went out through the far wall of the shed. Knowing her, that was always a possibility, he grinned mirthlessly.

He knocked once on the screen door of the kitchen and went straight in. There was a coffee pot beside the range, and he touched it as he passed. It was still warm.

He went through into the living room, and called:

'Samantha!'

The bedroom door was ajar. He pushed it open. There was a suit of denims, and some pale transparent wisps of underwear thrown carelessly over the patchwork quilt.

The shack was deserted. He went down the steps of the front stoop and straight on to the beach. The tide had swept the sand smooth, and her prints were the only ones. She had dropped her towel above the high-water mark but he had to shade his eyes against the ruddy glare of the lowering sun before he could make out her bobbing head – five hundred yards out.

He sat down beside her towel in the fluffy dry sand and lit a cheroot.

He waited, while the sun settled in a wild, fiery flood of light, and he lost the shape of her head against the darkening sea. She was half a mile out now, but he felt no urgency, and the darkness was almost complete when she rose suddenly, waist-deep from the edge of the gentle surf, waded ashore and came up the beach, twisting the rope of her hair over one shoulder to wring the water from it.

Nicholas felt his heart flop over and he flicked the cheroot away and stood up. She halted abruptly, like a startled forest animal, and stood completely still, staring uncertainly at the tall, dark figure before her. She was so young and slim and smooth and beautiful.

'What do you want?' she faltered.

'You,' he said.

'Why? Are you starting a harem?' Her voice hardened and she straightened; he could not see the expression of her eyes, but her shoulders took on a stubborn set.

He stepped forward and she was rigid in his arms and her lips hard and tightly unresponsive under his.

'Sam, there are things I'll never be able to explain. I don't even understand them myself, but what I do know very clearly is that I love you, that without you my life is going to be flat and plain goddamned miserable—'

There was no relaxation of the rigid muscles. Her hands were still held stiffly at her sides and her body felt cold and wet and unyielding.

'Samantha, I wish I were perfect – I'm not. But all I am sure of is that I can't make it without you.'

'I couldn't take it again. I couldn't live through this again,' she said tightly.

'I need you. I am certain of that,' he insisted.

'You'd better be, you son of a bitch. You cheat on me one time more and you won't have anything left to cheat with – I'll take it off clean, at the roots.' Then she was clinging to him. 'Oh God, Nicholas, how I hated you, and how I missed you – and how long you took to come back,' and her lips were soft and tasted of the sea.

He picked her up and carried her up through the soft sand. He didn't trust himself to speak. It would be so easy to say the wrong thing now.

'Nicholas, I've been sitting here waiting for your call.' Bernard Wackie's voice was sharp and alert, the tension barely contained. 'How soon can you get yourself back here?'

'What is it?'

'It is starting to pop. I've got to hand it to you, baby, you've got a nose for it. You smelled this coming.'

'Come on, Bernie!' Nicholas snapped.

'This call is going through three open exchanges,' Bernie told him. 'You want chapter and verse, or did nobody ever tell you that it's a tough game you are in? There is a lot of competition cluttering up the scene. The cheese-heads have one lying handy.' Probably *Wittezee* or one of the other big Dutch tugs, Nicholas thought swiftly. 'They could be streaming a towing wire within a couple of days. And the Yanks are pretty hot numbers. McCormick has one stationed in the Hudson River.'

'All right,' Nick cut through the relish with which Bernie was detailing the threat of hovering competition.

'There is a direct flight at seven tomorrow morning – if I can't make that, I'll connect with the British Airways flight from Nassau at noon tomorrow. Meet me,' Nick ordered.

'You shouldn't have gone running off,' said Bernard Wackie, showing amazing hindsight. Before he could deliver any more pearls of wisdom, Nicholas hung up on him.

Samantha was sitting up in the centre of the bed. She was stark naked, but she hugged her knees to her chest with both arms, and under the gorgeous tangle of her hair her face was desolate as that of a lost child and her green eyes haunted.

'You're going again,' she said softly. 'You only just came, and now you're going again. Oh God, Nicholas, loving you is the toughest job I've ever had in my life. I don't think I have got the muscle for it.'

He reached for her quickly and she clung to him, pressing her face into the thick pad of coarse dark hair that covered his chest.

'I have to go – I think it's *Golden Dawn*,' he said, and she listened quietly while he told it to her. Only when he finished speaking did she begin to ask the questions which kept them talking quietly, locked in each other's arms in the old brass bed, until long after midnight.

She insisted on cooking his breakfast for him, even though it was still dark outside and she was more than half asleep, hanging on to the range for support and turning up the early morning radio show so that the music might shake her awake.

'Good morning, early birds, this is WWOK with another lovely day ahead of you. A predicted 85° at Fort Lauderdale and the coast, and 80° inland with a 10 per cent chance of rain. We've got a report on Hurricane Lorna for you also. She's dipping away south, towards the lesser Antilles – so we can all relax, folks – relax and listen to Elton John.'

'I love Elton John,' Samantha said sleepily. 'Don't you?'

'Who is he?' Nicholas asked.

'There! I knew right away we had a lot in common.' She blinked at him owlishly. 'Did you kiss me good morning? I forget.'

'Come here,' he instructed. 'You're not going to forget this one.'

Then, a few minutes later, 'Nicholas, you'll miss your plane.'

'Not if I cut breakfast.'

'It would have been a grotty breakfast anyway.' She was coming awake fast now.

She gave him the last kiss through the open window of the Cougar. 'You've got an hour – you'll just about make it.'

He started the engine and still she held on to the sill.

'Nicholas, one day we will be together – I mean all the time, like we planned? You and me doing our own thing, our own way? We will, won't we?'

'It's a promise.'

'Hurry back,' she said, and he gunned the Cougar up the sandy driveway without looking back.

There were eight of them crowded into Tom Parker's office. Although there was only seating for three, the others found perches against the tiered shelves with their rows of biological specimens in bottles of formaldehyde or on the piles of reference books and white papers that were stacked against the walls.

Samantha sat on the corner of Tom's desk, swinging her long denim-clad legs, and answered the questions that were fired at her.

'How do you know she will take the passage of the Florida Straits?'

'It's an educated guess. She's just too big and clumsy to thread the needle of the islands.' Samantha's replies were quick. 'Nicholas is betting on it.'

'I'll go along with that then,' Tom grunted.

'The Straits are a hundred miles wide—'

'I know what you're going to say,' Samantha smiled, and turned to one of the other girls. 'Sally-Anne will answer that one.'

'You all know my brother is in the Coast Guard – all traffic through the Straits reports to Fort Lauderdale,' she explained. 'And the coastguard aircraft patrol out as far as Grand Bahama.'

'We'll have a fix on her immediately she enters the Straits – we've got the whole US Coast Guard rooting for us.'

They argued and discussed for ten minutes more, before Tom Parker slapped an open palm on the desk in front of him and they subsided reluctantly into silence.

'Okay,' he said. 'Do I understand the proposal to be that this Chapter of Greenpeace intercepts the tanker carrying cad-rich crudes before it enters American territorial waters and attempts to delay or divert the ship?'

'That's exactly it,' Samantha nodded, and looked about her for support. They were all nodding and murmuring in agreement.

'What are we trying to achieve? Do we truly believe that we will be able to hold up the delivery of toxic crudes to the refinery at Galveston? Let's define our objectives,' Tom insisted.

'In order for evil men to triumph it is necessary only that good men do nothing. We are doing something.'

'Bullshit, Sam,' Tom growled. 'Let's cut down on the rhetoric – it's one of the things that does us more harm than good. You talk like a nut and you discredit yourself before you have begun.'

'All right,' Samantha grinned. 'We are publicizing the dangers, and our opposition to them.'

'Okay,' Tom nodded. 'That's better. What are our other objectives?'

They discussed that for twenty minutes more, and then Tom Parker took over again.

'Fine, now how do we get out there in the Straits to confront this vessel – do we put on our waterwings and swim?'

Even Samantha looked sheepish now. She glanced around for support, but the others were studying their fingernails or gazing with sudden fascination out of the windows.

'Well,' Samantha began, and then hesitated. 'We thought—'

'Go on,' Tom encouraged her. 'Of course, you weren't thinking of using University property, were you? There is actually a law in this country against taking other people's ships – it's called piracy.'

'As a matter of fact—' Samantha gave a helpless shrug.

'And as a senior and highly respected member of the faculty, you would not expect me to be party to a criminal act.'

They were all silent, watching Samantha, for she was their leader, but for once she was at a loss.

'On the other hand, if a party of graduate researchers

put in a requisition, through the proper channels, I would be quite happy to authorize an extended field expedition across the Straits to Grand Bahama on board the *Dicky*.'

'Tom, you're a darling,' said Samantha.

'That's a hell of a way to speak to your Professor,' said Tom, and scowled happily at her.

'They came in on the British Airways flight from Heathrow yesterday afternoon. Three of them; here is a list of the names,' Bernard Wackie slid a notepad across the desk, and Nicholas glanced at it quickly.

'Charles Gras – I know him, he's Chief Engineer at Construction Navale Atlantique,' Nicholas explained.

'Right,' Bernard nodded. 'He gave his occupation and employer to Immigration.'

'Isn't that privileged information?'

Bernard grinned. 'I keep my ear to the ground,' and then he was deadly serious again. 'All right, so these three engineers have a small suitcase each and a crate in the hold that weighs three hundred and fifty kilos, and it's marked "Industrial Machinery".'

'Don't stop now,' Nicholas encouraged him.

'And there is an S61N Sikorsky helicopter sitting waiting for them on the tarmac. The helicopter has been chartered direct from London by Christy Marine of Leadenhall Street. The three engineers and the case of machinery are shuttled aboard the Sikorsky so fast that it looks like a conjuring trick, and she takes off and egg-beats for the south.'

'Did the Sikorsky pilot file a flight-plan?'

'Sure did. Servicing shipping, course 196° magnetic. ETA to be reported.'

'What's the range of the 61N – 500 nautical miles?'

'Not bad,' Bernard conceded. '533 for the standard, but this model has long-range tanks. She's good for 750. But that's one way, not the return journey. The helicopter hasn't returned to Bermuda yet.'

'She could refuel aboard – or, if they aren't carrying avgas, she could stay on until final destination,' Nicholas said. 'What else have you got?'

'You want more?' Bernard looked aghast. 'Doesn't anything ever satisfy you?'

'Did you monitor the communications between Bermuda Control, the chopper, and the ship she was servicing?'

'Nix,' Bernard shook his head. 'There was a box-up.' He looked shamefaced. 'It happens to the best of us.'

'Spare me the details. Can you get information from Bermuda Control of the time the chopper closed her flight-plan?'

'Jesus, Nicholas, you know better than that. It's an offence to listen in on the aviation frequencies, let alone ask them.'

Nicholas jumped up, and crossed swiftly to the perspex plot. He brooded over it, leaning on clenched fists, his expression smouldering as he studied the large-scale map.

'What does all this mean to you, Nicholas?' Bernard came to stand beside him.

'It means that a vessel at sea, belonging to the Christy Marine fleet, has requested its head office to send machinery spares and specialist personnel by the fastest possible means, without regard to expense. Have you figured the air freight on a package of 350 kilos?'

Nicholas straightened up and groped for the crocodile-skin cheroot case.

'It means that the vessel is broken down or in imminent danger of breakdown somewhere in an area south-west of Bermuda, within an arc of four hundred and fifty miles –

probably much closer, otherwise she would have requested service from the Bahamas, and it's highly unlikely they would have operated the chopper at extreme range.'

'Right,' Bernard agreed. Nicholas lit his cheroot and they were both silent a moment.

'A hell of a small needle in a bloody big haystack,' said Bernard.

'You let me worry about that,' Nicholas murmured, still without taking his eyes from the plot.

'That's what you are paid for,' Bernard agreed amiably. 'it's *Golden Dawn*, isn't it?'

'Has Christy Marine got any other vessels in the area?'

'Not as far as I know.'

'Then that was a bloody stupid question.'

'Take it easy, Nicholas.'

'I'm sorry.' Nicholas touched his arm. 'My boy's on that pig.' He took a deep draw on the cheroot, held it a moment, and then slowly exhaled. His voice was calm and businesslike, as he went on:

'What's our weather?'

'Wind at 060° and 15 knots. Cloud three eighths stratocumulus at four thousand feet. Long-range projection, no change.'

'Steady trade winds again,' Nicholas nodded. 'Thank God for all small mercies.'

'There is a hurricane warning out, as you know, but on its present position and track, it will blow itself out to sea a thousand miles south of Grand Bahama.'

'Good,' Nicholas nodded again. 'Please ask both *Warlock* and *Sea Witch* to report their positions, course, speed and fuel conditions.'

Bernard had the two telex flimsies for him within twenty minutes.

'*Warlock* has made a good run of it,' Nicholas murmured, as the position of the tug was marked on the plot.

'She crossed the equator three days ago,' said Bernard.

'And *Sea Witch* will reach Charleston late tomorrow,' Nicholas observed. 'Are any of the opposition inside us?'

Bernard shook his head. 'McCormick has one in New York and *Wittezee* is halfway back to Rotterdam.'

'We are in good shape,' Nicholas decided, as he balanced the triangles of relative speeds and distances between the vessels.

'Is there another chopper available on the island to get me out to *Warlock*?'

'No,' Bernard shook his head. 'The 61N is the only one based on Bermuda.'

'Can you arrange bunkering for *Warlock*, I mean immediate bunkering – here in Hamilton?'

'We can have her tanks filled an hour after she comes in.'

Nicholas paused and then made the decision. 'Please telex David Allen on *Warlock*, TO MASTER WARLOCK FROM BERG IMMEDIATE AND URGENT NEW SPEED TOP OF THE GREEN NEW COURSE HAMILTON HARBOUR BERMUDA ISLAND DIRECT REPORT EXPECTED TIME OF ARRIVAL ENDS.'

'You're going to run, then?' Bernard asked. 'You are going to run with both your ships?'

'Yes,' Nicholas nodded. 'I'm running with everything I've got.'

*Golden Dawn* wallowed with the dead heavy weight of one million tons of crude oil. Her motion was that of a waterlogged hulk. Broadside to the set of the swells, her tank decks were almost awash. The low seas broke against her starboard rail and the occasional crest flopped over and spread like pretty patches of white lace-work over the green plastic-coated decks.

She had been drifting powerlessly for four days now.

The main bearing of the single propeller shaft had begun to run hot forty-eight hours after crossing the equator, and the Chief Engineer had asked for shutdown to inspect the bearing and effect any repairs. Duncan Alexander had forbidden any shutdown, overriding the good judgement of both his Master and Chief Engineer, and had only grudgingly agreed to a reduction in the ship's speed.

He ordered the Chief Engineer to trace any fault and to effect what repairs he could, while under reduced power.

Within four hours, the Chief had traced the damaged and leaking gland in the pump that force-lubricated the bearing, but even the running under reduced power setting had done significant damage to the main bearing, and now there was noticeable vibration, jarring even *Golden Dawn*'s massive hull.

'I have to get the pump stripped down or we'll burn her clear out,' the Chief faced up to Duncan Alexander at last. 'Then you'll *have* to shut down and not just a couple of hours either. It will take two days to fit new bearing shells at sea.' The Chief was pale and his lips trembled, for he knew of this man's reputation. The engineer knew that he discarded those who crossed him, and he had the reputation of a special vindictiveness to hound a man until he was broken. The Chief was afraid, but his concern for the ship was just strong enough.

Duncan Alexander changed direction. 'What was the cause of the pump failure in the first place? Why wasn't it noticed earlier? It looks like a case of negligence to me.'

Stung at last, the Chief blurted out, 'If there had been a back-up pump on this ship, we could have switched to secondary system and done proper maintenance.'

Duncan Alexander flushed and turned away. The modifications he had personally ordered to *Golden Dawn*'s design had excluded most of the duplicated back-up systems; anything that kept down the cost of construction had been ordered.

'How long do you need?' He stopped in the centre of the owner's stateroom and glared at his engineer.

'Four hours,' the Scot replied promptly.

'You've got exactly four hours,' he said grimly. 'If you haven't finished by then you will live to regret it. I swear that to you.'

While the engineer stopped his engines, stripped, repaired and reassembled the lubrication pump, Duncan was on the bridge with the Master.

'We've lost time, too much time,' he said. 'I want that made up.'

'It will mean pushing over best economic speed,' Captain Randle warned carefully.

'Captain Randle, the value of our cargo is 85 dollars a ton. We have on board one million tons. I want the time made up.' Duncan brushed his objection aside. 'We have a deadline to meet in Galveston roads. This ship, this whole concept of carrying crude is on trial, Captain. I don't have to keep reminding you of that. The hell with the costs, I want to meet the deadline.'

'Yes, Mr Alexander,' Randle nodded. 'We'll make up the time.'

Three and a half hours later, the Chief Engineer came up to the bridge.

'Well?' Duncan turned on him fiercely as he stepped out of the elevator.

'The pump is repaired, but—'

'What is it, man?'

'I've got a feeling. We ran her too long. I've got a nasty feeling about that bearing. It wouldn't be clever to run her over 50 per cent of power, not until it's been taken down and inspected—'

'I'm ordering revolutions for 25 knots,' Randle told him uneasily.

'I wouldn't do that, man,' the Chief shook his head rather mournfully.

'Your station is in the engine room,' Duncan dismissed him brusquely, nodded to Randle to order resumption of sailing, and went out to his customary place on the open wing of the bridge. He looked back over the high round stern as the white turbulence of the great propeller boiled out from under the counter and then settled in a long slick wake that soon reached back to the horizon. Duncan stood out in the wind until after dark, and when he went below, Chantelle was waiting for him. She stood up from the long couch under the forward windows of the stateroom.

'We are under way again.'

'Yes,' he said. 'It's going to be all right.'

The engine control was switched to automatic at nine o'clock local time that night. The engine room personnel went up to dinner, and to bed, all except the Chief Engineer. He lingered for another two hours shaking his head and mumbling bitterly over the massive bearing assembly in the long, narrow shaft tunnel. Every few minutes, he laid his hand on the massive casting, feeling for the heat and vibration that would warn of structural damage.

At eleven o'clock, he spat on the steadily revolving propeller shaft. It was thick as an oak trunk and polished brilliant silver in the stark white lights of the tunnel. He pushed himself up stiffly from his crouch beside the bearing.

In the control room, he checked again that all the ship's systems were on automatic, and that all circuits were functioning and repeating on the big control board, then he stepped into the elevator and went up.

Thirty-five minutes later, one of the tiny transistors in the board blew with a pop like a champagne cork and a puff of grey smoke. There was nobody in the control room to hear or see it. The system was not duplicated, there was no back-up to switch itself in automatically, so that when the temperature of the bearing began to rise again, there was no impulse carried to the alarm system, no automatic shutdown of power.

The massive shaft spun on while the overheated bearing closed its grip upon the area of rough metal, damaged by the previous prolonged running. A fine sliver of metal lifted from the polished surface of the spinning shaft, and curled like a silver hairspring, was caught up and smeared into the bearing. The whole assembly began to glow a sullen cherry red and then the oxide paint that was daubed on the outer surfaces of the bearing began to blister and blacken. Still the tremendous power of the engine forced the shaft around.

What oil was still being fed between the glowing surfaces of the spinning shaft and the shells of the bearing turned instantly thin as water in the heat, then reached its flash-point and burst into flame and ran in little fiery rivulets down the heavy casting of the main bearing, flashing the blistered paintwork alight. The shaft tunnel filled with thick billows of stinking chemical-tainted smoke, and only then did the fire sensors come to life and their alarms repeated on the navigation bridge and in the quarters of Master, First Officer and Chief Engineer.

But the great engine was still pounding along at 70 per cent of power, and the shaft still turned in the disintegrating bearing, smearing heat-softened metal, buckling and distorting under unbearable strains.

The Chief Engineer was the first to reach the central console in the engine control room, and without orders from the bridge he began emergency shutdown of all systems.

It was another hour before the team under the direction of the First Officer had the fire in the shaft tunnel under control. They used carbon dioxide gas to smother the burning paint and oil, for cold water on the heated metal would have aggravated the damage done by heat distortion and buckling.

The metal of the main bearing casting was still so hot when the Chief Engineer began opening it up, that it scorched the thick leather and asbestos gloves worn by his team.

The bearing shells had disintegrated, and the shaft itself was brutally scored and pitted. If there was distortion, the Chief knew it would not be detected by eye. However, even a buckling of one ten thousandth of an inch would be critical.

He cursed softly as he worked, making the obscenities sound like a lullaby; he cursed the manufacturers of the lubricating pump, the men who had installed and tested it, the damaged gland and the lack of a back-up system, but mostly he cursed the stubbornness and intractability of the Chairman of Christy Marine whose ill-advised judgement had turned this functionally beautiful machinery into blackened, smoking twisted metal.

It was mid-morning by the time the Chief had the spare bearing shells brought up from stores and unpacked from their wood shavings in the wooden cases; but it was only when they came to fit them that they realized that the cases had been incorrectly stencilled. The half-shells that they contained were obsolete non-metric types, and they were five millimetres undersized for *Golden Dawn*'s shaft; that tiny variation in size made them utterly useless.

It was only then that Duncan Alexander's steely urbane control began to crack; he raged about the bridge for twenty minutes, making no effort to think his way out of the predicament, but abusing Randle and his engineer in wild and extravagant terms. His rage had a paralysing effect on all *Golden Dawn*'s officers and they stood white-faced and silently guilty.

Peter Berg had sensed the excitement and slipped up

unobtrusively to watch. He was fascinated by his stepfather's rage. He had never seen a display like it before, and at one stage he hoped that Duncan Alexander's eyeballs might actually burst like overripe grapes; he held his breath in anticipation, and felt cheated when it did not happen.

At last, Duncan stopped and ran both hands through his thick waving hair; two spikes of hair stood up like devil's horns. He was still panting, but he had recovered partial control.

'Now sir, what do you propose?' he demanded of Randle, and in the silence Peter Berg piped up.

'You could have new shells sent from Bermuda – it's only three hundred miles away. We checked it this morning.'

'How did you get in here?' Duncan swung round. 'Get back to your mother.'

Peter scampered, appalled at his own indiscretion, and only when he left the bridge did the Chief speak.

'We could have spares flown out from London to Bermuda—'

'There must be a boat—' Randle cut in swiftly.

'Or an aircraft to drop it to us—'

'Or a helicopter—'

'Get Christy Main on the telex,' snapped Duncan Alexander fiercely.

It was good to have a deck under his feet again, Nicholas exulted. He felt himself coming fully alive again.

'I'm a sea-creature,' he grinned to himself. 'And I keep forgetting it.'

He looked back to the low silhouette of the Bermuda islands, the receding arms of Hamilton Harbour and the flecking of the multicoloured buildings amongst the cedar trees, and then returned his attention to the spread charts on the navigation table before him.

*Warlock* was still at cautionary speed. Even though the channel was wide and clearly buoyed, yet the coral reef on each hand was sharp and hungry, and David Allen's full attention was on the business of conning *Warlock* out into the open sea. But as they passed the 100 fathom line, he gave the order to his deck officer,

'Full away at 0900 hours, pilot,' and hurried across to join Nicholas.

'I didn't have much of a chance to welcome you on board, sir.'

'Thank you, David. It's good to be back.' Nicholas looked up and smiled at him. 'Will you bring her round on to 240° magnetic and increase to 80 per cent power?'

Quickly David repeated his order to the helm and then shifted from one foot to the other, beginning to flush under the salt-water tan.

'Mr Berg, my officers are driving me mad. They've been plaguing me since we left Cape Town – are we running on a job – or is this a pleasure cruise?'

Nicholas laughed aloud then. He felt the excitement of the hunt, a good hot scent in the nostrils, and the prospect of a fat prize. Now he had *Warlock* under him, his concern for Peter's safety had abated. Whatever happened now, he could get there very fast. No, he felt good, very good.

'We're hunting, David,' he told him. 'Nothing certain yet—' he paused, and then relented, 'Get Beauty Baker up to my cabin, tell Angel to send up a big pot of coffee and a mess of sandwiches – I missed breakfast – and while we are eating, I'll fill both of you in.'

Beauty Baker accepted one of Nicholas' cheroots.

'Still smoking cheap,' he observed, and sniffed at the four-dollar cheroot sourly, but there was a twinkle of pleasure behind the smeared lenses of his spectacles. Then, unable to contain himself, he actually grinned.

'Skipper tells me we are hunting, is that right?'

'This is the picture—' Nicholas began to spell it out to them in detail, and while he talked, he thought with comfortable self-indulgence, 'I must be getting old and soft – I didn't always talk so much.'

Both men listened in silence, and only when he finished did the two of them begin bombarding him with the perceptive penetrating questions he had expected.

'Sounds like a generator armature,' Beauty Baker guessed, as he puzzled the contents of the wooden case that had been flown out to *Golden Dawn*. I cannot believe that *Golden Dawn* doesn't carry a full set of mechanical spares.'

While Baker was fully preoccupied with the mechanics of the situation, David Allen concentrated on the problems of seamanship. 'What was the range of the helicopter? Has it returned to base yet? With her draught, she must be heading for the Florida Straits. Our best bet would be to shape a course for Matanilla Reef at the mouth of the Straits.'

There was a peremptory knock on the door of the guest cabin, and the Trog stuck his grey wrinkled tortoise head through. He glanced at Nicholas, but did not greet him. 'Captain, Miami is broadcasting a new hurricane alert. "Lorna" has kicked northwards, they're predicting a track of north north-west and a speed over the ground of twenty knots.'

He closed the door and they stared at each other in silence for a moment.

Nicholas spoke at last.

'It is never one single mistake that causes disaster,' he said. 'It is always a series of contributory errors, most of them of small consequence in themselves – but when taken with a little bad luck—' he was silent for a moment and then, softly, 'Hurricane Lorna could just be that bit of bad luck.'

He stood up and took one turn around the small guest cabin, feeling caged and wishing for the space of the Master's suite which was now David Allen's. He turned back to Beauty Baker and David Allen, and suddenly he realized that they were hoping for disaster. They were like two old sea wolves with the scent of the prey in their nostrils. He felt his anger rising coldly against them, they were wishing disaster on his son.

'Just one thing I didn't tell you,' he said. 'My son is on *Golden Dawn*.'

The immense revolving storm that was code-named Lorna was nearing full development. Her crest was reared high above the freezing levels so she wore a splendid mane of frosted white ice particles that streamed out three hundred miles ahead of her on the jet stream of the upper troposphere.

From one side to the other, she now measured one hundred and fifty miles across, and the power unleashed within her was of unmeasurable savagery.

The winds that blew around her centre tore the surface off the sea and bore it aloft at speeds in excess of one hundred and fifty miles an hour, generating precipitation that was as far beyond rain as death is beyond life. Water filled the dense cloud-banks so that there was no clear line between sea and air.

It seemed now that madness fed upon madness, and like a blinded and berserk monster, she blundered across the confined waters of the Caribbean, ripping the trees and buildings, even the very earth from the tiny islands which stood in her path.

But there were still forces controlling what seemed uncontrollable, dictating what seemed to be random, for, as she spun upon a spinning globe, the storm showed the primary trait of gyroscopic inertia, a rigidity in space that was constant as long as no outside force was applied.

Obeying this natural law, the entire system moved steadily eastwards at constant speed and altitude above the surface of the earth, until her northern edge touched the landmass of the long ridge of land that forms the greater Antilles.

Immediately another gyroscopic law came into force, the law of precession. When a deflecting force is applied to the rim of a spinning gyro, the gyro moves not away from, but *directly towards* that force.

Hurricane Lorna felt the land and, like a maddened bull at the flirt of the matador's cape, she turned and charged towards it, crossing the narrow high strips of Haiti in an orgy of destruction and terror until she burst out of the narrow channel of the Windward Passage into the open beyond.

Yet still she kept on spinning and moving. Now, barely three hundred miles ahead of her, across those shallow reefs and banks prophetically named 'Hurricane Flats' after the thousands of other such storms that had followed the same route during the memory of man, lay the deeper waters of the Florida Straits and the mainland of the continental United States of America.

At twenty miles an hour, the whole incredible heaven-high mass of crazed wind and churning clouds trundled north-westwards.

Duncan Alexander stood under the bogus Degas ballet dancers in the owner's stateroom. He balanced easily on the balls of his feet and his hands were clasped lightly behind his back, but his brow was heavily furrowed with worry and his eyes darkly underscored with plum-coloured swollen bags of sleeplessness.

Seated on the long couch and on the imitation Louis Quatorze chairs flanking the fireplace, were the senior officers of *Golden Dawn* – her Captain, Mate and Chief Engineer, and in the leather-studded wing-backed chair across the wide cabin sat Charles Gras, the engineer from Atlantique. It seemed as though he had chosen his seat to keep himself aloof from the owner and officers of the crippled ultra-tanker.

He spoke now in heavily accented English, falling back on the occasional French word which Duncan translated quickly. The four men listened to him with complete attention, never taking their eyes from the sharp, pale Parisian features and the foxy bright eyes.

'My men will have completed the reassembly of the main bearing by noon today. To the best of my ability, I have examined and tested the main shaft. I can find no evidence of structural damage, but I must emphasize that this does not mean that no damage exists. At the very best, the repairs must be considered to be temporary.' He paused and they waited, while he turned deliberately to Captain Randle. 'I must urge you to seek proper repair in the nearest port open to you, and to proceed there at the lowest speed which will enable you efficiently to work the ship.'

Randle twisted uncomfortably in his seat, and glanced across at Duncan. The Frenchman saw the exchange and a little steel came into his voice.

'If there is structural distortion in the main shaft, operation at speeds higher than this may result in permanent and irreversible damage and complete breakdown. I must make this point most forcibly.'

Duncan intervened smoothly. 'We are fully burdened and drawing twenty fathoms of water. There are no safe harbours on the eastern seaboard of America, that is even supposing that we could get permission to enter territorial waters with engine trouble. The Americans aren't likely to welcome us. Our nearest safe anchorage is Galveston roads, on the Texas coast of the Gulf of Mexico – and then only after the tugs have taken off our pod tanks outside the 100-fathom line.'

The tanker's First Officer was a young man, probably not over thirty years of age, but he had so far conducted himself impeccably in the emergencies the ship had encountered. He had a firm jaw and a clear level eye, and he had been the first into the smoke-filled shaft tunnel.

'With respect, sir,' and they all turned their heads towards him, 'Miami has broadcast a revised hurricane alert that includes the Straits and southern Florida. We would be on a reciprocal course to the hurricane track, a directly converging course.'

'Even at fifteen knots, we would be through the Straits and into the Gulf with twenty-four hours to spare,' Duncan stated, and looked to Randle for confirmation.

'At the present speed of the storm's advance – yes,' Randle qualified carefully. 'But conditions may change—'

The Mate persisted. 'Again, with respect, sir. Our nearest safe anchorage is the lee of Bermuda Island—'

'Do you have any idea of the value of this cargo?' Duncan's voice rasped. 'No, you do not. Well, I will inform you. It is $85,000,000. The interest on that amount is in the region of $25,000 a day.' His voice rose a note, again that wild note to it. 'Bermuda does not have the facilities to effect major repairs—'

The door from the private accommodation opened silently and Chantelle Alexander stepped into the stateroom. She wore no jewellery, a plain pearl silk blouse and a simple dark woollen skirt, but her skin had been gilded by the sun and she had lightly touched her dark eyes with a make-up that emphasized their size and shape. Her beauty silenced them all and she was fully aware of it as she crossed to stand beside Duncan.

'It is necessary that this ship and her cargo proceed directly to Galveston,' she said softly.

'Chantelle—' Duncan began, and she silenced him with a brusque gesture of one hand.

'There is no question about the destination and the route that is to be taken.'

Charles Gras looked to Captain Randle, waiting for him to assert the authority vested in him by law. But when the young Captain remained silent, the Frenchman smiled sardonically and shrugged a world-weary dismissal of further interest. 'Then I must ask that arrangements be made for my two assistants and myself to leave this ship immediately we have completed the temporary repairs.' Again Gras emphasized the word 'temporary'.

Duncan nodded. 'If we resume our sailing when you anticipate, and even taking into consideration the low fuel condition of the helicopter, we will be within easy range of the east coast of Florida by dawn tomorrow.'

Chantelle had not taken her eyes from the *Golden Dawn*'s officers during this exchange, and now she went on in the same quiet voice.

'I am quite prepared to accept the resignation of any of the officers of this ship who wish to join that flight.'

Duncan opened his mouth to make some protest at her assumption of his authority, but she turned to him with a small lift of the chin, and something in her expression and the set of her head upon her shoulders reminded him forcibly of old Arthur Christy. There was the same toughness and resilience there, the same granite determination; strange that he had not noticed it before.

'Perhaps I have never looked before,' he thought. Chantelle recognized the moment of his capitulation, and calmly she turned back to face *Golden Dawn*'s officers.

One by one, they dropped their eyes from hers; Randle was the first to stand up.

'If you will excuse me, Mrs Alexander, I must make preparations to get under way again.'

Charles Gras paused and looked back at her, and he

smiled again, as only a Frenchman smiles at a pretty woman.

'*Magnifique*!' he murmured, and lifted one hand in a graceful salute of admiration before he stepped out of the stateroom.

When Chantelle and Duncan were alone together, she turned to him slowly, and she let the contempt show in her expression.

'Any time you feel you have not got the guts for it, let me know, will you?'

'Chantelle—'

'You have got us into this, me and Christy Marine. Now you'll get us out of it, even if it kills you.' Her lips compressed into a thinner line and her eyes slitted vindictively. 'And it would be nice if it did,' she said softly.

The pilot of the Beechcraft Baron pulled back the throttles to 22″ of boost on both engines, and slid the propellers into fully fine pitch, simultaneously beginning a gentle descending turn towards the extraordinary-looking vessel that came up swiftly out of the low early morning haze that spilled over from the islands.

The same haze had blotted the low silhouette of the Florida coast from the western horizon, and even the pale green water and shaded reefs of little Bahamas Bank were washed pale by the haze, and partially obscured by the intermittent layer of stratocumulus cloud at four thousand feet.

The Baron pilot selected 20° of flap to give the aircraft a nosedown attitude which would afford a better forward vision, and continued his descent down through the cloud. It burst in a brief grey puff across the windshield before they were out into sunlight again.

'What do you make of her?' he asked his co-pilot.

'She's a big baby,' the co-pilot tried to steady his binoculars. 'Can't read her name.'

The enormously wide low bows were pushing up a fat sparkling pillow of churning water, and the green decks seemed to reach back almost to the limits of visibility before rising sheer into the stern quarters.

'Son of a gun,' the pilot shook his head. 'She looks like the vehicle-assembly building on Cape Kennedy.'

'She does too,' agreed his co-pilot. The same square unlovely bulk of that enormous structure was repeated in smaller scale by the navigation bridge of the big ship. 'I'll give her a call on 16.' The co-pilot lowered his binoculars and thumbed the microphone as he lifted it to his lips.

'Southbound bulk carrier, this is Coast Guard November Charlie One Fife Niner overhead. Do you read me?'

There was the expected delay; even in confined and heavily trafficked waters, these big bastards kept a sloppy watch and the spotter fumed silently.

'Coast Guard One Fife Niner, this is *Golden Dawn*. Reading you fife by fife. Going up to 22.'

Two hundred miles away the Trog knocked over the shell-casing, spilling damp and stinking cigar butts over the deck, in his haste to change frequency to channel 22 as the operator on board *Golden Dawn* had stipulated, at the same time switching on both the tape recorder and the radio direction-finder equipment.

High up in *Warlock*'s fire-control tower, the big metal ring of the direction-finding aerial turned slowly, lining up on the transmissions that boomed so clearly across the ether, repeating the relative bearing on the dial of the instrument on the Trog's cluttered bench.

'Good morning to you, *Golden Dawn*,' the lilting Southern twang of the coastguard navigator came back. 'I would be mightily obliged for your port of registry and your cargo manifest.'

'This ship is registered Venezuela.' The Trog dexterously made the fine tuning, scribbled the bearing on his pad, ripped off the page and darted into *Warlock*'s navigation bridge.

'*Golden Dawn* is sending in clear,' he squeaked with an expression of malicious glee.

'Call the Captain,' snapped the deck officer, and then as an afterthought, 'and ask Mr Berg to come to the bridge.'

The conversation between coastguard and ultra-tanker was still going on when Nicholas burst into the radio room, belting his dressing gown.

'Thank you for your courtesy, sir,' the coastguard navigator was using extravagant Southern gallantry, fully aware that *Golden Dawn* was outside United States territorial waters, and officially beyond his government's jurisdiction. 'I would appreciate your port of final destination.'

'We are en route to Galveston for full discharge of cargo.'

'Thank you again, sir. And are you appraised of the hurricane alert in force at this time?'

'Affirmative.'

From *Warlock*'s bridge, David Allen appeared in the doorway, his face set and flushed.

'She must be under way again,' he said, his disappointment so plain that it angered Nicholas yet again. 'She is into the channel already.'

'I'd be obliged if you would immediately put this ship on a course to enter the Straits and close with her as soon as is possible,' Nicholas snapped, and David Allen blinked at him once then disappeared on to his bridge, calling for the change in course and increase in speed as he went.

Over the loudspeaker, the coastguard was being politely persistent.

'Are you further appraised, sir, of the update on that hurricane alert predicting storm passage of the main navigable channel at 1200 hours local time tomorrow?'

'Affirmative.' *Golden Dawn*'s replies had become curt.

'May I further trouble you, sir, in view of your sensitive cargo and the special weather conditions, for your expected time of arrival abeam of the Dry Tortugas Bank marine beacon and when you anticipate clearing the channel and shaping a northerly course away from the predicted hurricane track?'

'Standby.' There was a brief hum of static while the operator consulted the deck officer and then the *Golden Dawn* came back, 'Our ETA Dry Tortugas Bank beacon is 0130 tomorrow.'

There was a long pause now as the coastguard consulted his headquarters ashore on one of the closed frequencies, and then:

'I am requested respectfully, but officially, to bring to your attention that very heavy weather is expected ahead of the storm centre and that your present ETA Dry Tortugas Bank leaves you very fine margins of safety, sir.'

'Thank you, coastguard One Fife Niner. Your transmission will be entered in the ship's log. This is *Golden Dawn* over and out.'

The coastguard's frustration was evident. Clearly he would have loved to order the tanker to reverse her course. 'We will be following your progress with interest, *Golden Dawn*. Bon voyage, this is coastguard One Fife Niner over and out.'

Charles Gras held his blue beret on with one hand, while with the other he lugged his suitcase. He ran doubled up, instinctively avoiding the ear-numbing clatter of the helicopter's rotor.

He threw his suitcase through the open fuselage door and then hesitated, turned and scampered back to where the ship's Chief Engineer stood at the edge of the white-painted helipad target on *Golden Dawn*'s tank deck.

Charles grabbed the Engineer's upper arm and leaned close to shout in his ear.

'Remember, my friend, treat her like a baby, like a tender virgin – if you have to increase speed, do so gently – very gently.' The Engineer nodded, his sparse sandy hair fluttering in the down draught.

'Good luck,' shouted the Frenchman. '*Bonne chance!*' He slapped the man's shoulder. 'I hope you don't need it!'

He darted back and scrambled up into the fuselage of the Sikorsky, and his face appeared in one of the portholes. He waved once, and then the big ungainly machine rose slowly into the air, hovered for a moment and then banked away low over the water, setting off in its characteristic nose-down attitude for the mainland, still hidden by haze and distance.

Dr Samantha Silver, dressed in thigh-high rubber waders and with her sleeves rolled up above the elbows, staggered under the weight of two ten-gallon plastic buckets of clams as she climbed the back steps of the laboratory building.

'Sam!' down the length of the long passageway, Sally-Anne screamed at her. 'We were going to leave without you!'

'What is it?' Sam dumped the buckets with relief, slopping salt water down the steps.

'Johnny called – the anti-pollution patrol bespoke *Golden Dawn* an hour ago. She's in the Straits. She was abeam Matanilla reef when they spotted her and she will be abeam of Biscayne Key before we can get out there, if we don't leave now.'

'I'm coming.' Sam hefted her heavy buckets, and broke into a rubber-kneed trot. 'I'll meet you down on the wharf – did you call the TV studio?'

'There's a camera team on the way,' Sally-Anne yelled back as she ran for the front doors. 'Hurry, Sam – fast as you like!'

Samantha dumped the clams into one of her tanks, switched on the oxygen and as soon as it began to bubble to the surface, she turned and raced from the laboratory and out of the front doors.

*Golden Dawn*'s deck officer stopped beside the radar-scope, glanced down at it idly, then stooped with more attention and took a bearing on the little glowing pinpoint of green light that showed up clearly inside the ten-mile circle of the sweep.

He grunted, straightened, and walked quickly to the front of the bridge. Slowly, he scanned the green wind-chopped sea ahead of the tanker's ponderous bows.

'Fishing boat,' he said to the helmsman. 'But they are under way.' He had seen the tiny flash of a bow wave. 'And they are right in the main navigational channel – they must have seen us by now, they are making a turn to pass us to starboard.' He dropped the binoculars and let them dangle against his chest. 'Oh thank you.' He took the cup of cocoa from the steward, and sipped it with relish as he turned away to the chart-table.

One of the tanker's junior officers came out of the radio room at the back of the bridge.

'Still no score,' he said, 'and only injury time left now,' and they fell into a concerned discussion of the World Cup soccer match being played under floodlights at Wembley Stadium on the other side of the Atlantic.

'If it's a draw then it means that France is in the—'

There was an excited shout from the radio room, and the junior officer ran to the door and then turned back with an excited grin. 'England has scored!'

The deck officer chuckled happily. 'That will wrap it up.' Then with a start of guilt he turned back to his duties, and had another start, this time of surprise, when he glanced into the radarscope.

'What the hell are they playing at!' he exclaimed irritably, and hurried forward to scan the sea ahead.

The fishing boat had continued its turn and was now bows on.

'Damn them. We'll give them a buzz.' He reached up for the handle of the foghorn and blew three long blasts that echoed out mournfully across the shallow greenish water of the Straits. There was a general movement among the officers to get a better view ahead through the forward bridge windows.

'They must be half asleep out there.' The deck officer thought quickly about calling the Captain to the bridge. If it came to manoeuvring the ship in these confined waters, he flinched from the responsibility. Even at this reduced speed, it would take *Golden Dawn* half an hour and seven nautical miles to come to a stop; a turn in either direction would swing through a wide arc of many miles before the ship was able to make a 90° change of course – God, then there was the effect of the wind against the enormously exposed area of the towering stern quarters, and the full bore of the Gulf Stream driving out of the narrows of the Straits. The problems of manoeuvring the vessel struck a chill of panic into the officer – and the fishing boat was on collision course, the range closing swiftly under the combined speeds of both vessels. He reached for the call button of the intercom that connected the bridge directly to the Captain's quarters on the deck below, but at that moment Captain Randle came bounding up the private staircase from his day cabin.

'What is it?' he demanded. 'What was that blast on the horn?'

'Small vessel holding on to collision course, sir.' The

officer's relief was evident, and Randle seized the handle of the foghorn and hung on to it.

'God, what's wrong with them?'

'The deck is crowded,' exclaimed one of the officers without lowering his binoculars. 'Looks as though they have a movie-camera team on the top deck.'

Randle judged the closing range anxiously; already the small fishing vessel was too close for the *Golden Dawn* to stop in time.

'Thank God,' somebody exclaimed. 'They are turning away.'

'They are streaming some sort of banner. Can anybody read that?'

'They are heaving-to,' the deck officer yelled suddenly. 'They are heaving-to right under our bows.'

Samantha Silver had not expected the tanker to be so big. From directly ahead, her bows seemed to fill the horizon from one side to the other, and the bow wave she threw up ahead of her creamed and curved like the set of the long wave at Cape St Francis when the surf was up.

Beyond the bows, the massive tower of her navigation bridge stood so tall that it looked like the skyline of The Miami Beach, one of those massive hotel buildings seen from close inshore.

It made her feel distinctly uneasy to be directly under that on-rushing steel avalanche.

'Do you think they have seen us?' Sally-Anne asked beside her, and when Samantha heard her own unease echoed by the pretty girl beside her, it steeled her.

'Of course they have,' she announced stoutly so that everyone in the small wheelhouse could hear her. 'That's why they blew their siren. We'll turn aside at the last minute.'

'They aren't slowing down,' Hank Petersen, the helmsman, pointed out huskily, and Samantha wished that Tom Parker had been on board with them. However, Tom was up in Washington again, and they had taken the *Dicky* to sea with a scratch crew, and without Tom Parker's written authorization. 'What do you want to do, Sam?' And they all looked at her.

'I know a thing that size can't stop, but at least we're going to make them slow down.

'Are the TV boys getting some stuff?' Samantha asked, to delay the moment of decision. 'Go up, Sally-Anne, and check them.' Then to the others, 'You-all get the banner ready. We'll let them get a good look at that.'

'Listen, Sam.' Hank Petersen's tanned intelligent face was strained. He was a tunny expert, and was not accustomed to handling the vessel except in calm and uncluttered waters. 'I don't like this, we're getting much too close. That thing could churn us right under, and not even notice the bump. I want to turn away now.' His voice was almost drowned by the sudden sky-crashing blast of the tanker's foghorns.

'Son of a gun, Sam, I don't like playing chicken-chicken with somebody that size.'

'Don't worry, we'll get out of their way at the last moment. All right!' Samantha decided. 'Turn 90° to port, Hank. Let's show them the signs. I'm going to help them on deck.'

The wind tore at the thin white canvas banner as they tried to run it out along the side of the deckhouse, and the little vessel was rolling uncomfortably while the TV producer was shouting confused stage directions at them from the top of the wheelhouse.

Bitterly Samantha wished there was somebody to take

command, somebody like Nicholas Berg – and the banner tried to wrap itself around her head.

The *Dicky* was coming around fast now, and Samantha shot a glance at the oncoming tanker and felt the shock of it strike in the pit of her stomach like the blow of a fist. It was huge, and very close – much too close, even she realized that.

At last she managed to get a turn of the thin line that secured the banner around the stern rail – but the light canvas had twisted so that only one word of the slogan was readable. 'POISONER', it accused in scarlet, crudely painted letters followed by a grinning skull and crossed bones.

Samantha dived across the deck and struggled with the flapping canvas; above her head the producer was shouting excitedly; two of the others were trying to help her; Sally-Anne was screaming 'Go back! Go back!' and waving both arms at the great tanker. 'You poison our oceans!'

Everything was becoming confused and out of control. The *Dicky* swung ahead into the wind and pitched steeply, the person next to her lost his footing and knocked painfully into Samantha, and at that moment she felt the change of the engine beat.

*Tricky Dicky*'s diesel had been bellowing furiously as Hank opened the throttle to its stop, using full power to bring the little vessel around from under the menace of those steel bows.

The smoking splutter of the exhaust pipe that rose vertically up the side of the deckhouse had made all speech difficult – but now it died away, and suddenly there was only the sound of the wind.

Even their own raised voices were silenced, and they froze, staring out at *Golden Dawn* as she bore down on them without the slightest check in her majestic approach.

Samantha was the first one to recover, then she ran across the plunging deck to the wheelhouse.

Hank Petersen was down on his knees beside the bulkhead, struggling ineffectually with the conduit that housed the controls to the engine room on the deck below.

'Why have you stopped?' Samantha yelled at him, and he looked up at her as though he were mortally wounded.

'It's the throttle linkage,' he said. 'It's snapped again.'

'Can't you fix it?' and the question was a mockery. A mile away, *Golden Dawn* came down on them – silent, menacing, unstoppable.

For ten seconds Randle stood rigid, both hands gripping the foul weather rail below the sill of the bridge windows.

His face was set, pale and finely drawn, as he watched the stern of the wallowing fishing boat for the renewed churning of its prop.

He knew that he could not turn nor stop his ship in time to avoid collision, unless the small vessel got under way immediately, and took evasive action by going out to starboard under full power.

'Damn them to hell,' he thought bitterly, they were in gross default. He had all the law and the custom of the sea behind him; a collision would cause very little damage to *Golden Dawn*, perhaps she would lose a little paint, at most a slightly buckled plate in the reinforced bows – and they had asked for it.

He had no doubts about the object of this crazy, irresponsible seamanship. There had been controversy before the *Golden Dawn* sailed. He had read the objections and seen the nutcase environmentalists on television. The scarlet-painted banner with the ridiculously melodramatic Jolly Roger made it clear that this was a boatload of nutters who were attempting to prevent *Golden Dawn* from entering American waters.

He felt his anger boiling up fiercely. These people always made him furious. If they had their way, there would be no tanker trade, and now they were deliberately threatening him, placing him in a position which might prejudice his own career. He already had the task of taking his ship through the Straits ahead of the hurricane. Every moment was vital – and now there was this.

He would be happy to maintain course and speed, and to run them down. They were flaunting themselves, challenging him to do it – and, by God, they deserved it.

However, he was a seaman, with a seaman's deep concern for human life at sea. It would go against all his instincts not to make an effort to avoid collision, no matter how futile that effort would be. Then beside him one of his officers triggered him.

'There are women on board her – look at that! Those are women!'

That was enough. Without waiting for confirmation, Randle snapped at the helmsman beside him.

'Full port rudder!'

And with two swift paces he had reached the engine room telegraph. It rang shrilly as he pulled back the chromed handle to 'Full Astern'.

Almost immediately, the changed beat came up through the soles of his feet, as the great engine seven decks below the bridge thundered suddenly under all emergency power, and the direction of the spinning main propellor shaft was abruptly reversed.

Randle spun back to face ahead. For almost five minutes, the bows held steady on the horizon without making any answer to the full application of the rudder. The inertia of a million tons of crude oil, the immense drag of the hull through water and the press of wind and current held her on course, and although the single ferro-bronze propeller bit deeply into the green waters, there was not the slightest diminution of the tanker's speed.

Randle kept his hand on the engine telegraph, pulling back on the silver handle with all his strength, as though this might arrest the great ship's forward way through the water.

'Turn!' he whispered to the ship, and he stared at the fishing boat that still lay, rolling wildly, directly in *Golden Dawn*'s path. He noticed irrelevently that the tiny human figures along the rear rail were waving frantically, and that the banner with its scarlet denunciation had torn loose at one end and was now whipping and twisting like a Tibetan prayer flag over the heads of the crew.

'Turn,' Randle whispered, and he saw the first response of the hull; the angle between the bows and the fishing boat altered, it was a noticeable change, but slowly accelerating and a quick glance at the control console showed a small check in the ship's forward speed.

'Turn, damn it, turn.' Randle held the engine telegraph locked at full astern, and felt the sudden influence of the Gulf Stream current on the ship as she began to come across the direction of flow.

Ahead, the fishing boat was almost about to disappear from sight behind *Golden Dawn*'s high blunt bows.

He had been holding the ship at full astern for almost seven minutes now, and suddenly Randle felt a change in *Golden Dawn*, something he had never experienced before.

There was a harsh, tearing, pounding vibration coming up through the deck. He realized just how severe that vibration must be, when *Golden Dawn*'s monumental hull began to shake violently – but he could not release his grip on the engine telegraph, not with that helpless vessel lying in his track.

Then suddenly, miraculously, all vibration in the deck under his feet ceased altogether. There was only the calm press of the hull through the water, no longer the feel of the engine's thrust, a sensation much more alarming to a mariner than the vibration which had preceded it, and simultaneously, a fiery rash of red warning lights bloomed on the ship's main control console, and the strident screech of the full emergency audio-alarm deafened them all.

Only then did Captain Randle push the engine telegraph to 'stop'. He stood staring ahead as the tiny fishing boat disappeared from view, hidden by the angle from the navigation bridge which was a mile behind the bows.

One of the officers reached across and hit the cut-out on the audio-alarm. In the sudden silence every officer stood frozen, waiting for the impact of collision.

*Golden Dawn*'s Chief Engineer paced slowly along the engine-room control console, never taking his eyes from the electronic displays which monitored all the ship's mechanical and electrical functions.

When he reached the alarm aboard, he stopped and frowned at it angrily. The failure of the single transistor, a few dollars' worth of equipment, had been the cause of such brutal damage to his beloved machinery. He leaned across and pressed the 'test' button, checking out each alarm circuit, yet, while he was doing it, recognizing the fact that it was too late. He was nursing the ship along, with God alone knew what undiscovered damage to engine and main shaft only kept in check by this reduced power setting – but there was a hurricane down there below the southern horizon, and the Chief could only guess at what emergency his machinery might have to meet in the next few days.

It made him nervous and edgy to think about it. He searched in his back pocket, found a sticky mint humbug, carefully picked off the little pieces of lint and fluff before tucking it into his cheek like a squirrel with a nut, sucking noisily upon it as he resumed his restless prowling up and down the control console.

His on-duty stokers and the oilers watched him surreptitiously. When the old man was in a mood, it was best not to attract attention.

'Dickson!' the Chief said suddenly. 'Get your lid on. We are going down the shaft tunnel again.'

The oiler sighed, exchanged a resigned glance with one of his mates and clapped his hard-hat on his head. He and the Chief had been down the tunnel an hour previously. It was an uncomfortable, noisy and dirty journey.

The oiler closed the watertight doors into the shaft tunnel behind them, screwing down the clamps firmly under the Chief's frosty scrutiny, and then both men stopped in the confined headroom and started off along the brightly-lit, pale grey painted tunnel.

The spinning shaft in its deep bed generated a high-pitched whine that seemed to resonate in the steel box of the tunnel, as though it was the body of a violin. Surprisingly, the noise was more pronounced at this low speed setting. It seemed to bore into the teeth at the back of the oiler's jaw like a dentist's drill.

The Chief did not seem to be affected. He paused beside the main bearing for almost ten minutes, testing it with the palm of his hand, feeling for heat or vibration. His expression was morose, and he worried the mint humbug in his cheek and shook his head with foreboding before going on up the tunnel.

When he reached the main gland, he squatted down suddenly and peered at it closely. With a deliberate flexing of his jaw he crushed the remains of the humbug between his teeth, and his eyes narrowed thoughtfully.

There was a thin trickle of seawater oozing through the gland and running down into the bilges. The Chief touched it with his finger. Something had shifted, some balance was disturbed, the seal of the gland was no longer watertight – such a small sign, a few gallons of seawater, could be the first warning of major structural damage.

The Chief shuffled around, still hunched down beside the shaft bed, and he lowered his face until it was only inches from the spinning steel main shaft. He closed one eye, and cocked his head, trying once again to decide if the faint blurring of the shaft's outline was real or merely his over-active imagination, whether what he was seeing was distortion or his own fears.

Suddenly, startlingly, the shaft slammed into stillness. The deceleration was so abrupt that the Chief could actually see the torque transferred into the shaft bed, and the metal walls creaked and popped with the strain.

He rocked back on to his heels, and almost instantly the shaft began to spin again, but this time in reverse thrust. The whine built up swiftly into a rising shriek. They were pulling emergency power from the bridge, and it was madness, suicidal madness.

The Chief seized the oiler by the shoulder and shouted into his ear, 'Get back to control – find out what the hell they are doing on the bridge.'

The oiler scrambled away down the tunnel; it would take him ten minutes to negotiate the long narrow passage, open the watertight doors and reach the control room and as long again to return.

The Chief considered going after him, but somehow he could not leave the shaft now. He lowered his head again, and now he could clearly see the flickering outline of the shaft. It wasn't imagination at all, there was a little ghost of movement. He clamped his hands over his ears to cut out the painful shriek of the spinning metal, but there was a new note to it, the squeal of bare metal on metal and before his eyes he saw the ghost outline along the edge of the shaft growing, the flutter of machinery out of balance, and the metal deck under his feet began to quiver.

'God! They are going to blow the whole thing!' he shouted, and jumped up from his crouch. Now the deck was juddering and shaking under his feet. He started back along the shaft, but the entire tunnel was agitating so violently that he had to grab the metal bulkhead to steady himself, and he reeled drunkenly, thrown about like a captive insect in a cruel child's box.

Ahead of him, he saw the huge metal casting of the main bearing twisting and shaking, and the vibration chattered his teeth in his clenched jaw and drove up his spine like a jackhammer.

Disbelievingly he saw the huge silver shaft beginning to rise and buckle in its bed, the bearing tearing loose from its mountings.

'Shut down!' he screamed. 'For God's sake, shut down!' but his voice was lost in the shriek and scream of tortured metal and machinery that was tearing itself to pieces in a suicidal frenzy.

The main bearing exploded, and the shaft slammed it into the bulkhead, tearing steel plate like paper.

The shaft itself began to snake and whip. The Chief cowered back, pressing his back to the bulkhead and covering his ears to protect them from the unbearable volume of noise.

A sliver of heated steel flew from the bearing and struck him in the face, laying open his upper lip to the bone, crushing his nose and snapping off his front teeth at the level of his gums.

He toppled forward, and the whipping, kicking shaft seized him like a mindless predator and tore his body to pieces, pounding him and crushing him in the shaft bed and splattering him against the pale metal walls.

The main shaft snapped like a rotten twig at the point where it had been heated and weakened. The unbalanced weight of the revolving propeller ripped the stump out through the after seal, as though it were a tooth plucked from a rotting jaw.

The sea rushed in through the opening, flooding the tunnel instantly until it slammed into the watertight doors

– and the huge glistening bronze propeller, with the stump of the main shaft still attached, the whole unit weighing one hundred and fifty tons, plummeted downwards through four hundred fathoms to embed itself deeply in the soft mud of the sea bottom.

Freed of the intolerable goad of her damaged shaft, *Golden Dawn* was suddenly silent and her decks still and steady as she trundled on, slowly losing way as the water dragged at her hull.

Samantha had one awful moment of sickening guilt. She saw clearly that she was responsible for the deadly danger into which she had led these people, and she stared out over the boat's side at the *Golden Dawn*.

The tanker was coming on without any check in her speed; perhaps she had turned a few degrees, for her bows were no longer pointed directly at them, but her speed was constant.

She was achingly aware of her inexperience, of her helplessness in this alien situation. She tried to think, to force herself out of this frozen despondency.

'Life jackets!' she thought, and yelled to Sally-Anne out on the deck, 'The life jackets are in the lockers behind the wheelhouse.'

Their faces turned to her, suddenly stricken. Up to this moment it had all been a glorious romp, the old fun-game of challenging the money-grabbers, prodding the establishment, but now suddenly it was mortal danger.

'Move!' Samantha shrieked at them, and there was a rush back along the deck.

'Think!' Samantha shook her head, as though to clear it. 'Think!' she urged herself fiercely. She could hear the tanker now, the silken rustling sound of the water under its hull, the sough of the bow wave curling upon itself.

The *Dicky*'s throttle linkage had broken before, when they had been off Key West a year ago. It had broken between the bridge and the engine, and Samantha had watched Tom Parker fiddling with the engine, holding the lantern for him to see in the gloomy confines of the smelly little engine room. She had not been certain how he did it, but she remembered that he had controlled the revolutions of the engine by hand – something on the side of the engine block, below the big bowl of the air filter.

Samantha turned and dived down the vertical ladder into the engine room. The diesel was running, burbling away quietly at idling speed, not generating sufficient power to move the little vessel through the water.

She tripped and sprawled on the greasy deck, and pulled herself up, crying out with pain as her hand touched the red-hot manifold of the engine exhaust.

On the far side of the engine block, she groped desperately under the air filter, pushing and tugging at anything her fingers touched. She found a coil spring, and dropped to her knees to examine it.

She tried not to think of the huge steel hull bearing down on them, of being down in this tiny box that stank of diesel and exhaust fumes and old bilges. She tried not to think of not having a life jacket, or that the tanker could tramp the little vessel deep down under the surface and crush her like a matchbox.

Instead, she traced the little coil spring to where it was pinned into a flat upright lever. Desperately she pushed the lever against the tension of the spring – and instantly the diesel engine bellowed deafeningly in her ears, startling her so that she flinched and lost the lever. The diesel's beat died away into the bumbling idle and she wasted seconds while she found the lever again and pushed it hard against its stops once more. The engine roared, and she felt the ship picking up speed under her. She began to pray incoherently.

She could not hear the words in the engine noise, and she was not sure she was making sense, but she held the throttle open, and kept on praying.

She did not hear the screams from the deck above her. She did not know how close the *Golden Dawn* was; she did not know if Hank Petersen was still in the wheelhouse conning the little vessel out of the path of the onrushing tanker – but she held the throttle open and prayed.

The impact, when it came, was shattering, the crash and crackle of timbers breaking, the rending lurch and the roll of the deck giving to the tearing force of it.

Samantha was hurled against the hot steel of the engine, her forehead striking with such a force that her vision starred into blinding white light; she dropped backwards, her body loose and relaxed, darkness ringing in her ears, and lay huddled on the deck.

She did not know how long she was unconscious, but it could not have been for more than a few seconds; the spray of icy cold water on her face roused her and she pulled herself up on to her knees.

In the glare of the single bare electric globe in the deck above her, Samantha saw the spurts of water jets through the starting planking of the bulkhead beside her.

Her shirt and denim pants were soaked, salt water half blinded her, and her head felt as though the skull were cracked and someone was forcing the sharp end of a bradawl between her eyes.

Dimly she was aware that the diesel engine was idling noisily, and that the deck was sloshing with water as the boat rolled wildly in some powerful turbulence. She wondered if the whole vessel had been trodden under the tanker.

Then she realized it must be the wake of the giant hull which was throwing them about so mercilessly, but they were still afloat.

She began to crawl down the plunging deck. She knew

where the bilge pump was, that was one thing Tom had taught all of them – and she crawled on grimly towards it.

Hank Petersen ducked out of the wheelhouse, flapping his arms wildly as he struggled into the life jacket. He was not certain of the best action to take, whether to jump over the side and begin swimming away from the tanker's slightly angled course, or to stay on board and take his chances with the collision which was now only seconds away.

Around him, the others were in the grip of the same indecision; they were huddled silently at the rail staring up at the mountain of smooth rounded steel that seemed to blot out half the sky. Only the TV cameraman on the wheelhouse roof, a true fanatic oblivious of all danger, kept his camera running. His exclamations of delight and the burr of the camera motor blended with the rushing sibilance of *Golden Dawn*'s bow wave. It was fifteen feet high, that wave, and it sounded like wild fire in dry grass.

Suddenly the exhaust of the diesel engine above Hank's head bellowed harshly, and then subsided into a soft burbling idle again. He looked up at it uncomprehendingly, now it roared again, fiercely, and the deck lurched beneath him. From the stern he heard the boil of water driven by the propeller, and the *Dicky* shrugged off her lethargy and lifted her bows to the short steep swell of the Gulf Stream.

A moment longer Hank stood frozen, and then he dived back into the wheelhouse and spun the spokes of the wheel through his fingers, sheering off sharply, but still staring out through the side glass.

The *Golden Dawn*'s bows filled his whole vision now, but the smaller vessel was scooting frantically out to one side, and the tanker's bows were swinging majestically in the opposite direction.

A few seconds more and they would be clear, but the bow wave caught them and Hank was flung across the wheelhouse. He felt something break in his chest, and heard the snap of bone as he hit, then immediately afterwards there was the crackling rending tearing impact as the two hulls came together and he was thrown back the other way, sprawling wildly across the deck.

He tried to claw himself upright, but the little fishing boat was pitching and cavorting with such abandon that he was thrown flat again. There was another tearing impact as the vessel was dragged down the tanker's side, and then flung free to roll her rails under and bob like a cork in the mill race of the huge ship's wake.

Now, at last, he was able to pull himself to his feet, and doubled over, clutching his injured ribs. He peered dazedly through the wheelhouse glass.

Half a mile away, the tanker was lazily turning up into the wind, and there was no propeller wash from under her counter. Hank staggered to the doorway, and looked out. The deck was still awash, but the water they had taken on was pouring out through the scuppers. The railing was smashed, most of it dangling overboard and the planking was splintered and torn, the ripped timber as white as bone in the sunlight.

Behind him, Samantha came crawling up the ladder from the engine room. There was a purple swelling in the centre of her forehead, she was soaking wet and her hands were filthy with black grease. He saw a livid red burn across the back of one hand as she lifted it to brush tumbled blonde hair out of her face.

'Are you all right, Sam?'

'Water's pouring in,' she said. 'I don't know how long the pump can hold it.'

'Did you fix the motor?' he asked.

Samantha nodded. 'I held the throttle open,' she said, and then with feeling, 'but I'll be damned to hell if I'll do it again. Somebody else can go down there, I've had my turn.'

'Show me how,' Hank said, 'and you can take the wheel. The sooner we get back to Key Biscayne, the happier I'll be.'

Samantha peered across at the receding bulk of *Golden Dawn*.

'My God!' she shook her head with wonder. 'My God! We were lucky!'

*'Mackerel skies and mares' tails,*
*Make tall ships carry short sails.'*

Nicholas Berg recited the old sailor's doggerel to himself, shading his eyes with one hand as he looked upwards.

The cloud was beautiful as fine lacework; very high against the tall blue of the heavens it spread swiftly in those long filmy scrolls. Nicholas could see the patterns developing and expanding as he watched, and that was a measure of the speed with which the high winds were blowing. That cloud was at least thirty thousand feet high, and below it the air was clear and crisp – only out on the western horizon the billowing silver and the blue thunder-heads were rising, generated by the land-mass of Florida whose low silhouette was still below their horizon.

They had been in the main current of the Gulf Stream for six hours now. It was easy to recognize this characteristic scend of the sea, the short steep swells marching close together, the particular brilliance of these waters that had been first warmed in the shallow tropical basin of the Caribbean, the increased bulk flooding through into the Gulf of Mexico and there heated further, swelling in volume until they formed a hillock of water which at last rushed out through this narrow drainhole of the Florida Straits, swinging north and east in a wide benevolent wash, tempering the climate of all countries whose shores it touched and warming the fishing grounds of the North Atlantic.

In the middle of this stream, somewhere directly ahead of *Warlock*'s thrusting bows, the *Golden Dawn* was struggling southwards, directly opposed to the current which would clip eighty miles a day off her speed, and driving directly into the face of one of the most evil and dangerous storms that nature could summon.

Nicholas found himself brooding again on the mentality of anybody who would do that; again he glanced upwards at the harbingers of the storm, those delicate wisps of lacy cloud.

Nicholas had sailed through a hurricane once, twenty years ago, as a junior officer on one of Christy Marine's small grain carriers, and he shuddered now at the memory of it.

Duncan Alexander was a desperate man even to contemplate that risk, a man gambling everything on one fall of the dice. Nicholas could understand the forces that drove him, for he had been driven himself – but he hated him now for the chances he was taking. Duncan Alexander was risking Nicholas' son, and he was risking the life of an ocean and of the millions of people whose existence was tied to that ocean. Duncan Alexander was gambling with stakes that were not his to place at hazard.

Nicholas wanted one thing only now, and that was to get alongside *Golden Dawn* and take off his son. He would do that, even if it meant boarding her like a buccaneer. In the Master's suite, there was a locked and sealed arms cupboard with two riot guns, automatic 12-gauge shotguns and six Walther PK.38 pistols. *Warlock* had been equipped for every possible emergency in any ocean of the world, and those emergencies could include piracy or mutiny aboard a vessel under salvage. Now Nicholas was fully prepared to take an armed party on board *Golden Dawn*, and to take his chances in any court of law afterwards.

*Warlock* was racing into the chop of the Gulf Stream and scattering the spray like startled white doves, but she was running too slowly for Nicholas and he turned away impatiently and strode into the navigation bridge.

David Allen looked up at him, a small frown of preoccupation marring the smooth boyish features.

'Wind is moderating and veering westerly,' he said, and Nicholas remembered another line of doggerel:

*'When the wind moves against the sun*
*Trust her not for back she'll run.'*

He did not recite it, however, he merely nodded and said:

'We are running into the extreme influence of Lorna. The wind will back again as we move closer to the centre.'

Nicholas went on to the radio room and the Trog looked up at him. It was not necessary for Nicholas to ask, the Trog shook his head. Since that long exchange with the coastguard patrol early that morning, *Golden Dawn* had kept her silence.

Nicholas crossed to the radarscope and studied the circular field for a few minutes; this usually busy seaway was peculiarly empty. There were some small craft crossing the main channel, probably fishing boats or pleasure craft scuttling for protection from the coming storm. All across the islands and on the mainland of Florida the elaborate precautions against the hurricane assault would be coming into force. Since the highway had been laid down on the spur of little islands that formed the Florida Keys, more than three hundred thousand people had crowded in there, in the process transforming those wild lovely islands into the Taj Mahal of ticky-tacky. If the hurricane struck there, the loss of life and property would be enormous. It was probably the most vulnerable spot on a long exposed coastline. For a few minutes, Nicholas tried to imagine the chaos that would result if a million tons of toxic crude oil was driven ashore on a littoral already ravaged by hurricane winds. It baulked his imagination, and he left the radar and moved to the front of the bridge. He stood staring down the narrow throat of water at a horizon that concealed all the terrors and desperate alarms that his imagination could conjure up.

The door to the radio shack was open and the bridge was quiet, so that they all heard it clearly; they could even catch the hiss of breath as the speaker paused between each sentence, and the urgency of his tone was not covered by the slight distortion of the VHF carrier beam.

'Mayday! Mayday! Mayday! This is the bulk oil carrier *Golden Dawn*. Our position is 79° 50′ West 25° 43′ North.'

Before Nicholas reached the chart-table, he knew she was still a hundred miles ahead of them, and, as he pored over the table, he saw his estimate confirmed.

'We have lost our propeller with main shaft failure and we are drifting out of control.'

Nicholas' head flinched as though he had been hit in the face. He could imagine no more dangerous condition and position for a ship of that size – and Peter was on board.

'This is *Golden Dawn* calling the United States Coast Guard service or any ship in a position to afford assistance—'

Nicholas reached the radio shack with three long strides, and the Trog handed him the microphone and nodded.

'*Golden Dawn*, this is the salvage tug *Warlock*. I will be in a position to render assistance within four hours—'

Damn the rule of silence, Peter was on board her.

' – Tell Alexander I am offering Lloyd's Open Form and I want immediate acceptance.'

He dropped the microphone and stormed back on to

the bridge, his voice clipped and harsh as he caught David Allen's arm.

'Interception course and push her through the gate,' he ordered grimly. 'Tell Beauty Baker to open all the taps.' He dropped David's arm and spun back to the radio room.

'Telex Levoisin on *Sea Witch*. I want him to give me a time to reach *Golden Dawn* at his best possible speed,' and he wondered briefly if even the two tugs would be able to control the crippled and powerless *Golden Dawn* in the winds of a hurricane.

Jules replied almost immediately. He had bunkered at Charleston, and cleared harbour six hours previously. He was running hard now and he gave a time to *Golden Dawn*'s position for noon the next day, which was also the forecast time of passage of the Straits for Hurricane Lorna, according to the meteorological up-date they had got from Miami two hours before, Nicholas thought as he read the telex and turned to David Allen.

'David, there is no precedent for this that I know of – but with my son on board *Golden Dawn* I just have to assume command of this ship, on a temporary basis, of course.'

'I'd be honoured to act as your First Officer again, sir,' David told him quietly, and Nicholas could see he meant it.

'If there is a good salvage, the Master's share will still be yours,' Nicholas promised him, and thanked him with a touch on the arm. 'Would you check out the preparations to put a line aboard the tanker?'

David turned to leave the bridge, but Nicholas stopped him. 'By the time we get there, we will have the kind of wind you have only dreamed about in your worst nightmares – just keep that in mind.'

'Telex,' screeched the Trog. '*Golden Dawn* is replying to our offer.'

Nicholas strode across to the radio room, and read the first few lines of message as it printed out.

> OFFER CONTRACT OF DAILY HIRE FOR TOWAGE THIS VESSEL FROM PRESENT POSITION TO GALVESTON ROADS

'The bastard,' Nicholas snarled. 'He's playing his fancy games with me, in the teeth of a hurricane and with my boy aboard.' Furiously he punched his fist into the palm of his other hand. 'Right!' he snapped. 'We'll play just as rough! Get me the Director of the US Coast Guard at the Fort Lauderdale Headquarters – get him on the emergency coastguard frequency and I will talk to him in clear.'

The Trog's face lit with malicious glee and he made the contact.

'Colonel Ramsden,' Nicholas said. 'This is the Master of *Warlock*. I'm the only salvage vessel that can reach *Golden Dawn* before passage of Lorna, and I'm probably the only tug on the eastern seaboard of America with 22,000 horsepower. Unless the *Golden Dawn*'s Master accepts Lloyd's Open Form within the next sixty minutes, I shall be obliged to see to the safety of my vessel and crew by running for the nearest anchorage – and you're going to have a million tons of highly toxic crude oil drifting out of control into your territorial waters, in hurricane conditions.'

The Coast Guard Director had a deep measured voice, and the calm tones of a man upon whom the mantle of authority was a familiar garment.

'Stand by, *Warlock*, I am going to contact *Golden Dawn* direct on Channel 16.'

Nicholas signalled the Trog to turn up the volume on

Channel 16 and they listened to Ramsden speaking directly to Duncan Alexander.

'In the event your vessel enters United States territorial waters without control or without an attendant tug capable of exerting that control, I shall be obliged under the powers vested in me to seize your vessel and take such steps to prevent pollution of our waters as I see fit. I have to warn you that those steps may include destruction of your cargo.'

Ten minutes later the Trog copied a telex from Duncan Alexander personal to Nicholas Berg accepting Lloyd's Open Form and requesting him to exercise all dispatch in taking *Golden Dawn* in tow.

'I estimate we will be drifting over the 100-fathom line and entering US territorial waters within two hours,' the message ended.

While Nicholas read it, standing out on the protected wing of *Warlock*'s bridge, the wind suddenly fluttered the paper in his hand and flattened his cotton shirt against his chest. He looked up quickly and saw the wind was backing violently into the east, and beginning to claw the tops of the Gulf Stream swells. The setting sun was bleeding copiously across the high veils of cirrus cloud which now covered the sky from horizon to horizon.

There was nothing more that Nicholas could do now. *Warlock* was running as hard as she could, and all her crew were quietly going about their preparations to pass a wire and take on tow. All he could do was wait, but that was always the hardest part.

Darkness came swiftly but with the last of the light, Nicholas could just make out a dark and mountainous shape beginning to hump up above the southern horizon like an impatient monster. He stared at it with awful fascination, until mercifully the night hid Lorna's dreadful face.

The wind chopped the Gulf Stream up into quick confused seas, and it did not blow steadily, but flogged them with squally gusts and rain that crackled against the bridge windows with startling suddenness.

The night was utterly black, there were no stars, no source of light whatsoever, and *Warlock* lurched and heeled to the patternless seas.

'Barometer's rising sharply,' David Allen called suddenly. 'It's jumped three millibars – back to 1005.'

'The trough,' said Nicholas grimly. It was a classic hurricane formation, that narrow girdle of higher pressure that demarcated the outer fringe of the great revolving spiral of tormented air. 'We are going into it now.'

And as he spoke the darkness lifted, the heavens began to burn like a bed of hot coals, and the sea shone with a sullen ruddy luminosity as though the doors of a furnace had been thrown wide.

Nobody spoke on *Warlock*'s bridge, they lifted their faces with the same awed expressions as worshippers in a lofty cathedral and they looked up at the skies.

Low cloud raced above them, cloud that glowed and shone with that terrible ominous flare. Slowly the light faded and changed, turning a paler sickly greenish hue, like the shine on putrid meat. Nicholas spoke first.

'The Devil's Beacon,' he said, and he wanted to rationalize it to break the superstitious mood that gripped them all. It was merely the rays of the sun below the western horizon catching the cloud peaks of the storm and reflected downwards through the weak cloud cover of the trough – but somehow he could not find the right words to denigrate that phenomenon that was part of the mariner's lore, the malignant beacon that leads a doomed ship on to its fate.

The weird light faded slowly away leaving the night even darker and more foreboding than it had been before.

'David,' Nicholas thought quickly of something to

distract his officers, 'have we got a radar contact yet?' and the new Mate roused himself with a visible effort and crossed to the radarscope.

'The range is very confused,' he said, his voice still subdued, and Nicholas joined him at the screen.

The sweeping arm lit a swirling mass of sea clutter, and the strange ghost echoes thrown up by electrical discharges within the approaching storm. The outline of the Florida mainland and of the nearest islands of the Grand Bahamas bank were firm and immediately recognizable. They reminded Nicholas yet again of how little sea-room there was in which to manoeuvre his tugs and their monstrous prize.

Then, in the trash of false echo and sea clutter, his trained eye picked out a harder echo on the extreme limits of the set's range. He watched it carefully for half a dozen revolutions of the radar's sweep, and each time it was constant and clearer.

'Radar contact,' he said. 'Tell *Golden Dawn* we are in contact, range sixty-five nautical miles. Tell them we will take on tow before midnight.' And then, under his breath, the old sailor's qualifications, 'God willing and weather permitting.'

The lights on *Warlock*'s bridge had been rheostatted down to a dull rose glow to protect the night vision of her officers, and the four of them stared out to where they knew the tanker lay.

Her image on the radar was bright and firm, lying within the two mile ring of the screen, but from the bridge she was invisible.

In the two hours since first contact, the barometer had gone through its brief peak as the trough passed, and then fallen steeply.

From 1005 it had crashed to 900 and was still plummeting, and the weather coming in from the east was blustering and squalling. The wind mourned about them on a forever rising note, and torrential rain obscured all vision outside an arc of a few hundred yards. Even *Warlock*'s twin searchlights, set seventy feet above the main deck on the summit of the fire-control gantry, could not pierce those solid white curtains of rain.

Nicholas groped like a blind man through the rain fog, using pitch and power to close carefully with *Golden Dawn*, giving his orders to the helm in a cool impersonal tone which belied the pale set of his features and the alert brightness of his eyes as he reached the swirling bank of rain.

Abruptly another squall struck *Warlock*. With a demented shriek, it heeled the big tug sharply and shredded the curtains of rain, ripping them open so that for a moment Nicholas saw *Golden Dawn*.

She was exactly where he had expected her to be, but the wind had caught the tanker's high navigation bridge like the mainsail of a tall ship, and she was going swiftly astern.

All her deck and port lights were burning, and she carried the twin red riding lights at her stubby masthead that identified a vessel drifting out of control. The following sea driven on by the rising wind piled on to her tank decks, smothering them with white foam and spray, so that the ship looked like a submerged coral reef.

'Half ahead both,' Nicholas told the helmsman. 'Steer for her starboard side.'

He closed quickly with the tanker, staying in visual contact now; even when the rain mists closed down again, they could make out the ghostly shape of her and the glow of her riding lights.

David Allen was looking at him expectantly and

Nicholas asked, 'What bottom?' without taking his eyes from the stricken ship.

'One hundred sixteen fathoms and shelving fast.' They were being blown quickly out of the main channel, on to the shallow ledge of the Florida littoral.

'I'm going to tow her out stern first,' said Nicholas, and immediately David saw the wisdom of it. Nobody would be able to get up into her bows to secure a towline, the seas were breaking over them and sweeping them with ten and fifteen feet of green water.

'I'll go aft—' David began, but Nicholas stopped him.

'No, David. I want you here – because I'm going on board *Golden Dawn*.'

'Sir,' David wanted to tell him that it was dangerous to delay passing the towing cable – with that lee shore waiting.

'This will be our last chance to get passengers off her before the full hurricane hits us,' said Nicholas, and David saw that it was futile to protest. Nicholas Berg was going to fetch his son.

From the height of *Golden Dawn*'s towering navigation bridge, they could look directly down on to the main deck of the tug as she came alongside.

Peter Berg stood beside his mother, almost as tall as she was. He wore a full life-jacket and a corduroy cap pulled down over his ears.

'It will be all right,' he comforted Chantelle. 'Dad is here. It will be just fine now.' And he took her hand protectively.

*Warlock* staggered and reeled in the grip of wind as she came up into the tanker's lee, rain blew over her like dense white smoke and every few minutes she put her nose down and threw a thick green slice of sea water back along her decks.

In comparison to the tug's wild action, *Golden Dawn* wallowed heavily, held down by the oppressive weight of a million tons of crude oil, and the seas beat upon her with increasing fury, as if affronted by her indifference. *Warlock* edged in closer and still closer.

Duncan Alexander came through from the communications room at the rear of the bridge. He balanced easily against *Golden Dawn*'s ponderous motion but his face was swollen and flushed with anger.

'Berg is coming on board,' he burst out. 'He's wasting valuable time. I warned him that we must get out into deeper water.'

Peter Berg interrupted suddenly and pointed down at *Warlock*.

'Look!' he cried.

Until that moment, the night and the storm had hidden the small huddle of human shapes in the tug's high forward tower. They wore wet, glistening oilskins and their life jackets gave them a swollen pregnant look. They were lowering the boarding gantry into the horizontal position.

'There is Dad!' Peter shouted. 'That's him in front.'

At the extremity of her roll, *Warlock*'s boarding gantry touched the railing of the tanker's quarterdeck, ten feet above the swamped tank deck – and the leading figure on the tug's upperworks ran out lightly along the gantry, balanced for a moment high above the roaring, racing green water and then leapt across five feet of open space, caught a hand hold and then pulled himself over *Golden Dawn*'s rail.

Immediately the tug sheered off and fell in fifty yards off the tanker's starboard side, half hidden in the rain mists, but holding her station steadily, despite all the wind's and the sea's spiteful efforts to separate the two vessels.

The whole manoeuvre had been performed with an expertise which made it seem almost casual.

'Dad's carried a line across,' Peter said proudly, and Chantelle, looking down, saw that a delicate white nylon thread was being hove in by two seamen on the tanker's quarter deck, while from the tug's fire-control tower a canvas bosun's chair was being winched across.

The elevator doors slid open with a whine and Nicholas Berg strode on to the tanker's bridge. His oilskins still ran with rainwater that splattered on to the deck at his feet.

'Dad!' Peter ran to meet him and Nicholas stooped and embraced him fiercely before straightening; with one arm still about his son's shoulders, he confronted Chantelle and Duncan Alexander.

'I hope both of you are satisfied now,' he said quietly, 'but I for one don't rate our chances of saving this ship very highly, so I'm taking off everybody who is not needed on board to handle her.'

'Your tug,' burst out Duncan, 'you've got 22,000 horse-power, and can—'

'There is a hurricane on its way,' said Nicholas coldly, and he shot a glance at the roaring night. 'This is just the overture.' He turned back to Randle. 'How many men do you want to keep on board?'

Randle thought for a moment. 'Myself, a helmsman, and five seamen to handle the towlines and work the ship.' He paused and then went on, 'And the pump-room personnel to control the cargo.'

'You will act as helmsman, I will control the pump room, and I'll need only three seamen. Get me volunteers,' Nicholas decided. 'Send everybody else off.'

'Sir,' Randle began to protest.

'May I remind you Captain, that I am salvage master, my authority now supersedes yours.' Nicholas did not wait for his reply. 'Chantelle,' he picked her out, 'take Peter down to the quarterdeck. You'll go across first.'

'Listen here, Berg,' Duncan could no longer contain himself, 'I insist you pass the towing cable, this ship is in danger.'

'Get down there with them,' Nicholas snapped. 'I'll decide the procedures.'

'Do as he says, darling,' Chantelle smiled up at her husband vindictively. 'You've lost. Nicholas is the only winner now.'

'Shut up, damn you,' Duncan hissed at her.

'Get down to the afterdeck,' Nicholas' voice cracked like breaking ice.

'I'm staying on board this ship,' said Duncan abruptly. 'It's my responsibility. I said I'd see it out and by God I will. I am going to be here to make sure you do your job, Berg.'

Nicholas checked himself, studied him for a long moment, and then smiled mirthlessly.

'Nobody ever called you a coward,' he nodded reluctantly. 'Other things – but not a coward. Stay if you will, we might need an extra hand,' Then to Peter, 'Come, my boy.' And he led him towards the elevator.

At the quarterdeck rail, Nicholas hugged the boy, holding him in his arms, their cheeks pressed tightly together, and drawing out the moment while the wind cannoned and thrummed about their heads.

'I love you, Dad.'

'And I love you, Peter, more than I can ever tell you – but you must go now.'

He broke the embrace and lifted the child into the deep canvas bucket of the bosun's chair, stepped back and windmilled his right arm. Immediately, the winch party in *Warlock*'s upperworks swung him swiftly out into the gap between the two ships and the nylon cable seemed as fragile and insubstantial as a spider's thread.

As the two ships rolled and dipped, so the line tightened and sagged, one moment dropping the white canvas bucket almost to the water level where the hungry waves snatched at it with cold green fangs, and the next, pulling the line up so tightly that it hummed with tension, threatening to snap and drop the child back into the sea, but at last it reached the tug and four pairs of strong hands lifted the boy clear. For one moment, he waved back at Nicholas and then he was hustled away, and the empty bosun's chair was coming back.

Only then did Nicholas become aware that Chantelle was clinging to his arm and he looked down into her face. Her eyelashes were dewed and stuck together with the flying raindrops. Her face ran with wetness and she seemed very small and childlike under the bulky oilskins and life jacket. She was as beautiful as she had ever been but her eyes were huge and darkly troubled.

'Nicholas, I've always needed you,' she husked. 'But never as I need you now.'

Her existence was being blown away on the wind, and she was afraid.

'You and this ship are all I have left.'

'No, only the ship,' he said brusquely, and he was amazed that the spell was broken. That soft area of his soul which she had been able to touch so unerringly was now armoured against her. With a sudden surge of relief, he realized he was free of her, for ever. It was over; here in the storm, he was free at last.

She sensed it – for the fear in her eyes changed to real terror.

'Nicholas, you cannot desert me now. Oh Nicholas, what will become of me without you and Christy Marine?'

'I don't know,' he told her quietly, and caught the

bosun's chair as it came in over *Golden Dawn*'s rail. He lifted her as easily as he had lifted his son and placed her in the canvas bucket.

'And to tell you the truth, Chantelle, I don't really care,' he said, and stepping back, he windmilled his right arm. The chair swooped out across the narrow water, swinging like a pendulum in the wind. Chantelle shouted something at him but Nicholas had turned away, and was already going aft in a lurching run to where the three volunteers were waiting.

He saw at a glance that they were big, powerful, competent-looking men.

Quickly Nicholas checked their equipment, from the thick leather gauntlets to the bolt cutters and jemmy bars for handling heavy cable.

'You'll do,' he said. 'We will use the bosun's tackle to bring across a messenger from the tug – just as soon as the last man leaves this ship.'

Working with men to whom the task was unfamiliar, and in rapidly deteriorating conditions of sea and weather, it took almost another hour before they had the main cable across from *Warlock* secured by its thick nylon spring to the tanker's stern bollards – yet the time had passed so swiftly for Nicholas that when he stood back and glanced at his watch, he was shocked. Before this wind they must have been going down very fast on the land. He staggered into the tanker's stern quarters, and left a trail of sea water down the passageway to the elevators.

On the bridge, Captain Randle was standing grim-faced at the helm, and Duncan Alexander snapped accusingly at him.

'You've cut it damned fine.' A single glance at the

digital printout of the depth gauge on the tanker's control console bore him out. They had thirty-eight fathoms of water under them now, and the *Golden Dawn*'s swollen belly sagged down twenty fathoms below the surface. They were going down very swiftly before the easterly gale winds. It was damned fine, Nicholas had to agree, but he showed no alarm or agitation as he crossed to Randle's side and unhooked the hand microphone.

'David,' he asked quietly, 'are you ready to haul us off?'

'Ready, sir,' David Allen's voice came from the speaker above his head.

'I'm going to give you full port rudder to help your turn across the wind,' said Nicholas, and then nodded to Randle. 'Full port rudder.'

'Forty degrees of port rudder on,' Randle reported.

They felt the tiny shock as the tow-cable came up taut, and carefully *Warlock* began the delicate task of turning the huge ship across the rising gusting wind and then dragging her out tail first into the deeper water of the channel where she would have her best chance of riding out the hurricane.

It was clear now that *Golden Dawn* lay directly in the track of Lorna, and the storm unleashed its true nature upon them. Out there upon the sane and rational world, the sun was rising, but here there was no dawn, for there was no horizon and no sky. There was only madness and wind and water, and all three elements were so intermingled as to form one substance.

An hour – which seemed like a lifetime – ago, the wind had ripped away the anemometer and the weather-recording equipment on top of the navigation bridge, so Nicholas had no way of judging the wind's strength and direction.

Out beyond the bridge windows, the wind took the top off the sea; it took it off in thick sheets of salt water and lifted them over the navigation bridge in a shrieking white curtain that cut off visibility at the glass of the windows. The tank deck had disappeared in the racing white emulsion of wind and water, even the railing of the bridge wings six feet from the windows was invisible.

The entire superstructure groaned and popped and whimpered under the assault of the wind, the pressed aluminium bulkheads bulging and distorting, the very deck flexing and juddering at the solid weight of the storm.

Through the saturated, racing, swirling air, a leaden and ominous grey light filtered, and every few minutes the electrical impulses generated within the sixty-thousand-foot-high mountain of racing, spinning air released themselves in shattering cannonades of thunder and sudden brilliance of eye-searing white lightning.

There was no visual contact with *Warlock*. The massive electrical disturbance of the storm and the clutter of high seas and almost solid cloud and turbulence had reduced the radar range to a few miles, and even then it was unreliable. Radio contact with the tug was drowned with buzzing squealing static. It was possible to understand only odd disconnected words from David Allen.

Nicholas was powerless, caged in the groaning, vibrating box of the navigation bridge, blinded and deafened by the unleashed powers of the heavens. There was nothing any of them could do.

Randle had locked the ultra-tanker's helm amidships, and now he stood with Duncan and the three seamen by the chart-table, all of them clinging to it for support, all their faces pale and set as though carved from chalk.

Only Nicholas moved restlessly about the bridge; from the stern windows where he peered down vainly, trying to get a glimpse of either the tow-cable and its spring, or of the tug's looming shape through the racing white storm, then he came forward carefully, using the foul-weather rail to steady himself against the huge ship's wild and unpredictable motion, and he stood before the control console, studying the display of lights that monitored the pod tanks and the ship's navigational and mechanical functions.

None of the petroleum tanks had lost any crude oil and in all of them the nature of the inert gas was constant. There had been no ingress of air to them; they were all still intact then. One of the reasons that Nicholas had taken the tanker in tow stern first was so that the navigation tower might break the worst of wind and sea, and the fragile bloated tanks would receive some protection from it.

Yet desperately he wished for a momentary sight of the tank deck, merely to reassure himself. There could be malfunction in the pump control instruments, the storm could have clawed one of the pod tanks open, and even now *Golden Dawn* could be bleeding her poison into the sea. But there was no view of the tank decks through the storm, and Nick stooped to the radarscope. The screen glowed and danced and flickered with ghost images and trash – he wasn't too certain if even *Warlock*'s image was constant, the range seemed to be opening, as though the towline had parted. He straightened up and stood balanced on the balls of his feet, reassuring himself by the feel of the deck that *Golden Dawn* was still under tow. He could feel by the way she resisted the wind and the sea that the tow was still good.

Yet there was no means of telling their position. The satellite navigational system was completely blanketed, the radio waves were distorted and diverted by tens of thousands of feet of electrical storm, and the same forces were blanketing the marine radio beacons on the American mainland.

The only indication was the ship's electronic log which gave Nicholas the speed of the ship's hull through the water and the speed across the sea bottom, and the depth finder which recorded the water under her keel.

For the first two hours of the tow, *Warlock* had been able to pull the ship back towards the main channel at three and a half knots, and slowly the water had become deeper until they had 150 fathoms under them.

Then as the wind velocity increased, the windage of *Golden Dawn*'s superstructure had acted as a vast mainsail and the storm had taken control. Now, despite all the power in *Warlock*'s big twin propellers, both tug and tanker were being pushed once more back towards the 100-fathom line and the American mainland.

'Where is *Sea Witch?*' Nicholas wondered, as he stared helplessly at the gauges. They were going towards the shore at a little over two knots, and the bottom was shelving steeply. *Sea Witch* might be the ace that took the trick, if she could reach them through these murderous seas and savage winds, and if she could find them in this wilderness of mad air and water.

Again, Nicholas groped his way to the communications room, and still clinging to the bulkhead with one hand he thumbed the microphone.

'*Sea Witch. Sea Witch.* This is *Warlock.* Calling *Sea Witch.*'

He listened then, trying to tune out the snarl and crackle of static, crouching over the set. Faintly he thought he heard a human voice, a scratchy whisper through the interference and he called again and listened, and called again. There was the voice again, but so indistinct he could not make out a single word.

Above his head, there was a tearing screech of rending metal. Nicholas dropped the microphone and staggered through on to the bridge. There was another deafening banging and hammering and all of them stood staring up at the metal roof of the bridge. It sagged and shook, there was one more crash and then with a scraping, dragging rush, a confused tangle of metal and wire and cable tumbled over the forward edge of the bridge and flapped and swung wildly in the wind.

It took a moment for Nicholas to realize what it was.

'The radar antennae!' he shouted. He recognized the elongated dish of the aerial, dangling on a thick coil of cable, then the wind tore that loose also, and the entire mass of equipment flapped away like a giant bat and was instantly lost in the teeming white curtains of the storm.

With two quick paces, he reached the radarscope, and one glance was enough. The screen was black and dead. They had lost their eyes now, and, unbelievably, the sound of the storm was rising again.

It boomed against the square box of the bridge, and the men within it cowered from its fury.

Then abruptly, Duncan was screaming something at Nicholas, and pointing up at the master display of the control console. Nicholas, still hanging on to the radarscope, roused himself with an effort and looked up at the display. The speed across the ground had changed drastically. It was now almost eight knots, and the depth was ninety-two fathoms.

Nicholas felt icy despair clutch and squeeze his guts. The ship was moving differently under him, he could feel her now in mortal distress; that same gust which had torn away the radar mast had done other damage.

He knew what that damage was, and the thought of it made him want to vomit, but he had to be sure. He had to be absolutely certain, and he began to hand himself along the foul-weather rail towards the elevator doors.

Across the bridge the others were watching him intently, but even from twenty feet it was impossible to make himself heard above the clamorous assault of the storm.

One of the seamen seemed suddenly to guess his intention. He left the chart-table and groped his way along the bulkhead towards Nicholas.

'Good man!' Nicholas grabbed his arm to steady him, and they fell forward into the elevator as *Golden Dawn* began another of those ponderous wallowing rolls and the deck fell out from under their feet.

The ride down in the elevator car slammed them back and forth across the little coffin-like box, and even here in the depths of the ship they had to shout to hear each other.

'The tow cable,' Nicholas yelled in the man's ear. 'Check the tow cable.'

From the elevator they went carefully aft along the central passageway, and when they reached the double storm doors, Nicholas tried to push the inner door open, but the pressure of the wind held it closed.

'Help me,' he shouted at the seaman, and they threw their combined weight against it. The instant that they forced the jamb open a crack, the vacuum of pressure was released and the wind took the three-inch mahogany doors and ripped them effortlessly from their hinges, and whisked them away, as though they were a pair of playing cards – and Nicholas and the seaman were exposed in the open doorway.

The wind flung itself upon them, and hurled them to the deck, smothering them in the icy deluge of water that ripped at their faces as abrasively as ground glass.

Nicholas rolled down the deck and crashed into the stern rail with such jarring force that he thought his lungs had been crushed, and the wind pinned him there, and blinded and smothered him with salt water.

He lay there helpless as a newborn infant, and near him he heard the seaman screaming thinly. The sound steeled him, and Nicholas slowly dragged himself to his knees, desperately clutching at the rail to resist the wind.

Still the man screamed and Nicholas began to creep

forward on his hands and knees. It was impossible to stand in that wind and he could move only with support from the rail.

Six feet ahead of him, the extreme limit of his vision, the railing had been torn away, a long section of it dangling over the ship's side, and to this was clinging the seaman. His weight driven by the wind must have hit the rail with sufficient force to tear it loose, and now he was hanging on with one arm hooked through the railing and the other arm twisted from a shattered shoulder and waving a crazy salute as the wind whipped it about. When he looked up at Nicholas his mouth had been smashed in. It looked as though he had half chewed a mouthful of blackcurrants, and the jagged stumps of his broken front teeth were bright red with the juice.

On his belly, Nicholas reached for him, and as he did so, the wind came again, unbelievably it was stronger still, and it took the damaged railing with the man still upon it and tore it bodily away. They disappeared instantly in the blinding white-out of the storm, and Nicholas felt himself hurled forward towards the edge. He clung with all his strength to the remaining section of the rail, and felt it buckle and begin to give.

On his knees still he clawed himself away from that fatal beckoning gap, towards the stern, and the wind struck him full in the face, blinding and choking him. Sightlessly, he dragged himself on until one outstretched arm struck the cold cast iron of the port stern bollard, and he flung both arms about it like a lover, choking and retching from the salt water that the wind had forced through his nose and mouth and down his throat.

Still blind, he felt for the woven steel of *Warlock*'s main tow-wire. He found it and he could not span it with his fist – but he felt the quick lift of his hopes.

The cable was still secured. He had catted and prevented it with a dozen nylon strops, and it was still holding. He crawled forward, dragging himself along the tow-cable, and immediately he realized that his relief had been premature. There was no tension in the cable and when he reached the edge of the deck it dangled straight down. It was not stretched out into the whiteness, to where he had hoped *Warlock* was still holding them like a great sea anchor.

He knew then that what he had dreaded had happened. The storm had been too powerful; it had snapped the steel cable like a thread of cotton, and *Golden Dawn* was loose, without control, and this wild and savage wind was blowing her down swiftly on to the land.

Nicholas felt suddenly exhausted to his bones. He lay flat on the deck, closed his eyes and clung weakly to the severed cable. The wind wanted to hurl him over the side; it ballooned his oilskins and ripped at his face. It would be so easy to open his fingers and to let go – and it took all his resolve to resist the impulse.

Slowly, as painfully as a crippled insect, he dragged himself back through the open, shattered doorway into the central passageway of the stern quarters – but still the wind followed him. It roared down the passageway, driving in torrents of rain and salt water that flooded the deck and forced Nicholas to cling for support like a drunkard.

After the open storm, the car of the elevator seemed silent and tranquil as the inner sanctum of a cathedral. He looked at himself in the wall mirror, and saw that his eyes were scoured red and painful-looking by salt and wind, and his cheeks and lips looked raw and bruised, as though the skin had been rasped away. He touched his face and there was no feeling in his nose nor in his lips.

The elevator doors slid open and he reeled out on to the navigation bridge. The group of men at the chart-table seemed not to have moved, but their heads turned to him.

Nicholas reached the table and clung to it. They were silent, watching his face.

'I lost a man,' he said, and his voice was hoarse and

roughened by salt and weariness. 'He went overboard. The wind got him.'

Still none of them moved nor spoke, and Nicholas coughed, his lungs ached from the water he had breathed. When the spasm passed, he went on.

'The tow-cable has parted. We are loose – and *Warlock* will never be able to re-establish tow. Not in this.'

All their heads turned now to the forward bridge windows, to that impenetrable racing whiteness beyond the glass, that was lit internally with its glowing bursts of lightning.

Nicholas broke the spell that held them all. He reached up to the signal locker above the chart-table and brought down a cardboard packet of distress flares. He broke open the seals and spilled the flares on to the table. They looked like sticks of dynamite, cylinders of heavily varnished waterproof paper. The flares could be lit, and would spurt out crimson flames, even if immersed in water, once the self-igniter tab at one end was pulled.

Nicholas stuffed half a dozen of the flares into the inner pockets of his oilskins.

'Listen,' he had to shout, even though they were only feet away. 'We are going to be aground within two hours. This ship is going to start breaking up immediately we strike.'

He paused and studied their faces; Duncan was the only one who did not seem to understand. He had picked up a handful of the signal flares from the table and he was looking inquiringly at Nicholas.

'I will give you the word; as soon as we reach the twenty-fathom line and she touches bottom, you will go over the side. We will try and get a raft away. There is a chance you could be carried ashore.'

He paused again, and he could see that Randle and his two seamen realized clearly just how remote that chance was.

'I will give you twenty minutes to get clear. By then, the pod tanks will have begun breaking up—' He didn't want this to sound melodramatic and he searched for some way to make it sound less theatrical, but could think of none. 'Once the first tank ruptures, I will ignite the escaping crude with a signal flare.'

'Christ!' Randle mouthed the blasphemy, and the storm censored it on his lips. Then he raised his voice. 'A million tons of crude. It will fireball, man.'

'Better than a million-ton slick down the Gulf Stream,' Nicholas told him wearily.

'None of us will have a chance. A million tons. It will go up like an atom bomb.' Randle was white-faced and shaking now. 'You can't do it!'

'Think of a better way,' said Nicholas and left the table to stagger across to the radio room. They watched him go, and then Duncan looked down at the signal flares in his hand for a moment before thrusting them into the pocket of his jacket.

In the radio room, Nicholas called quietly into the microphone. 'Come in, *Sea Witch* – *Sea Witch*, this is *Golden Dawn*.' And only the static howled in reply.

'*Warlock*. Come in, *Warlock*. This is *Golden Dawn*.'

Something else went in the wind, they heard it tear loose, and the whole superstructure shook and trembled. The ship was beginning to break up; it had not been designed to withstand winds like this.

Through the open radio room door, Nicholas could see the control console display. There were seventy-one fathoms of water under the ship, and the wind was punching her, flogging her on towards the shore.

'Come in, *Sea Witch*,' Nicholas called with quiet desperation. 'This is *Golden Dawn*. Do you read me?'

The wind charged the ship, crashing into it like a monster, and she groaned and reeled from the blow.

'Come in, *Warlock*.'

Randle lurched across to the forward windows, and clinging to the rail he bowed over the gauges that monitored the condition of the ship's cargo, checking for tank damage.

'At least he is still thinking.' Nicholas watched him, and above the Captain's head, the sounding showed sixty-eight fathoms.

Randle straightened slowly, began to turn, and the wind struck again.

Nicholas felt the blow in his stomach. It was a solid thing, like a mountain in avalanche, a defeaning boom of sound and the forward bridge window above the control console broke inwards.

It burst in a glittering explosion of glass shards that engulfed the figure of Captain Randle standing directly before it. In a fleeting moment of horror, Nicholas saw his head half severed from his shoulders by a guillotine of flying glass, then he crumpled to the deck and instantly the bright pulsing hose of his blood was diluted to spreading pale pink in the torrent of wind and blown water that poured in through the opening, and smothered the navigation bridge.

Charts and books were ripped from their shelves and fluttered like trapped birds as the wind blustered and swirled in the confines of glass and steel.

Nicholas reached the Captain's body, protecting his own face with an arm crooked across it, but there was nothing he could do for him. He left Randle lying on the deck and shouted to the others.

'Keep clear of the windows.'

He gathered them in the rear of the bridge, against the bulkhead where stood the Decca and navigational systems. The four of them kept close together, as though they gained comfort from the close proximity of other humans, but the wind did not relent.

It poured in through the shattered window and raged

about the bridge, tearing at their clothing and filling the air with a fine mist of water, flooding the deck ankle deep so that it sloshed and ran as the tanker rolled almost to her beam ends.

Randle's limp and sodden body slid back and forth in the wash and roll, until Nicholas left the dubious security of the after bulkhead, half-lifted the corpse under the arms, and dragged it into the radio room and wedged it into the radio operator's bunk. Swift blood stained the crisply ironed sheets, and Nicholas threw a fold of the blanket over Randle and staggered back into the bridge.

Still the wind rose, and now Nicholas felt himself numbed by the force and persistence of it.

Some loose material, perhaps a sheet of aluminium from the superstructure, or a length of piping ripped from the tank deck below, smashed into the tip of the bridge like a cannon ball and then flipped away into the storm, leaving a jagged rent which the wind exploited, tearing and worrying at it, enlarging the opening, so that the plating flapped and hammered and a solid deluge of rain poured in through it.

Nicholas realized that the ship's superstructure was beginning to go; like a gigantic vulture, soon the wind would begin stripping the carcass down to its bones.

He knew he should get the survivors down nearer the water line, so that when they were forced to commit themselves to the sea, they could do so quickly. But his brain was numbered by the tumult, and he stood stolidly. It needed all his remaining strength merely to brace himself against the tearing wind and the ship's anguished motion.

In the days of sail, the crew would tie themselves to the main mast, when they reached this stage of despair.

Dully, he registered that the depth of water under the ship was now only fifty-seven fathoms, and the barometer was reading 955 millibars. Nicholas had never heard of a reading that low; surely it could not go lower, they must be almost at the centre of the revolving hurricane.

With an effort, he lifted his arm and read the time. It was still only ten o'clock in the morning, they had been in the hurricane for only two and a half hours.

A great burning light struck through the torn roof, a light that blinded them with its intensity, and Nicholas threw up his hands to protect his eyes. He could not understand what was happening. He thought his hearing had gone, for suddenly the terrible tumult of the wind was muted, fading away.

Then he understood. 'The eye,' he croaked, 'we are into the eye,' and his voice resounded strangely in his own ears. He stumbled to the front of the bridge.

Although the *Golden Dawn* still rolled ponderously, describing an arc of almost forty degrees from side to side, she was free of the unbearable weight of the wind and brilliant sunshine poured down upon her. It beamed down like the dazzling arc lamps of a stage set, out of the throat of a dark funnel of dense racing swirling cloud.

The cloud lay to the very surface of the sea, and encompassed the full sweep of the horizon in an unbroken wall. Only directly overhead was it open, and the sky was an angry unnatural purple, set with the glaring, merciless eye of the sun.

The sea was still wild and confused, leaping into peaks and troughs and covered with a thick frothy mattress of spindrift, whipped into a custard by the wild winds. But already the sea was subsiding in the total calm of the eye and *Golden Dawn* was rolling less viciously.

Nicholas turned his head stiffly to watch the receding wall of racing cloud. How long would it take for the eye to pass over them, he wondered.

Not very long, he was sure of that, half an hour perhaps – an hour at the most – and then the storm would be on them again, with its renewed fury every bit as sudden as its passing. But this time, the wind would come from exactly the opposite direction as they crossed the hub and went into the far side of the revolving wall of cloud.

Nicholas jerked his eyes away from that racing, heaven-high bank of cloud, and looked down on to the tank deck. He saw at a single glance that *Golden Dawn* had already sustained mortal damage. The forward port pod tank was half torn from its hydraulic coupling, holding only by the bows and lying at almost twenty degrees from the line of the other three tanks. The entire tank deck was twisted like the limb of an arthritic giant. It rolled and pitched out of sequence with the rest of the hull.

*Golden Dawn*'s back was broken. It had broken where Duncan had weakened the hull to save steel. Only the buoyancy of the crude petroleum in her four tanks was holding her together now. Nicholas expected to see the dark, glistening ooze of slick leaking from her; he could not believe that not one of the four tanks had ruptured, and he glanced at the electronic cargo monitor. Loads and gas contents of all tanks were still normal. They had been freakishly lucky so far, but when they went into the far side of the hurricane he knew that *Golden Dawn*'s weakened spine would give completely, and when that happened it must pinch and tear the thin skins of the pod tanks.

He made a decision then, forcing his mind to work, not certain how good a decision it was but determined to act on it.

'Duncan,' he called to him across the swamped and battered bridge. 'I'm sending you and the others off on one of the life-rafts. This will be your only chance to launch one. I'll stay on board to fire the cargo when the storm hits again.'

'The storm has passed,' suddenly Duncan was screaming at him like a madman. 'The ship is safe now. You're going to destroy my ship – you're deliberately trying to break me.'

He was lunging across the heaving bridge. 'It's deliberate. You know I've won now. You are going to destroy this ship. It's the only way you can stop me now.' He swung a clumsy round arm blow. Nicholas ducked under it and caught Duncan around the chest.

'Listen to me,' he shouted, trying to calm him. 'This is only the eye—'

'You'd do anything to stop me. You swore you would stop me—'

'Help me,' Nicholas called to the two seamen, and they grabbed Duncan's arms. He bucked and fought like a madman, screaming wildly at Nicholas, his face contorted and swollen with rage, sodden hair flopping into his eyes. 'You'd do anything to destroy me, to destroy my ship—'

'Take him down to the raft deck,' Nicholas ordered the two seamen. He knew he could not reason with Duncan now, and he turned away and stiffened suddenly.

'Wait!' he stopped them leaving the bridge.

Nicholas felt the terrible burden of weariness and despair slip from his shoulders, felt new strength rippling through his body, recharging his courage and his resolution – for a mile away, from behind that receding wall of dreadful grey cloud, *Sea Witch* burst abruptly into the sunlight, tearing bravely along with the water bursting over her bows and flying back as high as her bridgework, running without regard to the hazard of sea and storm.

'Jules,' Nicholas whispered.

Jules was driving her like only a tugman can drive a ship, racing to beat the far wall of the storm.

Nicholas felt his throat constricting and suddenly the scalding tears of relief and thankfulness half-blinded him – for a mile out on *Sea Witch*'s port side, and barely a cable-length astern of her, *Warlock* came crashing out of the storm bank, running every bit as hard as her sister ship.

'David,' Nicholas spoke aloud. 'You too, David.'

He realized only then that they must have been in radar

contact with him through those wild tempestuous hours of storm passage, hovering there, holding station on *Golden Dawn*'s crippled bulk and waiting for their first opportunity.

Above the wail and crackle of static from the overhead loudspeaker boomed Jules Levoisin's voice. He was close enough and in the clear eye the interference allowed a readable radio contact.

'*Golden Dawn*, this is *Sea Witch*. Come in, *Golden Dawn*.'

Nicholas reached the radio bench and snatched up the microphone.

'Jules.' He did not waste a moment in greeting or congratulations. 'We are going to take the tanks off her, and let the hull go. Do you understand?'

'I understand to take off the tanks,' Jules responded immediately.

Nicholas' brain was crisp and clear again. He could see just how it must be done. '*Warlock* takes off the port tanks first – in tandem.'

In tandem, the two tanks would be strung like beads on a string, they had been designed to tow that way.

'Then you will take off the starboard side—'

'You must save the hull.' Duncan still fought the two seamen who held him. 'Goddamn you, Berg. I'll not let you destroy me.'

Nicholas ignored his ravings until he had finished giving his orders to the two tug masters. Then he dropped the microphone and grabbed Duncan by the shoulders. Nicholas seemed to be possessed suddenly by supernatural strength, and he shook him as though he were a child. He shook him so his head snapped back and forth and his teeth rattled in his head.

'You bloody idiot,' he shouted in Duncan's face. 'Don't you understand the storm will resume again in minutes?'

He jerked Duncan's body out of the grip of the two

seamen and dragged him bodily to the windows overlooking the tank deck.

'Can't you see this monster you have built is finished, finished! There is no propeller, her back is broken, the superstructure will go minutes after the wind hits again.'

He dragged Duncan round to face him, their eyes were inches apart.

'It's over, Duncan. We will be lucky to get away with our lives. We'll be luckier still to save the cargo.'

'But don't you understand – we've got to save the hull – without it—' Duncan started to struggle, he was a powerful man, and quickly he was rousing himself, within minutes he would be dangerous – and there was no time, already *Warlock* was swinging up into her position on *Golden Dawn*'s port beam for tank transfer.

'I'll not let you take off—' Duncan wrenched himself out of Nicholas' grip, there was a mad fanatic light in his eyes.

Nicholas swivelled; coming up on to his toes and swinging from the shoulders he aimed for the point of Duncan's jaw, just below the ear and the thick sodden wedge of Duncan's red-gold sideburns. But Duncan rolled his head with the punch, and the blow glanced off his temple, and *Golden Dawn* rolled back the other way as Nicholas was unbalanced.

He fell back against the control console, and Duncan drove at him, two running paces like a quarterback taking a field goal, and he kicked right-legged for Nicholas' lower body.

'I'll kill you, Berg,' he screamed, and Nicholas had only time to roll sideways and lift his leg, scissoring it to protect his crotch. Duncan's kick caught him in the upper thigh. An explosion of white pain shot up into his belly and numbed his leg to the thigh, but he used the control console and his good leg to launch himself into a counter-punch, hooking with his right again, under the ribs – and the wind went out of Duncan's lungs with a whoosh as he doubled. Nicholas transferred his weight smoothly and swung his left fist up into Duncan's face. It sounded like a watermelon dropped on a concrete floor, and Duncan was hurled backwards against the bulkhead, pinned there for a moment by the ship's roll. Nicholas followed him, hobbling painfully on the injured leg, and he hit him twice more. Left and right, short, hard, hissing blows that cracked his skull backwards against the bulkhead, and brought quick bright rosettes of blood from his lips and nostrils.

As his legs buckled, Nicholas caught him by the throat with his left hand and held him upright, searching his eyes for further resistance, ready to hit again, but there was no fight left in him.

Nicholas let him go, and went to the signal locker. He snatched three of the small walkie-talkie radios from the radio shelves and handed one to each of the two seamen.

'You know the pod tank undocking procedures for a tandem tow?' he asked.

'We've practised it,' one of them replied.

'Let's go,' said Nicholas.

It was a job that was scheduled for a dozen men, and there were three of them. Duncan was of no use to them, and Nicholas left him in the pump control room on the lowest deck of *Golden Dawn*'s stern quarter, after he had closed down the inert gas pumps, sealed the gas vents, and armed the hydraulic releases of the pod tanks for undocking.

They worked sometimes neck-deep in the bursts of green, frothing water that poured over the ultra-tanker's foredeck. They took on board and secured *Warlock*'s main cable, unlocked the hydraulic clamps that held the forward pod tank attached to the hull and, as David Allen eased it clear of the crippled hull, they turned and lumbered back along the twisted and wind-torn catwalk, handicapped by the heavy seaboots and oilskins and the confused seas that still swamped the tank-deck every few minutes.

On the after tank, the whole laborious energy-sapping procedure had to be repeated, but here it was complicated by the chain coupling which connected the two half-mile-long pod tanks. Over the walkie-talkie Nicholas had to co-ordinate the efforts of his seamen to those of David Allen at the helm of *Warlock*.

When at last *Warlock* threw on power to both of her big propellers and sheered away from the wallowing hull, she had both port pod tanks in tow. They floated just level with the surface of the sea, offering no windage for the hurricane winds that would soon be upon them again.

Hanging on to the rail of the raised catwalk Nicholas watched for two precious minutes with an appraising professional eye. It was an incredible sight, two great shiny black whales, their backs showing only in the troughs, and the gallant little ship leading them away. They followed meekly, and Nicholas' anxiety was lessened. He was not confident, not even satisfied, for there was still a hurricane to navigate – but there was hope now.

'*Sea Witch*,' he spoke into the small portable radio. 'Are you ready to take on tow?'

Jules Levoisin fired the rocket-line across personally. Nicholas recognized his portly but nimble figure high in the fire-control tower, and the rocket left a thin trail of snaking white smoke high against the backdrop of racing, grey hurricane clouds. Arching high over the tanker's tank-deck, the thin nylon rocket-line fell over the catwalk ten feet from where Nicholas stood.

They worked with a kind of restrained frenzy, and Jules Levoisin brought the big graceful tug in so close beside them that glancing up Nicholas could see the flash of a gold filling in Jules' white smile of encouragement. It was only a glance that Nicholas allowed himself, and then he raised his face and looked at the storm.

The wall of cloud was slippery and smooth and grey, like the body of a gigantic slug, and at its foot trailed a glistening white slimy line where the winds frothed the surface of the sea. It was very close now, ten miles, no more, and above them the sun had gone, cut out by the spiralling vortex of leaden cloud. Yet still that open narrow funnel of clear calm air reached right up to a dark and ominous sky.

There was no hydraulic pressure on the clamps of the starboard forward pod tank. Somewhere in the twisted damaged hull the hydraulic line must have sheared. Nicholas and one of the seamen had to work the emergency release, pumping it open slowly and laboriously by hand.

Still it would not release, the hull was distorted, the clamp jaws out of alignment.

'Pull,' Nicholas commanded Jules in desperation. 'Pull all together.' The storm front was five miles away, and already he could hear the deadly whisper of the wind, and a cold puff touched Nicholas' uplifted face.

The sea boiled under *Sea Witch*'s counter, spewing out in a swift white wake as Jules brought in both engines. The tow-cable came up hard and straight; for half a minute nothing gave, nothing moved – except the wall of racing grey cloud bearing down upon them.

Then, with a resounding metallic clang, the clamps slipped and the tank slid ponderously out of its dock in *Golden Dawn*'s hull – and as it came free, so the hull, held together until that moment by the tanks' bulk and buoyancy, began to collapse.

The catwalk on which Nicholas stood began to twist and tilt so that he had to grab for a handhold, and he stood frozen in horrified fascination as he watched *Golden Dawn* begin the final break-up.

The whole tank deck, now only a gutted skeleton, began to bend at its weakened centre, began to hinge like an enormous pair of nutcrackers – and caught between the jaws of the nutcracker was the starboard after pod tank. It was a nut the size of Chartres Cathedral, with a soft liquid centre, and a shell as thin as the span of a man's hand.

Nicholas broke into a lurching, blundering run down the twisting, tilting catwalk, calling urgently into the radio as he went.

'Shear!' he shouted to the seamen almost half a mile away across that undulating plane of tortured steel. 'Shear the tandem tow!'

For the two starboard pod tanks were linked by the heavy chain of the tandem, and the forward tank was linked to *Sea Witch* by the main tow-cable. So *Sea Witch* and the doomed *Golden Dawn* were coupled inexorably, unless they could cut the two tanks apart and let *Sea Witch* escape with the forward tank which she had just undocked.

The shear control was in the control box halfway back along the tank deck, and at that moment the nearest seaman was two hundred yards from it.

Nicholas could see him staggering wildly back along the twisting, juddering catwalk. Clearly he realized the danger, but his haste was fatal, for as he jumped from the catwalk, the deck opened under him, gaping open like the jaws of a steel monster and the seaman fall through, waist deep, into the opening between two moving plates, then as he squirmed feebly, the next lurch of the ship's hull closed the plates, sliding them across each other like the blades of a pair of scissors.

The man shrieked once and a wave burst over the deck, smothering his mutilated body in cold, green water. When it poured back over the ship's side there was no sign of the man. The deck was washed glisteningly clean.

Nicholas reached the same point in the deck, judged the gaping and closing movement of the steel plate and the next rush of sea coming on board, before he leapt across the deadly gap.

He reached the control box, and slid back the hatch, pressing himself into the tiny steel cubicle as he unlocked the red lid that housed the shear button. He hit the button with the heel of his hand.

The four heavy chains of the tandem tow lay between the electrodes of the shear mechanism. With a gross surge of power from the ship's generators and a flash of blue electric flame, the thick steel links sheared as cleanly as cheese under the cutting wire – and, half a mile away, *Sea Witch* felt the release and pounded ahead under the full thrust of her propellers, taking with her the forward starboard tank still held on main tow.

Nicholas paused in the opening of the control cubicle, hanging on to the sill for support and he stared down at the single remaining tank, still caught inextricably in the tangled moving forest of *Golden Dawn*'s twisting, contorting hull. It was as though an invisible giant had taken the Eiffel Tower at each end and was bending it across his knee.

Suddenly there was a sharp chemical stink in the air, and Nicholas gagged on it. The stink of crude petroleum oil gushing from the ruptured tank.

'Nicholas! Nicholas!' The radio set slung over his shoulder squawked, and he lifted it to his lips without taking his eyes from the *Golden Dawn*'s terrible death throes.

'Go ahead, Jules.'

'Nicholas, I am turning to pick you up.'

'You can't turn, not with that tow.'

'I will put my bows against the starboard quarterdeck rail, directly under the forward wing of the bridge. Be ready to jump aboard.'

'Jules, you are out of your head!'

'I have been that way for fifty years,' Jules agreed amiably. 'Be ready.'

'Jules, drop your tow first,' Nicholas pleaded. It would be almost impossible to manoeuvre the *Sea Witch* with that monstrous dead weight hanging on her tail. 'Drop tow. We can pick up again later.'

'You teach your grandfather to break eggs,' Jules blithely mangled the old saying, giving it a sinister twist.

'Listen Jules, the No. 4 tank has ruptured. I want you to shut down for fire. Do you understand? Full fire shut down. Once I am aboard, we will put a rocket into her and burn off cargo.'

'I hear you, Nicholas, but I wish I had not.'

Nicholas left the control cubicle, jumped the gaping, chewing gap in the decking and scrambled up the steel ladder on to the central catwalk.

Glancing over his shoulder, he could see the endlessly slippery grey wall of racing cloud and wind; its menace was overpowering, so that for a moment he faltered before forcing himself into running back along the catwalk towards the tanker's stern tower half a mile ahead.

The single remaining seaman was on the catwalk a hundred yards ahead of him, pounding determinedly back towards the pick-up point. He also had heard Jules Levoisin's last transmission.

A quarter of a mile across the roiling, leaping waters, Jules Levoisin was bringing *Sea Witch* around. At another time Nicholas would have been impressed by the consummate skill with which the little Frenchman was handling his ship and its burdensome tow, but now there was time and energy for one thing only.

The air stank. The heavy fumes of crude oil burned Nicholas' pumping lungs, and constricted his throat. He coughed and gasped as he ran, the taste and reek of it coated his tongue and seared his nostrils.

Below the catwalk, the bloated pod-tank was punctured in a hundred places by the steel lances of the disintegrating hull, pinched and torn by moving steel girders, and the dark red oil spurted and dribbled and oozed from it like the poisonous blood from the carcass of a mortally wounded dragon.

Nicholas reached the stern tower, barged in through the storm doors to the lowest deck and reached the pump control room.

Duncan Alexander turned to him, as he entered, his face swollen and bruised where Nicholas had beaten him.

'We are abandoning now,' said Nicholas. '*Sea Witch* is taking us off.'

'I hated you from that very first day,' Duncan was very calm, very controlled, his voice even, deep and cultured. 'Did you know that?'

'There's no time for that now.' Nicholas grabbed his arm, and Duncan followed him readily into the passageway.

'That's what the game is all about, isn't it, Nicholas, power and wealth and women – that's the game we played.'

Nicholas was barely listening. They were out on to the quarterdeck, standing at its starboard rail, below the bridge, the pick-up point that Jules had stipulated. *Sea Witch* was turning in, only five hundred yards out, and Nicholas had time now to watch Jules handle his ship.

He was running out the heavy tow cable on free spool, deliberately letting a long bight of it form between the tug and its enormous whalelike burden, and he was using the slack in the cable to cut in towards *Golden Dawn*'s battered, sagging hulk. He would be alongside for the pick-up in less than a minute.

'That was the game we played, you and I,' Duncan was still talking calmly. 'Power and wealth and women—'

Below them *Golden Dawn* poured her substance into the sea in a slick, stinking flood. The waves, battering against her side, churned the oil to a thick filthy emulsion, and it was spreading away across the surface, bleeding its deadly poison into the Gulf Stream to broadcast it to the entire ocean.

'I won,' Duncan went on reasonably. 'I won it all, every time—' He was groping in his pockets, but Nicholas hardly heard him, was not watching him. ' – until now.'

Duncan took one of the self-igniting signal flares from his pocket and held it against his chest with both hands, slipping his index finger through the metal ring of the igniter tab.

'And yet I win this one also, Nicholas,' he said. 'Game, set and match.' And he pulled the tab on the flare with a sharp jerk, and stepped back, holding it aloft.

It spluttered once and then burst into brilliant sparkling red flame, white phosphorescent smoke billowing from it.

Now at last Nicholas turned to face him, and for a moment he was too appalled to move. Then he lunged for Duncan's raised hand that held the burning flare, but Duncan was too fast for him to reach it.

He whirled and threw the flame in a high spluttering arc, out over the leaking, stinking tank-deck.

It struck the steel tank and bounced once, and then rolled down the canted oil-coated plating.

Nicholas stood paralysed at the rail staring down at it. He expected a violent explosion, but nothing happened; the flare rolled innocently across the deck, burning with its pretty red twinkling light.

'It's not burning,' Duncan cried. 'Why doesn't it burn?'

Of course, the gas was only explosive in a confined space, and it needed spark. Out here in the open air the oil had a very high flashpoint; it must be heated to release its volatiles.

The flare caught in the scuppers and fizzled in a black pool of crude, and only then the crude caught. It caught with a red, slow, sulky flame that spread quickly but not explosively over the entire deck, and instantly, thick billows of dark smoke rose in a dense choking cloud.

Below where Nicholas stood, the *Sea Witch* thrust her bows in and touched them against the tanker's side. The seaman beside Nicholas jumped and landed neatly on the tug's bows, then raced back along *Sea Witch*'s deck.

'Nicholas,' Jules' voice thundered over the loud hailer. 'Jump, Nicholas.'

Nicholas spun back to the rail, and poised himself to jump.

Duncan caught him from behind, whipping one arm around his throat, and pulling him backwards away from the rail.

'No,' Duncan shouted. 'You're staying, my friend. You are not going anywhere. You are staying here with me.'

A greasy wave of black choking smoke engulfed them, and Jules' magnified voice roared in Nicholas' ears.

'Nicholas, I cannot hold her here. Jump, quickly, jump!'

Duncan had him off-balance, dragging him backwards, away from the ship's side, and suddenly Nicholas knew what he must do.

Instead of resisting Duncan's arm, he hurled himself backwards and they crashed together into the superstructure – but Duncan bore the combined weight of both their bodies.

His armlock around the throat relaxed slightly and Nicholas drove his elbow into Duncan's side below the ribs, then wrenched his body forward from the waist, reached between his own braced legs and caught Duncan's ankles. He straightened up again, dragging Duncan off his feet and the same instant dropped backwards with his full weight on to the deck.

Duncan gasped and his arm fell away, as Nicholas bounced to his feet again, choking in the greasy billows of smoke, and he reached the ship's side.

Below him, the gap between *Sea Witch*'s bows and the tanker's side was rapidly widening and the thrust of the sea and the drag of the tug pulled them apart.

Nicholas vaulted on to the rail, poised for an instant and then jumped. He struck the deck and his teeth cracked together with the impact; his injured leg gave under him and he rolled once, then he was up on his hands and knees.

He looked up at *Golden Dawn*. She was completely enveloped now in the boiling column of black smoke. As the flames heated the leaking crude, so it burned more readily. The bank of smoke was shot through now with the satanic crimson of high, hot flame.

As *Sea Witch* sheered desperately away, the first rush of the storm hit them, and for a moment it smeared the smoke away, exposing the tanker's high quarterdeck.

Duncan Alexander stood at the rail above the roaring holocaust of the tank-deck. He stood with his arms extended, and he was burning; his clothing burned fiercely and his hair was a bright torch of flame. He stood like a ritual cross, outlined in fire, and then slowly he seemed to shrivel and he toppled forward over the rail into the bubbling, spurting, burning cargo of the monstrous ship that he had built – and the black smoke closed over him like a funeral cloak.

As the crude oil escaping from the pierced pod tank fed the flames, so the heat built up swiftly, still sufficient to consume only the volatile aromatic spirits which constituted less than half the bulk of the cargo.

The heavy carbon elements, not yet hot enough to burn, boiled off in that solid black column of smoke, and as the returning winds of the hurricane raced over the *Golden Dawn* once more, so that filthy pall was mixed with air and lifted into the cloud bank of the storm, rising first a thousand, then ten, then twenty thousand feet above the surface of the ocean.

And still *Golden Dawn* burned, and the temperatures of

the gas and oil mixture trapped in her hull rocketed steeply. Steel glowed red, then brilliant white, ran like molten wax, and then like water – and suddenly the flashpoint of heavy carbon smoke in a mixture of air and water vapour was reached in the womb of this mighty furnace.

*Golden Dawn* and her entire cargo turned into a fireball.

The steel and glass and metal of her hull disappeared in an instantaneous explosive combustion that released temperatures like those upon the surface of the sun. Her cargo, a quarter of a million tons of it, burned in an instant, releasing a white blooming rose of pure heat so fierce that it shot up into the upper stratosphere and consumed the billowing pall of its own hydrocarbon gas and smoke.

The very air burst into flame, the surface of the sea flamed in that white fireball of heat and even the clouds of smoke burned as the oxygen and hydrocarbon they contained exploded.

Once an entire city had been subjected to this phenomena of fireball, when stone and earth and air had exploded, and five thousand German citizens of the city of Cologne had been vaporized, and that vapour burned in the heat of its own release.

But this fireball was spawned by a quarter of a million tons of volatile liquids.

'Can't you get us further away?' Nicholas shouted above the thunder of the hurricane. His mouth was only inches from Jules Levoisin's ear.

They were standing side by side, hanging from the overhead railing that gave purchase on this wildly pitching deck.

'If I open the taps I will part the tow wire,' Jules shouted back.

*Sea Witch* was alternately standing on her nose and then

her tail. There was no forward view from the bridge, only green washes of sea water and banks of spray.

The full force of the hurricane was on them once more, and a glance at the radarscope showed the glowing image of *Golden Dawn*'s crippled and bleeding hull only half a mile astern.

Suddenly the glass of the windows was obscured by an impenetrable blackness, and the light in *Sea Witch*'s navigation bridge was reduced to only the glow of her fire-lights and the electronic instruments of her control console.

Jules Levoisin turned his face to Nicholas, his plump features haunted by green shadows in the gloom.

'Smoke bank,' Nicholas shouted an explanation. There was no reek of the filthy hydrocarbon in the bridge, for *Sea Witch* was shut down for fire drill, all her ports and ventilators sealed, her internal air-conditioning on a closed circuit, the air being scrubbed and recharged with oxygen by the big Carrier until above the main engine room. 'We are directly downwind of the *Golden Dawn*.'

A fiercer rush of the hurricane winds laid *Sea Witch* over on her side, the lee rail deep under the racing green sea, and held her there, unable to rise against the careless might of the storm for many minutes. Her crew hung desperately from any hand hold, the irksome burden of her tow helping to drag her down further; the propellers found no grip in the air, and her engines screamed in anguish.

But *Sea Witch* had been built to live in any sea, and the moment the wind hesitated, she fought off the water that had come aboard and began to swing back.

'Where is *Warlock?*' Jules bellowed anxiously. The danger of collision preyed upon him constantly, two ships and their elephantine tows manoeuvring closely in confined hurricane waters was nightmare on top of nightmare.

'Ten miles east of us.' Nicholas picked the other tug's image out of the trash on the radarscope. 'They had a start, ahead of the wind—'

He would have gone on, but the boiling bank of hydrocarbon smoke that surrounded *Sea Witch* turned to fierce white light, a light that blinded every man on the bridge as though a photograph flashlight had been fired in his face.

'Fireball!' Nicholas shouted, and, completely blinded, reached for the remote controls of the water cannons seventy feet above the bridge on *Sea Witch*'s fire-control tower.

Minutes before, he had aligned the four water cannons, training them down at their maximum angle of depression, so now as he locked down the multiple triggers, *Sea Witch* deluged herself in a pounding cascade of sea water.

*Sea Witch* was caught in a furnace of burning air, and despite the torrents of water she spewed over herself, her paintwork was burned away in instantaneous combustion so fierce that it consumed its own smoke, and almost instantly the bare scorched metal of her exposed upper-works began to glow with heat.

The heat was so savage that it struck through the insulated hull, through the double glazing of the two-inch armoured glass of her bridge windows, scorching and frizzling away Nicholas' eyelashes and blistering his lips as he lifted his face to it.

The glass of the bridge windows wavered and swam as they began to melt – and then abruptly there was no more oxygen. The fireball had extinguished itself, consumed everything in its twenty seconds of life, everything from sea level to thirty thousand feet above it, a brief and devastating orgasm of destruction.

It left a vacuum, a weak spot in the earth's thin skin of air; it formed another low pressure system smaller, but much more intense, and more hungry to be filled than the eye of Hurricane Lorna itself.

It literally tore the guts out of that great revolving storm, setting up counter winds and a vortex within the established system that ripped it apart.

New gales blew from every point about the fireball's vacuum, swiftly beginning their own dervish spirals and twenty miles short of the mainland of Florida, hurricane Lorna checked her mindless, blundering charge, fell in upon herself and disintegrated into fifty different willy-nilly squalls and whirlpools of air that collided and split again, slowly degenerating into nothingness.

On a morning in April in Galveston roads, the salvage tug *Sea Witch* dropped off tow to four smaller harbour tugs who would take the *Golden Dawn* No. 3 pod tank up the narrows to the Orient Amex discharge installation below Houston.

Her sister ship *Warlock*, Captain David Allen commanding, had dropped off his tandem tow of No. 1 and No. 2 pod tanks to the same tugs forty-eight hours previously.

Between the two ships, they had made good salvage under Lloyd's Open Form of three-quarters of a million tons of crude petroleum valued at $85.50 US a ton. To the prize would be added the value of the three tanks themselves – not less than sixty-five million dollars all told, Nicholas calculated, and he owned both ships and the full share of the salvage award. He had not sold to the Sheikhs yet, though for every day of the tow from the Florida Straits to Texas, there had been frantic telex messages from James Teacher in London. The Sheikhs were desperate to sign now, but Nicholas would let them wait a little longer.

Nicholas stood on the open wing of *Sea Witch*'s bridge and watched the four smaller harbour tugs bustling importantly about their ungainly charge.

He lifted the cheroot to his lips carefully, for they were still blistered from the heat of the fireball – and he pondered the question of how much he had achieved, apart from spectacular riches.

He had reduced the spill from a million to a quarter of a million tons of cad-rich crude, and he had burned it in a fireball. Nevertheless, there had been losses, toxins had been lifted high above the fireball. They had spread and settled across Florida as far as Tampa and Tallahassee, poisoning the pastures and killing thousands of head of domestic stock. But the American authorities had been quick to extend the hurricane emergency procedures. There had been no loss of human life. He had achieved that much.

Now he had delivered the salvaged pod tanks to Orient Amex. The new cracking process would benefit all mankind, and nothing that Nicholas could do would prevent men from carrying the cad-rich crudes of El Barras across the oceans. But would they do so in the same blindly irresponsible manner that Duncan Alexander had attempted?

He knew then with utter certainty that it was his appointed life's work from now on, to try and ensure that they did not. He knew how he was to embark upon that work. He had the wealth that was necessary, and Tom Parker had given him the other instruments to do the job.

He knew, with equal certainty, who would be his companion in that life's work – and standing on the fire-scorched deck of the gallant little vessel he had a vivid image of a golden girl who walked forever beside him in sunlight and in laughter.

'Samantha.'

He said her name aloud just once, and suddenly he was very eager to begin.